4

omega

jack mcDevitt

2003
50TH
ANNIVERSARY

ace books, new york

An Ace Book
Published by The Berkley Publishing Group
A division of Penguin Group (USA) Inc.
375 Hudson Street
New York, New York 10014

First edition: November 2003

Library of Congress Cataloging-in-Publication Data

McDevitt, Jack.
    Omega / Jack McDevitt.—1st ed.
        p.   cm.
    Sequel to: The engines of God.
    ISBN 0-441-01046-6
    1. Life on other planets—Fiction.   I. Title.

PS3563.C3556O46 2003
813'.54—dc22

                                                                    2003057927

PRINTED IN THE UNITED STATES OF AMERICA

10   9   8   7   6   5   4   3   2   1

Acknowledgments

I'm indebted to Sara and Bob Schwager for their work with the manuscript; to Walter Cuirle, physicist and writer, for technical assistance; to Ginjer Buchanan, for editorial guidance; to Ralph Vicinanza, for being there; and to Maureen McDevitt for showing the way.

Dedication

For Jean and Scotty Parrish, USN

"Scientists have today confirmed that one of the omega clouds is indeed approaching Earth. First, I want to reassure everyone that it poses no danger to us. It is not expected to arrive in our vicinity for almost a thousand years. So neither we, nor our children, nor our children's children, need be fearful.

"However, we are now aware that these objects have visited the Earth in the past, at intervals of approximately eight thousand years. Apparently, they destroy cities and will attack other kinds of construction. No one knows why. No one knows whether they are natural objects or the results of a perverted science.

"Our generation faces only one danger, that we might say to ourselves this is not our problem, and that we will pass it off to the distant future. That we might shrug and say to ourselves that a thousand years is a long time. That we will become complacent and conclude that this problem will take care of itself.

"But I say to you, we should take no satisfaction in the fact that we ourselves are in no physical danger. This is a hazard to our world, to everything we hope to pass on to future generations. And it is clear that we should act now, while we have the time.

"Therefore, I am directing that the full resources of the Council of Nations be brought to bear. We will learn how this cloud operates, and we will shut it down."

—MARGARET ISHIRO, GENERAL SECRETARY, WCN
SEPTEMBER 9, 2213

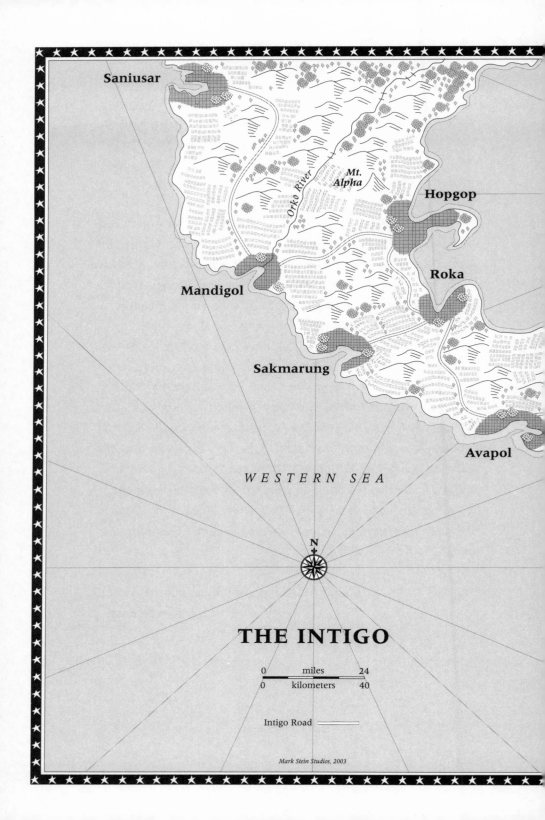

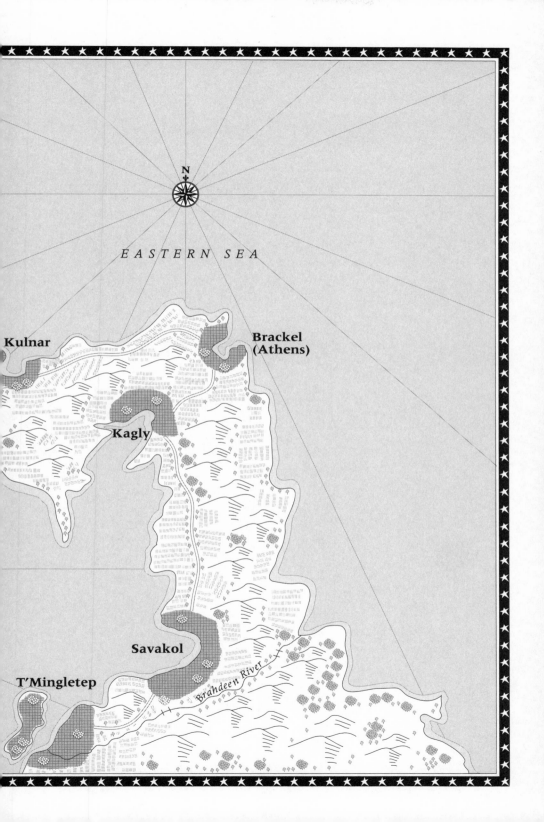

prologue

On the surface at Brinkmann IV
("Moonlight"), in IC4756, 1300
light-years from Earth.
Autumn 2230.

IT WAS THE most majestic series of structures David Collingdale had ever seen. Steeples and domes and polygons rose out of ice and snow. Walkways soared among the towers, or their remnants. Many had collapsed. There were pyramids and open squares that might once have been parks or courtyards. An obelisk anchored the center of the city. It was a place out of time, frozen, preserved for the ages, a landscape that might have been composed by Montelet. A place of crystal and glass, and, in a kinder age, of flowering trees and shaped hedges and beckoning forest. Catch it at the right time, when its giant moon, half again as big as Luna, was in the sky, and one might have thought that here was the celestial city, Valhalla, Argolis, El Dorado by night.

It looked too ethereal to have actually served as a home for a thriving population. Rather, Collingdale could not get away from the sense that it had been intended by its builders as a work of art, to remain unused, to stand as a monument rather than a city. Several of the towers had collapsed, broken fragments rising out of a thick carpet of snow. Its name was unknown, so they called it Moonlight, the city and the world and the sense of something lost.

A bleak wind howled down the empty streets, chilling him even in the e-suit, which was apparently not functioning properly. He'd see to getting it adjusted when he got back to the dome. Wouldn't want to have it fail out here at twenty below.

The sun was struggling to get above a flat mountain range. Several thousand years ago, something had gone wrong with it. Abrams had explained it to him, a surfeit of metals or some such thing. Just temporary, he'd insisted. Be back to normal, he expected, in another few thousand years. Not that it would matter.

He was at the equator, where the remnants of the once-global civilization had fled. There were other cities, most in areas that had once been equatorial, some buried in snowfields, still others frozen behind walls of ice.

He and his team knew little yet about the race that had lived here, except that they were a long time dead, and their architecture rivaled anything man had produced. Crystal bridges thrown across mighty rivers, hyperbolic domes, broad walkways in the sky. All frozen now, the bridges as well as the rivers, the crystal as well as the spirit.

It was perhaps a hard irony that Moonlight, which had thrived and died about the time humans were rolling stones out of quarries to build the first pyramids, would probably have remained undiscovered indefinitely had it not been that it was about to receive an unwelcome visitor. A survey ship, the *Harry Coker*, had been watching an omega, one of the monstrous clouds that drifted in waves out of the galactic core, and which seemed bent on destroying any civilization in their path. The *Coker* was anxious to see how the cloud would fare in the complex gravity field of a planetary system, when it spotted evidence of cities on the fourth planet.

Collingdale squinted into the hard gray sky. The cloud was visible from late afternoon until shortly after midnight. It was up there now, partially obscured in the glare of the sunset. In the daytime it looked utterly harmless, a large dark thunderstorm, perhaps, like a million others he had seen in his lifetime. But this one rose and set with the sky beyond the atmosphere. It always described the same path across the heavens and it kept getting bigger.

The omega clouds were old news. They'd been discovered a quarter century earlier. Although no one had ever seen them attack a city, they were tied to massive destruction in ancient times on Quraqua, Beta Pacifica III, and two other worlds. Objects with a wide range of geometric shapes had been floated in front of the omegas, and humans now knew beyond any question that designs not found in nature could expect to draw lightning bolts.

Nobody understood how or why. No one knew where they came from. And few seemed to feel it was likely we would ever find out.

Until now, no one had seen a cloud change course and glide into a planetary system. No one had seen a city under attack.

It was fortunate nobody lived on Moonlight. The inhabitants had obviously been overwhelmed by the ice age brought on by the instability of their sun. Best estimates were that there'd been no one there for about two thousand years.

COLLINGDALE HAD GROWN up in Boston with an alcoholic mother and a missing father, who, his mother insisted until the day of her sodden teary death, had gone west on business and would be back any day. He'd spent two years in an orphanage, been adopted by a pair of religious fanatics, run away so many times they'd eventually implanted a tracker, and—despite everything—won a scholarship from the University of Massachusetts. He'd taken a degree in archeology, taken private flying lessons on a whim, and, as he liked to think of it, never again touched ground. Eventually he'd decided that flights between Chicago and Boston were too confining. He'd learned to pilot the superluminals, had taken the command seat for several major corporations and the Academy, had gotten bored hauling people and supplies back and forth through the void, gone back to school, and specialized in a discipline that, at that time, lacked subject matter: xenology.

In the meantime he'd attended the funerals of both his foster parents, who'd died a year apart, the one unable to live without the other. They'd refused longevity treatments on the grounds they were not God's plan. They'd never given up on him, even though they disapproved of the directions his life had taken. He'd stopped going home during the last years of their lives because they kept telling him they forgave him and were sure God would as well.

He didn't know why they intruded on his thoughts while he gazed across the city. He would have liked them to see Moonlight. Surely they would have been caught up in its majesty, and they might have understood what his life was about.

THE OMEGAS ROUTINELY hurled lightning bolts at perpendiculars. Any object designed with right angles, or sharp departures from nature's natural arcs, could expect to become a target.

It had seemed an old wives' tale when the stories first came back. Collingdale recalled that the scientific community, almost to a person, had scoffed at the reports. The notion that clouds could somehow navigate on their own seemed absurd. That they could bump up to high velocities more absurd still. Most had not accepted the idea until the one approaching Moonlight, the Brinkmann Cloud, had changed course, begun to slow down, and headed insystem. That was four years ago.

The claims had been so outlandish that nobody who cared about his reputation had even tested them. But once the Brinkmann showed its ability to navigate, researchers had come, and an attempt to explain the impossible had begun. It had begun with the discovery of nanos in samples taken from the omega.

Were the clouds natural objects? Or artificial? Did the universe disapprove of intelligent life? Or was there a psychotic force in existence somewhere? Or, as his parents had thought, was God sending a warning?

"You coming, Dave?"

They'd cut their way into the base of the northeastern tower, and Jerry

Riley was standing aside, leaving for Dave the honor of being first person to enter the structure. He clapped a few shoulders, strode down between banks of dug-out snow, paused at the entrance, put his head in, and flashed his lamp around.

The interior was as large as New York's main terminal. The ceiling soared several stories. Benches were scattered throughout the area. Sleek metal columns supported balconies and galleries. Alcoves that might once have been shops were set into the walls. And there was a statue.

He took a few steps inside, scarcely daring to breathe. They knew what the natives looked like because they'd found remains. But they'd never seen any depictions of them. No sculptures, no graphics, no engravings. How odd it had seemed that a species so given to art had given them no copies of its own image.

The others filed in and spread out around him, all enamored of the statue. Jerry raised his lamp slowly, almost reverently, and played the light across it. It was a feline. Claws were replaced by manipulative digits, but the snout and fangs remained. Narrow eyes, in front. A predator. But it wore a hat, rather like an artist's beret, angled down over one eye. It was decked out in trousers, a shirt with long fluffy sleeves, and a jacket that would not have looked out of place in Boston. A bandanna was tied around its neck. And it sported a cane.

One of the women giggled.

Collingdale couldn't suppress a smile himself, and yet despite its comic aspect, the creature displayed a substantial degree of dignity.

There was an inscription on the base, a single line of characters, executed in a style reminiscent of Old English. It was probably a single word. "Its name?" someone suggested.

Collingdale wondered what the subject had done. A Washington? A Churchill? A Francis Bacon? Perhaps a Mozart.

"The architect," said Riley, short and generally cynical. "This is the guy who built the place." Riley didn't like being out here, but needed this last mission to establish his *bona fides* with the University of Something-or-Other back home. He'd be an inspiration to the students.

It was odd how the intangibles carried over from species to species. Dignity. Majesty. Power. Whether it was seen in an avian or a monkey, or something between, it always had the same look.

His commlink vibrated against his wrist. It was Alexandra, who'd arrived two days before on the *al-Jahani* with a cargo of nukes, which she'd been instructed to use in an effort to blow away the cloud. Nobody believed it could be done, but no other course of action offered itself. The cloud was simply too big, thirty-four thousand kilometers in diameter. A few nukes would have no effect.

"Yes, Alex. What've you got?"

"It's still slowing down, Dave. And it's still on target."

"Okay."

"It's coming in on your side of the world. Looks as if it's homed in on your city. We're going to set the bombs off tonight. In about six hours."

The omega was slowing down by firing jets of dust and hydrogen forward. Riley thought it might also be twisting gravity, but there was no evidence yet to support that idea. The only thing that mattered was that, however it was managing things, the cloud was going to arrive right on top of Moonlight.

THEY WANDERED FOR hours through the underground. There was a network of smaller chambers connected to the large area. They found an endless number of chairs, bowls, radios, monitors, plumbing fixtures, conference tables. Artifacts they couldn't identify. Much of it was in surprisingly good condition. There were boxes of plastic disks, undoubtedly memory storage units. But electronic records were fragile. Early civilizations carved their history onto clay tablets, which lasted virtually forever. More advanced groups went for paper, which had a reasonable shelf life, provided it was stored in a dry place and not mishandled. But electronic data had no staying power. They had not yet been able to recover a single electronic record.

There were some books, which had *not* been stored properly. Nevertheless, they gathered them into plastic containers. They'd been in the area several weeks, but there was a special urgency about this visit. The cloud was coming. Anything they did not carry off today might not survive.

The walls were covered with engravings. Collingdale assigned one of his people to record as many of them as she could. Some of it was symbolic, much was graphic, usually with bucolic themes, leaves and stems and branches, all of which, when the sun came back, might grow on this world again.

Stairways and shafts rose high into the structure and descended to lower floors, which were encased in ice. "But that might be a huge piece of good luck," Collingdale told Ava MacAvoy, who looked unusually attractive in the reflected light. "It should survive the cloud, whatever happens to the rest of the city."

They went back outside. It was time to leave, but Collingdale delayed, taking more pictures, recording everything. Ava and Riley and the others had to pull him away.

The cloud was setting by then, and Collingdale wished it was possible to halt the planet on its axis, keep the other side between the omega and the towers. Hide the city.

Damn you.

He stood facing it, as if he would have held it off by sheer will.

Ava took his arm. "Come on, Dave," she said. "It's getting late."

THEY RETREATED TO the dome, which had served as their base for the better part of a year. A lander waited beside it. The dome was small, cramped, uncomfortable. They'd brought out too many people, and could in fact have brought several shiploads more. Everyone had wanted to come to Moonlight. The Academy, under time pressure, had tried to accommodate the requests as best it could. It should have said no. That was partly Collingdale's own fault for not demanding they cut things off.

They'd filled the dome with artifacts and shipped them topside to the *al-Jahani,* which now carried a treasure trove of mugs and plates and table lamps and electronic gear, and materials far more esoteric, objects whose function defied analysis. Other pieces were now being loaded. There was more than the lander could handle, but they'd stacked the rest in the dome, hoping that it would be safe there.

Collingdale waited until everybody else was on board—there were seven of them, excluding the pilot—took a last look around, and climbed in. The omega was almost down. Only a black ridge of clouds was visible in the west, and a few streaked plumes soared above the horizon. The pilot started the engines, and the lander rose. Nobody said much.

Jerry commented how scary it was, and Collingdale couldn't restrain a smile. He himself was of the old school. He'd started his archeological career in Iraq, had been shot at, threatened, deported. When archeology went interstellar, as it had a half century ago, it had become, curiously enough, *safer.* There were no deranged local populations defending sacred tombs, no warlords for whom the security payment might be insufficient, no national governments waiting to collapse with dire consequences to the researchers, who might be jailed, beaten, even killed. There were still hazards, but they tended to be less unpredictable, and more within the control of the individual. Don't take foolish chances, and you won't get burned. Don't stay too long in the submerged temple, as had famously happened to Richard Wald twenty-some years earlier, when you know the tidal wave's coming.

So Collingdale was getting his people out in plenty of time. But it didn't prevent them from thinking they were having a narrow escape from something dire. In fact, of course, at no time were they in danger.

He was looking down at the receding city when the pilot informed him he had an incoming transmission from the *al-Jahani*. He opened the channel, turning up the volume so everybody could hear. Alexandra's blond features appeared on-screen. *"We've launched, Dave,"* she said. *"All twelve running true. Detonation in thirty-eight minutes."*

The missiles were cluster weapons, each carrying sixteen nukes. If the plan worked, the missiles would penetrate two thousand kilometers into the cloud and jettison their weapons, which would explode simultaneously. Or they would explode when their electronics failed. The latter provision arose from the inability of researchers to sink probes more than a few kilometers into the clouds. Once inside, everything tended to shut down. Early on, a few ships had been lost.

"Good luck, Alex," he said. "Give it hell."

The lander, powered by its spike technology, ascended quickly, traveling west. The cloud began to rise also. The flight had been planned to allow the occupants a view of the omega when the missiles reached the target.

Collingdale ached for a success. There was nothing in his life, no award, no intellectual breakthrough, no woman, he had ever wanted as passionately as he wanted to see Alexandra's missiles blow the son of a bitch to hell.

They climbed into orbit and passed into sunlight. Everyone sat quietly, not talking much. Riley and Ava pretended to be examining an electronic device they'd brought up, trying to figure out what it was. Jerry was looking through his notes. Even Collingdale, who prided himself on total honesty, gazed steadfastly at a recently recorded London conference on new Egyptian finds.

The cloud filled the sky again.

"Three minutes," said Alex.

THEY COULDN'T SEE the *al-Jahani* directly. It was too far, and it was lost somewhere in the enormous plumes that fountained off its surface like so many tendrils reaching toward Moonlight. But its position was known, and Bill, the ship's artificial intelligence, had put a marker on the screen. They could see the cloud, of course, and the positions of the missiles were also marked. Twelve blinking lights closing on the oversize gasbag. Collingdale amused himself by counting the weapons.

"Thirty seconds to impact," said the pilot.

Collingdale let his head fall back. He wondered whether one could achieve *impact* with a cloud.

Ava watched the time, and her lips were moving, counting down the seconds.

"They're in," she said. Someone's hand touched his shoulder. Gripped it. Good luck.

Riley adjusted his harness.

Collingdale, knowing his foster parents would have been proud, muttered a prayer.

"They've gone off." Alexandra's voice. *"Too soon."*

There were a few glimmerings along the surface of the cloud. But he saw no sign of disruption.

"It might take a while before we can really see anything," said Riley, hopefully.

The hand on his shoulder let go.

"You're right," said one of the others. "I mean, the cloud is *so* big."

"The bombs had to do *some* damage. How could they not?"

"Maybe just screw up the steering mechanism. Hell, that would be enough."

The glimmering got brighter. Collingdale thought he saw an explosion. Yes, there was no doubt of it. And there. Over there was a second eruption of some kind. They watched several patches grow more incandescent. Watched the cloud pass overhead. Watched it begin to sink toward the rim of the world.

The explosive patches darkened.

On a second orbit, they were still visible, smoldering scars on the otherwise pacific surface of the omega.

"I don't think it's going to work," said the pilot.

ON THE THIRD orbit, they rendezvoused with the *Quagmor*, the vessel that had transported them to the system. The mood on the ship was dark, and everybody was making comments about having made a good effort. Just so much we can do.

Alexandra reported that the omega was still on course for Moonlight. *"We didn't get much penetration. There's still a chance we might have done some damage that just doesn't show. I mean, if we blew up the internal skunk works, how would we know? So don't give up, Doc."*

He didn't. But the view was unsettling. The jets reached out, arcing as if to encircle the planet. The omega was a malignant force, a thing out of religious myth, a force beyond understanding.

The *al-Jahani* maneuvered around the fringes of the cloud, trying to record as much of the event as it could. Collingdale went to his quarters, slept, got up, slept some more. The cloud closed and, as the city rotated into position, made contact directly above. Winds howled. Lightning ripped through the skies. Tornadoes formed.

It was just after sunset.

Collingdale could hardly bring himself to watch. Electrical discharges had been growing in the cloud, had become more intense as it drew nearer. The storm gathered force, but the towers stood, and the planet rotated, moving the city directly to ground zero and then past. And for a while he hoped it would get clear. But without warning a gigantic bolt tore though the cloud and hammered the city. The chess-piece structures seemed to melt and blacken and sink into the ice. Sprays of pebbles rattled against them, and something blasted into the base of one of the corner towers. The tower shuddered and began to lean precipitously. Other buildings collapsed or were blown away. Once, twice, they lost the picture as satellites were neutralized. Lightning ripped out of the night, scorched the diamond steeples and the crystal polygons. Hurricane-force winds hurled black dust across the snowscape. A few rocks fell from the sky, plowing into glass and crystal. It needed only a few minutes, and when it was over, a ground blizzard buried everything.

Collingdale was hardly a violent or even a confrontational man. He hadn't been in a loud argument as far back as he could remember. But in those moments he would have killed. Rage spilled out of his soul, sheer fury driven to excess by his helplessness.

The cloud wrapped itself around the world, around Moonlight, and it found the other cities. It struck them in a display of sheet lightning, forked lightning, chain lightning, and fireballs. Collingdale couldn't get away from it. He wandered through the ship, downing glasses of rum, extreme behavior for a man who seldom drank. He couldn't stop moving, from the bridge to the mission center to the common room to his cabin to Riley's quarters. ("Hey, Dave, look at what this damned thing is doing in the north.") It fed his rage to watch, and for reasons he would never understand, it gave him a twisted pleasure to hate so fiercely.

When finally the cloud grew dormant, pieces of it broke off and began to drift away, as if there were no gravity near the planet to hold on to them. The skies began to clear.

The cities were charred and wrecked, wreathed in black smoke. Ava was in tears. Most of the others were in a state of shock. The devastation was more complete than anything they had imagined.

Collingdale was drinking black coffee, trying to clear his head, when a couple of the technicians created a commotion. "Look," one of them said, pointing at a screen.

At a city. Intact.

Untouched.

Its towers still stood tall. Its hanging walkways still connected rooftops.

A monument was down, and, on its southern flank, a minaret had collapsed. Otherwise, it had escaped.

It was halfway around the globe from where the intersection with the cloud had happened. The safest possible place. But that alone wouldn't have been enough. Other cities, equally distant, had been leveled.

They went back and looked at the record.

Collingdale saw it right away: snow. The surviving city had been experiencing a blizzard when the cloud hit.

"It never saw this place," said Ava.

FIELD REPORT: Moonlight

The only aspects of this civilization that survive are the city that suffered a timely blizzard, and the bases the inhabitants had established on the moon and on the third planet. And in the artifacts that we've managed to haul away.

The loss is incalculable. And I hope that someone, somewhere, will realize that it is time to devise a defense against the omegas. Not to wait until our turn comes, when it might be too late. But to do it now, before the next Moonlight happens.

—David Collingdale,
Preliminary Post-omega Report
December 11, 2230

PART ONE

hedgehogs

chapter 1

HAROLD TEWKSBURY WOKE from one of those curious disjointed dreams in which he was wandering down endless corridors while his heart fluttered and he had trouble breathing. Damned thing wouldn't go away anymore.

The doctors wanted to give him a synthetic heart. But he was over a hundred years old, and even if they could fix things so his body wouldn't be tired, *he* was. His wife was long dead, his kids had grown up sixty years ago. Somehow he'd been too busy for his family, and he'd allowed himself to get separated from his grandchildren and great-grandchildren. Now none of them knew him.

The commlink was chiming, and he heard Rhonda's soft voice. *"Harold,"* she was saying. *"The lab."* Rhonda was the house AI. *"I don't like waking you for these calls, and I think you should let me deal with them."*

"Can't, Rhonda. Just patch it through."

"At the very least, you should take your medication first. Are you all right?"

"Yes," he said, pushing up to a sitting position. "I'm fine. Just a little short of breath." He dumped a pill into his hand and swallowed it. And felt better almost immediately.

It was 3:17 A.M.

"Put them on," he said. And he knew, of course, why they were calling. The only reason they *ever* called at this hour except the time that Josephine had tripped over a rumpled carpet, broken an arm, and had to be taken off to the hospital.

"Harold." Charlie's voice.

"Yes, Charlie? It happened again?"

"Yes, sir."

"Same as the others?"

"Right. No record there was ever a star there anywhere."

"Same signature?"

"We don't quite have the details down yet, but it looks like it."

A nova. But not really. Not the right intensity. Not the right spectroscopic reading. And no evidence of a star having been in the neighborhood. He shook his head. Can't have a nova without a star. "Where?"

"Near the Golden Crescent."

"On a line with the others?"

"Yes."

And that was what really chilled him. There had been three earlier events. On a line, as if something were marching through the sky.

"Did we catch it at the beginning? Or was it running when the package opened up?"

"At the beginning, Harold."

"Okay. Pipe it through."

He rearranged his pillows. A starfield winked on. The Golden Crescent, nursery to a thousand newborn stars, floated over his dresser. To his left, great smoky walls fell away to infinity. The Mogul, a small, dim class-G, was close enough to illuminate the clock. And the long arm of the Milky Way passed through the center of the room.

"Five seconds," said a recorded voice.

He pushed himself higher and watched a dazzling light appear over the dresser. Brilliant and blinding, it overwhelmed everything else in the sky.

It looked like a nova. Behaved like a nova. But it was something else.

He ran it a few more times before closing the record. They had this one from the beginning. If it was like the others, the light would sustain itself for sixty-one days before shutting down.

THROUGH HIS WINDOW the lights of the Washington Monument were a distant blur. The White Eagle Hotel, usually a bright beacon in the night, had been swallowed by an unseasonable fog. He sat quietly, allowing full rein to a rush of sheer pleasure. He was caught up in one of the great mysteries of the age, had no clue what was happening, suspected there would not be a reasonable explanation during his lifetime. And he could not have been happier. The universe, it seemed, was smart enough to keep them all guessing. Which was as it should be.

They'd started trying to sell Weatherman fifteen years ago. The idea was to use their FTL capability to put automated observation packages in strategic locations. They'd presented the program as a means for observing omega clouds, finding out what they were, and possibly learning how to combat them. Fifteen years earlier that had been a very big deal. The clouds had still been relatively new. The news that one was headed toward Earth, even though it wouldn't arrive for roughly nine hundred years, had scared the pants off the general public. But that fear had long since subsided.

The technology had never been right; the program was expensive, and superluminals were needed to make the deliveries. Then there had been a huge piece of luck: the discovery of an alien vehicle at the Twins a few years before provided new technology: a way to build compact self-contained FTL engines and install them as part of the observation package. Push a button, and the Weatherman was on its way.

It had been a long time getting there, but it was on the job at last.

A month ago, the first long-range Weatherman package had arrived in the neighborhood of M68, a globular cluster thirty-one thousand light-years away. Since then, several dozen units had unfurled their sails and powered up scopes and sensors and hyperlight transmitters. More units were en route to hundreds of sites.

The first pictures had come in, and they'd popped the champagne. Sylvia Virgil, the director of operations, had come down and gotten wobbly. But that night nobody cared. They'd stood around looking at a sky filled with dusty clouds like great walls, vast star nurseries that rose forever. It was eerie, gothic, ominous, illuminated by occasional smears of light, like the Monument and the White Eagle. The "walls" were, of course, thousands of light-years across. And they'd watched everything through the eye of the Weatherman. Soon, he'd told himself, they would be everywhere.

MOST OF HAROLD'S colleagues had been blasé about the kind of results they expected. At the time they thought they understood everything, knew how galaxies formed, had a lock on the life cycles of suns, grasped the general nature of the beasts that haunted the dark reaches between the stars. But right out of the box they'd gotten a surprise.

The first phase of the Weatherman Project consisted of the simultaneous launch of more than six hundred probes. When they all arrived at their stations, the Academy would have coverage of sites ranging from within two thousand light-years of the core all the way out to the rim, from Eta Carina to the Lagoon, from the Ring Nebula to the M15 cluster. They would take the temperature of dust clouds and nebulas, track down gravitational anomalies, and provide pictures of the controlled chaos around the supermassive black hole at the center of the galaxy. With luck, it would all happen during Harold's lifetime.

Actually, there'd been several surprises, from black jets to the galactic wind. But the great anomaly was the quasi nova. Behind his back, his people were already calling them *tewks*. Starlike explosions, eruptions of enormous energy in places where there were no stars. And almost in a line. Not quite, but *almost*. It made his hair stand on end.

There was no use trying to go back to sleep. He disentangled himself from the sheets, wandered into the kitchen, got out two pieces of farm bread, and slugged some strawberry jelly on them. One of his many guilty pleasures.

The explosions, though they were less than nova force, were nevertheless of sufficient intensity to be visible across tens of thousands of light-years. Probably all the way out to Andromeda. They were far away, and for that he felt grateful. Explosions of their magnitude, for which one couldn't account, were disquieting.

Light from the four events would reach Earth toward the end of the millennium. They would be visible in the southern hemisphere, where they'd blaze across the sky, in Libra and Scorpius, not quite lining up. But close.

THIS WAS PRISCILLA Hutchins's second tour in the Academy bureaucracy. She'd served two years as transport chief, gotten bored, returned to piloting, gotten married, and accepted a tempting offer: assistant director of operations. She was at last content to leave the superluminals behind, to get away from the long voyages, to get out of the ships with their virtual beaches and their virtual mountainscapes and their virtual everything-else. The oceans and the breezes and the sand were real now. She had a man who loved her, and a daughter, and a house in the suburbs, and life was good.

But Sylvia Virgil was leaving for a lucrative position in private industry. She was effectively gone, and Hutch had found herself assigned as Acting D.O. With an inside shot at getting a permanent appointment.

But the view from the top was turning out to be a bit more complicated than she'd expected. The days in which she made decisions of no consequence to anyone, invested countless hours formulating policy for the record, attended conferences at establishments with convenient golf courses, reviewed reports from the field, and took extraordinarily long lunches abruptly ended.

Hutch was now responsible for coordinating the movements of all Academy vessels, for deciding who piloted those vessels, and for determining passenger transportation. That sounded simple enough. In the old days, when Professor Hoskinson wanted to bump Dr. O'Leary from a flight to Pinnacle, Hutch had simply passed the issue along and let Sylvia make the call. Now *she* was in the middle of every food fight, and she had discovered that her clients, for the most part, owned substantial egos and were not above bringing to bear whatever pressure they could manage. Because they were inevitably the top people in their respective fields, the pressure they could bring was considerable.

She had also become responsible, within monetary constraints, for determining which projects the Academy pushed and which it neglected, and for establishing their priority, and the level of resources to be devoted to each. All, of course, controlled by guidelines from the commissioner. She had a staff of scientific advisors, but the decisions tended more often than not to be based on political considerations. Who had clout with Congress? Who had been supportive of the Academy during the previous fiscal year? Whom did Asquith like?

Michael Asquith was the Academy commissioner, her boss, and a man who believed that scientific considerations were necessarily secondary to rewarding the Academy's supporters and punishing its critics. He called it taking the long view. "We have to give preference to our friends," he told her in strictest secrecy, as if it weren't a transparent policy. "If a little science doesn't get done as a consequence, that's a price we're willing to pay. But we have to keep the Academy in business and well funded, and there's only one way to do that."

The result was that when a program that deserved support on its own merits didn't get it, Hutch took the heat. When a popular initiative went through and provided serious results, the commissioner got the credit. During the three months since she'd accepted the assignment, she'd been bullied, threatened, harassed, and hectored by a substantial representation of the scientific community. Many of them seemed to believe they could take her job. Others promised reprisals, and there'd even been a couple of death threats. Her once benign view of academics, formed over more than two decades of hauling them around the Orion Arm, had gone downhill. Now, when they contacted her, she had to make a conscious effort not to get hostile.

She'd had a modicum of vengeance against Jim Albright, who'd called her to threaten and complain when his turn at one of the Weatherman units had been set back. She'd responded by indiscreetly mentioning the incident to Gregory MacAllister, an editor who'd made a long and happy career of attacking academics, moralists, politicians, and crusaders. MacAllister had gone after Albright with a bludgeon, depicting him as a champion of trivial causes and his program as "one more example of squandering the taxpayers' money counting stars." He hadn't mentioned Hutch, but Albright knew.

That didn't matter, because the bottom line was that she didn't hear from Albright again, although she learned later that he'd tried to have her terminated. Asquith understood what had happened, though, and warned her to call off the big dog. "If it comes out that we're behind any of that, we'll all be out on the street," he told her. He was right, and Hutch was careful not to use the MacAllister weapon again. But she'd enjoyed watching Albright go to ground.

She was in the middle of trying to decide how to persuade Alan Kimbel, who was currently at Serenity doing research on stellar jets, that he could not stay beyond the original timetable and would have to come home. Kimbel had appealed to her on the ground that there'd been a breakthrough discovery, and he and his team needed a few more weeks. *Please.* The man had been almost in tears.

The problem was that it happened all the time. Space on the outlying stations was scarce, and there were already people en route and more in line. Extensions could be granted under certain conditions, and her advisors had told her that Kimbel was correct in his assessment. But if she granted the extension, she'd have to tell another group already a week into their mission that, when they arrived at Serenity, they wouldn't be able to stay. She couldn't very well do that. And the only alternative was to cut someone else short. She'd looked at the possibilities and, for various reasons, there was no easy pick. In the end, she'd denied the request.

She was recording a response to Kimbel when her link chimed. Harold Tewksbury on the circuit.

Harold was the senior member of the astrophysics staff. He'd been with the Academy when Hutch had toured the place as a high school senior. He was an organization freak, a fussy little man with a penchant for order and procedure. His reputation in the field wasn't good. His colleagues thought him quarrelsome and uncommunicative, but no one seemed to doubt his capabilities. And he was always nice to Hutch.

"Yes, Harold," she said. "What are you up to this morning?"

"You busy at the moment?"

She had a hatful of problems. "It isn't like the old days," she said. "But I can make time."

"Good. When you can, stop by the lab."

SHE FOUND HIM sitting at his desk staring out into the courtyard. He shook his head when he saw her, signaling bewilderment. But he also managed a smile. "Something odd's going on," he said.

She thought he was talking about equipment. There *had* been recent problems with spectrometers. Replacing them would have been expensive, so they'd gone with upgrades. Harold didn't like upgrades, didn't like not having the top-of-the-line. "Spend all this money to send out packages," he'd grumbled to her just a few days earlier, "and then skimp on the retrieval-and-analysis gear."

But he surprised her. "You know about the quasi novas," he said.

The tewks. She knew, more or less. It seemed a bit esoteric to her, events a thousand light-years away. Hardly a matter of concern for any but the specialists.

He leaned toward her. His white hair was plumped up and one wing of his collar stuck out sideways. He presented the classic image of a researcher. His blue eyes became unfocused rather easily; he frequently lost his train of thought: and he was inclined often to stop in the middle of a sentence when some new idea occurred to him. In the bright midday sunlight, he looked like an ultimate innocent, a man for whom physical law and mathematics were the only realities. Two cups of coffee arrived.

"They're almost in a line," he said.

"And the significance of that is—?"

"It shouldn't happen naturally."

She just didn't know where to go with it. "What are you telling me, Harold?"

"I don't really know, Hutch. But it scares me."

"You're sure they're not novas?"

"Positive." He tried his coffee, examined the cup, sighed. "Among other things, there's too much energy in the visible spectrum, not enough in the X-ray and gamma."

"Which means—?"

"You get more visible light for the amount of energy expended. A ton more. It's brighter. By a lot."

"A lightbulb."

"You could almost say that."

"All right," she said. "I'll pass it on. You recommend any action?"

He shook his head. "I'd give quite a lot to have a Weatherman in place the next time one goes off."

"Can we do that? Can you predict the next one?"

Now he was looking at the spoon. "Unfortunately not. I can take a stab."

"A stab? What are the odds?"

"Not good."

"Harold, let's do this: Let's watch for a while. If you reach a point where we know an event is coming, where you can give me a target with a reasonable degree of certainty, we'll take a serious look. Okay?"

IT WASN'T SOMETHING she could get excited about. She made a mental note to suggest that Eric Samuels, the public relations director, get in touch with Harold to see whether the Academy couldn't squeeze some publicity out of it. Meantime, she was looking at a busy afternoon.

She had lunch with the president of the SPA, the Superluminal Pilots' Association. They wanted more money, a better retirement system, better career opportunities, you name it. She knew Ben Zalotski well, from her own days on the bridge. Ben was a decent guy, and a hard charger for the pilots. The problem was that he had no compunctions about taking advantage of their long association to get what he wanted. In reality, it wasn't even Hutch's area of responsibility. Jill Watkin in Personnel was supposed to handle all this stuff, but Ben had framed the hour as an opportunity for old friends to get together. She'd known what was coming, but couldn't very easily refuse to see him. She might have simply gotten busy, but she didn't like being devious. In the end she had to tell him she couldn't help, refused even to concede that she sympathized with his objectives, even though she did. But she was part of the management team and her loyalties lay in a different direction. Ben quoted some of her past comments back at her, the pilots are overworked, they can't keep their families together, and nobody gives a damn for them. They're just glorified bus drivers and that's the way they get treated. He allowed himself to look disappointed, and even implied that she'd turned her back on her old comrades.

So she returned to her office in a foul mood, listened to an appeal from Hollis Gunderson, "speaking for the University of the Netherlands," to have his pet project put on the docket. The project was a hunt for a white hole, which Hutch's scientific team had advised her didn't exist, couldn't exist, and would be a waste of resources. Gunderson had gotten past the appointments secretary by claiming someone had misunderstood his intentions. Hutch had made time to talk with him, on the assumption it was easier to see him while he was here than to call back and cancel him. Anyhow, there was something to be said for not making enemies unnecessarily. Her now-retiring boss, Sylvia Virgil, had commented on Priscilla's most recent evaluation that she had a tendency to put off confrontations. She'd suggested Hutch was too timid. Hutch had wondered how Virgil would have done on Deepsix, but let it go.

She heard Gunderson out and concluded the "misunderstanding" to which he'd referred was semantic rather than substantive. Call it by any other name, he still wanted to go looking for a white hole. She told him that, to have the project even considered, he'd have to provide a written statement supporting his views from two of the thirteen physicists certified by the Academy to rule on such matters. "Until you can satisfy two of them, Professor," she said, "I'm afraid we can't help you."

A young man had a complaint concerning one of the pilots. He'd been gruff, he said, and rude and generally not very talkative. All the way back from Outpost. Did Hutch have any idea what it was like to ride for weeks with a ship's captain who kept to himself? He was talking about Adrian Belmont, whom she'd like to get rid of because there were always com-

plaints, but the SPA would come down hard on the Academy if she terminated him. Better to hire a hit man. Cleaner.

In any case, it wasn't an operational matter. "I'm terribly sorry," she told
him. "You should be aware that the pilots frequently make those voyages
alone. Some of them have simply learned to get along without a social life.
We ask the passengers to be understanding. But if you really want to press
the matter, I'm afraid you have the wrong department. You'll want Personnel. End of the corridor, turn right, thank you very much."

She gave an interview to a journalist working on a book about Moonlight,
arranged special transportation to Paradise for Abel Kotanik, who'd been
requested by the field team, juggled shipping schedules to get a load of
medical supplies (which had been mistakenly dropped and left on the pier
at Serenity) forwarded to the Twins, and decided to fire the chief engineer
at Pinnacle for sins of commission and omission that stretched back three
years.

Her final meeting of the day was with Dr. Alva K. Emerson. It was another example of granting an interview she would have liked to hand off
to someone else. *Anyone* else. Hutch didn't intimidate easily, but she was
willing to make an exception on this occasion.

Alva Emerson was an M.D., well into her eighties, and one of the great
figures of the age. She had founded and led the Children's Alliance, which
had brought modern medical care to hundreds of thousands of kids world-
wide during the past forty years. She'd mobilized the wealthy nations, gotten legislation passed by the World Council and in sixty countries around
the globe to provide care for the forgotten peoples of the Earth. While we
reach for the stars, she'd said in her celebrated remarks twenty years before
at the Sudan Memorial, a third of our children cannot reach for a sandwich.
The comment was engraved in stone over the entrance to Alliance Headquarters in Lisbon.

The world loved her. Political leaders were terrified of her. Everywhere
she went, good things happened. Hospitals rose, doctors poured in, corporate donations swelled the coffers. (No one wanted to be perceived as stingy
or mean-spirited when Dr. Alva came knocking.) She was credited with
saving millions. She'd won the Peace Prize and the Americus, was on first-
name terms with the pope and the president of the NAU, and had stopped
a civil war in Argentina simply by putting her body in the way. And there
she was to see Hutch. Not the commissioner. Not Asquith. But Priscilla
Hutchins. By name.

Asquith had asked her why, but Hutch had no idea.

"Whatever she wants," Asquith had instructed her, "don't commit the
Academy to *anything*. Tell her we'll take it under advisement."

He didn't offer to sit in.

*   *   *

HUTCH HAD SEEN Dr. Alva numerous times, of course. Everyone had. Who could forget the blood-soaked images of her kneeling over a dying girl during the aftershocks of the Peruvian earthquake of '21? Or leading the Counselor himself through the wreckage of Bellaconda after the Peacekeepers finally put down the rebels? Or charging out of the flyer in plague-ridden South Africa?

But when she came through the door, Hutch would not have recognized her. She seemed smaller somehow. The windblown hair was under control. There was no sign of the no-nonsense attitude that was such a large part of the legend. She was reserved, polite, almost submissive. A woman, perhaps, headed out shopping.

"Dr. Emerson," said Hutch, rising to greet her, "it's a privilege to meet you." Her voice went a few decibels higher than normal.

"Priscilla?" Alva stretched out her hand. "It's my pleasure."

Hutch directed her to a wing chair and sat down beside her. "I hope you didn't have any trouble finding the office."

Alva wore a pleated navy skirt and a light blue blouse beneath a frayed velomir jacket. Part of the image. Her hair had gone white, "in the service of the unfortunate," as Gregory MacAllister had once put it. She was probably the only public figure for whom MacAllister had ever found a kind word.

"None at all, thank you." She arranged herself, glanced around the office, and smiled approvingly. It was decorated with several of Tor's sketches, images of the Twins and of the Refuge at Vertical, of the illuminated *Memphis* gliding through starlight, of Hutch herself in an antique Phillies uniform. She smiled at that one, and her eyes settled on Hutch. They were dark and penetrating. Sensors, peering *through* the objects in the room. This was not a woman to be jollied along.

"What can I do for you, Doctor?" she asked.

"Priscilla, I need your help."

Hutch wanted to shift her weight. Move it around a bit. Force herself to relax. But she sat quite still. "In what way?"

"We need to do something about the omega."

At first Hutch thought she'd misunderstood. Alva was of course talking about the one headed toward Earth. When people said *the* omega, that was always the one they meant. "It won't become a problem for almost a thousand years," she said uneasily. "Were you suggesting—?"

"I was suggesting we find a way to stop it."

That was easy to say. "We've been doing some research."

"It's been more than twenty years, Priscilla. Or is it *Hutch*?"

"Hutch is good."

"Hutch." Her tone softened. "Somehow, in your case, it is a very feminine name."

"Thank you, Doctor."

"Alva."

Hutch nodded and tried the name. It was a bit like sitting with Washington and calling him *George.*

Alva leaned forward. "What have we learned so far?"

Hutch shrugged. "It's loaded with nanos. Some of our people think it can create gravity fields. To help it navigate."

"And it doesn't like artificial objects."

"Yes."

"Anything else?"

"There's a lot of dust and hydrogen. The clouds vary in size by a factor of about 30 percent. They coast along at a pretty good clip. In the range of 20 million klicks an hour."

"That's how fast it's coming? *Our* cloud?"

"Yes." Hutch thought for a minute. "Oh, and they seem to come in waves. We don't know how wide the waves are because we can't see the end of them. The local waves are 160 light-years apart, give or take, and one of them rolls through the solar system approximately every eight thousand years."

"But they're not always the same distance apart? The waves?"

"No. It's pretty erratic. At the beginning, we assumed that the local pattern held everywhere, and that there were literally millions of clouds drifting throughout the Orion Arm. But of course that's not true. Fortunately."

"Anything else?"

"The waves are arcing outward in the general direction that the galaxy is turning. Joining the flow, I suppose."

"And that's it?"

"Pretty much."

"It strikes me there's not much we didn't know twenty years ago. As to the questions that come to *my* mind, we don't know where they come from. Or why they behave the way they do. We don't even know if they're natural objects."

"That's correct."

"Or how to disable them."

Hutch got up. She could feel energy radiating out of the woman. "They're not easy to penetrate," she said.

Alva smiled. "Like a virgin."

Hutch didn't reply.

For a long moment, neither spoke. The commlink blinked a couple of times, then shut off. Incoming traffic. Hyperlight from Broadside, personal for her.

Alva smiled politely and fixed Hutch with those dark eyes. The woman looked simultaneously amused and annoyed. "Are we making a serious effort?"

"Well," said Hutch. "Of course."

"But we've nothing to show. After twenty years. Thirty years, actually."

"We're working on it." She was floundering.

Alva nodded. "We have to do better."

"Alva—" She had to struggle to say the word. "There's no hurry. I mean, the thing's a thousand years away."

Alva nodded again. But it wasn't a concession, an acknowledgment that she had a point. Rather it was a recognition that Hutch was behaving exactly as expected, saying precisely what Alva had known all along she would say. She straightened her collar. "Hutch, you've been to Beta Pac."

Home of the Monument-Makers, the lost race that had left majestic relics of their passing across several thousand light-years. Star-travelers while the Sumerians were learning to bake bricks. Nothing more than savages now, wandering through the ruins of their once-proud cities. "Yes, I've been there."

"I have *not*." Her eyes clouded. "I've seen quite enough decimation here at home." Another long silence ensued. Then: "I understand the Monument-Makers knew about the omegas. Well in advance of their appearance at Beta Pac."

"That's correct. They even tried to divert the things at Quraqua and at Nok. To save the local inhabitants."

"With no success."

Hutch saw where this was going. "They cut cube moons and inserted them in orbit around Nok hoping the cloud would go for them instead of the cities." She shrugged.

"In the end," said Alva, "they couldn't even save themselves."

"No. They couldn't. There's evidence they packed up a substantial chunk of the population and cleared out."

"Yet they had how long to prepare? Two thousand years?"

"A little longer, we think."

She was on her feet now, moving to the window, drawn by the sunlight, but still not looking at anything. "How do you think that could have happened? Are the clouds so irresistible that even the Monument-Makers, given two millennia, couldn't do something?"

"It's probably not easy. To stop one of the omegas."

"Hutch, I would suggest to you that two thousand years was too much time to get ready. That they probably put it off. Somebody else's problem. Get to it next year. Or sometime during the next century. And they continued delaying until it became too late."

"Maybe it's too late already," suggested Hutch. But she knew as soon as the words were out of her mouth that it had been the wrong thing to say.

Alva was a diminutive woman, but her presence filled the office. Overwhelmed it and left Hutch feeling like an intruder in her own space. "Maybe it is," Alva said. "But we'd best not make that assumption."

The office grew briefly darker, then brightened again. A cloud passing over the sun.

"You think," said Hutch, "we're going to let the situation get away from us."

Alva's eyebrows came together. "I *know* we are. What's going to happen is that people are going to talk and think exactly as you do. And, Hutch, *you've* seen these things in action. You know what they do." Her gaze turned inward. "Forgive me. I mean no offense. But the situation calls for honesty. We, too, are looking at the omegas as somebody else's problem. But when it comes, it will be *our* children who are here."

She was right, of course. Hutch knew that. Anyone who thought about the issue knew it.

Alva reached for a pad, scratched something on it, furrowed her brow. "Every day," she said, "it advances on us by a half billion kilometers."

It was late. It was past five o'clock and it had been a horribly long day. What did this woman want anyhow? "You understand," Hutch said, "I don't make Academy policy. You should be talking to Dr. Asquith."

"I wasn't trying to influence Academy policy. It's too far down the scale to worry about, Hutch. Any serious effort to do something about the omegas is going to require political will. That doesn't get generated here."

"Then I don't see—?"

"I didn't come looking to get Academy support for this. It's *your* support I want."

"Mine?"

"You're the public face of the Academy."

"No. You've got the wrong person. Eric Samuels is our public affairs chief."

"*You*, Hutch. You found the first cloud. You and Frank Carson and the others. Incidentally, someone told me you actually did the math. It was *you* who figured it all out. Is that true?"

"Yes," she said.

"And you're the woman from Deepsix. The woman who rescued her husband from that antique starship, the, what did you call it?"

"The *chindi*. But he wasn't my husband then."

"No matter. The point is you've been in the public eye for quite some time." She was back in her seat, leaning toward Hutch, old friends who had been in combat together. "Hutch, I need you."

"To—?"

"—become the public persona of the Omega Society."

Well, it didn't take a mathematician to figure out what the Omega Society was going to be doing. "Why don't *you* do it, Alva? You're a bit better known than I am." She managed a weak smile.

"I'm the wrong person."

"Why?"

"Because I'm associated with charities. With medical care. Nobody's going to take me seriously when I start talking about long-range destruction. *You* aren't taking me seriously and yet you know I'm right and I'm sitting in the same room with you."

"No, that's not true," said Hutch. "*I'm* taking you seriously."

The woman had an infectious smile. She turned it on Hutch, who bathed in its warmth and suddenly realized the secret of her success. The mental agility, the worthiness of her causes, her single-mindedness, none of it would have mattered without that pure living charm. *Nobody ever says no to me. Nobody turns away. This is the moment of decision.*

"I'd stay in the background, of course," she said. "Board of directors stuff. But I'd be there if needed. We'd have a couple of major league scientific people out front to direct things, to run the organization. To provide the muscle. But *you* would be its face. Its voice."

Alva was right. In a moment of startling clarity Hutch saw the centuries slipping away while the cloud drew closer. *Not our problem. There'll be a breakthrough. Don't worry.* How many times had she heard that already? But there probably wouldn't be. Not without a concerted effort. And maybe there was a window that might close. There'd been talk of an all-out program when we'd first learned about the clouds. But when the initial shock wore off, and people began thinking how far away the thirty-second century was . . . Well, it was like worrying about the sun exhausting its fuel.

If she accepted, Hutch would have to give up all claim to being taken seriously ever again. The few who worried about the omegas, even if they were backed by Alva, provided the material for late-night comedians. They were greeted in academic circles with amused smiles and people shaking their heads. And *she'd* be out front.

Alva saw she was reluctant. "Before you answer," she said, "I want to remind you that the public knows you're a hero. You've put yourself at risk on several occasions, and you've saved a few lives. You've gotten credit for your acts." The Academy's Johanssen Award, which she'd received after Deepsix, hung on one wall. Other plaques commemorated her accomplishments at the Twins and in the rescue of her husband. And, of course, there'd been the sim, in which Hutch had been portrayed by the smoky-voiced, statuesque Ivy Kramer. "This time," Alva continued, "there'll be no credit and no applause. No sim and probably no books. No one will ever really know what you've accomplished, because you'll have saved a world that's quite far away. And we do have short memories. You have a heroic past, Hutch. But *this* time, there isn't just *one* life, or a few lives, in the balance. Unless people like you come forward and act, we're all going the same way as the Monument-Makers."

The silence between them stretched out. The room seemed unsteady. "I'm sorry," said Hutch at last. "But I can't do this. It would involve a conflict of interest."

Don't look at me like that. It's true.

"My obligations to the Academy—I can't take up a cause like this and keep my job here. There's no way I can do it."

"We have adequate funding, Hutch. I'm sure you would find the compensation sufficient."

"I really can't do it," said Hutch. "I have responsibilities here."

Alva nodded. Sure. Of course you do. How could I not have seen it? Perhaps I misjudged you.

She gave Hutch time to reconsider her decision. Then she rose, and a business card appeared in her hand. "If you change your mind," she said, holding it out for her.

"I won't," said Hutch. "But I thank you for asking." And how hollow did *that* sound?

"I appreciate your hearing me out. I know you're a busy woman." Her gaze dissected Hutch and found her wanting. Not who I thought you were, it appears. Then she was gone, leaving Hutch with a feeling of rejection as overwhelming as any lover could have engendered.

THE TRANSMISSION THAT had come in during the interview was from Broadside, the newest of the deep-space bases maintained by the Academy. At a distance of more than three thousand light-years, it was three times as far as Serenity, which had for years been the most remote permanent penetration. Its operational chief was Vadim Dolinsk, an easygoing former pilot who was past retirement age but for whom she'd bent the rules because he was the right man for the job.

Vadim was seated at his desk, and his usual blasé expression had lengthened into a frown. *"Hutch,"* he said, *"we're getting a reading on one of the clouds. It's changing course."*

Hutch was suddenly aware of the room. Of the cone of light projecting down from the desk lamp, of the flow of warm air from the vents, of someone laughing outside in the corridor.

Ironic that this would happen on the day that Alva had asked for help and Hutch had brushed her aside. Even Alva had not seen the real danger, the *immediate* danger. A few years ago, one of the clouds had drifted through the Moonlight system, had spotted the ruins on the fourth world, and had gone after them like a tiger after a buck. What would have happened had they been populated? Millions would have died while the Academy watched, appropriately aghast, unable to help. In the end, they would have shaken their heads, made some philosophical remarks, and gone back to work.

Within the next ten years, clouds would approach seven planetary systems that the Academy knew about. All were presumed empty, because virtually all systems *were* empty. But who could be sure? The systems in question were outside the range of finances rather than technology, so she simply didn't know.

"Data's attached," Vadim continued. *"I've diverted the Jenkins to take a look. They were about to start home, so they won't be happy. But I think this is too important to let slide. I'll notify you when I have more.*

"How's life in Woodbridge these days?"

Not as good as it was an hour ago.

She looked at the numbers. The cloud in question was another five hundred light-years beyond Broadside. It was approaching a class-G sun known to have three gas giants, but that was all that *was* known about the system. The star was located in the direction of the Dumbbell Nebula.

There were images of the cloud, and she recognized the streamers exploding away from it, trying to continue along the original course while the cloud turned a few degrees onto a new vector.

It had spotted something.

NEWSDESK

MOB CHIEF ASSASSINATED IN PHILLY
Hobson Still Insists There Is No Mob

SALUTEX CEO INDICTED FOR INSIDER TRADING
McBrady Could Face Ten Years

MIRROR STRAIN SPREADING IN CENTRAL AMERICA
Dr. Alva Headed for Managua
Outbound Flights Halted

ECONOMY WORSENS
Recession Is Now Official

DEMONSTRATORS OUT IN FORCE AT POSTCOMM SUMMIT
Morrison Has No Sympathy
"They're Against Us, but They Have No Suggestions"

WASHINGTON AREA VOLCANO BECOMING ACTIVE AGAIN?
Disaster Center Issues Warning

ARAB PACT DEMANDS REPARATIONS
Claim Oil Supplies Sold At Fraction of Value To Keep West Afloat
Al-Kabarah: "Without Our Sacrifice, the World Would Still Be
in the 18th Century"

IS THERE REALLY A MULTIVERSE?
Gunderson Proposes Hunt for White Hole
"It's Out There Somewhere."

SYRACUSE COPS ARRESTED IN LIGHTBENDER CASE
ACLU Will File Suit To Ban Invisibility

TIME TRAVEL MAY BE POSSIBLE
Technitron Claims to Have Sent Stop Watch Forward Ten Seconds
Hoax or Error, Say Most Experts

GIANTS FAVORED IN TITLE GAME
Jamieson Says He Is Okay to Play

chapter 2

THE ARTIFICIAL INTELLIGENCE in all Academy ships had been given the name *Bill*. His demeanor, and his appearance, tended to change from vessel to vessel, depending on his relationship with the captain. Whatever seemed to work with a given personality type, under whatever local circumstances might prevail. He could be paternal in the best sense, quarrelsome, sympathetic, persistent, quiet, even moody. Bill was sometimes a young and energetic companion, sometimes a gray eminence.

The *Quagmor*'s version reminded Terry Drafts of his garrulous and mildly ineffectual uncle Clete. The AI took everything very seriously, and seemed a bit on the frivolous side. Terry had been asleep when Bill got him up and asked him to come to the bridge. Jane was waiting.

"What is it?" Terry Drafts was the most senior physicist on the Academy staff among those who had worked actively at trying to solve the various problems associated with the omega clouds. He had been with the Frank Carson group during the initial encounter, had watched that first cloud attack the decoy shapes that Carson had set out for it on the lifeless world now celebrated as Delta.

Terry had been so entranced by what he'd seen that he had dedicated his life to the omegas. He'd appeared before Congress, had done interviews, had written the definitive account, *Omega*, which had caused a brief stir, all in the hope of rallying public opinion.

But the problem was almost a thousand years away, and he'd never been able to get past that. In the end, he'd given up, and settled for spending his time on monitoring missions. It was Terry who'd discovered that the clouds incorporated nanotechnology, who'd theorized that they manipulated gravity to navigate, that their primary purpose was something other than the destruction of cities. "Horribly inefficient if that's what they're supposed to do," he'd argued in *Omega*. "Ninety-nine point nine percent of the things never *see* a civilization. They're something else—"

But what else, he didn't know.

Terry was tall, quiet, self-effacing. A believer. He was from the Ivory Coast, where they'd named a high school and a science wing at Abidjan University after him. He'd never married because, he'd once told an interviewer, he liked everybody.

At the beginning of his career, he'd formulated a series of ambitions, which awards he hoped to win, what level of prestige he hoped to achieve, what he wanted to accomplish. It had all narrowed down to a single unquenchable desire: to find a way to throttle the clouds.

One of them was currently on the ship's scanners. As was something else.

"I have no idea what it is," said Jane. It was an object that looked vaguely like an artistically exaggerated thistle, or a hedgehog. It was enormously larger than the *Quagmor*. "Just spotted it a couple minutes ago."

Jane Collins was the ship's captain, and the only other person on board. She was one of Terry's favorite people, for reasons he'd have had trouble putting into words. She was in her sixties, with grandchildren out there somewhere. Pictures of them decorated the bridge. She was competent, he could trust her, and she was good company.

"It looks artificial," he said. But not like any kind of vessel or package he'd ever seen. Spines stuck out all over it. They were rectangular and constructed with geometric precision.

"There's somebody else out here," said Terry, barely able to contain his excitement. Someone else worrying about the omegas.

"*It has a low-level magnetic field,*" said Bill. "*And it is running on the same course as the cloud.*"

"You're sure, Bill?" asked Jane.

"*No question.*"

"Is it putting out a signal?"

"*Negative,*" said Bill. "*At least, nothing I can detect.*"

"Odd," said Jane. "Range to the cloud, Bill?"

"*Sixty thousand kilometers.*" In their rear. "*Something else: It is moving at the same velocity as the cloud. Or if not, it is very close to it.*"

"Pacing it."

"*Yes. It appears so.*"

"Somebody's keeping an eye on the thing," said Terry. "Bill, is the cloud likely to enter any system in the near future?"

"*I have been looking. I cannot see that it could pose a near-term threat to anyone.*"

"How about long-term?"

"*Negative. As far forward as I can track with confidence, I see no intersection with, or close passage past, any star system.*"

"How far forward," asked Jane, "can you project? With confidence?"

"One point two million years."

Then what was it doing here? In a half century, no one had yet run into any living creatures with star travel. They'd hardly run into any living creatures, period. "Bill, what are we getting from the sensors?"

"The exterior is stony with some nickel," said the AI. *"But it's hollow."* He put a picture of the object on-screen. The projections were blunted triangles. There was a wide range of sizes. They were similar to each other, although of different designs, some narrow, some wide, all flat on top. The overall effect was of a hedgehog covered, not with spines, but with sculpted polygons.

"Can you tell what's inside?"

"Not clearly. Seems to be two chambers in the base unit. And shafts in the spines. Beyond that I can't make out any details."

"The spines?" asked Jane.

"Some of them measure out to a bit over two kilometers." Taller than the world's tallest skyscraper. *"If we consider it as a globe, with the tips of the longest spines marking the limits of the circumference, the diameter is six and a half kilometers. The central section is about two kilometers."* Bill's image appeared, seated in a chair. Although he could summon whatever likeness he wished, he usually showed up in his middle-aged country lord demeanor. Beige jacket with patched elbows, cool dark eyes, black skin, silver cane, receding silver hair. *"It's a polyhedron,"* he said. *"Specifically, a rhombicosidodecahedron."*

"A what?"

"It has 240 sides."

"It's an odd coincidence," he said.

"What is?"

"We know the clouds rain down fire and brimstone on anything that has right angles."

"Okay."

Terry pointed an index finger at the image on the screen. "This thing is loaded with right angles. That's what it is: An oversize complex of right angles."

They looked at one another. "Is it designed to be a target?" Jane asked. "Or are the clouds intended specifically to kill these things?"

"IT IS UNDER power," said Bill. *"There's only a trace, but we're getting an electronic signature."* It was rotating. The spines caught and manipulated light from the Bumblebee. *"Once every seven minutes and twelve seconds,"* Bill continued helpfully.

They had drawn within a hundred meters of the object. The spines turned slowly past them. Bill switched on the navigation lights so they could see better. Terry was reminded of the puzzles he used to do as a boy, enter here, find your way through the labyrinth, come out over there.

There were no sharp points anywhere. The tops of all the spines were flat. Ninety degrees.

Jane submitted a report to Serenity. While she talked, Terry studied the object. It had no thrusters, no visible communication devices, no sign of a hatch. It had enough dents and chips to suggest it was old. A couple of the spines had been broken off. Otherwise, the surface was smooth, as if it had come out of a mold. "Bill," he said, "train the lights into the notches. Let's see what it looks like down there."

It was a long way. No central surface was visible; the spines seemed simply to rise out of each other. Jane took them in almost close enough to touch.

The *Quagmor* was dwarfed.

"Still no reaction of any kind, Bill?"

"*Negative, Terry.*"

They approached the top of one of the spines. It was rectangular, about the dimensions of a basketball court, perfectly smooth save for a couple of chunks gouged out by collisions. The *Quagmor* passed over it, the ship's navigation lights sliding across the surface, over the edge and into a chasm. Then he was looking down the slanted side until the lights lost themselves in the depths, to reappear moments later coming back up another wall, wider and shorter and angled differently.

"Bill," he asked, "do you see any more of these things in the neighborhood?"

"*Negative. I haven't been able to do a complete sweep, but I do not see anything else.*"

Jane finished recording and sent her message on to Serenity. Then she got up and stood beside him, her hand on his shoulder. "I've always assumed the universe made sense, Terry," she said. "I'm beginning to wonder."

"I've been looking for a hatch."

"See anything?"

"Nope."

"Just as well. I don't think I'd want to go calling. Maybe we should try talking to it."

"You serious? From the looks of it, there hasn't been anything alive in there for the last few million years."

"That's an interesting estimate. It's derived from—?"

"It looks old."

"Good. In the end, I can always count on you to fall back on hardheaded logic." Her eyes sparkled. "You know, it might be programmed to respond to a signal."

"It's a thought." He swung around in his chair and gazed up at the AI's image. "Bill, we'll use the multichannel. Audio only."

"Ready when you are, Terry. The circuit is open."

"Okay." He leaned forward, feeling foolish, and allowed a glib tone to creep into his voice. "Hello out there. Is anybody home?"

Another spine rotated past.

"Hello. This is us out here talking to you over there." He looked at Jane. "Why are you laughing?"

"I was just thinking how you'd react if somebody answered."

He hadn't even considered the possibility. "We getting anything, Bill?"

"There is no response. No reaction of any kind."

He stayed with it a few minutes before giving up. The hedgehog sparkled and glowed in the lights of the *Quagmor*. His own interstellar artifact. "Going to have to break in," he said.

She shook her head. "Not a good idea. Serenity will have the information in a few hours, and they'll be sending somebody right out. Let's wait for them."

There was no way he was going to be sitting on his rear end when they got there, and have to confess he didn't know any more than he and Jane put in the report. "I want to see what's inside."

"We don't know what it is."

"That's why I'd like to see the inside."

"Let's let the experts do it."

"You know any experts on interstellar artifacts? Jane, nobody knows anything about this stuff. Nobody's better qualified to open it than you and I."

She made a face. Don't like the idea. Not a good move. "You know," she said, transparently trying to change the subject, "it's one of the loveliest things I've ever seen."

"You're kidding."

"No. I mean it."

"Jane, it has all the lines of a porcupine."

"No." She was looking past him, out the viewport at the bizarre landscape passing by. "It's a rhombi-whatever. It's magnificent." She turned a sympathetic smile on him. "You really don't see it, do you?"

"No." Terry followed her gaze, watched the shadows from the navigation lights creep up, down, and across the artifact's planes and angles. "I don't like the clouds. And I don't like these things." He got out of his chair and headed for the storage locker. "You want to come along?"

*   *   *

THEY STRAPPED ON e-suits, which would project a Flickinger field around them, protecting them from the void. The field was flexible, molded to the body except for a hard shell that arced over the face, providing breathing space.

They went down to the launch bay, picked up laser cutters and air tanks, and turned on the suits. While the bay depressurized, they did a radio check and strapped on wristlamps.

There was no launch vehicle in the bay, but it didn't matter because it wouldn't have been useful anyhow in the current situation. They pulled go-packs over their shoulders, and Terry hung an imager around his neck. "Bill," he said, "I'll record everything. Transmit live to Serenity."

"Do you really think it's that dangerous, Terry? Maybe we should reconsider what we're doing," said Bill.

"Just a precaution," he said.

Bill opened the airlock and admonished them to be careful.

They had left Serenity seven months earlier and had spent the entire time studying the omega. It had a numerical designation, as all the clouds did. But they'd gotten into the habit of referring to this one as George. George was apparently a onetime boyfriend of Jane's, although she refused to provide details. But it amused her to ridicule him. The cloud, she'd said, was inflexible, windy, and took up a lot of space. And it kept coming. No matter what you said or did, it kept coming.

George hung ominously in the background as Terry picked out a spine and directed Bill to match rotation with it, so that it became a stable fixture a few meters from the airlock.

The *Quagmor*, which was affectionately referred to by almost everyone as the *Quagmire*, was the first research vessel designed specifically to operate near the clouds without fear of drawing the lightning. Unlike the polygon object it was inspecting, it had no right angles. The ship's hull, her engine mounts, her antennas, sensing, and navigation equipment, everything, was curved.

They'd even penetrated George's surface mists, gone a few hundred meters into the cloud, taken samples, and tried to listen for the heart of the beast. That was a joke between them, a reaction to the insistence of one school of thought that the clouds were *alive*. It was not a view that Terry took seriously. Yet plunging into it had given him the eerie sensation that there might be some truth to the notion. It was a view easily dismissed when they'd emerged. Like laughing at ghosts when the sun was high.

"Ready?" asked Jane.

"All set." He was standing at the edge of the airlock trying to decide on a trajectory. This was the first time they'd been outside the ship on this run, except for a brief repair job on the forward sensor pods; Terry nevertheless had long experience working in the void. "There," he said, pointing.

One of the higher spines. Nice broad top for them to land on. Easy spot to start. Jane shook her head, signifying that she'd done dumber things but was having trouble remembering when. They exchanged looks that were supposed to register confidence, and he pushed out of the lock, floated across the few meters of space that separated the ship and the spine, and touched down on his target. But the stone surface was slippery, slippery even for the grip shoes, and momentum carried him forward. He slid off the edge, blipped the go-pack, did a 360, and came down smoothly atop the crest.

"Nice maneuver, Flash," said Jane.

"Be careful," he said.

She floated over and drifted gently onto the surface, letting him haul her down. "It's all technique," she said.

Terry rapped on the stone with the handle of the cutter. "Feels solid," he said. "See any way in?"

She shook her head. No.

He looked into the canyon. Smooth rock all the way down, until the beam faded out. The spine widened as it descended. It looked as if they all did.

"Shall we see what's below?" he asked.

She was wearing a dark green pullover and light gray slacks. A bit dressy for the work. "Sure," she said. "Lead the way."

He stepped into the chasm and used the go-pack to start down. Jane followed, and they descended slowly, examining the sheer wall as they went.

Plain rock. Smoother than on the roof, because the lower areas took fewer hits. But there was nothing exceptional, all the way to the bottom.

BILL MANEUVERED THE *Quagmire* directly overhead, leaving the spotlights off because they would have been a distraction. But the navigation lights were on.

There was nothing in Terry's experience to which he could compare the place. The spines did indeed grow out of one another. There was no flat or curved surface at the center of the object that could have been described as housing the core. It was dark, surreal, the *Quagmire* no more than a few lights overhead, and the rest of the world walled out.

Terry felt light-headed. Even in the vacuum, he was accustomed to having a flat space underfoot, a moonscape, a ship's hull, *something*. Something to relate to. Here, there was no up or down, and everything was at an angle. "You okay?" she asked.

"I'm fine," he said.

He took the cutter out of his harness. "There's a chance," he said, "that this thing is under pressure. I'm just going to cut a narrow hole until we know. But stand clear anyhow. Just to be safe."

She nodded and backed off a few meters. Told him to be careful. Not to stand in front of it.

Terry grinned. How could he make the cut standing over to one side? He pressed the activator and watched the amber lamp come on, felt the unit vibrate as it powered up. "Big moment," he said. The lamp turned a bright crimson. He punched the button, and a long red beam of light blinked on. He touched it to the wall.

It cut in. He knew not to lean on it, but simply held it steady while it went deeper.

Jane advanced a few steps. "How's it going?"

He was about to suggest she try a little patience when it broke through. "Bingo," he said.

Somewhere deep in the hedgehog, he sensed movement, as if an engine had started. Then the ground murmured. It trembled. Rose. Shook violently. He told Jane to get out, for God's sake get out, and he stabbed at the go-pack and the thrusters ignited and began to take him up.

And the world went dark.

ARCHIVE

Sky, we lost contact with the *Quagmire* moments ago. Divert. Find out what happened. Render assistance. Report as soon as you have something.

—Audrey D'Allesandro,
Hyperlight transmission to the *Patrick Heffernan*

chapter 3

THE *CHINDI* HAD finally begun giving up its secrets. The gigantic alien starship, apparently fully automated, continued its serene slower-than-light voyage toward a class-F star whose catalog number Hutch could never remember. It had taken a major effort, because of its velocity, to get researchers on board. But the Academy had begun to get a good look at its contents, artifacts from hundreds of cultures. And live visual recordings over a span of tens of thousands of years. The ship itself was thought to be more than a quarter million years old.

Its pictures of lost civilizations were opening up whole new areas of knowledge. The vast distances that separated sentient species tended to create the illusion that civilizations were extremely rare. It now appeared they were simply scattered, in time and in space. And, disconcertingly, they did not seem to last long.

They were sometimes suicidal. They were often destroyed by economic, political, or religious fanaticisms; by the selfishness and corruption of leaders; by an inability to stop ever-more-deadly wars. They sometimes simply behaved in stupid ways. Two that had avoided the more obvious pitfalls were swept away by something that should not have been there: the clouds.

Hutch had always felt a special kinship with the Monument-Makers, who'd roamed this section of the galaxy for thousands of years, who'd tried to save others from the omegas. She had been to their home world, and had seen the remnants of a race reduced to savagery, unaware of their proud history. They'd been on her mind recently because the *chindi* had, a week ago, provided a record of another demolished culture. She'd sat during the course of a bleak wintry day looking at pictures of smashed buildings and ruined cities. And she'd recognized some of the images. It was the home of the Hawks, the race that had come to the rescue centuries ago on Deepsix when the inhabitants of that unlucky world had faced a brutal ice age.

The images haunted her, the broken columns, the brave symbols scrolled across monuments and public buildings, the overgrown roads, the shattered towers, the cities given over to forest. And perhaps most compelling, the starship found adrift in a solar orbit.

The Hawks and the Monument-Makers. And the human race. It was hard not to dwell on what might have been, had they been allowed to sit down together, to pool their knowledge and their speculations. To cooperate for the general good. To become allies in the great adventure.

As has happened with the Monument-Makers, a few individual Hawks had survived. But their civilization was gone. Their racial memory consisted only of a cycle of myths.

Kellie Collier had been there, had been first to board the Hawk starship, and had complained later to Hutch about the cost imposed by the existence of the clouds. There had been tears in her eyes when she described what she'd seen.

KELLIE AND THE broken cities and the clouds were never far from Hutch's mind. The chilling possibility that they were about to experience another wipeout had kept her awake these last two nights. It would be the most painful of ironies if they had finally found a living civilization, someone other than the Noks, that they could actually talk to, just in time to say good-bye.

The cloud in question was at a substantial distance, more than thirty-one hundred light-years. Nine months away. The *Bill Jenkins* was enroute, diverted from its survey mission by the station at Broadside. But they'd need a month to get there. Add another week for the report to reach her. It would be April before she knew whether she had a problem.

Prudence, and experience, suggested she expect the worst.

She arrived at the Academy bleary-eyed and in a foul mood. She'd talked it over at home with Tor, but all he could think of was to suggest she ease the pressure on herself by quitting. *We can live comfortably on my income,* he'd suggested. He was a commercial artist, and the money was decent, although they weren't going to wind up with a chalet in the Rockies and a beach home on Sea Island.

She needed to talk to somebody. The commissioner wasn't the right person either, so she put in a call to Harold as soon as she arrived at her desk. He wasn't in yet, his watch officer explained, but they would contact him. Five minutes later he was on the circuit. Just leaving home.

"Harold," she asked, "have you had breakfast yet?"

"*No,*" he said. "*I usually eat in the Canteen.*"

"How about eating with me this morning? My treat."

"*Is there a problem?*" he asked cautiously.

"I need your advice."

"Okay. What did you have in mind?"

"Meet me at Cleary's," she said. "Twenty minutes okay?"

CLEARY'S WAS THE small, posh coffee shop overlooking the Refuge, the alien habitat that had been hauled in from the Twins and reconstructed on a platform at the edge of the Potomac in Pentagon Park. The sun was warm and bright, and the sky full of lazy clouds. When Harold walked in, Hutch was sitting in a corner booth, stirring coffee and staring out the window, her mind gone for a gallop. She didn't see him until he slid in across from her.

"This is a pleasant surprise, Priscilla." He smiled shyly.

She knew that she intimidated him, but didn't know why. She'd noticed it years before when she'd provided transportation for him on a couple of occasions. It didn't seem to be all women, just her. "It's always good to get away for a bit," she said. She asked him a few questions about Weatherman, and the tewks, to put him at his ease.

Cleary's used human waiters. A young woman brought more coffee, and some orange juice.

"So what did you actually want to talk to me about?" he asked.

She told him about the report from Broadside that a cloud was changing course. Heading insystem.

His eyes dropped to the table. "That's unsettling." He picked up his spoon, fiddled with it, put it back down, gazed out at the Potomac. "Well," he said finally, "with any kind of luck, it'll be a false alarm."

She looked at him.

"Priscilla," he said, "it doesn't matter. Whatever it turns out to be, there'll be nothing you can do."

"There might be somebody out there."

"—In its path. I understand that." He tasted his coffee, patted his lips with a napkin, shrugged. "If there is someone there, they'll have to look out for themselves."

He was trying to be detached, but she heard the resignation in his voice. "To be honest, Hutch," he continued, "it's not worth worrying about. Not if we can't intervene. Anyway, at most it will probably turn out to be more ruins. That's all they ever find out there anyhow." The waitress was back. "Bacon and eggs," he said. "Home fries and toast."

She'd heard that he was supposed to be on a diet, egg whites and bran flakes, that sort of thing. But she said nothing, and ordered French toast. What the hell.

When the waitress was gone, he sat back and made himself comfortable. She liked Harold. He got the job done, never complained, and on Family Day had made a big fuss over Maureen. "Is that why you asked me here?" he said. "The omega?"

Hutch nodded. "Assume the worst happens. Somebody's in the way. Is there really nothing we can do to disable this thing? Blow it up? Scatter it? Something?"

It was a lovely morning, crisp and clear. The Potomac, which had risen considerably during the last century, and was still rising, was not unlike a small inland sea. The Capitol, the White House, most of the monuments, were islands now. Hutch had been around long enough to remember when Rock Creek Park could be reached on foot, when you didn't need a boat to get to the Washington Monument. You could stand out there now on one of the piers, and watch the river, and look out toward Sagitta, which was where the local cloud was, the one with Arlington's number on it, and you got a sense that despite everything, despite the extended life spans and the superluminals and the virtual disappearance of organized violence on the planet, civilization was still losing ground.

"If it had a physical core of some sort," Harold was saying, "a vital part, then *yes*. We could go after it. Take a hammer to it. But it seems to be holistic. Throw as many nukes at it as we like and it simply seems to pull itself back together."

"We don't know how it does that?"

His jaws worked. "It's not my field. But no, as far as I'm aware, we have no idea. The technology is well beyond anything *we* know about. It uses nanos, but we haven't been able to figure out how they work, what they do, even how they guide the cloud." He took a long sip of orange juice. "I look at what those things can do, and I look at the fact they seem to be only dust and hydrogen, and I feel as if I should be sitting off somewhere beating a drum. It's a whole new level of technology."

Their food came. Harold dumped a substantial amount of catsup on his potatoes.

"Of course," he continued, "the real problem is that we can't seem to penetrate the cloud. Ships don't come back. Probes disappear. Even scans and sensors don't give us much." He sampled the eggs, smiled with satisfaction, covered his toast with strawberry jam, and bit off a piece. "Good stuff," he said. "This where you normally eat?"

"Usually at home," she said.

"Yes." He studied her. "You survived one of those things, Hutch," he continued. "You were actually inside it, weren't you? When it came down on Delta?"

Hutch had been with Frank Carson that day. Thirty years ago—my God, had it really been that long?—when they'd deliberately baited a cloud, had structured some plateaus to look artificial, and had watched with horror as the monster came after them. "Yes," she said. "I was there."

"You survived it."

"Heaviest weather I've ever seen. Lightning. Tornado winds. Meteors. Not the way you'd want to spend a weekend."

He used his toast and a fork to finish off the eggs. "Well, I can understand you might be worried. Where did you say this thing is?"

"Out near the Dumbbell."

"My God. It's really over in the next county, isn't it? Well, look, your role, it seems to me, is simple. These things attack cities. If it turns out there are actually inhabitants, you just sail in, tell them what's coming, and they can head for the hills. Or maybe they could build themselves some underground shelters."

Out along the pier a gaggle of kids were trying to get a kite in the air and not having much luck. Beyond, a few sails drifted on the river.

The kite was red, and it had a dragon on it.

She needed a dragon.

WHEN SHE GOT back to her office, she called the Lunar Weapons Lab, which had been founded twenty years earlier for the express purpose of developing something that could be used against the omega clouds. The weapons lab was under the control of the Science Advisory Commission, which was a quasi-independent group overseen by the World Council. Like the Academy, it was underfunded.

Arky Chan, the assistant director, was an old friend. He greeted her with a cheery good morning. "We hear," he said, "you're taking over permanently up there."

"They don't tell me anything, Arky." Thirty-three years ago, on her first flight beyond the solar system, Arky had been one of her passengers. His black hair had grayed only slightly since then, and his smile was as infectious as ever.

"What can I do for you, Hutch?" he asked.

"Find me the key." It was code for a way to neutralize the clouds.

He nodded. "Anything else while I'm at it? Maybe produce the universal solvent? Or a time machine?"

"I'm serious. What's on the table?"

"Why? What's happening?"

"One of the damned things changed course."

"I heard. You have anything yet on what's in its path?"

"A G-class sun. Presumably a planetary system to go with it. We're still waiting. I'm hoping it just picked up some natural formations and got confused." That had happened once. A group of remarkably straight stress fractures on a satellite had been attacked. Whatever else the damned things were, they were *not* bright.

"I hope so too. But no, Hutch, I'm sorry to say we haven't really made any progress."

"Nothing at all?"

"They don't give us any money, love. And the Academy doesn't give us any ships." That was pointed at her.

"You have *one*."

"The Rajah *spends more time in the garage than it does in the field."*

"That'll change," said Hutch. She'd been trying to free up some money for more than a year.

"Well, I'm glad to hear it, but to tell you the truth, I'll believe it when I see it. What we need is for the cloud to be sitting up over the Capitol. Put a couple of bolts down the pants of the Congress. Then they'd damn soon get serious."

"You have anything at all we can use, if it becomes necessary?"

"Not really."

"How about nukes?"

"We tried that at Moonlight."

"How about something bigger? A supernuke? Or maybe we shovel a load of antimatter into it?"

"The problem we keep having is that the thing seems always able to reconstitute itself. Somewhere it has a heart, a control pod, an AI, probably. But we don't know where it is, we can't probe it, we're blind—" He held out his hands. *"If you have an idea, I'd love to hear it."*

"Arky, if that thing's bearing down on somebody, I don't want to be in the position of having to just sit here and watch."

"I understand completely."

"Find me something. Just in case."

"Look." His voice got cold. *"It's easy enough for you to demand a miracle. But you people are the ones who keep saying there's plenty of time, don't worry about it, we have other priorities right now."*

SHE HAD LUNCH with Tom Callan, her number two guy. Tom was assistant director of operations for special projects. He'd been, in her opinion, the most capable of the applicants for the D.O.'s job, except herself, of course. Tom was young, ambitious, energetic, and if he hung around long enough, would undoubtedly succeed her. That would be as high as he could go in the Academy, however. The commissioner was a political appointment, and the position never went to anybody in-house.

Tom held a license to pilot superluminals, he could work under pressure, and he didn't mind making decisions. He was about average size, with clean-cut good looks, but without the intensity one usually found in able young people who'd already climbed pretty high. Probably because he knew he was good. "I was thinking maybe," he said, "if we had to, we could decoy the damned thing."

"How would you go about it? A projection?"

"That's what I had in mind."

"Throw a big cube out there for it to chase."

"Yes." He bit into a turkey sandwich. "It might work. We've never experimented with it, so we don't really know. It would help if we knew what kind of sensory system it uses."

If it were strictly visual, then a big picture of a box might be enough. "Let's look into it," she said. "Check the literature. See if you can find anything that either supports the idea or negates it."

"Okay."

"And, Tom. Priority. If there's a problem, we won't have much time."

"Consider it done." He took a long pull at his iced tea and went after the sandwich again. The kid had an appetite. "There *is* a good chance it wouldn't be fooled by a holocast."

"I know."

"We might try a backup."

"What did you have in mind?"

"Be ready to put a *real* box out there."

THAT BROUGHT HER back to the kite with the dragon. Her first afternoon call went to Rheal Fabrics. Rheal specialized in producing a range of plastics, films, and textiles for industry. (They also had a division that operated a chain of ice-cream outlets.) Hutch had, on a number of occasions, taken their executives out to Serenity, and she had kept in contact with several over the years.

One of them was Shannon McKay, who had something to do with R&D. Shannon was tall, redheaded, and very much in charge.

They did a couple of minutes' small talk, during which Hutch got congratulated on her forthcoming promotion. She was surprised that Shannon knew. "We keep track of the important stuff," Shannon said. The Academy was a major customer for Rheal, so it made sense that they would.

"I need a feasibility study," Hutch said. She explained what was happening, emphasized that it would probably amount to nothing, but that if a difficult situation arose, she wanted to be ready to deal with it. "I might need a kite," she said. "A big one."

Shannon nodded. "Give me the dimensions."

Who knew? Who had the slightest idea? She tried some numbers and Shannon said okay. They could do it.

"How long will it take?" A blue lamp blinked on. And Harold's name. He was on the line, waiting to talk to her.

"How long do we have?"

"From the time you get the go-ahead, not much more than a week. At best."

"You're kidding."

"Can you manage it?"

"Let me look into it. I'll get back to you."

"YES, HAROLD."

"Thought you'd like to know. We've got another one."

"Another *what?*"

"Another tewk." A quasi nova. It was the first time she'd heard him use the term his people had coined. Short for Tewksbury Object. The pride in his voice was evident.

"Okay."

"Different spectrogram. Different color. But the same essentials."

"Same area?"

"Other side of the sky. Different Weatherman."

"Okay. You're sure it's a tewk and not a nova?"

"We're sure."

"All right, Harold. Keep me posted."

"It's very strange."

"When you want to make an announcement, let me know."

SHE DIRECTED THE AI to get Marge Conway for her at the International Bureau of the Climate in London. Twenty minutes later Marge was on the circuit. *"Been a long time,"* she said. *"What can I do for you, Hutch?"*

Marge and Hutch had been friends at Princeton a long time back, had once competed for a boyfriend, now best forgotten, and had kept in touch over the years. Marge had been thin and quiet in those days. Later she'd become a bodybuilder. She'd gone through several husbands. Wore them out, people said behind her back.

"Is there a way to generate a cloud cover?" Hutch asked. "For maybe a few days. Hide some stuff."

"Cloud cover?"

"Yes. I'm talking about a terrestrial atmosphere—"

"Not Earth."

"No."

"Okay. How big would the coverage be?"

"Planetary."

She shook her head. *"No. A few thousand square klicks, maybe, yes. But that's about the limit."*

"What would it take?"

"You'll need some landers."

"Okay. That's no problem."

"Four of them. Plus a hauler. An AV3 would probably be best."

"All right. What else?"

"How much time do we have?"

"To put it together? Ten days. Maybe a week. No more than that."

"That's a bit of a rush."

"I know."

"And we'd need a helicopter."

"A helicopter? What's that?"

"Antique aircraft. Propellers on top."

"Marge, where am I supposed to get a helicopter?"

"Work it out. Keep it small, by the way. The helicopter."

"I'll see what I can do."

"Okay. Let me take a look at things on this end. I'll get back to you."

Marge broke the connection and Hutch called Barbara, the Academy AI. "Find out where there's an air show. Antique aircraft. I'll want to talk to whoever's in charge."

SHE DISPOSED OF her routine work, handing most of it over to assistants. Eric called to remind her that she'd be expected to make a few remarks at Sylvia Virgil's retirement.

That was tonight! She'd forgotten. *"And you'll be handing out one of the awards,"* he added.

"Okay."

She had started making notes on what she would say when the commlink blipped again. This time it was the commissioner's three short bursts. She answered, was asked to wait, the commissioner would be with her momentarily, then Asquith's plump, smiling features filled the screen.

"Hutch," he said, *"do you have a minute?"*

"Yes, Michael. What can I do for you?"

"Why don't you come over to the office? I need to talk to you."

When she got there, the blinds were drawn. Asquith waved her in, got up, and came around to the front of his desk. It was a substantial walk because the thing was the size of a soccer field. The office was ringed with leather chairs and walnut side tables. The walls were decorated with pictures of the Andromeda Galaxy and the Twins and the North American Nebula and the Refuge sitting out on the Potomac. Several lamps glowed softly.

"Hutch." He angled one of the chairs for her. "How are you doing today?"

"Fine, Michael," she said, warily.

He waited until she'd sat down. "Well, last day for Sylvia, I guess." He managed to look wistful while adjusting the blinds, brightening the room somewhat. Then he went back behind his desk. "The Academy's going to miss her."

"Yes, we will."

"Pity about—" He stopped midsentence, shrugged, and she knew exactly what he was implying. Virgil was retiring under pressure after a couple of major embarrassments. Three people had died a year ago when the *Yves Vignon* had collided with Wayout Station. The problem had been traced to equipment maintenance, and ultimately to a negligent supervisor, but some of it had inevitably washed off on the director of operations at the Academy. And then, just a few months later, a breakdown in scheduling had left the Berkeley mission temporarily stranded at Clendennon III. Not Sylvia's fault, but she'd taken the hit anyhow, just as she had six years ago when Renaissance Station had been destroyed by a massive flare. Renaissance had remained operational for political reasons, and against her continued protests. But none of it had mattered. "Should have kept an eye on things myself," Asquith had told a group of Academy researchers. "Sylvia tried to get it right. Not really her fault. Bad luck."

Truth be told, Hutch's opinion of Sylvia hadn't been all that high, but that didn't change the reality that she'd been left hanging in the wind. And that Hutch herself now worked for a guy who would go missing at the first sign of trouble.

"Hutch," he said, "I know you're busy, so I won't take your time."

"It's okay, Michael. What can I do for you?"

He opened a drawer and brought out a cream-colored folder, which he opened and placed on his desk. She couldn't see what it was. "You've done a good job here over the last couple of years." He extracted a document from the folder and gazed fondly at it. It crackled in his hands. "Congratulations," he said, holding it out for her.

She looked down at it. Saw the Academy's coat of arms. And her name.

Priscilla Maureen Hutchins. Promoted to grade fifteen. Director of Operations. Effective Tuesday, March 4, 2234.

In eight days.

He extended a hand across the desk and beamed at her. "I wish you a long and happy career, Priscilla."

"Thank you." It felt good.

"There'll be a formal presentation early next week. But I wanted you to know." He took the document back and returned it to its drawer. "We'll give it to you then."

"I appreciate your confidence, Michael." While there had been a selection panel, she knew she would not have been chosen without the commissioner's approval.

He broke out a bottle. "Vintage pavlais," he said. And, reading the label, "Twenty-one ninety."

Expensive enough to pay the mortgage for a month.

He produced an opener, wrestled the cork out of the bottle, and filled two glasses. She was tempted to embrace him. But the formality of the occasion overwhelmed the impulse. "To you, Hutch," he said. "Never let go."

It was an echo of the now-celebrated comment by Randall Nightingale, when, with bleeding and broken hands, he'd pulled her out of the clouds over Deepsix. *I'd never have dropped you, Hutch.* It had become a kind of informal Academy watchword.

Their eyes met over the rims of the glasses. Then the moment passed, and it was back to work. He handed her a disk and a sheaf of documents. "You'll want to look at these," he said. "It's all administrative stuff, position description, personnel considerations, and so on. And there are a few operational issues in there you'll need to do something with."

Hutch was no connoisseur, but she knew good wine when she tasted it. He held out the bottle for her. Did she want more?

Yes! But she was too well bred to drink up the man's expensive store. As a compromise, she accepted a half glass. "Michael," she said, "did you know one of the clouds has changed course?"

"Yes," he said. "I heard."

"I'm concerned there might be somebody out there."

He beamed. Not to worry. "Let's wait and see," he said.

"If there is, would the Academy support intervention?"

His face wrinkled and he made growling noises in his throat. "That could get a little uncomfortable, couldn't it?"

"We'd probably have to violate the Protocol."

He waved the problem away. "No," he said. "Don't worry about it. There's no one there."

"How can you be sure?"

"There's *never* anybody there." He smiled paternally at her and studied his glass. "I've been in this office, or otherwise associated with the Academy, for more than twenty years. Do you know how many times we've gotten reports that somebody thought they'd found someone? And you know how many times it actually happened?"

"Once," she said. That would be the Angels. Airborne forest creatures on Paradise.

"That's right. And you were there for that one. Now if we go back another twenty-five years, there's another. That makes *two*. In all that time. Out of thousands of systems visited. *Two*. I suggest we put it aside and find more important things to worry about."

The door opened behind her, as if by magic, and he was ushering her out of the room.

"If it happens," she persisted, "we're going to be pressed for time."

"We'll worry about it when it does, Priscilla." His smile disappeared as if someone had thrown a switch.

HUTCH CALLED UP the archive files on the *Pasquarella*, the first vehicle lost researching the clouds. That had been twenty years before. It was a voice-only, the voice belonging to Meg Campbell, the only person on the ship. Hutch had seen Meg once, from the back of a lecture hall. She'd been a tall woman, dark hair, lots of presence. Very sure of herself.

Hutch played it through, listened to the voice she remembered, not from the long-ago presentation, but because she'd played that same record any number of times before. Meg had gone three times into the cloud, each descent deeper, each time encountering more electronic interference.

She hadn't come back from the third descent. A search had revealed nothing, and on July 14, 2211, the *Pasquarella* was officially designated lost.

In the middle of the recording, Barbara's voice broke in. "*Transmission for you, ma'am. From Serenity.*"

She switched off the recording. "Put it up, Barb."

As soon as she saw Audrey's face, she knew there was bad news. "*Hutch,*" Audrey said, "*we lost contact with the* Quagmor *at 0014 hours 24 February. The AI went down without warning. They found an artifact yesterday in the vicinity of the Bumblebee and were investigating. The* Heffernan *has been diverted and will arrive in the area in three days. Record from* Quagmor *is attached.*"

Her stomach churned. It was possible there was nothing more to it than a communication breakdown. Then she watched the attached report.

NEWSDESK

PITCHERS, CATCHERS REPORT TO SPRING TRAINING
Forty-six Teams Start Today

STRANDED ORCA RESCUED IN PUGET SOUND

AMERICAN HIGH SCHOOL STUDENTS STILL LOSING GROUND
Who Was Churchill? Nobody Knows

GOMORRAH COUNTY RESIDENTS SUE TO CHANGE NAME

MASKED ROBBER WEARS NAME ON ARM
Tattoo Leads to Arrest

ORBITAL AMUSEMENT PARK GETS OKAY
ZeroGee Will Open in Two Years

UNN SURVEY: HALF OF ALL AMERICANS BELIEVE ASTROLOGY WORKS

WHO WILL BE ONE-HUNDREDTH PRESIDENT?
Campaign Gets Under Way in Utah, Ontario

BASEBALL: MOVE TO OUTLAW ENHANCEMENTS GAINS STEAM
Evidence Mounts of Long-term Damage

GREAT GATSBY FIRST EDITION SELLS FOR 3.6 MILLION

IBC WARNS OF STRONGER HURRICANES
Southern Coast Overdue for Big One

chapter 4

EXCEPT FOR ONE person, the research team on the *Jenkins* was delighted to be diverted. The fact that an omega had veered into a planetary system might mean they were close to finding the grail, a living alien civilization. A real one, something more exotic than the Angels, who were pretechnological barbarians, or the Noks, who were industrial-age barbarians. The exception was Digby Dunn, who would ordinarily have joined in the general elation. But Digby was in love with the captain. Her name was Kellie Collier, and Digby's passion for her was both intense and unrelenting.

On the whole, it had been a painful experience. Love affairs always include an element of discomfort; it is part of what makes them life-changing ventures. But this one had been extraordinarily difficult. Passengers may not touch the captain. Bad for morale and all that. Impossible situation, Digger. We'll just have to wait until we get clear. Be patient and everything'll be fine.

She smiled, that gorgeous, alluring smile, rendered even more seductive because she was trying to make it impersonal, friendly, understanding. Lose my job, she'd added on occasion when he'd tried to press her.

They'd been headed back to the station when the call came. We've got an omega changing course. Turn left and find out what's going on. See what it's after.

So Digby, an anthropologist by trade, but riding as a volunteer with a survey mission that was gathering information about local stars and planetary systems, pretended to be pleased, exchanged platitudes with everybody, and aimed pained glances at Kellie.

"Sorry," she told him. "But look, it'll be quick. In and out, see what's there, and then back to Broadside. We're only talking a couple of extra weeks."

She was tall and lovely with soft black skin and luminous eyes and she made every other woman in his life seem hopelessly dull. Ah yes, how he'd like to take her out on an expedition to unearth a few ancient cookpots.

But he resigned himself to making an occasional grab, which she usually—but not always—declined with stern disapproval. "Be patient," she told him. "Our time is coming."

The *Jenkins* was more than three thousand light-years out, and they held the current record for going farther from Earth than any other ship. They'd been away from Broadside almost a year. It had been a long and lonely voyage by any standard, broken only by an occasional rendezvous with a supply vessel.

A rendezvous was always a special occasion. There had been a push at the Academy to automate replenishment, to send the sandwiches in a ship directed only by an AI. Asquith had been unable to see the point of sending a captain along since it cost a great deal more, and it was hard to visualize a situation in which human judgment might be needed. But somebody apparently understood what seeing a fresh face could mean when you were out in the deeps.

Jack Markover had thrown his weight into the fight by threatening to quit and hold a news conference if they took the human captains off the run. The commissioner had backed down, pretended it had been someone else's idea, and it had been quietly put aside.

Jack was the chief of mission. He was a little man with a hawk face and too much energy. He loved his work and, if he'd been forced to follow through on his threat, would not have survived. He talked about retirement a lot, usually during the gray hours when the *Jenkins* was in hyperflight, and the hours were long and quiet. But Digger knew he'd never step down, that one day they'd have to haul him off and lock him away.

Digger had never quite figured out what Jack's specialty was. He was from the American Midwest, a quiet, dedicated type with doctorates in physics and literature. There seemed to be no field of human knowledge in which he did not speak as an expert. Acquainted with all, he was fond of saying, knowledgeable in none.

The comment could hardly have been less true. Where Digger knew the ground, the man inevitably had his facts down. He was the only person Digger knew who could explain Radcliffe's equations, quote *Paradise Lost*, discuss the implications of the *Dialogues*, play Mozart with panache, and hold forth on the history of the Quraquat.

Kellie loved him, Digger thought of him as the grandfather he'd never known, and Mark Stevens, who usually piloted the supply ship, was fond of saying the only reason he agreed to keep doing the flights was to spend a few hours with Jack Markover every couple of months.

The fourth member of the research team was Winnie Colgate. Winnie had been through a couple of marriages. Both had expired, according to

Winnie, amiably under mutual agreement. But there was an undercurrent of anger that suggested things had not been so amiable. And Digger suspected that Winnie would be slow to try the game again.

She had begun her professional life as a cosmologist, and she periodically commented that her great regret was that she would not live long enough to see the solutions to the great problems: whether there was a multiverse, what had caused the Big Bang, whether there was a purpose to it all. Digger thought they were adrift in a cosmic bingo game; Jack could not believe stars and people had happened by accident. Winnie kept an open mind, meaning that she changed her opinions from day to day.

She was blond, quiet, affable. It was no secret that she was entranced by Jack, would have taken him into her bed, but Jack was something of a Puritan about sex, didn't believe you should do it outside marriage. In any case, he behaved like Kellie, apparently convinced that his position as head of mission would in some way be compromised if he started sleeping with the staff.

Digger wished for it to happen, because it would have eased his way with Kellie. But, unhappily, Jack held his ground and respected Wendy's virtue.

JACK MARKOVER HAD spent half his career on these missions, and had come to doubt the wisdom of his choice. He'd staked everything on the glorious possibility of making the first major contact. There was a time when it had seemed easy. Almost inevitable. Just get out there and do it. But that had been during an era of overt optimism, when the assumption had been that every world on which life was possible would inevitably develop a biosystem, and that once you got a biosystem you would eventually get tribal chiefs and math teachers. It was true that the habitable worlds orbiting the sun's immediate neighbors had been sterile, but that had seemed like no more than a caprice.

Now he wondered whether they'd all simply read too much science fiction.

He knew what his reputation was. Hi, Jack, find any little green men yet? He had, after each of the last two missions, gone home determined not to come out again. But it was like a siren call, the sense that he might quit just one mission too soon. So he knew that, whatever happened this time, whatever he might think about retiring to Cape Cod, he'd be back out again, poking a new set of worlds. Hoping to find the big prize.

To date, during the past year, they had looked at seventy-nine systems, all with stable suns. The stated purpose of the mission was strictly survey. They were accumulating information and, especially, noting planets that might become future habitats without extensive terraforming. They'd found one life-supporting world, but the life-forms were microscopic. In his entire career, across thirty-five years, Jack had seen only nine worlds on which life had gotten a foothold and been able to sustain itself. There'd been two others on which conditions had changed, an atmosphere grown too thin, a passing star scrambling an orbit, and the life-forms had died out. And that was it.

On each of the living worlds, the bioforms were still microscopic. He had never gone to a previously unvisited world and seen so much as a blade of grass.

The omega was approximately 41,000 kilometers through the middle, big as these things went. It *had* turned, had adjusted course, was *still* turning. It was also decelerating. You could *see* it because the cloud had lost its spherical shape. As it decelerated, sections of mist broke loose and fountained forward.

The turn was so slight as to be barely discernible. Jack was surprised it had been detected at all. Observers must have been watching the object over a period of months to make the determination. Then he realized that, because it was approaching a planetary system, the Academy would have been paying special attention.

The *Jenkins* spent several days doing measurements and collecting readings, sometimes standing off at thousands of kilometers, sometimes pushing uncomfortably close to the cloud front. The numbers confirmed what Broadside had: It *was* angling into the planetary system.

It wasn't hard to find the target.

If the braking continued at the present level, and the turn continued as it was going, the omega would shortly line up on a vector that would bring it to a rendezvous with the third planet.

The *Jenkins* was still too far away to see details. But Jack reported to Broadside. "Looks like a December 14 intersect, Vadim," he told them. "We'll head over there and take a look."

IT WAS THEIR custom to name each terrestrial world they investigated. Although the names were not official, and each planet would continue to be referred to in formal communications by a numerical designator attached to its star's catalog number, unofficially it was easier to think in terms of Brewster's World, or Backwater, or Blotto. (Brewster had been Winnie's companion in her first foray to the altar. The world got its name because it had achieved tidal lock, so the sun, viewed from the surface, "just sat there, doing nothing.")

It was Kellie's turn to name the new one. "This might turn out to be a special place," she said. "When I was a kid we lived near Lookout Point in northern New York. I loved the place. We used to go there and have picnics. You could see the Hudson in the distance."

"So you want to call it Lookout Point?"

"Lookout would be good, I think."

And so Lookout it became.

The ship made a jump to get within an AU, and began its approach. They were still much too far for the telescopes to make out any detail. But they discovered immediately that no electronic envelope surrounded the world.

That news produced mixed feelings. Like everyone else, Digger would have liked to see a world with an advanced civilization. It had never happened, and it would be a huge achievement. On the other hand, there was the cloud. Better, he told himself, it should be empty, and the cloud being drawn by unusual rock formations. Or by ruins, like at Moonlight.

By the third day, the disk that represented Lookout was still only a bright sprinkle of light to the naked eye. In the scopes, however, it was covered with clouds. The only visible surface was blue. An ocean. "It has a big moon," said Winnie, watching the data come in from the sensors. "Two moons, in fact."

The presence of a large moon was thought to be critical to the development of civilizations. Or, for that matter, of large land animals.

The filters reduced the reflection and they were watching two disks and a star, the larger several times the diameter of its companion. The star was the second moon, which was probably a captured asteroid. They brought the images up to full mag and concentrated on the big moon, looking for signs that someone had been there. But they were still too far away. A building the size of Berlin's Bergmann Tower would not have been visible at that range.

It was a strange feeling. How many times had they approached worlds like this, literally praying for an earthwork, for a wall, for a light on the sea? And tonight—it was just short of midnight GMT—Digger hoped they would see only the usual barren plains.

The clarity of the images grew. Lookout had white cumulus clouds. Continents. Archipelagoes.

The continents were *green*.

They shook hands when they saw that. But it was a muted round of celebration.

The poles were white, the oceans blue.

"Looks like Earth," Wendy said, as if she were pronouncing sentence.

ON THE FOURTH day they were able to pick up physical features, mountain ranges, river valleys, large brown patches that might have been plains. A section of the night side was visible, and they searched it eagerly for lights, but saw nothing.

They slept in shifts, when they slept at all. Usually, they dozed off in the common room, and left only to head for the washroom or to get something to eat. They began imagining they saw things. Someone would sit before a monitor tapping it with a pen, observing that there are lines here, looks like a building, or something there, in the harbor, maybe improvements. At one point, Winnie was convinced she could make out a mountain road, and Digger claimed he saw wakes at sea, maybe from ships. Kellie wondered whether she hadn't spotted a dam on one of the rivers, and Jack saw changes in the color of the land that suggested agricultural development.

But in the growing clarity of the telescopes, everything faded, save forest, jungle, rivers, and coastline. The arc of the night side remained dark.

THERE WAS A substantial cloud cover, and storms were everywhere. Blizzards covered the high northern and low southern latitudes, a hurricane churned through one of the oceans, and lightning flickered in the temperate zones. Rain seemed to be falling on every continent. Bill did the usual measurements and posted the results. The planet was about 6 percent smaller than the Earth. Axial tilt twenty-six degrees. (Axial tilt was another factor that seemed to be significant if a world was to develop a biosystem. All known living worlds ranged between eighteen and thirty-one degrees.)

According to Bill, the atmosphere would be breathable, but they'd be prudent to use bottled air. The air at sea level was notably richer in oxygen content than the standard mix. Gravity was .92 standard.

The smaller moon had a retrograde movement. Both satellites were airless, and both were devoid of evidence that anyone had ever landed on them. Seventy percent of the surface was liquid water. And Lookout had a rotational period of twenty-two hours, seventeen minutes.

They went into orbit, crossed the terminator onto the night side, and almost immediately saw lights.

But they weren't the clear hard-edged lights of cities. There was smoke and blurring and a general irregularity. "Forest fires," said Jack. "Caused by lightning, probably." He smiled. "Sorry." Though probably he wasn't.

Thirty minutes later they were back on the daylight side. There were no major cities. The night was dark as a coal sack. Jack sat down, visibly relieved, visibly disappointed, and sent off yet another report to Vadim, information to the Academy. "No sign that the world is occupied. No lights. Will look more closely."

"So why is the cloud coming this way?" asked Winnie.

* * *

THEY MADE SEVERAL orbits and saw nothing. They zeroed in on numerous harbors and rivers, looking for any sign of improvement and finding none. There was no visible shipping, no indication of a road anywhere.

They were about to send off another message informing Broadside that the Academy need not concern itself with Lookout when Digger heard Jack's raspy uh-oh. He glanced at the screens, which were showing nothing but night. "I saw lights," said Jack.

"Where?" Digger knew that Jack had written the world off. He was not going to get excited again. Not about Lookout.

"They're gone," said Jack. "We passed over. They're behind us. But they were there."

"Bill?"

"Realigning the scopes now."

The alpha screen, the prime operational monitor, went dark, and then came back on. *"I've got it,"* said the AI.

Several lights, like lingering sparks. But they didn't go out.

"Fires?"

"What are we getting from the sensors?" asked Winnie.

Bill switched over, and they saw several hazy, luminous rings. "Somebody's got the lights on," said Digger. He looked over at Kellie.

"Could be," she said.

It wasn't London, thought Digger. But it was sure as hell something.

"What's the ground look like?" asked Winnie.

Bill put the area on display.

The biggest of the continents stretched from pole to pole, narrowing to an isthmus in the southern temperate latitudes before expanding again. The lights were located on, or over, the isthmus.

It was about four hundred kilometers long, ranging between forty and eighty kilometers wide. It was rough country, with a mountain range running its length, lots of ridges, and three or four rivers crossing from one ocean to the other.

Digger didn't know what he was supposed to feel. He was along on the mission, and he was dedicated to it like Jack and Winnie. But unlike them, he hadn't expected to see anything. Nobody ever saw anything. It was a rule.

"How could we have missed that?" asked Winnie.

"It's still raining down there," suggested Bill. *"Visibility hasn't been very good."*

"Lock it in, Bill. I don't want to have trouble finding it again when it gets out into the daylight." Digger went back to the viewport and stared out at the long dark curve of the planet. There wasn't a light anywhere to be seen. Well, they'd come around again a few more times before it would be dawn over the target area. Maybe the cloud cover would go away and they'd get a good look.

And then they'd zero in by daylight.

THEY DIDN'T SEE the lights again. But the weather cleared toward dawn, the target area rotated out into the sun, and Digger looked down on a long jagged line that traveled the length of the isthmus. A *road*! It couldn't be anything else.

Simultaneously Kellie announced she could see a city. "One of the harbors," she said, bringing it up on the monitor.

"Here's another one." Winnie pointed at the opposite side of the isthmus. And another here, where the isthmus widens into the southern continent. And two more, where it reaches up into the northern land mass.

Cities crowded around harbors, cities spread out along an impossibly crooked shore line, cities straddling both sides of rivers. There was even a city on a large offshore island in the western sea.

The telescope zoomed in, and they saw creatures on the road, large awkward beasts of burden that looked like rhinos. And humanoids, equally awkward, wide around the middle, waddling along, with reins in their hands and hats that looked like sombreros.

"I'll be damned," said Jack. "They're actually there."

They had pale green skin, large floppy feet (had their ancestors been ducks?), and colorful clothing. It was red and gold and deep sea blue and emerald green. Winnie counted six digits rather than five, and thought their scalps were hairless. They wore baggy leggings and long shirts. Some had vests, and everything was ornamented. There were lots of bracelets, necklaces, feathers. Many wore sashes.

"My first aliens," said Kellie, "and we get Carpenter." That was a reference to Charlie Carpenter, the creator of the Goompahs, an enormously popular children's show. And the aliens did, in fact, look like Goompahs.

"Incredible," said Winnie.

Somebody laughed and proposed a toast to Charlie Carpenter, who'd gotten there first. They were looking at the traffic on the central road just outside a city that stood on the eastern coast. While they shook their heads in amusement, Jack switched the focus and brought up a building atop a low ridge near the sea. It stopped the laughter.

The building was round, a ring of Doric columns supporting a curved roof. It glittered in the sunlight, which was just reaching it, and it looked for all the world like a Greek temple.

"Say what you like," said Digger. "But these people know their architecture."

THEY COUNTED TWELVE cities in all, eight through the isthmus, two on the northern continent, one in the south, and one on the island. It was sometimes difficult to determine where one city ended and another began because, remarkably, they saw no walls. "Maybe it's a *nation*," said Kellie, who'd come down from the bridge to share the moment of triumph. "Or a confederacy."

There was a similarity in design among all of them. They'd clearly not been planned, in the modern sense, but had grown outward from commercial and shipping districts, which were usually down near the waterfront. But nevertheless the cities were laid out in squares, with considerable space provided for parks and avenues. The buildings were not all of the elegance of the temple, but there was a clean simplicity to the design, in contrast to the decorative accoutrements worn by individuals.

The cities were busy, crowds jostling through the commercial areas, hordes of the creatures doing that curious duck-walk, little ones chasing one another about, individuals relaxing near fountains. And Jack realized with a shock that the natives had running water.

"Can we tell how big they are?" asked Winnie.

"*Smaller than they look*," said Bill. "*They would on average come up to Jack's shoulders.*"

There were a variety of structures, two-story buildings that might have been private dwellings, others that looked like public buildings, shops, markets, storage facilities. Three ships were tied up at the piers, and a fourth was entering the harbor as they watched. Its sails were billowing in the wind, and sailors scrambled across its decks.

The architecture was similar everywhere. If it lacked the Doric columns of the seaside temple, it possessed the same simple elegance, straight lines, vaulted roofs, uncluttered cornices. *Just the thing*, Digger thought, *that would attract an omega*. And he was struck by how much better the cloud's sensing equipment was than the *Jenkins*'s.

THE CITIES WERE surrounded by agricultural areas, squares of land given over to one crop or another, orchards, silos, barns. A few rhinos, and other smaller creatures, grazed contentedly.

Gradually the farms gave way to forest.

Beyond the northern cities, the woods grew thick, and broke on the slopes of a mountain range that rivaled the Alps. Beyond the peaks lay jungle, and the jungle, as it approached the equator, became desert. In the south, the cities stood on the edge of more mountains, which proceeded unbroken for thousands of kilometers, all the way to the ice cap.

Where were the other cities?

Digger didn't realize he'd asked the question aloud until Jack commented that it looked as if the isthmus was the only populated section on the planet. The other continents looked empty. The land above and below the isthmus looked equally empty.

They searched the oceans for ships and found none other than those in the coastal waters near the cities. "Looks," said Kellie, "as if they stay in sight of land."

"Look at this." Digger pointed at two of the rivers that crossed the isthmus. "A lock."

They zoomed in and saw that it was so. "They have to get ships over the high ground in the middle of the isthmus," said Jack. "So they use a system of locks to raise them, then get them back down to sea level."

Kellie raised a congratulatory fist. "The Goompahs are engineers," she said. "Who would've thought?"

Jack was getting ready to make his report. "They'll want to know about the population." He looked around at his colleagues. "What do you think?"

Anybody's guess. Winnie brought the cities up one by one. The northernmost was on the western coast, and it was probably the smallest of the group. It could lay claim to a couple of spectacular buildings. The larger of the two was set in front of a pool and looked very much like the main admin building on the Academy grounds. It was long, low, only three levels, made of white stone. It was probably a bit smaller, but the same architect might have designed both.

The other structure was round, like the temple by the sea, but bigger, with more columns. It appeared to be open to the elements. And something that might have been a sun disk stood at the apex of its roof. It looked out across a park.

Crowds were pressed into the commercial section, which was too narrow. The avenues curved and wandered off in all directions. They were lined with buildings of all sizes and shapes. *Minimum twenty thousand*, Digger thought. *Probably closer to twenty-five*. The other cities appeared to be larger. Say an average population fifteen to twenty percent more. Make it thirty thousand for each. That was a conservative estimate. And it gave, what?

"Three to four hundred thousand," Winnie told Jack.

He nodded. Kellie said the estimate was a bit low, but Digger thought she had it about right. Jack agreed and went across the corridor to record his report.

One of the sailing vessels was making its way northward up the coast on the western sea. It was under full sail, and it looked like an eighteenth-century frigate. No Roman galleys for these guys. Or Viking boats. They clearly had no use for oars.

On the other hand, they hadn't learned the value of an outboard motor.

"THE QUESTION," SAID Jack, "is what we do now?"

It was night on the isthmus again, but a clear night this time, and they could see the cities spotted with lights. They were barely discernible, flickering oil lamps probably, but they *were* there.

"We wait for instructions," said Jack. "They'll probably send some contact specialists."

"I hate to bring this up," said Digger, "but where are the contact specialists coming from?"

"The Academy, I assume."

"It's a nine-month flight."

"I know."

"The cloud is only nine months away. When they get here there won't be anybody to contact."

Jack looked uncomfortable. "If they get underway without wasting any time, they'll have a couple of weeks before the cloud hits. In any case, Hutch can get back to us within a couple of weeks and let us know what she intends. Meantime, I don't think there's much for us to do except sit tight."

Kellie frowned. "You don't think we should go down and say hello?"

"No," said Jack. "The Protocol requires us to keep hands off. No contact."

"Nothing anybody can do," said Winnie.

Digger frowned. "Doesn't the policy say something about extraordinary circumstances?"

"As a matter of fact, no."

ARCHIVE

Vadim, we have a lowtech civilization on Lookout. On the third world. It's confined to a small area in the southern hemisphere. What do you want us to do?

—Jack Markover
February 26, 2234

LIBRARY ENTRY

"Where are you going, Boomer?"

"I'm headed to the Chocolate Shop."

"Can I go along? It's my favorite place in the whole town."

"Sure. As long as you promise not to eat any. It's not good to eat between meals."

"I know, Boomer. You can count on me." (Wink, wink at the audience.)

—*The Goompah Show,*
All-Kids Network
February 25

chapter 5

"NOTHING," SAID SKY. They'd been searching the *Quagmire*'s last known position for six hours. There was no sign of the ship, and none of the hedgehog.

"It couldn't just have disappeared," said Emma.

He wasn't sure whether the "it" she was referring to meant the ship or the hedgehog. But whichever, there didn't seem to be any of either in the neighborhood.

Schuyler Capabianco was one of only two of the Academy's twenty-three captains who were currently married, and the only one whose wife was part of the onboard team. She was an astrophysicist out of the University of Arizona who claimed she'd never have started taking Academy assignments had it not been for the chance to be with her husband. He didn't believe it, but he was happy to hear her say so.

Em had been optimistic for a happy outcome to the rescue mission. She had never witnessed a fatal off-Earth incident, and could not bring herself to believe one had happened there. A rationale was hard to find, though. The most likely seemed to be that a power failure had occurred, leaving the ship adrift, without its long-range communication functions. Sky knew it was possible, but only remotely so.

When they'd arrived near the cloud and heard no distress signal, no radio call, they had both realized that the chance of rescue had become vanishingly small. Superluminals were designed so that the radio transmitter would be pretty much the last thing that went down.

There just weren't many things that could account for the silence other than catastrophe. Nevertheless they looked, but Bill reported no sign of the ship. "*It is not in the search area,*" he said.

Em and Sky didn't know either of the people on the *Quagmire*, but that didn't soften things any. There was a brotherhood among those who traveled the great deeps. A tradition had developed much like that among mariners in the dangerous early days on the seas: They were a band, they looked out for each other, and they grieved when anyone was lost.

The *Quagmire* was lost. The mission had become salvage rather than rescue.

"Must have been an explosion," Emma said.

Sky looked off to starboard, where the omega drifted, dark and quiet. But it was too far away to be the culprit.

Emma folded herself into his arms. "Damn," she said.

"We knew all along it might be like this," said Sky.

"I suppose." She snuffled, wiped her eyes, pulled away from him, and cleared her throat. "Well," she said, "there's probably no point hanging around here. What we should do is try to get a look at what happened."

That got his attention. "How do you suggest we do that?"

THEY SLIPPED INTO hyperspace, rode the quiet mists, and jumped out again before Sky could finish his coffee. *"Right on target,"* Bill announced. They had traveled 104 billion kilometers, had gotten in front of the light wave from the search area, and could now look back at the place where the hedgehog and the *Quagmire* had been. Bill unfolded the array of dishes that served as the ship's telescope and aimed it at the region.

They were seeing the area as it had been four days earlier. Had the telescope been more efficient, they could have watched the *Quagmire* approach the hedgehog, could have watched Terry Drafts and Jane Collins leave their ship and descend into the spines.

Emma posted the time at the *Quagmire* site, late evening on the twenty-third, exactly twenty-five minutes before communications had stopped.

It was after midnight on the *Heffernan*. He felt weary, tired, numb, but not sleepy. While they waited he sent off a preliminary report to Serenity. No sign of the *Quagmor*. Continuing investigation.

They talked about the incident. Odd that they'd just vanish. You don't think they might have just taken off? Or been grabbed by something? Sounded wild, but no stranger than simply dropping out of sight. Sky laughed at the idea, but asked Bill whether anything unusual was moving in the area.

"Negative," said Bill.

Watching too many horror sims.

Emma gently pressed his arm. "Coming up," she said. He was watching the time. Just a minute or so.

The cloud was, of course, invisible at that range. (He couldn't help connecting the event with the cloud. Knew it would somehow turn out to be responsible.) But they were well away from it now. The distance between their present position and the site of the incident was seven times as great as the diameter of the solar system. "I can't imagine what we'd expect to see at this range," he said.

"We won't see anything, Sky. But there's a chance—"

"*Photons*," Bill reported. "*Just a sprinkle. But they were right on schedule.*"

"So what's it tell us?" asked Sky.

"Explosion," said Em. "Big one."

"Big enough to obliterate the ship? And the rock?"

"If we can pick up traces of it out here. Oh, yes, I'd say so."

LIBRARY ENTRY

. . . Few of us now alive can remember when we looked at the stars and wondered whether we were alone. We have had faster-than-light transport for almost a half century, and if we have not yet encountered anyone with whom we can have a conversation, we know nevertheless they are out there, or have *been* there in the past.

More than a hundred people have given their lives to this effort. And we are now informed that, during the last fiscal year, roughly 2 percent of the world's financial resources have gone into this exploration of the outer habitat in which we live.

Two percent.

It does not sound like much. But it could feed 90 million people for a year. Or provide housing for 120 million. It could pay all the medical costs in the NAU for sixteen months. It could provide a year's schooling for every child on the planet.

So what do we have for our investment?

Sadly, we have nothing to put into the account books. It's true we have improved our plumbing methods and created lighter, stronger materials. We can now pack more nourishment into a convenience meal than we ever could before. Our electronics are better. We have lightbenders, which have proved of some use in crime prevention, and also of some use to criminals. We have better clothing. Our engines are more fuel-efficient. We have learned to husband energy. But surely all of this could have been had, at far less cost, by direct investment.

Why then do we continue this quest?

It is too easy to think that we go because of the primal urge, as Tennyson said, *to sail beyond the sunset.*

We pretend that we are interested in taking the temperatures of

distant suns, of measuring the velocity of the winds of Altair, of presiding over the birth of stars. Indeed, we have done these things.

But in the end, we are driven by a need to find someone with
whom we can have a conversation. To demonstrate that we are not
alone. We have already learned that there have been others before
us. But they seem to have gone somewhere else. Or passed into
oblivion. So the long hunt continues. And in the end, if we are successful, if we actually find somebody out there, I suspect it will be
our own face that looks back at us. And they will probably be as
startled as we.

—Conan Magruder
Time and Tide, 2228

chapter 6

University of Chicago.
Thursday, March 6.

IT HAD BEEN almost four years, but David Collingdale had neither forgotten nor forgiven the outrage at Moonlight. The sheer mindlessness of it all still ate at him, came on him sometimes in the depths of the night.

Had it been a war, or a rebellion, or anything at all with the most remote kind of purpose, he might have been able to make peace with it. There were times when he stood before his classes and someone would ask about the experience and he'd try to explain, how it had looked, how he had felt. But he still filled up, and sometimes his voice broke and he fell into a desperate silence. He was not among those who thought the omegas a force of nature. They had been designed and launched by somebody. Had he been able to gain access to that somebody, he would have gladly killed and never looked back.

A blanket of snow covered the University of Chicago campus. The walkways and the landing pads had been scooped out; otherwise, everything was buried. He sat at his desk, his class notes open before him, Vivaldi's "Spring" from *The Four Seasons* drifting incongruously through the office. He'd spent the night there not because he knew the storm was coming, although he did, but simply because he sometimes enjoyed the spartan ambience of his office. Because it restored reason and purpose to the world.

The classes were into their first period. Collingdale had an appointment with a graduate student at nine thirty, leaving him just enough time to get himself in order—shower and fresh clothes—and get down to the faculty dining room for a quick breakfast.

Life should have been good there. He conducted occasional seminars, served as advisor for two doctoral candidates, wrote articles for a range of journals, worked on his memoirs, and generally enjoyed playing the campus VIP. He was beginning to get a reputation as something of an eccentric, though. He'd discovered recently that some of his colleagues thought he was a bit over the side. Believed that the experience at Moonlight had twisted him. Maybe it was true, although he would have thought *intensified* to be the more accurate verb. His sensitivity to the subject seemed to be growing deeper with time. He could, in fact, have wept on cue, had he wished to do so, merely by thinking about it.

He'd become sufficiently oppressed by conditions that he worried he might be having an unfortunate effect on his students. Consequently, he'd tried to resign in midsemester the year before, but the chancellor, who saw the advantage of having someone with Collingdale's stature on the faculty, had taken him to a local watering hole for an all-night session, and he'd stayed on.

The chancellor, who was also a longtime friend, suggested a psychiatrist, but Collingdale wasn't prepared to admit he had a problem. In fact, he had acquired an affection for his obsession. He wouldn't have wanted to be without it.

Things got better for him this past Christmas when Mary Clank had walked into his life. Tall, angular, irrepressible, she had heard all the jokes about her name and laughed all of them off. Trade *Clank* for *Collingdale*? she'd asked the night he proposed. You must think I have a tin ear.

He loved her with as much passion as he hated the clouds.

She refused to be caught up in his moods. When he wanted to watch a sim, she insisted on a stroll through the park; when he suggested a fulfilling evening at a concert, she wanted to bounce around at the Lone Wolf.

Gradually, she became the engine driving his life. And he found the occasional day when he did not see her to be an empty time, something to be gotten through as best he could.

He'd always assumed that the romantic passions were practiced exclusively by adolescents, women, and the slow-witted. Sex he could understand. But together forever? That's our song? It was for children. Nevertheless he'd conceived a passion for Mary Clank the first time he'd seen her—at a faculty event—and had never been able to let go. To his delight, she returned his feelings, and Collingdale became happier and more content than he had ever been.

But his natural pessimism lurked in the background and warned him she would not stay. That the day would come when he would walk into the Lone Wolf alone, or with another woman on his arm.

Enjoy her while you can, Dave. All good things are transient.

Well, maybe. But she had said *yes*. They hadn't set a date, although she'd suggested that late spring would be nice. June bride and all that.

He squeezed into his shower. He had private accommodations, a bit cramped, but sufficient. Collingdale liked to think he was entitled to much more, that he was demonstrating to the university that he was really a self-effacing sort by settling for, in fact by insisting on, much less than someone in his position would customarily expect. A lot of people thought modesty a true indicator of greatness. That made it, at least, a prudent tactic.

When he'd finished he laid out fresh clothes on the bed. The sound system was running something from Haydn, but the HV was also on, the sound turned down, two people talking earnestly, and he was pulling on a shirt when he became aware that one of them was Sigmund Halvorsen, who usually got called out when a major scientific issue was in the news. He turned the volume up.

"*—is unquestionably,*" Halvorsen was saying in his standard lecture mode, "*a group of cities directly in its path.*" He was an oversize windbag from the physics department at Loyola. Mostly beard, stomach, and overbearing attitude.

The interviewer nodded and looked distressed. "*Dr. Halvorsen,*" he said, "*this is a living civilization. Is it at risk?*"

"*Oh, yes. Of course. The thing is already tracking them. We don't have much experience with the omegas, but if our analyses of these objects are correct, these creatures, whatever they are, do not have much time left.*"

"*When will the cloud get there?*"

"*I believe they're talking about December. A couple of weeks before Christmas.*" His tone suggested irony.

Collingdale hadn't been near a newscast since the previous evening. But he knew right away what was happening.

A picture of the cloud replaced the two men. It floated in the middle of his bedroom, ugly, ominous, brainless. Malevolent. Silent. Halvorsen's voice droned on about "a force of nature," which showed what he knew.

"*Is there anything we can do to help them?*" asked the interviewer.

"*At this time, I doubt it. We're lucky it isn't us.*"

From his angle near the washroom door, the omega seemed to be closing in on his sofa-bed. "Marlene," he said, calling up the AI.

"*Dr. Collingdale?*"

"Connect me with the Academy. Science and Technology. Their headquarters in Arlington. Audio only. I want to talk with Priscilla Hutchins."

Her whiskey voice informed him that the connection had been made and a young woman's voice responded. "*Can I help you, Dr. Collingdale?*"

"Director of operations, please."

"*She's not available at the moment. Is there someone else you wish to speak with?*"

"Please let her know I called." He sat down on the bed and stared at the cloud. It blinked off, and was replaced by a scattering of lights. The cities by night.

"*—any idea what we're looking at?*" the interviewer asked.

"Not yet. These are, I believe, the first pictures."

"And this is where?"

"The third planet—just like us—of a star that has only a catalog number."

"How far is it?"

"A bit more than three thousand light-years."

"That sounds pretty far."

"Oh, yes. That's about as far out as we've gone. I'd venture to say the only reason we're there now is because somebody spotted the cloud moving."

Collingdale's line blinked. He took it in his sitting room. *"Dave."* Hutch materialized standing on the throw rug. She was framed by a closet door and a plaque awarded him by the Hamburg Institute. *"It's good to hear from you. How've you been?"*

"Good," he said. "The job pays well, and I like the work." Her black hair was shorter than it had been the last time he'd seen her. Her eyes were dark and intelligent, and she obviously enjoyed being an authority figure. "I see things are happening."

She nodded. *"A living civilization, Dave. For the time being. We released it this morning."*

"How long have you known?"

"We got the news two days ago, but we've suspected it for a while now."

"Well," he said, unsure how to get where he wanted to go, "congratulations. I assume there's a major celebration going on down there."

"Not exactly."

No, of course not. Not with a cloud closing in on somebody. "What kind is it?" he asked, referring to the type of civilization.

"Green deuce."

Nontechnological. Agricultural. But organized into cities. Think eastern Mediterranean, maybe four thousand years ago. "Well," he said, "I'm delighted to hear it. I know there'll be some complications, but it's a magnificent discovery. Who's getting the credit?"

"Looks like a technician at Broadside. And Jack Markover on the Jenkins.*"*

That was a surprise. In the old days, it would have been someone higher up the chain. "The cloud led you to it?"

"Yes." She looked discouraged.

"They're saying December on the HV."

"Yes."

"Are you going to try to do anything for them? For the inhabitants?"

"We're putting together a mission."

"Good. I thought you would. Do you have anything going, anything that can take out the cloud?"

"No."

Yeah. That's what makes it all such a bitch. "What are you going to try to do? What's the point of the mission?"

"We'll decoy it. If we can."

"How?"

"Projections. If that doesn't work, a kite." She allowed herself a smile.

"A kite?" He couldn't suppress a grin himself.

"Yes."

"Okay. I'm sure you know what you're doing."

"Ask me in nine months." She tilted her head and her expression changed. Became more personal. *"Dave, what can I do for you?"*

He was trembling. The smartest thing he could do, the only thing he could do, was to stay out of it. The mission, round trip, would take close to two years. And it was likely to fail. When it did, he would be happily married to Mary. "When are they leaving?"

"A few days. They'll be on their way as soon as we can get everybody on board."

"They won't have much time after they get there."

"We figure about ten days."

"Who's running it?"

"We're still looking at the applications."

He ran over a few names in his memory, thought he knew who'd be trying to get on board. Couldn't think of anyone with better qualifications than he. "What happens if the decoy doesn't work?"

"We have some other ideas."

Decision time. "Hutch—" he said.

She waited.

Two years away. Mary Clank, farewell.

"Yes, Dave?" she prompted.

"I'd like to go."

She smiled at him, the way people do when they think you're kidding. *"I understood you were pretty well settled."*

"I'd like to do this, Hutch. If you can see your way clear."

"I'll add your name to the candidates' lists."

"Thanks," he said. "I'd consider it a personal favor."

She turned away momentarily and nodded to someone out of the picture. *"Dave, I can't promise."*

"I know. What kind of creatures are they?"

She vanished and a different image appeared, an awkward, roundish humanoid that looked like something out of a Thanksgiving parade. Complete with vacuous eyes and a silly grin. Baggy pants, floppy shoes, bilious shirt. Round, polished skull. No hair save for eyebrows. Long thin ears.

Almost elfin. They were the saving grace in an otherwise comic physiognomy.

"You're kidding," he said.

"No. This is what they look like."

He laughed. "How many of them are there?"

"Not many. They all seem to be concentrated in a group of cities along a seacoast." Again, something off to the side distracted her. *"Dave,"* she said, *"I have to go. It was good to talk with you. I'll get back within twenty-four hours. Let you know, up or down."*

HE HAD LUNCH with Mary, and she knew something had happened. They were in the UC faculty lounge, he with only twenty minutes before he was due to conduct a seminar, she with an hour to spare. His intention had been to say nothing until he had the decision from the Academy. But she sat there behind a grilled cheese and looked into him and waited for him to explain what was going on.

So he did, although he made it sound, without actually lying, as if Hutch had called him and asked whether he was available.

"They might pick somebody else," he concluded. "There's a lot at stake. It would be hard to say no."

She looked back at him with those soft blue eyes, and he wondered whether he had lost his mind. "I understand," she said.

"I don't really have a choice in something like this, Mary. There's too much riding on it."

"It's okay. You have to do what you think is right." Steel in the ribs.

"I'm sorry. The timing isn't very good, is it?"

"You'll be gone two years, you say?"

"If I get picked, it would be closer to a year and a half." He tried a smile but it didn't work. "If it happens, I can probably arrange space for you. If you'd want to come."

She nibbled at the sandwich. Considered it. He saw her wrestle with it. Saw those eyes harden. "Dave, I'd like to, but I can't just take two years off."

"It wouldn't be two years."

"Close enough. It would wreck my career." She was an instructor in the law school. There was a tear. But she cleared her throat. "No. I just can't do it." And there was a message there somewhere, in her voice, in her expression. I'm yours if you want me. But don't expect me to hang around.

In that moment, filled with the smell of fresh-brewed coffee and cinnamon, he hoped that Hutch would pass over him, pick someone else. But he also understood he'd driven a spike into his relationship with Mary, that whatever happened now, things would never again be right.

* * *

HUTCH CALLED THAT night. *"You still want to go?"*

"When do we leave?"

"A week from tomorrow."

"I'll be ready."

"I'm attaching a folder. It has all the information on the mission. Who'll be there. What we plan to do. If you have any ideas, get back to me."

"I will."

"Welcome aboard, David."

"Thank you. And, Hutch—"

"Yes?"

"Thanks for the assignment."

He signed off and looked out across the lake. He lived on the North Shore. Nice place, really. Hated to leave it. But he'd already arranged to sublet.

ARCHIVE

Jack, for planning purposes, we will assume that we'll be unable to stop the cloud. The cloud will target the cities. See if you can come up with a way to move the population out into the country, preferable to higher ground, since they're all vulnerable to the ocean. We are going to try to master their language. To that end, we need recordings. Raw data should be forwarded to the *Khalifa al-Jahani* as soon as it becomes available.

Anything you can do without compromising the Protocol will help. I'm informed you don't have lightbenders. We're sending a shipment from Broadside, but I'd be grateful if you didn't wait for their arrival to get started. Find a way to make things happen. Everyone here understands the difficulty that implies. Therefore, be advised that your primary objective is to get the job done. If it becomes necessary to set the Protocol aside, this constitutes your authority to do so.

We also need you to collect and run analyses of food samples. Forward any information you can get. What do they eat? Fruit, pizza, whatever. Any other data that might help us get them through this.

Time is of the essence. In view of the lag between Lookout and your other points of contact, you are free to use discretion.

—P. M. Hutchins,
Director, Operations
March 6, 2234

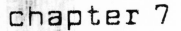

chapter 7

Arlington.
Friday, March 7.

HUTCH FOUND A note on her desk, requesting she report to the commissioner's office immediately on arrival. She found him packing. "Heading for Geneva," he said. "Right after the memorial service."

"What's happening?" she asked.

"Political stuff. But they want me there. You'll be acting the rest of the week."

"Okay."

He looked at her. "That's it," he said.

"No special instructions?"

"No. Just use your best judgment."

SHE'D BEEN HIT hard by the loss of Jane Collins and Terry Drafts. Hutch had known both, had partied with Jane and risked her neck with Terry. Standing on the lawn by the Morning Pool, listening to the tributes, she couldn't get the notion out of her head that both would show up, walk into the middle of things, and announce it was all a mistake. Maybe if they had found the bodies, it would have been easier.

The commissioner conducted the event with his usual charm and aplomb. Their friends and colleagues recalled fond memories of one or the other, and there was a fair amount of laughter. Hutch glanced up at the south wall, on which were engraved the names of all who had lost their lives over the years in the service of the Academy. Or, as she'd have preferred to put it, in the service of humanity. The list was getting long.

When her turn to speak came, she filled up. Tom Callan handed her a glass of water but she stood there, shaking her head impatiently. Poor way for a leader to behave. She began by saying that Jane and Terry were good people, and her friends. "They were bright, and they went to a place that was dark and deadly and nobody knew. Now we know.

"I'm proud they were my colleagues."

*   *   *

THE HEDGEHOG AND the cloud had been on the same course, moving at the same velocity. The cloud was programmed to attack objects with perpendiculars, or even sharp edges. The hedgehog had been all perpendiculars. If Terry's surmise that someone else was monitoring the cloud was correct, why do it with a package designed in that particular way? Why not just throw an ordinary set of sensors out there?

What was going on?

The two objects had been separated by sixty thousand kilometers. Why put a surveillance package in front instead of alongside? And why so far away?

She made some calls. Everybody she could think of who'd been involved with the omegas. She put the same question to each: Was it possible that there'd been other hedgehogs accompanying other clouds? And that they hadn't been observed?

The answers: It was certainly possible. And at sixty thousand klicks, it was unlikely they'd have been noticed. The research vessels had been intent on the omegas. It had not been part of the routine to do long-range sweeps of the area.

By midafternoon she was satisfied it was worth an investigation. "Barbara," she said, "record transmissions for Serenity and Broadside."

"Ready, Ms. Hutchins."

She looked into the imager. "Audrey, Vadim: Let's find out if some of the other clouds have a hedgehog. Assign whoever's available to take a look. Just nearby stuff. A few samples. Tell them if they find one, or anything remotely like it, to stay away from it. We don't want to lose anybody else. Let me know results ASAP."

THE VARIOUS WEATHERMAN packages had sighted five more tewks, for a total of ten. They were concentrated in two widely separated areas, three near the Golden Crescent, four near the Cowbell.

The Golden Crescent, home to millions of aging stars, floated over her couch. Great smoky walls fell away to infinity. A class-G dominated the foreground, close enough to illuminate the clock. A luminous river of gas and dust ran across the back of the room.

She activated the program, and three bright objects appeared, one at a time, inward from the Crescent. One up here, one over there, one down center.

Then the image rotated, the Golden Crescent sank, the vast clouds moved around the walls, and the three stars lined up.

She had just watched the same process happen with the four tewks at the Cowbell. Except that there only three of the four had lined up. But it was enough.

It was almost choreographed. And it chilled her.

They were no closer to figuring out what was happening than they'd been when the first sightings came in a few weeks earlier. She suspected that, with Weatherman packages becoming operational on a regular basis, they were going to see more of these things.

She checked the time and shut the program down. Leave it to Harold to figure out. As acting commissioner she had more pressing matters to attend to.

Asquith had taken her aside after the memorial. It was her first experience as the Academy's chief decision maker, and he had apparently thought better of his intention to pass along no special instructions. "Don't make any decisions," he'd told her, "other than those directly in line with Academy policy. Anything that requires judgment, defer it, and I'll take care of it when I get back." He'd looked at her, realized what he'd said, and added, "No offense."

None taken. Asquith was too shallow for her to take his opinion of her capabilities seriously. The problem, of course, was that he wrote her evaluation.

She pushed it aside, called Rheal Fabrics, and told them to assemble the kite. They gave her the dimensions it would have while stored, which she added to the space requirements Marge's weathermaking gear would need.

The Lookout mission would require two ships. One would carry Collingdale and his team. The other would have to be a freighter, which meant she'd have to charter it. Oddly, the Collingdale ship was the problem. She needed something that could transport upward of twenty people, and the only thing available was the *al-Jahani*, currently undergoing a refitting. She'd have to hurry it along.

She'd briefed Asquith on what she intended to do. "Maybe even worse than the direct attack by the omega," she told him, "is the aftermath. We don't know what it'll do to the atmosphere. Might be years before things will grow. That means a possibility of starvation for the natives. We're going to need to send out relief supplies."

He'd sighed. "Not our job, Hutch."

But it would become theirs, and they both knew it. When the pictures starting coming back of starving and dying Goompahs, the public would get upset, and the politicians would turn to the Academy. "When it happens," she'd told him, "we better be ready."

Next day he'd announced his Geneva trip. It hardly seemed a coincidence.

The *al-Jahani* was supposed to leave Friday. The logistics were set, and Collingdale and his people were en route. But Jerry Hoskins, the Academy's chief engineer, had been dubious. Not enough time. The ship was due for a major overhaul, and Hutch wanted to send her on a two-year mission? But he'd see what he could do. So when Barbara informed her that Jerry was on the circuit, she got a bad feeling. *"Hutch,"* he said, *"we can't really get her ready in a few days."*

"How much time do you need, Jerry?"

"If we drop everything else—?"

"Yes."

"Three weeks."

"Three weeks?"

"Maybe two. But that's the best we can do."

"That won't work. They wouldn't get there in time. Might as well not go." She had nothing else available. Damned stuff was all out in the boondocks. "What's the worst that can happen if we go through with the launch?"

"You mean Friday?"

"Yes."

"It might blow up."

"You're kidding."

"Of course. But I wouldn't guarantee it'll get where it's going."

"Okay. No guarantee. Other than that, what are my chances?"

"It'll probably do fine."

"Any safety concerns?"

"We'll do an inspection. Make sure. No, they'll be okay. They might get stranded. But otherwise—"

"—No guarantees."

"—Right."

"Okay. Jerry, I'm going to send a record of this conversation to Dave Collingdale. You inform the captain."

Collingdale hadn't come in yet, so she left a message, describing the chief engineer's concerns. She told him reluctantly that it should add some spice to the flight. Then she sighed and headed for the commissioner's office to assume her new duties.

HER FIRST APPOINTMENT was with Melanie Toll of Thrillseekers, Inc.

Despite the capabilities of existing technology to create images that could not be distinguished from the originals, allowing virtual face-to-face conversations between people thousands of kilometers apart, people with business propositions still found the personal touch indispensable. Making the effort to cross some geography at personal inconvenience sent a message about how serious one was.

Serious. And here came Ms. Toll of Thrillseekers.

Hutch gazed at her over the vast expanse of Asquith's desk. (The commissioner insisted she use his office when exercising his function.) She was young, attractive, tall, quite sure of herself. She wore a gold necklace and a matching bracelet, both of which acquired additional sparkle in the sheen of her auburn hair.

"Nice to meet you, Dr. Hutchins," she said.

"You're giving me more credit than I deserve." Hutch shook her hand, listened to the light tinkle of the gold, and led her to a seat by the coffee table.

They talked briefly about weather, traffic, and how lovely the Academy grounds were. Then Hutch asked what she could do for her visitor.

Toll leaned forward, took a projector from her purse, and activated it. An image appeared of a young couple happily climbing the side of a mountain. Below them, the cliff fell away five hundred meters. Hutch could see a river sparkling in the sunlight.

Thrillseekers, Inc., took people on actual and virtual tours around the world and let them indulge their fantasies. Aside from dangling from cliffs, they rode golly balls along treacherous rivers, rescued beautiful women (or attractive men) from alligators, mounted horses and fought mock battles with bandits in the Sahara.

The projector displayed all this in enhanced colors, accompanied by an enthusiastic score, and over-charged titles. *Danger for the Connoisseur. The Ultimate Thrill-Ride.* The latter was a wild chase in a damaged flyer pursued by a man-eating cloud.

Moments later Hutch was racing down a ski slope, approaching a jump that seemed to have no bottom. *"Hold on to Your Socks!"* read the streamer. She couldn't help pushing back into her chair and gripping the arms.

"Well," said Toll, snapping off the image just before Hutch would have soared out into space, "that's what we do. Although, of course, you knew that."

She smirked at Hutch, who, despite herself, was breathing hard. "Of course, Ms. Toll." Steady yourself. "That's quite a show."

"Thank you. I'm glad you liked it."

"How can I help you?"

"We're interested in Lookout. The place where the Goompahs are."

"Really. In what way?"

"We'd like to put it on our inventory." She crossed one leg over the other. The woman oozed sex. Even with no male in the room.

Marla, the commissioner's secretary, came in with a coffee service and pastries. She glanced at Hutch to see if she could proceed. Hutch nodded, and the woman filled two fine china cups and asked if there was anything else. There wasn't, so she withdrew. (Asquith didn't use an AI for secretarial duties because having a human signified his elite status within the organization. Very few people other than CEOs and heads of state had them. But there was no question that Marla added to the ambience.)

"How do you mean," Hutch asked, "put it on your 'inventory'?"

"We'd like to make the experience available to our customers. We'd like them to be on the ground when the cloud comes in, watch the assault, feel what it's like."

"Ms. Toll, Lookout is three thousand light-years away. Your customers would be gone for almost two years. Maybe gone permanently."

"No, no, no. We don't mean we'd literally ship them out. What we'd like to do is send a couple of our technicians to Lookout to record the attack, get the sense of what really happens. Then we'd construct an artificial experience." She tried the coffee and nodded. It met with her approval. "We think an omega program would do quite nicely."

"And you'd like permission from me?" She wondered about that detail. Any world shown to have sentient life automatically came under the purview of the World Council, but its agent in such matters was the Academy.

"Permission and transportation," said Toll.

Her instincts pushed her to say no, but she couldn't see a reason to refuse. "Thrillseekers would have to pay their share of expenses."

"Of course."

"You'd have to agree not to make contact with the natives. But that shouldn't be a problem. We'd simply set you down on the other side of the globe."

She shook her head. "No, Ms. Hutchins. I don't think you understand. The natives and their cities are the critical part of the equation. We'll want to record them up close. But I can promise we'll stay out of the way. They won't see us."

Representatives from two of the major news organizations had appointments with her during the afternoon, and she suddenly realized why they were there. There was going to be more of this. *Let's get good shots of the Goompahs running for their lives.*

"I'm sorry, Ms. Toll, but I don't think we can do it."

Her pretty brow furrowed and Hutch saw that she had a vindictive streak. "Why not?" she asked, carefully keeping her voice level.

Common decency, you blockhead. "It puts the Protocol at risk."

"I beg your pardon." She tried to look baffled. "They won't see us."

"You can't guarantee that."

She tried to debate the point. "We'll keep out of the way. No way they'll know we're there. Our people will be in the woods."

"There's also a liability problem," Hutch said. "I assume you expect these people to stay during the bombardment."

"Well, of course. They'd have to stay."

"That makes us liable for their safety."

"We'll give you a release."

"Releases have limited value in this kind of case. One of your people doesn't come back, his family sues you, and then sues us. The piece of paper isn't worth a damn in court if it can be shown we willingly transported him into an obviously dangerous situation."

"Ms. Hutchins, I would be grateful if you could be reasonable."

"I'm trying to be."

Toll quibbled a bit longer, decided maybe she needed to talk with the commissioner, the *real* commissioner. Then she shook her head at Hutch's perversity, shook hands politely, and left.

SHE HAD A brief conversation with maintenance over contracts with suppliers, then went down to the conference room for the commissioner's weekly meeting. That was usually a scattershot affair, attended by the six department heads. Asquith was neither a good planner nor a good listener. There was never an agenda, although he'd left one for her this time. It was all pretty routine stuff, though, and she got through it in twenty minutes.

It didn't mention the Goompahs. "Before I let you go," she concluded, "you all know what the situation is at Lookout."

"The Goompahs?" said the director of personnel, struggling to keep a straight face.

She didn't see the humor. "Frank," she said, "in December, a lot of them are going to die. Maybe their civilization with them. If anybody has an idea how we might prevent that, I'd like to hear it."

"If we had a little more time," said Life Sciences, Lydia Wu-Chen, "we could set up a base on their moon. Evacuate them. At least get some of them out of harm's way."

Hutch nodded. "It's too far. We need nine months just to get there."

"I don't think it's possible," said Physics, Wendell McSorley.

"Did you see the pictures from Moonlight?" asked Frank, looking around at his colleagues. "You have to find a way to stop the cloud. Otherwise, it's bye-bye baby."

"There's nothing we can do about the cloud," said Wendell.

"No magic bullet?" asked Lydia. "Nothing at all?"

"No."

Hutch described Tom Callan's idea. Wendell thought there was a possibility it might work. "It would have helped if we'd been out there with it a couple of years ago, though. We've waited until the thing has *seen* the Goompahs."

"The same thing," said Hutch, "could happen somewhere else next month. We need a weapon."

"Then we need money," said Wendell. "Somebody has to get serious about the program." He looked dead at her.

AND THAT BROUGHT her back to the issue of food and blankets for survivors. She'd like to send medical supplies, too, but saw no quick way to find out what would be useful. So forget the medical stuff. The food would have to be synthesized, after they'd discovered what the natives would eat. But who would do it?

She had Marla put in a call to Dr. Alva. Very busy, they told her. Not available. Who is Priscilla Hutchins again? But ten minutes later Marla informed her that Dr. Alva was on the circuit. She looked impressed. "And by the way," she added, "your three o'clock is waiting."

Alva was wearing fatigues and seemed to be inside a makeshift lab. "*What can I do for you, Hutch?*" she asked. She did not sound annoyed, but there was no preliminary talk.

"You know about Lookout, Alva?"

"*Only what I've read.*"

"They're going to get decimated."

"*Are you going to warn them? At least let them know what's coming?*"

"There's a mission leaving next week with linguists."

"*Well, thank God for that. I don't suppose that means we already have people on the ground who can speak with them?*"

"Not yet. We just got there, Alva. But we're trying."

"*I was concerned you'd want to keep hands off. You want my help overturning the Protocol?*"

"Actually, that's not why I called. We're going to ship supplies to them. We don't have any samples yet to work from, but as soon as I can get them, we're going to send food and blankets. And medical, if it's feasible. Whatever seems appropriate."

"*Good. Maybe you'll be able to save some of them. What do you need from me?*"

"Advice. After I get the formulas, who would be willing to synthesize the food?"

"*Gratis?*"

"Probably. I'm going to try to get the Academy to spring for some cash, but I have my doubts."

"Your best bet is Hollins & Groat. Talk to Eddie Cummins over there."

"Where'll I find him?"

"Call Corporate. Tell him you talked with me. That I'd consider it a personal favor. In fact, wait until tomorrow and I'll try to reach him and set things up. You've no idea what you're going to need, right?"

"Not at this point."

"Okay. Let me see what I can do. If you don't hear from me, call him tomorrow afternoon. Your time."

HER THREE O'CLOCK appointment was with the Rev. George Christopher, M.A.D.S., S.T.D. He represented the Missionary Council of the Church of Revelation. His group was currently the largest and most powerful of the Fundamentalist organizations in the NAU.

Christopher was right out of Nathaniel Hawthorne. Tall, severe, pious, eyes forever searching the overhead as if communicating with a satellite. The drawn-out diction that comes from too many years in the pulpit and causes people to think *God* has two syllables. He was pale, with a lean jaw and a long nose. He told her how glad he was to meet her, that in his view they needed some fresh young blood in the Academy hierarchy, and he implied he was tight with Asquith.

In fact, he was. The Church was of course not a donor, but it had influence over people who were, and it wielded considerable political clout. The Rev. Christopher was an occasional guest at Asquith's retreat on Chesapeake Bay. "Good man, Michael," he said. "He's done a superb job with the Academy."

"Yes," she agreed, wondering if there was a special penalty for lying to a man of the cloth. "He works very hard."

He settled back in one of the armchairs, adjusting his long legs, adjusting his smile, adjusting his aura. "Ms. Hutchins," he said, "we are concerned about the natives on Lookout." His lips worked their way around the verb and the two nouns. "Tell me, is that really the name of the place?"

"No," she said. "It doesn't have a designator other than a number."

"Well, however that may be, we are concerned."

"As are we all, Reverend."

"Yes. Of course. Are we going to be able to head off the disaster?"

"Probably not. We're going to try. But it doesn't look as if we have much chance."

He nodded, suggesting that was the usual human condition. "We'll ask our people to pray."

"Thank you. We could use a little divine intervention."

He looked up, tracked his satellite, and nodded again. "I wonder whether you've ever considered how the clouds originated? Who sent them?"

Her flesh chilled. *Who?* Well, whatever. The truth was that hardly a day had gone by that she *hadn't* wondered about it, since that terrible afternoon thirty years ago when she'd watched the first cloud rip into Delta, rip into it because she and Frank Carson and the others had carved a few squares to entice it. And the thing had come like a hound out of hell.

"A lot of good people know what this is about," he said. "They've looked at the clouds, and they know exactly what is happening."

"Which is—?"

"God is losing patience with us."

Hutch didn't really have any comment, so she simply cleared her throat.

"I know how this sounds to you, Ms. Hutchins—may I call you *Priscilla*?"

"Of course."

"I know how this sounds, Priscilla, but I must confess that I myself find it hard to understand why God would have designed such an object into the universe."

"It may not be a natural object, Reverend."

"I suppose that's possible. It's hard to see how, but I suppose it could happen. I'm not a physicist, you know." He said that as if he might easily have been mistaken for one. "When you get an answer, please let me know. Meantime, I have to tell you what *I* think it is."

"And what's that?"

"A test."

"It's a pretty severe one."

"There've been pretty severe ones before."

Well, she couldn't deny that. Wars, famines, holocausts. It could be a tough world. "May I ask how I can help you, Reverend?"

"Of course." He rearranged his legs and studied her, and she understood he was making a judgment about how honest he could be. "You're not a person of faith, I take it?"

Hutch didn't know. There had been times when she'd almost felt the presence of a greater power. There'd been times when things had gotten desperate and she'd prayed for help. The fact that she was sitting in this office suggested the prayers might have been answered. Or she might have been lucky. "No," she said finally. "It looks pretty mechanical out there to me."

"Okay. That's fair enough. But I want you to consider for a moment what it means to be a person who believes, who *really* believes, there is a Creator. Who believes without question that there is a judgment, that we will all one day have to face our Maker and render an accounting of our lives." His voice had taken on a controlled passion. "Think of this life as being only a taste of what is to come." He took a deep breath. "Priscilla, do these creatures know about God?"

For a moment she thought he was talking about Academy employees. "The Goompahs?" she said. "We don't have any information on them yet, Reverend."

He looked past her toward the window, gazing at the curtains. "They face decimation, and they probably do not have the consolation of knowing there is a loving God."

"They might argue that if they had a loving God they wouldn't be facing decimation."

"Yes," he said. "You would think that way."

She wondered where this was going. "Reverend Christopher," she said, "it's hard to see what we can do about their religious opinions."

"Priscilla, think about it a moment. They obviously have souls. We can see it in their buildings. In their cities. And those souls are in jeopardy."

"At the moment, Reverend, I'm more worried about their *bodies*."

"Yes, I'm sure." Note of sympathy. "You'll understand if I point out there's far more to lose than simply one's earthly life."

She resisted pointing out that the Goompahs had no earthly life. "Of course."

"It's strictly short-term."

"Nevertheless—"

"I want to send a few missionaries. While there's still time." His manner remained calm and matter-of-fact. He might have been suggesting they have a few pizzas delivered. "I know you don't agree with all this, Priscilla. But I'm asking you to trust me."

"The Protocol prevents it, Reverend."

"These are special circumstances."

"That's true. But there's no provision, and I have no authority to override."

"Priscilla. Hutch. They call you *Hutch*, don't they?"

"My friends do, yes."

"Hutch, I'm asking you to show some courage. Do the right thing." He looked on the verge of tears. "If need be, the Church will back you to the hilt."

Right. That's exactly what the Goompahs need right now, to hear about hellfire and damnation. "I'm sorry, Reverend." She got up, signaling the end of the interview. "I wish I could help."

He got to his feet, clearly disappointed. "You might want to talk this over with Michael."

"His hands would be tied also."

"Then I'll have to go to a higher authority." She wasn't sure, but the last two words sounded capitalized.

JOSH KEPPLER REPRESENTED Island Specialties, Inc., a major player in communications, banking, entertainment, and retailing. Plus probably a few other areas Hutch didn't recall at the moment.

Anyone who sought an appointment with the director of operations was required to state his business up front. She assumed the commissioner ran things the same way, but if so, he hadn't passed the information along. It was becoming a long day, and she couldn't imagine anything Keppler would have to say that she was interested in hearing.

"Costume jewelry," he said.

"I beg your pardon?"

"The Goompahs wear a lot of costume jewelry. It looks pretty good. Sort of early Egyptian."

"I'm sorry. I don't think I'm following you."

"The original stuff would be worth enormous money to collectors."

"Why? Nobody's interested in what the Noks wear."

"Nobody *likes* the Noks. People *love* the Goompahs. Or at least they will after we launch our campaign. And anyhow, the Goompahs are going to get decimated. That provides a certain nostalgia. These things are going to be instant relics."

Keppler wore a white jacket and slacks, and he had a mustache—facial hair was just coming back into style after a long absence—that did nothing for him. Add close-set dark eyes, hair neatly parted down the center of his skull, and a forced smile, and he looked like an incompetent con man. Or a failed lothario. Care to swing by my quarters tonight, sweetie?

"So Island Specialties is going to—?"

"—We're sending a ship out. It'll be leaving in about a week. Don't worry. We'll take care of everything, and we'll stay out of the way." He was carrying a folder, which he opened and laid before her. "This constitutes official notification. As required by law."

"Let me understand this," she said. "You're sending a ship to Lookout. And you're going to—"

"—Do some trading."

"Why not just reproduce the jewelry? You know exactly what it looks like."

"Authenticity, Ms. Hutchins. That's what gives it value. Each piece will come with a certificate of origin."

"You can't do it." She pushed the document back across the desk without a glance.

"Why not?"

"First of all, Lookout is under Academy auspices. You need permission to do this."

"We didn't think there'd be a problem about that."

"There is. Secondly, it would be a violation of the Protocol."

"We're willing to accept that."

"What do you mean?"

"We don't think it would stand up in court. The Protocol has never been tested, Ms. Hutchins. Why would anyone suppose the Court of the Hague has jurisdiction out around Alpha Centauri?"

Well, he was probably right there. Especially if the Academy granted *de facto* rights by accepting his notification. "Forget it," she said.

Keppler tried to smile at her, but only his lips moved. "Ms. Hutchins, there would be a considerable financial advantage for the Academy." He canted his head to let her know that Island Specialties was prepared not only to buy off the Academy, but her as well.

"Makes me wonder," she said, "if the cloud doesn't constitute one of the Goompahs' lesser problems."

His expression continued to imply he was trying hard to be her friend. He grinned at her little joke. Flicked it away harmlessly to show he hadn't taken offense. "Nobody will get hurt," he said. "And we'll all do very nicely."

"Mr. Keppler, if your people go anywhere near Lookout, we'll act to defend our prerogatives."

"And what precisely does that mean?"

"Show up and find out." In fact, she knew that Island would not be able to get a superluminal for that kind of voyage unless they could show Academy approval, or at least Academy indifference.

THE COMMISSIONER CONSIDERED public relations his primary responsibility. Eric Samuels, his PR director, routinely scheduled a press conference every Friday afternoon at four. Shortly before the hour she heard his cheery hello to Marla, then he rolled into the office, bubbly and full of good cheer, affecting to be surprised to find Hutch behind the desk, and did a joke about how the commissioner had never looked better.

He wanted her to sign off on a couple of press releases on matters of no real concern. She was surprised he didn't have the authority to handle them on his own. One of the world's top physicists was scheduled to visit the Academy the following week, and Eric wanted to make it an Event. Several new artifacts were going on display in the George Hackett Wing of the library. (That one brought a twinge. Thirty years ago George had stolen her heart and lost his life.) There was also an announcement of new software being installed throughout the Academy buildings to make them friendlier to visitors.

"Okay," she said, signing with a flourish. She liked the feeling of power it brought. "Good."

"Did Michael leave anything for me?" he asked. "You know, the Goompahs? They'll be all over me today about Lookout." Eric was tall, and would have been quite good-looking had he been able to convey the impression somebody was home. The truth was that he wasn't vacuous, but he did look that way.

"No," she said. "Michael didn't leave anything. But *I* have something for you."

"Oh?" He looked suspicious, as if she were about to hand him an assignment. "What's that?"

She activated the projector and a Goompah appeared in the middle of the office. "Her name's Tilly."

"Really?"

"Well, no. Actually we don't know what her name is." She changed the picture, and they were in one of the streets of the city with the temple. Goompahs were everywhere. Behind shop counters, standing around talking, riding beasts that were simultaneously ugly and attractive (like a bulldog, or a rhino). Little Goompahs ran screaming after a bouncing ball.

"Marvelous," he said.

"Aren't they?"

"How much of this stuff do we have?"

She shut the sound off, extracted the disk, and held it out for him. "As much as your clients could possibly want."

"Yes," he said. "The networks'll love it."

More than that, she thought. If the public reacted the way Hutch knew they would, it would become politically very difficult for the government to decide the Goompahs were more trouble than they were worth and simply abandon them.

AT THE END of the day, she wandered down to the lab. Harold was in his office, getting ready to leave. "Anything more on the tewks?" she asked.

"Well," he said, "we do have another one."

"Really?"

"In the Cowbell again."

"Still no star it could have been?"

"This was already lit when the package went operational. And we don't have a good picture of the area beforehand, so we really don't know. But it's a tewk. The spectrogram is right. Incidentally, one of the older ones shut down."

"Okay."

"The one that shut down: We don't know how long it was active because we don't know when it first began. Might have been a couple of weeks before the package started operating." He tugged at his jacket, as though a piece of lint were hanging on. Finally, he gave up. "There's something odd about that, too. About the way they switch off.

"Usually, a true nova will fade out. Maybe come back to life a couple times in any given cycle. Burn some more. But these things—" He looked for the right word. "When they're done, they're done. They go off, and nobody hears from them again."

"Like a light going out?"

"Yes. Exactly like that." He frowned. "Is it cold out?"

Hutch hadn't been outside since morning. "Don't know," she said.

"There's something else." He looked pleased, puzzled, amused. "The clouds tend to run in waves."

"Old news, Harold."

"Sometimes they don't, but the ones we've seen usually do. Now, what's interesting, we've detected some clouds near the tewks. If we assume they are also running in waves, then at least four of the tewks, and maybe all of them, happened along wave fronts."

She looked at him, trying to understand the implications. "You're telling me these are all attacks? We're watching worlds get blown up?"

"No." He shook his head. "Nothing like that. There's far too much energy being expended for that kind of scenario. All I'm saying is what I said: Wherever one of these explosions has happened, we're pretty sure a cloud has been present."

"No idea as to what's going on?"

"Well, it's always helpful when you can connect things. It eliminates possibilities." He smiled at her, almost playfully. "I was wandering through the Georgetown Gallery last night." He was checking his pockets for something. Gloves. Where were his gloves? "I got to thinking." He found them in a desk drawer, frowned, wondering how they could have gotten there, and put them on. He seemed to have forgotten the Georgetown Gallery.

"And—?" prompted Hutch.

"What was I saying?"

"The Georgetown Gallery."

"Oh, yes. I have an idea what the omegas might be."

She caught her breath. Give it to me. Tell me.

"It's only an idea," he said. He glanced at the time and tried to push past her. "Hutch, I'm late for dinner. Let me think about it some more and I'll get back to you."

She seized his arm. "Whoa, Harold. You don't drop a line like that and walk off. Have you _really_ figured it out?"

"Give me a few days. I need to do some math. Get more data. If I can find what I'm looking for, I'll show you what they might be."

LIBRARY ENTRY

"Go, therefore, and teach all nations." The requirement laid on us by the Gospels is no longer as clear as it once was. Do the creatures we call Goompahs constitute a nation in the biblical sense? Are they, like ourselves, spiritual beings? Can they be said to have souls?

For the third time in recent years, we are facing the issue of an extraterrestrial intelligence, beings that seem to have a moral sense, and might therefore qualify as children of God. To date, we have delayed, looked the other way, and avoided the question that is clearly being put to us: Was the crucifixion a unique event? Does it apply only to those born of terrestrial mothers? Or has it application on whatever worlds the children of Adam may visit?

What precisely is our responsibility? It is no easy question, and we must confess we find no ready answer in the scriptures. We are at a crossroad. And while we ourselves consider how to proceed, we would remind those ultimately tasked with the decision, who have delayed more than thirty years since the first discovery on Inakademeri, that failure to act *is* a decision. The cloud is bearing down on the Goompahs, while we bide our time. The entire Christian community is watching. And it is probable that whatever precedent is set in these next few months will determine the direction of missionary efforts well into the future. If indeed we determine that the Gospels are not applicable off Earth, we should so state, loudly and clearly, along with the reasons why. If, on the other hand, they *do* apply, then we should act. And quickly. The clock is running.

—*Christianity Today*, April 2234

chapter 8

HUTCH SAT QUIETLY in the back of the briefing room while Collingdale talked to his people. There were twenty-five of them, xenologists, sociologists, mathematicians, and technicians. And, primarily, a team of twelve language specialists, whose job it would be to interpret the raw data sent back by the *Jenkins* crew, and to become proficient in basic Goompah.

The *Khalifa al-Jahani* was visible through the viewports. It was one of the Academy's older ships, and she recalled the engineer's cautions with misgivings. Probably be okay, but no guarantees. Collingdale had not been happy. But he'd accepted the reality of their position, and they'd passed the information on to the volunteers. None had opted out.

He was telling them that he planned to break new ground and he was pleased to have them with him.

"I've asked the *Jenkins* to get as many recordings as possible," she'd told Collingdale earlier in the day. "They're going to plant A/V pickups wherever they can. I've advised them to get the data and not worry too much about the Protocol unless the natives prove hostile. In which case they're just going to hunker down until you get there."

"If they turn out to be hostile," Collingdale had said, "I doubt we'll be able to do much for them."

That had brought up the question of equipment. How many pickups did the *Jenkins* group have to work with? It couldn't be many. They'd been doing routine survey work and, in the ordinary course of things, had little use for recording devices. They'd have to jury-rig some spare parts. In any case, there wouldn't be more than a handful.

She'd ordered a shipment sent over to the *Jenkins*, along with some light-benders, including a capital unit that could be used to conceal their lander. None of that, however, would arrive for weeks. So it would be left, for the time being, to Jack Markover's imagination. She knew Markover, and could think of no one she'd rather have in the present position.

Collingdale had already talked individually with his team members, of course. But this was the first time they'd all been together. She was pleased to see that he refused to use the term *Goompahs*.

That had raised the question of a proper reference. Had it been visible from Earth, Lookout would have been located in Draco. But *Draconians* would never do. They were close to the Dumbbell Nebula but that didn't help much either. In the end, knowing she had no control over the matter, hearing the media going on endlessly about *Goompahs,* she put it aside. It was already too late.

Collingdale finished his preliminary remarks, which consisted mostly of an orientation and welcome aboard. He invited them to get ready to depart, but asked the linguists to stay a moment. They were, to Hutch's mind, the heart and soul of the operation. And she was pleased to see a substantial level of enthusiasm.

Judy Sternberg would be their director. Judy was an Israeli, a specialist in the intersection between language and culture, and a born leader. He introduced her, and she said all the right things. Proud to be working with them. An opportunity to make a major contribution. She knew they'd perform admirably.

Judy was no taller than Hutch, but she had presence. "Ladies and gentlemen," she concluded, "we are going to rescue the Goompahs. But first we are going to *become* Goompahs."

So much for getting rid of the terminology. She wished Jack Markover had come up with something else on those initial transmissions.

Collingdale thanked Judy and shook her hand. "While we're en route to Lookout," he told the linguists, "we are going to break into their language. We are going to *master* it. And when we get there we are going to warn the natives what's coming. We'll help them evacuate their cities and head for the hills." He allowed himself a smile at the expression. "And we are going to help them. If it comes to it, we may be with them. We'll do what is necessary to save their rear ends."

One of them raised a hand. Hutch recognized him from the manifest as Valentino Scarpello, from Venice. "How," he asked, "are we going to do this? Why would they believe us?"

Valentino had a dazzling smile and leading-man features. Half the women in the group were already drooling in his direction.

"By the time we arrive on the scene," Collingdale said, "the cloud will be hanging over their heads. I don't think it'll be hard to persuade anyone."

That brought applause. Someone had hung on the bulkhead a picture of a Goompah, with its saucer eyes and large vacuous smile. They were pets, and the Academy people, and maybe the whole world, were adopting them.

"It might be," he added, "that we won't need to hide behind the disguises.

Hutch back there—Hutch, would you stand a moment please?—Hutch is doing what she can to get us past the Protocol. It's possible that, by the time we get to Lookout, we'll be able to walk in, say hello, and suggest that everybody just get out of town. But however that plays out, we *will* not stand by and watch them die."

More applause.

"Thank you." He exuded confidence.

When the linguists had gone up the ramp to the *al-Jahani*, she took Collingdale and Judy aside. "I appreciate your spirit," she said. "But nobody stays on the ground when the omega gets there." She looked both in the eye. "We are not going to lose anyone out there. You guys understand that?"

"I was speaking metaphorically," said Collingdale. "We'll take care of them." He looked at Judy for confirmation and Judy gazed at Hutch.

"Don't worry," she said. "We won't let anything like that happen."

Then they were shaking hands. Good-bye. Good luck. See you in a couple of years. Hugs all around.

She was thinking about Thrillseekers, Inc., and the Church of Revelation, and Island Specialties. Yesterday there'd been four more, a clothing retailer who wanted to bring back some of the natives to use as models for a new line of Goompah fashions ("—and we'd save the lives of the models, don't forget that—") which, incidentally, looked not very much like the originals; a representative from the media giants, who were demanding an opportunity to record the destruction; a games marketer who wanted to develop a game that would be called *Omega*; and an executive from Karman-Highsmith who wanted to send a crew to get location shots for a sim that was already in the works. Major people involved.

Collingdale lingered while Judy boarded. Then he looked down into her eyes. "Wish you were coming?"

"No," she said. "I've gotten too old for this sort of thing."

WHILE WAITING FOR departure, she checked in with ops and got the latest status report from the *Jenkins*. It was a week old, of course, the time needed for hyperlight traffic to reach her from Lookout. That was another mistake, allowing the name *Lookout* to get around. It had become a joke for late night comedians, as well as a predictor of disaster. She saw now that they should have gotten on top of that right away. Should have given the sun a name, something like Chayla, and then they could have called the world Chayla III. And the inhabitants would have become Chaylans. All very dignified. But it was too late for that. It was her fault, but a smart Academy public relations section would have picked up on it right away.

There was nothing new from the *Jenkins*. They were still debating how best to go down and look around. She didn't envy Jack, who had some tough decisions in front of him. The ops officer pressed his earphones and signaled her to wait. He listened, nodded, and looked up. "Commissioner on the circuit for you, ma'am."

That was a surprise. "I'll take it in the conference room," she said.

He was seated on the deck of a yacht, a captain's cap pulled low over his eyes. *"Just thought I'd check in,"* he said. *"How are we doing?"*

"Fine. I see you didn't quite make Geneva."

He smiled innocently. *"Will the* al-Jahani *get away on schedule?"*

"Yes, sir. They're packed and ready to go." She paused. "Why?"

"Why do I want to know about the al-Jahani?"

"Why run me through the parade?"

"I thought it would be a good idea if you learned why there's a Protocol."

She sat down. "You made your point."

"Good. Hutch, it's not just the Goompahs. We're talking about a precedent. If we break it at Lookout, wherever we find anyone we'll be baptizing, selling motorized carts, and dragging critters back to perform in circuses. You understand?"

"You really think that would happen?"

"It's hard to see how it wouldn't. I take it you told them no deal."

"All except the media. They're getting limited access. But not on the ground. How'd you know?"

"I've already heard rumblings of formal protests. Good. I'm proud of you."

She'd always thought of Asquith as a man who'd avoid a fight at any cost. "What chance do you think they have, Michael? The protests."

"Zero to poor. Unless you give the game away."

SHE JUST MISSED a flight to Reagan and, rather than wait three hours, she caught one to Atlanta, and then took the glide train to D.C. Just south of Richmond they ran into a snowstorm, the first in that area in ten years or more. It got progressively heavier as the train moved north.

It was late evening by the time she reached home, descending onto the landing pad through a blizzard. Tor was waiting on the porch.

She got out of the taxi and hurried through the storm. The door swung open, and he handed her a hot chocolate. "Well," he said, "did we get everybody off safely for Goompah country?"

"I hope so. How's Maureen?"

"Asleep. She missed her mommy. I don't think she likes the way I read George." That was a reference to George Monk, the garrulous chimp.

The hot chocolate was good. Inside, he had a blazing fire going. She set the cup down and shook the snow off her jacket.

"It's all over the networks," he said. "The talking heads don't think much of your chances."

"They're probably right." She was about to sit when the house AI (named for the chimp, or maybe it was the other way round) sounded the chime that indicated an incoming call.

"Who is it, George?" Tor asked.

"Academy watch officer. For Hutch."

"That's odd," she said. "I can't imagine what that would be about." Actually she could: Her first thought was that the *al-Jahani* had developed a problem already.

Jean Kilgore's face appeared on-screen. *"Hutch?"*

"Yes. What do you have, Jean?"

"I wanted to let you know Harold is in the hospital. Apparently it's serious."

She needed a moment to understand. "What happened?" she asked. "How is he?"

"Heart attack. They took him to Georgetown. It happened this afternoon."

"Do you have anything on his condition?"

"No, ma'am. Only what I told you."

"Okay."

"He went home early. Said he wasn't feeling well."

"Thanks, Jean." She was headed toward her closet for a fresh jacket.

"Jenny Kilborn says he's been on heart medication for years."

"Yes," she said. "I know."

"But they didn't think it was that serious. If he was having trouble, he doesn't seem to have told anyone. Jenny talked with somebody at the hospital. Or maybe the police. I'm not sure which. They said his neighbor couldn't get her front door open because of the snow. He went over to help her dig out."

Great. Guy with a heart condition. "Thanks, Jean." She'd have to change her shoes. "George, get me a cab. And connect me with that aunt of his, the one who lives in Wheaton."

SHE COULDN'T GET through to the aunt, whom she'd met once, years before. She was, as far as Hutch knew, Harold's only relative in the area. But the traffic director informed her she was offline. Apparently one of those people who did not carry a commlink. Well, Hutch could understand it. If she ever got clear of the Academy, she'd think about ditching hers.

All attempts to get information from Georgetown also went nowhere. *"He's been admitted,"* the hospital told her. *"Other than that we don't have anything at the moment."*

Twenty minutes after leaving Woodbridge she settled onto the roof of the Georgetown Medical Center. She climbed out, momentarily lost her balance on the snow-covered ramp, and hurried down to the emergency room receiving desk.

The aunt was there, standing in a small circle of worried-looking people. *Mildred*. Her eyes were red.

Hutch introduced herself. Mildred smiled weakly, stifling tears. There was also a female cousin, a neighbor, a clergyman, and Charlie Wilson, one of the people from the lab. "How is he?" she asked.

Charlie looked steadily at Hutch and shook his head.

N E W S D E S K

RECORD COLD IN MIDWEST
Temperature Hits Fifty Below in St. Louis

WCN SENDS PEACEKEEPERS TO MIDDLE EAST
Train Bombed by Iniri Rebels

TIDAL WAVE KILLS HUNDREDS IN BANGLADESH
Triggered by Collapsing Island

SINGH DEFEATS HARRIGAN FOR HUMAN CHESS CHAMPIONSHIP
First Off-Earth Title Match

DOCTOR ALVA ACCEPTS PERUVIAN MEDAL
Honored for Efforts During Bolus Outbreak

WOMAN KILLS FOUR IN NEW HAMPSHIRE BAR
Claims Devil Was On the Way to Snatch Their Souls

RECESSION ENTERS THIRD QUARTER
Unemployment Up Seventh Straight Month

SIX KILLED AT BELGRADE CONCERT
Grandstand Gives Way During Beethoven Fair

DEALY GUILTY
Billionaire Convicted On All Counts
Victims Demonstrate Outside Court
Civil Suits Pending
Faces Character Reconstruction

SANASI CALLED BEFORE CONGRESS
Expected to Take Fifth
Martin Says No to Deal

ALIENS IN DRACO
Primitive Civilization Under Cloud
Natives Resemble Goompahs

PART TWO

goompahs

chapter 9

Arlington.
Saturday, March 15.

HAROLD NEVER REGAINED consciousness, and was pronounced dead at 4:32 A.M.

Hutch was still there when the word came, trying to provide what support she could to Mildred and the cousin. She notified the lab watch officer and listened while the doctor said he was sorry, there was really nothing they could have done.

He was 106. Mildred explained that the doctors had wanted to give him a synthetic heart a few years back, but he'd refused. She wondered why. He'd always seemed rational. And he had everything to live for: He seemed content with his work and was respected around the world.

"He was alone," Mildred said. Tears leaked out of her eyes. She looked relatively young, but she was Harold's aunt so she, too, was past the century mark.

Hutch came out of the hospital under a sky still dark and cold, wondering why she hadn't seen it coming, why she hadn't stepped in. She'd never invited him to the house. Not once. Despite the fact they'd eaten lunch countless times, that she'd confided in him when she'd gotten frustrated with the job. And he'd always told her to calm down, everything would be okay. It'll pass. It was his favorite line. Everything passes.

Tor's parents lived in Britain, and her own father was long dead. Harold would have made a superb substitute grandfather for Maureen, if Hutch had only known. Had only *thought*.

So she stood in the access station, watching the last few flakes drifting across the rooftop. Probably windblown, she decided, suspecting the snow had stopped. Banks of the stuff were piled up around the landing pads.

Harold gone. It was hard to believe.

Her link sounded. It was Tor. *"What's happening?"*

"We lost him."

"I'm sorry."

"About a half hour ago."

"You okay?"

"Yes. I'm on my way home now."

"All right. I'll have some breakfast waiting."

"No. Nothing for me, thanks. I'm not hungry."

A taxi descended, a woman got out, and Hutch's commlink sounded, alerting her it was *her* cab. She climbed in, and the harness descended on her. And the thought she'd been pushing aside for the last two hours settled in beside her. Harold, what are the omegas?

A medical unit drifted down onto the far end of the roof, where the emergency pad was located. She gave the taxi her address and settled back.

It lifted off, turned south, and picked up speed toward the Potomac.

SHE USUALLY WORKED a half day Saturdays, especially when things were happening, which was pretty much all the time. She'd been at her desk less than an hour when the report came in. The *Gallardo* had inspected a cloud out near Alpha Cassiopeiae and found another hedgehog. The circumstances were the same: It was out front, same course, same velocity. Six and a half kilometers in diameter. Preliminary scan suggested it was an identical object. The only thing different was its range from the cloud, only fifteen thousand klicks.

The two sites were hundreds of light-years apart.

She'd barely digested the information when the watch officer called with more. The local cloud had one too. Again it was identical in everything except range, which was forty-two hundred kilometers. Even the spines were set in an identical pattern. As if the objects had come out of the same mold. There was some minor damage, probably caused by collisions.

It looked harmless.

She sat several minutes studying the images and went down to the lab. Harold's office was empty, but Charlie Wilson was there, and a few of the technicians. It had been Hutch's experience that bosses are rarely loved, and whatever the employees might say, there was inevitably a sigh of relief when they moved on. Even when the movement was to a better world. But everyone had liked Harold. And the mood in the lab was genuinely depressed.

"You know why we needed him?" Charlie told her after she'd sat down to share a glass of pineapple juice. "He was as big as any of the people who try to shoulder their way to the equipment. Which meant he could say *no.* He could keep things orderly. Who's going to refuse time on the systems now to Stettberg? Or to Mogambo?"

"You will, Charlie," she said. "And I'll back you up." He looked doubtful, but she smiled. "You'll do fine. Just don't show any hesitation. You tell them no, that's it. Let them know we'll call them if we get available time. Then thank them kindly and get off the circuit."

He took a long pull at the juice without saying anything.

"Charlie." She changed her tone so he'd see the subject was closed. "I want to talk with you about the omegas."

"Okay."

"Last week, Wednesday, I think, Harold told me he thought he knew what they were."

Charlie tilted his head, surprised. The reaction was disappointing. She'd hoped Harold had confided in him. "He didn't say anything to you?"

"No, Hutch. If he had any ideas, he kept them to himself."

"You're sure."

"Of course. You think I'd forget something like that?" Harold's office was visible through a pane of glass. The desk was heaped with paper, disks, magazines, books, and electronic gadgets. Waiting for someone to clear them away, box them and ship them home. "I just don't know what he was thinking, Hutch. But I can tell you one thing you might not know."

"What's that, Charlie?"

"We matched the tewks with the omegas. With the waves. Or at least with the places where the waves should be if they're consistent."

"He told me that. So there's a connection."

"Apparently."

And two of them with hedgehogs. Did all the clouds have hedgehogs? "Charlie," she said, "these objects that we've spotted running in front of the omegas: They seem to be booby traps. Bombs. Is it possible that what you've been seeing is hedgehogs exploding?"

"No." He shook his head.

"How can you be sure?"

"Did you look at the pictures from the *Heffernan*?"

Hutch hadn't. She'd read the report.

"The explosion that destroyed the *Quagmor*—Is that right? I keep hearing two different names for the ship—is nothing like what we see when one of the tewks goes off. It's on the order of difference between a firecracker and a nuke."

"Okay," she said. "Just a thought."

THEY WENT INTO Harold's office and looked through the stacks of documents. But nothing presented itself as particularly relevant. "Charlie," she said, "I need you to go over everything he was working on. See if you can find anything new on the clouds. Or the tewks."

"Okay."

"Let me know if you find something."

"Actually," he said, "we've already started." Charlie was tall and rangy, with sandy hair and clear blue eyes. Unlike most of the researchers who came to the Academy, Charlie kept himself in decent physical condition. He played basketball with his kids on weekends, swam an hour a day in the Academy pool, and played occasional tennis. He lacked his boss's brilliance, but then so did pretty much everybody else.

"Okay," she said. "Stay with it. Let me know if anything turns up." She started to leave but stopped short. "What about the nova patterns, Charlie? Anything new on those?"

"You mean, about the way they line up?" He shook his head. "Maybe if more of them get sighted, we'll have a better idea. But I think the notion there's a pattern is an illusion."

"Really. Why?"

"They tend to bunch up in a relatively small space. When that happens, you can almost always rotate the viewpoint and get a pattern."

"Oh."

"And the sightings are probably confined to those two areas not because that's the only places they are, but because we don't have that many packages up yet and functioning. Give it time. There will probably be more. If there are, I think you'll see the patterns go away."

LIBRARY ENTRY

Harold Tewksbury

. . . His achievements over an eighty-year career have been adequately chronicled elsewhere. He is one of the fortunate few whose work will survive his lifetime. But that is also on the record elsewhere. What mattered to me was his essential decency, and his sense of humor. Unlike many of the giants in our world, he was never too busy to talk to a journalist, never too busy to lend a hand to a friend. It is entirely fitting that he died helping a neighbor.

Everyone who knew him feels the loss. We are all poorer this morning.

—Carolyn Magruder
UNN broadcast,
Sunday, March 16, 2234

chapter 10

TWICE TO THE Wheel in a weekend.

Standing with Julie Carson, the ship's captain, Hutch watched the people from Rheal Fabrics pack the kite onto the *Hawksbill*. Eight large cylinders, each more than thirty meters in diameter and maybe half again as long, were clamped to the hull. These were described on the manifest as chimneys. They were, in fact, rainmakers. Four landers had been stored in the cargo bays, along with an antique helicopter whose hull was stenciled CANADIAN FORCES. There was also an AV3 cargo hauler; a shuttle reconfigured to accommodate an LCYC projector, like the big ones used at Offshore and other major theme parks; a half dozen pumps; and lengths of hose totaling several kilometers. A second LCYC was already mounted on the underside of the ship.

The *Hawksbill* was not part of the Academy fleet; it was a large cargo carrier on loan from a major shipping company which had donated it for the current project with the understanding that they would get all kinds of good publicity. Plus some advantages in future Academy contracts. Plus a tax break.

Like all ships of its class, it wasn't designed to haul passengers, and was in fact limited to a pilot plus two. Or three, in an emergency.

The workers from Rheal were in the after cargo hold, running a final inspection on the kite before closing the doors. A cart carrying luggage appeared on the ramp and clicked through the main airlock. "Dave Collingdale will direct the operation," Hutch was explaining. "Anything that has to do with the *Hawksbill*, you're in charge. Kellie will be there with the *Jenkins*. Do you know her? Yes? Good. She'll be switching places with you so you can help Marge get the rainmakers set up."

"Which means," said Julie, "that she'll be taking the *Hawksbill* out to play tag with the omega?"

"Yes."

"Okay," she said. "Whatever you guys want."

Julie was an Academy pilot, about the same age Hutch had been when she'd taken her first superluminal out of the solar system. She'd had her license for a year, but she'd already acquired a reputation for competence.

Hutch felt a special kinship with her. She was the daughter of Frank Carson, who had dodged the lightning with her during their original encounter at Delta.

She was tall, like her father, same military cut, brown eyes, her mother's red hair. She also had her mother's conviction that there was no situation she could not handle. It was one of the reasons Hutch had offered her the assignment. She was facing a long time away with a limited social life, but it was a career-enhancing opportunity and a chance to show what she could do. The other reason was that she could pilot the AV3 hauler.

One of her passengers appeared at the top of the ramp. Avery Whitlock was one of a long line of philosophical naturalists who had come to prominence originally in the nineteenth century with Darwin and Thomas Huxley, and continued with Loren Eiseley, Stephen Jay Gould, and Esther Gold. He had silver hair, a long nose, and a timid smile. He was a black man, had grown up with all the aristocratic advantages, gone to the right schools, mixed with the right people. But he had a populist talent that shone through his work, and made him the most widely read scientific writer of his era. Eventually, Hutch knew, he would produce a history of the attempt to rescue the Goompahs. Succeed or fail, Whitlock liked the human race and would ensure that it, and the Academy, got just due for the effort it was making.

He looked out at the ship, and Hutch saw his jaw drop a bit. "It's a behemoth," he said. "Really only room for two of us?"

Hutch grinned and shook his hand. "Good to see you, Whit. And actually, if you count the captain, it holds three." She introduced him to Julie, who surprised her by commenting that she was familiar with Whitlock's work. "I especially liked *The Owl and the Lamp*," she said. Whitlock beamed, and Hutch saw again that there was no quicker way to a writer's heart than by expressing admiration for his work.

Julie had her own views, it turned out, about avian evolution. Hutch listened for a couple of minutes, then pointed out that it was getting late. "Of course," said Julie.

"You'll have plenty of time on the flight," she added.

"I had no idea," Whitlock said, returning his gaze to the ship, "that it would be so big."

"It's pretty much all storage space," said Julie. "Living quarters are on the top deck." A line of viewports was visible. "Most of the rest of it has no life support."

"Incredible. What are we carrying?"

"Some rainmakers and a kite," said Hutch.

Marge Conway showed up moments later. She was a big woman, a one-time ballet dancer, though Hutch would have liked to see the guy who would catch her in his arms and give her a quick spin. More to the point, she was an accomplished climatologist. The years had caught up with her somewhat since the last time Hutch had seen her. Her hair had begun to show patches of gray, and a few lines had appeared around her eyes. But there was still something feline in the way she got around.

Julie took them on board and showed them their compartments. Avery here, Marge there, sorry folks, they're a little cramped, but they're comfortable.

Hutch had been surprised when Marge announced she would make the flight personally. She didn't seem to mind that it would be a two-year mission. "Once in a lifetime you get to do something like this," she said, "if you're lucky. No way I'm sending somebody else." Her kids were grown, her husband had not renewed, and she'd explained she wanted to get as far from him as she could.

Hutch stayed with them until it was time to leave. This was of course a different kind of social arrangement from the *al-Jahani*, which had been a small community setting out. The onboard interplay there would be vastly different. Cliques would form, people would make friendships, find others with shared attitudes, and they'd have no real problem.

The *Hawksbill* would be nine months in flight with three people. At the far end, if they were sick of each other, Collingdale could make other arrangements to get them home. But for the better part of a year they'd be sealed together and they would *have* to get along. Hutch had interviewed Marge a couple of days earlier, to reassure herself, and she knew Whitlock well enough to have no qualms about him. They should be all right. But it would be a long trip, and she knew they'd be glad to see daylight at the other end.

While they got settled, she repaired to the bridge with Julie. "One critical thing you should pass on to Kellie," she said. "This ship wasn't designed to go anywhere near omegas. The architecture isn't right, and it could draw the lightning. You hear what I'm saying?"

"Yes, ma'am. I will tell her."

"She'll be captain during that phase of the operation. I don't care what anybody tells her, she will keep minimum range from the cloud. She'll have it in writing from me long before then, but it's maybe a little more convincing coming from you."

"I doubt that," Julie said. "What's minimum range?"

"Two hundred kilometers is standard for this kind of vessel."

"Two hundred klicks. Okay. I'll tell her."

Hutch asked permission to sit in the pilot's seat, and inquired about Julie's parents. Her father was semi-retired, teaching at the University of Maine and still serving as a consultant to the Margaret Tufu Foundation. Her mother Linda was curator of the Star Museum, which contained the third largest collection of extraterrestrial artifacts in North America, behind the Academy Museum and the Smithsonian.

"Say hello for me," Hutch said.

"I will."

"I hope you're as good as they are."

"Yes, ma'am. I am."

It was the right reply. Hutch shook her hand and gazed at the console, at the navigation monitor to the pilot's right, at the orange ready lamp indicating energy buildup, and she felt again the awesome power of the drive units. Finally, realizing Julie was waiting for her to leave so she could get to her check list, she said good-bye.

She wished Marge and Whitlock success, and strode up the ramp and back into the Wheel.

GREGORY MACALLISTER WAS waiting when she got home. Tor, who was a better chef than she was, had dinner on. Maureen was entertaining Mac by running in circles while a black kitten watched.

MacAllister was a big man in every sense of the word. He took up a lot of space. He was an intellectual linebacker. When he walked into a room, everyone inevitably came to attention. Mac was an international figure, an editor and essayist whose acquaintance with Hutch had begun when they were stranded together on Deepsix.

He'd become interested in the Goompahs and had called, asking whether he could talk with her about what the Academy intended to do on Lookout.

Hutch explained over the pork chops. She told him about the limitations imposed by the Protocol, about her fears as to what would happen if they set the wrong precedent, about the hedgehogs.

When they finished, they retired to the living room and Hutch put up some pictures of the Goompahs. These were long-range, taken from telescopes on the *Jenkins* and on satellites. There were shots of temples, of the isthmus road and some of its traffic, of farms, of parks and fountains. "Not bad," Mac remarked from time to time, obviously impressed with Goompah culture. Hutch understood he was impressed because he hadn't expected much. Hadn't done his homework. "I thought they were primitives," he said.

"Why would you think that?" The screen had paused on a picture of three Goompahs, mom, dad, and a kid, probably, almost as if Jack had asked them to pose. A tree like nothing that ever grew on Earth rose behind them, and the images were filled with sunlight.

Mac made a face, suggesting the answer should be obvious. "Because—" He looked up at one of Tor's paintings, a depiction of a superluminal cruising through moonlight, and paused, uncertain. "Well, they look dumb. And they have a fifth-century society." He glanced over at Maureen playing with her dollhouse. "She has her mother's good looks, Hutch."

"Thank you."

"I guess the question at issue is whether the Goompahs are worth all the fuss being made over them."

"They're worth the fuss," said Tor. "They're intelligent."

MacAllister smiled. "That puts them ahead of us."

Gregory MacAllister was not the best-known journalist of the age, but he was certainly the most feared. Acerbic, acid-tongued, not given to taking prisoners, he liked to think of himself as a champion of common sense and a dedicated opponent of buffoonery and hypocrisy in high places. During the course of an interview the previous evening regarding the drive to make lightbenders available to the general public, he'd commented that while people have the right to commit suicide, he saw nothing in the Constitution requiring the government to expedite matters. "Invisible drunks," he'd said. "Think about it." Then he'd added, "The original sin was stupidity, and it is with us still."

"Maybe it does," said Tor. "That's all the more reason to give them a chance."

Hutch produced a cold beer for Mac, and wine for herself and Tor. Mac took a pull at the beer, expressed himself satisfied, and asked Tor why he thought the creatures were intelligent.

Tor rolled his eyes. "You've seen their architecture. And the way they've laid out their cities. What more do you need?"

Mac's eyes usually darkened when he considered the issue of intelligent behavior. They did so now. "Tor," he said, "the bulk of the human race shouldn't be allowed out by themselves at night. A lot of them live near parks, fountains, and even spaceports. But that's assigning worth by reflection."

"You're not serious."

Mac had liberated some chocolate cookies from the kitchen. He held one out for Maureen, who took it happily and told Mac he wasn't supposed to give any to Babe. That was the kitten, who showed no interest anyhow. "Tor," he said, "most generations produce a handful of rational people who, so far, have been able to keep us going while everyone else spends his time falling into the works. Most people are programmed by the time they're six, and learn nothing worthwhile afterward."

Tor made a sound indicating he was in pain. In fact, of course, he was used to Mac's exaggerations and would have expected no less.

But Hutch never got used to it. "Are you suggesting," she asked, "that we should give an IQ test before rescuing someone, or some*thing*, in trouble?"

"Not at all. By all means, we should help anyone if we can reasonably do it. And the Goompahs do look worth saving. But I think you're facing a no-win situation."

That surprised her. "How do you mean?"

"You'll probably have to break the Protocol to do anything for them. I mean, you're even going to be shipping relief supplies. How do you possibly get them to these creatures without announcing your presence?" A look of genuine concern passed over his craggy features. "If you *don't* succeed in helping them and a lot of them get wiped out, or they *all* get wiped out, you won't forgive yourself. And the Academy will take a beating."

Tor nodded reluctantly. "He's probably right, Hutch."

She looked at Mac across the top of her wineglass. And then leveled her gaze at her husband. "What would you two have me do? Just ignore them? Let them die by the thousands and not lift a finger?"

For a time no one spoke. Maureen looked at her oddly, as if Mommy had misbehaved. Babe the kitten came over and tried to chew on her ankle.

"I take it," said Mac, "that there really *is* no way of shutting down the cloud?"

"None that we've been able to figure out. There's never been enough money to fund a serious effort."

Mac laughed. "But there's enough money to underwrite the farming industries. And to provide tax breaks for General Power and Anderson & Goodbody." He growled. "The truth is that it's hard to justify spending money on a hazard that's so far off, Hutch. Or that's threatening somebody else. Still, I can understand the reluctance."

She knew that. Mac had remained silent while major pundits laughed at Senator Blasingame, when he'd put together a bill demanding an extensive effort to find a way to neutralize the omegas. Blasingame had even made Hal Bodley's annual Boondoggle List. Mac might have been able to stem the tide had he gotten into the fight.

"We could have used you," she said.

"Hutch, the sun's going to expand in a few billion years and wipe out all life on Earth. Maybe we should do something about that, as well."

"Try to keep it serious, Mac," she said.

"Okay." He emptied his glass, trundled out to the kitchen, and came back with a refill. It was an uncomfortable moment, and Hutch suspected she shouldn't have said anything, but damn it, Mac's point of view was short-sighted. Maureen got a pulltoy out and she and the kitten retreated into the den.

Rachmaninoff's Concerto Number Two was playing softly in the background. Light swept briefly through the window as a flyer descended onto the landing pad they shared with the Hoffmanns.

"It strikes me," Mac said, easing back into his chair, "that it's not true. Or at least, it's not a *universal* truth."

"What isn't, Mac?"

"That cultures get swamped when they encounter a more developed civilization."

"Can you name an exception?"

"Sure," he said. "India."

"They weren't swamped," said Tor. "But they were taken over."

"That doesn't count. The Brits at the time were imperialists. That wouldn't apply on Lookout. But my point is that Indian culture survived pretty well. The essentials, their music, their marital patterns, their self-image, didn't change at all."

"What about the Native Americans?"

He smiled. "It's a myth, Hutch. They didn't collapse because they were faced with an intrinsically stronger culture. They were beaten down by a superior military. And maybe because their own cultural habits wouldn't allow them to unite.

"Priscilla, if I felt the way you do, I wouldn't mess around with all these half measures."

"What would you do, Mac?"

"I'd send the Peacekeepers out there and get them all out of the cities when the damned thing gets close. Get them behind rocks or in caves or whatever else they have until it passes. It only takes a day or so, right?"

"Mac, I can't do that."

"Then you don't have the courage of your convictions."

She glanced over at Tor. He was shaking his head at her. You know better than to take Mac seriously. Relax. Let it go.

"There is this," pursued Mac. "If you called out the troops, you'd have the satisfaction of knowing you gave it your best shot."

Maureen had finished her cookie, leaving crumbs everywhere. Hutch let her head drift back for a moment, then got up and took Maureen's hand. "Time for bed, Mo."

"Too early, Mommy," said the child, who began to fill up. She hated going to bed when they had company. She especially liked Mac. What on Earth was there about him that a child could love?

"We'll read for a while," she said. "Say good night to Uncle Mac."

Maureen made a sad face at Mac. "Good night, Uncle Mac," she said. And she reached for him, and kissed his cheek.

"Good night, darling," said Mac.

HUTCH COULD HEAR them chattering away downstairs while she read to Maureen. Benny Rabbit makes friends with Oscar the Cat. Hutch would believe it when she saw it. But Maureen giggled and Babe the kitten joined them and stayed when Maureen fell asleep and Hutch turned out the lamp and went downstairs.

They were talking about Paxon Carbury's latest novel, *Morley Park*. It had gotten strong reviews, and Tor had liked it, but Mac was consigning it to the unwashed. "It's just more adultery in the suburbs," he said.

And that seemed to settle it. Tor made a few objections, tried to explain what he had liked about the book, then backed off. Mac asked Hutch whether she'd read it.

"No," she said. "I've been a little pressed lately."

In the background, the commlink chimed. Hutch excused herself and went into the dining room. "Who is it, George?"

"*Academy watch officer,*" said the AI.

She was beginning to hate these calls. A screen lit up. Actually it was Charlie. "*I hate to bother you at home,*" he said.

"Yes, Charlie, what have you got?"

"*You wanted to hear anything that came in on the hedgehogs.*"

"What happened?"

"*They found another one.*"

"Who?"

"*The* Santiago. *We don't have any details yet. But it's beginning to look as if they all have them. All the clouds, I mean.*"

"Yes, Charlie, I think you're right. Thanks. Let me know if you hear anything else."

"*There is something else.*"

"Yes?"

"*We don't think the hedgehogs and the clouds are actually running at the same velocity.*"

"Oh? I didn't think any questions had been raised about that."

"*They hadn't. The difference is so slight, it's hard to measure. Even now, we're not really certain. But it looks as if the hedgehogs are moving a bit slower.*"

"How much?"

"Almost too little difference to measure. It's why we didn't pick it up at first. I mean, a cloud's not a solid object, so you don't really get—"

"How much difference, Charlie?"

"The escorts are slower by between four and five meters an hour."

"All of them?"

"Two of them. We're still trying to get measurements on the others."

SHE DIDN'T KNOW what to make of it. It didn't sound especially important until she found herself telling Tor and Mac about it. And suddenly the lights went on and a chill ran through the room. "Dumb," she said, breaking into the middle of a sentence.

"What is?" asked Tor.

"Me. *I* am."

"In what way, Priscilla?" said Mac.

"You know about the tewks. We think they all happen where there are clouds."

"And—?"

"If each cloud has a hedgehog, and each hedgehog is running at a slightly slower speed so that the cloud eventually overtakes it—"

"Oh," said Mac.

"The escorts are exactly the sort of things that the clouds seem to want to attack. Lots of right angles. Couple hundred of them."

Tor was nodding. "They're designated targets."

"I think so," she said. "Has to be."

Mac couldn't accept the idea. "Not at those rates of closure. You're talking a couple of thousand years before the clouds catch the damned things."

"But what's the point?" asked Tor. "I don't get it."

She reactivated her link. "Charlie?"

"Yes, Hutch?"

"Contact Serenity. Tell Audrey the hedgehogs may be triggers."

"Triggers?"

"Right. They go boom. And they initiate something."

"Like what?"

"Like a tewk. Listen, I'll be in touch with her tomorrow. Meantime, I want her to start looking at sending a mission to push one of the damned things into a cloud. See what happens."

"I'll tell her."

"Explain that we'll want the whole thing done by robot. Nobody is to go anywhere near any part of the operation. Okay?"

"Yes, ma'am. I'll pass it on."

She switched off. "When you talk to her tomorrow—" said Tor.

"Yes—?"

"Tell her to pick a cloud that's well away from anybody's neighborhood."

LIBRARY ENTRY

The stores are filling up with Goompah dolls, and we are becoming increasingly aware of the existence of these terminally cute offworld wobblies. Children cannot resist them. They are showing up in games and books. There is already an activist society devoted to their welfare. Yet they face possible extinction.

It may be necessary to lay the Noninterference Protocol aside. Indeed, it's hard to see how we can go to their rescue without doing so. But it would help if we defined the exception as a one-time only affair. Make it clear that we are not setting a precedent, and draw a line across which interested manufacturers, religious groups, charitable organizations, trading companies, and everybody else who'd like to use these creatures to play out their own fantasies and ambitions, may not venture.

—Gregory MacAllister,
"How's the Jihad Going?"
Lost on Earth Interview, Monday, March 17

chapter 11

*. . . Be advised that your primary objective is to get the job done. If you find it
necessary to set the Protocol aside, this constitutes your authority to do so. . . .*
    . . . Collect and run analyses of food samples. . . .
    *. . . Time is of the essence. In view of the lag between Lookout and your
other points of contact, you are free to use discretion.*

IN FACT, JACK didn't like the idea of using discretion. Not in this kind of
situation. It was purely political. No matter what he did, and how things
turned out, he would be criticized. Any blame to be assigned would come
his way, and credit would go to the Second Floor at the Academy. He'd
been around too long not to know how these things worked.

After watching Hutchins's transmission, Winnie was exasperated, too.
"How," she demanded, "do they expect us to record conversations down
there? For a start, where are we going to get recording equipment?"

"We might be able to rig some pickups," said Digger.

It had required more than two weeks for their report to cross the interstellar gulfs, and the answer to come back. And their instructions had been
a surprise. They were to attempt to establish contact with the Goompahs.
They were to record conversations, if in fact these creatures actually conversed, and send the results back, where a team of linguists would work to
break into the language. They were to get visuals of the creatures as they
spoke, so that nonverbal cues could be included in the translation effort.
And they were to provide whatever additional information they could to
help ferret out meaning. And they were to do all this, preferably, while
respecting the Protocol.

Preferably.

Bureaucratic double-talk.

Translation: Get the job done without compromising the Protocol. If you
compromise the Protocol, and things go badly, you will be asked why you
found it necessary to do so.

Markover knew Hutchins, had always thought he could trust her, but he'd been around too long not to understand how these things went.

There was good news: The air sample analyses they'd transmitted to Broadside had undergone additional tests. No dangerous bioagents had been found, and no toxins. That was no surprise: So far, experience indicated that diseases from one world generally had no effect on life-forms from another. (Just as creatures operating outside their own biosystem would have a hard time finding anything digestible.) They could, if necessary, operate for a short time outside the e-suits.

Jack and Winnie both had notebooks, which were, of course, equipped with audio recorders and projectors. These could be used as pickups. Kellie said she thought the ship could contribute three more units.

"So how do we go about this?" asked Winnie.

Jack could see only one way. "I think," he said, "if you read between the lines, we just go down and say hello. See how they react."

Digger reread the message. "*That's* not what I see between the lines."

"What do *you* see?"

"The message literally says that we can ignore the Protocol. But she'd like us to use our imagination and find a better way."

Jack liked to think of himself as the kindly old director. Patient, easy-going, willing to listen. And to an extent he was correct. But it wasn't true that he had no temper; he was simply quite good at not letting people see it. This business with Hutch's message, though, was exactly the sort of thing that drove him up the wall. Because she was laying out contradictory propositions. If she could think of a way to accomplish what she wanted without talking directly to the Goompahs, why didn't she say so? Or, if she couldn't, why not just tell him flat out to take care of things. "Do you know of a better way?" he asked.

"No," said Digger.

Winnie looked out the viewport, peering down into the sun-streaked atmosphere, as though she could find an answer out there somewhere.

"Well," said Jack, "barring any other ideas, I think what we do is go down and say hello. See how they react. Then we plant some pickups so we can start recording their conversations." He swung around in his seat and looked at the transmission again.

"FIRST THING WE want to do," said Jack, "is to create an avatar. One of us to say hello."

"All right," said Winnie. "You don't think we'd do better to have someone just step out and wave?"

"Too dangerous. Let's see what they do when they see the avatar." He looked around. "We need pictures of somebody who looks friendly."

Winnie studied each of them as if that was no easy task. "Who do you suggest?"

"One of the women," said Digger. "They'll be less threatening."

Kellie was watching him carefully, her nose wrinkled, trying to restrain a smile. "I think *you'd* be our best bet, Dig."

"Me? Why?"

But he knew. Nobody had to say it. Digger possessed a slight approximation to their size and shape. He was a bit overweight, and somewhat less than average height.

"I think that'll work fine," said Jack. "So we let them take a look at the avatar. It waves and says hello, and if things go well, we shut off the visuals and, Digger, you step out of the underbrush and continue the conversation. Make friends on the spot."

"First ambassador from Earth," said Winnie.

Digger sucked in his belly.

Kellie beamed at him. "I'm proud of you, Dig." She circled him, measuring his dimensions. "We should give him a large shirt. Yellow, I think. Green leggings. Nice floppy hat. Get you looking a little bit like one of the locals."

That hurt. "You think I look like a Goompah?"

"No." Kellie laughed and gave him a hug. "You're cuter than they are. And you have a great smile." She paused and must have seen he was embarrassed. Her tone changed: "Digger, you're easy to like." She gripped his arm. "If they'll respond to any of us, it'll be you."

Digger conceded. "Doesn't fool me for a minute," he grumbled. "And I don't waddle, you know."

Kellie embraced him again. Longer this time. "We know that, Dig." Her eyes told him she meant it. Or, if he did waddle, it didn't matter to her. Either way, he guessed it was all right.

They produced the appropriate clothing, floppy everything, and he put it on, a bright yellow shirt that felt as if it was made from sailcloth, and baggy green leggings and sandals three sizes too big. Most of it, Kellie informed him, was made from blankets. The sandals had belonged to the previous skipper. A woman's red hat, origin unknown, came out of storage. Looked as if it had been with the ship for years.

When he was dressed they took pictures of him. "Why not make me look like a Goompah?" he suggested. "Why stop here?"

He half expected someone to remark that he already did. But Jack, reading his mind, only smiled. "Because eventually," he said, "we'll have to be able to talk to them. The avatar needs to look like you. Not them."

They made up the visuals and jury-rigged a projector by removing the heart of one of the VRs and connecting it to the power cells from a laser cutter. In the same way, they constructed three audiovisual pickups. They were clumsy and bigger than they'd have preferred. But the things worked, and that was sufficient for the moment. "All set," said Kellie, after they'd tested everything.

Below, it was early morning on the isthmus, a couple of hours before dawn. "Who wants to come?" asked Jack.

"I guess I'm going," said Digger.

And Kellie would pilot. "Winnie," he said, "you hold the fort."

She shook Digger's hand solemnly as he started toward the cargo bay. Good luck, Dig, the body language said. I'm with you, kid.

THE CARGO BAY also served as the launch area. Digger's pulse picked up a few notches as they descended through the ship. He was telling himself to relax, don't worry, we're about to make history. Hello, Goompahs.

The lander was a sleek, teardrop craft. It had less capacity than the older, boxy vehicles, but it provided a smoother ride. They climbed in, and Kellie started the launch process.

Jack began dispensing advice. He was a good guy, but he was a bit too helpful. If we decide it's okay for you to show yourself, don't make any sudden moves. Try to smile. Nonverbals are different from culture to culture, but the Noks and the Angels both recognize smiles, so it can't hurt. Unless, of course, things are different here.

He continued in that vein despite all Digger's efforts to change the subject, until finally Dig simply asked him to stop. "You're getting me rattled," he complained.

"I'm sorry. Listen, Dig, everything'll be okay."

Digger sat there in his native finery, feeling both foolish and scared. The Goompahs looked friendly. But he'd read about the Angels on Paradise, how harmless they'd looked, how *angelic*, before they tore two members of the Contact Society to shreds.

"I'm fine, Jack," he said. "I just wish I knew the language."

They dropped through a cloudless sky. The ground was dark despite innumerable individual lights. But they were mere sparks in the night, like distant stars, a few in the cities, some on the isthmus road, and a handful along the docks and on anchored ships.

They had no way of concealing the lander, and though Kellie turned off all the lights, they were nonetheless descending through a cloudless moonlit sky. Kellie, up front in the pilot's seat, held up five fingers to signify everything was okay. "All in it together," she said.

Jack sat lost in thought. "I wonder," he said, "if we could do this strictly through the use of avatars."

"How do you mean, Jack?" asked Digger.

"Produce a native avatar and stick with it. We stay out of sight altogether."

Digger thought about it. "Eventually," he said, "it would have to talk to them."

Jack made a pained sound. The avatar could not be made spontaneous. It could be programmed to deliver lines, but unless they knew how the Goompahs would react, there was no way to have it respond to them.

"Just as well," Jack said. "You look so good it would be a pity not to put you out there." Har-har.

Digger sat in his chair, thinking how this was the gutsiest thing he'd done in his life. Except maybe for the time in high school when he'd gotten his courage together and asked Veronica Keating for a date. Veronica had passed—thanks but I'm tied up for the next couple years—but he'd tried. Next time out of the barn he'd done better. With somebody else, of course.

They picked up some wind as they descended. Digger would have liked to open a window to get a sense of what the sea and the forest smelled like. Of course, they couldn't do that. The atmosphere was breathable, but it was oxygen-rich. He didn't know what the effect of that would be over an extended period, but it couldn't be good.

Jack was looking at the map, trying to decide where they should set down. "Here," he said at last, indicating the isthmus road a short distance north of the city with the temple by the sea.

The temple, lost in darkness now, looked Greek. That made the city Athens. He smiled at the notion. Athenians as oversize green critters waddling around.

He couldn't see anything out the windows other than the stars and the lights on the ground.

"You all set?" asked Jack, trying to relieve the tension.

"I'll be okay." He wasn't used to riding in the lander with the navigation lights out. It was hard to say why, but it was disquieting, as if they were sneaking up on an enemy stronghold. Kellie had done something to render the vehicle quieter than usual, had made it virtually silent.

"Be on the ground in two minutes, gentlemen," she said. "Activate your suits."

Digger checked his harness and his converter, and complied. One advantage of a relatively earthlike atmosphere was that they didn't have to haul air tanks around. The converter would provide an air supply from the existing atmosphere. Jack switched his on, and Digger momentarily caught the glow of the Flickinger field in the moment of ignition. Then it faded.

He activated his suit, pulled on a vest, attached his converter, and wondered briefly if he should have brought some trinkets to hand out to the natives.

Below, lanterns floated through the dark, spread out, and vanished. Trees rose around him. Kellie held the vehicle aloft for a moment to ensure that the ground was solid, then let the weight settle. They were down in a glade, the first streaks of light showing in the east.

IT WAS DIGGER'S first time on a world that could really be said to be alive. He squeezed Kellie's shoulder and shook hands with Jack. They were now eligible to join the Corbin Society, whose membership was limited to people who had made a first landing on a world with life-forms big enough to be visible. The Society was named for the director of the Tarbell mission, who, forty-five years before, had been the first to look out a window across extraterrestrial soil and see a live animal. In his case, it had been a large reptile, still the biggest land creature on record. It had inspected, then tried to eat, the lander.

Kellie turned on her e-suit. Her voice sounded in his link. "It's almost dawn. By the time we get out to the road, it should be daylight."

Jack's notebook would provide the projector. He pushed it into a vest pocket and handed the avatar disk to Digger. "You hang on to this," he said.

Digger nodded, released his restraints, and started for the airlock.

Kellie got out of her seat and pocketed the second notebook. "You might want to use the washroom before we leave. It'll be a while before we get back here." Their e-suits had no provision for disposing of bodily waste. Attachments were available but no one saw any need for them on this trip. Just get out, go to the road, say hello, and see how the locals respond. Then hustle back to the lander. Simple enough.

THEY WENT THROUGH the airlock and stood momentarily in the outer hatch. There was some fluttering in the trees, and the steady clacking of insects, but otherwise the forest remained quiet. They switched on dark lights. Digger would have preferred a regular lamp, but who knew what might be wandering around in the woods.

"Everyone ready?" asked Jack, climbing down onto sawtooth grass. He knelt, reacted with an *ouch*, and said, "Be careful. It's sharp."

In fact it was like a field of daggers. Digger squared his shoulders the way he had seen Jack Hancock do when facing danger in a dozen sims. He cautioned Kellie and stepped aside to let her pass. Then he fell in behind to bring up the rear.

They all wore pistols, just in case. Digger was qualified but unpracticed. He'd never before been on ground where there was a risk from local wildlife.

The line of trees was dark and quiet. Jack paused, looking for a break in the forest. Shrubbery, blossoms, vines, thorns, dead leaves, and misshapen trees crowded on them. Jack picked a spot and plunged in. Kellie followed, and Digger watched her plow through a spiderweb. Or something's web. Digger remembered reading somewhere that, so far, spiders had been found only on Earth. Even safely enveloped in the Flickinger field, he felt queasy about them.

It was slow going. The vegetation was thick, and the e-suits provided no defense against thorns and needles. The road was less than a half klick away from the landing site, but after an hour's time they were still struggling through heavy growth.

Winnie called from the ship twice to ask why it was taking so long. Jack, who usually stayed cool, told her that next time she should come and her grasp of the situation would improve.

Then he felt badly about growling at her and apologized. On his private circuit, he told Digger that he understood why she was worried, that anything could happen, that nobody really knew what kind of creatures might be loose in this forest.

That did nothing for Digger's state of mind.

Through breaks in the canopy of overhead branches and leaves, they saw the ship, a bright star moving through the fixed constellations. That alone, he realized, in a low-tech culture, could be enough to cause a major reaction.

The eastern horizon was getting bright. Behind him, in the bushes, something moved, and there was a brief scuffle. But Digger never saw anything.

"Road," said Jack.

At last. Digger came up beside him and looked out at it. It was really only a trail. But it had been laboriously cut through the forest, and it was wide enough for two wagons to pass side by side.

There was a low hill directly opposite. "He should stand up there," said Jack, referring to the avatar. "On the crest. I'd say under the tree would be good."

The tree looked more like an overgrown mushroom. Digger surveyed the area. To his left, north, the road proceeded another fifty meters or so before disappearing over the top of a hill. To his right, toward Athens, he could see for a considerable distance, maybe the length of a football field, before it curved off into the forest.

They crossed the road, climbed the hill, and hid themselves behind a clump of bushes with bright red blossoms. Digger handed over the disk, which Jack inserted into his notebook. "Test run, Holmes?" he asked.

"Indubitably, old chap."

The notebook was equipped with a projector on its leading edge. Jack aimed it toward the tree, which was about ten meters away, and punched a button. Digger's image, in green and gold and with his bright red hat, blinked on. He was standing a half meter in the air. Jack adjusted the picture, focused it, and brought the feet to Earth. Then he turned to Digger. "Okay," he said. "I think we're in business."

THERE WERE GREEN trees, and pale gray growths like the big mushroom at the top of the hill. The wind sucked at them all, and when Digger closed his eyes, it sounded like any forest back home. Avery Whitlock had once written that all forests were alike in their essence, that there was a kind of universal forest that was a prerequisite for intelligent life. *Wherever sentience is found*, he'd predicted, *it will have come to fruition in a deep wood.*

Kellie produced the second notebook and assured Digger she would take pictures and record everything for his grandchildren. She apparently thought remarks like that would put everybody off the trail of what was really happening (or not happening) between the two of them. But Jack was too excited wondering what was going to come around the curve in one direction or over the hill in the other, to give a damn about onboard romance.

"Traffic on the road." Winnie's voice. As planned, she was watching through the ship's scopes and satellites. (The ship by then was over the horizon and somewhere on the other side of the world.) As long as the sky stayed clear, the *Jenkins* would have them constantly in view. *"Looks like two of them. And a cart."*

"Thanks, Winnie."

"And a few more behind. Three on foot. And a second cart. Make that two, no, three, more carts. They're coming from the south. About a half kilometer from you."

Around the curve.

They waited, listening to the wind until they heard the sounds of creaking wheels, snorting, heavy clop-clops. And music. Pipes and stringed instruments, Digger thought. And thumping on a drum. And voices in allegro, maybe a little high-pitched.

The song, if that was what it was, lacked the easy rhythms of human melodies. "They're not exactly Ben and the Warbirds," Kellie observed.

Well, no. The voices were a bit lacking. But the critical news was that Digger hadn't heard anything yet that wasn't within the range of human capabilities.

"But you'll need women to do it," commented Kellie.

A large animal rounded the bend, hauling a cart, and lumbered toward them. It was one of the rhinos they'd spotted from orbit, big, heavy, with long tusks, and a body shaped like a barrel. The eyes were larger than a rhino's, though; they were saucer-shaped and had the same sad expression that was so prominent a part of the inhabitants' physiognomy. The eyes turned their way, and Digger got the distinct impression the beast could see them through their screen of shrubbery.

"Maybe it can smell us," said Digger.

"No." Kellie's voice had gone flat. The way it might if she perceived danger. "Not through the e-suit."

Jack activated the recorder in the notebook.

The cart was loaded with plants. Vegetables, maybe? Two Goompahs sat in the vehicle, singing at the top of their lungs. It was all off-key.

"I'm tempted to take my chances," said Jack, "and just go out and say hello."

"Don't do it," said Kellie.

And there came the three on foot. And the other three wagons. They were filled with passengers. Everybody was singing. They plucked on instruments that looked like lutes, blew into pipes, and pounded on the sides of the carts. They were having a roaring good time.

"They know how to travel," said Kellie.

There were eleven Goompahs in all. "Too many," said Jack. "Let them go."

"Why?" asked Digger. "They're in a good mood. Isn't that what we want?"

"If they turn out to be hostile, there are too many. I want to be able to get clear if things take a bad turn."

Some had mammaries. All were clumsy. Hadn't evolution worked at all on this world? Digger couldn't imagine how they'd avoided predators.

The convoy passed, gradually climbed to the crest of the hill and disappeared beyond.

TEN MINUTES LATER they got their chance. They heard the crunch of footsteps coming over the hill. A lone pedestrian appeared at the top. He carried a staff and swung it jauntily from side to side as he started down.

He wore boots and red leggings and a shirt made of hide. A yellow cap was pulled almost rakishly over one saucer eye. "Ladies' man," said Kellie.

The sky was clear. "Anybody else on the road?" Jack asked Winnie.

"Not anywhere near you."

It struck Digger that the fact the creature was traveling alone said a great deal about the kind of society in which it lived. In early Europe, strolling about the highways without an armed escort would have been an exercise in recklessness.

Digger felt Kellie's hand on his shoulder. Here we go.

Jack waited until the traveler was immediately adjacent. Then he switched on the projector. Digger's avatar appeared gradually atop the crest opposite, as if striding up from the far side, paused on its summit, and waved.

The traveler swung his large head in the avatar's direction. *"Hello, friend,"* the avatar said cheerfully, in English. *"How are you doing?"*

The Goompah stared.

The avatar raised its hand and waved again.

The Goompah's eyes widened, grew enormous.

The avatar started slowly down the slope.

The Goompah growled and showed a set of incisors Digger hadn't seen before. It retreated a step, but quickly found its back against a tree.

"How are you today?" the avatar asked. *"What a lovely day this is. I just happened to be in the neighborhood and thought I'd pop by. Say hello."*

"Careful," said Kellie.

The Goompah edged away from the tree, back in the direction from which it had come. It bowed its head, and Digger could see its lips moving although he couldn't hear any sounds. It was, if he was reading the signs correctly, terrified.

"What's happening?" asked Winnie.

Kellie told her to wait a minute.

The creature was shaking its head from side to side. It moaned and choked and spasmed. It threatened the avatar with its staff. It waved its hands, odd gestures, signs almost.

"This isn't going well," said Jack.

"Where are you headed, friend?" asked the avatar, oblivious of the effect it was having. *"By the way, my name's Digger."* It waved yet again, in the friendliest possible fashion.

The Goompah opened its mouth and said *"Morghani,"* or something very much like it. Then it turned and sprinted back the way it had come, moving far more quickly than Digger would have thought possible. It swayed wildly from side to side, tumbled but picked itself up without breaking stride, charged up the hill at the end of the road, and disappeared behind it.

When it was gone, the avatar said, *"It's been good talking with you."*

Kellie couldn't resist snickering. "You *are* pretty fearsome," she said, "now that I think of it."

*   *   *

DIGGER THOUGHT THEY should go back to the lander and rethink things. But getting back there would be a battle, and Kellie told him he was giving up too easily. Jack agreed and that was the vote that counted.

"The problem," Jack argued, "was that the image wasn't responsive. The thing got scared, and the avatar can't shrug, and say, 'Hey buddy, it's okay, don't worry.' "

"But who here can speak Goompah?" asked Digger.

"Don't have to," said Jack. "All we need is a rational reaction. A sign that we can deal with them on a one-to-one basis. Nonverbals will do it."

"What are you suggesting?"

"We dispense with the avatar."

IT DIDN'T MATTER. The second attempt, with Digger in the flesh trying to be friendly, went pretty much the same way. They passed on a couple of single travelers, selecting instead a group of four, bouncing along in a wagon pulled by one of the rhinos. Should have been enough to grant a sense of security to the proceedings. But they took one look at Digger, the real Digger, safely perched atop his hill so that a quick retreat was feasible, and went screaming back down the road, abandoning their wagon and the rhino.

"Well," he told Kellie, "I'm beginning to wonder if I'm not quite as charming as I always thought."

"Eye of the beholder," she said, turning to Jack. "What do we do now?"

"I'm not sure."

"How about walking in through the front door? Just stroll right into the city."

"I don't think so."

He asked Winnie to send a report to Hutch, informing her that initial attempts at contact had been unsuccessful.

"Do you want to say that we'll try again?"

"Yes," he said, but Digger knew that tone. He'd decided it wasn't a good idea.

"Having successfully completed phase one," said Kellie, "we should turn our attention to figuring out how to plant the pickups."

They brought up images of the cities and looked through them one by one. All had waterfront areas, and that's where the shops tended to be. And where the population clustered. "I say we go into downtown Athens," Digger said. "How many pickups do we have? Six?"

"Five," said Kellie. "Including the notebooks."

There was one other assignment: The Academy wanted information on

Goompah nutrition. During the past two weeks, they'd seen the Goompahs eating a variety of fruits, vegetables, meat, and fish. (At least, that's what it looked like through the telescopes.) Some of the fruit they'd seen hung on trees in their immediate area. Red pears, large golden melons that looked delicious, small silver apples. They picked up samples of everything.

In addition to buildings that appeared to be ordinary cabins or dwellings for housing individuals or small families, there were structures clearly intended to be living quarters, but they were big, rambling places, with wings and upper floors, large enough to provide shelter to fifty or more. And the places looked occupied and busy.

When they had seen enough, they retired to the lander to await the coming of dark.

IT DIDN'T TAKE long. A twenty-two-hour rotational period created a short day. Jack napped, while Kellie watched for intruders and Digger watched Kellie. But the woods stayed quiet, and the afternoon passed without incident. Winnie informed them that there was still occasional traffic on the highway, in case they "wanted to try again." She sounded serious. Digger half expected that the palace guard and the local militia would arrive to put a volley of arrows into whatever the thing was that had been seen terrifying travelers along the isthmus road. But the area remained quiet, and Winnie observed nothing that looked like a militia response.

Clouds gathered, and rain began to fall. By sunset it was a steady downpour. Ideal weather for strange creatures that needed to get out and do some lurking.

When night came, it grew absolutely dark. Back-of-the-basement locked-in-the-storage-bin dark. There wasn't a speck of light out there anywhere. There was no way to judge, of course, the quality of the locals' ability to see at night, but they did have large eyes.

Jack, however, had a substantial advantage: night goggles. Kellie got them out of the supply locker, and ten minutes later the lander, operating in silent mode, drifted through heavy rain over Athens and its harbor.

Athens was medium-sized, compared with the other Goompah cities. It was located on the eastern side of the isthmus. Four piers jutted out into the harbor, where a few ships lay at anchor. Tumbledown storage facilities lined the waterfront. Lights flickered in one or two of them. The streets were deserted. "A part of Athens you don't usually hear about," said Digger.

Jack smiled in the glow of the instrument panel. "Nobody uses Doric columns to build warehouses," he said. His tone suggested it was wisdom for the ages.

Kellie brought them down alongside one of the piers. Jack turned in his seat and looked back at Digger. "Listen, if you want, *I'm* willing to do this."

Digger would have been happy to turn the job over to him. But Kellie would never have approved, would have seen it as an act of cowardice. Jack was not young, was slow afoot, and would have a difficult time if the mission went wrong. This was a rare chance for Digger to show off. And he suspected there was no real danger. Goompahs were terrified of him, so what did he have to fear? "You don't have the build," he said laconically. "Or the clothes."

He stuffed the pickups and the notebooks into a bag and headed for the airlock. "Be careful," Kellie said. She surprised him with a quick embrace.

He slipped through the hatch, looked around, saw nothing moving, and stepped out onto the pier.

The sea was high, and the wind tried to push him into the water. The e-suit kept him comfortable but he knew it was cold out there.

He signaled to Kellie, and she began to pull away. *"Good luck, Champ,"* she said.

Digger hurried off the pier and slipped into a narrow street. There were small wooden buildings on either side, mostly sheds. But there was noise ahead: music and loud gargling sounds and pounding like the pounding he'd heard on the road. He rounded a corner and saw an open-front café.

It was half-empty, but the Goompahs inside were drinking, eating, dancing, and having a good time. The café was located in a dreary four-story stone building. A stout wooden canopy was erected to protect daytime patrons from the sun. He stood beneath it, peering into the interior, when two Goompahs he had not seen passed behind him and wandered into the café without giving him a second look.

He strolled closer, squeezing down inside his shirt and pulling his wide-brimmed hat down over his face.

The pickups, because they were jury-rigged, were of different sizes and shapes. Each had a strip of adhesive affixed that would allow him to attach it to a flat surface.

The café was an ideal spot, and the obvious flat surface was in the juncture of cross-fitting wooden beams supporting the canopy. Digger wandered casually close to it, and was able to stay out of sight of the customers while he put one of the notebooks in place. He'd have preferred to install it higher, where it would be less visible and out of everyone's reach. But it was reasonably well hidden, and he thought it would probably be okay for a while.

He withdrew into the shadows and away from the noise. "Jack," he said. "I just planted number four. How's it look?"

"Good. Perfect. One thing, we won't have any problem hearing them."

The area was lined with wooden stalls hung with skins. Rain poured down on them. Somewhere, down the street and around a corner, there was more noise. Another drinking establishment, obviously. He tried to look in a couple of the shops, but they were locked.

The streets were becoming a swamp. Occasionally, figures hurried along, bundled against the downpour, too intent on keeping dry to think much about strangers. One of these came out from behind a wall without warning and almost collided with Digger. The creature said something, glanced at him, and its eyes went wide. Digger smiled back and said, "Hi," in his best falsetto.

The creature shrieked.

Digger broke into a run, turned left behind a shed, cut across a muddy expanse of open ground, and found himself in a quiet street of stone-and-brick houses. He listened for a long moment, heard sounds of commotion behind him, but there was no evidence of pursuit.

"How you doing?" asked Kellie. He jumped at the sound of the voice.

"I just crashed into one of them."

"You're kidding."

"I never kid. I think the thing saw enough of me to realize I wasn't a local." He couldn't altogether keep the pride out of his voice.

"Are you okay now?"

He found an alley and turned into it. "I think so."

"If he gets too curious, just show him what you really look like."

"Har, har." The sounds behind him were dying down. And the street remained empty.

"Maybe you should just plant the pickups and get back here."

"Relax," he said. "Everything's under control." But something was coming. Two animals, large-jawed, trimmer than the rhinos, sort of like fat horses. Two Goompahs rode them, bent against the storm. He hurried to the other end of the alley and came out on a street that was given over to more shops.

He found occasional bits of vegetable and meat or fish lying about. He recovered them and dropped them into sample bags, grateful for the Flickinger field that prevented his having to touch them. Some of the stuff looked repulsive.

He broke into a storage building, found an office, and planted one of Kellie's pickups. He got it up on a shelf, between vases, where it seemed relatively safe. The truth was that none of these devices could really be hidden. Later, when the shipment they'd been promised from Broadside showed up, they'd be working with units not much bigger than coins.

He hid the third pickup in a tree near a meat shop. And the fourth in a park, aimed at a couple of benches.

Two blocks away, there were buildings whose architecture had been taken seriously and which were therefore probably either public or religious. Or both.

Several of them had signs outside. The signs contained some hand-drawn pictures, of Goompahs, and of a boat, and, on another, of a torch. There was writing on all of them, delicate, slender characters that reminded him of Arabic.

He took pictures, then tried a door. It opened, and he stepped into a long, high-ceilinged hallway. No lights anywhere. No sounds.

The floor might have been made of marble. The walls were dark-stained wood, and suggested that the authorities were not without resources. Several sets of large doors lined the corridor. He opened one and looked in.

It might have been a theater-in-the-round. Or possibly an auditorium. A platform stood in the center of a large room, surrounded by several hundred oversize seats.

Perfect. Digger found a column, climbed atop a seat, and attached the last pickup, the remaining notebook, as high as he could, aiming it at the platform.

They tested it on the lander, and Jack pronounced it satisfactory.

Time to go back.

THE RAIN HAD finally stopped, and Digger was within a block of the waterfront, moving through the shadows, when a pair of doors directly across the street banged open, light spilled into the night, and a crowd began to pile out. It was too late to duck, so he tried to squeeze down, to minimize his height, and kept going. But several were looking at him already. And the voices died off completely. "I've attracted attention, Jack."

"*You need help?*"

Sure. A lot of help Jack would be. "No. Stay put. I think they they're wondering about my size."

"*Yeah. It's probably not de rigueur in that neighborhood.*"

Digger wished he had a bigger collar to pull up. He stared at the street and kept walking, but he could feel their eyes on him until he got past them. He wanted to break into a run. He heard nothing behind him. No movement, no sound. It was eerie.

A Goompah appeared in front, coming in his direction. On the same side of the street. There was no way to get around him, no way to avoid being seen. The Goompah's eyes reacted, in a reflex that was becoming painfully familiar. It squealed, turned, and fled. The shriek triggered the crowd, which joined in the screaming, but they were coming after him. Something sailed past his head.

That put Digger in the impossible position of seeming to chase the fleeing Goompah, whose cries must have been audible all over the waterfront.

They reached the end of the street, the Goompah barreling along in abject terror, Digger right on its heels. It turned right, the direction Dig needed to go to get to the pier where the rendezvous was to take place. But the creature, out of its mind with fear, fell down and rolled out of the way.

Digger was distancing the crowd. "Jack," he said, "pier in three minutes."

ALL FIVE PICKUPS passed their field tests, and they were recording that night. Digger watched and listened with satisfaction as the day's customers haggled and pleaded, criticized and pressed their hands to the tops of their skulls in dismay. They watched a supervisor behind a desk working with subordinates and occasionally reporting to others to whom he was responsible. They watched young Goompahs romp in a park while older ones sat on benches and carried on animated conversations. And they watched a seminar of some sort conducted from the stage in the public building. Digger was surprised how easy it became to interpret substantial passages of the conversation.

Meantime a fresh transmission came in from Hutch. When Jack saw it, he ran it for all of them.

"*Help is coming. The* al-Jahani *will have left by the time you receive this. Dave Collingdale is heading up the operation, and he needs as much information as you can get him. Particularly anything that will allow him to gain access to the language.*

"*Also, we're dispatching the* Cumberland *from Broadside to take supplies and equipment to you. It'll take off anybody who wants to go home. But it won't be able to leave for a few days yet. It looks as if it'll be about seven weeks before you'll see it. I hate to ask this of you, but it's essential that we keep somebody at the scene to learn whatever we can. So I need you to hang on there until it arrives. I know that's not exactly the mission plan, and it's an inconvenience to you. But you'll understand this is a special circumstance.*

"*Also, I need to know what you want to do. We have to maintain an Academy presence until the* al-Jahani *gets there. But that won't be until December. Do you want to stay on? Or do you want me to organize a relief mission? Jack, I'd prefer to have you stay, but I understand if you feel enough is enough. Let me know.*

"*The* Cumberland *will be carrying shipments of lightbenders and pickups. Plant as many of the devices as you can. It's essential that we get the language down.*

"All data relating to the Goompahs should be designated for relay by Broadside directly to the al-Jahani, and I'd appreciate it if you included me as an information addee.

"Thanks, guys. I know this doesn't make you happy, but if it means anything, I'm grateful."

There was a long silence when the Academy logo appeared on-screen. They looked at one another, and Kellie grinned. "The aliens are lunatics," she said. "And the cloud is coming. Is there anyone who *wants* to go home?"

It wasn't exactly what Digger had hoped to hear.

IN FACT, THERE was one. "I don't plan to spend the next year or so of my life out here," Winnie told Jack. "It'd be different if there were something constructive I could do. But I'm not needed. I'm ready to head out."

So was Digger. But Kellie wouldn't be leaving, so he wasn't about to go anyplace. Digger let her see that he wanted to stay on, wanted to be part of a major achievement, and all that. The truth was, he wanted Kellie, and everything else was a sideshow. But with Kellie watching, he had no choice but to play the selfless hero. He knew her too well and understood clearly what would happen to her respect for him if he didn't stand up and do his duty.

He wished, as a compromise, he could think of a way to persuade Jack to go back to Broadside while he stayed here with Kellie. Don't worry about the details, big fella. We'll take care of anything that comes up. You go ahead and take some time off.

LIBRARY ENTRY

"You should never talk to strangers, Shalla."

"Why not, Boomer? Some of the nicest people I know are strangers."

"But if you know them, they're not strangers."

"Oh."

"Do you see what I mean?"

"Not really, Boomer. I mean, you were a stranger once. Should I not have spoken to you?"

"Well, that's different."

"How?"

"I'm a nice person."

"But how can I find out if I don't talk to you?"
"I'm not sure, Shalla. But I know it's not a good idea."

—The Goompah Show
All-Kids Network
March 19

chapter 12

BILL DID AN overnight analysis of the food samples and told Digger he probably wouldn't like any of the local cuisine. They forwarded the results to Broadside and the *al-Jahani*.

They were having breakfast in the common room when Winnie carried her tray in. "I just saw something odd," she said, sitting down at the table with the other three. "There's a parade of some sort out on the road. Near where you were yesterday."

"Really?" Jack rolled up a biscuit, dipped it into his egg yolk, and finished it off. "How do you mean, a parade?"

"Well, not really a parade. But a bunch of locals look as if they're headed for the spot where you showed up."

"Are you serious?" asked Digger.

"They're coming from the north. About twenty of them. The guy in front is wearing a black robe."

"They're probably just going through to Athens," said Digger.

Jack looked interested. "It's the first black robe we've seen. These folks like bright colors."

Kellie had been trying to finish her breakfast without getting caught up in the latest bout of Goompah mania. But she sighed. "You think they came to see where the critter was?"

"Maybe. There's a bunch of wagons parked up the road a bit. We didn't have coverage this morning because of clouds, but I think these guys rode in on them. There are still a few back there. With the wagons. Looks as if they're waiting,"

"Bill—?" said Jack.

The screen lit up. There was indeed a Goompah in a black robe. He was approaching the spot where the avatar had appeared. Approaching in the sense, Digger thought, that he was coming up on it with great care. The crowd was trailing, but giving him plenty of room.

He carried a staff, and when he'd reached the spot on the road in closest proximity to the hill on which the avatar had stood, he stopped, planted the staff, leaned on it, and appeared to survey his surroundings. After a minute he looked behind, and one of the onlookers came forward. There was a conversation and some pointing.

"Looks as if Digger may have stirred something up," Jack said.

Right. Digger did it.

A cloud drifted into the field of view.

"What do you think?" asked Kellie.

"It looks ceremonial."

Winnie wondered whether anybody recognized any of the Goompahs.

Digger smothered a laugh. "They all look alike. Can *you* tell them apart?"

"I haven't seen them up close. Not the way you have. I thought you might recognize one of the guys you talked to yesterday." She put a slight emphasis on the verb, and she was obviously talking about the one who had been traveling alone and whom Digger now saw was indeed there, carrying a javelin.

"I have no idea," Digger said.

"He's saying something," said Kellie, meaning the one in the robe.

"I think he's singing," said Jack. "We should have left a pickup in the area."

The marchers spread out on either side of the black robe, forming an arc centering on him.

"It's a chant," said Winnie. "Look at them." They had all begun doing a kind of coordinated swaying.

"They're looking for *me*," said Digger.

Jack leaned forward, intrigued. Digger, whose training should have produced the same curiosity, felt only a chill. "It's a religious ceremony," Jack said.

"Maybe we need to go back down," said Winnie. "Explain to them it's okay."

Kellie's eyes shone. "I'll be damned," she said. "They think they saw a god."

"I doubt it," said Jack.

The one in the robe shook down long sleeves and pulled a hood over his head. The javelin was held out for him to take. He made signs over it, lifted it, and waved it in a threatening gesture at the top of the hill. The chant ended.

Everyone stood quietly for another minute or so. Then he climbed the hill while the others watched with—Digger thought—no small degree of anxiety, and came finally to the spot where the avatar had stood. The one who'd been on the road, who'd carried the weapon, called out to him and he moved a couple of steps to his right. They seemed to agree that was the correct location. And without further delay, he brandished the javelin with practiced ease and plunged it into the ground.

He made more signs, drew his hands together, and looked at the sky. They all bowed their heads and closed their eyes. Their lips moved in unison. One of them crept up the hill and recovered the javelin. And they withdrew.

Down the hill and back along the road until they reached the waiting wagons. Into the wagons and headed north.

"I think," said Digger, "we've just seen a declaration of war."

Jack was still looking ecstatic. "I don't think so," he said. "I believe we've just watched an exorcism."

THEY SPENT MUCH of the next few days watching and listening to Goompah conversations. Winnie hung a sign on the bulkhead that said *It's Greek to me.* Each of the five channels allotted to the pickups had been routed in, but one had gone inactive. They'd seen a Goompah hand close over it, and then for a while all they could see was the grass. And finally the unit shut down. Somebody had probably hit it with a stick.

But they still had four links.

They listened and marked down phonetic impressions and bounced phrases off each other while Bill recorded everything, collapsed the signals into compressed transmissions, and fired them off every six hours by way of Broadside to the *al-Jahani.*

The language seemed straightforward enough. Some of the sounds were odd, lots of grunts and gargles, a load of aspirates and diphthongs. And nobody rolled their *l*'s like these guys. There was an overall harshness to the diction, but Digger didn't hear much that a human tongue couldn't reproduce. And they'd even deciphered a couple of words.

Challa, collanda appeared to be the universal greeting. Two Goompahs met, morning or evening, male or female, it didn't seem to matter: "*Challa, collanda,*" they would say.

Hello, friend. Kellie took to greeting her passengers with it, and soon they were all using it. *Challa,* Jack.

Digger discovered the sheer pleasure in reproducing some of the sounds he was hearing. He could roll his *l*'s and grunt with the best of them. He also began to discover something he hadn't known about himself: He had a facility for language. Next time he ran into some Goompahs he'd be ready. He wondered if things might have gone a bit differently had he been able to raise his hand and, in his jolliest demeanor, send the proper greeting: "*Challa, collanda.*"

But there wouldn't be a next time. Lightbenders were on the way, so when they went back down to set up more listening posts they'd be invisible.

Well, there was nothing to be done about it now. But he knew he'd be tempted to walk up to one of the Goompahs, no more than a voice in the wind, and say hello. Just whisper it and watch him jump.

He'd never worn a lightbender. They were prohibited to private ownership. A few had gotten out and become invaluable tools for criminals. But there was a National Lightbender Association claiming that people had a constitutional right to the devices. It struck Digger that once they became generally available everyone would have to wear infrared glasses to protect himself. Even imagining himself invisible bestowed a sense of both power and recklessness.

About a week after they'd gone down to the surface, Jack announced that a message had arrived from the Academy. "We've got something else to look for," he said.

Hutch's image appeared on-screen.

"*Jack,*" she said, "*This is a hedgehog.*" The screen divided and produced a picture of an object with triangular spikes sticking out all over it. An accompanying scale indicated it was six and a half kilometers in diameter.

"*To date, we have three reports of these objects. We have no idea what they are or what their purpose is. We do know that one of them exploded while it was being inspected by the* Quagmor. *If you can take a look around without compromising your main objectives, please do so. We'd like very much to know if your cloud has one. It'll be directly out front, running on the same course, at the same speed. The ranges between the objects and the clouds have varied out to sixty thousand klicks.*

"*So far, the things are identical. They have 240 sides. Lots of right angles. If you see one, keep a respectful distance. Don't go near it. We don't want an inspection; we just want to know whether it's there.*" She allowed herself a smile but Digger could see she was dead serious. "*Thanks,*" she said. "*Be careful. We don't want to lose anybody else.*"

The hedgehog remained a few seconds after Hutch's image blanked, and then it, too, was gone, replaced by the Academy logo.

All those spines. Like stalagmites. But with flat tips. "What is it?" asked Winnie. "Do they have any idea?"

"You heard as much as I did," said Jack.

Kellie looked thoughtful. "I'll tell you what it might be," she said. "It looks designed to attract the clouds. Maybe somebody's been using them to get rid of the damn things. A cloud shows up and you give it a whatzis to chase."

They all looked at her. "It's possible," said Digger. "That might be *it*."
Kellie's eyes shone. It was a pleasure to be first to solve a puzzle.
"Well," said Jack, "let's go see if we've got one."

THE CLOUD'S SHAPE had changed during the few weeks since they'd first
seen it. It had become distorted, and was throwing jets forward and to one
side, blown off by gee forces as it continued to decelerate and to turn. At
the rate the thing was braking, Digger had trouble understanding how it
managed to hold together at all. He was not a physicist, but he knew enough
to conclude that the stability of the gas and dust, in the face of those kinds
of stresses, demonstrated that this was no natural phenomenon. There were
widespread claims by mystics, and even some physicists, who should know
better, that the omegas were an evolutionary step, a means by which the
galaxy protected itself from the rise of the supercivilization, the one entity
that could raise havoc, that could eventually take control and force it away
from its natural development.

It was a notion very much in play these days, fitting perfectly with the
idea that the present universe was simply a spark in a vast starry sky, one
of countless universes, afloat in a cosmos that was perhaps itself an infini-
tesimal part of an ever-greater construct. Grains of sand on a beach that
was a grain on a much bigger beach . . .

Where did it all end?

Well, however that might be, the omega clouds were too sophisticated
to have developed naturally.

"How do you know?" asked Kellie, sitting quietly looking out at the monster, while Digger went on about stars and universes.

He explained. How it held together. How it had long-range sensors far
better than anything the *Jenkins* had. How it had spotted Athens from a
range of 135 billion kilometers when they couldn't find it from orbit.

She listened, nodding occasionally, apparently agreeing. But when he'd
finished, she commented that there were people around who'd argue that
Digger couldn't have happened simply as a result of natural evolution. "I
think," she said, "you're doing the argument from design."

"I suppose. But this is different."

"How?"

"It's on a bigger scale."

"Dig, that's only a difference in degree. Size doesn't count."

He couldn't find an adequate response. "You think these things are natural objects?"

"I don't know." The cloud was misshapen, plumes thrown forward and
to one side. It was a dark squid soaring through the night. "I'm keeping my

mind open." Neither spoke for a minute. Then she said, "I'm not sure which scares me more."

"Which what?"

"Which explanation. Either they're natural, which leads to the conclusion that the universe, or God, however you want to put it, doesn't approve of intelligence. Or they're built and set loose. That means somebody who's very bright has gone to a lot of trouble to kill every stranger he can find."

AT THEIR CURRENT range, Lookout's sun was only a bright star.

The *Jenkins* had begun a sweep when it had approached within 12 million klicks of the cloud. They moved steadily closer over the next three days but saw nothing.

On the fourth day of the hunt Kellie suggested they terminate.

"You're sure there's nothing there?" said Jack.

"Absolutely. There are a few rocks but that's it. Nothing remotely resembling the dingus." She waited for instructions.

"Okay." Jack's attitude suggested the hell with it. "Let's go back to Lookout."

Kellie directed them to belt down and began angling the *Jenkins* onto its new course. It was going to be a long turn and they'd be living with gee forces for the better part of a day. Consequently, she wasn't particularly happy. "If I'd used my head," she told Digger, "I'd have arranged things differently. We could have been on a more efficient course at the end of the pattern. But I assumed we were going to find something."

"So did I," he said. "If you're right, though, that the hedgehogs are lures, they won't be everywhere. Only close to clouds that are threatening something their makers are interested in."

Jack sent off a message to Hutch, information copies to the *al Jahani*: "*No hedgehog at Lookout. Returning to orbit.*"

While they made the long swing, they decided to watch a sim together, and Kellie, at their request, brought up a haunted house thriller. Digger didn't have much taste for horror, but he went along. "Scares me though," he told them, making a joke of it, as if the idea were ridiculous, but in fact it did. He took no pleasure watching a vampire operate, and there'd been times even here, in the belly of a starship, maybe *especially* here, when he'd gone back through a dimly lit corridor to his quarters after that kind of experience and heard footsteps padding behind him.

The problem with the superluminal was that, even though it was an embodiment of modern technology, a statement that the universe is governed by reason, a virtual guarantee that demons and vampires do not exist, it was still quite small. Almost claustrophobic. A few passageways and a handful of rooms, with a tendency toward shadows and echoes. It was a place you couldn't get away from. If something stalked you through the ship's narrow corridors, there would be nowhere to run.

His problem, he knew, was that he suffered from an overabundance of imagination. Always had. It was the quality that had drawn him into extraterrestrial assignments. Digger was no coward. He felt he'd proved it by going down on Lookout and sticking his head up. He'd worked on a site in the middle of the Angolan flare-up, had stayed there when everybody else ran. On another occasion he'd gotten a couple of missionaries away from rebels in Zampara, in northern Africa, by a mixture of audacity, good sense, and good luck. But he didn't like haunted houses.

The plot always seemed to be the same: A group of adolescents looking for an unusual place to hold a party decide to use the abandoned mansion in which there reportedly had been several ghastly murders during the past half century. (It wasn't a place to which Digger would have gone.)

There was always a storm, rain beating against the windows, and doors opening and closing of their own volition. And periodically, victims getting cornered by whatever happened to be loose in the attic.

He tried to think about other things. But the creaking doors, the wild musical score, and the tree branches scraping against the side of the house kept breaking through. Jack laughed through much of the performance, and energetically warned the actors to look out, it's in the closet.

Midway through, strange noises come from upstairs. Shrieks. Groans. Unearthly cries. Two of the boys decide, incredibly, they will investigate. *Only in the sims*, Digger thinks. But he wants them to stay together. The boy in the lead is tall, good-looking, with a kind of wistful innocence. The kid next door. Despite the silliness of the proceedings, Digger's heart is pounding as he and his companion climb the circular staircase, while the tempo builds to a climax. As they arrive at the top, another shriek rips through the night. It comes from behind the door at the end of the hallway.

The door opens, apparently unaided, and Digger sees a shadowy figure seated in an armchair facing a window, illuminated only by the flickering lightning. The second boy, prudently, is dropping behind.

Stay together. Digger shakes his head, telling himself it's all nonsense. No sensible kids would do anything like this. And if they did, they'd certainly stick close to each other.

And he found himself thinking about the hedgehog. They'd overlooked the obvious.

"WHAT WOULD IT be doing way out there?" asked Jack.

Digger has used a cursor to indicate where he thought the object could be found. "We assumed the cloud and the hedgehog were a unit. Where one goes, the other follows. But here, we've got a cloud that has thrown a right turn.

"The cloud's been turning and slowing down for a long time. Maybe over a year. But there's no reason to assume the hedgehog wouldn't keep going."

"Original course and velocity?" said Jack.

"Probably."

"Why would it do that?" asked Winnie.

"Why *any* of this? I don't know. But I bet if we check it out, we'll find it where the cloud would have been if it hadn't decided to go for a walk."

Kellie's dark eyes touched him. Go to it, big boy.

"Why not take a look?" he asked. "It's not as if we have to be anywhere tomorrow."

THEY FOUND IT precisely where Digger had predicted. It was moving along at a few notches under standard omega velocity. As if the great cloud still trailed behind.

LIBRARY ENTRY

The discovery of escort vehicles with the omegas reveals just how little research has been done over the past thirty years on this critical subject. What other surprises are coming? And how many more lives will be sacrificed to bureaucratic inertia?

—The London *Times*
March 23

chapter 13

On board the *Heffernan*, near Alpha
Pictoris, ninety-nine light-years
from Earth.
Friday, April 4.

THE PICTORIS HEDGEHOG made it six for six. They all have one.

It was twenty-eight thousand kilometers in front of the cloud. Its diameter was the standard six and a half kilometers. "Report's away," Emma said.

Sky didn't like going anywhere near the damned thing. But they'd asked for volunteers, told him they'd probably be okay, but to be careful, don't take any unnecessary chances, and keep your head down. Emma had said not to hesitate on her account, and the *Heffernan* was the only ship in the neighborhood.

Ordinarily Sky loved what he did for a living. He enjoyed cruising past ringed giants, lobbing probes into black holes, delivering people and supplies to the ultimate out-of-the-way places. But he didn't like the clouds. And he didn't like the hedgehogs. They were things that didn't belong.

They were far enough away from Pictoris that the only decent illumination on the object was coming from their probe.

"*Its magnetic field matches the signature of the other objects,*" said Bill.

"Ajax is ready to go," said Emma.

There was no known entry hatch anywhere, so Drafts would have chosen a spot at random. Which is what the *Heffernan* would do.

Emma and Sky were looking forward to celebrating their sixteenth anniversary the next day, although they hadn't been married precisely sixteen years. Participating in experiments with the new hypervelocity sublight thrust engines had alternately speeded them up and slowed them down, or maybe just one or the other. He'd never been able to figure out relativity. He just knew the numbers didn't come together in any way he could understand. But it didn't matter. He'd had a lot of time with Emma, and he was smart enough to appreciate it. She'd told him once, when they were still a few months from their wedding, and were eating dinner at the Grand Hotel in Arlington, that he should enjoy the moment because the day would come when they'd give anything to be able to return to that hour and relive that dinner.

It was true, of course. Everything was fresh and young then. They hadn't yet learned to take each other for granted. When he was tempted to do so now, he reminded himself that the life he had wouldn't be forever, and if he couldn't go back to the Grand Hotel when his romance with Emma was still new, when the entire world was young and all things seemed possible, it was equally true that he'd remember the hedgehog, and how they'd stood on the bridge together, watching it come close, a piece of hardware put together by God knew what, for purposes no one could imagine. A *bomb*. But it was still a moment that he savored, because he knew that, like the Grand Hotel, he would one day give much to be able to return.

Sixteenth anniversary. How had it all gone by so quickly?

"Relativity." She laughed.

"*Recommend Ajax launch*," said Bill.

"Okay, Bill. Keep in mind that we want it to snuggle up very gently. Just kiss it, right?"

"*Just a smooch*," said Bill. He appeared beside them, wearing a radiation suit and a hard hat. Protection against explosions. His idea of a joke.

"Okay," Sky said. "Launch Ajax."

Warning lamps blinked. The usual slight tremor ran through the ship. "*Ajax away. Time to intersection: thirty-three minutes.*"

"Okay, Bill. Let's leave town."

THEY ACCELERATED OUT. Sky directed the AI to maintain jump capability, which required firing the main engines throughout the sequence to build and hold sufficient charge in the Hazeltines.

It was the first time in all these years that he'd been in this kind of situation, not knowing well in advance whether he'd have to jump.

"Out of curiosity—" she said.

"Yes?"

"On the jump, can you override Bill? If you had to?" The jump engines couldn't be used until they were charged. That usually required twenty-eight minutes off the main engines. Any attempt to do a jump prior to that risked initiating an antimatter explosion, and consequently would be refused by the AI.

"We could do a manual start if something happened to Bill."

"You know," she said, "I suspect that's what the hedgehog is loaded with, too."

"Antimatter?"

"Yes. That would explain the magnetic field."

"In what way?" asked Sky.

"Containment envelope. It's probably what happened to Drafts. He did something that impaired its integrity."

Sky shook his head. Who'd have expected anything like that out here?

EMMA WAS AN astrophysicist. When he'd warned her that marrying someone who took a superluminal out for months at a time might not be a smart move for her, she'd said okay, that she'd really wanted a tall blond guy anyhow, good-bye. And he'd tried to recover ground, said he wasn't entirely serious, didn't want to lose her, just wanted to be sure she knew what she was getting into.

It had taken almost two years to get the joint assignment to the *Heffernan*, but it had happened, largely because the Academy had a policy of trying to keep its captains happy.

They were both on the bridge, sharing, after all these years, their first moment of danger. The danger was remote, fortunately, but it added a dash of spice to the experience.

"Ajax has closed to four klicks," said Bill. *"Contact in eleven minutes."*

They could see Ajax, which looked like an insect, wings and legs spread, angling toward the spiked surface.

"Is it going to work?" asked Sky.

"If it's what we think it is, Ajax will find the frequency and interfere with the magnetic belt. That should be enough. If it isn't, it'll start cutting the thing up with its lasers. One way or another, yes, it should work."

Sky listened to the innumerable sounds the ship's systems routinely make, whispers and sighs and clicks and the ongoing background thrum of the engines, boosting them to ever-higher velocities.

They talked occasionally about retirement, about her getting a job at home, maybe having the child they'd always promised themselves. Can't really do that if you're bottled up inside a container all the time. Virtual beaches are all right for adults, but a kid needs real sand.

Emma, reading his thoughts, nodded. "Time for something new?" she suggested.

"I don't know," he said uncertainly.

"There *is* this, Sky. Where else could we be this useful?"

Can't hug her. Not while under acceleration. So he reached over and took her hand.

"Five minutes," said Bill. *"We are ready to jump on command."*

One of the screens carried the cloud, its image captured live through the telescopes. Sky thought the omegas possessed an ethereal kind of beauty. Not this one, because it was too dark, there wasn't enough light hitting it.

But when they got lit up by sunlight, they were actually very striking. He grinned at the unintentional pun.

Emma couldn't see it. She thought they were the embodiment of pure malevolence. A demonstration that there were devils loose in the universe. Not the supernatural kind, of course. Something far worse, something that really existed, that had left its footprint among the stars, that had designed booby traps and sent them out to kill strangers.

Sky had grown up with the notion that evil inevitably equated to stupidity. The symbol of that idea was embodied in the fact that superluminals were not armed, that no one (other than fiction writers) had ever thought of mounting a deck gun on an interstellar vessel.

It was a nice piece of mythology. But mythology was all it was.

"*Two minutes.*" Bill loved doing countdowns. There was a picture of him on the auxiliary screen, sitting in an armchair, still safely tucked inside his suit, and with his helmet visor down.

"Bill, ready to bail if we have to." There was no way to be sure the energy levels of the hedgehog were all the same.

"*We are QBY,*" he said. Ready to go. Bill favored the official terminology. He sometimes admitted to Sky that he regretted that starship life was so peaceful. He talked occasionally, and wistfully, of running missions against alien horrors that were determined to destroy civilization, to overrun Berlin and all it stood for. (Sky could never tell for sure when Bill was kidding.) The AI wished for pirates and renegade corporations, hiding in the dust of giant clouds. Clouds, he added, hundreds of light-years across, clouds that would make the omegas look like puffs of mist on a summer breeze.

Bill, *this* Bill, had a poetic streak. Sometimes he went a bit over the top, but he did seem to have a passion for flowers and sunsets and the wind in the trees. All a facade, of course. Bill had never experienced any of that, wasn't even self-aware if you believed the manual. Furthermore, although the Academy AIs were compatible, and in fact most people thought there was really only *one* Academy AI, which sometimes simply got out of contact with its various parts, Sky knew that Bill was different on different ships. Sometimes the manifestation was withdrawn and formal, seldom showing up visually, and then usually in dress whites; on other vessels, on the *Quagmire*, for example (which Sky had piloted on a couple of missions), he'd been young, energetic, always advancing his opinion, usually in a jumpsuit with the ship's patch on his shoulder. The *Heffernan* AI was philosophical, sometimes sentimental, inclined to quote Homer and Milton and the Bible. And apparently a fan of melodrama.

Sky was one of the few Academy captains who believed that a divine force functioned in the universe. He'd heard Hutch say one time that the notion of a God was hard to accept out here because of the sheer dimensions of the cosmos. Richard Feynman had made a comment to that effect. *"The stage is just too big."* Why create something so enormous? Why make places so far away that their light will never reach the Earth?

But that was the reason Sky believed. The stage is *immense* beyond comprehension. The fallacy in Hutch's reasoning, he thought, was the assumption that the human race was at the center of things. That *we* were what it was all about. But Sky suspected the Creator had made everything so large because He simply liked to create. That's what creators do.

"Twenty seconds," said Bill.

He watched the package move in. The hedgehog was rotating, slowly, once every thirty-seven minutes. The others rotated at different rates. It depended on the gravity fields they'd passed through.

"Ten."

It closed and snuggled in against one of the object's 240 sides.

"Contact."

"Very good, Bill."

"Thank you, sir."

He looked over at Emma.

"Bill," she said, "proceed with Ajax."

"Proceeding." And, a moment later: *"Lockdown."* The magnetic couplers took hold. There had been a possibility that might have been enough to detonate the thing, but Emma hadn't thought so. If it had no more stability than that, it would have gone up long ago. Objects drifting through interstellar space are bathed by particles and gravitons and you name it.

"You know," said Emma, "I think I'm going to enjoy blowing this son of a bitch to hell."

"There's nobody in it."

"Doesn't matter." She looked over at him. Her eyes were green, and they were smoldering. She didn't share his faith in a benign creator, but she felt that the universe should be a place of pristine beauty and wonder. And most of all it should be neutral, and not loaded against intelligence. We're the only reason there's any point to it, she believed. Unless there's someone smart enough to look at it, and appreciate its grandeur, *and do the science,* the universe is meaningless.

"Are we ready to pull the trigger?" Sky asked.

"Just enjoying the moment," she said.

"Fire when ready, babe."

She checked the status board. All green. "Bill," she said.

"Locked and loaded."

"Proceed to degauss."

"Activating." His image vanished. He was all business now.

Sky watched the time tick off. "Would the reaction be instantaneous?" he asked.

"Hard to say. But I'd think so."

"I do not detect a change in the object's magnetic signature."

"Doesn't work?" asked Sky.

"Let's give it a little more time."

The hedgehog was getting smaller as the *Heffernan* continued to withdraw.

"Still no change," said Bill.

"Maybe it's not antimatter?"

"It might be that we don't have enough energy to shut it down. Or that we haven't calibrated correctly. Or who knows what else? It's not exactly my field." She took a deep breath, "You ready to go to phase two, Sky?"

"Yes. Do it."

"Bill?"

"Yes, Emma?"

"Activate the blade." The laser.

"Activating blade."

"Can you enhance the picture?" Sky asked.

"Negative. We are at maximum definition now."

Emma had told him it would probably take time, but Sky kept thinking about Terry Drafts poking a laser into its shell. The record showed that once you did that, things happened pretty quickly. But some parts of the object might be more vulnerable than others.

Sky was beginning to amuse himself thinking how the Academy might say okay, it's obviously not going to work, go back in and retrieve the unit when it went, erupted in a white flash.

ARCHIVE

No one denies that the effort to find a way to dispose of the omega clouds is of value. But they do not constitute a clear and present danger. They are in fact so remote a hazard that it remains difficult to understand why so many continue to get exercised over the issue. At a time when millions go hungry, when repairing environmental damage is exhausting vast sums of money, when the world population steams ahead, we can ill afford to waste our resources on a threat that remains so far over the horizon that we cannot even imagine what the planet will look like when it arrives. The Council and the

Prime Minister need to set their priorities, and live with them despite the shifting political winds.

—Moscow International
April 5

chapter 14

ASQUITH NEVER REALLY looked happy, except when VIP visitors were present. This morning, which was rainy, gloomy, and somehow tentative, was
momentarily devoid of VIPs. The commissioner was making the kinds of
faces that suggested he was tired of hearing about problems that didn't go
away. "So we know the hedgehogs—can't we get a better name for them,
Hutch?—are bombs. Tell me about the one that's going to pass close to us.
Tony's going to be over this afternoon, and I need some answers. What
happens if it goes off?"

Tony was the ultimate VIP: the NAU's funding liaison with the Academy.

"You don't have to worry about it, Michael. It's as far away as the cloud
is. It can't hurt us."

"Then why are we worried about it?"

"We aren't worried in the sense that it can do any damage to us. Not at
its current range. Maybe in a few centuries."

"Then why do we care about it?"

"Because we don't know its purpose."

"So we're talking a purely academic issue? Nobody's at risk?"

"No."

He'd gotten up when she came into the room. Now he eased himself
back into his chair. "Thank God for that," he said. He motioned her to a
chair. "Why would anybody be putting bombs out there?"

"We think they're *triggers*."

"Triggers. Bombs. We're arguing terminology." He rolled his eyes. "What
do they trigger?"

"The clouds."

"What's that? How do you mean? The clouds blow up?"

"We don't really know yet, Michael. But I think it's something like that.
I think you get a special kind of explosion."

"How many kinds of explosions are there?"

She sat down and tried to get the conversation onto a level at which she could handle it. "The reason they're important," she said, "is that if these things turn out to be what they seem to be, they may give us a way to get rid of the clouds."

"By blowing them up."

"Yes. Maybe. We don't know." She felt good this morning. Had in fact felt pretty good for the last few days. "We need to find out."

"So what precisely do you propose?

"We need to run a test."

He nodded. "Do it."

"Okay."

"But not with the cloud." The local one.

"We won't go near it."

"Good." He took a deep breath. "I'd be grateful if it worked."

"As would I, Michael."

"I guess you've noticed the Goompahs have been getting popular." His tone suggested that was a problem.

Of course she'd noticed. Everywhere she looked there were Goompah dolls, Goompah games, Goompah bedding. People loved them. Kids especially loved them. "Why is that bad news?" she asked innocently. But she knew the reason.

"There's a growing body of opinion that the government hasn't done enough to help them."

"I'm sorry to hear it."

"They'd like to keep the media away. In case things go badly."

"*They* being the president and the Council."

He nodded. Who else? "They're afraid there'll be graphic pictures of Goompahs getting killed in large numbers."

"Too bad they're not insects."

He didn't pick up the sarcasm. "Anything but these terminally cute roll-over critters."

"The media say they'll be there."

He made a sound in his throat that resembled a gargle going awry. "I know. But there's no way to stop them. If our little experiment works out, though, the problem will be solved." He looked happy. As if the sun had come out in the office. "Make it happen, Hutch."

"Wait a minute," she said. "Michael, I think we've had a communication breakdown. Even if it works, we aren't going to be able to use the technique to help the Goompahs."

Shock and dismay. "Why not? I thought that was the whole point."

"The whole point is to get control of the clouds. To forge a weapon." She tried to sound reassuring. "I'm sorry I misled you. But the cloud at Lookout is too close."

"How do you mean?"

"If we get the result we expect, we're going to learn how to destroy the damned things. But we expect a very big bang. Trigger the cloud at Lookout, and you'd fry them all."

"How can you know that before you've run the test?"

"Because I'm pretty sure I've seen other clouds explode. I know what kind of energy they put out."

And suddenly he understood. "The tewks."

"Yes." She'd put it all in the reports, but it was becoming clear he didn't read the reports.

"All right," he said. He was still disappointed and he let her see it. "Let me know how it turns out."

"Okay." She started to get up, but he waved her back down. Not finished with you yet.

"Listen, Hutch. I've gone along with everything you've wanted to do. We sent out Collingdale and his people. We sent out the kite. And we're sending meals, for God's sake. We'll be broke for three years after this. Now you owe me something.

"We've gotten some help from the Council on this. So we need to play ball with them. I'm going to tell Tony we'll go all out to save the poor bastards. That's what they want, by the way. Save them. Divert the goddam cloud. If you can't blow it up, make your kite work. Make it happen.

"If you don't, if the cloud hammers them, we'll all be in the soup."

Hutch kept her voice level. "Michael," she said, "we've had thirty years to figure out how to do something about the omegas. The Council felt safe because the danger seemed so far away. It didn't occur to them that political fallout might come from a different direction. I personally don't care if they all get voted out. But we are trying to save the Goompahs. We were trying to do it before it became politically popular."

She was at the door, on her way out, when he called her back. "You're right, Hutch," he said. "I know that. Everybody knows it. Which is why the Academy will look so good if we can pull these fat little guys out of the fire."

"Right," she said, and let it drop.

ARCHIVE

"Senator, we've all seen the pictures of the cloud at Moonlight. Is there anything at all we can do for the Goompahs?"

"Janet, we are moving heaven and earth to help. Unfortunately, we haven't yet learned how to turn these things aside. The first ship-load of supplies will be leaving day after tomorrow. We're doing everything we can."

—Senator Cass Barker,
Press Conference, April 4

chapter 15

THERE WERE TOO many people on the mission. Collingdale had heard that
the entire scientific community had wanted to go, despite the distance to
Lookout. And Hutch had accommodated as many as she possibly could. That
was a mistake. They were going to have to work as a team, and he had the
unenviable task of trying to organize, mollify, control, and entertain a task
force that included some of the biggest egos on the planet. There were his-
torians and xenologists and mathematicians and specialists in other lines of
inquiry of which he'd never heard. Every one of whom thought of him/
herself as a leading light in his or her field. And they were going to be locked
up together until late November.

Frank Bergen was a good example of the problem. Frank expected everyone to take notes whenever he spoke. Melinda Park looked stunned if anyone took issue with any of her opinions, even those outside her area of
expertise. Walfred Glassner ("Wally" behind his back) thought everyone
else in the world was a moron. Peggy Malachy never let anyone else finish
a sentence. The others, save Judy Sternberg's linguists, were no better. Before it was over he was convinced there'd be a murder.

They comprised the Upper Strata, the scientific heavyweights.

Bergen was, in his view, the only one of them who really mattered. After
everybody else had debarked onto the *Jenkins*, he would make the flight
with Kellie Collier to try to distract the omega. Bergen, who was short,
dumpy, arrogant, was sure the plan would succeed if only because anything
he touched always succeeded. They had at their disposal visual projections,
and if those didn't do the job, they had the kite. One way or the other, he
assured anybody who would listen, they'd get rid of the thing. He sounded
as if he thought the cloud wouldn't dare defy him.

In fact, it seemed to Collingdale that the only other ones crucial to the
mission were the linguists. They were all kids, all graduate students or post-
docs, save for their boss, Judy Sternberg.

They were already at work with the data forwarded by the *Jenkins*, trying to decipher and familiarize themselves with basic Goompah. He'd have preferred to double their number and get rid of the giants-in-their-field. But he understood about politics. And Hutch had maintained that it was impossible to find, in a few days' time, an adequate supply of people, no more than five and a half feet tall, with the kind of specialized skill they needed, who were willing to leave home for two years. She had done the best she could and he'd have to make do.

They were indeed of minimal stature. Not one of the twelve, male or female, rose above his collarbone.

It had been an ugly scene, those last few days before departure. He'd never seen Hutch lose her temper before, but it was obvious she was under pressure. You have to understand the reality, he'd told her, and she'd fired back that politics *was* the reality.

Nonetheless, they were doing as well as could be expected. The Upper Strata had settled in and seemed to have achieved an amicable standoff with each other. And the linguists were hard at work on the daily flow of recordings. They were both enthusiastic and talented, and he expected that, by the time they arrived on-station, he'd have people able to speak with the natives.

He'd been trying to master the language himself but had already fallen far behind the young guns. His lack of proficiency surprised him. He spoke German and Russian fluently and, despite his fifty-six years, had thought he'd be able to pace the help. Within the first two weeks he'd seen it wasn't going to happen. But maybe it was just as well. Staying ahead of the old man provided an incentive for them.

The incoming data consisted of audiovisual recordings. The pictures weren't very good. Sometimes the conversations took place entirely out of view of the imager. On other occasions, the Goompahs walked out of visual range while they talked. Even when the subjects stayed still, the angles were usually less than ideal. At this early stage, in order to have a reasonable chance to understand, the linguists needed to be able to *see* what was happening. But they were getting enough to match actions with talk and, still more important, with gestures.

Most of the Upper Strata were looking forward to putting on lightbenders and walking unseen among the population. They would try to do what they'd done on Nok, penetrate the libraries, eavesdrop on conversations, observe political and religious activities. But Nok was a long time ago. They'd all been young then. And Collingdale had already noticed a reluctance among them to learn the language. He knew what would happen: They'd put it off, finding one pretext or another to avoid the effort. And when they got to Lookout they'd be asking to borrow one of the linguists, somebody to go down and interpret.

It was clear that whatever was to be accomplished on this mission would be done by Judy's team.

When he'd heard the conditions under which he would be making the flight, he'd almost changed his mind about going. But he had asked Hutch for the assignment, and he didn't feel he could back away. Moreover, he hoped that Bergen was right, that the cloud would be turned aside, and that they would beat the thing. He desperately wanted to be there if it happened.

THEY WERE MAKING some progress in figuring out the syntax, and they had already begun to compile a vocabulary. They had words for *hello* and *good-bye*, *near* and *far*, *ground* and *sky*, *come* and *go*. They could sometimes differentiate among the tenses. They knew how to ask for a bolt of cloth, or to request directions for *Mandigol*. (Nobody had any clue where *that* was.)

There was some confusion about plurals, and they were mystified by pronouns. But Judy was there, reassuring them that time and patience would bring the solutions. Her plan called for the establishment of a working vocabulary of at least one hundred nouns and verbs by the end of their first month on board, and a basic grasp of syntax by the end of the second. They'd achieved the first goal, but the second was proving elusive. At the end of the second month, no English would be permitted in the workroom. At the end of the third month, they would speak Goompah exclusively, everywhere on the ship, except when communicating with home.

Several objected to that provision. How were they to talk with their fellow passengers? To Collingdale's immense satisfaction, Judy replied that was the problem of the passengers. It would do Bergen and the others good, she said, to begin hearing the native language. They're supposed to be learning it anyhow.

The Upper Strata, when it heard the idea, dismissed it out of hand. Utterly unreasonable. They had more important things to do. Not that it mattered. But Collingdale didn't want more division and in the end he was forced to intervene and insist, in the interests of peace, that Judy back down. The surrender was disguised as a compromise: English, or other non-Goompah languages, would be spoken by the linguists outside work hours when members of the Upper Strata or the captain were present, or at anytime during any emergency.

Collingdale did his best to appease Judy by including in the declaration that he henceforth considered himself a member of the language team, and would be bound by their rules, except when his duties made it impractical.

* * *

THE ONLY OTHER functioning culture that had been found during the decades of interstellar travel was on Nok. It was the right name for the world. The inhabitants were in the middle of an industrial age, but they'd been up and down so many times they'd exhausted most of their natural resources. They were always at war, and they showed no talent whatever for compromise or tolerance.

The research teams had experienced massive problems there during the first couple of years because everybody who wanted a lightbender just checked one out and went down to the surface. They were forever running landers up and down with consequent waste of fuel. They had people fighting over e-suits, trying to monopolize the language specialists, and arguing constantly about the no-contact policy. A substantial number maintained it was immoral for the Academy to stand by while the idiots made war on one another, and huge numbers of noncombatants were killed. It happened all the time, the wars never really ended until everybody was exhausted, and as soon as they got their breath back they started up again.

The level of animosity among the researchers rose until it became apparent that the human teams weren't able to rise much above the level of the Noks. It was as if the Protocol should have been working the other way, shielding humans from the less advanced culture.

There was no evidence of conflict at Lookout, but once again they were facing the intervention issue. Except this time they were prepared to confront the natives, if it seemed prudent.

Not everyone on board was in agreement with that policy. Jason Holder, who described himself as the world's only exosociologist, had wasted no time taking Collingdale aside to warn him that contact would cause extensive harm in the long run, that if the Goompahs could get past the Event on their own, they'd be far better off if we kept out of it. "Sticking our noses in," he'd said, "all but guarantees they'll be crippled."

When Collingdale asked how that could be, he'd trotted out the usual explanation about the clash of civilizations, and how the weaker one always, *always*, went down. "The effects might not be immediately noticeable," he'd said, "but once they understand there's a more advanced culture out there, they lose heart. They give up, roll over, and wait for us to tell them the Truth, provide dinner, and show them how to cure the common cold."

"But we won't let them become dependent," Collingdale had said. "We won't be there after the Event."

"It'll be too late. They'll know we exist. And that will be enough."

Maybe he was right. Who really knew? But the natives weren't human, so maybe they'd react differently. And maybe Holder didn't know what he was talking about. It wouldn't be the first time an authority had gotten things wrong.

JUDY STERNBERG WAS a little on the bossy side, and she ran her operation like a fiefdom. She laid out each day's assignments in detail, added projects if time permitted, and expected results. She might have run into some resentment except that she didn't spare herself.

Her specialty was, she explained, the interrelationship between language and culture. "Tell me," she was fond of saying, "how people say *mother* and I'll tell you how their politics run."

Like Hutch, she was a diminutive woman, barely reaching Collingdale's shoulders. But she radiated energy.

They'd been out more than five weeks when she asked whether he had a moment to stop by Goompah Country, which was the section of the ship dedicated to the linguists, housing their workrooms and their individual quarters. "Got something to show you," she said.

They strolled down to B Deck, started along the corridor, and suddenly a door opened and a Goompah waddled out and said hello. Said it in the native tongue. "*Challa,* Professor Collingdale."

Collingdale felt his jaw drop. The creature was realistic.

"Meet Shelley," Judy said, trying to restrain a smile.

Shelley was even shorter than her supervisor. In costume she was wide, green, preposterous. Her saucer eyes locked on him. She adjusted her rawhide blouse, tugged at a yellow neckerchief, and held out a six-fingered hand.

"*Challa,* Shelley," he said.

She curtsied and pirouetted for his inspection. "What do you think?" she asked in English. The voice had an Australian lilt.

"We haven't done much with the clothing yet," said Judy, "because we're not really sure about texture. We'll need better data. Preferably samples. But by the time we get there, we'll have our own team of Goompahs."

"Well," he said, "it looks good to me, but I'm not a native."

She smiled. "Have faith. When we go down, nobody will be able to tell us from the locals."

Shelley took off her mask, and Collingdale found himself looking at an amused young blonde. Her figure in no way resembled Goompah anatomy. And he was embarrassed to realize he was inspecting her.

"I suspect you're right," he told Judy.

*   *   *

HE SENT A twenty-minute transmission to Mary, describing what they were doing, and telling her how much he'd have enjoyed having dinner with her tonight on the *al-Jahani*. "It's very romantic," he said, smiling into the imager. "Candlelight in the dining room, a gypsy violinist, and the best food in the neighborhood. And you never know whom you're going to meet."

None of it made much sense, except that she would understand the essential message, that he missed her, that he hoped she'd wait for him. That he regretted what had happened, but that it was a responsibility he really couldn't have passed off.

He had been getting messages from her every couple of days. They were shorter than he'd have preferred, but she said she didn't want to take advantage of Hutch's kindness in providing the service and run up the bill on the Academy. It was enough to satisfy him.

This was the only time in his life that he'd ever actually believed himself to be in love. Until Mary, he'd thought of the grand passion as something adolescents came down with, not unlike a virus. He had his own memories of June Cedric, Maggie Solver, and a few others. He remembered thinking about each of them that he had to possess her, would never forget her, could not live without her. But none of it had ever survived the season. He'd concluded that was how it was: A lovely and charming stranger takes your emotions for a ride, and the next thing you know you're committed to a relationship and wondering how it happened. He'd even suspected it might turn out that way with Mary. But each day that passed, every message that came in from her, only confirmed what now seemed true. If he lost her, he would lose everything.

WHILE HE WAS composing the transmission to Mary, Bill had signaled him there was a message from Hutch.

"*Dave,*" she said, "*you know about the hedgehogs.*" She was seated behind her desk, wearing a navy blouse, open at the neck, and a silver chain. "*It's beginning to look as if all the clouds have one. Jenkins tells us there's one at Lookout. The cloud has fallen away from it since it angled off to go after the Goompahs.*" The imager zoomed in on her until her face filled the screen. Her eyes were intense. "*It gives us a second arrow. When Frank uses the projectors, instead of just giving it a cube to chase, let's also try showing it a hedgehog. If one doesn't work, maybe the other will.*"

"*Hope everything's okay.*"

HE WAS APPALLED to discover that some of his colleagues were actually looking forward to the coming disaster. Charlie Harding, a statistician, talked openly about watching a primitive culture respond to an attack that would certainly seem to them "celestial."

"The interesting aspect," he said, "will come afterward. We'll be able to watch how they try to rationalize it, explain it to themselves."

"If it were a human culture," commented Elizabeth Madden, who had spent a lifetime writing books about tribal life in Micronesia, "they would look for something *they'd* done wrong, to incur divine displeasure."

And so it went.

It would be unfair to suggest they were all that way. There were some who applauded the effort to get the natives out of the cities, get them somewhere beyond the center of destruction. But anyone who'd seen the images from Moonlight and 4418 Delta (where the first omega had hit) knew that a direct strike by the cloud might render irrelevant all efforts to move the population.

Most nights, before retiring, he sent angry transmissions off to Hutch, damning the clouds and their makers.

She seemed curiously unresponsive. Yes, it was a disaster in the making. Yes, it would be helpful if we could do something. Yes, getting them out of the cities might not be enough. She knew all that, lived with it every day. But she never mentioned giving the Academy a kick in the rear to try to jump-start something.

THEY HAD GOOD pictures of several of the isthmus cities, identified by latitude. Their names were not considered a critical order of business by the linguists, but since they would probably not survive the Event, it seemed appropriate to get past the numbers. Collingdale wondered which of them would turn out to be *Mandigol*.

The cities were attractive. They were spacious and symmetrical, the streets laid out in a pattern that suggested a degree of planning mixed in with the usual chaotic growth that traditionally started at a commercial area and spread out haphazardly in all directions. Unfortunately, the patterns of the Goompah cities were exactly what would draw the cloud.

Markover's people had commented on a general style of design that had approximated classical Greek. They were right. Whatever one might say about the clownishness of these creatures, they knew how to lay out a city, and how to build.

The center of activity in the cities was usually near the waterfront area. But he saw parks and wide avenues and clusters of impressive structures everywhere. Bridges crossed streams and gulleys and even, in a couple of places, broad rivers. Roads and walkways were laid out with geometric precision.

Buildings that must have been private homes spread into the countryside, thinning out until forest took over. He spent hours studying the images coming from the *Jenkins*. The place wasn't Moonlight, but it was worth saving.

LIBRARY ENTRY

The notion that a primitive race, or species, is best served by our keeping away from it, is an absurdity. Do we refrain from assisting remote tribes in South America or Africa or central Asia when they are in need? Do we argue that they are best left to starve on their own when we have wheat and vegetables to spare? To die by the tens of thousands from a plague when we have the cure ready to hand?

Consider our own blighted history. How much misery might we have avoided had some benevolent outsider stepped in, say, to prevent the collapse of the Hellenic states? To offer some agricultural advice? To prevent the rise to power of Caligula? To suggest that maybe the Crusades weren't a good idea, and to show us how to throw some light into the Dark Ages? We might have neglected to create the Inquisition, or missed a few wars. Or neglected to keep slavery with us into the present day.

The standard argument is that a culture must find its own way. That it cannot survive an encounter with a technologically superior civilization. Even when the superior civilization wishes only to assist. That the weaker society becomes too easily dependent.

The cultures pointed to as examples of this principle are inevitably *tribal*. They are primitive societies, who, despite the claims made for their conquerors, are usually imposed on by well-meaning advocates of one kind or another, or are driven off by force. One thinks, for example, of the Native Americans. Or the various peoples of Micronesia.

However one may choose to interpret terrestrial experience, it is clear to all that the Goompahs are an advanced race. It is true that their technology is at about the level of imperial Rome, but it is a gross error to equate civilization with technology. They are, for the most part, peaceful. They have writing, they have the arts, they appear to have an ethical code which, at the very least, equals our own. A case can be made that the only area in which we excel is in the production of electrical power.

There is in fact no reason to believe that a direct intervention on behalf of the Goompahs would not be of immense benefit to them. Especially now, when they face a lethal danger of which they are not even aware. To stand by, and permit the massive destruction of these entities in the name of a misbegotten and wrongheaded policy, would be damnable.

The Council has the means to act. Let it do so. If it continues to dither, the North American Union should take it upon itself to do something while there is yet time.

—*The New York Times*, Wednesday, April 23, 2234

chapter 16

JULIE, MARGE, AND Whitlock had become friends. The women called him
Whit, and they talked endlessly about omegas and cosmology, elephants
and physicists, Goompahs and God. The days raced by, and Julie began to
realize she had never been on a more enjoyable journey. It was almost as
though her entire life had been spent preparing for this epochal flight.

Whit consistently delivered odd perspectives. He argued that the best
form of government was an aristocracy, that a republic was safest, and that
a democracy was most interesting. Mobs are unpredictable, he said. You
just never know about them. He pointed out that during the Golden Age,
the worst neighbor in the Hellespont had been Athens. On the major knee-
bending religious faiths, he wondered whether a God subtle enough to have
invented quantum mechanics would really be interested in having people
deliver rote prayers and swing incense pots in His direction.

Marge had been reserved at first, had seemed always buried with work.
But gradually she'd loosened up. Now the three of them plotted how to
save the Goompahs, and make sure that the Academy was funded afterward
so that it could learn to deal decisively with the omegas.

Julie wanted to see an expedition put together to track the things to their
source. There'd been plans for years to do just that. The old Project Scythe,
for one. And then Redlight. And finally, in its early stages, Weatherman.
But it was expensive, the target was thought to be near the core, thirty
thousand light-years away, and the resources were simply not there.

"We'll only get one chance to beat these things," Whit said, referring to
the omegas. "The time spans are so great that people get used to having
them around. Like hurricanes or earthquakes. And eventually we'll try to
learn to live with them. So if we don't succeed on the first effect on, the
window will close and it won't get done."

"But why does it have to be us?" Julie asked. "Why not somebody six
centuries from now?"

"Because we're the ones who lived through the shock of discovery. For everybody else, it'll be old stuff. Which means people will still be sitting in London and Peoria complaining about why the government didn't do something when the cloud shows up to shut *them* down."

Although he lived in a society of renewable marriages and, in many places, multiple spouses, Whit was a romantic. At least, that was the impression Julie had gotten after reading *Love and Black Holes*, his best-known collection of commentaries on the human condition. True love came along only once in a lifetime, Whit maintained. Lose her, or him, and it was over. Everything after that was a rerun. Julie assumed that Whit, who wasn't married, had suffered just such a loss and never recovered. She was careful not to ask about it, but she wondered who it had been, and what had happened. And, eventually, if the woman had any idea what she'd let get away.

Whitlock was tall, with a lined face, one of those faces that had been lived in. He had white hair, and exuded dignity. The rejuvenation treatments had come along too late to do him much good, but he didn't seem to mind. He told her he'd lived the life he wanted and had no regrets. (That was clearly a falsehood, but a brave one.) He was on board because Hutch liked him and liked his work. There'd been a battle about his coming, apparently. Whit wasn't a serious scientist, in the view of many, and consequently was not on the same level as others who would have liked the last seat on the mission. Julie had heard that Hutchins had taken some heat for giving it to him.

He asked Julie whether a lightbender would be made available to him when they got to Lookout because he wanted to go down to the surface and actually *see* the Goompahs. He was even working with some of the people on the *al-Jahani*, trying to familiarize himself with their language, but he confessed he wasn't having much luck picking it up. "Too old," he said.

He had turned out to be a dear. He did not assume a superior attitude, as she'd expected when she first saw his name on the manifest. He was already taking notes, not on what was happening on the *Hawksbill*, but on his own reaction to learning that an intelligent species was at risk. At Julie's request, he'd shown her some of his work, and had even gotten into the habit of asking for her comments. She doubted he really needed her editorial input, but it was a nice gesture, and she had quickly learned he wanted her to tell him what she really thought. "Doesn't do any good to have you just pat me on the head and say the work is great," he'd said. "I need to know how you really react, whether it makes sense. If I'm going to make a fool of myself, I'd prefer to keep the fact in the ship's company rather than spread it around the world."

He had a habit of referring to humans as smart monkeys. They were basically decent, he told her one evening in the common room when they were talking about the long bloodbath that human history had been. "But their great deficiency is that they're too easily programmed. Get them when they're reasonably young, say five or six, and you can make them believe almost anything. Not only that, but once it's done, the majority of them will fight to the death to maintain the illusion. That's why you get Nazis, racists, homophobes, fanatics of all types."

Marge Conway's assignment was to assume the cloud would arrive over the isthmus precisely on schedule, and to find a way to hide the cities. She would do so by generating rain clouds. If a blizzard had concealed a city on Moonlight, there was no reason to think storm clouds wouldn't have the same effect on Lookout.

If the mission to shoo the cloud away succeeded, her job would become unnecessary. Marge was one of those rare persons who was primarily concerned with overall success, and didn't much care who got the credit. In this case, though, she couldn't conceal that she longed to see her manufactured clouds in action.

Marge admitted that she'd gotten the appointment not because she was particularly well thought of in her field, but because of her connection with Hutchins. She'd worked on a number of projects for the Academy, but had never before been on a superluminal. She didn't even like aircraft. "The ride up to the station," she told Julie, "was the scariest experience of my life." Julie wasn't sure whether to believe her or not because the woman didn't look as if *anything* could scare her.

"We have one major advantage," Marge commented. "Nobody expects us to get the job done."

"Hutch does," said Julie.

Marge didn't think so. "Hutch puts on a good show. She knows that Moonlight might have been an anomaly. She's seen the clouds in action, and I doubt she thinks anything can turn them aside."

"Then why are we being sent out?"

"You want the truth?" said Whit.

"Please."

"Because the politicians want to be able to say they made a serious effort. If we don't try this, and a lot of Goompahs die, which they almost certainly will, the public's going to be looking for whose fault it is."

Whit's statement cast a pall over things because he was usually so optimistic.

Marge asked him why he thought the decoy wouldn't work.

"Because somebody else tried it. We don't really know who, although we suspect it was the Monument-Makers. Somebody tried to save Quraqua at one time by building a simulated, and very square, city on its moon. At Nok, they put four cube-shaped satellites, each about two kilometers wide, in orbit. Both places got hit anyhow."

"Sounds definitive to me," said Marge.

"Maybe they waited too long," said Julie.

"How do you mean?" asked Whit.

"At both places, the decoys were too close to the targets. By the time the cloud picked them up, it would already have been locked on its objectives. Lots of cities on both worlds."

Whit considered it. "I'm sure you're right," he said. "But we'll be showing up at the last minute, too. It's not as if we're getting there with a year to spare."

Dead and buried, she thought. He must have seen her disappointment because he smiled. "But don't give up, Julie. I think the rain makers will work."

WHIT WANTED TO look at the cloud-making equipment, so in the morning Julie took them down to the cargo bay, which required everyone to get into an e-suit because it was in vacuum.

The bay itself looked like a large warehouse. Marge and Whit had not been off A Deck, which was the only area of the ship maintaining life support. It had therefore been easy for them to forget how big the *Hawksbill* was until they stood gazing from prow to stern, down the length of an enclosure filled with four landers, an AV3 heavy-duty hauler, and an antique helicopter. The rainmakers were attached to the hull. Julie took them into the airlock and opened up so they could see them. They resembled large coils.

"They're actually chimneys," Marge said. "When they're deployed, they'll be three kilometers long. Each of them."

"That's pretty big."

"As big as we could make them."

Avery Whitlock's Notebooks

One of the unfortunate side effects of organized religion is that it seeks to persuade us that we are inherently evil. Damaged goods.

I've watched volunteers work with kids injured in accidents; I've seen sons and daughters give over their time to taking care of elderly parents. There are a thousand stories out there about people who have given their lives for their children, for their friends, and sometimes for total strangers. We go down to the beach to try to push a stranded whale back into the ocean.

Now we are trying to help an intelligent species that cannot help itself. Whether we will pull it off, no one knows. But of one thing I am certain: If we ever start to believe those who think God made a race of deformed children, then that is what we will become.

And who then would help the Goompahs?

chapter 17

On board the *Heffernan*, near Iota
Pictoris, 120 light-years from
Earth.
Monday, April 28.

SKY STAYED WELL clear of the hedgehog. Since he'd watched the one at
Alpha Pictoris explode, he'd gained a lot of respect for the damned things.

Emma was beside him, enjoying a mug of beef stew. The aroma filled
the bridge. "Bill," he said, "send the packages."

He sensed, rather than heard, the launch. *"Packages away,"* said Bill.

The hedgehog was forty-four thousand kilometers in front of the cloud.

"Withdraw to five thousand kilometers."

Bill swung the *Heffernan* around and retreated as directed.

"Keep the engines running."

The AI smiled. He was on-screen, seated in his armchair. *"We are ready to
accelerate away, should it become necessary."* He looked off to his left. *"Sky,"* he
said, *"we are receiving a transmission from the Academy. From the DO."*

Emma smiled. "That'll be another warning to play it safe," she said.

"Let's see what she has to say for herself, Bill."

The overhead screen blinked on, first the Academy seal, a scroll and lamp
framing the blue Earth of the United World, and then Hutch. She was seated
on the edge of her desk.

"Emma," she said, *"Sky, I thought you'd be interested in the preliminary results
we're getting. It looks as if, when these things blow up, they're not ordinary explosions. I can't explain this exactly, but I suspect Emma will be able to. The energy
release is sculpted. That's the term the researchers are using. They think it's designed
for a specific purpose.*

*"We hope, when you're finished out there, we'll have a better idea what the
purpose is. And we appreciate what you've been doing. I know it's not the most
rousing assignment in the world."*

She lifted a hand in farewell, the seal came back, and the monitor shut
down. Sky looked at his wife. *"Sculpted?"*

"Just like the lady says," said Emma. "Think of it as a blast in which the
energy doesn't just erupt, but instead constitutes a kind of code."

"To do what?"

She gazed at the image of the omega, floating serenely on the auxiliary screen. "Sometimes," she said, "to excite nanos. Get them to perform."

THE PACKAGES ARRIVED in the vicinity of the hedgehog and opened up. Twelve sets of thrusters assembled themselves, collected their fuel tanks, and circled the hedgehog. At a signal, each located the specific site it had been designed for and used its set of magnetic clamps to attach itself. The twelve sites had been carefully chosen, because on this most uneven object, the thrusters lined up almost perfectly parallel with each other. They would function as retrorockets.

"Everything's in place," said Bill. *"Ready to proceed."*

"Execute, Bill."

The thrusters fired in unison. And continued to fire.

Satisfied, Sky got himself a mug of Emma's soup.

"You do good work, darling," she said.

"Yes, I do." He reclaimed his seat and slowly put away the soup. Bill screened the figures on deceleration rate, the fuel supplies left in the retros, and attitude control.

There had been some concern that the magnetic clamps would set the device off, but that had happily not occurred.

They were in a dark place, in the well between stars, where no sun illuminated the sky. It wasn't like a night sky seen from Earth. You knew you were far out in the void. There was no charm, no bright sense of distant suns and constellations. The only thing he felt was distance.

"Retro fuel running low," said Bill. *"Two minutes."*

The important thing was to shut them all down simultaneously, and not let one or more run out of fuel and cause the others to push the thing off-course.

"Bill, where will we be if we shut down with thirty seconds remaining?"

"The hedgehog will have shed 30 kph."

"Okay. That means the cloud will overtake it when?"

"In sixty days. June 27."

"Good. Let's do it."

"I DON'T LIKE these things, Em." He pushed himself out of the chair.

"Nor do I," she said.

He gazed down at the navigation screen, which had set up a sixty-day calendar and clock, and begun ticking off the seconds.

"I'm going to turn in."

She nodded. "Go ahead. I'll be along in a minute." She was looking at the cloud. It was dark and quiet. Peaceful. In the vast emptiness, it would not have been possible to realize it was racing through the heavens.

"What are you thinking, Em?"

"About my dad. I remember one night he told me how things changed when people found out about the omegas."

"In what way?"

"Until then," he said, "people always thought they were at the center of things. The universe was made for us. The only part of it that thinks. Our God was the universal God and He even paid a visit. We were in charge.

"I never really thought that way. I more or less grew up with the clouds." She touched the screen, and the picture died. "I wish we could kill it," she said.

LIBRARY ENTRY

The omegas are a footprint, a signal to us that something far greater than we is loose in the galaxy. Once we used our churches to demonstrate that we were kings of creation, the purpose for it all. Now we use them to hide.

—Gregory MacAllister,
"The Flower Girl Always Steals the Show,"
Editor at Large, 2220

ALSO BY BENTON RAIN PATTERSON

The Generals: Andrew Jackson, Sir Edward Pakenham,
and the Road to the Battle of New Orleans

Washington and Cornwallis: The Battle for America, 1775–1783

Harold and William: The Battle for England, A.D. 1064–1066

A Reporter's Interview with Jesus

WITH THE HEART

OF A KING

ELIZABETH I OF ENGLAND, PHILIP II OF SPAIN,

AND THE FIGHT FOR A NATION'S

SOUL AND CROWN

BENTON RAIN PATTERSON

ST. MARTIN'S PRESS ✷ NEW YORK

www.stmartins.com

Book design by Claire Naylon Vaccaro

Library of Congress Cataloging-in-Publication Data

Patterson, Benton Rain, 1929–
    With the heart of a king : Elizabeth I of England, Philip II of Spain, and the fight for a nation's soul and crown / Benton Rain Patterson. — 1st ed.
        p. cm.
    Includes bibliographical references and index.
    ISBN-13: 978-0-312-34844-1
    ISBN-10: 0-312-34844-4
    1. Elizabeth I, Queen of England, 1533–1603. 2. Philip II, King of Spain, 1527–1598. 3. Great Britain—History—Elizabeth, 1558–1603. 4. Great Britain—Foreign relations—Spain. 5. Spain—Foreign relations—Great Britain. 6. Queens—Great Britain—Biography. I. Title.

DA355.P38 2007
942.05'5092—dc22
[B]   2006050141

First Edition: February 2007

10   9   8   7   6   5   4   3   2   1

Dedicated to

the memory of my loving parents,

Palmer and Jess Wood Patterson

 CONTENTS

Contents

WITH the HEART
OF a KING

·⚬· I. THE PRINCE

In the year 1527, the most powerful man of the Western world was the Holy Roman emperor, Charles V, emperor of Austria and Germany, king of Spain and Sicily, and lord over a dozen or more other states in Italy and the Netherlands, which included Belgium. A rare confluence of noble family connections had made him sovereign over the largest realm in Europe, made still larger by explorers and conquistadors who had claimed for Spain lands of the vast New World and beyond it as far as the Philippines.

Charles was twenty-seven years old in 1527, not tall but well built, blond and blue eyed, with a long face, aquiline nose, and the thick lower lip that ran in his father's family, the Habsburgs. When single, he had fathered an illegitimate daughter (Margaret of Parma), but now he was married to the beautiful, blond, twenty-four-year-old Portuguese princess Isabel, who was also his cousin (both were grandchildren of the late King Ferdinand and Queen Isabella of Spain). He had reneged on an agreement to marry Mary Tudor, the future queen of England, who was only a child at the time, so that he could wed Isabel.

The wedding had been held in Seville on March 10, 1526, and the following August Isabel had become pregnant, a fact over which virtually the entire population of Spain, where the couple resided, apparently rejoiced, the birth of a royal heir being always a huge cause for celebration.

The ninth month of Isabel's pregnancy, May 1527, arrived with the fragrance of orange blossoms in the warm Castilian air but with international problems looming dangerously before Charles. If God in His mercy would grant him a son, a male heir to his empire and kingdoms, that advent would be such glad news to Charles that the gloomy clouds of threats from France and England and the pope might for a time be burst with brightness. Deeply serious about his Catholic faith (though not a friend of the pope), Charles doubtless was earnestly praying that Isabel would deliver a son, a successor, healthy and whole.

About three o'clock in the morning of May 21, 1527, in the royal palace in Valladolid (then Spain's capital), Isabel began a difficult labor, which she stoically endured, telling the midwife who attended her, "I may die, but I will not cry out." Thirteen hours later, at four o'clock that afternoon, Isabel's eagerly awaited baby arrived. Charles, who remained with his wife throughout her ordeal, had received the happy answer to his prayer. He was the father of a son.

He took the infant in his arms, praying as he held him: "May our Lord God make you a good Christian. I beg our Lord God to give you His grace. May it please our Lord God to enlighten you, that you may know how to govern the Kingdom you shall inherit."

As news of the baby's birth rippled out from the palace, church bells pealed in gleeful annunication, first in Valladolid, then in nearby towns and villages, then throughout the land. In Castile's protective forts, cannons were fired in thunderous salute to the blessed event. Many of the country's important persons, members of the royal court, noblemen, government officials, and high-ranking clergy, began making their way to the Valladolid palace to offer their congratulations and join the celebration.

Charles, meanwhile, in a pouring rain that had come sweeping through Valladolid, made his way on foot from the palace to the Church of Saint Paul (San Pablo) to give thanks for the prayed-for blessing that God had bestowed upon him.

Two weeks later, on Sunday, June 2, the royal infant was carried from the palace to the Church of Saint Paul, along a path scattered with rose petals and lemon and orange blossoms, to be baptized according to the Catholic tradition and to receive his name, one that history would forever remember. According to one account, many of those close to Charles wanted him to name the boy Fernando (Ferdinand), after the child's famous great-grandfather. One of those closest to Charles, the duke of Alba, while standing at the baptismal font during the ceremony, went so far as to insist that Charles name him Fernando.

Charles, however, had already made up his mind about what his son would be called and he couldn't be dissuaded. The infant prince would be named for Charles's father. He would be Philip, grandson of Philip the Handsome. And so was he baptized by the primate of Spain, the archbishop of Toledo, Don Alonso de Fonseca, who drew the baptismal water from a large silver font and pronounced the baby's name. The child's godparents were the duke of Bejar, who cradled the baby in his arms during the ceremony, and Charles's older sister Eleanor, queen of France. Upon the infant's baptism, a royal herald announced to the onlookers, "*Oyd, oyd, oyd, Don Philipe, principe de Castilla por la gracia de Dios!*"

That solemn ceremony having been concluded, the joyous celebrations began, nights of banquets and days of feasts, celebratory bullfights and tournaments, jousts that featured some two hundred knights. Members of the royal court put aside other concerns and gave themselves to the celebration. "There is consequently a great lull in politics," the ambassador from Bohemia wrote in an official report, "and the courtiers think of nothing save the rejoicings."

Within days, however, the festivities were abruptly aborted on receipt of alarming news from Italy. An army of Pope Clement VII, who had allied himself with the French king, Francis I, Charles's hostile brother-in-law, had challenged Charles's forces based in Milan. Charles's army had brushed aside the challenge and, marching south on Rome, had assaulted the Vatican on May 6, 1527, and had sent the pope and his cardinals fleeing for their lives, the pope narrowly escaping capture or worse. Out of control after their commander had been killed in the assault, Charles's troops, many of them German mercenaries, had, according to one report, slaughtered some six to eight thousand men of Rome and had sacked the city, leaving much of it in ruins. News of the peril to the pope and the atrocities committed against the capital of Christendom ignited a firestorm of outrage throughout Western Europe.

Charles learned of the events about the middle of June and, persuaded that the festive mood was now inappropriate, he called off the celebrations of his son's birth. Strong reaction to the atrocities in Rome had burst through Spain as it had done elsewhere in Europe. Defiantly denouncing Charles from their pulpits, many Spanish priests had demanded an end to the celebrations, and many of the members of Charles's Spanish court who had been joyfully celebrating went into mourning over the deeds of their sovereign's army.

For the newborn prince it was an inauspicious beginning to his public life, which officially began when at age one year he was, on May 10, 1528, recognized as heir to the throne of Castile, Spain's major province, by Castile's legislature, the Cortes. The Cortes then also recognized Philip's mother, the Empress Isabel, as regent whenever Charles was out of the country, which he soon would be. Isabel was likely thinking little about becoming regent, how-ever. She was then pregnant with a second child, who was born on June 21, 1528, in Madrid and was named Maria.

Deciding that he could no longer stay in Spain, that he needed to take charge of developing events in other parts of his realm, Charles set sail from Barcelona on July 27, 1529, when Philip was two years old. It was the last the boy would see of his father for nearly four years.

There was no question of Isabel and the children going with Charles. Nine years earlier, in 1520, there had been a widespread rebellion in Spain against Charles, who was born and raised in Flanders and whom a great many in Spain considered an outsider. He had made some concessions to the rebels in the course of bringing the revolt to an end. The rebels, called *comuneros,* had asked Charles to spend more time in Castile and less time in other parts of his empire. They had also asked him to learn to speak Spanish. Further, they had asked him to marry a Portuguese princess. All of those things he had done. They had also asked that whatever children he had with the princess be brought up as Spaniards and be educated in Spain. Now, no doubt remem-bering the *comunero* revolt and the promises made, Charles left his young son and baby daughter in Spain with his wife as he sailed away to attend to his af-fairs outside Spain.

Little Philip, fair skinned, blond haired, and blue eyed, was turned over by his mother to the care of a Portuguese nurse, Leonor Mascarenhas, for whom Philip developed a lasting affection. He managed to survive several childhood illnesses, all of which his mother, who kept a watchful eye on him, fretted over. "The prince my son is ill with fever," she wrote to a friend during one of Philip's sicknesses, "and though the illness is not dangerous it has me very worried and anxious." Philip recovered, but three weeks later he fell sick again. "I'm very anxious," Isabel wrote to her absent husband.

The doings of the royal siblings were reported to their father in letters. "The infanta [Maria] grows bigger and fatter by the day," the boy's governor, Pedro González de Mendoza, wrote to Charles, "and the prince entertains her like a genteel gallant." The prince also had other moments. "He is so mis-chievous that sometimes Her Majesty gets really angry," another report reads. "She spanks him, and the women weep to see such severity."[1]

When Philip was seven years old, Charles appointed a tutor for him, forty-eight-year-old Juan Martínez Silíceo, a priest who was a professor at the

University of Salamanca. He was described by one of Philip's biographers as "a man of piety and learning and of an accommodating temper, too accommodating . . . for the good of his pupil."[2] The result of the tutor's easygoing attitude, Charles believed, was that young Philip was not absorbing all the learning that was available from Siliceo.

In 1535, when Philip was eight years old, his father appointed a new governor for him, Juan de Zúñiga, one of Charles's close associates, and Zúñiga and Siliceo mapped out the prince's education, Siliceo handling the book learning and Zúñiga handling the extracurricular activities, such as riding and hunting, as well as character building.

Philip progressed through basic reading and writing and began to take on more difficult assignments. "He has made a lot of progress in reading and learning prayers in Latin and Spanish," Siliceo wrote to Charles in February 1536, and during the following September Siliceo reported that Philip "knows the [Latin] conjugations and some other principles; soon he will start to study authors, the first of whom is Cato." Other subjects that he studied, however assiduously, included mathematics, science, French, Italian, art, and the principles of architecture. Though he did well enough with Latin, learning to speak and write it acceptably, which he often did in later years, he didn't do as well with Italian or French. Science and math he liked, and over the years he acquired such a knowledge of architecture, painting, and sculpture that he became a credible critic of them.

Philip also learned to appreciate music. Luis Narvaez, a composer from Granada, was appointed Philip's music tutor, and he taught the prince to play the guitar. The boy was said to be a talented musician, though he had not much of a singing voice. He developed such a fondness for organ music, which was played for him in his private chapel, as well as for music in general, that when he traveled, he took with him an organ, an organist, and a choir, so that he could always have good-listening music.

He was showing increased interest in extracurricular activities, too. "Though hunting is at present what he is most inclined to, he doesn't neglect his studies a bit," Siliceo wrote reassuringly to Charles. And aware of the boy's advancing adolescence, the tutor-priest observed that "we have to be grateful that at this age of fourteen when the weakness of the flesh begins to assert itself, God has given the prince such a passion for hunting that he spends most of his time in this and in his studies."[3]

The time the prince was spending hunting was more of a concern to Zúñiga than it was to Siliceo. "He went on horseback into the hills for a good six hours," Zúñiga told Charles. "It only seemed like two hours to him, but it seemed more than twelve to me. . . . His only real pastime is shooting game with the crossbow." The game he shot included rabbits, deer, wolves, and bears, and he became so skilled at shooting them that restrictions were imposed lest he overkill his father's game.

In one of his reports to Charles, Zúñiga said that Philip was happiest when he was outdoors. He was content to do almost anything "provided he could do it in the countryside," Zúñiga wrote. The boy had developed a love of nature and he collected birds that he kept in cages, so many of them that a mule was needed to transport them when Philip's household was moved periodically. Indoors, he played with toy soldiers and played cards and quoits. He also painted pictures in a large book of blank pages.

In 1539 Philip suffered the most tragic event of his young life, the death of his mother. She had had a miscarriage in late April and died on May 1, three weeks before Philip's twelfth birthday. Becoming ill while he walked in the funeral procession, Philip returned to his rooms and was put to bed. His mother's body was taken to Granada and buried in the royal tombs, where King Ferdinand and Queen Isabella were buried. Charles was so stricken with grief that he isolated himself in mourning for the next seven weeks.

Following his mother's death, Philip spent two years in official mourning, wearing only black, unadorned with jewelry. In May 1541 Charles let him begin wearing colorful clothing again and gave him permission to wear gold jewelry.

The loss of his mother deprived Philip of nearly all expressions of parental love, and he grew through his teenage years largely dependent on his sisters, Maria and Juana (born to Isabel on June 24, 1535, two years before her death), for mutual feelings of affection.

Ever since he was seven years old, Philip had been living in his own separate quarters. He was being attended by his own servants and receiving guidance from his own advisers. He also had his own friends, or special companions, all of them selected for him. His six-year-old cousin Maximilian, son of Charles's brother Ferdinand, was brought from Vienna to be tutored with Philip. The two boys played and studied together, although Maximilian never became one of Philip's best friends. He and Philip's other companions, or pages, most of them the sons of noble families, formed a sort of boys' court, over which Philip presided, rehearsing the role of his future. By 1540 the members of Philip's household totaled 191,[4] including 51 pages, 8 chaplains, a physician, a crew of kitchen workers, plus miscellaneous maids, grooms, stable workers, and others who kept the boy's mansion humming and maintained and the prince himself well served. In 1541 he was given his own personal secretary, Gonzalo Pérez, a somewhat imperious priest who ended up serving Philip for the next twenty-four years.

Charles was becoming increasingly dissatisfied with Siliceo as the boy's main tutor. He wrote to Philip to prepare him for Siliceo's dismissal. "[He] has not been nor is the most suitable teacher for you; he has given in to you too much."[5] (Later Philip would choose the priest Siliceo, to whom he felt close, as his official confessor. On learning of the choice, Charles wrote to his son: "I hope he will not want to appease you as much in matters of conscience as he did in matters of study."[6]) In 1541, the year that Philip made his first communion, Charles appointed three new tutors for Philip, one to teach Latin and Greek, one to teach math and architecture, and another to teach geography and history. Charles may have given up on the likelihood that his son could learn modern languages, for he appointed no tutor to make further attempts at teaching them to Philip.

The new tutors, who also taught Philip's pages, were provided funds to acquire a library for the prince. Over time the books of Philip's library included works by Aquinas, Boccacio, Copernicus, Dante, Dürer, Erasmus, Machiavelli, Petrarch, Savonarola, Sophocles, Virgil, and Vitruvio. The book collection assembled by his tutors, some of which he undoubtedly read, at least in part, apparently inspired Philip to add his own eclectic selections to his library. They included books on art, architecture, music, theology, warfare, and magic.

Discipline, which once had been administered to the prince by his mother, was now the responsibility of the boy's governor, Zúñiga, whose strictness Philip protested to his absent father. Charles, however, thought Zúñiga's rigor was just what the boy needed. "If he gave in to your every caprice," Charles wrote to his son, "you would be like the rest of mankind and would have no one to tell you the truth."

In Charles's absence, Philip's valet was given the job of buying gifts for the boy. The valet received thirty ducats a month to buy things he thought would please the prince. During the months of 1540, those pleasing things included fencing swords, jousting lances, jewels, perfume, and a glass cup from Venice.

Despite the seeming robustness required for his riding, hunting, fencing, jousting, and other physical activities, Philip remained sickly. According to one report, his blond hair and pale complexion gave him "an almost albino coloring."[7] Except for an attack of what was apparently salmonella poisoning, however, he suffered no serious illnesses.

His diet was limited because of his digestive problems. He took two meals a day, lunch and dinner, and the fare was the same for both. His choices of entrees were chicken, partridge, pigeon, beef, and venison and other game. On Fridays there was no choice: As other good Catholics did for centuries, he ate fish. (He later received special dispensation from the pope to eat meat on Fridays, which he did, except on Good Friday.) He was also served soup and bread at every meal. Few vegetables made it to his table, perhaps by his own instructions. Fruit was served to him at lunch, and salads at dinner.

His health became a continuing concern to Philip. When he asked the pope for permission to eat meat on Fridays, he told his holiness his reason for asking was that "we do not wish to risk changing our diet." One of his most troublesome problems was chronic constipation, which the royal physicians treated with doses of oil of turpentine and enemas and emetics. He later suffered from hemorrhoids.

To accommodate his needs, a new chamber pot was purchased and placed in the prince's privy every two weeks. His other personal items, accumulated over time, included an ebony toothbrush inlaid with gold, a gold toothpick, bowls that contained tooth powder and toothpaste, ear-cleaning instruments, a hairbrush and a brush to clean combs, a manicure set, and a special silver goblet that he used to take his medications.

Apparently not handicapped by his health problems, which included asthma, Philip was an active teenager. At age sixteen he was described by Zúñiga as "the most accomplished man of arms in this court, and this can be said without flattery. This week he and the duke of Alba put on a contest in the country." Philip, Zúñiga said, was "very good at fighting both on foot and on horseback." The prince also showed his accomplishments inside the palace, where he often held dances, his sister Maria being his dancing partner, and other festivities.

At age sixteen Philip's life as a carefree boy ended. For one thing, he became officially betrothed. The bride his father selected for him was Princess Maria Manuela of Portugal, one of Philip's cousins (her father, Juan III of Portugal, was the brother of Philip's mother). In a letter dated May 4, 1543, just before his father once more departed Spain, Charles gave his son some advice about marriage. He cautioned Philip about overindulgence in sex: "When you are with your wife . . . be careful and do not overstrain yourself at the beginning, in order to avoid physical damage, because besides the fact that it [intercourse] may be damaging both to the growth of the body and to its strength, it often induces such weakness that it prevents the siring of children and may even kill you."[8]

The point of being married, Charles told Philip, was not to have sex but to produce heirs. "For this reason," Charles wrote, "you must be careful when you are with your wife. And because this is somewhat difficult, the remedy is to keep away from her as much as you can. And so I beg and advise you strongly that as soon as you have consummated the marriage, you should leave her on some pretext, and do not go back to see her too quickly or too often. And when you do go back, let it be only for a short time."[9] (In a separate letter to Zúñiga, Charles instructed him to make sure Philip followed this advice.)

Avoidance of his wife, furthermore, was no excuse to take up with other women, Charles said. "Apart from the discomfort and ills that may ensue from it between you and her [his wife], it will destroy the effect of keeping you away from her."

The other life-changing event, also in May 1543, was Philip's appointment by his father as regent in Spain, leaving Philip, as Charles wrote, "in my place during my absence, to govern these realms." The emperor also gave his son some advice concerning that responsibility. "Keep God always in mind," he wrote, and "accept good advice at all times." Charles told Philip to make service to God his first priority and "never allow heresies to enter your realms. Support the Holy Inquisition," Charles instructed, ". . . and on no account do anything to harm it."[10]

As a ruler, Charles wrote, Philip must be "an upholder of justice" and must root out all corruption among his government's officials. He should avoid flatterers and make sure his advisers feel free to give him their honest opinions. "You must also find time to go among and talk with the people," Charles told him. Philip should strive to be "temperate and moderate in all you do," his father said. "Keep yourself from anger, and do nothing in anger."[11]

Charles braced him for the difference the new role would make in his life. "Till now your company has been that of children. . . . From now on, you must not associate with them. . . . Your company will be above all that of grown men."

In a second letter of advice about governing, dated May 6, 1543, Charles cautioned about allowing one official to attach himself to Philip, to the exclusion of others. He mentioned specific individuals.

> The duke of Alba is the ablest statesman and the best soldier I have in my dominions. Consult him, above all, in military affairs; but do not depend on him entirely in these or in any other matters. Depend on no one but yourself.
>
> The grandees will be too happy to secure your favor and through you to govern the land. But if you are thus governed, it will be your ruin. The mere suspicion of it will do you infinite prejudice. Make use of all; but lean exclusively on none.
>
> In your perplexities, ever trust in your Maker. Have no care but for Him.[12]

Philip immediately responded to the new responsibilities his father placed on him. "His Highness received the Instructions, together with the powers which Your Majesty sent for governing these realms and those of Aragon," Zúñiga promptly reported to Charles. "After he had read it all, he sent the special instructions to the tribunals and councils. He has begun, conscientiously and with resolution, to study what he has been ordered to do. He is in touch always with the duke of Alba and the grand commander of Léon [Francisco de los Cobos]."

Feeling the role in which he had been suddenly cast by his father, Philip in the summer of 1543 started adding these words to his scrawled signature on official correspondence: *Yo el Príncipe*. I the Prince.

In October 1543 Philip got to see his bride-to-be for the first time. Accompanied by a considerable number of Portuguese nobles and attendants, as well as the archbishop of Lisbon, Maria had set out from her father's palace in Lisbon on the long, slow trip to Salamanca, in Castile, where the wedding was to be held. Riding out to meet the Portuguese procession and escort it was a party of Spanish dignitaries led by the duke of Medina Sidonia, described in one account as the wealthiest and most powerful lord in the Spanish province of Andalusia. The duke was borne in a sumptuous litter carried by mules that were shod with gold. The members of his household and his retainers, including his private band, swelled the escort to an estimated three thousand persons, most of them mounted and liveried. About six miles from Salamanca, that impressive procession was joined by a small group of riders who looked very much like a party of hunters.

One of the ostensible hunters was Philip. He was wearing a velvet slouch hat and a gauze mask over part of his face so that he wouldn't be recognized. He had ridden out with several attendants so that he could take a good, furtive look at the girl he was going to marry.

Maria, five months younger than sixteen-year-old Philip, was neither short nor tall; she had a good figure, though she was a bit on the plump side, and had a pleasing expression to her face. She wore a dress made of cloth of silver embroidered with gold flowers. On her shoulders was a *capa*, a mantle, made of violet velvet with gold figures in it. She wore a hat of the same velvet material, with a white and blue plume atop it. She sat on a silver saddle, riding a mule caparisoned in rich brocade.

Philip rode with the procession until nightfall. He later wrote to his father that "I saw her without her being able to see me." Philip returned to Salamanca to make a ceremonial entry on November 12, and Maria arrived several hours later.

Maria's procession was met by the rector and professors of the University of Salamanca, dressed in their academic gowns, and behind the professors came officials of the city and other public officers, wearing their robes of office, followed by contingents of cavalry and infantry in their dress uniforms. By that colorful entourage and amid shouts from the crowd of spectators who turned out for the spectacle and the sounds of celebratory music, Princess Maria was extravagantly ushered into the city.

She rode on to the palace of the duke of Alba, where a lavish reception was held for her. That evening, Monday, November 12, 1543, she and Philip were married. Each went forward from a group of attendants and, when they met, Philip kissed her hand and embraced her. The ceremony was performed under a resplendent canopy, the archbishop of Toledo, Cardinal Tavera, officiating. The emperor, Philip's father, was absent as usual. The duke and duchess of Alba stood as sponsors. Following the ceremony, a royal ball began, and the city erupted in celebration, which lasted well into the next morning.

A week later, on November 19, after days of fiestas and celebratory tournaments and bullfights, the newlyweds moved to Valladolid. On their way, through towns gaily decorated in honor of the couple, they made a stop at Tordesillas to visit Philip's grandmother, Queen Juana, mother of Charles. Juana, daughter of the late King Ferdinand and Queen Isabella, suffered from mental problems, popularly believed to have been caused by the unexpected death of her husband, Philip the Handsome, and was known as Juana *la loca*— Juana the Crazy. Her behavior following her husband's death perhaps justified the name. One stormy November night she was found outside, half naked, shrieking into the wind. Night after night in an open field she had sat in the darkness with her husband's corpse. Finally she had been locked away in a castle. For fifty years she had been held, in effect, a prisoner of her dementia. On the day that Philip and Maria visited her, however, she seemed more or less normal. She asked them to dance for her, and when they did, she sat gazing on them admiringly.

From Tordesillas, Philip and Maria continued on to Valladolid, where they would settle into the routine of married life and he would resume his responsibilities as regent. Some things would not quickly change. Philip would still attend daily sessions with his tutors and he would still pursue his riding, hunting, and jousting. The affairs of government, though, would gradually come to occupy more of his time and thoughts.

His father was pleased. "Up till now," he wrote to Philip, "thanks be to God, there is nothing obvious to criticize in you."

⤙ 2. THE PRINCESS

It was in the year 1527 that Anne Boleyn began to feel from England's king, Henry VIII, the gratifying warmth of royal attention. Delighted as she was by it, she was determined not to respond as her sister had, by becoming one of the king's mistresses. Anne's ambitions were supremely grander than sharing Henry's bed. What she had in mind was sharing his crown. She let him know that marriage was the only way he would get what he wanted from her.

She was a cute thing, petite, with unusually expressive dark eyes, a dark complexion, and long black hair that fell past her waist, beguiling in her gestures and body movements, smartly dressed, bright, witty, sophisticated, effervescent, entirely charming, more charming than good-looking, actually. Henry found her irresistible.

Her father was Sir Thomas Boleyn, who came from wealth (the family fortune having been founded by Anne's great-grandfather, Sir Geoffrey Boleyn, a hugely prosperous textile merchant who became mayor of London), and Thomas had used it to help advance a career of service to the king. Anne's mother, Elizabeth, was the daughter of the second duke of Norfolk and was the sister of the third duke of Norfolk. Thomas placed Anne, as a child, in the care of the Archduchess Margaret of Austria (aunt of Emperor Charles V), whose household in the Netherlands was like a finishing school for select, privileged youngsters from various countries. So impressed with Anne after she had got to know her, the archduchess wrote to Thomas that, "I find her so well behaved and agreeable for her young age, that I am more obliged to you for sending her than you are to me [for accepting her]."[1]

Under the guidance of a tutor who was a member of Margaret's household, Anne learned to write and speak fluent French, and when her father became England's ambassador to the court of France's King Francis I, Anne, joining him, quickly assimilated the manners, habits, and dress of a young

French lady. She learned to sing and dance and play the lute. More signifi-cantly, she also learned to play the flirt, French style, and did it so well that by the time she was a young teenager, "many men," according to one report, "were hers to command." Among those whose notice she captured was King Francis himself, and when Anne was recalled home to England in 1521, Fran-cis wrote to the English minister of state, Cardinal Thomas Wolsey, to protest the withdrawal of "the daughter of Mr Boullan [Boleyn] . . . who was in the service of the French Queen."

Back in England, at the court of King Henry, Anne was appointed a lady-in-waiting to Henry's queen, Catherine of Aragon, and soon attracted admir-ers. At least one of them, young Lord Henry Percy, wanted to marry her (and she may have been willing), but he was prevented from doing so by opposi-tion from his family and hers and by the politically powerful Cardinal Wolsey, in whose service Percy was then employed. Another admirer, the poet Thomas Wyatt, who already had a wife, became absolutely passionate in his pursuit of Anne, memorializing her—and his wife—in a sonnet ("If Waker Care"), but all in vain as she merely toyed with him.

By then King Henry also had become infatuated with Anne. It was he, ap-parently, who had given Cardinal Wolsey the task of breaking up the romance between Anne and Henry Percy, and Wolsey had used all his browbeating prowess to accommodate the king, whose lustful eyes were fixed on Anne and who would brook no competition. Henry courted her relentlessly, writing her letters that declared his love and that urged her to yield to it. "Henceforward my heart shall be dedicated to you alone," he told her, "with a strong desire that my body could also be thus dedicated."

Anne boldly wrote back to tell him he had her heart, but that was all, for now. Her body would wait for wedding bells.

Unused to such frustration of his desires, inflamed with growing passion, and at last persuaded of Anne's resolve, lovesick Henry started thinking about how he might give her what she wanted, so that he could get what he desperately wanted.

The manifest answer was somehow to end his marriage to Catherine of Aragon so he would be free to marry Anne. He had no qualms about casting off Catherine. She had outlived her usefulness to him. She had failed to give him—and the nation—a male heir to the throne, and it was by now obvious that she never would. Marrying Anne would not only give him the woman he desired but also provide a new opportunity to have a royal son and heir.

Catherine, five years older than Henry, had been the wife of Henry's older brother, Arthur, the prince of Wales and heir apparent to the throne, who had died of tuberculosis in April 1502, five months after marrying Catherine. Henry's father, King Henry VII, had then betrothed Henry, at age twelve, to Catherine, and seven years later, as he lay dying, Henry VII had advised his son to go through with the marriage.

Catherine was still living in England at the time and was then, in 1509, twenty-three years old, petite, dainty (less than five feet tall), graceful, with reddish blond hair, blue eyes, and fair skin, having evidently inherited the looks not of her Spanish forebears but of her English great-grandmother, for whom she was named. (Catherine's parents were King Ferdinand and Queen Isabella; Isabella's grandmother was Catherine, daughter of John of Gaunt, duke of Lancaster.)

Henry in 1509 was eighteen, tall (six foot two), well built, fair skinned, auburn haired, vigorously athletic and, according to one observer, "altogether the handsomest potentate I have ever set eyes upon."[2] He was also apparently smitten with Catherine—or, as some biographers have suggested, he was, with his adolescent hormones surging, perhaps more in love with love and with the idea of being adult enough to be married. In addition, Henry may have been particularly interested in marrying Catherine because the marriage would keep Spain as England's ally in the expected conflict with France. In any case, Henry wanted her as his wife and wrote to her father, King Ferdinand, to tell him so. "Even if we were still free [to marry whoever], it is she, nevertheless, that we would choose for our wife before all other." Catherine, moreover, had fallen in love with handsome Henry.

Their proposed nuptials having received the blessing of Pope Julius II, the two were married in a private ceremony in Greenwich on June 11, 1509, six weeks after Henry's father's death. On June 24, 1509, Midsummer Day, in Westminster Abbey, Henry was crowned king, and Catherine was crowned queen.

For a time, everything went well, and the couple enjoyed a long honeymoon. "Our time is spent in continual festival," Catherine wrote to her father. Within a couple of months of their wedding, Catherine became pregnant.

Then came a series of misfortunes. In January 1510 she suffered a miscarriage. She soon became pregnant again and in January 1511 gave birth to a boy, whom his joyful father named Henry. Six weeks later, the child died. Several more heartbreaking miscarriages and infant deaths followed.

On February 18, 1516, Catherine at last bore a child who survived, a girl, whom the parents named Mary. Two years later Catherine became pregnant once more, and Henry's heart rose again in hope for the birth of a prince. On November 10, 1518, Catherine gave birth to another girl, who died not long after.

His hopes completely crushed, Henry despaired of ever having a son by Catherine, who was then thirty-two years old. His feelings toward her turned cold, and he sought comfort and pleasure in the arms of his mistresses. One of them, Elizabeth Blount, gave him a bastard son, Henry Fitzroy, born in 1519, whom Henry in 1525 created duke of Richmond.

Eager to get on with his romance with Anne Boleyn and to marry her, Henry in 1527 assembled a group of legal and religious experts to help him shed Catherine. The ploy used to accomplish Henry's purpose was an effort to establish that his marriage to Catherine was unlawful and therefore null. The grounds for such a claim were found in the Old Testament book of Leviticus, which prohibited a man from marrying his brother's widow: "And if a man shall take his brother's wife, it is an unclean thing: he hath uncovered his brother's nakedness; they shall be childless."

Pope Julius, according to the argument made by Henry and his advisers, had erred in granting Henry dispensation to marry Catherine. Proof of the error lay in the fact that Henry and Catherine had indeed been childless, or at least sonless, which Henry considered the same thing as childless. "All such issue males as I have received of the Queen," Henry stated, "died immediately after they were born, so that I fear the punishment of God in that behalf." Henry's plea was that the current pope, Clement VII, recognize his predecessor's wrong and right it by declaring Henry's marriage to Catherine nullified.

Henry's case was not quite cut-and-dried, however. The prohibition in Leviticus was partly set aside by a provision in Deuteronomy, another of Moses's law books: "If brethren shall dwell together, and one of them die, and have no child, the wife of the dead shall not marry without unto a stranger: her husband's brother shall go in unto her, and take her to him to wife, and perform the duty of an husband's brother unto her." Henry and his advisers argued that the Deuteronomy provision was for Jews alone, but that the prohibition in Leviticus was a statement of natural law, applicable to everyone, and that not even the pope could overrule or suspend it.

There were other complications in getting Pope Clement to dissolve the marriage. The pope had his own problems at the time: The armies of Emperor Charles V, which had dispossessed him of much of his papal holdings, had driven him from Rome and in effect held him prisoner in the remote, ramshackle palace where he had taken refuge. Charles was Catherine's nephew, and he had a political as well as an emotional stake in seeing his aunt remain queen and Mary, his young cousin, remain heir apparent. Pope Clement would only increase the danger he faced from the emperor by nullifying Catherine's marriage, thereby dethroning and disgracing her and bastardizing her child.

The arguing and maneuvering dragged on for months, then stretched, agonizingly for Henry, into years, with Catherine and her backers opposing Henry every step of the way toward a resolution. Catherine meanwhile apparently held the sympathy of most of Henry's subjects, while Anne held their contempt and in public was shouted at with such scornful epithets as "Witch!" and "Harlot!"

At last, feeling that Henry would indeed make her his queen, Anne decided to provide him more encouragement to make the marriage happen sooner. After five years of holding him off, she got into bed with him, and by the end of 1532 she had become pregnant.

By now Cardinal Wolsey, largely because of his failure to win a favorable judgment from the pope, had been replaced by Thomas Cromwell as Henry's chief minister. Cromwell advised Henry to short-circuit the pope by declaring himself, in place of the pope, head of the church in England, making it a national church, apart from Rome. Henry accepted the advice and pronounced himself "Supreme Head of the Church, in so far as the Law of Christ allows." The pope responded by excommunicating Henry. Henry then turned to his recently appointed archbishop of Canterbury, Thomas Cranmer, to take the next step—to make an official ruling, obligingly delivered by Cranmer, that Henry's marriage to Catherine of Aragon was null and void and that therefore Henry was free to marry Anne.

All barriers having been circumvented, Henry and Anne were married in a secret ceremony in January 1533. Five months later, after an elaborate, days-long celebration, Anne was crowned queen in Westminster Cathedral on Whitsunday, June 1, 1533, her bulky robe concealing her otherwise obvious pregnancy. (Catherine then became once again dowager princess of Wales. She was provided two manors where she resided till she died of cancer in January 1536 at age fifty.)

On August 26, 1533, pregnant Queen Anne secluded herself for the traditional lying-in, for which the royal couple chose the palace in Greenwich, where Henry had been born, and in early September a royal announcement reported that Anne had gone into labor.

Henry was confident the baby would be a boy. Those who were considered experts in such matters—the king's physicians, astrologers, and possibly a few wizards—were agreed in their predictions: The queen would bear a son. In anticipation of such a monumental event, Henry began planning celebrations and ordered birth announcements heralding the "deliverance and bringing forth of a Prince." He was still deciding on a name for the child, the choice being between Henry and Edward.

Between three and four o'clock in the afternoon on Sunday, September 7, 1533, Anne and Henry's baby arrived, healthy and whole. It was a girl.

Henry abandoned his plans for the jousting tournament he had intended to celebrate the birth of a son. He would make do with a Te Deum, which he ordered sung at Saint Paul's Cathedral, and bonfires and the ringing of church bells. The elegant birth announcements were altered with a couple of curlicues of the pen that turned "Prince" into "Princes[s]." Henry—and probably Anne, too—decided the baby's name would be Elizabeth, which was the name of his mother, Elizabeth of York, as well as her mother, Elizabeth Howard Boleyn. The christening was scheduled for Wednesday, September 10, at the Church of the Observant Friars in Greenwich.

In accordance with the custom of the times, little Elizabeth's parents were not present for the christening. She was attended instead by her godparents, Archbishop Cranmer and Anne's grandmother, the dowager duchess of Norfolk. All available nobility turned out for the occasion. The dowager duchess, under a portable canopy that was the centerpiece of a glittering procession that inched through the crowded church, carried Elizabeth, who was elaborately done up in a purple velvet mantle with a long train trimmed in ermine, which was ceremonially held by Anne's father. Anne's uncle, the duke of Norfolk, and her brother, Viscount Rochford, also participated in the ceremony.

When the ritual was over, the garter king of arms, one of Henry's court officials, declaimed before the audience in a loud voice, "God, of his infinite goodness, send prosperous life and long to the high and mighty princess of England, Elizabeth!" That statement, declaring Elizabeth to be England's princess, meant that her father the king had made little Elizabeth first in line to succeed him, replacing her recently bastardized half sister, Mary.

After the formalities, refreshments were served to the congregants—"wafers, comfits [sugared fruits] and hypocras [spiced wine] in such plenty that every man had as much as he would desire," according to the official chronicler of the event, Edward Hall.

Elizabeth was carried to Anne's chambers, where she was returned to her parents following the ceremony, but she didn't stay with them long. She was placed in the care of the so-called lady mistress of the nursery, a gentle, motherly widow named Margaret Bryan, who headed a considerable staff of nursery attendants who would take care of all Elizabeth's needs, including wet-nursing her. Lady Bryan had similarly presided over the care of Mary when she was a child. The nursery was housed in a special suite of rooms in the Greenwich palace, and there little Elizabeth was kept for three months, until December 1533, when she was moved to a house, actually a palace, of her own, complete with an elaborate household, at Hatfield, twenty miles north of London. Her journey to Hatfield, routed through London, became something of a public spectacle and a public relations device, designed to parade her before the king's subjects, to let them get a glimpse of her and establish her as *the* royal child.

Anne visited her at Hatfield at least once, bringing her pretty things to wear and some other niceties. All the tasks of nurturing her, though, were left to the members of Elizabeth's household, all royal employees.

In March of the following year, 1534, when she was six months old, Elizabeth was moved again, this time to Eltham, Henry's primary residence when he was a boy, about five miles southeast of Greenwich. Two weeks after Elizabeth had been moved into her new quarters, Henry and Anne, accompanied by a party of courtiers, came to see her. At that tender age, she was reported by one of the courtiers to be "a goodly child as hath been seen, and her Grace is much in the King's favour, as a goodly child should be, God save her."[3] Elizabeth had inherited some of her father's good looks, including the fair skin and reddish hair.

In February 1535, when Elizabeth was seventeen months old, the French king's representatives—after viewing her in her birthday suit, apparently to make sure she was normal—began negotiating with Henry for Elizabeth's marriage to the French king's younger son (who was therefore *not* heir to the French throne), the boy duke of Angoulême. Both Henry and the French negotiators asked for more than the other was willing to grant. Henry's position was that "when he offered the heiress of a kingdom to a younger son, they ought rather give him something than ask." After several months, the negotiations ended fruitlessly. Elizabeth would not be marrying King Francis's son.

Anne, meanwhile, had become pregnant about three months after Elizabeth's birth and had suffered a miscarriage. In late 1535, when Elizabeth was two years old, Anne became pregnant again. In January 1536 she miscarried again. This time the unborn child was a boy. In despair, Henry lamented, "I see that God will not give me male children."

Other things were happening with Anne. She had lost her husband's love. The perkiness—or perhaps more accurately, her brassiness—that had seemed charming in a mistress came to seem shrewish in a wife. Her abrasive self-assertiveness, caustic tongue, fiery disposition, and insulting behavior made enemies in Henry's court and became an embarrassment to him. Rumor had it that by the time she secluded herself in the Greenwich palace to await Elizabeth's birth, Henry had already taken another mistress, setting off at least one angry quarrel in which Henry told Anne she would just have to "shut her eyes and endure as those better than herself had done."

A year later, in September 1534, when Anne tried to cope with Henry's attentions to one of her ladies-in-waiting by dismissing her, Henry had overruled Anne and sent her a note telling her that "she ought to be satisfied with what he had done for her; were he to commence again, he would certainly not do as much."[4]

By January 1536, when Anne had miscarried the son Henry craved, he had become enamored of another one of Anne's ladies-in-waiting, Jane Seymour. Entirely disenchanted with Anne and convinced she would never give him a son (and freed by Catherine's death from any sort of tie to his former queen, whom the pope had finally ruled was his lawful wife), Henry decided to rid himself of the woman he had found so fascinating eight years earlier.

In April 1536 a commission was formed to collect evidence that could be used against Anne in a trial, the outcome of which had already been determined by the king. Thomas Cromwell, now Henry's hatchet man, was given the odious task of discovering enough evidence to convict her of whatever offense would allow Henry to get rid of her. Adultery was that offense. She was charged with fornication with one of Henry's court musicians, Mark Smeaton, and five others, and with committing incest with her brother, George, the Viscount Rochford. The accused men were taken to the Tower of London, there to face the king's interrogators and their instruments of torture. Five of the men, including Anne's brother, were tried, convicted, and condemned to death for fornicating with the queen.

On May 2, 1536, Anne herself was taken to the Tower. On May 15 she was tried, and although she managed a courageous defense, "excusing herself," according to one account, "with her words so clearly as though she had never been faulty,"[5] which she almost certainly was not, she was nevertheless found guilty of adultery, as Henry and Cromwell intended, and was sentenced "to be burned or beheaded as shall please the King."

The king was indeed pleased to have her beheaded. On Friday, May 19, 1536, on Tower Green, Anne was publicly decapitated with a sword by an executioner brought from France just for that purpose. Her head was wrapped in a cloth and carried away, her body quickly interred at the Chapel of Saint Peter ad Vincula, within the Tower grounds.

On Saturday, May 20, the day after Anne's execution, Henry became engaged to Jane Seymour. On May 30 he and Jane were married. On June 4 she was proclaimed queen.

Elizabeth was then two years and eight months old.

Anne's fall took her daughter down as well. Four days before Anne's execution, Cranmer, the archbishop of Canterbury, who had pronounced Henry's marriage to Catherine invalid, had annulled, undoubtedly at the king's command, Henry's marriage to Anne, on whatever grounds—now unknown for certain—that could be trumped up. The annulment automatically made a bastard of Elizabeth, and when a new act of succession, passed by Parliament, was issued in July 1536, two months following Anne's death, it specified that Elizabeth was "illegitimate . . . and utterly foreclosed, excluded and banned to claim, challenge or demand any inheritance as lawful heir." Under the new act, the right to succession was given only to the children Henry would have by Jane Seymour, or by some subsequent wife.

Elizabeth had been moved from Eltham in late January 1536 and was living at Hunsdon House, in Hertfordshire, north of London, still in the care of Lady Bryan. Elizabeth had also been given a steward, presumably the head of her household. He was John Shelton, pompous, overbearing, and self-serving. One of his ideas for Elizabeth's care was to provide a daily feast of adult food and drink for her, enough to feed his friends, who dined with the child in a public atmosphere and ate well at no cost to themselves. Lady Bryan complained to Thomas Cromwell about that practice. "Master Shelton," she wrote, "would have my Lady Elizabeth to dine and sup every day at the board of estate. Alas! my Lord, it is not meet for a child of her age to keep such rule yet. I promise you, my Lord, I dare not take it upon me keep her in health, and she keep that rule. For there she shall see divers meats and fruits, and wine, which would be hard for me to restrain Her Grace from it. Ye know, my Lord, there is no place of correction here. And she is too young to correct greatly."[6]

Elizabeth's diminished status was resulting in some official neglect. She had outgrown her clothes, and no new clothes were being provided. Lady Bryan mentioned that matter to Cromwell, too. "She hath neither gown nor kirtle, nor petticoat, nor no manner of linen, nor foresmocks, nor kerchiefs, nor sleeves, nor rails [nightgowns], nor bodystichets, nor handkerchiefs, nor mufflers, nor biggens [nightcaps]. . . . [I am] beseeching you, my Lord, that you will see that Her Grace may have that [which] is needful for her."[7]

Lady Bryan also mentioned to Cromwell Elizabeth's difficulty in teething, but all in all, she reported, the child was doing well. "[She is having] great pain with her teeth, and they come very slowly forth, and causeth me to suffer Her Grace to have her will more than I would. I trust to God, and her teeth were well graft, to have Her Grace after another fashion that she is yet; so I trust the King's Grace shall have great comfort in Her Grace, for she is as toward a child, and as gentle of conditions, as ever I knew any in my life, Jesu preserve her Grace."[8]

The letter to Cromwell had some effect, at least about meals. Shelton was told that the king wanted Elizabeth to eat in her own rooms.

Henry saw Elizabeth again in the autumn of 1536, when, faced with a Catholic rebellion in the northern provinces, he ordered both Mary and Elizabeth brought to his court for their protection. According to one eyewitness account, "The Lady Mary is now first after the Queen, and sits at table opposite her. . . . The Lady Elizabeth is not at that table, though the King is very affectionate to her. It is said he loves her much."[9]

When Elizabeth was four, she was allowed to participate in the christening ceremony for the son that Jane bore to Henry on October 12, 1537. The ceremony was held in the royal chapel at Hampton Court in London on Monday, October 15, and Elizabeth, who was herself carried in the arms of Jane's brother, carried the train of the white chrisom robe in which the christened infant would be wrapped. Mary, now twenty-one years old, was the godmother. Following the christening, the garter king of arms proclaimed to the assembled throng the baby's name and titles: "God of His almighty and infinite grace give and grant good life and long to the right high, right excellent and noble prince, Prince Edward, duke of Cornwall and earl of Chester, most dear and beloved son to our most dread and gracious lord, King Henry the Eighth!"

Henry's jubilation, and that of his court and the nation, over the birth of a prince, at last, soon turned to solemn public and private prayers when Jane was stricken with puerperal fever days after the christening. The prayers were unavailing; she died during the night of October 24, 1537.

Edward's birth meant changes in Elizabeth's life. One of the first was the loss of the attentions of Lady Bryan, who was reassigned to care for Edward as she had done for Mary and Elizabeth. Lady Bryan's replacement was a well-educated young woman named Katherine Champernowne, whom Elizabeth called "Kat." Kat became Elizabeth's teacher as well as her governess, and it was from her that Elizabeth took her first Latin and penmanship lessons and began other parts of her formal education.

So precocious was Elizabeth that when she was six years old, one of her visitors, Thomas Wriothesley, Henry's secretary, sent by the king to check on the child at Christmastime, came away from his conversation with her at Hertford Castle, where she was then living, observing that, "If she be no worse educated than she now appeareth to me, she will prove of no less honour to womanhood than shall beseem her father's daughter." Wriothesley reported that Elizabeth "gave humble thanks [for the visit], inquiring again of his Majesty's welfare, and that with as great a gravity as she had been forty years old."

By 1543, when she was ten years old, Elizabeth had had four stepmothers, the first of whom was the tragic Jane Seymour. On January 6, 1540, Henry, at age forty-eight, had reluctantly married Anne of Cleves, twenty-four-year-old sister of the duke of Cleves, who ruled several states in northern Germany and with whom Henry desired an alliance to help check the alliance recently created by Europe's two most powerful rulers, Charles V, emperor of the

Holy Roman Empire, and Francis I, king of France. Henry could never warm up to Anne, however, and in July 1540 his unconsummated marriage to Anne, having lasted six months, ended in a divorce. Henry provided her with two houses and an income, and she chose to remain in England rather than return to Germany.

Henry then, on August 8, 1540, married one of Anne of Cleves's former ladies-in-waiting who was also Anne Boleyn's cousin. She was Catherine Howard, about twenty years old, pretty, pleasingly plump, and amorously experienced enough to know how to effect Henry's arousal, which had become a problem for him. Apparently not satisfied by the king, however, Catherine shared her favors with others, flagrantly so, and on February 13, 1542, having been judged guilty of treasonous adultery, she was beheaded in the Tower.

On July 12, 1543, Henry married for the sixth and last time. His bride this time was thirty-three-year-old Catherine Parr, twice a widow, childless, wealthy, attractive, affectionate, and sweet dispositioned. Henry, although fifty years old, grossly obese, and suffering from a host of maladies, nevertheless apparently had great expectations going into the marriage. He made a new will that stated the offspring of his marriage to Mrs. Parr would stand in front of Mary and Elizabeth in the line of succession to the throne. (Mellowing at last, Henry in April 1543 had let it be known that he intended to restore Elizabeth to the succession list.)

Elizabeth and Mary were invited to come to Henry's court in June, before the wedding, to meet Catherine Parr, which they did, and they were also guests of honor at the wedding in July. Mary, twenty-seven years old then, remained at Henry's court after the wedding, but Elizabeth, along with Edward, returned to St. James's Palace to resume their studies. Elizabeth would not see her new stepmother again for about a year. Perhaps disappointed that she was not getting opportunities to become closer to Catherine, Elizabeth on July 31, 1544, at age ten, carefully penned in her own hand, in flawless Italian, the following letter, forceful evidence of her precocity and doubtless intended to show herself off:

> Inimical Fortune, envious of all good, she who revolves things
> human, has deprived me for a whole year of your most illustri-
> ous presence, and still not being content with that, has robbed
> me once again of the same good: the which would be intolerable

to me if I did not think to enjoy it soon. And in this my exile I know surely that your highness' clemency has had as much care and solicitude for my health as the king's majesty would have had. For which I am not only bound to serve you but also to revere you with daughterly love, since I understand that your most illustrious highness has not forgotten me every time that you have written to the king's majesty, which would have been for me to do. However, heretofore I have not dared to write to him, for which at present I humbly entreat your most excellent highness that in writing to his majesty you will deign to recommend me to him, entreating ever his sweet benediction and likewise entreating the Lord God to send him best success in gaining victory over his enemies [Henry had launched an offensive against France a month earlier] so that your highness, and I together with you, may rejoice the sooner at his happy return. I entreat nothing else from God but that He may preserve your most illustrious highness, to whose grace, humbly kissing your hands, I offer and commend myself. From Saint James on the thirty-first of July.

Your most obedient daughter and
most faithful servant, *Elizabeth*[10]

Henry, who had the reputation of being Europe's best-educated monarch, evidently wanted a good education for his children, male or female. At age ten, Elizabeth was sharing a tutor with her little brother, who was then six, and was learning French and Italian, both of which she mastered. When she was eleven, she was given her own private tutor, William Grindal, a Greek and Latin scholar and member of the faculty of St. John's College at Cambridge. She soon became so proficient at Latin that she could not only read and write it but speak it fluently. She loved reading the classics, feasting on Cicero, Livy, Sophocles, and Isocrates and the Greek New Testament. She made a hobby of translating Latin literary works, some of which she presented as gifts to those close to her, particularly her new stepmother. Her studies covered a wide range of subjects, including history, mathematics, geography, architecture, music, astronomy, Spanish, Flemish, and Welsh. It was said that she could hold her own in conversation on any intellectual subject.

Kat Ashley (she had recently married), furthermore, saw to it that Elizabeth's lessons were not academic only. She also learned to sew, embroider, dance, and ride. She proved an apt and gifted student and a voracious reader, reading on her own several hours daily.

By the time Elizabeth wrote that somewhat turgid letter to Catherine at the end of July 1544, young Prince Edward had been moved from St. James's Palace to Hampton Court and there placed in the care not of motherly women but of men who could help prepare the boy for the throne that awaited him. In 1546 Elizabeth, too, was moved to Hampton Court. King Henry was gathering his family together under one roof. Now Elizabeth and her stepmother could become close.

Strong of mind and of character, well educated and articulate—and steadfastly devoted to the religion of the Protestant reformers—Catherine soon became to Elizabeth a powerful role model and, like Kat Ashley, an enduring influence.

Something of a zealot, Catherine regularly read the Scripture and took formal instruction on it. She wrote prayers and meditations and had a couple of volumes published. She had others join her in the sessions of Bible study and religious discussion that she held in her suite. Every afternoon she had a service in which one of her chaplains preached to her and an audience made up of members of her household and anyone else who cared to attend. It was as if Catherine were operating her own little Protestant Bible school in the royal palace. Elizabeth was the most important student there.

Included in those study sessions and sermons, naturally, was criticism of the church of Rome, its doctrines, practices, and abuses. The differences between the theology of the reformers and that of the church of Rome were undoubtedly defined for those attending. Fundamental to the reformers' beliefs were the authority of Scripture—an authority above that of the Catholic church—and the doctrine of justification by faith. It was especially those basic beliefs that less than thirty years earlier had driven Martin Luther to separate himself from the established church and set off the Protestant Reformation. Luther's reading of Saint Paul's epistle to the first-century Christians in Rome, particularly Romans 1:17 and 3:27–28, had persuaded him that Catholicism had it all wrong. It was not what people *did* that saved them, or justified them, as Catholic theology had it; instead, it was their *faith* that saved them, that made them righteous in the eyes of God.

Now those words were sounding in the mind of young Elizabeth. S̲ come so caught up with those revolutionary religious ideas that for a time, as she later said, exaggeratedly, "I studied nothing else but divinity."

Catherine's attempts to draw Henry into her Bible school failed. The king's quarrel with the pope and the church of Rome was much more about politics than about theology—a subject in which the enormously egotistical Henry considered himself something of an expert. Henry's attitude was that he knew all he wanted or needed to know about religion.

Another royal person who disdained the sessions was Mary, who, following the model of her mother, Catherine of Aragon, remained vehemently conservative and Catholic.

It was not only in the matter of religion that Elizabeth was affected by her stepmother. While Henry was with his troops in France, Catherine governed as regent and she more than held her own with the king's male ministers and advisers, capably dealing with affairs of state, making her voice heard and her opinions respected. Elizabeth observed her. Her stepmother was a competent woman in charge.

Elizabeth herself was becoming a young woman, no longer a child. She turned thirteen on September 7, 1546. It was when she was thirteen that her first portrait was painted. It shows a slender, serious, oval-faced, bejeweled girl, not especially pretty but not at all unattractive, with pale skin, large dark eyes, red hair parted down the middle, noticeably long slim fingers, and the clear, soft curves of a maiden's bosom. In the words of one of Henry's officials, Elizabeth was "a very witty and gentyll young lady." At least some of those who were her own age, however, found her "proud and disdainful," to the extent that those unattractive qualities "blemished the handsomeness and beauty of her person."[11]

During the Christmas season following Elizabeth's thirteenth birthday, Henry's poor health, aggravated by his gross obesity, took a turn for the worse. Looking into a future where he was no longer present, Henry in December rewrote his will. It provided for the succession of Edward, Mary, and Elizabeth, in that order, and further stipulated the succession in the event each of his children died without offspring. It also provided an income for Mary and Elizabeth—three thousand pounds annually until they married and a final payment of ten thousand pounds if they married, amounts that were not exactly princely sums. What was more, Henry's will decreed that if Elizabeth married without the approval of the king's Privy Council, she would forfeit her place in the succession to the crown, "as though the said Lady Elizabeth were then dead." It was Henry's attempt to control the life of his daughter, even from his grave.

The seriously ill Henry spent that Christmas at his palace in London, while Catherine, for whatever reason, perhaps not knowing how sick her husband was, spent the holiday in Greenwich. She still was not with him a month later, on the evening of January 28, 1547, when the king was told he was dying and he sent for Archbishop Cranmer. Henry was unable to speak, but he grasped Cranmer's hand as the archbishop assured him of his salvation. Around two o'clock the next morning, January 29, 1547, King Henry VIII died, at age fifty-five, still holding onto his archbishop's hand.

Edward was summoned, and with Elizabeth standing by him, he and his sister were told the solemn news: The king was dead; Edward was the new king. Nine-year-old Edward burst into tears. Elizabeth, too. They clung to each other, weeping.

3. THE PREPARATION
FOR A CROWN

Prince Philip may have been a bit overscrupulous in following his father's instructions about his conjugal activity. His case of scabies not long after his wedding had provided a good reason for his sleeping apart from his bride, Maria, for more than a month, but when he was over that, he seemed no closer to her. "The prince is somewhat distant with the princess," his absent father, Charles, was informed in January 1544, "and in Portugal they feel strongly about it."[1] The report drew a response from Charles, who expressed his displeasure with "the coldness the prince adopts to his wife in public, which distresses me very much."

Other aspects of Philip's behavior also troubled Charles. The inordinate amount of time Philip took preparing for bed and for arising, the lavish parties he threw or attended, the numerous nights he spent out and frequent tournaments in which he participated—all were reported by the watchful Juan de Zúñiga, Philip's governor, giving Charles causes for concern. Believing that Philip was spending too many hours at his favorite pastime, Charles particularly cautioned the prince to "moderate the great lust you always had for hunting."

By the fall of 1544 Philip had rewarmed to Maria enough for Francisco de los Cobos, one of the advisers Charles had appointed for the prince, to report to Charles that Philip and Maria "get on together very well." In fact, they were getting on so well that Maria had become pregnant. After an especially difficult labor, which lasted two days, Maria on July 8, 1545, gave birth to a boy with an abnormally large head. The child was named Carlos, after Philip's father, and became known as Don Carlos.

At first, both mother and baby did well, but within hours Maria developed a rising fever, then went into convulsions and became delirious. Cobos wrote to the emperor on July 16 to apprise him of the unhappy turn of events:

... seeing that the malady had now become so grave as to be almost hopeless, the physicians decided to bleed the patient at the
ankle. This was done, and the Princess again became conscious,
and seemed somewhat better. The improvement, however, lasted
but a very short time, and the attack became so severe that in a
few hours Extreme Unction was administered at the Princess' request. The attack still increased until God took her to Himself on
that day [Sunday, July 12, 1545] between four and five in the afternoon, amidst universal grief, such as Your Majesty may imagine.
Her end was tranquil and Christian.[2]

"The Prince was extremely grieved," Cobos told Charles. "As to prove that
he loved her . . . he at once decided to go the same night to the monastery of
Abrojo, where there was a fairly good lodging for him in the house they had
repaired. He was so sad that he will allow no one to visit or see him."

Maria's body was interred in the cathedral at Granada, later to be moved
to the Escorial, the magnificent palace/monastery/mausoleum that Philip
was to build.

After several days of refuge at the Abrojo monastery, Philip, now a widower and father at age eighteen, returned to Valladolid, there to face the
awaiting cares of his government and of his infant son.

Philip had been serving as Spain's regent since May 1543, when his father
had begun what would be a fourteen-year absence from Spain. Decisions on
the most important matters, such as financial affairs, were still made in con-
sultation with Charles through a communication system that took weeks to
get messages to and from the emperor. The day-to-day workings of Spain's
government, however, were more efficient, being handled by a small group
of administrators headed by Cobos and Cardinal Juan de Tavera, who was
president of the royal council, archbishop of Toledo, and also Spain's inquisitor general, the leader of the Inquisition. Philip's circle of counselors divided
itself into two factions, at times openly antagonistic toward each other, one
guided by Cobos's influence, the other by Tavera's. Philip listened and
learned while his counselors reached their decisions.

One of the biggest issues that faced Philip and his counselors during that
time of his regency was which territory was more important to Spain, the
Netherlands or Milan. It became an issue in late 1544 because Charles was

thinking of arranging a marriage between either his daughter Maria or his niece Anne of Hungary and the duke of Orléans, second son of France's King Francis. If Maria were to become the duke's bride, her dowry would be the Netherlands, which the duke would possess after Charles's death. If it were Anne, her dowry would be Milan, which would become the duke's a year after the marriage. To help him decide between the two girls—and the two territories—Charles asked for the advice of his counselors in Spain and the Netherlands.

Philip presided over the debate of the question in Spain and established a procedure for reaching a decision. The first step was to have the council members meet several times and discuss the matter. Philip spelled out the steps taken after the initial discussions:

> Afterwards when I came, the council met immediately in my presence, and I wished to hear all that they had discussed and debated. They debated again and discussed the matter at length, and although they were settled in their views, I ordered them to think more about it. On the third day I said they they should meet again in council and come to it with their minds made up so we could arrive at a decision. It was so done. Since we learned from our contacts that their opinions were divided, I ordered each member to express his view.[3]

The duke of Alba and Cobos, both military men, contended that Milan was strategically essential to the defense of Spain, Sicily, and Naples. The majority on the council, however, including Tavera and Zúñiga, argued that the Netherlands were too important to the economy of Spain ever to be relinquished or lost. Charles accepted the majority's decision, but the matter became an empty issue when the duke of Orléans died in September 1545 while the marriage negotiations were still going on. The debate and decision-making process, however, had provided Philip the means by which he would reach decisions in the future.

The self-reliance that Charles had urged upon Philip was soon forced to take root in his decision making. On August 1, 1545, less than three weeks after he had lost his wife, Philip lost the counsel of Cardinal Tavera, who died at age seventy-three. His importance was expressed, somewhat unfeelingly, by Charles, who said that "by his [Tavera's] death Philip had suffered a greater loss than by that of Maria; for he could get another wife, but not another Tavera." During the eight months that followed Tavera's death, three more senior members of the royal council died. Then, on June 27, 1546, Philip suffered another huge loss with the death of Zúñiga, who was as much of a father to him as was Charles. On May 10, 1547, Cobos died, making the forty-year-old duke of Alba Philip's most senior adviser.

Charles, keeping for himself the power to appoint, named two council members to replace Tavera. One was Juan Martínez Siliceo, Philip's former tutor, who was also appointed to succeed Tavera as archbishop of Toledo. The other was García de Loaysa, who succeeded Tavera as inquistor general but died shortly after his appointment. Charles then appointed Fernando de Valdés to succeed Loaysa. Those appointments would prove critical in the life of Spain and to the course of its history, for Siliceo and Valdés were rigid, remorseless ultraconservatives in matters of religion and the Catholic church. Not long after his appointment as archbishop of Toledo, the leading archdiocese of Spain, Siliceo decreed that conversos, Jews who had become Christians, and anyone else who had Jewish ancestry or was accused of having Jewish ancestry were prohibited from holding a church office in his archdiocese, thereby setting off a wave of anti-Semitism as well as one of reaction to it. Valdés, as inquisitor general, expanded the reach of the Inquisition so as to leave no one safe from its horrors.

About that same time, Philip was also having to deal with rebellious Spanish settlers in South America. In November 1543 Charles had signed new laws that liberalized the treatment of Indians of the New World, and when the government tried to enforce the new laws, settlers who had been exploiting the Indians resisted the changes. In Peru the attempts of the Spanish viceroy, Blasco Núñez de Vela, to impose the new laws sparked a revolt led by Gonzalo Pizarro, the conquistador who with his brother Francisco had defeated the Incas and conquered Peru some fifteen years earlier. Pizarro's army of rebels confronted the government's forces in January 1546 and killed the viceroy in the ensuing battle.

When news of the widespread rebellion reached Philip in 1545, he had called a meeting of his council, and only one of its members, Alba, had recommended sending a strong force to crush it. The other members preferred to make concessions, believing it impracticable to marshal a sufficient army and transport it across the Atlantic. Instead, Philip's councilors proposed dispatching a one-man delegation to attempt to pacify the rebels. To do the job, they picked a priest with military experience, Pedro de la Gasca, a member of the council of Inquisition.

Gasca reached the New World in July 1546 and began seeking support for his mission. Unsure of exactly how Gasca should proceed, Philip wrote to him in May 1547, expressing his hope "that the land be pacified through the path of clemency, without any need for severity and punishment." Becoming more determined in his attitude, Philip wrote to Gasca two weeks later and told him that if the rebels failed to yield, "it seems that an exemplary punishment may be exercised on the leaders and on the most guilty." The resourceful Gasca managed to raise a formidable army that defeated Pizarro's forces in April 1548. Pizarro was executed. From the experience, Philip gained a clear idea of how to handle rebellious subjects.

In the meantime, Philip's father was handling opposition in Germany, where a coalition of Lutheran princes, called the Schmalkaldic League, had presented a growing challenge to the emperor's authority and had launched a campaign of terror that had begun as a resistance movement and had exploded into a war on Catholic churches, monasteries, and convents. With Alba's help, Charles and his army defeated the coalition forces at the battle of Mühlberg in Saxony on April 23, 1547, restoring peace and the emperor's authority in Central Europe. Philip sent an embassy to his father in Brussels, to which he had withdrawn, to congratulate him on his achievement.

Triumphant but exhausted, "pale as death and thin as a skeleton,"[4] Charles was feeling a need to see his son, whom he had not seen in almost six years. In failing health, prematurely aged, worn out by the toils of battle and the cares of his office, Charles was seriously thinking of abdicating, turning his burden of responsibility over to Philip. To prepare Philip, Charles instructed him to come join him so that he could show him the Netherlands and introduce him to his future subjects there.

Philip left his new brother-in-law, his cousin Maximilian (who had recently married Philip's sister Maria, as arranged by Charles), in charge of Spain's government in his absence and rode out from Valladolid on October 2, 1548, bound for Saragossa and Barcelona at a leisurely pace and then heading for the port city of Rosas. From there he and his entourage of traveling companions, which included not only luminaries such as the duke of Alba and

Philip's good friend Ruy Gómez de Silva and other distinguished members of Spanish society but a company of musicians as well, for Philip's entertainment and to create a public spectacle. Borne on a fleet of fifty-eight vessels provided by Genoa, Naples, and Sicily and commanded by the venerable admiral Andrea Doria, the party of travelers sailed from Rosas on October 19.

It was Philip's first sea voyage. Bad weather made it an uncomfortable trip. The ships hugged the coastline, and the vessel that carried Philip landed each afternoon so that he could spend a comfortable night in a bed ashore. In Genoa, where he spent two weeks, he was the guest of the Dorias, lodged in their magnificent mansion and royally entertained. There he received embassies bringing greetings and homage from the various Italian states, one of them coming from Pope Paul III. From Genoa, Philip and his party traveled overland to Pavia, then on to Milan, the wealth and luxuries of which were splendidly displayed for the royal guest. From fifteen miles out of the city "the road was spanned by triumphal arches, garlanded with flowers and fruits and bearing inscriptions, both in Latin and Italian, filled with praises," according to one account. "As he drew near the town, two hundred mounted gentlemen came out to escort him into the place. They were clothed in complete mail of the fine Milanese workmanship and were succeeded by fifty pages in gaudy livery, devoted to especial attendance on the prince's person during his residence in Milan."[5]

Philip reciprocated the hearty welcome and hospitality by liberally handing out gifts to his hosts and those who helped entertain him, including the musicians who played at the balls or otherwise for his enjoyment. To the churches of the city, he gave more substantial examples of his generosity.

As he was about to leave Milan, his entourage was joined by a contingent of two hundred mounted, yellow-uniformed soldiers armed with musketlike harquebuses, sent by his father to escort him. He then proceeded to Trent, traveling mostly on horseback, the roads frequently being too rugged for carriages. Along the way, the official welcomes and gifts were acknowledged by the more socially adept Alba, who rode beside Philip.

At Trent, Philip stayed five days, and there was a banquet for him and his traveling companions every night. At the banquet on the first night, an eyewitness reported, "the dinner was joyous and very German because everyone drank a lot; it ended at ten, and then the celebrations began."[6] The celebrations included dancing, and "the first to dance was the prince, who was picked out by the most beautiful of the Italian ladies."[7] The next two nights, however, Philip chose to dine alone, a practice that was to become a habit over the years, as if the company of others could be tolerated for only so long.

On February 3, 1549, Philip's party reached the Brenner Pass and on February 4 it arrived at Innsbruck, where Philip spent a day hunting in nearby woods. From Innsbruck the party traveled by boat down the River Inn to Rosenheim and from Rosenheim they rode overland to Ebersberg, where they stayed at an abbey, and then proceeded on to Munich, arriving there on February 13. On the second day in Munich, Philip and his companions went hunting and were treated to a picnic in the country. That night Philip and his party attended a dinner with "sweet music and ladies."[8] It was an occasion that Philip evidently enjoyed. "During all these entertainments, his Highness was as happy, relaxed and sociable as if he understood the language; as a result everyone was enchanted, above all the duke's [of Bavaria] daughter."[9]

On February 21, Philip and his entourage reached Augsburg, entering into Lutheran country. Philip managed to conceal whatever feelings he had toward heretics. Since leaving Trent, he had been accompanied by Maurice of Saxony, the German elector who was a close ally of Philip's father and who was also a leading Lutheran. Charles had learned to coexist when it was politically expedient, and Philip was learning also. The travel was proving broadening.

After six months, the procession at last reached Brussels. At the outskirts of the city, large crowds gathered to greet him, and additional military units came out to escort him as artillery salutes were fired and church bells pealed in accompaniment. His aunt, Charles's sister Mary, queen of Hungary and regent of the Netherlands, staged a reception for the visitors, and following that, on the evening of April 1, Philip made a formal entrance into the city, greeted by more than fifty thousand welcomers. At the royal palace he was formally received by Mary and another of Charles's sisters, Eleanor, queen of France, and was led by his aunts to the chamber where Charles was waiting for him.

Philip was now twenty-one years old, and his father, after embracing him, must have taken notice of his appearance, having last seen him when he was still a teenager. He had not grown tall, but was probably only about five foot six. He was slight of build, fair complexioned, with light blond hair and beard, blue eyes, his eyebrows set a little too close together, and with a thin, aquiline nose, a lanternlike lower jaw, and a thick lower lip. All in all, he re-sembled his father, although without the quality that gave Charles the look of an intellectual. Philip's demeanor was solemn, even dull seeming, perhaps re-flective of his phlegmatic temperament.

Philip's stay in the Netherlands was to be a long one, and Charles, in failing health and doubtless eager to pass on as much knowledge and wisdom as he could while Philip was with him, worked out a schedule for him to make sure his hours were well spent. Philip would spend time every day in meetings with Charles's cabinet or attending sessions of Charles's Council of State or simply engaged by Charles in conversation on public affairs, all parts of the practicum in political science that the emperor was putting on for his son and heir. Ac-cording to one account, Charles required Philip to come "every day for two or three hours to his study to instruct him person to person."[10] Not all his hours were spent in instruction, though. Also on the prince's program were banquets, dances, masked balls, hunting parties, and tournaments in which he partici-pated, jousting with notables such as William, prince of Orange, and Lamoral, count of Egmont, men who would play important roles in his future.

After about two months with his father in Brussels, Philip set out on a se-ries of trips that took him deep into each of the seventeen provinces that made up the Netherlands, or Low Countries, which until 1548 were unified mainly by their common allegiance to the ruler of the Holy Roman Empire, Charles. To make certain that the Netherlands passed on to his son, assuring Spain that the economic and political advantages of possessing the Nether-lands would continue, Charles separated the seventeen provinces from the empire but kept them under his rule. As Philip visited the provinces, each of them swore in Philip as Charles's heir.

What he saw in the Netherlands impressed Philip. Their wealth, coming from trade in the northern provinces and from industry and agriculture in the southern provinces, had allowed Netherlanders to build handsome cities characterized by elegant architecture and formal gardens. One of Philip's traveling companions, Calvete de Estrella, who on the trip had already seen much of the splendor of Europe's cities, described Antwerp, whose popula-tion of eighty thousand made it the Netherlands' largest city, as "the very richest" of cities. The art and music of the Netherlands also drew Philip's ad-miration, so much so that he had several pieces of art sent back to Spain and added Netherlands musicians and their instruments to his household.

Although there was much that he found attractive in the lives of the people there, he was less than accepting of their attitudes. The Netherlanders were more freethinking, more independent in spirit than what he was used to in the people of Spain. In Spain, he was the ruler, and the people were expected to accept his word as final, his power as absolute. It was not so in the Netherlands, he was discovering as he traveled from city to city. The people's devotion to their sovereign was contingent on his performance as a just and benevolent ruler. In the Netherlanders' mind, the ruler owed the people something; they held him accountable for their welfare. Philip rejected such ideas. In his view the ruler was meant to rule, and the people were meant to be ruled. That was what he was used to. Charles, born in the Netherlands, had struggled to understand and accommodate the independent spirit of the people there; Philip, a son of Spain, rejected it altogether.

From the accounts it is hard to say with certainty what the Netherlanders thought of Philip. He apparently was not comfortable with the ceremonial pomp and show that were popular in the royal courts of Northern Europe, including that of Brussels, but were foreign to Spain and thus to him. His was a quiet, private style that would let him spend hours in his chambers alone or with a few of those closest to him. He thus seemed cold and aloof to others. According to one account,[11] it was only with his fellow Castilians that he felt he had anything in common, and when he engaged in conversation, he talked of nothing, and seemed to think of nothing, other than Spain, making him seem provincial and disinterested. It was not a good way to win over his Netherlands subjects. Further contributing to the distance from them was Philip's lack of conviviality. He had no taste for beer, a favorite social drink in the Netherlands, and drank wine mainly with his meals.

At least one chronicler of Philip's visit, his contemporary biographer Luis Cabrera de Córdoba, saw good results despite Philip's solemn taciturnity. Cabrera concluded that Philip made a special effort to please the people of Brussels and that they liked and admired him, "even if he said little and laughed less." The most glowing—and flattering—report of Philip's Brussels visit was written by seventeenth-century biographer Gregorio de Leti, whose account told of the prince's being received with extraordinary affection by the people of Brussels, "and all the more since they saw him at the age of twenty-two, endowed with grave discourse, skillful in his replies, mature in his deliberations, easily comprehending the most difficult matters, prudent in speaking his opinion in affairs of importance, judicious, and no less informed of the intrigues of the world than any other politician of long experience, possessing, in fact, all the qualities of a great king."[12]

Philip's departure from Brussels, to begin a slow trip home, accompanied by his father part of the way, was scheduled for May 31, 1550. On the evening before he was to leave, a huge celebration was held to bid him farewell. His steward, Vicente Álvarez, described the all-night party: "That night His Highness did not go to bed. He stayed in the main square, conversing with the ladies as they sat at their windows. A few gentlemen, young and even some old, accompanied him. The talk was of love, stories were told, there were tears, sighs, laughter, jests. There was dancing in the moonlight to the sound of orchestras that played all night."[13]

Despite having kept late hours, Charles and Philip and their entourage left the next day as planned. Their first stop was nearby Louvain, and on arriving there, Philip mysteriously turned around and galloped back to Brussels, where he apparently spent the night, returning to Louvain the following day, "very worn out," Álvarez, his steward, reported. "I do not know," Álvarez wrote, yielding none of the prince's secrets, "if he slept under the stars or under a roof."

From Louvain the royal party traveled to Maastricht, then on to Aachen, where Philip, like any tourist, visited the tomb of Charlemagne. The next big stop was Cologne, which they reached on June 10 and where they stayed four days before leaving for Bonn. At Bonn on June 15 they boarded boats and sailed up the Rhine River, stopping each evening to spend the night ashore, until they reached Mainz. From Mainz they made their way overland, through Worms and Speyer and on to Augsburg, where they arrived on July 8, 1550.

It was there that Charles had called together the members of the Imperial Diet, the parliament of his German dominions. The main item on his agenda, which included the solicitation of help to combat a possible invasion up the Danube by Turks, was to effect the Diet's election of Philip as the so-called king of the Romans, a title whose holder enjoyed the right to succeed to the office of emperor. The title was at the time held by Charles's brother, Ferdinand. Charles wanted to place Philip first in line to succeed him as emperor. To do so he would need Ferdinand to relinquish the title. What Ferdinand had in mind, though, was for the title—and the emperor's crown—to pass to his son, Maximilian, who had married Philip's sister Maria and was filling in as regent of Spain while Philip was away.

Charles's attempts to persuade Ferdinand went on for months, and the Diet continued to meet. Neither was inclined to go along with Charles's plan for Philip. The exchanges between Charles and Ferdinand generated so much bitterness that for a while the two brothers refused to speak further to each other. Charles suggested that Maximilian leave Valladolid and come to Augsburg and give his opinion. He did come, but, according to one account, he artfully dodged the question by responding that he had no right to interfere in the matter since it was the Diet's business to decide.[14]

In fact, Maximilian was as opposed to surrendering his rights to Philip as was his father, Ferdinand, but he felt safe in leaving it to the members of the German Diet to decide, knowing they wanted a fellow German, as he was, as their ruler. Philip in particular was unacceptable to them. In the words of one official, they would prefer a Turk to Philip, who was even more unpopular with the Germans than he was with the Netherlanders. Besides his being a Spaniard, and therefore foreign, he impressed them as haughty and unlikable. An example of his offensive manners is given by a nineteenth-century biographer: "When Charles returned to his palace, escorted, as he usually was, by a train of nobles and princes of the empire, he would courteously take them by the hand and raise his hat as he parted from them. But Philip, it was observed, on like occasions, walked directly into the palace, without so much as turning round or condescending in any way to notice the courtiers who had accompanied him."[15]

The insistent Charles, unaccustomed to being thwarted, eventually got part of what he wanted. Through a compromise to which Ferdinand acquiesced, Ferdinand retained the right to succeed Charles as emperor, Philip gained the right to succeed Ferdinand, and Maximilian was given the right to succeed Philip. That agreement, however, collapsed within two years, as Charles suffered a series of military defeats that removed much of Central Europe from his control and reduced his prestige as well as his power. In May 1552 he narrowly managed to escape capture or worse at the hands of the elector Maurice of Saxony, a former ally, by being hurriedly carried through the night on a litter, fleeing from his imperial territory into Italy.

Philip stayed on in Germany until May 1551, mixing his princely work with pleasures that included sightseeing in Munich, hunting in the woods, and participating in tournaments in which Maximilian and Prince William of Orange also participated. On May 25 he left Augsburg with his party of fellow travelers and made his way through the Tyrolean mountains to Innsbruck, where he spent several days. Late in the day on June 6, he arrived in Trent, where the Catholic church's historic Council of Trent was meeting to standardize the Mass and define Catholic doctrines on salvation, the sacraments, and the biblical canon—thereby distinguishing them from doctrines being promulgated by Protestant reformers. At his approach to the city, the prelates who were there for the council came out to greet Philip and during his stay in Trent they helped entertain him with masked balls, theatrical performances, and jousts.

From Trent Philip traveled to Mantua and there spent an afternoon with Pedro de la Gasca, who was on his way to deliver his report to Charles on the suppression of the rebellion in Peru and who briefed Philip on South American matters. Milan was Philip's next destination, and from there he passed through Padua en route to Genoa, which he reached on July 1, 1551. There he and his party boarded ships again commanded by Andrea Doria and, after a stop in Nice, sailed into Barcelona on July 12. In contrast to his stormy passage when he left Spain, the return voyage was, Philip reported, "the most perfect voyage that one could wish for."

One account reports that Philip dallied in Barcelona so that he could enjoy the city's festivities, enlivened by musicians who performed in the streets, and more especially, Barcelona's young women.[16] Finally, on July 31, he left Barcelona and rode to Saragossa, there to meet Maximilan, who had left Augsburg in a separate party, and Maria, Philip's sister and Maximilian's wife. On August 15 Maria and Maximilian, his service for Philip having ended with Philip's return to Spain, left for Barcelona to catch a ship for Italy, and Philip departed for Navarre, where the governing council, the Cortes, swore fealty to him. From Navarre he turned south, bound first for Soria and then for Valladolid and home.

On September 1, accompanied by his sister Juana and six-year-old Don Carlos, who had come to meet him, Philip arrived back at Valladolid after having been gone seven weeks short of three years. He had traversed a vast expanse of Europe, seen the people and places of the empire his father intended him to inherit, learned an unreckonable amount, and, despite many gaffes and ruined opportunities, had evidently enjoyed himself. The feasts and other entertainments, the young women especially, had been particularly enjoyable. It would take him a while to get back into a governing mood, back to his normal seriousness.

There were important matters coming to his attention. In January 1552, four months after Philip's return, France formed an alliance with the political leaders in Germany, including the turncoat, Maurice of Saxony, to block Charles's attempt to impose on Europe his plans for the empire. In the spring of 1552 France's King Henry II sent an army into Lorraine and captured Metz, Toul, and Verdun. Maurice of Saxony meanwhile led his army into southern Germany in an effort to capture Charles. Enraged by that news, Philip determined to go to his father's aid in person. Alba and others had already set out to help. In June Philip wrote to Andrea Doria, whose ships were then transporting Alba's troops, to arrange passage: "I have decided to go to serve His Majesty, and to this effect I am writing the present letter to implore you. When you arrive in Genoa, you will do me a very great favor by coming back at once with the galleys, without losing a moment, so that I can cross over."[17]

Charles, however, apprised of Philip's intentions, discouraged him from acting on them. And so instead of going to his father, Philip stayed in Spain and spent his efforts raising desperately needed men and money to aid his father's cause. He also visited his sister Juana at Toro and stayed with her until the middle of June, when she left for Portugal for her marriage to Portugal's Prince João.

In October 1552 Charles attempted to strike back at his enemies by laying siege to Metz. The siege failed to force the city's surrender, and Charles, humiliated once more, lifted the siege in January 1553 and withdrew to Brussels. It was now that he decided to do what he had for some time been thinking of doing. Sick and worn and thinking of death, he would abdicate and pass the burden to his son, even though Philip still needed, Charles thought, preparation for the responsibilities. From Brussels he wrote to Philip: "I have represented to you many times how you need to win the confidence and affection of these states [the Netherlands], giving them through your presence and contact more satisfaction than they had in your last stay here, since they were not able to get to know you as well enough as was required to keep them happy and gain their good will. . . . I very much doubt whether these states, of whose importance you are aware, can be sustained without your presence and aid."[18]

Sick as he was, Charles was nevertheless thinking also of a new marriage to be arranged for Philip. Charles's first choice as a suitable bride was Princess Maria of Portugal, Philip's cousin. But before marriage negotiations could begin, Charles changed his mind about Maria. An enormously tragic death had occurred in England, and Charles now thought of a new prospective bride. Fifteen-year-old King Edward VI, successor to his father, King Henry VIII, after months of agony, had succumbed to tuberculosis on July 6, 1553, and not long after his death, word reached the rest of Europe that the crown of England had passed to the late King Henry's elder daughter, Mary Tudor, who was unmarried.

Mary was thirty-seven years old, eleven years older than Philip, sixteen years younger than Charles, who was her cousin. Her maternal grandparents, like Charles's, were King Ferdinand and Queen Isabella. Charles once had been betrothed to her, when she was a child, but he broke off the engagement to marry Princess Isabel of Portugal. In her youth, portraits showed an attractive young woman, "handsome" and "exceedingly well made," in the words of Venice's ambassador to Mary's court, Giovanni Micheli. Advancing years and illness, however, had taken away that youthful attractiveness.

Her looks, though, mattered little for what Charles had in mind. What he was envisioning was his son with the crown of the king of England upon his head, wedding England to Spain, to the Netherlands, to the realms of Italy and the Holy Roman Empire and the lands beyond the Atlantic— the vision of an awesome extension of empire. He was also seeing the acquisition of a powerful new ally to meet the continual threat from France. Charles promptly issued instructions to his ambassador at Mary's court in London, Simon Renard, to sound out the new queen about the possibility of a marriage to Philip.

Charles wrote to Philip, too, sounding him out as well. Philip wrote back:

> I very well see the advantages that might accrue from the successful conclusion of this affair. . . . All I have left to say about the English affair is that I am rejoiced to hear that my aunt [Mary Tudor, actually a cousin] has come to the throne of the kingdom, as well out of natural feeling as because of the advantages mentioned by Your Majesty where France and the Low Countries are concerned. . . .

... if you wish to arrange the match for me, you know that I am so obedient a son that I have no will other than yours, especially in a matter of such high import. Therefore I think it best to leave it all to Your Majesty to dispose of as shall seem most fitting.[19]

When Renard brought up the subject of marriage to Mary, she responded, Renard reported to Charles, by "laughing, not once, but several times, and giving me a significant look, which showed that the idea was very agreeable to her, plainly intimating at the same time that she had no desire to marry an Englishman." In a later conversation, Renard took the next step and suggested to Mary that the prince of Spain might be a good match for her. She interrupted him and, according to Renard, said that "she had never felt the smart of what people called 'love,' nor had ever so much as thought of being married, until Providence had raised her to the throne; and that, if she now consented to it, it would be in opposition to her own feelings, from a regard to the public good."

However, she went on, Renard should assure the emperor that she wished to please him, in the same way she would wish to please her father. She said that even if her father were alive, she would accept Charles's choice as a husband for her. She more or less invited Charles to broach to her council the subject of her marriage, implying that she could not do so herself.

Charles interpreted those remarks as Mary's signal for him to pursue the matter of a marriage to Philip. The pursuit, though, must be kept secret, for Charles's representatives were still negotiating for a marriage between Philip and the Portuguese princess, Maria, and if Queen Mary proved at last unwilling to wed Philip, Charles's next choice for him would be the princess, whose representatives would doubtless end the negotiations if they knew that Charles was also attempting to arrange Philip's marriage to Mary. Charles therefore instructed Renard to dissuade Mary from seeking the advice of her council but instead to rely on Charles for guidance.

Preventing the Portuguese from learning about his interest in Mary was actually only one of the two big reasons for secrecy. The other was that Charles wanted time to win over some of the important members of Mary's council. He realized that English public opinion was against the queen marrying a foreigner, that the English generally were predisposed to dislike all foreigners, particularly Spaniards, and that he would have to court Mary's advisers and sell them on the idea.

On October 10, 1553, his emperor apparently feeling that the time was ripe for Mary's acceptance, Renard presented to Mary Charles's formal proposal of marriage to Philip, with the extravagantly courtly assertion that but for his age and ill health, he—Charles—would be proposing for himself rather than for his son.

By then Renard and Charles's attempts at secrecy had failed. Inevitably the content of the messages passing between them leaked out, setting off rumors among Mary's ministers and at least one foreign member of her court, the French ambassador, Antoine de Noailles. He quickly saw the disadvantage to France of such an English-Spanish connection. Following instructions from his government, Noailles began using his influence in London to incite English opposition to the proposed marriage and in doing so, he found an ally in Stephen Gardiner, the bishop of Winchester, who was also Mary's chancellor and the head of her council. Opposition to the marriage soon grew to the extent that Parliament's House of Commons voted to send the queen a petition requesting that she not marry someone from abroad, but instead select a husband from among her subjects.

The opposition seemed only to harden Mary's decision to accept Charles's proposal. She told Renard, who by now had become her confidant, that she had been informed of the efforts of Gardiner and Noailles to thwart the marriage. "But," she said, "I will be a match for them." On the evening of October 30 she invited Renard to join her in her private chapel and there in his presence and attended by Susan Clarencieux, a longtime member of her household, she knelt in front of the Eucharist, invoked it as her protector, guide, and counselor, and recited the *Veni Creator*.

Then, her little ceremony finished, she stood and announced that God, having already performed many miracles for her, had just performed another. He had led her to make a solemn vow in the presence of the Eucharist. She would marry Philip, and there was no way that she would ever change her mind.

4. THE BLOODY QUEEN

At age thirty-seven, Mary could still dream of having a husband and children, something she had thought about and heard about for a long time. Ever since she was two years old, her marriage to some suitable mate had been the subject of negotiations or at least serious conversation by her father or his representatives. First it was the dauphin of France who was to be her husband. Her betrothal to him, effected in elaborate ceremonies in England and France, was broken off three years later. Next, when she was six years old, her intended husband was her cousin Charles, the emperor, who was then twenty-two. They were to marry, according to the agreement with her father, when she was twelve. Charles waited four years for her, then decided to marry the Portuguese Princess Isabel instead. Then followed a succession of talked-about matches, which included, among others, King Francis I of France; King James of Scotland; the duke of Cleves; the vaivode (governor) of Poland; Luiz, son of the king of Portugal; the duke of Orléans, second in line to succeed to the French throne; and Duke Philip of Bavaria. Even an Englishman, Thomas Cromwell, her father's influential secretary, was for a time a possibility.

For one reason or another, all those as well as other possible marriages had fallen through, and Mary had begun to despair. At age twenty-seven, she was, she said, "a young maid and willing to continue so." However, being "a maid for life," as she put it, would have been an enormous disappointment for a young lady prepared as she was to assume a wifely role. Mary had been educated in the Greek and Latin classics and had learned to speak Latin, Spanish, French, and Italian, as well as her native English. She had also been schooled in science and music and by the time she was four years old had learned to master the virginal, a small harpsichordlike instrument. But much of her education, influenced by her Spanish mother, concerned the proper attitudes for a young woman. They were laid out for her, at the request of her mother, in a curriculum designed for her by Juan Luis Vives, the Spanish scholar and writer whose works included *On the Instruction of a Christian Woman*. In it he instructed that a young woman must always remember, as a guiding principle, that she is "the devil's instrument, not Christ's." To combat her natural proclivity toward immorality, Vives taught, a woman must keep her mind "ever bent toward Christ." To help Mary do so, he ordered her to read Scripture every morning and evening and also to read the works of Christian writers, including Jerome, Ambrose, and Augustine. Vives's ideal woman kept submissively quiet and stayed modestly out of the public eye by remaining at home, where there would be "few to see her and none at all to hear her."

According to Scripture and the times, women were to submit to the men in their lives, a theme repeated by the apostle Paul in his New Testament writings. "Wives should submit themselves to their husbands," he wrote forthrightly in his letter to the church at Colossae. His other teachings include the premises that "the head of every man is Christ, and the head of a woman is her husband," "man was not created for the benefit of woman, but woman was created for man's benefit," and "wives should submit to their husbands as they do to the Lord, for a husband is the head of his wife in the same way that Christ is the head of his church. . . . Therefore as the church is subject to Christ, so should wives be subject to their husbands."

It was such sentiments, which had pervaded society, as well as the tradition of having men as rulers, that made Mary's choice of Philip odious to the English people. The English had a dislike for foreigners in general and for the Spanish in particular. To the English, the Spanish seemed repugnantly remorseless in their wars of conquest waged both on the Continent and against the peoples of the New World. Worse, they seemed horrifyingly fanatical in the campaign of slaughter and suppression waged by the Inquisition in their own land. A Spanish husband for England's queen, a prince who had already permitted the Inquisition's terrors in his own country, against his own people, could conceivably impose upon England even more terrible atrocities, too abhorrent to imagine, all with a submissive wife's acquiescence. Furthermore, members of the queen's council and others in her government were fearful that Philip would, through Mary, involve England in Spain's wars.

On November 17, 1553, less than three weeks after Mary had sworn her vow to marry Philip, she met with about twenty members of the House of Commons who had come to let her know that although they were in favor of her getting married, they had misgivings concerning her marriage to Philip. When they attempted to dissuade her, she put them down by telling them it was by God's authority she held her crown and it was to Him alone she would turn for counsel on a matter so important as her marriage. She said, however, that in choosing a husband, she would regard the happiness of her subjects as much as she would her own happiness. When the group left, its members apparently were either reassured or resigned and offered no further resistance to the marriage.

Meanwhile, members of Mary's council, particularly those who had objections to Philip, were being plied with gifts—"bribes" is probably not too strong a term—of gold jewelry, gold coins, and other valuables from the Spanish ambassador. Finally their objections diminished to the point where they were ready to receive Philip's special envoy, Count Egmont, who in December 1553 came over from Brussels with a small group of counselors to make the official proposal to Mary and to work out the details of what was in effect a prenuptial agreement between the parties. He arrived in London on January 2, 1554, and was lavishly entertained while he awaited an audience with Queen Mary, which occurred on January 12. Dealing with a stranger now, not the familiar Renard, Mary assumed an air of royal reserve. "It was not for a maiden queen thus publicly to enter on so delicate a subject as her own marriage," she remarked. "This would be better done by her ministers, to whom she would refer him. But this she would have him understand: her realm was her first husband, and none other should induce her to violate the oath which she had pledged at her coronation."[1]

Under the direction of Mary's chancellor, Bishop Stephen Gardiner, who was himself opposed to her choice of Philip, a marriage contract was meticulously drafted. Its most important provisions stipulated that Philip must respect the laws of England (as opposed to the laws of Spain) and leave English subjects in possession of their rights; that the power to confer titles, honors, emoluments, and offices of all kinds was to be reserved to the queen; and that foreigners were to be excluded from office. If Mary and Philip had a son, he was to succeed to the English crown and to Spain's possessions in Burgundy and the Netherlands; and if Philip's son, Carlos, were to die, the son of Mary and Philip would also succeed to the crown of Spain and Spain's other territories. Furthermore, Mary was never to leave England without her express desire, and her children were not to be taken out of the country without the consent of England's government leaders. The agreement stipulated that Philip should not involve England in his wars with France but should strive to maintain the existing amicable relations between England and France. In the event of Mary's death, Philip was not to claim a right to participate in England's government.

The agreement attempted to protect the nation from the worst foreseeable dangers of the queen's marriage to Philip, but it had a critical weakness, which was raised in Parliament by a member who stood to ask, "But if the bond be violated, who is there to sue the bond?" The question seemed unanswerable.

When the news was issued that an agreement had been concluded, providing confirmation of the queen's impending marriage to Philip, it set off an explosion of public reaction, ranging from ridicule to rebellion. Within weeks, in late January 1554, insurrections broke out in parts of the country, the most threatening of which was led by Thomas Wyatt, whose father was one of England's best-known poets. Wyatt raised a force of insurgents in Kent and assembled them in Rochester, some two to four thousand men, whose numbers included soldiers of the royal army who had deserted their units after being ordered out to suppress the rebellion. Wyatt's aim, he told his followers, was to force a change in the queen's council and give her better advice. To do so, he began a march on London.

In London the duke of Norfolk hurriedly raised an army of Londoners to resist the advancing force of rebels and marched out to confront them. Disastrously, some five hundred of the duke's men defected to Wyatt, and Norfolk's force then broke and fell back to London in disarray as Wyatt's troops continued their march. London itself remained guarded against an attack, as armored warriors were posted at each of the city's entrances and artillery was emplaced at the drawbridge. The queen's council fearfully debated what she should do, whether to take refuge behind the protective walls of the Tower of London or flee to Windsor or across the Channel to Calais or simply fade into the countryside, abandoning London to the rebels.

Mary considered none of those alternatives. With an escort, she resolutely proceeded to London's Guildhall, where many of the city's residents had gathered to decide what measures to take to resist Wyatt. Inside the hall, she stood upon the platform facing the gathered throng and addressed the people in a loud, low-pitched voice that reached to the rear of the hall. "I am come unto you in mine own person," she proclaimed, "to tell you that which you already see and know. That is, how traitorously and rebelliously a number of Kentishmen have assembled themselves against us and you." She accused Wyatt of using her marriage to Philip as a pretext for seizing control of the government. "What I am ye right well know," she told the crowd. "I am your queen, to whom at my coronation, where I was wedded to the realm . . . you promised your allegiance and obedience unto me. And that I am the right and true inheritor of the crown of this realm of England, I take all Christendom to witness. My father, as ye all know, possessed the same regal state, which now rightly is descended unto me."[2] She assured the people that she was marrying for the prime purpose of producing an heir to succeed her.

"Certainly, if I did either know or think that this marriage should either turn to the danger or loss of any of you, my loving subjects, or to the detriment or impairing of any part or parcel of the royal estate of this realm of England, I would never consent thereunto, neither would I ever marry while I live. . . . Now as good and faithful subjects," she urged the crowd, "pluck up your hearts and like true men stand fast with your lawful prince against these rebels, both our enemies and yours, and fear them not, for I assure you that I fear them nothing at all."[3]

Mary's speech, delivered extemporaneously, worked a powerful effect on her listeners. To shouts of "God save Queen Mary!" Mary left the Guildhall, and within hours some twenty thousand of her subjects, responding to her address, which was quickly printed and publicly posted in London, volunteered to join her army of defenders. On Saturday, February 3, 1554, Wyatt's force drew up to the edge of the Thames in Southwark and positioned two artillery pieces at London Bridge. Facing them at the opposite side of the river were four artillery pieces emplaced by the city's defenders and the guns of the Tower, the menace of which caused Wyatt to shift his army upriver to Kingston Bridge, where on the night of February 6–7 he crossed the Thames, marched on London, and invaded it from the west. Throughout February 7 the battle for the city raged until defenders stopped the rebels' advance at Ludgate. When Wyatt attempted to withdraw his men, he discovered that all routes from the city were blocked by its defenders. He then surrendered.

Wyatt was taken prisoner, as was his army of rebels. Hundreds of his followers were executed, and their corpses were left hanging on gallows in the streets. Those who had deserted the royal army to join the rebellion were hanged outside their houses. Wyatt himself was beheaded two months later, his head mounted for public display and his corpse boiled, then quartered and its parts displayed in four sections of London. The bulk of his men, however, were forced to kneel in the mud at Westminster, their hands bound with rope, nooses about their necks, and there thus humbled they received Mary's pardon, after which they were cut free.

Thanks to her heroic rallying of her loyal subjects, Mary had survived the threat to her crown. It was the second time in her so far brief reign that she had done so. The first had come during the previous summer, after John Dudley, duke of Northumberland, had manipulated the dying young King Edward into naming as his successor Lady Jane Grey, Dudley's daughter-in-law and a niece of Henry VIII. Jane had been proclaimed queen following Edward's death, but the country had refused to accept her. As a result, Jane's accession had been revoked, and Mary had been proclaimed queen in July 1553. Mary then had had John Dudley executed, and following the failure of Wyatt's rebellion, she also had the seventeen-year-old Lady Jane and Jane's husband, Guilford Dudley, put to death. They had not participated in Wyatt's plot, but in Mary's mind, they posed a continuing threat to her crown. Jane's father, Henry Grey, duke of Suffolk, who had participated in the plot, was also executed.

With the rebellion quashed, Mary moved ahead with her marriage plans, although objections to it continued. One of the functionaries of Reginald Pole, the self-exiled English cardinal who had refused to support Henry VIII's divorce from Mary's mother, took it upon himself to write Mary a letter warning that she "would fall into the power and become the slave of her husband," and besides that, "at her advanced age she cannot hope to bear children without the peril of her life." The letter reached her on her thirty-eighth birthday. Even Simon Renard seemed to be having second thoughts, vaguely suggesting to Philip that the whole matter of the marriage might be reconsidered. Renard of course was thinking of Philip's interests. He feared that some violence to Philip might occur once he was in England. Renard recommended that Philip put off coming to England for the wedding until the fall of 1554, allowing time for popular feelings there to ameliorate. In discussing his fears of violence, Mary tearfully told Renard that she herself would personally guarantee Philip's safety, that she would rather have not been born than have some harm come to him. Philip, she said, should not postpone the wedding.

Meanwhile, Philip was writing letters to practically everyone concerned with arranging the wedding, except Mary. His message to her, saying he was looking forward to the marriage, was conveyed to her orally by Renard.

In March 1554 Count Egmont, representing Philip again, returned to England to exchange the ratifications of the marriage agreement and finalize the arrangements in a formal ceremony. In the presence of the queen's council, Mary knelt and solemnly called upon God to be her witness that in contracting the marriage, she was not motivated by any carnal impulse or any other worldly consideration, but by a desire to secure the welfare of her kingdom. It was to the kingdom, she said, that her faith had first been plighted and she hoped that heaven would so strengthen her that she would keep the oath she had taken at her coronation. According to Simon Renard, who attended the ceremony, Mary's words were spoken with such feeling that all who heard her were moved to tears.

After the ratifications had been exchanged, Mary knelt again and asked the witnesses to join her in praying that God would help her keep the provisions of the agreement and that He would give her a happy marriage. That done, Egmont presented her with a diamond ring, which Mary slipped onto her finger and held out for all to admire. The ring was a gift from Charles, not Philip.

As Egmont then was about to leave, he asked Mary if she had any message she would like him to carry to Philip. Mary told him that he might convey to the prince her most affectionate regards and assure him that she would always be ready to show him all the kindnesses that a loving and obedient wife could bestow. And when Egmont asked her if she would write to him, she replied, "Not till he had begun the correspondence." Philip still had not troubled himself to pen so much as a note to his bride-to-be. It was not until May 1554, two months before the scheduled wedding, that he at last wrote to her. With that letter he also sent her several pieces of exquisite jewelry.

In June he began preparations for the voyage to England to claim his bride. His father had instructed him to make his arrival in England as unostentatious as possible, but even so, Philip gathered for the trip some three thousand grandees, courtiers, wives, attendants, servants, minstrels, mummers, and men-at-arms and, to transport them following their arrival, about fifteen hundred horses and mules. He was also taking with him a king's ransom in gold to finance himself and his entourage. All would be carried to England in a fleet that included seventy large vessels, a number of smaller ships, and an escort of thirty warships.

Evidently suspecting that Philip might not follow all his instructions, both present and past, and worried that his son might embarrass him, Charles commissioned the duke of Alba to oversee Philip's conduct. "For the love of God," Charles told Alba in a letter, "see to it that my son behaves in the right manner, for otherwise, I tell you I would rather never have taken the matter in hand." From Charles's ambassador in Rome came a letter further revealing the emperor's anxieties. It directed Philip, whose reputation for off-putting haughtiness was well established, to be as ingratiating to the English as possible and yield to them in whatever issue came up. Furthermore, the ambassador implored, "For God's sake, appear to be pleased."

As Charles had ordered, Philip turned over the running of Spain to his sister Juana, young widow of the late heir to Portugal's throne, who had died the previous January, and on July 12 Philip and his entourage set sail from La Coruña, bound for Britain. Seven days later, after a rough voyage through choppy seas, the fleet anchored at Southampton.

Probably remembering his father's caution against making too big a show, Philip decided to take ashore with him, on the royal barge sent out to fetch him, only nine of his nobles, among them Alba and Egmont. On landing, Philip was greeted by a delegation of English nobles and presented with a spectacularly caparisoned white horse on which to ride, through a steady rain, to Southampton's ancient Church of the Holy Rood for a celebratory Mass. For the next three days Philip stayed at Southampton, riding out from the town occasionally with an English escort to show himself to the people of the area, as if campaigning to gain their goodwill, an effort that met with some success.

On July 23, escorted by a contingent of two hundred brightly clad horsemen, he and his Spanish companions—including the wives of some of them—left Southampton on horseback, in a heavy rain, headed for Winchester, about twelve miles to the northeast, where he would meet his bride and where the wedding would be held. He and his party arrived late that afternoon, sodden and spattered, and were met at the city gates by the mayor and aldermen, who braved the rainstorm to welcome Philip and present to him the keys to the city. They then ushered him and his companions to their lodgings. Philip would stay at the home of the dean of Winchester Cathedral. At the cathedral, crowded with curious onlookers, a special service, at which

Winchester's bishop, Stephen Gardiner, and four other bishops officiated, was held for Philip not long after his arrival.

Mary met him that evening. With her entourage she had arrived earlier in the day and was waiting for him in Bishop Gardiner's residence, across the cloister from where Philip was staying. Accompanied by several of his courtiers, including his good friend and confidant Ruy Gómez de Silva, he ascended a winding staircase and entered a long, narrow chamber to stand smiling before her. She took his hand, and he greeted her with a kiss on the lips. His companions greeted her with a kiss on her hand. They and Philip also greeted each of her ladies-in-waiting with a kiss.

A Scottish witness to the meeting described Philip: "Of visage he is well-favored, with a broad forehead and grey eyes, straight-nosed and manly countenance. From the forehead to the point of his chin, his face groweth small; . . . with a yellow head and a yellow beard. . . . He is so well-proportioned of body, arm, leg, and every other limb to the same as nature cannot work a more perfect pattern."[4] He wore a white kid doublet and trunk hose, a cloak woven with gold and silver threads, and a matching plumed cap. Altogether, he appeared an elegant figure of a man. Mary surely would have been pleased.

Philip's impression of Mary, however, may have been much different. Small, almost ghostly pale, she wore a plain, tight-fitting, unadorned, black velvet gown that contrasted woefully with Philip's sartorial splendor. Ruy Gómez commented that she looked "rather older than we had been told," and another of Philip's companions reported, "The queen is not at all beautiful. Small and flabby, rather than fat, she is of white complexion and fair and has no eyebrows."[5] To Philip she very likely seemed a lusterless jewel, drably mounted.

The two of them chatted amiably for an hour or more, speaking in Castilian, she more than holding her own in his—and her mother's—native language. As their meeting was drawing to a close, she attempted to teach him to say "good night" in English, and he managed a version of it before leaving her.

The next day, July 24, Philip, accompanied by a group of his grandees, offered himself to public display by walking through Winchester's streets, preceded by his minstrels, to meet Mary at the royal residence. Upon his entrance into the reception hall, she came forward and welcomed him with a kiss, then led him to a canopy under which thronelike chairs had been placed, and she took a seat in one and he in the other. There they conversed for more than an hour while their courtiers attempted to become acquainted with one another.

It was the following day, July 25, the feast day of Saint James, Spain's patron saint, that the wedding was held. Philip wore white, except for a cloth-of-gold mantle trimmed in crimson velvet and lined with crimson satin, which Mary had given him. Mary, who arrived at the cathedral about a half hour after Philip, wore a white satin gown adorned with diamonds, a black velvet mantle, and bright red slippers. As she proceeded, the earl of Derby strode before her, bearing an unsheathed sword in his hands, a symbol of royalty. Behind her came the marchioness of Winchester and Sir John Gage, Mary's lord chamberlain, carrying the train of her gown.

The words of the ceremony were spoken in both English and Spanish, and the bride was given away by the earls of Pembroke and Derby in the name of the people of the whole nation. After a Mass was said, the royal herald stood and presented the newlyweds to the audience in a loud voice: "Philip and Mary, by the grace of God king and queen of England, France, Naples, Jerusalem, and Ireland, defenders of the faith, princes of Spain and Sicily, archdukes of Austria, dukes of Milan, Burgundy, and Brabant, counts of Habsburg, Flanders and Tyrol!"

After about four hours, the ceremony was finally ended, and Philip led his bride out of the cathedral and into the great hall of Bishop Gardiner's palatial residence. Behind the couple trooped the wedding guests, preceded by the earls of Derby and Pembroke, each bearing an unsheathed sword, dual symbols of royalty. Philip and Mary took their seats at the dais, under an elegant canopy, and their guests took their assigned places, according to rank and status, at four long tables set for the sumptuous banquet that followed. At the far end of the chamber an orchestra provided music for the happy occasion. After the banquet came a ball, which lasted until nine o'clock that evening. The royal couple then retired to their quarters, where Bishop Gardiner blessed their bed and then left them alone to further enjoy their wedding night.

The honeymoon, at Winchester and then Windsor, lasted until August 28, when Mary and Philip made their way on horseback to London, which they entered in a colorful procession that let their English subjects see them and join in a public celebration of their marriage, which was so well consummated that in September, two months after the wedding, her physicians pronounced Mary pregnant.

As she resumed her normal activities, Philip seemed at first to make a point of staying in the background, leaving the affairs of government, as far as anyone could tell, to Mary and her ministers. His presence was soon felt, however, and by September he seemed in control of Mary and her government. He was especially noticed by the clergy. "He was as punctual in his attendance at Mass, and his observance of all forms of devotion, as any monk," commented one observer. "More so, as some people thought, than became his age and station. The ecclesiastics, with whom Philip had constant intercourse, talk loudly of his piety."[6]

No one seemed to doubt his sincerity in spiritual matters. Furthermore, he felt that what was good for him in such matters was good for all his subjects. "Better not [to] reign at all," he remarked on more than one occasion, "than reign over heretics." And so when Cardinal Pole, whom Pope Julius III had appointed as his legate to England following Mary's accession, made known that he was eager to come back to England from exile and get on with the task of restoring the country's strayed sheep to Rome's fold, Philip began lobbying the queen's ministers and influential nobles in an effort to smooth the way for Pole's successful return. The lobbying provided Philip opportunities to show his generosity, in the form of handsome pensions awarded to the queen's ministers, paid from the golden hoard that Philip had received from Peru and had deposited in the Tower's vaults.

Pole arrived in late November 1554. He came up the Thames in an elaborately appointed barge, on the prow of which was mounted a large silver cross, emblematic of his authority as the pope's representative, and when he stepped ashore in London, Mary and Philip and members of their court were on hand to welcome him.

Queen Mary and Cardinal Pole would see eye to eye on many things. Both were victims of the cruelty of Henry VIII, and the bitterness that each felt toward him would be reinforced by the other. Pole's mother, Margaret Pole, once Mary's governess, and Pole's brother had been beheaded as Henry's retaliation for Pole's opposition to his proposed divorce. Pole viewed his mother not merely as a victim of Henry's wrath but also as a martyr to her Catholic faith. He saw Henry's break with the pope, Henry's rejection of the authority of the pope and the church, as the cause of all the wrongs done him and his family. In Pole's mind Henry's outrages and Protestantism, which Henry had fostered for his own reasons, were intricately intertwined. Pole's mission was to extricate the nation from its heretical plight, brought on by Henry's papal defiance, and deliver the people from Protestant evil.

On November 28, 1554, Cardinal Pole stood before Parliament at Whitehall and after recounting the persecution he had suffered for his faith and reviewing the spiritual change that had swept over the country, he urged his audience to repent of their mistaken ways and come home to the faith they had left. "I come to reconcile, not to condemn," he assured Parliament. "I come not to compel, but to call again. . . . Touching all matters that be past, they shall be as things cast into the sea of forgetfulness." Two days later, Parliament accepted his call. The members petitioned Philip and Mary to ask Pole, on behalf of the pope, to grant them pardon. As they knelt en masse, Cardinal Pole declared their absolution.

Parliament then enacted legislation to restore to the church of Rome its former status in England and to remove all legal hindrances to it and to the authority of the pope. Also restored by Parliament, in a unanimous vote, were the old laws decreeing that heretics convicted by church courts were to be turned over to civil authorities for execution.

By messengers dispatched to Rome and other major cities of Christendom, Philip quickly spread the good news. England, four months after his arrival, was back in the fold.

But not entirely. Ordinary people in England, particularly those vulnerable to rumors and prone to violence, made known their objections to Mary's restoration of Catholicism, often by assaulting Catholics verbally and physically. And many other dissenters, perhaps thousands, including tradesmen, merchants, farmers, skilled workers of every kind, as well as Protestant clergymen and professional men, left the country rather than submit to Mary's imposition of Catholicism. Many of those who stayed behind but refused to submit paid a terrible price.

John Rogers, vicar of Saint Sepulchre's Church in London, whose sermons warned his congregation against popery, idolatry, and superstition—all associated with the practice of Catholicism—was imprisoned at Newgate Prison, then burned at the stake at Smithfield, in northeast London, in February 1555, the first religious martyr of Mary's reign.

Lawrence Saunders spoke against Catholic doctrine as a guest preacher in

Northampton and was seized, examined by the bishop of London, and burned alive at Coventry on February 8.

John Hooper, bishop of Worcester and Gloucester, preached about the Catholic church's abuses, was arrested, refused to recant, and was burned at the stake at Gloucester on February 9.

Rowland Taylor, vicar of Hadley in Suffolk, refused to have Mass said at his church, was personally denounced by Stephen Gardiner, accused of blasphemy, bound to the stake, killed by a stroke on the head with a halberd, and burned in February.

William Hunter, nineteen years old, refused to receive communion, was arrested, placed in stocks for two days, tortured, then burned at the stake in February.

Robert Farrar, bishop of Saint David's in Wales, preached Protestant doctrine, criticized Catholic practices, was arrested, condemned, and burned in Carmathen, Wales, on March 30.

The list went on. Rawlins White, a commercial fisherman from Cardiff, Wales, was burned for refusing to recant his Protestant opinions. George Marsh, a curate, for refusing to recant his beliefs, was burned alive on April 24. John Cardmaker, John Warne, John Simpson, and John Ardely, for refusing to recant, were all burned on the same day, May 25, two at Smithfield, one at Rochford, one at Railey. Thomas Haukes and Thomas Watts, both laymen, were pronounced heretics and burned in June. Also burned in June were Thomas Osmond, William Bamford, and Nicholas Chamberlain. In July John Bradford and John Leaf were burned at Smithfield. John Bland, John Frankesh, Nicholas Shetterden, and Humphrey Middleton were burned together on July 12 at Canterbury. Dirick Carver, a brewer, was burned on July 22 at Lewes. John Launder, a farmer, was burned on July 23 at Stening. Still the list went on: James Abbes, John Denley, John Newman, Patrick Packingham, W. Coker, W. Hooper, H. Laurence, R. Colliar, R. Wright, W. Stere, Elizabeth Warne—the widow of the martyred upholsterer John Warne—George Tankerfield, a London cook, Robert Smith, a clergyman, Stephen Harwood, Thomas Fust, Robert Samuel, also a clergyman.

On October 16, Hugh Latimer, the new bishop of Worcester, and Nicholas Ridley, bishop of London, went to the stake together, Latimer exhorting his comrade as the flames swept up their bodies, "We shall this day, by God's grace, light up such a candle in England as, I trust, will never be put out." On the same day that Latimer and Ridley were burned, Queen Mary's lord chancellor, the controversial Bishop Stephen Gardiner, was stricken while eating dinner. He died two weeks later.

On December 18, a bright young scholar, John Philpot, whom Gardiner had marked for execution, was burned at Smithfield, which by then had become a loathsome symbol of Mary's suppression of Protestants. On January 31, 1556, in a new year of persecution, five Protestants—four women and one man—were burned at two stakes in one huge fire. Others, more fortunate, died in prison of their torture or mistreatment before they could be taken to the stake.

In all, Mary—who for her deeds became known then and to history as Bloody Mary—burned to death nearly three hundred people, sixty of them women, over a period of three years. Of them, none was more famous, nor more hated by Mary, than Thomas Cranmer. He had become Henry VIII's archbishop of Canterbury largely as a reward for his arguments advancing the invalidity of Henry's marriage to Mary's mother—and thus the bastardization of Mary—and Henry's eligibility to marry Anne Boleyn. He was hugely instrumental in the establishment of the Church of England, authoring its Book of Common Prayer and separating the Anglican church from the Catholic church in doctrine, ritual, and law. Offered a pardon if he would recant and embrace Catholicism once more, Cranmer thought to save himself from the flames and wrote out his recantation. But Mary was determined he should die at the stake anyway, and when he learned his recantation was to no avail, he resigned himself to a martyr's death and publicly repudiated his recantation. He was burned to death on March 21, 1556, in Oxford.

Philip tried to give the appearance of noncomplicity in Mary's burnings. Not long after they had begun, he had his confessor, Alfonso de Castro, a Spanish friar, preach a sermon denouncing the burnings, saying they were contradictory to the spirit of Christianity, which stood for love and forgiveness. Instead of seeking punishment for errancy, the sermon went on, church officials should point out the sinner's errors and seek his repentance. The sermon had little effect in the campaign to purge England of heretics, but it may have served what was apparently its real purpose—to prevent public hostility toward Philip and his fellow Spaniards, known for their association with the Inquisition. Philip's father, moreover, the biggest influence on Philip, in 1555 was executing Protestants in the Netherlands at a rate of seventy to eighty a month. None of Charles's guilt, however, was in the English public mind attached to Philip.

The blame fell on the queen, and rightly so. She openly espoused the burnings.

> Touching the punishment of heretics, I believe it would be well to inflict punishment at this beginning, without much cruelty or passion, but without however omitting to do such justice on those who choose by their false doctrines to deceive simple persons, that the people may clearly comprehend that they have not been condemned without just cause, whereby others will be brought to know the truth and will beware of letting themselves be induced to relapse into such new and false opinions. And above all, I should wish that no one be burned in London, save in the presence of some member of the Council; and that during such executions, both here and elsewhere, some good and pious sermons be preached.[7]

Meanwhile, the goodwill of the English people toward the queen they had saved from rebellion had, with the victims of her burnings, also gone up in smoke.

⤙⚭ 5. THE SUSPECT PRINCESS

The circumstantial evidence looked bad for twenty-year-old Lady Elizabeth. It made her appear guilty of involvement in the conspiracy that had failed with the defeat of Thomas Wyatt's rebel army on the streets of London. The major goal of the conspirators had been to depose Catholic Mary and put Protestant Elizabeth on the throne in her place. That fact alone was reason enough to make Elizabeth suspect in Mary's mind. But there were other reasons.

One of the chief conspirators, William Pickering, was known to have had a suspicious private meeting with Elizabeth for two hours in late October 1553, about three months before the insurrection erupted. Another principal conspirator, James Croft, a close friend of Elizabeth, had told the French ambassador, Antoine de Noailles, who had met with the plotters—France being keen to forestall the English-Spanish alliance that would result from Mary's marriage to Philip—that Elizabeth had agreed to move to a safer residence before the insurrection was to occur, implying that Elizabeth knew what was coming and had at least acquiesced in it.

Actually, Croft had ridden to Ashridge, where Elizabeth was then living, having received Mary's permission to leave her court, and had advised Elizabeth to move to one of her more distant properties, Donnington Castle, which was virtually beyond Mary's reach. There she would be safe from possible attempts by Mary to take her hostage when the insurrection started. Wyatt had given her similar advice in a letter. But Elizabeth, suffering a malady—perhaps nephritis—that caused parts of her body to swell, had felt too ill to be moved. (Ever eager to disparage her, Simon Renard, Charles V's ambassador and Mary's confidant, had passed along the rumor that Elizabeth was pregnant, the result of a "vile intrigue," he said.) To Wyatt, Elizabeth had sent a vague oral reply, delivered by one of her functionaries, William St. Loe, that "she did thank him much for his good will and she would do as she should see cause." Wyatt, moreover, under interrogation following his arrest, had claimed that in a letter to Elizabeth he had told her he planned to depose Mary and put Elizabeth on the throne. Another conspirator, Francis Russell, under interrogation claimed that he had delivered letters from Wyatt to Elizabeth.

Another damning piece of circumstantial evidence was the copy of a letter that Elizabeth had written to Mary, found in the French ambassador's seized diplomatic pouch. In itself the letter was not incriminating, but its presence among the ambassador's dispatches to his government suggested that Elizabeth was in contact with French officials, who may have been aiding the conspiracy against Mary.

On the day after Wyatt's rebellion had begun, January 26, 1554, Mary had written Elizabeth a not unfriendly letter telling her to return to London for her safety and assuring her that she would "be most heartily welcome" and could stay as long as she liked. In the letter, Mary also mentioned that she had heard Elizabeth was thinking of moving to Donnington Castle, an indication that the queen's intelligence agents were on the job and that Elizabeth's safety was not all that worried her about Elizabeth.

In her written reply, Elizabeth, no doubt suspicious of her sister's intentions for her, had pleaded illness, saying she was too sick to travel, and had refused Mary's summons, providing further circumstantial evidence of guilt. It was a copy of that letter that was found among the French ambassador's dispatches.

On February 9, two days after Wyatt's defeat, Mary had sent three of her council members—William Howard (the queen's lord admiral and Elizabeth's great-uncle), Edward Hastings, and Thomas Cornwallis—backed by a cavalry contingent, to fetch Elizabeth back to London, sick or no. According to Renard, who so informed the emperor, Mary at that point had already concluded that Elizabeth was guilty of conspiring against her and had decided to have her executed. On the councilors' arrival at Ashridge, Elizabeth steadfastly maintained that she was still too sick to travel, but two royal physicians sent to examine her declared her illness not life threatening and said she was well enough to make the trip.

Clothed in white, she was carried in a litter, the curtains of which she had had pulled back so that her countrymen could see her, "proud, lofty, defiant," Renard reported, as she passed by with her mounted escort, a hundred scarlet-uniformed horsemen riding in front of her litter and another hundred behind it. At the councilors' instructions, the procession moved so carefully and slowly, because of Elizabeth's illness, that it traveled only six to seven miles a day. It had left Ashridge, in Hertfordshire, on February 12 and reached London on February 23, passing through Smithfield, the site of so many of Mary's Protestant burnings, and Fleet Street and on to Whitehall Palace.

The queen refused to see Elizabeth, and she was confined to quarters in a remote part of the palace. Meanwhile, Thomas Wyatt continued to be questioned and after interrogation was brought to trial. During the trial, which occurred on March 15, Wyatt disclosed no more than was already known about his contact with Elizabeth. Even so, on March 17 members of the queen's council came to Elizabeth's quarters in a group and informed her that she was being charged with involvement in the conspiracy and that the investigation of her activities would continue. The council members also informed her that the queen had decided she should be sent to the Tower, the massive, sprawling, centuries-old fortress that had become associated with torture and death.

Apparently expecting Elizabeth to attempt an escape to avoid the Tower, her captors isolated her from most of her servants and posted armed guards in the palace gardens, courts, and other access points. Two of the councilors, the earl of Sussex and the marquess of Winchester, took her to the Tower, the trip made by water to avoid the streets of London and a possible public demonstration sympathetic to Elizabeth, or even a riot to free her.

Steadfastly maintaining her innocence, Elizabeth pleaded for a delay. When that was refused, she asked permission to write Mary a note. The marquess of Winchester was ready to refuse that request as well, but the earl of Sussex, Thomas Radcliffe, perhaps fearful of being too harsh to a possible future queen, decided to let her write the note and ordered pen and ink and paper brought to her.

Elizabeth had reached a crucial moment. It was to the Tower that her mother had been sent, first to be confined, then to be tried, and finally to be executed. In Elizabeth's mind the Tower would have invoked awful images of her mother's ordeal, which Elizabeth realized she herself now faced. What she was about to write to Mary, she knew, might truly be the letter of her life. She began by urging Mary to give her a chance to plead her case in person, reminding her that Mary had once promised not to punish her without allowing her to answer whatever charges were brought against her. She prodded Mary to honor that promise. "A king's word," she wrote boldly, quoting something King John of France had once said, "[is] more than another man's oath." She protested her incarceration in the Tower. "I am by your Council from you commanded to go unto the Tower, a place more wonted for a false traitor than a true subject."

She asserted her innocence, declaring "afore God" that she had "never practised, counselled, nor consented to anything that might be prejudicial to your person in any way, or dangerous to the state by any means." She appealed to Mary's conscience. "Let conscience move your highness to take some better way with me than to make me be condemned in all men's sight afore my desert known." She emphasized the importance of making her case herself before Mary. "I have heard in my time of many cast away for want of coming to the presence of their prince." She made a personal plea that Mary's judgment not be unduly influenced by her councilors. "I pray God as evil persuasion persuade not one sister against the other," she urged. She begged for an audience with Mary. "Therefore once again kneeling with humbleness of my heart, because I am not suffered to bow the knees of my body, I humbly crave to speak with your highness, which I would not be so bold to desire if I knew not myself most clear as I know myself most true."

She rebutted evidence against her. "And as for the traitor Wyatt, he might peradventure write me a letter, but on my faith I never received any from him; and as for the copy of my letter sent to the French king, I pray God confound me eternally if ever I sent him word, message, token or letter by any means, and to this truth I will stand it to my death."

The letter ended at the top of a page, and lest someone forge additional words to what she had written, she drew diagonal lines down through the bottom two-thirds of the page, leaving just enough room to write a final request: "I humbly crave but one word of answer from yourself." Then she signed the letter, "Your highness's most faithful subject that hath been from the beginning and will be [until] my end, Elizabeth."[1]

The letter was delivered to Mary, who received it with anger that Elizabeth had been allowed to write it. She refused to read it all, and it ended up making no difference in the decision to send Elizabeth to the Tower. The forces impelling her to that grim destination were more than the queen's prejudices. The influential Simon Renard, who had the queen's ear, was convinced, as he wrote to the emperor, that "if [Mary and her council] do not punish [Elizabeth] now that the occasion offers, the queen will never be secure." That view was shared by a number of the members of Mary's council. Spain's ambassador, furthermore, believed Elizabeth should be executed because "while she lives it will be very difficult to make the prince's [Philip's] entry here safe."

Elizabeth's writing of her letter had accomplished one good effect, though minor. It had so delayed her departure that the tide had turned, and the barge on which she was to be transported to the Tower could not safely pass beneath London Bridge. The next favorable tide was not till midnight. The councilors decided against a nighttime trip because of the dangers and instead would wait until morning to move her.

The next day was Palm Sunday, which the queen had ordered her subjects to observe in the traditional Catholic fashion by carrying palm fronds to church. So as the faithful among Mary's subjects commemorated Jesus' joyous, final entry into Jerusalem before his arrest and execution, Elizabeth, already under arrest, was quietly hauled away to face possible execution. About nine o'clock that morning her escort arrived to take her and her attendants from her quarters at Whitehall, through the palace garden, past the gate, and down the steps that descended to the riverbank, where the barge awaited, floating on the outgoing tide. From the gray skies a steady, soaking rain fell, adding to the dreariness of the occasion.

Elizabeth was ushered to the barge's cabin, along with the six women and two men who were her attendants, and there they all were sheltered from the rain. As it moved downriver toward the Tower, the barge ran into the pilings beneath London Bridge and became stuck, forcing its crew to work for some time to free it. According to one contemporary account,[2] as the vessel approached the Tower, Elizabeth could see they were headed for the landing called Traitors' Stairs, or Traitor's Gate, apparently named for the sort of prisoners entering the Tower there, and she protested by exclaiming as she stepped from the barge, "Here lands as true a subject, being prisoner, as ever landed at these stairs; and before Thee, O God, I speak it, having no friend but Thee alone!"

A contradictory source says she was landed at Tower Wharf and was led into the Tower across the drawbridge there.[3] At first she refused to leave the barge, but eventually consented. Then, coming ashore, she sat down on the wet flagstones of the walkway and would not move. The lieutenant of the Tower, John Brydges, on whom now rested the responsibility for the royal captive, sought to talk her into getting up by herself and proceeding to her quarters to get out of the rain. "It is better sitting here than in a worse place," she replied. Apparently moved by pity at her plight, one of Elizabeth's male attendants began crying, and Elizabeth, letting him and the others know that her sit-down was an act of defiance rather than fear, rebuked him for his tears, telling him, "Alas! What do you mean? I took you to comfort, not to dismay me; for my truth is such that no one shall have cause to weep for me." She then rose and continued on.

Two ranks of the Tower's uniformed guards lined her path, and as she passed between them, she took objection to their presence. "Are all these harnessed men here for me?" she asked. She was told they were not. She refused that answer. "If it is on account of me," she said, "I beseech you that they may be dismissed. It needed not for me, being, alas, but a weak woman." At that, some of the guards reportedly were so moved that they dropped to their knees, took off their headgear, and cried out, "God save your grace!" Those who did were the next day fired from their jobs.

The sources differ in their descriptions of the quarters to which Elizabeth was taken, ranging from regal to mean. However, the sources agree that she was generally treated with deference. The earl of Sussex in particular never lost sight of the fact that she was King Henry's daughter, and he warned others, "Let us take heed, my lords, that we go not beyond our commissions, for she was our king's daughter." The likelihood is that she was quartered, as one source has it, in a palatial apartment in the southeast part of the Tower. The frightfulness of her accommodations lay not in their lack of comfort, for there was none, but in the worrisome fact that this was the same suite twice occupied by her mother, first to await her coronation and then, three years later, to await her execution. Its significance would not have been lost on Elizabeth.

John Brydges, the officer directly in charge of her, heeded Sussex's advice about remembering whose daughter Elizabeth was, and he treated her with respect and kindness, letting her take her meals in his recently completed house within the Tower grounds, allowing her attendants to bring her food and other items from outside the Tower, and allowing her to take walks, accompanied by her attendants, atop the Tower's battlements. The constable of the Tower, John Gage, Brydges's superior, thought Brydges was too lenient and he ended those privileges, saying he did so "more for love of the pope than for hate of her person."

When the lack of exercise and fresh air began to affect her health, Gage relented somewhat and permitted her to walk in the nearby walled garden, escorted by a guard. The four-year-old son of one of the guards came to see her every day and handed her a little nosegay until Gage put a stop to that, too. The boy was threatened with a whipping, and his father was ordered to keep him away from Elizabeth's quarters.

She was not living undisturbed in her captivity. She underwent repeated interrogation by council members, particularly by the queen's chancellor, Bishop Stephen Gardiner. One line of questioning sought to discover her reasons for her proposed move from Ashridge to Donnington Castle, which Gardiner felt sure was an indication of her complicity in Wyatt's rebellion. At first Elizabeth acted as if she didn't know she had a place called Donnington Castle. Then she remembered it but couldn't remember considering moving to it, saying that she had never in her life spent a night there. Gardiner and the other councilors had the conspirator James Croft, their informant, brought in to confront her. Then her memory improved. "And as concerning my going unto Donnington Castle," she conceded, "I do remember that Mister Hoby and mine officers and you, Sir James Croft, had such talk." She then blithely dismissed the matter by turning on her questioners with a question of her own. "What is that to the purpose, my lords," she demanded, "but that I may go to mine own houses at all times?"

Most of the councilors were unwilling to press her for the answers that Gardiner hoped would certify her guilt and at last he gave up in frustration. When the session was over, one of the councilors, Henry Fitzalan, earl of Arundel, knelt in front of Elizabeth and apologized for having troubled her over such a small matter. "You sift me narrowly," she responded, "but of this I am assured, that God has appointed a limit to your proceedings, and so God forgive you all."

Not all of the council members, though, were mollified by Elizabeth's histrionics and righteous words, nor was Mary. She told Renard that, "From day to day they [the council members] are finding new proofs against [Elizabeth]. . . . They had several witnesses who deposed as to the preparation of arms and provisions which she made for the purpose of rebelling with the others, and of maintaining herself in strength in a house [Donnington Castle] to which she sent the supplies."

Some of Mary's close confidants, Gardiner and Renard among them, remained certain that Elizabeth had been part of the plot, which proposed, among other things, to wed Elizabeth to young Edward Courtenay, the earl of Devonshire and a distant cousin of Mary and Elizabeth, and thereby make him England's king after Mary had been deposed and Elizabeth crowned. Renard told Mary she should have both Elizabeth and Courtenay beheaded. "It seems to me," he wrote to the emperor, "that she ought not to spare [them], for while they are alive there will always be plots to raise them to the throne, and it would be just to punish them, as it is publicly known that they are guilty and so deserve death." Thinking of the upcoming wedding of Philip and Mary, Spain's ambassador declared that "while she [Elizabeth] lives it will be very difficult to make the prince's [Philip's] entry here safe."

Wyatt went to the executioner's block on the morning of April 11 and before submitting himself to the ax proclaimed to the gathered throng Elizabeth's innocence. "Whereas it is said and whistled abroad that I should accuse my lady Elizabeth's grace and my lord Courtenay," he declared, addressing the crowd from the scaffold, "it is not so, good people. For I assure you neither they nor any other now in yonder hold [in the Tower] . . . was privy of my rising or commotion before I began. As I have declared no less to queen's council. And this is most true."[4] Wyatt's statement took the queen's officers by distressing surprise, coming as it did as a public relations calamity for all those who wanted Elizabeth put under the ax. The dean of Westminster, Hugh Weston, who was on the scene ostensibly to minister to Wyatt, from the scaffold attempted to negate Wyatt's remarks by claiming that Wyatt earlier had in writing implicated Elizabeth in his plot, but Wyatt's words of exculpation had already made their impression on the crowd.

After a month of questioning Elizabeth and interrogating others, some no doubt upon the Tower's rack, Mary's desire to have Elizabeth condemned was no closer to fulfillment. Many on the queen's council—a body divided between nobles who had served under Henry VIII, who tended to support Elizabeth, and the newcomers appointed by Mary—believed a trial was useless because the evidence was insufficient to convict her. In Parliament there was not enough support to pass an Act of Attainder, which could pronounce her guilty without a trial. Mary was stymied.

On May 5, about a month after he had received his royal prisoner, John Gage was relieved of his job as Elizabeth's keeper. His replacement was

Henry Bedingfield, whose chief credential for the job was his dogged loyalty to Mary. Not long after his arrival, massive replacements were made among the Tower guards, creating fresh consternation in Elizabeth's mind. She worried that her new custodian, whose reputation as the queen's willing agent she knew, commanding a new blue-uniformed cohort, had come with orders to do away with her secretly. The actual cause of the changes became known when on May 13 Elizabeth was moved out of the Tower and, escorted by Bedingfield and the troop of new guards, taken to the royal manor at Woodstock, near Oxford, there to be held under house arrest. Along the way to Woodstock she continued to worry that Bedingfield's mission was a sinister one. She dispatched one of her attendants to give a message to some of her former servants whom she had spotted watching her procession pass by. "Go to them," she directed, "and say these words from me: 'Tamquam ovis,' that is, like a sheep to the slaughter," an allusion to the messianic passage in Isaiah 53:7.

Well-wishers turned out along her route to glimpse her, bring gifts, and salute her with cries of "God save your grace!" as she passed through the towns and countryside. In at least one village bells of celebration were rung, apparently in the belief that she had achieved some sort of triumph. Angered by that display of public support for her, Bedingfield ordered the bell ringers seized and placed in stocks.

On May 16, having spent three nights in the homes of cordial hosts along the way, Elizabeth, with Bedingfield and his company of guards, arrived at Woodstock, a once palatial manor that had been updated by Elizabeth's grandfather, King Henry VII, but now stood in need of repairs, particularly to its roof and windows. Bedingfield soon learned that the place presented security problems, for he found only three doors that could be locked. To prevent an escape, he posted a detail of guards on a nearby hill.

The queen's written instructions to Bedingfield ordered him to guard Elizabeth closely, but at the same time he was to exercise "regard to use her in such good and honourable sort as may be agreeable to our honour and her estate and degree." Inflexible, obtuse, and a stickler for rules, Bedingfield could see that in handling Elizabeth he would have to walk a fine line, a performance for which he was ill suited. Other parts of his orders were slightly more specific. He was not to allow Elizabeth to have "conference with any suspected person outside of his hearing . . . As for [a] stranger," he was told, "ye must foresee that no persons suspect have any conference with her at all, and yet to permit such strangers whom ye shall think honest . . . to speak with her in your hearing only." Furthermore, he was not to allow Elizabeth to receive or send any "message, letter or token to or from any manner of person." His task would prove virtually impossible. Although Elizabeth's contacts with strangers (to Bedingfield) and "persons suspect" were severely restricted, the contacts of her servants and other attendants were less so, and there was no way her private conversations with them could all be monitored by Bedingfield or his force of guards.

Other than her loss of freedom and her cramped accommodations—she was able to use only four rooms of the manor—it was the lack of communication with the outside world that bothered her most. Thomas Parry, her cofferer, who managed her financial accounts and needed to confer frequently with her, was not allowed to stay at the manor and so he rented accommodations at an inn in town and visited her at the manor as necessary. Through him she was able to keep in contact with her supporters and sympathizers as well as with matters of her estates. (One source says that Elizabeth was the second largest landowner in England, second only to the queen.) Parry was in daily contact with people who came to him at the inn, presumably on Elizabeth's business. It was a situation Bedingfield, as well as some council members, disliked, but barring Parry from contact with Elizabeth would have meant that Bedingfield would have to assume from her the burden of financing and managing the Woodstock household, which he was unwilling, probably unable, to do. The council had budgeted money to pay Bedingfield's blue-uniformed cohort, but all other expenses, including the cost of feeding not only Elizabeth and her attendants but also Bedingfield and his servants, were borne by Elizabeth. "I neither will nor dare intermeddle myself with [managing the household]," he wrote to the council. Simply trying to watch her, in keeping with his orders, was responsibility enough for Bedingfield.

Once she saw that her life was no longer in jeopardy, Elizabeth found other matters to fret over—and about which to harry Bedingfield, whom she called her jailer, which he resented. She complained that the four rooms she had been assigned were inadequate. She demanded that she be allowed to walk not only in the manor's garden (which she did, accompanied by Bedingfield or a guard) but throughout the manor's park as well. She importuned to have returned to her the servants that Mary and her council had replaced, especially Elizabeth Sandes, one of Elizabeth's favorites, a die-hard Protestant whom Mary called a woman "of evil opinion and not fit to remain about our sister's person." She asked for more maids. She asked for more books, including an English Bible. She wanted more writing paper and ink. She demanded to be allowed to write letters to the queen's council (the ban on her letter writing Bedingfield interpreted to include letters to Mary). She wanted to use couriers of her choosing to deliver messages to Mary's court. She demanded that when she wrote to the council, since she was not permitted a stenographer, Bedingfield must take her dictation and pen the letter for her. Her requests and demands were nearly inexhaustible.

Some Bedingfield granted. Some he put off, telling Elizabeth he would see what he could do. Many, if not most, he referred to the council, unwilling to make a decision himself. Each time he came to her to voice a complaint of his own or to deny one of her requests, he respectfully knelt before her while giving her the bad news. He otherwise treated her with respect, and in his reports, with a touch of sarcasm, he referred to Elizabeth as "this great lady." Elizabeth, on the other hand, treated him with unconcealed contempt, seeing him as a fool not to be suffered gladly. She told him he was thoroughly unqualified for his job, that he lacked the "knowledge, experience and all other accidents" necessary for the position he held. Bedingfield was not so insensitive as to be unmoved by her treatment of him or by the demands that she, along with the task of overseeing her, made on him. Fed up after several months, he begged the council to relieve him of his duties, telling council members that if he were granted that relief, its announcement would be "the joyfullest tidings that ever came to me." His petition to the council, like so many of Elizabeth's to him, was refused.

Increasingly frustrated and restive, Elizabeth decided it was to Mary that her petition must be made if she was ever to be freed from her captivity. At first Bedingfield refused to let her write to Mary, on the grounds that letters to the queen were among the contacts prohibited under the orders given him. At last she was allowed to write and was brought ink and paper to do so. (When Bedingfield permitted her to write a letter, she was given paper and ink, and when she had written it, he removed the remaining paper and ink so that she could write nothing else.) The letter to Mary does not survive, and so its words are not known, but they can be deduced from Mary's reply. Elizabeth evidently asserted anew her innocence and did so in a way that infuriated

Mary, who in response ordered that Elizabeth was not to write any more such "colourable letters" but instead spend time praying for God's grace. Dismissing Elizabeth's defensive arguments, Mary told her that she, Elizabeth, would be more believable if her declaration of innocence had "so well satisfied indifferent ears as it seemeth to satisfy . . . [Elizabeth's] own opinion." If Elizabeth had anything further to say to her, Mary wrote, she must communicate it through Bedingfield. Elizabeth was not permitted to see Mary's reply for herself, but instead it was read to her by Bedingfield, presumably on his knees.

In June 1554 Elizabeth fell ill once more, again with swelling on parts of her body. She wrote to the council asking that the queen's physicians come attend to her. She was told that couldn't be arranged and she should consult with a physician in Oxford instead. She angrily wrote back that "I am not minded to make any stranger privy to the state of my body, but commit it to God." Mary later had second thoughts about denying medical help to her and sent two of her doctors to see her. After examining her, they reported, "Her grace's body is replenished with many cold and waterish humours" and put her on a diet that seemed to help.

Growing desperate for a disposition of her case, Elizabeth on July 30, 1554, had Bedingfield write to the council members urging them to mediate with the queen to seek her freedom. She asked that she either be brought to trial or be allowed to come to the queen's court to exonerate herself. She told the councilors that she would not make such a proposal "were it not that she knoweth herself to be clear even before God for her allegiance." In case neither event were allowed, she begged that some of the council members come to Woodstock and talk with her so that "she may take a release not to think herself utterly desolate of all refuge in this world."[5] Her isolation and frustration were getting to her. But her plea for the councilors' attention would not help. Her letter went unanswered.

‑❊‑ 6. THE NEW SPANISH KING

On July 25, 1554, just five days before Elizabeth wrote her desperation letter, Mary had married Philip, and her mind then was not on her suspect sister. Once their honeymoon was over, though, at least one of the royal couple had thoughts of Elizabeth. Perhaps it was the news of Mary's pregnancy, announced in November 1554, that aroused them. Now more than ever Philip realized how old Mary was, and at a time when childbirth for any woman was known to be risky, at Mary's age it was downright dangerous. Her pregnancy could be a matter of life or death.

Never romantic in his feelings toward her, having married her only for political reasons, pragmatic Philip doubtless wondered how he and Spain would be affected by Mary's death. If the expected child survived, he or she would succeed to the throne, and Philip would expect to be named the child's regent, thus keeping England as his ally in Spain's continuing conflicts with France. But if the child also died, what then?

The baby supposedly was due sometime in April 1555. On April 17 Henry Bedingfield received orders to bring Elizabeth to Hampton Court, Mary's palace in London, freeing her at last from her confinement at Woodstock. The reason for her release isn't known for certain, but Philip is widely believed to have been the instigator. He had never been persuaded that eliminating Elizabeth was a good idea, for him or for Spain, despite whatever threat she might pose to Mary's reign. If she were executed, or removed from the line of succession, and if Mary died childless, the crown would pass to Mary Queen of Scots. Her Catholicism was in her favor, but her betrothal to the heir of the throne of France and French upbringing were bound to make England under her rule a partner with France in its competitions with Spain. Together England and France would control the English Channel, Spain's lifeline to the Netherlands, a disaster for Spain that Philip knew he absolutely must not allow to happen. Elizabeth might be a heretic, might even be guilty of conspiracy, but on the throne of England she would be far better for Philip and Spain than the French-sympathizing queen of Scots. Besides, if Mary's death in childbirth were to occur, news of it could destabilize the country, and in a political or religious turmoil, Philip wanted the sort of high-powered protection that Elizabeth, the heir apparent, could provide him while he resided in England.

Elizabeth's release from Woodstock certainly did not signal an acceptance by Mary of Elizabeth's persistent protestations of innocence, for after two weeks of ignoring her following her arrival at Hampton Court, Mary sent Stephen Gardiner and three other council members to see Elizabeth and attempt to induce her to make peace with the queen by confessing her complicity in Wyatt's plot. The queen would be good to her, they promised Elizabeth, if she would only admit her guilt. They, and Mary herself, still had not learned how resolute, how defiant, Elizabeth could be. Her answer to Gardiner was that she would lie in prison the rest of her life rather than declare she was guilty. Gardiner took her words back to Mary. The next day he went again to Elizabeth and told her that the queen was astonished that Elizabeth would persist in her claim that she was blameless. If she was indeed innocent, Gardiner pointed out, people would conclude that the queen had unjustly sent her to the Tower and had falsely kept her captive at Woodstock for a year, implying that even if she was innocent, she should say, for the queen's sake, that she was guilty. She would have to change her story, Gardiner told her, if she wanted to be given her freedom. "Then," Elizabeth shot back, "I had rather be in prison with honesty and truth than have my liberty and be suspected by her majesty. What I have said I will stand to. Nor will I ever speak falsehood!" Gardiner gave up at that point and left, locking her in her palace apartment once more. (Consistent in her denials, Elizabeth nevertheless at times did seem less than totally innocent, as when, shortly before she left Woodstock, she used the diamond in her ring to scratch these words on a windowpane: "Much suspected, by me, Nothing proved can be. Quoth Elizabeth, prisoner.")

A week after Gardiner's visit to her, Elizabeth was one night, at about ten o'clock, abruptly summoned to Mary's rooms and, in fear of what might await her, followed her escort through the palace's corridors by torchlight to be ushered into the queen's presence. It had been two years since the sisters had seen each other. Mary was not alone in her suite. Not only was Susan

Clarencieux, her favorite attendant, there, but hidden where Elizabeth could not see him was Philip, perhaps to monitor Mary's words, perhaps mostly to get a look at Elizabeth. Upon entering the chamber, Elizabeth slipped to her knees, prayed that God would preserve the queen, and asserted that Mary had no subject more loyal than she. Mary cut her off. "You will not confess your offense, but stand stoutly to your truth. I pray God it may so fall out," she told Elizabeth.

"If it doth not," Elizabeth answered, "I request neither favor nor pardon at your majesty's hands."

"Well, you stiffly still persevere in your truth," Mary told her. "Besides, you will not confess that you have not been wrongfully punished." (Mary was apparently sensitive to criticism that she had unjustly imprisoned Elizabeth.)

"I must not say so, if it please your majesty, to you."

"Why, then, belike you will to others."

"No," Elizabeth responded, "if it please your majesty. I have borne the burden and must bear it. I humbly beseech your majesty to have a good opinion of me and to think me to be your subject not only from the beginning hitherto but forever, as long as life lasteth." The meeting soon ended, with neither sister completely satisfied by the conversation, though they had apparently reached a reconciliation of some sort. Several weeks after that meeting with Mary, Elizabeth was given more freedom in Hampton Court, being allowed to attend court and to receive callers at her apartment, although most of the courtiers, not daring to risk the queen's displeasure, chose not to visit her. Among those who did come to see her, however, was Philip. Elizabeth later claimed she made a good impression on him. About the same time, her fellow suspect, Edward Courtenay, was exiled to the Continent, and Henry Bedingfield finally received what he had said would be "the joyfullest tidings," his discharge from his duties as Elizabeth's custodian.

By early May 1555 it had become obvious to Philip, and others, that Mary was not pregnant, that the signs of pregnancy she had exhibited were caused by something else, some unknown malady. Also by then Philip had taken a deeper interest in Elizabeth, becoming a repeat visitor. At age twenty-eight, Philip had developed a roving eye and had collected a great deal of experience with young women. Elizabeth, youthful, slender, shapely, with golden red hair and pale complexion, oval face and dark eyes, not beautiful but attractive, would have seemed to Philip a desirable, sweet young thing. And if something were to happen to Mary, Elizabeth would become queen, making her all the more attractive to him.

By the end of June, with no birth having occurred, it became generally known, within the palace and without, that there would be no new prince, or princess, that indeed the queen was not pregnant. Philip was one of the first to give up the idea that a child would be born to him and Mary. To his thinking, there was therefore no good reason for him to remain in England, which he did not enjoy. He was tired of hanging on in a land where, unlike in Spain and the rest of his father's dominions, he was less than lord, being in England a mere consort rather than a true king (which Parliament refused to make him). He started making plans to leave England—without Mary—to take care of business on the Continent. His father had announced he would begin abdicating his powers and titles in favor of Philip, and Philip needed to be with him for the expected occasions.

By early August, Queen Mary herself realized there would be no baby. She knew, too, that her husband would soon be gone, for just a few weeks, he guilefully told her. On August 26 Philip and Mary were carried, Mary in an open litter so that her sympathizing subjects could see her, in a regal procession that coursed through the streets of London to Tower Wharf. There they boarded the royal barge to be transported down the Thames to Greenwich, where Philip would embark on a sailing ship, bound for the Netherlands. With them in the stately procession to see Philip off was Elizabeth.

On August 29, the day of Philip's departure from Greenwich, Mary walked with him part of the way to the waiting ship in public view, managing to control her emotions and maintain her regal demeanor even as they parted, "constraining herself the whole way to avoid, in sight of such a crowd, any demonstration unbecoming her gravity,"[1] an eyewitness reported. Philip, on the other hand, seemed to enjoy himself as he kissed each of the queen's female attendants good-bye. Once he boarded the vessel and slipped out of sight, Mary returned to her royal apartment and in privacy sat at a window overlooking the river, weeping as she watched her husband's horses, baggage, and other belongings being loaded onto the ship. As the vessel left the wharf and began to glide downriver, Philip came up on the open deck, doffed his hat, and waved it, according to one account, in the direction of the royal apartment, from which Mary was watching. She saw him wave and lingered at the window until the ship at last disappeared from view down the Thames.

From Greenwich the vessel took Philip and his entourage to Sitting-bourne, where the travelers spent the night, then to Canterbury for another night's stay, and then to Dover, where they waited five days for a favorable wind and an escort of Flemish ships to make the channel crossing. During the wait, Mary sent him letters, carried on horseback, and by return riders he dispatched his replies to her. On September 4, the ship bearing Philip and his companions finally sailed into the channel and made it to Calais in three hours. Philip then wrote Mary again, telling her about his swift voyage and safe arrival. After that, his letters to her became fewer and farther between, although she wrote to him every day. He was finding other matters to occupy his thoughts and time.

On September 8 he was greeted in Brussels by his tearful, ailing father. Six weeks later, on October 22, in accordance with Charles's schedule of divesti-ture, Philip was installed to succeed his father as commander of the Order of the Golden Fleece, the prestigious order of knighthood that had become the symbol of influence in Burgundian society. To climax his relinquishment of power, on the afternoon of October 25, 1555, Charles staged a ceremony marked by pomp and emotion, held in the Great Hall of the Brussels palace. There he would publicly renounce his lordship over the Netherlands and cede his authority to Philip.

Charles was now fifty-five years old, slightly bent, his hair and beard gray, and as he walked to the platform in the Great Hall to take his seat, he sup-ported himself with a staff in one hand and his other hand resting on the arm of William of Orange. He was obviously a man of spent vigor and failing health. Once Charles was seated on his throne on the platform, Philip at his right and his sister Mary, his regent, at his left, the presiding officer of the nation's council rose and addressed the host of dignitaries and leaders in at-tendance at this solemn event. He gave them the emperor's reasons for ab-dicating and enjoined them to confer upon Philip, the emperor's lawful heir, the same allegiance they had sworn to Charles. After a pause in the proceed-ings, Charles rose and stood, with difficulty, bracing himself with his right hand on the shoulder of Prince William. In his left hand he held a sheet of pa-per on which were written notes of the remarks he wished to make. He put on his glasses and looked at his notes, then lifted his head to cast his eyes on his audience and began to speak.

He told his listeners, in French, that he could not leave them without first speaking to them in person. He said it had been forty years since he had become lord of the Netherlands, the land of his birth, and since then he had also become ruler of an empire that included Spain and Germany. It was a heavy responsibility, he said, particularly for one as young as he was at the time. But, he said, he had always earnestly tried to fulfill his responsibility to the best of his ability. He had always kept the interests of his countrymen in mind, but he had placed foremost in his thoughts and purposes the cause of Christianity, which he had striven to serve and defend against the onslaughts of infidels and heretics. It was a struggle, he confessed, in which he had not always been successful. His summary of his travels gave his listeners an idea of the wear and tear he had suffered: "I have been nine times to Germany, six times to Spain, and seven to Italy. I have come here to Flanders ten times and have been four to France in war and peace, twice to England and twice to Africa . . . without mentioning other lesser journeys. I have made eight voyages in the Mediterranean and three in the seas of Spain, and soon I shall make the fourth voyage when I return there to be buried."[2]

His failing health, he told his listeners, had deprived him of his ability to continue in his tasks as ruler and so it was necessary for him to pass his duties to his son. He concluded his remarks by asking for understanding and forgiveness. "I know well," he said, "that in my long administration I have fallen into many errors and committed some wrongs, but it was from ignorance. And if there be any here whom I have wronged, they will believe that it was not intended and grant me their forgiveness."

The audience of nobles and influentials sat rapt and silent, tears coursing down their faces as they heard his words. The English ambassador, who was in the audience, later commented that there was "not one man in the whole assemblie . . . that poured not oute abundantly teares." The moment of emotion reached Charles also, and he wept as he turned to Philip, standing respectfully near him, and asked him to kneel. He took Philip's hand and embraced him, then placed his hands on Philip's head and blessed him, as if in a scene from the Old Testament. He then delivered a solemn charge to Philip:

> If the vast possessions which are now bestowed on you had come by inheritance, there would be abundant cause for gratitude. How much more, when they come as a free gift in the lifetime of your father! But however large the debt, I shall consider it all repaid if

you only discharge your duty to your subjects. So rule over them, that men shall commend and not censure me for the part I am now acting. Go on as you have begun. Fear God. Live justly. Respect the laws. Above all, cherish the interests of religion. And may the Almighty bless you with a son, to whom, when old and stricken with disease, you may be able to resign your kingdom with the same good will with which I now resign mine to you.[3]

Charles then tugged Philip to his feet and, as the two men stood facing each other, Charles hugged his son, tears streaming from the eyes of both. Then, exhausted, Charles turned and sank into his seat, his eyes on his audience, his lips pronouncing his benediction—"God bless you! God bless you!"

Philip, in Spanish, thanked his father and then used his limited French to say that he was sorry he could not say all he wanted to in their language, but that he would have a spokesman speak for him. It may have been at that point that the people of his Netherlands audience realized for the first time, as one account has it, that their country had passed into foreign hands. Philip's spokesman was Antoine Perrenot de Granvelle, the bishop of Arras, who in fluent French gave the Netherlanders Philip's assurance that he would respect the laws and traditions of the country, and he called on the assembled nobles to assist him by giving him their counsel and by upholding lawful authority in their domains. Following an appropriate response from the audience, Charles's sister Mary then formally abdicated as regent (to be succeeded by a governor, Emmanuel Philibert, the duke of Savoy, an appointment made by Charles), and shortly thereafter the historic convocation came to a close. Philip was now sovereign of the Netherlands, duly installed.

Three months later, on January 16, 1556, much less publicly and with little or no ado, Charles abdicated his sovereignty over Spain and its dominions around the world, turning over to Philip the documents that transferred possession to him as perfunctorily as if he were giving him a real estate deed. Charles later also transferred to Philip authority over the Holy Roman Empire territories in Italy, and on February 5 he gave to Philip the Franche-Comté, a vital part of the duchy of Burgundy. On March 28, in Valladolid, while he was still in Brussels, Philip was proclaimed king of Spain. Now he was king of Naples and Sicily, duke of Milan, lord of the Franche-Comté and the Netherlands, king of England and king of Spain as well. His possessions included the Cape Verde Islands and the Canary Islands off the West African coast, Tunis and Oran on the North African coast, the Philippine Islands and the Spice Islands in Asia, and Mexico and Peru and territories in the West Indies in the Americas. He was, in fact, at age twenty-nine, master of the vastest, most far-reaching empire in the world.

There was one last abdication for Charles to execute, his resignation of sovereignty over Germany, which he would do in favor of his brother Ferdinand. At Ferdinand's request, Charles would put off that act for several months, keeping the title of emperor temporarily although actual power rested with Ferdinand. On August 28, 1556, Charles took his leave of Philip in Brussels and on September 16, accompanied by some 150 attendants selected from the 762 members of his imperial household, he sailed from the port of Flushing, he and his retinue borne in a fleet of fifty-six vessels. When the fleet reached Laredo, on the Bay of Biscay, Charles, suffering from gout, disembarked with his party and began an overland journey to Burgos, then to Torquemada, then to Valladolid, royally greeted and hailed as the procession made its way through the countryside. After a prolonged stay in Valladolid, overcoming the gout and regaining strength while he enjoyed the hospitality of his daughter Juana, Philip's regent in Spain, Charles finally set out on the last leg of his journey to the Jeronimite monastery at Yuste, stopping for a three-month stay at Jarandilla until renovations were completed on the building that was to house him. He arrived in February 1557 at the monastery, an ancient edifice surrounded by lush gardens and groves of orange and lemon trees, set against a backdrop of rocky hills from which cascaded streams of cool, clear water. There, in the midst of this beauty, he would retire to a life of peace and live out his remaining days restfully, rid of the cares of government and power.

Of the enemies that Charles had made over the years of his rule, probably none was more intense in his hatred of him that Gian Pietro Carafa, member of a noble family from Naples, one of Spain's Italian possessions. When young, Carafa had been drawn, or led by his family, to an ecclesiastical career, and his prodigious abilities as scholar, public speaker, and linguist had launched him upward in the church's administrative hierarchy. In 1513, when he was thirty-six years old, he was sent to England as papal nuncio, the pope's spokesman. In 1525, when he was forty-eight, he resigned his official appointments and founded a religious order, the Theatins, whose members devoted themselves both to the ascetic rigors of monasticism and to the pastoral duties of the priesthood and were especially zealous about instituting reform among Catholic clergy and combating the growing threat of Protestantism. In 1536, at age fifty-nine, Carafa was made a cardinal by Pope Paul III, who had become his patron.

Carafa was also a longtime member of the royal council of Naples, serving at Charles's pleasure. That pleasure ended when Carafa began lobbying the pope to assert papal claims to the sovereignty of Naples, pitting the interests of the church—and the Carafa family's nationalistic sympathies—against the interests of Spain. In reaction, Charles dismissed Carafa from the Naples council. Later, when Paul III proposed appointing Carafa archbishop of Naples, Charles opposed the appointment, though in vain. Those affronts, and others, engendered in Carafa, by nature arrogant, hot-tempered, and resentful, a deep and lasting hatred of Charles, which only exacerbated his fierce desire to drive Spain out of Italy.

In May 1555, following the death of Pope Marcellus II (who lived only three weeks after being named pope), the church's College of Cardinals, despite Philip's interference aimed at blocking Carafa's election, chose Carafa to be the new pope. As pope, Carafa took the name Paul IV. The cardinals were perhaps looking for a reformer, and Carafa met the requirement, though he lacked some of the graces ordinarily associated with the office of pope. In any case, the cardinals probably figured that at age seventy-nine, Carafa would not be around long enough to cause major harm. They were mistaken. His elevation to pope seemed to invigorate him, energizing him to indulge his old animosities. "The pope is a man of iron," the ambassador from Florence to the Vatican remarked, "and the very stones over which he walks emit sparks." His first objective as pope was to free Italy from Spain and the emperor, as he had long dreamed of doing. He let loose an irrational, vituperative attack on Charles, calling him a secret atheist, a lunatic son of a lunatic mother, a "cripple in body and soul." He called the people of Spain Semitic scum. He swore he would never recognize Philip as ruler of Milan. In December 1555 he entered into an alliance with King Henry II of France to drive from Italy all Spanish and imperial forces. When that goal was accomplished, the papacy was to acquire Siena, and France was to acquire Milan and hold Naples as a fief under the papacy, with two of King Henry's sons being granted lordships over the two territories. What Carafa could not attempt against Charles he planned to execute against Charles's son.

Philip was faced with a dangerous dilemma. He would either acquiesce to the pope's aggression and give up territory, or else make war on the papacy, an unthinkable act for so staunch a defender of Catholicism as Philip was. He decided not to acquiesce. "I am determined to maintain all my realms," he declared. He saw the pope's plan of aggression as a challenge to him personally, as an insult to his character, and he promised that he would wage war on the pope and the French king "for the sake of undeceiving the world, and especially his enemies, with regard to their opinion of his being cowardly and spiritless."

His first act of retaliation was to convene an assembly of theologians and legal experts and ask them to give him answers to several questions. He wanted their considered opinion on, among things, (1) whether, in the event of a defensive war with the pope, it would be perfectly lawful for him, Philip, to seize the revenues of persons who had benefices in Spain but who refused to obey him; (2) whether he could impose such restrictions on the church's Spanish revenues that would prohibit any money being sent from Spain to Rome; (3) whether a council might be called to determine the validity of Carafa's election as pope, which already had come under question; and (4) whether an investigation might be made into the gross abuses of papal patronage—Carafa's flagrant nepotism, for example, in appointing two unqualified nephews to high office, one becoming a duke and the other a cardinal—and what measures might be taken to redress those abuses. The conclave of legal and theological authorities came up with, as expected, a set of answers all favoring the king of Spain. Philip had sent a warning shot across the pope's bow.

Now armed with legality and righteousness, Philip next sent orders to the duke of Alba, his viceroy in Naples and his most effective general. Prepare to defend Naples, Philip told Alba. Alba was already prepared, having mustered an army of twelve thousand infantry and fifteen hundred cavalry, supported by twelve pieces of artillery. Most of his force was drawn from Naples, but its backbone, about a third of its strength, was battle-hardened Spanish veterans. To absolve himself from making war on the pope, and possibly to give the pope a chance to back down, Alba wrote to Paul IV and the church's cardinals detailing his sovereign's grievances, describing the horrors of war, blaming the pope for inflicting them on the country, and saying, in effect, that he—Alba—was bound to follow his sovereign's orders. He had been placed in Italy to maintain his sovereign's possessions, Alba wrote, and by God, he would maintain them. Alba dispatched his letter to the Vatican by special messenger, a respected citizen of Naples, and when the pope received the letter, infuriated, he had the messenger thrown into prison and tortured. Meanwhile Alba attempted to effect a peace between the pope and Philip through the good offices of the government of Venice.

On September 1, 1556, accompanied by a detail of cavalry, Alba left the city of Naples and three days later joined his waiting army at San Germano, on the kingdom's northern frontier. He was not going to wait for the pope's troops to make the first move. The next day, September 5, he led his army across the border and marched on Pontecorvo, whose citizens opened the city's gates to admit him. From Pontecorvo he marched into one town after another, meeting no resistance, and in the major church of each town he had a notice nailed up, along with an escutcheon of the College of Cardinals, declaring that he was holding the town in the name of the college until a new pope was elected.

At the town of Anagni, walled and fortified, Alba met his first resistance. Its officials refused to surrender the town. For three days Alba's artillery pounded the town's walls until a breach was blasted out. His troops then stormed through the breach and overwhelmed the town, sacking it and slaughtering its inhabitants. The few other towns that resisted were similarly wasted. At each of the towns he captured, Alba left a small garrison to hold it, then with his remaining force marched on Tivoli, situated on high ground that commanded the eastern approaches to Rome. The city surrendered without a fight, and there Alba established a headquarters. In Rome, word of Alba's successes and his devastation of resisting towns set off a shock wave of terror. Panicked citizens fled the city to escape what they believed might be an imminent assault on it.

The pope, however, was not panicked. On receiving news of the sacking of Anagni, he made a public show of continuing with his business of the morning as if the town's destruction were nothing to concern him. Privately, though, he let loose his explosive temper on his visitors that day, one of whom was the representative from Venice who came seeking a way to make peace with Philip—and Alba. He haughtily told the Venetian envoy that if the Spanish wanted peace, Alba would have to withdraw across the frontier he had just invaded and then make a petition to the pope as any respectful child of the church would do. To two Frenchmen who, the pope supposed, had also come to propose peace he became bellicose and threatening. "Whoever would bring me into a peace with heretics is a servant of the devil. Heaven will take vengeance on him," he ranted. "I will pray God's curse may fall on him. If I find that you intermeddle in any such matter, I will cut your heads off your shoulders. Do not think this an empty threat. I have an eye in my back [an old Italian expression] on you and if I find you playing me false, or attempting to entangle me a second time in an accursed truce, I swear to you by the eternal God, I will make your heads fly from your shoulders, come what may come of it!"[4]

"In this way his holiness continued for nearly an hour," one of the two French dignitaries reported, "walking up and down the apartment and talking all the while of his own grievances and of cutting off our heads, until he had talked himself quite out of breath."

The pope did more than talk. He ordered Rome's defenses strengthened, imposed a tax to raise funds to pay the troops who would defend the city, called into the city the garrisons of nearby towns, organized a bodyguard of six hundred or more cavalry, and called out and equipped a levy of some six thousand infantry to oppose Alba's army. He then staged a review of his troops, splendidly uniformed as they passed his palace and received his blessing. Also among his force of defenders was a contingent of German Lutheran mercenaries, heretics hired by the papacy to fight Spanish Catholics on its behalf.

Alba, meanwhile, already commanding the eastern routes into Rome, moved his force across the Campagna, south of the city, and marched on the seaport town of Ostia to seize it and cut off Rome's communications with the coast, denying the city supplies from either direction. He reached Ostia in early November 1556 and placed his troops beside the Tiber River, where it divides into two branches. Ostia was protected by a formidable citadel, to which Alba prepared to lay siege after passing over a bridge that his troops built on captured boats. Once his heavy guns were in place, he opened fire on Ostia's fortifications and was answered by fire from the fortress. On November 17, his ammunition and his supplies running low, he decided to storm the citadel. On the morning of November 18, he sent a first wave of attackers to scale the town's walls. They were repulsed with heavy losses, and so a second assault, by Spanish infantry, was launched. Those attackers made it over the ramparts but were met by a fierce force of defenders inside the town. His losses mounting, Alba called a retreat as darkness set in. Two days later, while Alba's troops still lay before the town's walls, Ostia's beleaguered defenders, exhausted and hungry, surrendered. Rome was now without supply from east or west.

From the north the pope received word that his French allies were on their way. All he had to do now was stall Alba long enough to give the advancing French army, commanded by the duke of Guise, time to arrive and effect Rome's rescue. The pope's nephew, Cardinal Carafa, came to see Alba about a truce. To Alba a truce seemed a good idea (although Charles later criticized him for accepting it and not pressing the attack). He was not keen on fighting Guise's fresh troops with a force weakened by casualties and the fatigue of successive battles. He agreed to a forty-day cease-fire that let him keep the territory he had conquered, and he marched his army back across the frontier, back to the city of Naples.

Guise's army was composed of twelve thousand infantry and two thousand cavalry and included twelve artillery pieces. It left Paris and marched toward Rome without opposition. Guise's objective was Naples, and the pope urged him to speed his way to it. Guise's Italian father-in-law, however, the duke of Ferrara, commanding some six thousand Italian troops that were intended to reinforce Guise's army, argued with his son-in-law against proceeding south to Naples without first securing Spanish-held Milan in the north. When Guise refused Ferrara's pleading, Ferrara pulled his troops out of Guise's force, saying he needed them to protect his holdings against a possible attack from Milan. Guise proceeded down the Adriatic coast, passing through Ravenna and Rimini, then turning inland and stopping at Jesi, where he encamped his army while he went off to Rome to confer with the pope.

From the French army's presence Paul IV took new courage and renewed the war on Spain. His Roman troops attacked the towns where Alba had left only a weak garrison and quickly retook them, including Tivoli and Ostia. Guise and his army, according to the plan worked out by Guise and the pope, immediately marched across Naples's frontier and began the campaign against Alba by capturing the rich town of Campli, which they looted and burned after slaughtering all who resisted. From Campli, Guise's army marched on Civitella, a strategic hilltop town garrisoned by twelve hundred of Alba's men. There Guise laid siege to the fortified town, emplaced four of his big guns, and began bombarding the town's walls. The Spanish garrison promptly returned fire with its guns, inflicting considerable casualties on the French, who lay exposed in the field outside the town. When the French cannonades had at last breached the wall, Guise ordered a mass assault on the town, which was repulsed. Guise launched repeated assaults, all of them defeated as the town's women, fighting beside their husbands and brothers, helped turn back the French attackers. The besiegers and the besieged had reached an impasse, which stretched into many days, the French troops growing restive and Guise himself disgruntled and openly critical over the pope's failure to provide the promised men, ammunition, supplies, and money.

While the French lay before Civitella in northern Naples, Alba was in southern Naples, recruiting a new army that grew to some twenty-five thousand men. On April 11, 1557, he led his army out of the city of Naples, marching northward, reaching the town of Giulianova and seizing it from its French garrison. At the news of Alba's approach, Guise tried one more massive assault on the ramparts of Civitella and once more was repulsed, the town's defenders continuing to harass the French even as they gave up the siege and withdrew after having spent twenty-two days trying to take the town. As Alba moved closer to Guise's position, Guise promptly retreated with his entire army, crossing the Tronto River and moving out of the kingdom of Naples. Alba also crossed the Tronto and took a position not far from Ascoli, where the French were encamped.

When the town of Segni was besieged by an Italian force commanded by Philip's Italian ally, Marcantonio Colonna, the pope became alarmed enough to order Guise to fall back to Rome to protect it, and Guise withdrew his army to Tivoli, where he set up a headquarters. And when Segni at last fell, setting off a frenzy of plundering, rape, murder, and arson by the victors—as was the custom of the times—the pope went nearly wild with helpless fury. "They have taken Segni!" he exclaimed to his cardinals. "They have murdered the people, destroyed their property, fired their dwellings! Worse than this, they will next pillage Palliano. Even this will not fill up the measure of their cruelty. They will sack the city of Rome itself! Nor will they respect even my person! But, for myself, I long to be with Christ and await without fear the crown of martyrdom!"[5]

Alba marched his army to the town of Colona, in the Campagna, and encamped there. He then prepared a plan the objective of which is now unclear.

On the night of August 26, 1557, he led his troops toward Rome in a driving rain and halted in a field not far from the city. From there he sent out a patrol to reconnoiter the city, which lay quiet in the darkness. Suddenly, however, as the patrol drew nearer to the city walls, a great light appeared from within, like the illumination from many torches, and shortly after that, several horsemen emerged through the gates and rode off in the direction of the French army's camp at Tivoli. When he received that intelligence, Alba canceled his plan and withdrew his troops back to Colona, having concluded that his army had been spotted and Guise's army was being summoned to come to the city's aid, which could place Alba's men between two enemy forces.

Within the walls of Rome, the realization of the proximity of Alba's army set off a storm surge of consternation the next morning. The pope was beset with pleas and demands that he sue for peace, lest Rome and its citizens suffer the fact the Spanish army had already inflicted on neighboring towns. To make matters worse, the duke of Guise rode to the Vatican to tell Paul IV that he and his army were, on the command of Henry II, leaving immediately to return to France to protect Paris. The pope spitefully responded, "Go, then, and take with you the consciousness of having done little for your king, still less for the church and nothing for your own honor." Now, however, the pope would have to eat some crow.

Terms were worked out by Paul's nephew, Cardinal Carafa, and Alba at the town of Cavi, subject to the approval of Philip and the pope. The agreement included some stipulations objectionable to Alba but acceptable to Philip, who apparently was more eager than the pope to effect peace with the church. The worst was the requirement that Alba publicly ask the pope's pardon and receive absolution for having made war against the papacy, a provision on which the pope was unyielding, despite the weakness of his military position. "Sooner than surrender this point," he declared, "I would see the whole world perish—and this not so much for my own sake as for the honor of Jesus Christ."[6]

Philip caved in on that demand, causing Alba to remark that the peace treaty "seemed to have been dictated by the vanquished rather than by the victor. Were I the king, his holiness should send one of his nephews to Brussels [where Philip then was] to sue for my pardon, instead of my general's suing for his."

On September 27, 1557, the faithful Alba rode into Rome, where he was joined by an escort of colorfully uniformed papal guards and other Roman troops and led to the Vatican through streets thronged with well-wishing spectators. At the Vatican, Alba knelt before Paul IV and asked forgiveness for taking up arms against the church. The pope unhesitatingly granted him absolution and invited him to join him at his table.

Philip's war with the pope thus came to an end. He had let his best general be humiliated to gain peace with the church, but in waging war on the papacy to protect his domain, the new Spanish king and sovereign of Spain's far-flung territories had vigorously made a case for himself. He had let the world powers know that, as his father's successor, he would be no pushover.

7. THE END
OF REIGN

In March 1557, six months after the duke of Alba launched his campaign against the papacy on Philip's orders, Philip set out from the Netherlands to return to England. He would be returning also to Queen Mary, his wife, whom he had not seen since August 1555 and who longed for him to come back to her. She was not doing well. She continued to struggle with her illness but managed to marshal her strength each day to meet her responsibilities as queen and preserve her well-known piety. She had established a routine of praying in the morning, attending to government business in the afternoon, and writing long letters to her absent husband in the evening. Cardinal Reginald Pole, the archbishop of Canterbury, in a letter to Philip, using an allusion from Luke's gospel, reported that the queen passed her mornings "after the manner of Mary and in the afternoon admirably personates Martha by transacting business." Pole also told Philip that what the queen really needed to cure her illness was Philip's return. In her letters Mary told him the same thing, at times despairing that she would ever see him again.

What was bringing Philip back to England, however, was not his wife but his war with France. When France's King Henry II broke the peace treaty with Spain and sent the duke of Guise and his army across the Alps to help the pope run the Spaniards out of Italy, Philip, reacting with survival instincts, immediately ordered his troops in the north to assemble to defend the Netherlands and punish France by invading adjacent French territory. To help ensure success against the French, Philip wanted England to send troops across the channel to reinforce his army. Besides that, he wanted England to formally declare war on France and enter the conflict on his side. Getting the English to do so, he knew, would not be easy, particularly since English government leaders had foreseen the possibility of a Spanish effort to engage England in Spain's conflicts with France and had written into Mary and Philip's prenuptial agreement a provision that prohibited the very thing that Philip now sought. He would try anyway. Mary had written him that if he were to come and appear before her council in person, the council would grant him the war aid he desired.

From his palace in Brussels, Philip remained deeply involved in England's affairs. He stayed in contact with members of the queen's council and had the minutes of the council's meetings sent to him. He read them, made copious comments in the margins, and sent them back to the councilmen for them to act on his remarks. Once he even went so far as to demand that no important matter be taken to Parliament before the council submitted it to him. When Mary's chancellor, Stephen Gardiner, died in November 1555, Philip presumptuously wrote to Mary that she could appoint anyone she felt like to succeed him. For a long while Philip continued to harbor hopes that Parliament would crown him king, and when Mary let him know that was not going to happen, he suggested that she go over Parliament's head and make him king herself. She demurred.

Also from Brussels Philip had kept Mary informed about his war with the pope and France, giving her detailed accounts of Alba's actions. She seemed to come alive with his new burst of correspondence that reported on the war. She wrote back, sending him whatever information she had about the French. She reported on the meetings she was having with her council to implore its members to give Philip aid. She sent him money to help finance the war and promised naval support. In January 1557 the queen's council finally agreed to provide Philip with the six thousand infantry and six hundred cavalry that England was by treaty obligated to provide the Netherlands if attacked by France.

Philip left Brussels on March 8, 1557, traveling overland to Calais, which he reached, after several stops, on March 18. He immediately boarded a ship and crossed the channel, landing at Dover that evening. The next day he rode to Greenwich, where his jubilant wife waited to greet him. They arrived in London on March 23, escorted by the nation's nobles, hailed by pealing church bells and the booming salutes of the Tower's cannons, and officially welcomed by London's lord mayor and aldermen. Philip was back, and the city made a show of seeming glad to have him, as Mary was indeed.

To those who saw her up close, it was obvious that Mary was losing ground in her battle with her disease. At age forty-one she suffered depression, including lengthy spells of crying, and was frequently bled by her doctors, leaving her pale and emaciated. She had lost weight, and her face was drawn, with dark circles beneath her eyes. Her overall health was poor, and she was bothered by aching teeth and sleeplessness.

Philip, too, had changed. Now thirty years old, he was looking more like his father and acting more like him as well, in his habits and imperial lifestyle. He had become notorious for late-night partying and womanizing but had also gained a reputation as a grind in his daily attendance to his administrative duties. He had developed wrinkles in his brow and a slouch in his posture and no longer seemed as dashing as he once had. His odd eating habits had apparently caught up with him, too, for he suffered from attacks of indigestion and bowel troubles. Like Mary, he was beginning to seem old before his time.

Philip and Mary's reunion, which might have become a second honeymoon, got off to a poor start. She had a bad cold and a toothache, and he was still trying to recover from some sort of illness that he had acquired before leaving Brussels. On top of those difficulties, there were the two young women that Philip had brought with him. One was his sister, the duchess of Parma, and the other was his cousin, the duchess of Lorraine, who according to rumors was actually his mistress. Nevertheless, Mary and Philip went through with the banquets and dances that she had arranged to entertain him, and after several weeks the cousin departed, forced away by Mary, some said. Philip's sister stayed till early May and left complaining about how boring her stay in England was.

Not much time was wasted in getting to the point of Philip's visit. Mary called in the chief members of her council and made a speech to them about the French menace that England faced. If France succeeded against Spain, England would become a future target, she warned them. They needed to act now, providing troops and money and issuing a declaration of war against France, or else face a more serious situation later. She spoke with eloquence and reasoned arguments, according to an eyewitness, but failed to move the councilmen. They steadfastly opposed war with France, claiming that "their intention and their duty was to have no respect either for king or for queen, but solely for the public good of the kingdom."[1] Mary would have to try a different tactic.

As she continued to urge approval of the aid Philip sought, the councilmen did offer more funds and troops but would not okay the declaration of war. At the end of her patience—but not her resourcefulness—Mary threatened a wholesale dismissal of the council members and then summoned each member to appear before her, one at a time, and intimidated them into submission. Some she threatened with execution, some with forfeiture of their estates. Finally, with a further impetus provided by a failed revolt against Mary in the north of England, launched from France, the council members gave in. The declaration of war against France was issued on June 7, 1557.

Under an old international protocol, Mary dispatched an official herald, William Flower, to deliver the declaration of war to the French king, who was then at Reims. One account has it that on receiving the declaration, King Henry was urged to immediately hang Flower in protest. Henry, however, was more forgiving, hinting that he knew it was Philip, not Queen Mary, who was sending England into war. He dismissed Flower, telling him to leave France as quickly as he could.

Philip stayed on in England while he waited for the arrival of the troops he had ordered brought to the Netherlands from Spain, Mary enjoying his company while she was also engaged in preparations for the conflict with France. When at last Philip received reports that a Spanish fleet had entered the channel, presumably bearing the expected troops, he started making arrangements for his departure. When he left, Mary went with him part of the way to Dover, bidding him good-bye at Sittingbourne, where they spent the night, before he rode off for Canterbury and then on to Dover. Shortly before dawn on July 6, 1557, his ship sailed from Dover, bound for Calais. He would never see England or Mary again.

Once back in Brussels, Philip engrossed himself in the logistics of his war with France. He assumed not only the role of commander in chief but also of paymaster and, to some extent, quartermaster. He helped plan strategy with his generals, oversaw the movements of his troops and their supplies, and hired German mercenaries to bolster his army, which grew to some forty-eight thousand men. Germans accounted for about 53 percent of his force, Spaniards only about 12 percent. Twenty-three percent of his troops were from the Netherlands, and 12 percent were English. The German mercenaries were not all infantry. Many were the shock troops of their time, mounted schwarzreiters—black riders—each of whom carried five or six pistols in his belt and was protected by a cuirass, a vestlike piece of armor that extended from neck to waist. Schwarzreiters were superbly drilled in the execution of cavalry maneuvers and, with the firepower provided by their pistols, could sweep through the enemy with the effectiveness of modern light tanks. They were, according to one source, the most dreaded troops of their day.

Unlike his father, Philip did not see himself as a field general but as more of a strategist and planner. He entrusted field operations to handpicked commanders, such as the duke of Alba. To command this army of the north he appointed his cousin, Emmanuel Philibert, the duke of Savoy. Savoy was only twenty-nine years old but was already an experienced commander, having proved himself in combat under Charles V. His military ability recommended him for the job, but Savoy was especially suited for this command because of his desire to defeat the French and recover the domains that France had earlier taken from him.

In overall command of French troops was the constable (commander in chief) of France's armies, the sixty-four-year old Anne de Montmorency. Serving under him on the Netherlands front was, among other officers, the duke of Nevers, governor of the French province of Champagne. Montmorency's force totaled about eighteen thousand infantry and six thousand cavalry, plus artillery consisting of sixteen guns. The French had been keeping a watchful eye on the buildup of Philip's forces and had positioned troops at several places in Picardy and Champagne, provinces on France's frontier with the Netherlands.

Philip and his war council decided to besiege and take a key city near the northern border of Picardy, giving Philip's forces command of a main entry point into the Netherlands and into France. The first choice was the town of Rocroi, but the garrison there proved so strong and apparently so well supplied that Savoy decided its capture was not worth the effort or cost and that he should look for an easier target. On receiving Savoy's report, Philip convened his war council, then wrote to Savoy: "Taking into account all opinions, and the difficulties that you say exist over Rocroi, and the debates that we have had here, it was decided that the most convenient and suitable move is to invest St.-Quentin." The new target was an old town on Picardy's northern frontier, known chiefly as a point of deposit for goods traded between France and the Netherlands during peaceful times. It was strategically situated to bar a French advance into the Netherlands and to provide an invading army a clear route for a march on Paris, about seventy miles to the southwest. The town was protected by its fortifications, the masonry wall of which had begun to deteriorate, and by its natural setting, standing as it does on an eminence flanked on one side by an extensive swamp through which courses a branch of the River Somme. A wide fosse, above which rose a row of houses, helped protect the town's outer wall.

So that the French would not immediately realize that St.-Quentin was his objective, Savoy in late July made a feint at the nearby town of Guise, east of St.-Quentin, temporarily laying siege to it. He then quickly withdrew and marched on St.-Quentin. The governor of Picardy was Gaspard de Coligny, admiral of France and an experienced military commander. Seeing that Savoy's true objective was St.-Quentin, not Guise, Coligny swiftly gathered a force of some twelve hundred men, infantry and cavalry, and set out to race Savoy to the town to defend it. Coligny reached St.-Quentin ahead of Savoy, although his force had somehow been reduced to but seven hundred men by the time he entered the town's walls. Not long after Coligny's arrival, Savoy reached St.-Quentin and invested it with all the troops then at his command.

Philip, itching to be close to the action, moved from Brussels to Cambrai, about twenty-five miles north of St.-Quentin, arriving at the end of July; then, as a matter of courtesy, he waited there for the English troops to arrive before going with them to St.-Quentin. Anxious that the fighting would start before he could get there, he told Savoy in a note, "If there is no way to avoid an engagement before I arrive, I cannot enjoin you too strongly to inform me post haste, so as to give me the means and opportunity to arrive in time [to avoid missing the action]. . . . I beg you to have spare horses waiting day and night to be able to inform me." While Philip waited, he learned on August 9 that Montmorency's army was on the march, although its precise location was unknown. Philip decided to stay put until the French force could be located, lest he stumble into it.

From St.-Quentin, Coligny had sent a dispatch to Montmorency telling him that unless help came, he could not withstand the siege more than a few days. Montmorency resolved to relieve St.-Quentin's beleaguered defenders. Savoy's besieging army lay in a broad expanse between the river and the walls of the town, and Montmorency proposed to send a force in daylight across the river in small boats to attack Savoy's position. At nine o'clock on the morning of August 10, 1557, after managing to slip undetected into position on the riverbank, Montmorency launched his assault.

Savoy's army was encamped in tents and pavilions encircling the town, spread out as far as the eye could see, its banners stirred by the morning breeze. Suddenly Montmorency's artillery opened fire on Savoy's position, volleys of shot tearing through the encampment, one shot smashing into Savoy's own tent and sending the duke fleeing with his armor in his hands. He immediately ordered the position abandoned and swiftly moved his troops three miles downriver, to where his cavalry commander, Count Egmont, was encamped with his troopers.

The ground opposite him now cleared of the enemy, Montmorency ordered his troops to cross the river, a task not readily accomplished. It took two hours to round up several small boats, not nearly enough to quickly move his men across, thus necessitating many trips back and forth across the river to ferry his men. The overloaded boats repeatedly grounded in the soft mud off the bank on the far side of the river, and when some of the soldiers jumped from the boats to lighten them, they sank into the mire and disappeared beneath its surface. Meanwhile, a contingent of Spanish harquebusiers kept up a steady fire on the French troops from a rise that overlooked the crossing site.

On reaching Egmont's position, Savoy called a war council with his top officers to plan an attack on Montmorency, now occupying the area just evacuated by Savoy. Egmont was to take his cavalry and immediately engage Montmorency's troops before they had time to move from their position in the open field. The body of Savoy's army, mainly infantry, taking more time to reach the French position, would advance behind the cavalry and attack Montmorency's army with full force.

Eager for glory, the thirty-five-year-old Egmont, another who had proved himself in battle under Charles V (and who had been appointed governor of Flanders), decided not to wait for the infantry. The main body of Montmorency's force, Egmont discovered as he neared St.-Quentin, was already on the move, retreating toward La Fère, southeast of St.-Quentin, and Egmont worried that it would escape. He and his cavalrymen took off after the French column in hot pursuit. Late in the day, as he topped a hill, Egmont caught sight of the rear units of Montmorency's army, which was joined in its flight by a host of sutlers and other camp followers who, when they spotted Egmont's cavalry behind them, panicked and set off a loud commotion. Montmorency, at the head of his column, reacting to the disturbance at the rear, turned and saw for himself the imposing force of horsemen at his back.

He was caught, and there was nothing to do but have his army face about and take positions to defend itself.

Egmont formed his force into three divisions. One was to turn the left flank of Montmorency's line. The second, made up mainly of Germans, was to strike the center. The third, which Egmont would personally command, would attack Montmorency's right. Once the divisions were in position, Egmont gave the order to charge. His cavalry went pounding forward, lancers, swordsmen, and *schwarzreiters,* sweeping through the French cavalry formation and scattering it. The gallant old Montmorency, however, in the thick of the fighting with his troops, managed to rally them and to countercharge, turning the apparent rout into a vigorous pitched battle that waged back and forth until Savoy's reinforcements, both infantry and cavalry, arrived to present an overwhelming force. Confronted by dauntingly superior numbers, the French chevaliers at last gave ground, and their lines burst, precipitating their headlong flight in all directions in an effort to escape while closely pursued by *schwarzreiters.* The French infantry had formed itself into tight, phalanxlike squares, pikemen at the outer edges, harquebusiers at the centers, which proved impenetrable by Egmont's cavalrymen until Savoy's artillery came up and blasted great gaps in the squares, through which the cavalry then rushed and wreaked slaughter on the French infantrymen.

The battle, which went on for four hours, became a rout, French infantrymen abandoning their weapons and running for their lives, French chevaliers racing pell-mell through the shattered infantry formations, riding down their own comrades, riderless horses galloping aimlessly. Those who asked quarter from Savoy's troops were given it, but huge numbers of French soldiers fell to the slaughter. Only a relative few managed to escape to La Fère. French losses were estimated at between three and six thousand killed and six thousand captured. Among the prisoners was Montmorency, who was hit by a *schwarzreiter*'s pistol shot and suffered a fractured thigh. Most of the prisoners were later paroled, but some six hundred of them, members of the nobility, were held for ransom. Savoy's army's losses were estimated at not more than five hundred.

The defeat for France was enormous, the worst since the battle of Agincourt, where the French lost an estimated seven thousand to ten thousand men and some fifteen hundred members of the French nobility were captured and taken to England to be held for ransom, many of them never to return. To Queen Mary, the outcome at St.-Quentin was "miraculous," and Philip's good friend and confidant, Ruy Gómez de Silva, who had just returned from a mission for Philip in Spain, allowed that the victory must have been the work of God, since for Spain it had been gained "without experience, without troops, and without money."

Escorted by a troop of bodyguards, Philip arrived at Savoy's camp on August 13, impressively done up in armor from head to toe. He had missed the action but had come prepared nevertheless. He was received at the encampment with trumpet and artillery salutes and cheers from his troops. Savoy presented to him the trophies of the triumph—banners, arms, and other prizes—and knelt before him. Graciously urging him to stand, Philip embraced him and complimented him, as well as Egmont, on the victory. Philip also acknowledged the battle's losers. With his commanders he strode through the lines of the distinguished French prisoners, who had been formed up for his review, and offered his respects to each.

When Charles received Philip's letter telling of the victory, he immediately wanted to know, according to one account, whether Philip had entered Paris yet. (It was at this time that King Henry had summoned the duke of Guise and his army back from Italy to protect Paris.) If Philip had considered marching on to Paris, he had been dissuaded by his Netherlands council. He was out of money to pay his troops to continue the campaign, and he would soon lose the services of his German mercenaries, many of whom went over to the French for better pay. While Philip's army was shrinking, France stood ready with a large reserve to meet any threat to the French capital. Philip decided not to press the offensive beyond St.-Quentin.

The town had not yet fallen, and having rid himself of the harassing army at his back, Savoy now renewed the siege with determination. After two more weeks of investing the town, he decided to storm it. On August 27 he ordered the assault, preceded by a prolonged cannonade. Philip was apparently near the forefront as the attackers, including some eight thousand English troops, rushed through the jagged holes blasted into the town walls by Savoy's artillery and mines. He later reported the event. "In the afternoon of the twenty-seventh," he wrote, "we entered in strength . . . from every side, killing all the defenders." He had got his first taste of war. Actually, though, not all the defenders had been killed. Many were taken prisoner, including Admiral Coligny and his brother. Once in control of the town, the invaders set off on a rampage of murder, rape, pillage, and arson. The German mercenaries, according to an English eyewitness, the duke of Bedford, "showed such cruelty as the like hath not been seen." The cries of women and children, Bedford reported, were "so pitiful that they would grieve any Christian heart." Bloody as it was, the victory was seen by Philip as a gift from God. "Our Lord in his goodness," he wrote to his sister Juana, "has desired to grant me these victories within a few days of the beginning of my reign, with all the honor and reputation that follow from them."

Philip ordered the fortifications of St.-Quentin repaired, and leaving a Spanish garrison posted there, he and Savoy turned their attention toward the town of Le Catelet, about twelve miles north of St.-Quentin. It was a fortified town, but its defenders offered only token resistance before surrendering it on September 6. From Le Catelet, Philip's army marched on Ham, about ten miles southwest of St.-Quentin, then on to Noyon, south of Ham, and Chauny, east of Noyon. Both those towns were taken, and Chauny, which apparently had put up a stiffer resistance, was sacked. By now the English forces had concluded they were merely fighting Spain's battles, not their own, and urged to be relieved from further activity, a request that Philip, not wanting to injure relations with England, granted. Also by now many of the mercenaries had quit. The English troops left for home in October, and shortly thereafter, with bad weather coming on, Philip ended his campaign and marched his diminished army back to Brussels, where it went into winter quarters. All told, the campaign had been an outstanding success for Philip, confirming—following his success in Italy—that although he was not as aggressive as his warrior father, he was no less quick to respond to a threat and no less capable of defeating it.

Although Philip and his army had bowed out of the hostilities, at least for the present, King Henry was not ready to let France's army stand idle. Since Queen Mary had declared war on him, he would use the state of belligerence to settle an old, festering grievance against England. In the summer of 1346, during the Hundred Years War between England and France, King Edward III of England had led an army across the channel and invaded Normandy, ravaging the French countryside as the army advanced between the Seine and the Somme. Its marauding presence was challenged by an army led by French King Philip VI, which was soundly defeated by the English at the Battle of Crécy on August 26, 1346. From the victory at Crécy, King Edward marched his troops to the outskirts of Calais and laid siege to it. For eleven months Calais held out against the English besiegers but at last had to capitulate. Edward ordered the town's French inhabitants driven out, and he repopulated the town with people brought over from England, so that Calais became an extension of England onto the Continent. Possession of it ensured the free flow of trade, particularly in wool, tin, lead, and cloth, between England and the Continent and provided a disembarkation point for English troops bound for action in France or elsewhere on the Continent. When the French were brought to the negotiating table to make what turned out to be a temporary peace in 1360, the treaty they signed, the Treaty of Brétigny, provided that England was to rule Calais, as well as the nearby towns of Guînes and Marck, forever.

For two hundred years, then, Calais, standing opposite the English coast at the narrowest part of the channel, had belonged to England, and for two hundred years that fact had rankled in the French psyche. To take the town back from the English by force of arms, however, was a task so forbidding that it had not been attempted. Protecting Calais from attack by land were massive turreted double walls and a land-facing fort and a marsh that could be flooded by opening locks that allowed seawater into it. Another fort guarded the town's harbor from assault by sea. The English considered Calais so impregnable that they had mounted on the town's gates a sign that read: "Then shall the Frenchmen Calais win when iron and lead like cork shall swim." Over the years, however, Calais's fortifications had deteriorated, and the English government had neglected to appropriate funds to make repairs or to provide adequate troops to garrison the town. The French envoy to England, returning home after the declaration of war, had passed through Calais and noticed the decay in the defensive works of the town and the few troops that comprised its garrison. His report that passed along that information to his government was duly noted.

King Henry had called out the French levy, had ordered home his troops from abroad, and had hired a sizable force of German and Swiss mercenaries. He now had a powerful army at his command, without a threatening force to oppose it. He soon found a mission for it: Take Calais. The duke of Guise, promoted to lieutenant general, was appointed the army's commander. Having ordered a reconnaissance and verified the envoy's report, he planned his attack. He sent a division under the duke of Nevers to make a feint toward

Luxembourg, then marched the remainder of his force toward the towns that Philip and Savoy had recently captured. Suddenly turning northward, Guise then headed for Calais, meeting up with Nevers's force, which had swung westward, on the way. On January 2, 1558, aided by bitter cold that froze the marsh (which the garrison commander in Calais had failed to flood) and let his troops march across it with relative ease, Guise's army captured the fort that guarded the harbor. The next day Guise stormed the land-facing fort and took it, too. Calais was now cut off from relief by sea and by land.

Guise's artillery opened a round-the-clock cannonade against the town's thick walls, eventually breaching them. On January 5 he sent his troops surging through the breaches. On January 8 the commander of the over-whelmed garrison, the earl of Wentworth, surrendered the town to Guise. The two other English-held towns promptly capitulated as well. After two hundred years, England no longer had a French entrance onto the Conti-nent. Its foothold had been lost, its pride severely wounded.

Queen Mary was dismayed by the news. Her concern over Calais's fate had come a little late, though, for she had earlier, months before the French attack, failed to take action when the Calais commander had requested more troops and she was made aware of the need for repairs to the city's walls. When ap-prised of Guise's impending assault, she quickly wrote to landholders around Dover, asking them to marshal a force and send it across the strait to reinforce Calais's garrison, a response that was too little and much too late. Blame for Calais's neglect fell as well on Mary's government, which had dithered over pro-viding funds to bolster the town's defenses and had refused Philip's offer, made prior to the French attack, to provide Spanish troops to reinforce the Calais gar-rison. Nevertheless, Mary grieved over the loss of a prominent part of her realm. She was said to have remarked that when she was dead and her body cut open, Calais would be found lying on her heart.

Mary was having other problems, too. During the preceding autumn, in 1557, she had once again decided she was pregnant. She had so informed Philip, then in Brussels, and had calculated her due date to be sometime in March 1558. Philip, apparently elated, claimed that the expected birth was what he most desired. Mary came to hold a grimmer view. As her supposed due date drew nearer, she made out her will, "foreseeing," as she said, "the great danger which by God's ordinance remains to all women in their travail of children." Among her other instructions in the will, which distributed a considerable part of her wealth, she asked that her mother's remains be exhumed from their burial place in Peterborough and reinterred alongside her own remains. She also asked for monuments to memorialize her and her mother.

Philip's envoy to Mary's court, the count of Feria, was keeping Philip informed about the queen as well as about the affairs of England's government. Feria was not so sure that Mary was pregnant. He reported to Philip that he thought she was merely making herself believe that her symptoms—which included a distended abdomen and cessation of menstruation—were signs of pregnancy.

With good cause, Mary was becoming preoccupied with her health, neglecting her official duties. She allowed her council meetings to degenerate into sessions of chaotic arguing among the councilors, who, without strong leadership, got nothing done despite a desperate need to raise money to pay for the nation's defense—a situation brought on partly by Mary and Philip's insistence that England become involved in Spain's war with France—and to keep the government running. Turning her back on the financial crisis, she left London and traveled to Greenwich to seek refuge from her cares. There she received the comfort of friendly monks while she hoped for Philip's return.

Philip, though, was thinking about other things. By late spring of 1558 it was obvious that Mary was not pregnant but was instead a victim of some ailment (probably cancer) that might soon take her life. Philip's thoughts were of the future, when there would be no Queen Mary on England's throne. Those thoughts naturally led to his instructing Feria to go pay a visit to Elizabeth and offer her Philip's compliments.

There was also the continuing conflict with France to think about. Flush with success following the taking of Calais, the duke of Guise in May marched on the fortified town of Thionville, in Luxembourg, which surrendered after a three-week siege. He ordered one of his lieutenants, Marshal de Termes, to take a force of five thousand infantry and fifteen hundred cavalry and invade Flanders, which was promptly accomplished, his army moving north through St.-Omer. De Termes besieged Dunkirk, then stormed its defenses and overwhelmed the town. As summer came on, he marched deeper into Flanders, as far as Nieuport.

Philip's army commander, the duke of Savoy, sent orders to Count Egmont to muster as much of an army as he could and take a position to the rear of the French force, blocking its retreat, while Savoy gathered his army and attacked de Termes's force from its front. Eager to avenge the ravages of de Termes's army, Egmont swiftly recruited a force of some twelve thousand infantry and two thousand cavalry and set out after the French. As ordered, he threw a line of troops across the route by which de Termes had come. Unable to be relieved by Guise's force and eager to withdraw from his exposed position, de Termes decided to use an alternate escape route that would take him along the channel coastline, through Gravelines, a town midway between Calais and Dunkirk. He got his army across the River Aa, just east of Gravelines, but on reaching the opposite bank discovered that Egmont had beaten him to the crossing point and was lying in wait. With the river now at his back and the enemy in front of him, de Termes was left with little choice but to fight his way through Egmont's lines. As de Termes's troops moved from a column into battle forma-tion, Egmont ordered his cavalry to charge, hitting the center and left of the French line. For a time the battle went back and forth, Egmont withdrawing, then attacking again. His horse was killed beneath him, but he remounted and rallied his troops, shouting, "Those who love glory and their fatherland, follow me!" His men responded by charging once more and capturing de Termes's ar-tillery, quickly turning it on the French troops. While the struggle's outcome was still in doubt, an English naval squadron, which had been lying at a distance offshore, attracted by the noise of battle, drew in closer to shore and began fir-ing into the French formation, scattering de Termes's troops, who were soon routed by Egmont's swarming troopers.

For Egmont's army, composed mostly of Flemings, the victory was com-plete. French casualties amounted to some two thousand killed and three thousand taken prisoner. De Termes, who had suffered a head wound, was among the captured. Egmont's losses were put at not more than five hun-dred. News of the battle drew both Guise and Savoy to the vicinity, Guise to protect the French border and Savoy to confront him. Philip and Henry, too, were drawn to the site along the River Authie where the two armies lay within about twelve miles of each other. Except for several skirmishes, how-ever, they never engaged. Philip was apparently satisfied with what his armies had already accomplished, and Henry was unwilling to fight and risk a loss that would leave the road to Paris open to a triumphant invader. The battle at Gravelines, fought in July 1558, instead of provoking further conflict, pro-pelled Henry and Philip to the negotiating table. In October their representa-tives met at an abbey near Cambrai to work out a peace agreement.

With one eye on the war and the other on other matters, including money problems, Philip managed to stay in correspondence with his ailing wife, whose letters to him were becoming fewer. When they stopped altogether, around the end of September, his concern grew. "She has not written to me for some days past," he remarked, "and I cannot help being anxious." He soon learned that Mary, back in London at St. James's Palace, had taken a turn for the worse. Assuming that her death was near, he instructed Feria to talk to Mary about a successor. His choice was Elizabeth, who although expected to become openly Protestant once on the throne, might be manipulated by marriage, he believed. Mary, still reluctant even to admit that Elizabeth was her sister, much less recognize the daughter of Anne Boleyn as her successor, at last gave in to the urgings of Feria and her council and agreed to acknowledge that Elizabeth should succeed her, realizing, as they warned, that there was a great likelihood of civil war if Elizabeth were denied the crown.

As the days of early November passed, Mary continued to grow weaker. She told her attendants that she was having dreams of heavenly scenes and she was heard to pray that she would die with dignity, "that the weakness of my flesh be not overcome by the fear of death." Her prayers were apparently answered, for after hearing a private Mass said for her, she fell into a final sleep and died peacefully sometime between four and five o'clock on the morning of November 17, 1558.

From St. James's Palace the news was swiftly carried to Elizabeth at Hatfield, eighteen miles away. "This is the Lord's doing," she said, slipping to her knees and quoting from Psalm 118, "and it is marvelous in our eyes."

Philip, who had less than three weeks earlier learned of the death of his father, was on his way from Arras to Brussels when he received news of Mary's death. He sent word ahead that a quick memorial service should be held for her in Brussels and he asked the duke of Savoy to represent him, since he did not intend to enter Brussels before a funeral service for his father could be arranged. Honoring his father was of first importance to him. His wife's service was not to interfere. The memorial service for Charles, with Philip in attendance, was held on November 28. Three days later another service was held, for the late Queen Mary and for Philip's Aunt Mary, who had recently died in Spain.

In London, Mary's body lay in state at St. James's Palace for more than three weeks, until burial arrangements could be completed. Finally, on December 12, 1558, her funeral was held, the cortege bearing her corpse setting out from the palace and ceremoniously making its way to Westminster Abbey for the service, a throng of mourners leading the procession, followed by Mary's house servants, all dressed in black, walking in an orderly column, then a solemn group of noblemen, then heralds carrying personal tokens of the late queen—her sword and armor, her crest and mantle—then the carriage bearing the royal coffin, and behind it, the ladies of Mary's court, robed in black and mounted on horseback, then, last, members of the Catholic clergy, monks and bishops. The coffin was lifted from the carriage and carried by pallbearers into Westminster Abbey and there it rested in the great vaulted nave, under the watchful eyes of a body of black-robed attendants and members of the queen's guard, till the next day, when a requiem Mass was held.

The eulogy was delivered in Latin by the bishop of Winchester, John White, who, with courage or foolhardiness, praised Mary and, with obvious contempt for the Protestant Elizabeth, warned of dark days to come for the church. (The following day he was ordered to place himself under house arrest "for such offenses as he committed in his sermon at the funeral of the late queen.") When the eulogy had ended, the coffin was carried to Henry VII's Chapel (where the remains of all the Tudor monarchs save Henry VIII now lie) and placed in its tomb. Her heart, cut from her and contained in a silver casket, was separately entombed. Once the coffin was in place and the burial ceremony concluded, trumpeters gave the signal for the commencement of the funeral banquet, and the noble mourners turned from their dead queen and went off to dine and drink.

So ended the reign, at age forty-two, of bloody Queen Mary, pious in her faith, fanatic in its attempted preservation, embittered by ill treatment of her mother and herself, frustrated in marriage, thwarted by failure to give birth, yet ever stalwart in devotion to her high office and steadfast in personal courage. The final lines of her epitaph give eloquence to the summary of her anguished life:

> In greatest stormes she feared not, for God she made her shielde,
> And all her care she cast on him, who forst her foes to yelde.
> Her perfect life in all extremes her pacient hert dyd shoe,
> For in this worlde she never founde but dolfull dayes and woe.[2]

⋙ 8. THE NEW QUEEN

The transition of power had started long before Mary's death. "Frequent communications reach and leave her [Elizabeth] secretly in regard to the succession," Simon Renard, Emperor Charles's ambassador to England, reported in March, eight months before Mary died. And Feria, Philip's envoy, was only one of many who came calling on Elizabeth in the weeks prior to Mary's death. England's noblemen and other important persons came in a virtual stream to pay their respects, offer their support, or ingratiate themselves.

As Philip's representative, Feria had tried to ingratiate his master and had gone a bit too far, asserting to Elizabeth that it was Philip who was responsible for her impending accession, a claim that might have been somewhat true but that ignited a fiery retort from her. It was not Philip, she shot back, who had put her in her present position but rather the people of England. Like others who met with her, Feria was learning a lot about Elizabeth. "She is much attached to the people," he reported, "and is very confident that they are all on her side, which is indeed true." That was one of the nicer things he said about her. "She is a very vain and clever woman," he told Philip. "She must have been thoroughly schooled in the manner in which her father conducted his affairs, and I am very much afraid that she will not be well-disposed in matters of religion, for I see her inclined to govern through men who are believed to be heretics and I am told that all the women around her definitely are. Apart from this, it is evident that she is highly indignant about what has been done to her during the queen's [Mary's] lifetime."

Feria's foresight proved acute. The men who came to her at Hatfield tended to be Protestant sympathizers. Many had been in her coterie for years, having since the death of Edward looked forward to the day when England would have a Protestant queen. Many of them would be rewarded with positions in her government. The speed and care with which she made her first

appointments suggest that she had formed a sort of shadow cabinet in anticipation of the day when she would succeed to the throne. On the day Mary
died, several members of the queen's council had come to Hatfield to meet
with Elizabeth, and when she gave them an audience that afternoon, they
found sitting beside her thirty-eight-year-old William Cecil, a Protestant
lawyer and judge who had served as a member of Edward VI's council and in
a variety of other posts but whose career had withered during Mary's reign.
A Cambridge-educated commoner whose father had served Elizabeth's father, Cecil had been a financial adviser to Elizabeth and had otherwise
given her counsel for a number of years. It was obvious to the council
members who stood before her that he was going to be a key member of
her government.

After three days of official mourning, during which she continued to confer
informally with her advisers, Elizabeth convened a formal meeting on November 20 in Hatfield, attended by Mary's councilors and a large number of
other VIPs who had come to pay their respects. There Elizabeth gave her first
public speech and announced her appointment of Cecil as her secretary of
state, probably to no one's surprise. In administering the oath of office to him,
she told him that in his office and in her Privy Council "you will not be corrupted with any manner of gifts, and that you will be faithful to the state, and
that without respect of my private will, you will give me that counsel which
you think best." She then moved on to other appointments, swearing in
Nicholas Bacon as lord keeper of the great seal, and Nicholas Throckmorton
as chamberlain of the exchequer, and naming to her council, among others,
William Parr, the brother of her father's sixth wife, and Francis Knollys, a
Protestant zealot who had left the country to escape Mary's bloody purge and
had hurried back on news of Elizabeth's accession. Ten of the members of
Mary's council Elizabeth now appointed to her council, some of whom had
not supported her during Mary's reign but whose contributions to government Elizabeth apparently valued. Some others who had served on Mary's
council were excluded from Elizabeth's council, particularly those who were
ardent Catholic loyalists. Besides avoiding possible Catholic obstructionism in
her council, Elizabeth also hoped to bring more order to the council by reducing its size. Forty-four councilors, she said, the number who had served Mary,
"would make rather discord and confusion than good counsel."

Another of her first appointments, announced later that same day, was that of Robert Dudley as master of the horse, which carried a weightier responsibility than the title might connote in modern times. It put him, in effect, in charge of transportation for the queen, her court, and her household, horses being the prime motive power for land transport. It was Dudley, then, who would be responsible for royally conveying Elizabeth and her entourage from Hatfield into London to accept the good wishes of her subjects and the crown of her dominion. He and Elizabeth, born the same year or perhaps a year apart, had been friends since childhood, he having been selected to be one of her playmates. He was the fifth of the eight sons of John Dudley, whose father, Edmund Dudley, had been beheaded by Henry VIII for crimes allegedly committed in helping Henry VII amass a kingly fortune. John, who became the duke of Northumberland, had lost his head, too, for his part in the plot to remove both Mary and Elizabeth from the line of succession in favor of Lady Jane Grey. Robert and several of his brothers, as suspects in the plot, had spent time in the Tower—at the same time that Elizabeth was confined there—but remarkably had been released, and Robert had gone on to win the support of Philip and had served with distinction with the English troops who participated in the battle of St.-Quentin. Because of his family's association with treason, however, Robert remained, to many English influentials, a controversial figure.

In 1550, at age seventeen, he had married the daughter of Sir John Robsart and through her, who was her father's heiress, Robert had become a rather rich landowner in Norfolk County, in the east of England. An expert horseman, he was apparently well qualified for the job Elizabeth gave him. What was more, his brother John, who had since died, had held the same position when Edward VI was king. But Robert had other things going for him, which no doubt helped him a great deal in acquiring a vital position close to the new queen. He was by all accounts an unusually handsome young man, tall—about six foot—dark (so dark that he was called by some "the gypsy"), lean, and muscular, with reddish hair and beard. A dashing sportsman, he was an accomplished archer, tennis player, hunter, and fisherman, and a participant in jousts. He rode well, dressed well, spoke well—on a broad range of subjects—and was well read. He also sang well and danced well. He could speak fluent French and Italian. All told, he was an extraordinarily charming, even fascinating, man. Elizabeth certainly found him so. She rarely allowed him out of her sight.

On November 28 the people crowding the route of Elizabeth's London-bound procession were able to see Robert Dudley's first production of a moving spectacle, parades and entertainment being other parts of his responsibilities. Entering the city by way of Cripplegate, the queen's cavalcade, with an estimated one thousand persons in its train, was led by London's lord mayor and the garter king-at-arms, who bore the royal scepter, symbol of Elizabeth's new high office, riding together. Behind them came the queen's gentlemen-at-arms, uniformed in red damask and carrying gilded battle-axes, then heralds, and footmen arrayed in crimson and silver tabards with the initials "E.R." (Elizabeth Regina) on their chests and backs. Then came the earl of Pembroke, William Herbert, bearing the royal sword upright before him. Behind him rode Elizabeth herself, garbed in royal purple velvet, with an incongruous scarf around her neck, presumably added at the last minute to help her stave off the cold. Flanking her on both sides were protective sergeants-at-arms. Behind her, in the position to which he was entitled by virtue of his office, mounted on a black horse, rode the new master of the horse, Robert Dudley. After him came, at the very rear of the procession, the yeomen of the guard, armed with halberds. As the cavalcade proceeded through streets gaily decorated with banners and tapestries and lined with cheering onlookers, trumpeters sounded the announcement of the royal arrival, and cannons boomed in celebration.

The route took Elizabeth and her entourage east along the city wall to Bishopsgate, then south to the center of the city, then to the Tower, where Elizabeth would temporarily reside in the royal apartments. As she prepared to enter the massive old structure, the sight of it evidently brought back bad memories, and she commented to those around her, "Some have fallen from being princes of this land to be prisoners in this place. I am raised from being a prisoner in this place to be a prince of this land. That dejection was a work of God's justice. This advancement is a work of his mercy."

After six days at the Tower, Elizabeth left on December 5 and, to the sound of heralding trumpets, was rowed up the Thames and taken to Somerset House, the in-town residence she had occupied as princess. There she stayed until Mary's funeral had been held, clearing the royal palace, where Mary's body had lain in state, to receive the new queen. On December 23 Elizabeth at last moved into the majestic residence of the queen, Whitehall Palace, in time for the Christmas celebrations, made appropriately merry under Robert

Dudley's direction. On Twelfth Night, when Christmas gifts were exchanged, Elizabeth received as one of her presents a pair of silk stockings, her first, which so pleased her that, according to one account, she promised she would never wear cloth stockings again.

The next big event was her coronation, which she wanted to be held as soon as possible but on a propitious day. To help her choose one she consulted, at Dudley's suggestion, a longtime acquaintance, astrologer and scholar John Dee, who drew up Elizabeth's horoscope and decided that January 15 was the right date.

Preparations for the coronation had already begun. As early as November 30, the queen's council had ordered all imports of crimson silk to be held for Elizabeth to see so that she could take her pick. Other elegant fabrics had been ordered—cloth of gold, cloth of silver, crimson velvet, purple velvet, rich-hued damask, satin, and taffeta—as well as sumptuous furs and colorful plumes. Everyone who was to participate in the event, from the most prominent to the least, was to be provided with a set of clothes to fit the occasion and the wearer's role. Elizabeth herself, of course, would have more than one outfit, two of which had been Mary's, including the coronation mantle fashioned of cloth of gold and of silver and trimmed with ermine, along with the matching gown that went with it. Alterations to the bodice would have to be made to fit it to Elizabeth's trim figure instead of that of chunky Mary. The robe that Elizabeth would wear on her way to Westminster Abbey, where the coronation would be held, had also been Mary's, made of crimson velvet and trimmed in ermine, with a matching cap. The other robes, including one of purple velvet, would be created just for Elizabeth. Although strapped for cash, Elizabeth's government would foot the bill for all that coronation finery, plus the trappings for the occasion, which together totaled 16,741 pounds, 19 shillings, a considerable sum of deficit spending.

The big hitch in the coronation plans concerned authorized personnel. Who was going to crown the new queen? That job ordinarily fell to the archbishop of Canterbury, but there was none. Cardinal Reginald Pole, whom Mary had appointed archbishop of Canterbury (and who had been an ardent enemy of Elizabeth), had died in the afternoon of the same day that Mary had died. England's other archbishop, Nicholas Heath, archbishop of York, in a snit over Elizabeth's having walked out of the recent Christmas Mass when the Host was elevated, contrary to Elizabeth's wishes, told her he would not crown a heretic and refused to substitute for the late Cardinal Pole. The man who had actually elevated the Host at the Christmas service, Owen Oglethorpe, bishop of Carlisle and suffragan (assistant) to Archbishop Heath, was at last persuaded to do the honors, the rest of England's bishops having refused along with Heath. Elizabeth ordered the bishop of London, Edmund Bonner, whom she especially disliked, to lend Oglethorpe his best vestments to wear at the coronation.

Elizabeth returned to the Tower via the Thames on January 12 in preparation for the customary procession through the streets of London to Westminster on the day before the coronation, a ritual performance that gave all a chance to see and hail their new monarch. Two days later, on January 14, before setting out on the procession, she offered a prayer of thanksgiving. "I give Thee most hearty thanks that Thou hast been so merciful unto me to spare me to behold this joyful day," she prayerfully proclaimed. "Thou hast dealt as wonderfully and as mercifully with me as Thou didst with Daniel, whom Thou delivered out of the den from the cruelty of the raging lions. Even so was I overthrown and only by Thee delivered."[1] She then climbed into a satin-lined, satin-cushioned litter harnessed to two mules (also under Robert Dudley's jurisdiction) and, escorted by her uniformed gentlemen-at-arms and several hundred other ceremonial soldiers, handsomely clad attendants, and dignitaries, was carried through four miles of city streets, where she was gawked at, cheered, and entertained by a series of five outdoor allegorical pageants even as a light snow fell from gray skies.

At one point, as tradition required, she was presented with a satin purse filled with gold coins, which she accepted with moving gratitude. "I thank my lord mayor, his brethren and you all," she said solemnly. "And whereas your request is that I should continue your good lady and queen, be ye assured that I will be as good unto you as ever queen was to her people. No will in me can lack, neither, do I trust, shall there lack any power. And persuade yourselves that for the safety and quietness of you all, I will not spare, if need be, to spend my blood. God thank you all."[2] Her words touched off a loud and warm response from the crowd of onlookers. At another of the many stops she watched a figure depicting Truth receive, as if from heaven, an English Bible, which a youngster then presented to Elizabeth after delivering a recitation about how the Bible would help the queen in her efforts to bring needed prosperity to her nation. She took the Bible, kissed it, pressed it to her bosom in a warm show of appreciation, and promised she would be "a diligent reader thereof." As she was passing London's city limits to enter into adjoining Westminster, where she would spend the night, a choir of children sang a farewell to her, and she shouted back in response, "Be ye well assured I will stand your good queen!"

All in all the procession, the entire spectacle, was a huge public relations success. She had shown herself, her heart and her feelings, to her people, and they had given her their love and acceptance in return. Her rapport with ordinary people, throngs of whom enthusiastically cheered her as she moved along her route, was profound and obvious. She warmly acknowledged their cheers, smiling and shouting back to them, "God save you all!" Many times along the way she ordered her litter halted so that she could speak to those who were among the humblest of her subjects and to accept from them the modest gifts they offered, meager bouquets of flowers and, in one case, a simple branch of fragrant rosemary, which she still had with her when she arrived in Westminster. She had amply shown, and her subjects had joyfully seen, that she was truly the people's queen.

The next day, Sunday, January 15, 1559, cold and snowy, was the day of her coronation. As the bells of London's churches pealed in celebration and fifes and drums gave rhythm to her steps and those of the multitude of nobles and other dignitaries who preceded her in the lengthy, formal procession, she walked from Westminster Hall to the abbey wearing her crimson robe, striding beneath a handheld canopy borne by thirty-two barons, and atop a carpet of blue cloth that extended along the entire path. Flanking her and giving her support were the earls of Pembroke and Shrewsbury. Immediately behind her came the countess of Lennox, carrying the train of her regal robe, assisted by the lord chamberlain. Behind them came the young duchess of Norfolk. As soon as Elizabeth passed, souvenir-hunting onlookers dashed onto the carpet to cut off and carry away pieces of it, so swiftly that the duchess of Norfolk was nearly bowled over by them. Others in the crowd called out to her, "God save and maintain thee!" which drew Elizabeth's response: "God have mercy, good people!"

Inside the abbey the glow of hundreds of candles and torches lit the towering walls ornamented with rich tapestries hung for the occasion. The place was packed. Practically every peer of the realm was there as well as other dignitaries and many members of the church hierarchy. Conspicuously absent, however, were foreign representatives. Feria, Philip's representative to the English court, had refused to come, he, apparently like other foreign envoys, being too piously sensitive to witness the heretical innovations Elizabeth might make in the ceremony, which it had been rumored she would do.

Elizabeth was led to the platform before the high altar by Bishop Oglethorpe, who successively stood on each of the four corners of the platform and asked the people in the audience if they accepted her for their queen. Each time the shouted answer came back, "Yea! Yea!" to the accompaniment of trumpets, organ, and bells, and each time Oglethorpe pronounced her queen. Elizabeth and Oglethorpe then stepped down from the platform, toward the altar, and Elizabeth, after making the ceremonial oblation, a twenty-shilling gold piece and a crimson-and-gold pall to be placed over the paten, took her seat in the chair of estate, there to sit while the sermon was preached, then to kneel as the Lord's Prayer was recited. After that, Oglethorpe administered the coronation oath, which was written out for him and held up for him to read, like a cue card, by William Cecil, the newly appointed secretary of state. Elizabeth swore to keep the law and customs of the realm, to keep the peace of the church and the people, and to administer justice with mercy and truth.

On through the ceremony they plodded, Elizabeth leaving briefly after the anointing with oil and returning dressed in a different robe, a mantle of cloth of gold about her shoulders. This time she was seated in the traditional coronation chair, under which lay the ancient stone of Scone, on which Scottish kings had been crowned from the ninth century until its capture by King Edward I of England at the end of the thirteenth century. English sovereigns had been crowned on it since 1308. As trumpets blared, the royal ring that symbolized her being wedded to the nation was placed on the fourth finger of Elizabeth's slim right hand. The St. Edward's crown was placed on her head, then removed, and the seven-pound imperial crown of England was then put on her head, the official crowning act. Her nobles came forward to kneel and kiss her left cheek in an act of fealty to their new liege lord. After the nobles it was the clergy's turn to pledge their fealty. Elizabeth had reversed the traditional order of clergy first and then secular lords, perhaps out of spite for the bishops who, except for Oglethorpe, had refused to crown her.

That done, the first act of the new queen's mercy was, according to tradition, to pardon certain offenders. Oglethorpe read, in Latin, the proclamation of pardon. Excluded from the long list of the pardoned were those who had participated in "any conspiracy, confederation, abetting, or procurement made or had against our person, or for the imprisonment of our person in the time of our dearly beloved sister, Mary, formerly queen of England." Those omissions meant that those members of Mary's council who had ordered Elizabeth's imprisonment, those who had been her jailers, particularly Henry Bedingfield, and anyone who had acted to deprive Elizabeth of her right to the throne were all subject to the new queen's vengeance, should she choose to exercise it. The message sent was both clear and threatening.

At Bishop Oglethorpe's insistence, the coronation service was conducted in Latin (for the last time in English history), with a few exceptions. During the Mass that followed the coronation itself, the readings from the gospels and from the epistles were in both Latin and English. At least one of the prayers was also said in English. Those exceptions apparently were some of the innovations Elizabeth had ordered and to which Oglethorpe had agreed. He drew the line, however, at Elizabeth's wish to alter the Mass to suit her theology. Despite her objection, he would elevate the Host. When he did, as he had done at the Christmas Mass, Elizabeth made an exit, disappearing behind the altar, as she had done at the Christmas Mass, once more refusing to witness an act that she found offensive, signifying as it did the real presence of Christ's body in the wafer held out before the congregants. Her Protestant conscience simply would not permit her to tolerate the demonstration of that piece of Catholic doctrine. (Oglethorpe had perhaps agreed to officiate at the coronation on certain conditions, one being that he would be allowed to elevate the Host, and her departure at that point was expected by him and others in on the arrangements.) When the Mass was over, Elizabeth reappeared, having changed robes again, this time wearing violet velvet.

Now the participants in the royal procession started forming up for their march to Westminster Hall, where the coronation banquet would be held. The long, colorful column moved out of the west door of the abbey, Elizabeth taking her appointed place in it, holding the ceremonial orb and scepter and wearing a smaller, lighter crown than the seven-pounder used for the coronation. Seating for the banquet was by order of rank or status. The royal table, where Elizabeth and her favored few would sit, was at one end of the hall, on a dais. By three o'clock that afternoon, she was in her seat, and the feast began. While the estimated eight hundred privileged guests ate, Edward Dymoke, the designated queen's champion, clad in a bright suit of armor, flung down his gauntlet and rode his horse up and down the aisles of the great hall, daring anyone to dispute the new queen's right to the throne. It was all a traditional exhibition, of course, no one being expected to pick up the gauntlet and accept the challenge.

The celebration went on and on, as a seemingly inexhaustible supply of food and wine was brought in for the diners throughout the evening and from the hall's gallery court musicians provided background music. It was one o'clock Monday morning by the time the banqueting and the entertainment finally ended. Exhausted, Elizabeth decided to forgo the jousting tournament that had been scheduled for later in the day, and the event was postponed till Tuesday. Other festivities, including banquets, balls, and mummeries, followed the tournament, the celebrations stretching on through the next several days and evenings, turning into one huge party—to the point where a disapproving Italian guest criticized "the levities and moral licentiousness practiced at the court in dances and banquets."[3]

The reign of Elizabeth had thus begun, promising to be strikingly different from that of her grim sister. Her exhaustion from the coronation and its attendant activities, however, had helped her catch a cold, and her obligatory appearance at the opening of Parliament had to be postponed also. Originally scheduled for Monday, January 23, the opening session was moved to January 25.

On the day of the opening, Elizabeth, robed in crimson, strode in a procession from Whitehall Palace to Westminster Abbey to attend the religious service that traditionally preceded the opening of Parliament. At the entrance to the abbey she encountered a group of monks, there to greet her, holding lighted tapers. Candles, to the reformist Protestant mind, were objectionably Catholic, and Elizabeth took instant offense at the sight of them. "Away with these torches," she ordered, "for we see very well!" She then continued on into the abbey. The service featured a long sermon that its preacher, Richard Cox, a former tutor of Edward VI, used to inveigh against monks, accusing them of participating in the burning of Protestants. God had made Elizabeth queen, he declared, so that she could reverse the Catholic course of Mary, and he urged Elizabeth to do so. When the service was over, she again took her place in the procession of peers, and it made its way to the Parliament chamber in Westminster Palace. There she sat enthroned while the members of the House of Commons were called in to join the lords for the joint session.

With all in place, Nicholas Bacon, the bright, scholarly lawyer Elizabeth had recently appointed lord keeper of the great seal but who actually functioned as Elizabeth's chancellor, stood to read the opening address, according to custom. (According to one account, Elizabeth had withheld the title "chancellor" from Bacon because of his low birth. His father had been nothing grander than manager of an abbey's sheep flocks.) Elizabeth, meanwhile, sat silent, listening to the words from her lord keeper, many of which were hers, given to him in consultations. Money was one of the first topics. The need of it, Bacon said, required Parliament to raise taxes to supplement the Crown's usual income from customs duties, and Parliament needed to take care of that matter.

Its most important item of business, though, would be the resolution of religious issues. What was needed from Parliament in that regard was, as Bacon put it, "the well making of laws for the according and uniting of this realm into an uniform order of religion." Through Bacon's words Elizabeth was letting it be known that she was going to make religion her priority. As Mary had reversed Edward's Protestant direction, Elizabeth intended to reverse Mary's Catholic direction. As Mary had used Parliament to undo Edward's efforts, Elizabeth would use Parliament to undo Mary's. Elizabeth's tactics would be different, however. Her plan was to find middle ground, to reach consensus, so that great numbers of neither Catholics nor Protestants would be alienated by the changes. She intended, as Bacon said, a uniting of the realm, not the my-way-or-the-stake division of it that Mary had caused. Bacon told Parliament that as its members debated the religious issues they should avoid "all sophistical, captious and frivolous arguments . . . [that are] comlier for scholars than for councillors." Elizabeth wanted Parliament to produce useful results, not heated arguments. She was going to try to keep opposing tempers cool by having Bacon insist that those participating in the debate refrain from insults and from the use of such incendiary terms as "heretic," "papist," and "schismatic." By the time Bacon had finished his address, Parliament had a pretty good idea of what lay ahead.

Parliament's makeup promised both help and hindrance for Elizabeth's legislative agenda. The Commons, whose members were elected and thus at least to some extent reflected the sympathies of the people, was overwhelmingly Protestant, despite Mary's attempts to pack it with Catholics. Commons members who were on Elizabeth's Privy Council could be expected to provide effective leadership in moving the queen's proposals to passage. The House of Lords, on the other hand, was another matter. Its members were there by privilege not plebiscite. They tended to be conservative and opposed to change, most of them going along with the principle that England's church should be governed from England, not Rome, but unenthusiastic about any substantial change in the church's rituals or practices. What was more, each of England's bishops, by virtue of his office, was a member of the House of Lords, the total constituting as much as a third of its membership. That was a constituency from which Elizabeth could hardly expect support. The bishops furthermore wielded considerable influence over their fellow lords, being accepted by them as experts in religious matters and being articulate in making their case.

Parliament made finances its first order of business, enacting the tax measures that Elizabeth and Bacon had asked for. Then it turned its attention to religion. On February 9 a bill of supremacy, establishing England's monarch as head of the church in England, thereby reversing Mary's legislation that recognized the pope as head of the church, was introduced in the House of Commons. Over a period of nearly two weeks, the reform-minded, Protestant-dominated Commons overhauled the bill, adding, among other things, a provision that reinstated the 1552 prayer book, which had been written during Edward's reign and had eliminated certain worship practices that Protestants found offensive. By that prayer book's terms, the Catholic doctrine of transubstantiation—the belief in the real presence of Christ in the communion wafer—was rejected, and communion was celebrated as no more than a commemoration of Christ's Last Supper. The new supremacy bill, as altered by Commons, provided harsh penalties for individuals who refused to go along with the latest changes.

After Commons passed it, the bill was sent to the House of Lords on February 28. There it ran into trouble. It lay stalled until March 13, when it was bumped to a committee and underwent furious debate. Its critics, led largely by Archbishop Heath and Henry Montagu, attacked it on several counts, saying it would create a dangerous breach with the papacy, lead to excommunications, and destabilize the country. Besides all that, Heath argued, Parliament had no right to grant to a secular monarch authority over the church, and particularly to a monarch who was a woman, women being prohibited by Saint Paul from even speaking in church. In response to those arguments, the committee members gutted the bill. When their work was done, about all that remained of the Commons version was a provision that permitted the queen to become head of the church in England. The committee sent the butchered version to the full House of Lords on March 18, whereupon it was passed, although opposed by every bishop, and sent to the Commons.

In the Commons the amended bill presented a dilemma. It was unacceptable to the Protestant majority (and presumably to the queen), but refusal to adopt it would leave in place the anti-Protestant laws of Mary's reign. Swallowing hard, Commons on March 22 voted to accept the Lords' version. All it needed now to become law was the queen's approval. Elizabeth had planned to dissolve Parliament prior to Easter, which was March 26, but her hackles having risen over the Lords' butchery of her bill, she changed her plans and resolved to fight back. On Good Friday, March 24, instead of dissolving Parliament she prorogued it until April 3, giving it a ten-day intermission. During that time she would devise a scheme to overcome the bishops, whose influence in the House of Lords was seen as decisive. "The bishops," according to John Jewel, whom Elizabeth would later appoint bishop of Salisbury, "reign [in the House of Lords] as sole monarchs in the midst of ignorant and weak men and easily overreach our little party, either by their numbers or by their reputation for learning." Elizabeth had once promised the council, before Mary's death, that she would not overturn Catholicism in England if its tenets could be proved by Scripture. She now proposed—and the council apparently ordered—a public debate to test three Catholic beliefs, the debate to be held in Westminster Abbey during Parliament's recess. A team of eight learned Catholics, including four bishops, would face an equivalent Protestant team. The judges were to be members of Elizabeth's council. Bacon was to be the moderator.

The Catholic team requested that the debate be conducted in Latin, in the scholarly tradition. That request was denied. The debate would be conducted in English, so that its audience could understand what was being said. On each of the three questions to be debated, the Catholic team would speak first, then the Protestants. There would be no chance for rebuttal by the Catholics. When the Catholic team strenuously objected after the first day's debate, charging that the Protestant team was having the last word on each of the three issues, Bacon suggested canceling the remainder of the debate. Bishop John White of Winchester, who had already demonstrated his scorn for Elizabeth in his sermon at Mary's funeral, quickly responded, eager to call the whole thing off if the Catholic team were never allowed to speak last. "Let us be gone," he answered, "for we will not in this point give over." Bacon polled the Catholic team to find out what the others thought, whether the debate should continue with the Catholics presenting their case first and the Protestants then having their say. Of those responding, three followed White's lead and refused to continue the debate. Two, including Bishop Oglethorpe, who had presided at the coronation, agreed to continue, and one was noncommital. The Catholic team thus had voted to end the debate that had been ordered by the queen's council. Bacon then shut down the proceedings with a warning. "For that ye will not that we should hear you," he told the Catholic team members, "you may perchance shortly hear of us."

That evening Bishop John White and Thomas Watson, bishop of Lincoln, White's stoutest fellow in defiance, were arrested for contempt and confined to the Tower. The other members of the Catholic team were bound over. Elizabeth had determined not to be thwarted, particularly by her enemies.

When Parliament reconvened on April 3, it began with two newly written religious bills. One was a supremacy bill; the other dealt with uniformity of church practices and ritual. Elizabeth was determined to get at least one of the bills passed, to get at least one of those issues settled. In the supremacy bill she had made a concession. Instead of being designated "supreme head" of the church, the monarch would be "supreme governor" of the church, which was somehow more palatable to both Catholic and Protestant members of Parliament because of the present monarch's being a woman and the asserted fact that the true head of the church was Christ. That bill sailed through the House of Commons and was passed, over the dissent of the bishops, by the House of Lords as well.

The uniformity bill embodied several concessions by Elizabeth, the most important one being the insertion of a phrase from the 1549 prayer book into the words to be said by the priest during communion. The phrase, "The body of our Lord Jesus Christ, which was given for thee, preserve thy body and soul unto everlasting life," was added to the words of the 1552 prayer book, made mandatory by the bill, which had the priest say, "Take and eat this in remembrance that Christ died for thee, and feed on him in thy heart by faith with thanksgiving." Catholics, who believed in the real presence, and Protestants, who didn't, thus were both given expression in the communion.

The bishops in the House of Lords still objected. Despite their opposition, however, and with two of their number still in the Tower, two absent with illness, and another one having apparently deliberately absented himself to avoid voting, the Lords passed the uniformity bill by three votes. Elizabeth had prevailed, but the passage of the uniformity bill was not exactly a triumph for radical Protestants, those who felt the bill's provisions did not go far enough to reform worship practices. Elizabeth had rejected their views. After hearing Bacon congratulate its members for their efforts and warn that obedience to the new legislation would be required of all, Parliament formally closed on May 8.

Under the newly legislated Act of Supremacy all members of the clergy, as well as all magistrates and royal officials, were required to take an oath affirming their acceptance of Elizabeth as supreme governor of the church. The penalty for refusing the oath was the forfeiture of their office. The first to refuse and suffer the penalty was defiant Edmund Bonner, bishop of London, called Bloody Bonner for his brutal participation in Mary's Protestant persecutions. (John Foxe, in his *Book of Martyrs,* first published in 1559, called Bonner "the Catholic hyena.") Bonner not only rejected the oath but persisted in violating the Act of Uniformity. For that he lost his office and his freedom, too, becoming a captive in the Marshalsea prison. Bishops White and Watson, still in the Tower, also refused and were stripped of their office. Eventually all the bishops but one, Anthony Kitchin of Llandaff, refused and were deposed from their bishoprics, but in contrast to Mary's burning of dissenters, such as Archbishop Cranmer, Bishop Ridley, and Bishop Latimer, those who defied Elizabeth kept their lives. All but one of the deposed bishops spent time either in the Tower or the Fleet Street prison, their punishment for continued "declaiming and railing" against Elizabeth's changes, but all except Bonner (who died in prison in 1569) were freed after three years.[4]

The new prayer book mandated by the Act of Uniformity was ordered to be used starting June 24, 1559. To make sure that the clergy were following the requirements of the Act of Uniformity, royal commissioners acting as inspectors—so-called visitors—were appointed to check on the clergy during services. The visitors were empowered to seize everything banned by the act— proscribed vestments, crucifixes, altar cloths, images, superseded missals—and in London the confiscated items were destroyed in flaming piles throughout the city. Elizabeth's legislation prohibited, among other things, rosaries, most uses of candles, and most processions. It spelled out what the priests were to wear—copes during communion and surplices at other times. But it also retained much of the traditional Catholic service. It specified, for example, that worshippers were to kneel when prayers to God were made, worshippers were to bow at the mention of Jesus' name and, significantly, the use of wafers—rather than the Protestant preference of bread—was to continue during the celebration of communion.

In the parishes, priests were generally compliant. Only two hundred to four hundred of the estimated eight thousand clergy refused to take Elizabeth's oath. No doubt many who did take it did so merely to keep their jobs, but even so, their compliance meant that replacements would not have to be found for them. Replacing the dismissed bishops was trouble enough.

The first position that had to be filled was that of archbishop of Canterbury, which had been vacated with the death of Reginald Pole in November 1558. Elizabeth knew whom she wanted in that job. He was Matthew Parker, who had once been chaplain to Elizabeth's mother and later had been vice-chancellor of Cambridge University. He was also a good friend of Elizabeth's secretary of state and confidant, William Cecil, who considered the moderate, modest, and scholarly Parker the best person for the job. Parker was reluctant to accept the job, but responding to the continued urging of Elizabeth and Cecil, in August 1559 he finally agreed to take it.

Finding worthy men to fill the twenty-four vacant bishoprics was a much bigger problem. The most qualified candidates had fled from Bloody Mary's purge and exiled themselves on the Continent during the four years of her reign. Now they were back in England and available, but many were too radical, too vigorous in their protests, to suit Elizabeth's moderate taste. She culled out the most immoderate of them and made her selections from among those who were left. She ended up filling more than half of the bishoprics with former exiles, including some who believed Elizabeth's Act of Uniformity had not gone far enough in reforming traditional church practices. So swiftly did Elizabeth move that by May 1561 all but two of the vacated sees were occupied by new bishops. The church in England had been given a new direction, if not a conspicuous new look, which was as Elizabeth wished.

At the same time that she was beginning her refurbishing of the church, Elizabeth was also pursuing peace with France, seeking an end to the war into which Philip and Mary had plunged England. Those peace efforts had started before Mary's death, Mary having appointed a team of commissioners to work out a deal with the French. Elizabeth had fervently hoped that the return of Calais to England would be part of whatever treaty could be worked out, saying at one point that she would have the commissioners beheaded if they made peace without the return of Calais. It was more than could be managed, for even though the French agreed that after eight years it would either return Calais or compensate England for its loss, no one actually believed France would do so. But agreement on the terms of peace was achieved, and on April 2, 1559, the Treaty of Cateau-Cambrésis, ending hostilities, was signed by both countries.

With the religious issues and the war behind her, Elizabeth was ready to face what was really important to her people.

→ 9. THE NEW PROPOSAL

hilip, still in Brussels, was keeping up with developments in England mainly through Feria. Not long after Elizabeth became queen, Feria told Philip that "she seems to me incomparably more feared than her sister, and gives her orders and has her way as absolutely as her father did." When the House of Lords dismantled Elizabeth's first attempt at legislation, her first bill on supremacy and uniformity, which the Commons grudgingly accepted, Feria reported that "the heretics are very downcast in the last few days." And when Feria unhappily reported that Elizabeth had manipulated her new supremacy and uniformity bills to passage, he summed up the situation as "all roguery and injustice."

Philip also heard from Elizabeth herself. Shortly after her accession she had written him a letter in Latin, telling of her having become queen and expressing her hope that he and she would keep "the same friendly relations as their ancestors had done and, if possible, more friendly." Philip was open to a "more friendly" relationship, for more than one reason. He wanted England to remain an ally, mainly as protection against the ambitions of France. He also wanted to use his influence to preserve Roman Catholicism in England. Then, too, there was the matter of Elizabeth's nubility, which he considered with, perhaps, at least some degree of excitement.

Marriage for Elizabeth was a subject widely discussed and speculated upon in many European capitals and in England generally. Shortly after the opening of her first Parliament, the House of Commons had gone so far as to make an official request that she marry as soon as possible and on February 6, 1559, sent a delegation to deliver to her a petition setting forth the request. She had responded with what was to become typical obfuscation:

> I must tell you I have been ever persuaded that I was born by God
> to consider and, above all things, do those which appertain unto

his glory. And therefore it is that I have made choice of this kind of life, which is most free and agreeable for such human affairs as may tend to his service only. From which, if either the marriages which have been offered me by divers puissant princes or the danger of attempts made against my life could no whit divert me, it is long since I had any joy in the honor of a husband. And this is that I thought then that I was a private person. But when the public charge of governing the kingdom came upon me, it seemed unto me an inconsiderate folly to draw upon myself the cares which might proceed of marriage.

To conclude, I am already bound unto an husband, which is the kingdom of England. . . . And reproach me so no more that I have no children, for every one of you, and as many as are English, are my children and kinfolks. . . .

But in this I commend you, that you have not appointed me an husband, for that were unworthy the majesty of an absolute princess and the discretion of you that are born my subjects.

Nevertheless, if God have ordained me to another course of life, I will promise you to do nothing to the prejudice of the commonwealth. But as far as possible I may, will marry such an husband as shall be no less careful for the common good than myself. . . .

Lastly, this may be sufficient, both for my memory and honor of my name, if when I have expired my last breath, this may be inscribed upon my tomb: "Here lies interred Elizabeth, a virgin pure until her death."[1]

Despite what she said, hardly anyone believed she would remain unmarried. Certainly neither Feria nor Philip believed it. As feisty, flame-tongued John Knox, the influential Scottish Protestant preacher and former priest, said in his widely distributed pamphlet *First Blast of the Trumpet Against the Monstrous Regiment of Women*, "Being a maid, she must marry." He had said it about Mary, before she married Philip, but his argument, persuasive to many, applied equally to Elizabeth. Without a husband, a woman, "painted forth by nature to be weak, frail, impatient, feeble and foolish," according to Knox, would make a monstrous mess as a ruler. A woman, Knox claimed, needed someone "to relieve her of those labours which are fit only for men." Philip was willing to be that someone to Elizabeth as he had been to Mary.

"Everything," Feria told Philip, thinking of Spain and probably the church as well, "depends on the husband this woman chooses, for the King's will is paramount here in all things." But, Feria reported, having heard the court scuttlebutt, "Everybody thinks that she will not marry a foreigner, and they cannot make out whom she favors, so that nearly every day some new cry is raised about a husband." Feria was eager to get on with offering Elizabeth Philip's proposal, but Philip, characteristically cautious, was hesitating. Feria kept pressing. He told Philip that he would try to see Elizabeth and get her to talk about Philip and have her understand, as Mary had, that marrying an Englishman, a subject, would degrade her majesty. Feria pushed Philip for a decision, seeming to think that Philip was in a race for Elizabeth's hand. "I am afraid," he wrote, "that one fine day we shall find this woman married, and I shall be the last man in the place to know anything about it."

Philip seemed tortured by the matter. He professed great reluctance, which may have been genuine. Finally, though, on January 10, 1559, five days before Elizabeth's coronation, he told Feria, "I have decided to place on one side all other considerations that might be urged against it and am resolved to sacrifice my private inclination and render this service to God and offer to marry the Queen of England." He then authorized Feria to seek an audience with Elizabeth and to make a formal proposal on his behalf. Whatever his true feelings, he told Feria that "if it were not to serve God, I would not have got into this. Nothing would make me do it except the clear knowledge that it would gain the kingdom [of England] for his service and faith." His marriage to Elizabeth would, he said, be of "enormous importance to Christianity." But apparently feeling very much like a martyr—or wishing to be thought so—he told Feria that he felt "like a condemned man awaiting his fate."

There seemed no doubt in his mind that all he had to do was propose and Elizabeth would become his, even though he attached conditions to his offer to marry her. She would have to renounce her Protestant beliefs and become a bona fide Catholic. She would also have to receive absolution from the pope for the error of her previous ways. By so doing, Philip figured, she would make him look good. "It will be evident and manifest," he said, "that I am serving the Lord in marrying her."

Philip also stipulated that after their marriage he would be allowed to visit

Spain as often as he felt necessary and that, as in his prenuptial agreement with Mary, a child born to him and Elizabeth would not inherit the Netherlands, to which his son, Carlos, was heir.

Then it was time for Feria to go see Elizabeth and close the deal. He managed to obtain a private meeting with her and laid out the proposal. Apparently surprised that she didn't leap at the offer, he sat listening to her go on and on about the virtues of the single life. He ratcheted up his sales pitch by warning her that if she didn't marry and give England an heir, she would risk having the French king, Henry II, go to war against her and install Mary Stuart—Mary Queen of Scots, wife of Henry's heir—on the English throne in Elizabeth's place.

At that, Elizabeth went off like a rocket. She launched into a diatribe against Henry, against his sickly son and heir Francis, against Mary Stuart, Francis's wife, and against the French and Scots in general. Her ranting lasted so long and became so heated that she at last sank into a chair, apparently exhausted. She dismissed Feria by telling him that she needed time to think about Philip's proposal.

Several days later, having regained a cool head, she met again with Feria to discuss the proposal. This time she offered the arguments that could be made against her marriage to Philip. He had been married to her sister, and thus her marriage to him would be prohibited by the same scripture that her father had argued invalidated his marriage to Mary's mother, Catherine of Aragon, who had been married to Henry VIII's brother, Arthur. For that reason, an English court had ruled Henry's marriage to Catherine invalid, and another such marriage likely would be ruled invalid as well. Besides, she said, she would not do anything that violated Scripture, even if the pope gave her dispensation to do so. She claimed furthermore that such a marriage would dishonor her father, which she could not do. But, she told Feria, so that he would not leave empty-handed, she would consult her council and Parliament to have them consider the proposal and to receive their advice. While she did so, she said, Feria should tell his king that if she decided to marry, he would be her first choice.

Feria apparently was encouraged, as was Philip, who wrote to Elizabeth to tell her how much he hoped that Feria's mission would succeed. Elizabeth's councilors, however, were horrified. In answer to their pleas that she refuse the proposal, Elizabeth promised that, unlike her sister, she would not do anything against the interests of her country. "I am descended by father and mother of mere English blood," she told the council members, "and not of Spain, as my late sister was." But she was willing to keep Philip hoping.

She strung Feria along for a month. She told him that she would not give him an answer that was not a good one. She then let him try to guess what that meant. Finally, after the peace treaty with France had been negotiated—for which Elizabeth had evidently been stalling Feria and Philip—on March 14 she sent for Feria and gave him the bad news. She couldn't marry Philip. The reason, she said, was that she was a heretic.

Ever the diplomat, Feria assured her that Philip did not consider her a heretic, and neither did he.

She was a Protestant, she told him, and had no intention to change.

Now apparently stung, Feria, countered that, "My master will not change his religion for all the kingdoms in the world."

Elizabeth, enjoying the upper hand, shot back, "Then much less would he do it for a woman." She told Feria that she had no desire to marry anyone. As the meeting wound down, she assured Feria that she wanted their two countries to remain friends, to the same extent that a marriage between their two monarchs would have made them close friends.

Feria was then left with the joyless task of passing along the queen's decision. Philip seemed not at all disappointed. He wrote to Elizabeth to tell her he was sorry things had not worked out, but that their two countries would remain friendly. Then he quickly changed his marriage plans. In the diplomatic euphoria rising from negotiations for the treaty of Cateau-Cambrésis, which ended hostilities between Spain and France as well as between England and France, an agreement had been reached to further good Spanish-French relations by wedding the French king's fourteen-year-old daughter, Elizabeth of Valois, to Philip's son, Carlos, soon to turn fourteen. However, once Queen Elizabeth had rejected his proposal, Philip decided that instead of having his son marry the French princess, he, Philip, nearly thirty-two years old, would marry her.

Elizabeth pretended offense over that news when she saw Feria again. She claimed she had never given Philip a definite no and told Feria, "Your master must have been much in love with me not to be able to wait four months [for a definite answer]."

Feria failed to appreciate Elizabeth's humor. Fed up with her prevarications and histrionics, he wrote to Philip that England's government "has fallen into the hands of a woman who is a daughter of the Devil." No doubt he was pleased when later in March he received word that Philip was replacing him. Philip's new ambassador would be Alvaro de Quadra, bishop of Aquila, Spain.

On June 22, 1559, Philip, with the duke of Alba standing in for him as proxy groom, married the French princess Elizabeth in an elaborate ceremony at the Church of St. Mary in Paris. In a celebratory joust that followed the wedding, the French king, Henry II, forty-two-year-old father of the bride, was mortally wounded when an opponent's wooden lance splintered on impact with the king's helmet and a piece of the broken lance pierced Henry's temple. He died ten days later. His son Francis would now become king, and Mary Stuart, Queen of Scots, his wife, would become queen of France.

Philip had not been the first to propose to Queen Elizabeth. Even before she became queen, the crown prince of Sweden, Eric, proposed. She left him waiting interminably for an answer, but told Thomas Pope, who had brought the proposal to her, that she preferred being unmarried. Philip, furthermore, would not be her last opportunity for a husband. He had some suggestions for her in that regard, as a matter of fact. In an attempt to keep the Tudors in the Habsburg family and England as an ally, Philip on April 11 told Feria to offer Elizabeth either of two sons of Emperor Ferdinand, Philip's uncle, both of them Austrian archdukes. The obedient Feria tried to discuss the possibilities with Elizabeth, but she dazzled him with obfuscation, and he left the meeting frustrated. "I could not tell Your Majesty what this woman means to do with herself," he wrote to Philip, "and those who know her best know no more than I do."

The emperor himself had first had the idea of marrying one of his sons to Elizabeth, and in February he had dispatched an envoy to broach the matter to her, although he knew Philip had already proposed and was awaiting the queen's answer. He even sent to London a portrait of the older of the two sons, so Elizabeth could see what he looked like. When Ferdinand learned that Elizabeth had turned Philip down, he pressed his case. But now he had his envoy focus on just one of the sons, Charles, the younger of the two. The older son, also named Ferdinand, was, the father decided, too piously Catholic to abide Elizabeth. Charles, not so devout as his brother, seemed to the emperor a better match. Besides, Elizabeth had already rendered judgment on young Ferdinand, saying he was "fit only for praying for his own family." Religion mattered to the emperor, and he thought Charles could be more effective in winning Elizabeth into the Catholic fold. The emperor realized, though, that Elizabeth, instead of becoming a Catholic, might turn Charles into a Protestant—which some English officials thought would happen—but the father figured the political considerations were worth the risk of Charles's soul.

In May 1559 Emperor Ferdinand sent another envoy, Baron Caspar Breuner, to London to tender Archduke Charles's formal proposal of marriage. Elizabeth, receiving the offer, said she wished to thank the emperor for considering her to be worthy of his son. She then launched into her by now usual befogging remarks about marriage. On the one hand, she said, she was not inclined to marry anyone. But on the other hand, she said, she might change her mind. Later, when Quadra, Philip's new ambassador, came to see her about marrying Charles, she told him that she had heard that Charles had an unusually large head, that a portrait of him would not be good enough, since she did not trust portrait painters to render an accurate likeness, and that she would have to see and speak to anyone she might consider before agreeing to marry him. She hinted that Charles should come to England and let her look him over.

Quadra couldn't be sure she was serious, as he reported to Philip, but he thought she really wanted Charles to come to England in disguise. The emperor, though, was having none of it. He refused to send his son to Elizabeth on approval, in disguise or otherwise. Charles himself was opposed as well.

Elizabeth passed Charles's proposal along to her chief councilors. She promised she would take their advice, provided she could see and get to know the man before agreeing to marry him. At the same time, when Breuner came back to discuss the matter with her, she insisted that she was not going to marry anyone. But, she hedged, characteristically, God might cause her to change her mind. Over a period of days she continued to string him along. Finally, though, on June 5, guided by two of her top councilors, she wrote a tactful letter to Emperor Ferdinand, declining his son's proposal. It was not the end of Charles's pursuit, however.

In the meantime, other suitors were pushing or being pushed for acceptance, including Sweden's Prince Eric, who had not taken Elizabeth's lack of an answer to be a no. He kept writing her letters, declaring his love. He sent her a portrait of himself, which she apparently liked, and he renewed his proposal to her. She turned him down, but he refused to stay turned down. At one point he decided he would go to England and propose in person, but a storm at sea forced him to return home. Then he sent his younger brother, Duke John of Finland, to plead his case for him. John arrived in England in early October 1559, and after misunderstanding the warmth of his welcome to indicate Elizabeth's acceptance of Eric's proposal, he settled in to a long lobbying effort on Eric's behalf. In February 1560 Elizabeth tried again to turn Eric away, writing him that although she believed his professions of love for her were sincere, she did not feel the same way about him and so must refuse his proposal. Nevertheless, John stayed on in England for two more months, perhaps hoping she would change her mind, then sailed for home in April. Upon his father's death that same year, Eric became Sweden's king. He again proposed to Elizabeth in the fall of 1561. She at first encouraged him, then stalled, and he at last gave up the chase. (John, his brother, later deposed him from the throne and had him poisoned to death in 1577.)

Other foreign nobles were in the running for Elizabeth's hand, including the king of Denmark, the duke of Saxony, and the duke of Holstein, but Elizabeth was even less interested in them than she was in Archduke Charles and Prince Eric. Her councilors, although agreed that she should marry, were split on whether her choice should be a foreigner or an Englishman. Thomas Radcliffe, earl of Sussex, Thomas Howard, duke of Norfolk, and William Cecil, Elizabeth's secretary of state, all preferred a foreigner. But finding a suitable one would likely mean he would have to be a Protestant—a point in Eric's favor—or be willing to become one. He would have to come to England and let Elizabeth, in effect, interview him first, something that was highly unlikely to happen. Presumably she would also require him to reside in England after their marriage, since his having to live in his own country was one of the reasons she gave Eric for refusing him.

Probably the strongest argument against her marriage to a foreigner was that it would, as it had with Mary's marriage to Philip, entangle England in the foreign affairs of some other nation and would cost England at least some of its independence. Therefore, most of Elizabeth's councilors—with memories of Philip still fresh in their minds—wanted her to choose an Englishman. Marrying an Englishman, of course, meant marrying a subject, and she was not at all sure she should marry an inferior, whom she would have to raise to a suitable social level and who thus would become a creature of her own making. A creature so made by the queen would, according to some arguments, inevitably become a source of jealousy, controversy, contention, and power in Elizabeth's court and would set off destabilizing ill effects on the country. But at least a subject would be, presumably, someone she knew, someone whose looks, personality, and character were familiar to her, not the pig in a poke that a foreign noble would be. He might even be someone with whom she could fall in love, if she hadn't already.

She had several prospects. William Pickering was one. He was a tall, handsome bachelor in his early forties, popular with the ladies, who had known Elizabeth a long time and was believed to have been involved in the Wyatt rebellion that was aimed at deposing Mary. He had lived abroad for several years, had fallen ill, and had not been well enough to return to England until May 1559, whereupon he was promptly received by the new queen and was thought by many to be a likely candidate to marry her, although he believed she would never marry.

Henry Fitzalan, earl of Arundel, was another, or at least he considered himself to be. He was a member of Elizabeth's council, a widower in his late forties, wealthy, and from a long line of aristocrats, but lacking in looks and personality and having been described as "a flighty man of no ability, rather silly and loutish." He was available, but Elizabeth thought little of him. He was one of those she strung along, despite his defects.

The one she was really interested in—the only one—was her handsome master of the horse, Robert Dudley. Around April 1559 he became an obvious favorite. Elizabeth had him move from his former apartment in the palace into a suite next to hers. She took him riding with her almost every day. They spent evenings together, talking and laughing and singing to their own musical accompaniment. She also had her serious times with him, talking over matters of state, although he was not a member of her council, and letting him influence her about them, igniting further jealousy among her councilors. Feria, while he was still Philip's envoy, reported that Dudley "has come so much into favor that he does whatever he likes with affairs and it is even said that her majesty visits him in his chamber day and night." Of course, if Elizabeth was in love with Dudley and intended to marry him, his wife, Amy, would be a problem to be solved. Court scuttlebutt had the solution. "People talk of this so freely," Feria told Philip, "that they go so far as to say that his wife has a malady in one of her breasts and the queen is only waiting for her to die to marry Lord Robert."

Court scuttlebutt traveled from London to other capitals, and by June 1559 it had reached the ears of Emperor Ferdinand in Vienna. With his son Charles then awaiting an answer to his proposal to Elizabeth, Ferdinand began to wonder whether England's queen was still a bargain. He told his envoy, Breuner, to check out the rumor. Breuner reported back that he had done some investigating among the queen's ladies-in-waiting and they conceded that Elizabeth was paying too much attention to Dudley, but they insisted that she had "certainly never been forgetful of her honor."

Others were not so sure. Popular rumors, which reached into the countryside, said they were lovers. One even claimed that she had become pregnant by Dudley.

Elizabeth pooh-poohed such talk. When Katherine Ashley, her longtime friend and attendant, spoke frankly to her about the rumors, cautioning her, Elizabeth replied that it should be obvious there was nothing to them, "seeing that she was always surrounded by her ladies of the bedchamber, who at all times could see whether there was anything dishonorable between her and her master of the horse." But, she pointed out imperiously, "If she had ever had the will, or had found pleasure in such a dishonorable life—from which may God preserve her—she did not know of anyone who could forbid her." Nevertheless, she said, "She trusted in God that nobody would ever live to see her so commit herself." Mrs. Ashley suggested that the way to quiet the talk about her romantic adventures was for Elizabeth to get married and put Dudley out of her personal life. Elizabeth's reply was that she needed to keep Dudley close to her because he brought sunshine into her life, that "in this world she had so much sorrow and tribulation and so little joy." It was, especially for those who understood how little love there had been in her life, a touching confession.

Dudley was widely seen as an exploiter, using his relationship with Elizabeth, calculatedly cultivated by him, to further himself and his fortune. She had indeed showered him with position, privilege, and property. She gave him a mansion in Kew, near London, and land that had once been monastery property. She gave him Kenilworth Castle, which had belonged to his father and had been seized by the government on his father's execution. She gave him a license to export woollen cloth without having to pay duty on it, at which he turned a handsome profit by selling the license. She gave him the right to receive duties collected on imported silk and velvet and on sweet wine, which he turned into a significant cash flow. She gave him a government pension of a thousand pounds a year, in addition to his pay as master of the horse. She inducted him into the highly prestigious Order of the Garter, usually reserved for those who had rendered outstanding service to Crown or country. More gifts, including an earldom, were to come. Through Elizabeth's continuing largesse he had become both rich and powerful, a situation deeply resented at the queen's court. In the minds of many of England's influentials, he was, after all, the son and grandson of traitors, and had spent time in the Tower himself as a traitor till Queen Mary had pardoned him, and thus he was a person unworthy of so many royal favors. Thomas Radcliffe, earl of Sussex, one of those closest to Elizabeth, warned his friends about Dudley. "Beware of the gypsy [Dudley]," he cautioned, "for he will be too hard for you all. You know not the beast as well as I do." Enmity of him ran so deep that his murder was solicited, and two men of standing were arrested for attempted murder and sent to the Tower.

Still, Elizabeth was happy with him. But would she marry him? Would he become king? Those were the most bothersome questions. Some believed that Dudley was perfect for her to fall in love with because she would not be tempted to marry him, since he was already married. Elizabeth's notoriously willful father, however, had found ways to get around the barrier of an existing marriage, and she was perceived as no less willful than he.

Yet, although virtually everyone believed she would eventually marry *somebody,* there were her persistent declarations that she preferred to stay single. And what the queen preferred, she usually got. Dudley remembered Elizabeth's saying, when she was only eight years old, that she did not want to get married. Over the years, she had apparently retained that sentiment. Perhaps, since her accession, it had become even stronger, for she now had a more compelling reason for keeping it. James Melville, a Scots diplomat, divined that reason and told her he understood. "I know the truth of that [her desire to remain unmarried], madam," he said. "You need not tell it to me. Your majesty thinks if you were married, you would be but *queen* of England. And now you are both king *and* queen."

Others claimed that the reason she didn't want to marry was that she knew she was incapable of having children. Feria was one who bought into that rumor, reporting to Philip that, "If my spies do not lie which I believe they do not, for a certain reason which they have recently given me, I understand she will not bear children." Bishop Quadra, Feria's successor, repeated the rumor, telling Philip, "The common opinion, confirmed by certain physicians, is that this woman is unhealthy, and it is believed certain that she will not bear children." William Camden, one of her earliest biographers and a contemporary, states that "men cursed Huic, the queen's physician, for dissuading her from marriage for I know not what female infirmity." A mid-twentieth-century biographer, however, from correspondence between some of Elizabeth's chief advisers, including William Cecil, concluded that she did not have "any female infirmity more serious than a chronic inability to make up her mind."[2] Her later biographers seem agreed that the evidence that she had an infirmity conflicts with evidence that none existed and that, in the words of one, "the whole mass [of evidence] seems to add up to nothing."[3]

It was possible that far from being unable to become pregnant, pregnancy was what Elizabeth feared in marriage, childbirth being at the time a major killer of young women. The big reason for her getting married, as far as most people were concerned and perhaps in her mind, too, was for her to produce an heir. Once married, she would *have* to become pregnant and assure England a successor to the throne. Public pressure and the demands of her husband would require it. And that fact gave her one more reason for remaining unmarried. She did not want a rival, which an heir apparent—or any other designated successor—would instantly become. She had already witnessed how possible successors, herself and Jane Grey included, could be turned into rallying points for rebels bent on deposing a reigning monarch. Now that she was the reigning monarch, she was extremely reluctant to raise up someone who could be used by her enemies to threaten her crown, as France's King Henry II had already indicated he planned to do with his daughter-in-law, Mary Stuart, Queen of Scots, a possible successor to the English throne.

Elizabeth had been steadfastly resisting requests to name her successor, or define a line of succession, as Henry VIII had done, for just that reason. Besides Mary Stuart there were other possible successors, including the two sisters of the executed Lady Jane Grey, granddaughters of Henry VIII's sister Mary. There were also the half sister of Mary Stuart, Margaret Lennox, and her two sons; and there was Henry Hastings, earl of Huntingdon and a descendant of King Edward III through both his father and mother. Elizabeth showed no inclination toward any of them but let them all think they were candidates. She would allow the risk of whatever turmoil, including civil war, might follow her early death, if it should occur, and occur without her having produced an heir.

If Robert Dudley could have his way, however, Elizabeth would marry him and have a chance to give the country an heir. Rumors had it that he planned to get rid of his wife in one way or another so that he could marry the queen. Some thought he was waiting for her to die of a malignancy in her breast. Some said he was preparing a divorce. Others said he was plotting murder. Worse, rumor even had it that Elizabeth was a conspirator in the plot. That was one of the rumors that Quadra passed along. Quadra wrote, "I have heard from a person who is accustomed to giving me veracious news that Lord Robert has sent to poison his wife. Certainly all that the Queen will do with us in the matter of her marriage is only keeping the country engaged with words until this wicked deed is consummated." According to Quadra, "They [presumably meaning Dudley and Elizabeth] had given out that she [Dudley's wife] was ill, but she was not ill at all. She was very well and taking care not to be poisoned."

Quadra's source of that information was Elizabeth's secretary of state, William Cecil, who had suffered a humiliating loss of status in the queen's eyes, brought on by Dudley's dislike of him. The dislike was reciprocated by Cecil, who was certain the country was headed for doom if Elizabeth continued her relationship with Dudley, and worse if she married him. "Of Lord Robert," Quadra reported, "he [Cecil] said twice that he would be better in Paradise than here." Foxy as he was, Cecil knew that his accusation of Elizabeth's part in a plot to murder Amy Dudley would go from Quadra and be spread to the capitals of Europe, from which it would echo back to Elizabeth through her emissaries. Cecil apparently meant to deter her by having her realize the international community was aware of her unholy league with Robert Dudley. She would thus be warned that murdering Amy Dudley would have serious consequences. If Amy died, whether murdered or not, public opinion, enraged by reports of Elizabeth's complicity in a plot, would prevent her marriage to Dudley, which would only tend to confirm the rumor of her complicity.

Amy Dudley, who never visited Elizabeth's court, was living at Cumnor Hall, about four miles north of the town of Abingdon, near Oxford. The house had been leased by Robert Dudley's employee, Anthony Forster, who handled Dudley's financial affairs. It was a large, rectangular, two-story, gray stone structure built around a courtyard, its architecture reflecting its monastic past as the summer retreat of the abbots of Abingdon, and was picturesquely set among trees and ponds and terraced walkways. Looking out across the broad downs at the edge of the property, one could see a church spire rising in the distance. On the morning of Sunday, September 8, 1560, Amy arose early in her rooms at Cumnor Hall and instructed her several guests and their servants, as well as her own household staff, to leave her and go to the fair being held in Abingdon. When some objected to attending the fair on a Sunday, Amy emphatically insisted they go. Most of the servants and some of the guests left. Those who stayed retired to their rooms.

About eleven o'clock that morning Amy, who ordinarily couldn't stand being left alone, was joined at dinner by the elderly mother of the house's owner, who also lived there, as well as her son, William Owen. After Amy and Mrs. Owen had eaten, the house fell quiet and seemingly empty.

It was late afternoon when the servants returned from the fair. Entering the house, they made a horrifying discovery. Amy Dudley, her neck broken, lay dead at the foot of a stone stairway that descended from her rooms to the hall on the ground floor.

As the news seeped out, murder was quickly suspected.

Muddying the circumstances of the death were Elizabeth's remarks made to Bishop Quadra just the day before, September 7, which was Elizabeth's birthday. She had told Quadra, he later reported, "that Lord Robert's wife was dead, or nearly so, and begged me to say nothing about it." Quadra at the time apparently assumed she meant the malignancy in Amy's breast was about to kill her. But now the rumor that Dudley planned to murder his wife, with Elizabeth's complicity, which Quadra had also heard, took on new life.

There was at least one more bad piece of circumstantial evidence. On the day that Amy died, Dudley had dispatched one of his trusted servants, a distant relative named Thomas Blount, from Windsor Castle, where Elizabeth and her court were then residing, to Cumnor Hall on unspecified private business. On the way there, Blount on Monday had encountered another of Dudley's servants on the road, hurrying in the opposite direction. The two stopped long enough for the news of Amy's death to be told to Blount. On hearing it, and the attendant details, rather than turning back toward Windsor to inform Dudley or continuing on to Cumnor to see for himself, as might reasonably have been expected, Blount instead rode only as far as Abingdon and stopped for the night at an inn. He later explained that he "was desirous to hear what news went abroad." But his stop seemed suspicious, as if Blount, a confidant of Robert Dudley, had expected Amy's death and had no curiosity about it.

Dudley learned of his wife's death Monday morning. The servant who had met Blount on the road, a man named Bowes, delivered the news to him and Elizabeth at the same time. According to Quadra, who evidently was also there at the time, Elizabeth seemed to be struck speechless by the news. Dudley also seemed shocked and later that day dispatched a rider to carry a letter to Blount, telling him to begin a thorough investigation. "The greatness and suddenness of the misfortune doth so perplex me until I do hear from you how the matter standeth, or how this evil should light upon me, considering what the malicious world will bruit, as I can take no rest," he wrote, revealing more concern for the fallout than for his wife's demise. "And because I have no way to purge myself of the malicious talk that I know the wicked world will use, but one which is the very plain truth to be known, I do pray you, as you have loved me, and do tender me and my quietness, and as now my special trust is in you, that you will use all the devices and means you can possibly for learning of the truth, wherein have no respect to any living person."

Dudley told Blount he wanted the inquiry to be conducted by "the discreetest and most substantial men, such as for their knowledge may be able to search thoroughly the bottom of the matter, and for their uprightness will earnestly and sincerely deal therein. As I would be sorry in my heart any such evil should be committed, so should it well appear to the world my innocency by my dealing in the matter." He then dispatched riders to take the grim news to Amy's relatives and urged them to go to Cumnor Hall and witness the investigation.

Elizabeth, meanwhile, issued an order that the news of Amy's death be announced publicly. The announcement was to state that the death was caused by an accident. "She must have fallen down a staircase," Elizabeth reasoned. She further commanded that an inquest be held, and mindful of the appearance of things, she ordered Dudley to return to his house in Kew, so that there would be some distance between them when the news broke to the public.

By the time Blount finally showed up at Cumnor, on Tuesday, September 10, the coroner and the members of the coroner's jury were already on the scene, conducting their investigation. Waiting for Blount was the letter sent him by Dudley. Blount quickly wrote an up-to-date report to Dudley, telling him that the investigating jurymen seemed wise and able men, drawn from the community. But, he said, some were enemies of Anthony Forster and he expressed a hope that they could be indifferent to their feelings in determining the facts of the case. Their indifference was important because one rumor had it that Forster, who with his wife was living at Cumnor Hall, was involved in the plot to murder Amy.

The investigation, however, was moving toward the strong possibility of suicide. The facts, especially including Amy's insistence that everyone leave the house and go to the fair, her illness and her depression, pointed in that direction. Her maid, a Mrs. Pirto, although she claimed she thought the death was an accident, told Blount that she had at times "heard her [Amy] pray to God to deliver her from desperation."[4] Blount reported to Dudley, "Truly the tales I do hear of her maketh me to think she had a strange mind in her. . . ."

While the investigation continued, Elizabeth stayed out of public view, showing anxiety only to those who shared the privacy of her palace apartment. Dudley fretted away in his confinement at Kew, worried about not only what the inquest would determine but also what people were saying about him. He seemed to be hoping for a verdict of murder, so that he could assist in the apprehension of the killer and thereby establish his own innocence. "For as I would be sorry in my heart any such evil should be committed," he wrote to Blount, "so should it well appear to the world my innocency by my dealing in the matter."

Blount, keeping his ears open to the jury's proceedings, wrote back to Dudley on Friday, September 13, to tell him that the jury's investigation was being "kept very secret; and yet I do hear a whispering that they can find no presumption of evil. . . . And I think some of them be sorry for it, God forgive me." Blount felt good about the verdict he was expecting. He told Dudley that he was "much quieted" about the outcome. He was sure, after finding out as much as he could, that "only misfortune hath done it, and nothing else." Suicide, although possible, was now being ruled out.

Impatient for more than what Blount could tell, Dudley contacted the fore-man of the coroner's jury, a Mr. Smith, who perhaps was less explicit than Dud-ley desired but who assured Dudley that as far as he and his fellow members of the jury could now see, their verdict would be "death by misadventure."

Days later, in a document that has not survived, the coroner's jury did in-deed return that verdict. Dudley—and the queen—were absolved.

Murmurings about Dudley, though, persisted.

◆ 10. THE RELIGIOUS DIVIDE

Hans Luther, a German copper miner who rose from poverty by hard work to become a mine operator, had plans for his son. A gifted student, young Luther should use his gifts, his father decided, to study law. As a lawyer he would better himself, would be able to marry well, and would earn enough to provide for his parents when they were old. The young Luther, however, came up with a different idea. After buying some law books and studying them, he found he had little interest in the subject. An unusually pious young man, his major interest was religion, and he was nagged by thoughts that his spiritual condition was not what it should be, wondering if he should make a change in his life. As he was walking along a road one day he was severely frightened by a bolt of lightning that struck near him. He took it as a sign that he should seek God's acceptance by becoming a monk.

And so at age twenty-two, having already earned bachelor's and master's degrees, Martin Luther entered the monastery of the Augustinian Order of Hermits in Erfurt, Germany, in July 1505. In 1507 he was ordained as a priest. In later years he gave glimpses into his life as a monk. Here is one of them:

> I myself was a monk for twenty years and so plagued myself with prayers, fastings, wakings, and freezings that I almost died of cold, which hurt me so much that I would never want to attempt it again even though I were able. What else did I seek through this but God? Who was to see how I observed the rules and lived such a rigid life?[1]

Here is another:

> I have been a monk and waked at night, fasting, praying, chastising and tormenting my body, that I might remain obedient and

live chastely. I speak of those pious and sincere monks who take their vocation in this world seriously, not of whoremongers and rascals, who live an unchaste, loose life, but those who have made a real effort like myself, who have tried and striven to become like unto Christ that they might be saved. What did they accomplish by all this? Have they discovered him? Christ says here, "You will remain in your sins and die." That is what they have obtained.[2]

Life as a monk was not giving him what he was looking for. He felt no better off than he was before he entered the monastery. He later confessed his feelings:

When I was a monk, I believed that it was all up with my salvation. Each time I experienced the temptations of the flesh, that is to say, a number of evil desires, such as anger, hatred, jealousy in regard to a brother, etc., I tried all kinds of remedies. I confessed daily, but it was of no avail. The covetousness always returned. This is the reason I could find no peace, but was perpetually in torment, thinking, "You have committed such and such a sin. You are still the victim of jealousy and concupiscence. In vain you have joined the order. All your good works are useless."[3]

Further disillusionment came when he was one of two monks sent to represent the Erfurt monastery at a meeting in Rome, arriving there on foot in January 1511. During the month he was there, like the devout pilgrim that he was, he took in the sights and activities of the holy city, which was a lot less holy than what he was expecting. He was appalled by the corruption, licentiousness, hypocrisy, irreverence, and blasphemy, within the church and without.

After returning to Germany, he was transferred from the monastery in Erfurt to one in the village of Wittenberg, where there was also a university, newly founded. In Wittenberg he captured the attention and admiration of John Staupitz, the vicar general of the Augustinian Order and one of the founders of the University of Wittenberg, who told Luther he should work on a doctor of theology degree, which he could do at the university. To pay for the program of study, Luther agreed to teach at the university. He became the monastery's official preacher and was placed in charge of training novitiates.

He also became a frequent preacher at the parish church in Wittenberg. He received the doctoral degree on October 19, 1512, became a member of the university's theology faculty on October 22, and on Monday, October 25, began teaching.

His lectures covered a number of books of the Bible, including Psalms, Saint Paul's epistles to the Romans and the Galatians, and Hebrews. Oddly enough, his theological training thus far had not required him to study the Bible. Now, to prepare for his lectures, he was forced into an intensive study of the words of Scripture and he learned Hebrew and Greek, the languages in which they were originally written, to augment his readings in his Latin Bible. While poring over Saint Paul's letter to the first-century Christians in Rome—the New Testament book of Romans—Luther made a discovery that would change his life.

Up to this point he had believed that his acceptance by God depended on what he did. As Luther saw him, God was a stern judge, ready to pronounce judgment on sinners and to inflict harsh punishment on those judged unworthy of forgiveness and acceptance. To placate that fearsome God and avoid his punishment, an individual had to do something to make things right with God. That conception of God had long tormented Luther. It was what had driven him into the asceticism of a monk's life. Now, in the fall of 1515, he read in Romans 1:17 Saint Paul's quotation from the Old Testament prophet Habbakuk—"the just shall live by his faith." Luther wrestled with that passage until he was satisfied that he knew what it meant:

> My situation was that, although an impeccable monk, I stood before God as a sinner troubled in conscience, and I had no confidence that my merit would assuage him. Therefore I did not love a just and angry God, but rather hated and murmured against him. Yet I clung to the dear Paul and had a great yearning to know what he meant.
>
> Night and day I pondered until I saw the connection between the justice of God and the statement that "the just shall live by his faith." Then I grasped that the justice of God is that righteousness by which through grace and sheer mercy God justifies us through faith. Thereupon I felt myself to be reborn and to have gone through open doors into paradise. The whole of Scripture took

on a new meaning, and whereas before the "justice of God" had filled me with hate, now it became to me inexpressibly sweet in greater love. This passage of Paul became to me a gate into heaven. . . .

If you have a true faith that Christ is your Savior, then at once you have a gracious God, for faith leads you in and opens up God's heart and will, that you should see pure grace and over-flowing love. This it is to behold God in faith that you should look upon his fatherly, friendly heart, in which there is no anger nor ungraciousness.[4]

In an hour of momentous enlightenment, Luther had come to understand that, as he said, "the righteous are saved by God's grace, namely, through faith." This newfound theology of justification by faith, not works, which harked back to first-century Christianity, was to have ramifications in sixteenth-century Catholicism. It undercut the efficacy of the sacraments, and thus the power of the church. It invalidated much of the church's doctrine and diminished the church's authority over people's lives. Salvation became a personal, individual matter, gained entirely by God's grace through an individual's faith in Christ. Neither the church's priests nor its rituals were necessary. All believers in Christ were, in effect, priests. None other was needed for salvation.

The conclusions reached and preached by Luther were not all original with him. Some repeated the teachings of earlier reformers, especially including John Hus of Bohemia, burned at the stake in 1415 for being a heretic, and John Wycliffe of England, who died in 1384. Wycliffe, like Luther, had declared that the Bible, not the church, is the sole authority for Christian doctrine and he denied the Catholic doctrine of transubstantiation, which gave priests power to transform the communion elements into the body and blood of Jesus. Hus had been influenced by Wycliffe's writings, had preached his beliefs, and had decried the abuses and immorality of the clergy.

Luther became particularly critical of the church's practice of selling indulgences, which were, as one writer puts it, "the bingo of the sixteenth century."[5] The idea of indulgences rested on two foundational principles: (1) the Catholic belief that merely feeling sorry for one's sins and confessing them was not enough, that a person had to *do* something to prove that he or she was truly repentant; and (2) the belief that the Catholic saints had done so many good works, over and above what their own sins demanded, that they had built up a huge surplus of what might be considered good-works credits. Those credits, representing the saints' good works, were owned by the church, as were the good-works credits of Christ himself. And, most important, they could be sold by the church. For a sum of money, the church, through its representatives, would issue the indulgence buyer a sort of certificate, stating that the buyer's good-works requirement had been discharged out of the church's stockpile of good-works credits. Selling indulgences to persons who either had not the time or the inclination to do good works themselves turned out to be an enormous boon, an extremely lucrative source of income to the church. Income from indulgence sales was used to finance the construction of churches, cathedrals, monasteries, hospitals, and other medieval infrastructure, including a bridge across the Elbe River. Indulgences were used, too, to support the University of Wittenberg.

When an indulgence salesman, a Dominican monk working for Archbishop Albert of Mainz, arrived in the vicinity of Wittenberg in 1517 and in his sales pitch claimed that indulgences freed buyers from punishment for sins they had confessed and could even free souls from purgatory, among other claims, Luther angrily protested from his pulpit, denouncing the tactics and claims of the salesman, John Tetzel. Later, in the fall of 1517, after Tetzel had left the area, Luther obtained a copy of the instructions that had been issued by Archbishop Albert to the salesmen who were selling indulgences for him. Twenty-seven years old and holder of two other church offices (archbishop of Magdeburg and bishop of Halberstadt), Albert had had to pay an enormous fee to gain the appointment as archbishop of Mainz, outbidding other contenders for the position, and had to pay an additional sum to obtain dispensation to hold three church offices simultaneously, more than one being prohibited by the church. With the pope's authorization, he was selling indulgences to recoup what he had paid the pope, Leo X, through the pope's financial agent, the Fugger banking firm. Half of the indulgence proceeds reportedly were to go to the Fuggers to retire the loan Albert had made to pay the pope for the archbishopric, and half were to go to the pope to help finance the completion of the new St. Peter's Basilica in Rome, begun under the previous pope, Julius II.

Albert's instructions, bound in a book decorated with his coat of arms, directed his indulgence salesmen to emphasize four benefits granted by the pope and conveyed by the indulgences: (1) absolute forgiveness, even for souls in purgatory; (2) the choice of a confessor who was authorized to absolve even the most heinous offenses; (3) the availability of a permit to allow the dead to participate in the prayers, fasts, pilgrimages and Masses of the church; and (4) the remission of all good works required of souls in purgatory without their contrition or confession, except in extreme cases.[6] What Albert's salesmen were to promise went beyond the scope of ordinary indulgences.

Luther decided such abuses and the issues underlying them should be called to the attention of the university community. On October 31, 1517, he tacked to the main north door of the Wittenberg castle church, which served as a university bulletin board, a document, printed in Latin, that set forth ninety-five theses he was proposing for debate among his colleagues. The lengthy list was preceded by a prefatory paragraph: "Out of love and zeal for the elucidation of truth, the following theses will be debated at Wittenberg, the Reverend Father Martin Luther, Master of Arts and Sacred Theology, presiding. He begs that those who cannot be present at the oral discussion will communicate their views in writing. In the name of the Lord Jesus Christ. Amen."[7]

The theses disputed the whole idea of indulgences. In the very first thesis, Luther declared that penance is not the performance of a physical act but an attitude of mind, one that continues throughout life. In other theses he stated that the pope had no power to release souls from purgatory and, in an expression of German nationalism, he attacked the purpose for which the money derived from the indulgences was to be used, exaggeratedly asserting that:

> The revenues of all Christendom are being sucked into this insatiable basilica. The Germans laugh at calling this the common treasure of Christendom. Before long all the churches, palaces, walls and bridges of Rome will be built out of our money. First of all we should build living temples, not local churches, and only last of all Saint Peter's, which is not necessary for us. . . . Why doesn't the pope build the basilica of Saint Peter out of his own money? He is richer than Croesus. He would do better to sell Saint Peter's and give the money to the poor folk who are being fleeced by the hawkers of indulgences.[8]

Aside from such practical matters, Luther attacked the theology behind the indulgences:

> Papal indulgences do not remove guilt. Beware of those who say that indulgences effect reconciliation with God. The power of the keys [the pope] cannot make attrition into contrition. He who is contrite has plenary remission of guilt and penalty without indulgences. The pope can remove only those penalties which he himself has imposed on Earth, for Christ did not say, "Whatsoever I have bound in heaven you may loose on Earth."[9]

He disputed the idea of a storehouse of good-works credits:

> The saints have no extra credits. Every saint is bound to love God to the utmost. There is no such thing as [spiritual] supererogation. If there were any superfluous credits, they could not be stored up for subsequent use. The Holy Spirit would have used them fully long ago. Christ indeed had merits, but until I am better instructed I deny that they are indulgences. His merits are freely available without the keys of the pope. . . .
>
> If the pope does have the power to release anyone from purgatory, why in the name of love does he not abolish purgatory by letting everyone out? If for the sake of miserable money he released uncounted souls, why should he not for the sake of most holy love empty the place?[10]

By then warmed to his arguments, Luther further charged that:

> Indulgences are positively harmful to the recipient because they impede salvation by diverting charity and inducing a false sense of security. Christians should be taught that he who gives to the poor is better than he who receives a pardon. He who spends his money for indulgences instead of relieving want receives not the indulgence of the pope but the indignation of God. . . .

> Indulgences are most pernicious because they induce com-
> placency and thereby imperil salvation. Those persons are
> damned who think that letters of indulgence make them cer-
> tain of salvation.[11]

Luther's sharp-edged words, written by him in Latin, were, without his permission or knowledge, translated into German, and the German-language
version was printed and widely circulated. Within two weeks, according to a
contemporary account, Luther's theses had spread throughout all of Germany, and in four weeks other translations had spread throughout Christian
Europe. The time it took for Luther's words to reach such a large audience
was probably a lot longer than that account's writer had it, perhaps several
months, but reach it they did. In Germany the theses gave welcomed expression to the feelings of a great many people, Catholics who preferred to think
for themselves, who had already come to regard the Bible as *the* authority in
religious matters, who were deeply troubled by the church's abuses, and who
resented Rome's siphoning of German resources. Outside Germany as well,
Luther's words found agreement in the hearts of many others, souls made
restless as the new ideas of humanism—with its emphasis on the importance
of the individual and independent-mindedness—clashed with the old doctrines, statements, and practices of the church. Among the rising middle class
in Europe's urban areas the new ideas about the church and the clergy especially took hold, and there the words of reformers such as Luther found eager
acceptance.

Political feelings came into play as well. In Northern Europe particularly,
rulers and prosperous urbanites resented the fact that although the church
was exempt from paying taxes, it exercised a right to collect taxes, and much
of its tax income was sent out of the country and into the pope's treasury in
Rome. Rulers in much of Europe also resented the political power of the
pope, which tended to compete with, if not diminish, the power they held in
their own domains.

Some of Luther's ideas were shared by men of passion and conviction
in other European cities. In Zurich, Ulrich Zwingli, a priest two months
younger than Luther, preached that the Bible was *the* authority for Christian
living and urged that clergy be allowed freedom to preach from it (and that

clergy be permitted to marry, as he did). His influence became so widespread that the city fathers officially declared Zurich to be a Protestant city. In Geneva, John Calvin, the French-born son of a lawyer for the Catholic church, became the leader of a group of Protestant pastors after his influential work, *Institutes of the Christian Religion,* was published in 1536. Calvin espoused the Protestant beliefs that the Bible is the authority for Christian teaching, that salvation comes to an individual only by God's grace, that faith is preeminent over works, and that all believers are priests, needing no intermediary; he also advanced ideas about democratic government, the separation of church and state, and the right of the people to change their government—ideas that would find their way into the minds of the founding fathers of the United States of America and into the life of the new nation. From Calvin came also the ideas about church government that would result in the Presbyterian church. It was Calvin's words and ideas that inspired the Scottish Catholic-priest-turned-Protestant-preacher, John Knox, who brought Presbyterianism to Scotland and helped lead Scotland's conversion from Catholicism to Protestantism.

Luther of course made enemies as well as admirers, one of the first being the high-pressure indulgence salesman John Tetzel, who not only oversold the merits of his product but, claiming to be a heretic hunter for the church, intimidated his prospects into buying it. Tetzel tried to shut Luther up by exerting pressure on Luther's monastic order, the Augustinians, through the Dominicans, Tetzel's order, which turned into a failed effort. He also issued 106 countertheses to dispute Luther's 95. His Dominican order hastily conferred on him a doctoral degree to give him the necessary credential to have his countertheses published. When copies were distributed in Wittenberg, university students burned some eight hundred of them and threatened the man who had brought them to Wittenberg, an incident that embarrassed Luther, but not terribly. Tetzel issued a public threat that he would have Luther burned.

At the same time that Luther had posted his theses on the Wittenberg church door, he had sent a letter and a copy of the ninety-five theses to Albert, the young archbishop of Mainz. Luther at the time believed Albert had had no knowledge of Tetzel's sales pitch. After conferring with his theology experts in Mainz, Albert had forwarded the theses to the Curia, the papal court, in Rome. Efforts by the Curia to have Luther recant his statements proved futile and served only to widen the differences between him and the church of Rome. In January 1521, after Luther had published several influential works—*The Sermon on Good Works, The Papacy at Rome, The Address to the German Nobility, The Babylonian Captivity of the Church,* and *The Freedom of the Christian Man*—writings that detailed his views of Christianity and attacked the papacy and many of the church's traditional practices, including the Mass and the sacraments, Luther was formally excommunicated. Efforts to have him arrested and executed, however, were thwarted by Frederick the Wise, the imperial elector who ruled Saxony and had become Luther's steadfast protector.

King Philip's father, Emperor Charles V, had become another of Luther's enemies. In April 1521, two years after Charles, already king of Spain, had been elected emperor (by the seven German electors, including Frederick the Wise), he summoned Luther to the city of Worms to face a hearing into his heretical teachings. Assured of safe conduct to Worms, Luther dutifully reported, accompanied by three traveling companions and an imperial escort. He drew an enthusiastic, supportive crowd when he arrived in the city on April 16. In the second of a series of public hearings, Luther presented his case. When his interrogator, under Charles's direction, suggested that Luther recant, Luther movingly declared: "Unless I am convinced by the testimony of the scriptures or by clear reason—for I do not trust either in the pope or in councils alone, since it is well known that they have often erred and contradicted themselves— I am bound by the scriptures I have quoted, and my conscience is captive to the word of God. I cannot and I will not retract anything, since it is neither safe nor right to go against conscience. God help me. Amen."[12]

The crowd of onlookers erupted in shouts and cheers. According to one account, Charles's Spanish compatriots in the audience yelled, "To the fire with him!" One eyewitness, the papal nuncio in Germany, Jerome Aleander, claimed that nine-tenths of the Germans present were shouting, "Luther! Luther!" and the other tenth was shouting, "Death to the pope!" Charles, who could understand neither German nor Latin and had to have Luther's words translated for him, quickly decided when the commotion broke out that he had had enough and he stalked out of the chamber. The day's hearing then ended. After later attempts to proceed proved fruitless, the hearings, which came to be called the Diet [meeting] of Worms, concluded, and Luther set out for home. On the way, a mock kidnapping was staged by his supporters, and he was carried away to safety in the Wartburg castle, where he remained until December 1521, using the time there to translate the New Testament into German. He then returned to Wittenberg and resumed his duties, protected by those whose hearts and minds he had won.

Luther's influence continued to grow. In a letter written in 1522, Charles's brother, Archduke Ferdinand, told the emperor, "The cause of Luther is so deeply rooted in the whole empire that not one person in a thousand is free from it." In northern Germany, evangelical preachers inspired by Luther took over pulpits and inveighed against the pope and the bishops. Their sermons were replete with references to "God's word," the phrase that marked their adoption of the Bible as the sole authority for Christian teaching. Titled lords as well as peasants and burghers became converts to the reform movement, including Philip of Hesse, Casimir of Brandenburg, Ulrich of Württemburg, Ernest of Lüneburg, and John of Saxony. Even Emperor Charles's sister Isabella became a Lutheran. Clergy as well as laymen embraced Luther's teachings, priests and monks giving up their vows of celibacy to eagerly take wives.

Changes in the churches brought new problems in society. Sermons that gave German peasants a belief in their equality with priests gave them also a feeling of equality with their overlords. The New Testament book Acts, available in the German language, revealed the communal life of first-century Christians, and the Gospels showed Christ's concern for the poor and the oppressed. For radicals those passages became a signal for revolution. Pamphlets, widely distributed in Germany, demanded suffrage for every man and the popular election of councils to which the German princes and other government officials would be accountable. Pamphlets called for the abolition of all capitalist enterprises, the discontinuation of the collection of all tolls, duties, and fines, the institution of public education, the disqualification of all clergy from holding government offices, the confiscation of monasteries' property and the distribution of the proceeds to the poor. In 1524 those rebellious feelings struck Germany like a series of explosions as bands of peasants, up to three thousand strong, staged uprisings against the civil authorities. By spring of 1525, the revolt had spread over practically the entire empire as peasant bands took over towns and villages, inspiring local inhabitants to repudiate the authority of the landowners and town lords.

Luther deplored the revolt, taking the side of the princes and issuing a pamphlet titled *Against the Robbing and Murdering Hordes of Peasants,* which condemned the rebels and undercut their communalist motivation:

The Spanish Armada's course around England, Scotland, and Ireland. Map from a 1739 engraving.

Ferdinand Álvares, duke of Alba.

Elizabeth at age thirteen.

Elizabeth as a young woman.

Elizabeth in middle age.

Francis Drake.

King *James I of England, Elizabeth's successor.*

Mary, Queen of Scots.

Philip *as a young man, painted by Titian.*

The *young King Philip of Spain. Reproduced from the Collection of the Library of Congress.*

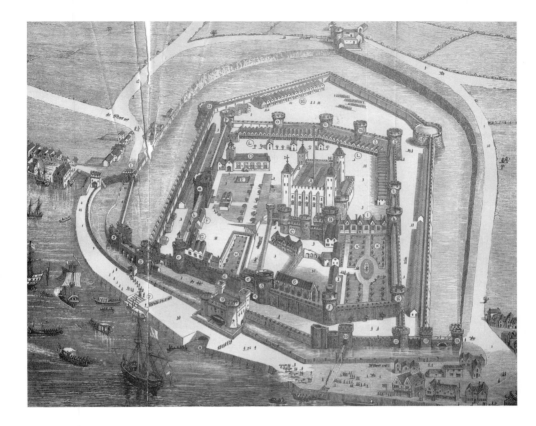

The Tower of London during the reign of Elizabeth.

Philip in middle age. Reproduced from the Collection of the Library of Congress.

Alexander Farnese, duke of Parma. Reproduced from the Collection of the Library of Congress.

Old London Bridge during the reign of Elizabeth. The earliest genuine full view, from a unique drawing in Pepys's Collection in Magdalen College, Cambridge, reproduced by W. Griggs in 1881 from a photo-chromo-lithograph for the New York Shakespeare Society.

Elizabeth signs the death warrant for Mary, Queen of Scots. Reproduced from the Collection of the Library of Congress.

John Hawkins. Reproduced from the Collection of the Library of Congress.

Elizabeth of Valois, Philip's third wife. Reproduced from the Collection of the Library of Congress.

Charles Howard, commander of the English fleet in 1588. Reproduced from the Collection of the Library of Congress.

Queen Mary I of England, known to history as Bloody Mary. Reproduced from the Collection of the Library of Congress.

Robert Dudley, Elizabeth's longtime favorite. Reproduced from the Collection of the Library of Congress.

Henry Stuart, Lord Darnley. Reproduced from the Collection of the Library of Congress.

Any man against whom sedition can be proved is outside the law of God and the empire, so that the first who can slay him is doing right and well. . . . For rebellion brings with it a land full of murder and bloodshed, makes widows and orphans, and turns everything upside down. . . .

The gospel does not make goods common, except in the case of those who do of their own free will what the Apostles and disciples did in Acts iv. They did not demand, as do our insane peasants in their raging, that the goods of others—of a Pilate or a Herod—should be common, but only their own goods. . . . I think there is not a devil left in hell; they have all gone into the peasants.[13]

The revolt was eventually crushed by the princes' armed forces in the summer of 1525, and the rebel peasants were ruthlessly slaughtered or cruelly punished, having their eyes gouged out or their hands chopped off. An estimated 130,000 peasants lost their lives in the defeat of their cause, the princes' carnage finally ceasing after the more moderate among them appealed to their self-interest, pleading, "If all the rebels are killed, where shall we get peasants to provide for us?"

About the same time, one of the most radical of the sects into which Protestants had splintered, the Anabaptists, made another attempt to institute communalism. The Anabaptists rejected the practice of infant baptism, believing that baptism had meaning only if it was administered following an individual's voluntary profession of his or her faith in Christ, and so those who had been baptized as infants were baptized again when they made their profession of faith—and thus they were called "again-baptizers," or Anabaptists. They were pacifists; they refused to swear allegiance to governmental authorities, insisted on adherence to a strict moral code, and lived and dressed conspicuously simply. The sect was established in Switzerland and first drew notice around 1524. In Zurich it proposed, among other things, abolishing taxes and compulsory tithes as well as doing away with military service, oaths, and interest charges. When Zwingli's form of Protestantism clashed with the Anabaptists', particularly over allegiance to the state and over infant baptism, the Zurich city council ordered that the parents of all unbaptized children must leave the city. The Anabaptists' public protests against the order resulted in their leaders being arrested and then banished from Zurich.

Their relocation to other cities and towns served only to spread their doctrines to a much larger area. Their following expanded rapidly throughout southern Germany.

The Anabaptists' doctrine of communalism drew fire in pamphlets that denounced it as a device to set the poor against the rich and subjects against rulers. The emperor, Charles, never letting himself rise above a religious controversy, decreed that rebaptism was a capital crime, to be punished accordingly. In some cities, reaction to the Anabaptists and their doctrines was much stronger. In 1529 the city of Spires in Bavaria issued a decree banning the dissemination of the new doctrines and ordered that Anabaptists were to be killed like wild animals whenever and wherever they were found. Many were. By the end of the next year, some two thousand Anabaptists had been executed. Still the sect grew, expanding into northern Germany, Prussia, Württemberg, Saxony, and the Netherlands. A group of Anabaptists took over the city of Münster in Westphalia by force in 1534, turned it into a commune they named the Kingdom of Zion, and legislated their doctrines and strict morality into law. A year later they were overcome by a military force launched against the city by Bishop Franz von Waldeck, but inspired by the Münster Anabaptists' example, another Anabaptist group attacked and captured a monastery in West Friesland, which was later recaptured, with an extensive loss of life.

Alarmed by the threat of continuing revolt, German Catholics and more moderate Protestants joined forces to suppress the militant Anabaptists, effecting a bloody purge that ended when the remaining Anabaptists accepted the fact that they would have to abandon their communalist ideas and restrict their religious and moral practices to those that the state would allow.

In France the Reformation and Protestantism largely took the form preached by John Calvin. Early attempts at protest and reform had met with quick squelching and punishment, usually at the stake, but Calvinism later came on strong. Calvinists in France were called Huguenots, for a reason not known for certain, the name itself being obscure in its origin, and by 1559 a number of towns—including Caen, Poitiers, La Rochelle, and many in Provence—were mostly Huguenot in their population. One Catholic priest estimated that in 1559 Protestants comprised nearly 25 percent of the French population. By 1561 there were two thousand Calvinist churches in France. In an attempt to suppress the Protestants, King Henry II ordered the Parliament of Paris to form a special commission to prosecute them, which resulted in the death by burning of sixty Protestants over a three-year period. Henry's persecution of Protestants ended with his accidental death at the joust celebrating his daughter's marriage to Philip in July 1559.

In Spain the church itself, with Philip's eager cooperation, assumed the task of exterminating Protestants, resorting to the devices of the so-called Holy Office, which Queen Isabella and King Ferdinand had introduced into Spain to rid the country of Jews and Moslems. The result was the continuation of the infamous Spanish Inquisition. In February 1558 Pope Paul IV directed the inquisitor general for Spain, Cardinal Fernando Valdés, the fanatical archbishop of Seville, to seek out and expunge heresy and those who espoused it. Sick as he was and nearing death, Emperor Charles managed to write a letter to Philip urging him to aid the pope in his efforts to eradicate the Protestant evil. Philip issued an edict for Spain, similar to one he had issued for the Netherlands, that commanded everyone who bought, sold, or read prohibited books or publications to be burned alive.

Upping the ante in the search for heretics, Pope Paul in January 1559 ordered all confessor priests to insist that their parishioners inform on anyone who might be guilty of heretical practices, no matter whether a family member or a close friend. Not to be outdone in zeal for the pursuit of heresy, Philip then reinstituted a law that awarded to the informant one-quarter of the heretic's confiscated property. The pope followed that move with a new bull that authorized Spanish inquisitors to deny pardon to recanting heretics if the inquisitors felt they were insincere. The pope also advanced money from the church's Spanish treasury to finance the heretic hunt, confident that the borrowed church funds would be replaced by the proceeds from the heretics' confiscated property.

Careful to avoid putting his prey to flight, Cardinal Valdés worked patiently and stealthily to spring his trap on suspects. He sent out a swarm of spies to discover the heretics, often covertly, by treachery, worming their way into the confidence of those suspected of embracing the ideas of the reformers, or by intimidation of informants. When the lists of targeted individuals were long enough, the inquisitors' agents struck a massive, sudden blow. Certain areas, such as Aragon and Valladolid and Seville, where the reformers' ideas had taken their strongest hold, were hit hardest. In Seville, the grand inquisitor's home diocese, some eight hundred individuals were arrested on the first day of the crackdown.

The arrest of one individual often led to the arrest of others, as the inquisitors' torturers extracted names from those already imprisoned. Subjected to the horrors of the rack and the pulley, their bodies broken and pulled asunder—all in the name of Christianity—many of the sufferers lost their will to the excruciating pain, telling their tormentors anything they wanted to hear. The new suspects were then arrested and secretly tried, without benefit of counsel, unable to face their accusers or even to know who they were.

Those rounded up by the Inquisition included people of all strata of Spanish society, ordinary folks, leading citizens, and men and women of wealth and status, as well as clergymen and church officials. At least nine bishops were among those convicted by the inquisitors. The most prominent prelate caught in the inquisitors' net was Bartolomé de Carranza, the archbishop of Toledo, a confidant of Emperor Charles, who had appointed him to be Philip's confessor when Philip was a youngster. Carranza had been part of Philip's entourage when Philip went to England to marry Mary and he had lived for some time in England, where he had participated in Bloody Mary's purge of Protestants. He had also spent considerable time in the Netherlands. According to his enemies, chief of which was Cardinal Valdés, Carranza's thinking—and thus his orthodoxy—had been corrupted by too much exposure to Protestants and Protestant writings during his lengthy sojourns in foreign lands. At midnight on August 22, 1559, agents of the Inquisition entered the episcopal palace in Torrelaguna, routed Archbishop Carranza from his bed, and under cover of darkness, presumably to evade notice by a sympathetic populace, hurried him off to the Inquisition's prisons in Valladolid. There he was held in captivity for two years. When the church's Council of Trent, of which Carranza had been a member, appealed to Philip to intervene on Carranza's behalf, Philip turned a blind eye, refusing to help the man in whose arms Philip's father had died. After eighteen years of imprisonment, Carranza was at last judged to be guilty of embracing Martin Luther's evil doctrines, and a list of penalties and penances was imposed upon him. Two weeks and two days after his sentencing, Carranza died, broken in body and spirit.

Carranza's case notwithstanding, the usual procedure of the Spanish Inquisition was for a trial to be held in secret, then the rendering of judgment and sentences were pronounced on the guilty, then the execution of the sentences was performed. The verdict of the inquisitors and the announcement of the sentences were delivered at a public spectacle wonderfully called an auto-da-fé (act of faith). The auto-da-fé was the most fearsome, the most loathsome ceremony of the Catholic church, more than a match for the gruesome spectacles contrived for the entertainment of the Romans and their emperors in the old days of the Coliseum. Crowds would gather as fascinated witnesses to the demonstration of religious bigotry and hatred. To mark it as a religious event, it would be held on a Sunday or some church holiday, and to help draw a crowd for it, the pope would issue an indulgence, good for forty days of absolution, to all who attended.

The prisoners, those who were to receive judgment, were herded together outside the Inquisition's prison and formed up to join a long procession. At the head of the column of participants marched a contingent of troops, clearing a path through the mass of onlookers. Behind them came bearers of pasteboard effigies and of muddy, foul-smelling coffins and wooden boxes recently disinterred and containing the remains of suspected heretics who failed to survive the rigors of their torture and imprisonment. Scorn for them was so intense that their bodies would not be allowed to escape the flames simply because they were dead and decayed. Some of the effigies represented heretics who had fled beyond the reach of the inquisitors and their agents before they could be arrested or who had somehow managed to escape captivity after their arrest. Other effigies represented those whom death, from disease, starvation, or torture, had spared further torment. Behind that grisly contingent came the prisoners, men in one group, women in another, all barefoot, ropes around their necks. Each was escorted by two officials of the Inquisition, called familiars, and also by two monks if the prisoner was to be executed. Those who had been condemned to the stake had been informed of their punishment the day before. As those facing death trudged forward, some weeping, some stoically silent, their escorting monks urged them to renounce their heresies. Most of the prisoners were conspicuous by their dress, being forced to wear apparel associated with shame—three-foot-tall conical pasteboard hats decorated with painted flames and sleeveless yellow gowns called sanbenitos, also decorated with flames and with devils fanning and feeding hellish fires.

Behind the prisoners came the civil magistrates, then members of the church's ecclesiastical orders, then members of the Spanish nobility, mounted on horseback. Next came the inquisitors themselves, those endowed with the power of life and death, and their fiscal, the one who performed as the Inquisition's prosecuting attorney. (Defendants were not allowed their own attorneys.) After him came a large group of mounted familiars, most of them local gentry who acted as ceremonial bodyguards for the Inquisition's officials. Finally came whoever else wished to be part of the procession.

The entire column proceeded to the city square, where the prisoners were made to stand beside a platform while a solemn Mass was held. At the Mass a church official delivered a sermon that outlined the tenets of the Catholic faith, set forth a definition of sin, and called on the spectators to search their hearts and repent of any sin found there. The grand inquisitor then administered an oath by which the crowd of onlookers swore to support the Inquisition, to keep the Catholic faith pure, and to turn in anyone who did not.

That done, an official called out the names of the prisoners, and as each name was called, the prisoner was led up to the platform to hear his or her sentence pronounced. Some would hear that they had been acquitted. Many more would learn that they had been convicted. Once the guilty verdict was read, the prisoner heard his or her punishment and required penance. Those who escaped the stake did so by recanting and repenting, in a way that is believed by the inquisitors to be sincere, and when their punishment and penance were completed, they would be allowed back into the good graces of the church. Any further misbehavior on their part, however, would have them condemned to the stake.

The mildest penalties were public service, fasting, and prayers. For others the punishment was to be stripped to the waist and receive a hundred or more lashes. The sentences of worse offenders varied. Their punishment could be months of house arrest, life in prison, years as oarsmen on Spanish galleys, forced pilgrimages to the Holy Land, exile from Spain, a lifetime of wearing the symbol of disgrace, the sanbenito, whenever they were out in public. Those forced to wear the sanbenito were to endure life as an outcast, they and their families, for the rest of their days; when they died, their sanbenitos, bearing their names and offenses, were hung in their parish church as lasting reminders of their disgrace. The penalties also included the confiscation of the offenders' property, reducing them to street beggars. In many cases the offenders and their descendants were also forever barred from holding any sort of public office. Though ruined, they had at least escaped the flames. They had been, to use the Inquisition's term, "reconciled."

The unreconciled, those who remained steadfast in their beliefs—or who did not recant credibly enough—were turned over (the official term was "relaxed") by the grand inquisitor to the corregidor, the city's chief magistrate, for execution at the stake, the church being prohibited by its own laws from carrying out a death sentence itself. Those who, stricken with horror at the sight or thought of their pyres, at the last minute confessed their errors were, as an act of mercy, garroted. The others became martyrs for their forbidden faith.

The first auto-da-fé of the Spanish Inquisition was held in Valladolid in May 1559[14] and was soon followed by similar ones in Granada, Toledo, Seville, and Barcelona. On October 8 a second auto-da-fé was staged in Valladolid. This one was attended by no less a majestic personage than the Spanish sovereign himself, King Philip, who, alarmed by the spread of Protestantism in his own land, had recently returned to Spain from the Netherlands. He was to be treated to the Inquisition's macabre spectacle as a part of the welcoming celebration of his return. It was at that auto-da-fé that Carlos de Seso, born of nobility in Florence and a resident of Valladolid since his marriage to a Castilian, was facing death for having become a convert to Martin Luther's doctrines and a proselytizer to his family and his neighbors. De Seso and a fellow prisoner, Domingo de Rojas, a Dominican monk, also affected by Luther's writings, had both refused to recant and both were to be burned alive. Of the twenty-eight others who were sentenced that day, sixteen had been reconciled, and twelve had recanted at the last minute and were to be garroted before their lifeless bodies were heaved into the flames.

The ceremony began at six o'clock that morning when the church bells of Valladolid began to toll and the grim procession started wending from the Inquisition's prison fortress, on its way to the square in front of the church of St. Francis. In the square had been constructed a stage, richly carpeted, on which seats bearing the arms of the Holy Office were arranged for the inquisitors and next to which had been built a special gallery to accommodate the royal guests, who would access their choice seats via a private entrance. In front of the gallery stood the platform where the unfortunate heretics would be led in clear view of all spectators, which that day numbered, according to the estimate of an eyewitness, about two hundred thousand.

With the inquisitors in place, Philip entered the gallery and took his seat. With him sat his son, Carlos, his sister Maria, who had been his regent while he was in the Netherlands, his nephew, Alexander Farnese (son of his half sister, Margaret of Parma), members of his household, a few foreign ambassadors, and a number of other VIPs and members of his court.

As de Seso, a man of some standing in the Spanish capital, wearing the degrading sanbenito, was ignominiously led in front of the royal gallery, he voiced a protest to Philip: "Is this the way that you allow your innocent subjects to be persecuted?"

As if rebuffing a heckler, Philip haughtily replied, "If my own son were as perverted as you are, I would bring the wood to burn him!"[15]

De Seso and de Rojas were then taken from the square to a spot outside the city wall where the execution would occur, a location called the *quemadero*— the burning place. Some, but not all, of the crowd followed to witness the horrid finale of the spectacle. Bound to the stake, both de Seso and de Rojas remained steadfast, the defiant de Rojas silenced by a gag in his mouth, but de Seso urging his executioners to pile on more wood to hasten the end of his agony, which they did.

The Spanish Inquisition was not to be limited to Philip's subjects. By the 1560s, according to one account, most of those whom the inquisitors accused of harboring, and in some cases disseminating, the ideas of Luther and Calvin were foreigners. Protestant publications were being brought into Spain and distributed by Protestant foreigners. Other foreigners arrested and sentenced by the inquisitors were simply Protestants who had come to Spain on business. At an auto-da-fé in Seville in December 1560, two English Protestants, William Brooks and Nicholas Burton, were executed. Burton was the supercargo on a ship that had landed in Seville. When one of the ship's owners sent a representative to take charge of the ship and return it, the representative, John Frampton, was arrested (for having an English translation of Cato in his luggage) and tortured until he agreed to become a Catholic; he was then, with great fanfare, baptized into the church. Protestant foreign sailors were in constant jeopardy while their ships were visiting Spanish ports. Protestant businessmen from England and elsewhere were also subject to arrest and execution by the Spanish inquisitors. In one year, 1565, twenty-six English subjects were burned to death in Spain, victims of the Inquisition.

One nineteenth-century historian described how the Inquisition menaced English seamen:

In their zeal to keep out heresy, the Spanish government placed their harbours under the control of the Holy Office. Any vessel in which an heretical book was found was confiscated, and her crew carried to the Inquisitional prisons. It had begun in Henry's time. The Inquisitors attempted to treat schism as heresy and arrest Englishmen in their ports. But Henry spoke up stoutly to Charles V, and the Holy Office had been made to hold its hand. All was altered now. It was not necessary that a poor sailor should have been found teaching heresy. It was enough if he had an English Bible and Prayer Book with him in his kit; and stories would come into Dartmouth or Plymouth how some lad that everybody knew—Bill or Jack or Tom, who had a wife or father or mother among them, perhaps—had been seized hold of for no other crime, been flung into a dungeon, tortured, starved, set to work in the galleys, or burned in a fool's coat, as they called it, at an auto de fe at Seville.[16]

The Inquisition also reached across the sea into America, into Mexico, where Protestant English sailors were arrested and imprisoned, some burned at Mexican autos-da-fé, others taken to Spain to suffer a similar fate there. News of the persecution's outrages, in Spain and elsewhere in the Spanish empire, inevitably found its way to the victims' homeland and into the hearts of their countrymen, inflaming public opinion and broadening the divide between Elizabeth's mostly Protestant England and Philip's militantly Catholic Spain.

~☙ 11. THE CATHOLIC RIVAL

She was only six days old when she became queen in December 1542, her dissolute father, King James V of Scotland, having died of his excesses at age thirty. She was his only legitimate child. Her mother was Mary of Guise, member of the politically powerful Guise family of France. Biographers and other writers generally describe her as beautiful, unusually so, but portraits of her show a rather ordinary face distinguished mainly by a prominent, pointed nose. Her best feature appears to be her youth. She had reddish hair, brown eyes, and the pale complexion considered so desirable in her times. She was tall, perhaps as much as five-ten, and by the time she was an older adolescent, she had grown appealingly shapely.

Precocious as a child, she was said to be able to entertain the king of France "with pleasant and sensible talk as if she were a woman of twenty-five."[1] Vivacity and charm came easily to her, as did generosity, which she showed to anyone she favored, especially her attendants. Ballroom dancing was one of the most noticeable skills she developed in becoming a socially adept young woman. She loved poetry, particularly French poetry, although she showed herself to be a better reader than writer of it. She admired the work of fine artists and became a patron of the arts. She also admired exquisite embroidery and developed a talent for needlework. She loved pets, dogs most of all, spaniels and terriers in particular. When young, she enjoyed making things to eat, such as candied fruit, in the kitchen with her friends. Her outdoor enjoyments included archery, falconry, riding, and hunting. She also played golf. Indoors she played chess and backgammon and was a good cardplayer. She sang some, often accompanying herself on the lute. She also learned to play the clavichord and the harp, but not especially well, music not being one of her gifts. She was not much of a student, either, although she was bright enough and quick-witted. Altogether, she was, as her uncle once said, "as perfect and accomplished . . . as is possible."

Her name was Mary Stuart. To history, she was Mary Queen of Scots.

Her paternal grandmother was Margaret Tudor, one of the two sisters of King Henry VIII of England. Thus she was the great-granddaughter of King Henry VII, his direct descendant. She was also the cousin (first cousin once removed) of Queen Elizabeth. Those consanguineous connections would dictate virtually the entire course of her life.

When she was still an infant, Henry VIII, seeking to wed Scotland to England and cut his northern neighbor loose from its French alliance, proposed that Mary be betrothed to his son, Edward, then five years old. His idea was to bring baby Mary to England and have her raised there until she and Edward were both old enough to marry. He devised a plan to that effect and dispatched a special ambassador, Ralph Sadler, to Scotland to work out the deal.

The man in charge in Scotland following James V's death was James Hamilton, earl of Arran and heir apparent to the Scottish throne if anything fatal happened to little Mary. Superficially sympathetic to the Protestant cause, which many of Scotland's nobles favored, as well as to the English—rather than the French—Arran had won the vote of the nobles to become regent, governing for the baby queen until she was able to do so herself. His rival for the job had been Cardinal David Beaton, archbishop of St. Andrews and archfoe of the Protestant movement. Beaton had wielded a strong influence during the late King James's regime and intended to maintain his position. To do so, he forged a will that purported to be King James's and that designated him and three of his associates "governors of the kingdom." Arran persuaded the nobles that the will was bogus, captured their vote, and had Cardinal Beaton thrown into prison. Arran, whom Henry VIII had courted by dangling the prospect of a marriage between Arran's son and the princess Elizabeth, was then in a position to follow Henry's program for the establishment of an English-Scottish union.

Little Mary's wily twenty-eight-year-old French mother, Mary of Guise, was following a different program. She was determined to keep Scotland in France's sphere of influence. When Sadler met with Arran in Edinburgh, he made little headway in his attempt to enlist him in King Henry's scheme, finding Arran to be frustratingly self-absorbed. Sadler then went to see Mary of Guise, who was staying with little Mary at the palace at Linlithgow, about fifteen miles west of Edinburgh. He wanted to see Mary of Guise, of course, to feel her out about Henry VIII's proposal to betroth the two royal children;

he also wanted to see little Mary, so that he could give a firsthand report to Henry. Mary of Guise had a nurse fetch the baby, then four months old, and when Sadler saw her, he asked the nurse to remove the baby's clothes so that he could inspect her naked. He also held her on his lap and, satisfied that the child was all she should be, he later reported to Henry, "I assure Your Majesty, it is as goodly a child as I have seen of her age, and as like to live, with the Grace of God."

To Sadler's presentation of Henry's plan for betrothing little Mary to Prince Edward and having her moved to London to keep her safe, Mary of Guise seemed surprisingly receptive. It was an act, of course, for as devoted as she was to French interests, she was not about to hand over Scotland's baby queen to England's king. She furthermore knew that Arran was sympathetic to the English and had planted spies in her house, and she suspected his complicity in King Henry's plan. She was plotting a move of her own, and before it was accomplished, she would do or say nothing that might put her adversaries on their guard. Sadler left beguiled by her, a truly attractive and clever young woman.

She had already begun moving clothes and furniture and other household articles from the Linlithgow palace, a structure vulnerable to siege, to her fortresslike and much more defensible castle at Stirling, about twenty miles northeast of Glasgow. There, according to her plan, she and young Mary would take refuge until further measures became necessary. Mary of Guise would be defying Arran in moving from Linlithgow, for he had decreed she and the child were to remain there. She had furthermore begun a campaign to undermine him, having planted in Sadler's mind the idea that Arran intended to double-cross Henry and keep Mary in custody in Scotland until Henry was dead and gone, then seize the Scottish throne for himself, having had, according to the supposed plan, Mary married off to his own son in the meantime.

Arran did indeed double-cross Henry, but not as Mary of Guise had imagined. When Matthew Stuart, earl of Lennox, an exiled Scottish royal family member who had become a naturalized French subject, came from France to meet with Mary of Guise, Henry VIII became alarmed that a conspiracy was under way to move little Mary beyond Arran's—and thus Henry's—reach. He instructed Arran to muster an army immediately and seize the child and take her to Edinburgh castle for safekeeping. Arran, however, was not so sure that following Henry's order was the best thing for him to do. To complicate matters for him, a number of Catholic nobles had rallied around Lennox, and Cardinal Beaton had managed to talk his prison guards into letting him escape. And so when Arran looked up, he saw an influential group of nobles solidly opposed to King Henry's proposition to betroth Mary to Edward and to marry Scotland to England. He promptly changed his mind about cooperating with Henry. He informed Sadler that the proposal was unacceptable.

Henry, furious, sent word back to Arran that unless he accepted the deal, Scotland could expect war with England. Arran and his fellow Scots then, on July 1, 1543, agreed to a somewhat altered version of the proposal, which came to be called the Treaty of Greenwich. It provided, among other things, that Mary would stay in Scotland until she was ten years old, then be moved to England and a year later would marry Edward.

Three weeks following that agreement, on July 24, Mary of Guise's Catholic and pro-French allies, Cardinal Beaton and the earl of Lennox, assembled an army at Linlithgow to escort little Mary and her mother and their retinue to the Stirling castle. Arran showed up in Linlithgow two days later with a force of his own, which was dangerously outnumbered. He stepped aside. On July 27 little Mary and her mother and their attendants, protected by a formidable force of twenty-five hundred cavalry and a thousand infantry, proceeded in a mile-long column to the stony refuge at Stirling. On September 9, in the castle's royal chapel, nine-month-old Mary Stuart was officially crowned queen of Scots, with Arran, Lennox, Cardinal Beaton, and the earl of Argyll, Archibald Campbell, four of the most influential men in Scotland, all participating in the ceremony. Three months later, in December 1543, a Scottish parliament dominated by Catholic nobles revoked the Treaty of Greenwich. There would be no marriage of Mary to Edward.

Henry's retaliation came in May 1544. He sent an army under the command of Edward Seymour, earl of Hertford (Jane Seymour's brother), across the Scottish border with orders to attack Edinburgh and its castle and scorch the earth from Edinburgh to Stirling and beyond. Henry's delusion was that by such action he would compel the Scots to accept his proposal of a marriage between Mary and Prince Edward. The invasion was therefore a sort of violent courtship of the little queen, which caused the whole brutal campaign to become known as "the rough wooing," a bit of sixteenth-century humor. Edinburgh castle proved invulnerable, but Hertford destroyed many other structures, including churches, palaces, abbeys, houses, and even entire towns. As he neared Stirling, Mary of Guise arranged for little Mary to be hurriedly carried off to Dunkeld, near the unassailable Highlands, about thirty miles north of Stirling.

After about three weeks of wholesale destruction, Hertford turned his army south and returned to England, in obedience to Henry's order to be back in time to invade France, which Henry had promised Emperor Charles V he would do as an ally in Charles's war with the French. When Charles later unilaterally made peace with France, Henry opened negotiations for peace as well, hoping that in the peacemaking process he might prevail upon the French king, Francis I, to use his influence to get the Scots finally to agree to Mary's betrothal to Edward.

Henry's rough wooing, which he temporarily resumed in September 1545, backfired on him and his plans for Mary. The Scots nobles turned their country away from England and back toward France, bringing it closer than ever to French and Catholic influence. Arran, the pro-English plotter and double-crosser, caught the blame for the English onslaught, resulting in the Scots Parliament rearranging the regency to have Mary of Guise become co-regent and to have Arran shifted to a lesser role as her adviser, though nominally a co-regent with her.

In January 1547 Henry VIII died. The earl of Hertford, Edward Seymour, uncle of England's new nine-year-old king, quickly assumed the position of England's regent, or protector, as the English called the office, and gave himself a new, grander title, duke of Somerset. He swiftly set about to impose the Treaty of Greenwich on the Scots and to accomplish Henry VIII's plan for uniting Scotland to England. In August he led fifteen thousand troops—infantry, artillery, and cavalry—supported by an English fleet, north and westward toward Edinburgh and in a massive battle on the eastern outskirts of the city soundly defeated a twelve-thousand-man Scottish army led by Arran, slaughtering some ten thousand of the Scots and routing the rest. Arran managed to survive and escape.

Though victorious in battle, Somerset—as Seymour was now called—lost his prey. From her castle at Stirling, Mary of Guise, under cover of night, hastily packed four-year-old Mary off to a remote priory on an island in the Lake of Menteith, forty-five miles from Edinburgh and Somerset's threatening

English army, which Somerset soon put to work building a network of forts preparatory to occupying Scotland.

Two months after the death of Henry VIII, France's King Francis I died and was succeeded by his son, who became King Henry II of France. Arran promptly threw in with Henry, who promised to run the English out of Scotland and, supplanting the English scheme, proposed to betroth Mary to his son the dauphin, who was a year younger than Mary, and wed Scotland to France. Henry began planning a French invasion of Scotland and put Mary's two Guise uncles, Claude, the duke of Guise, and his brother Charles, the cardinal of Lorraine, in charge of the campaign.

Mary of Guise, as part of Henry's plan, moved little Mary to Dumbarton Castle, some twelve miles northwest of Glasgow, and a contingent of French troops was landed there to secure the castle. In June 1548, a six-thousand-man French expeditionary force, with the Scots' consent, came ashore at Leith, at the edge of Edinburgh, to threaten Somerset's English forces. In July the Scottish Parliament approved a treaty that bound Scotland to France and promised little Mary to the French dauphin, Francis.

The French ships sent to transport Mary to France, seeking to avoid English ships, sailed around the northeastern and northern coasts of Scotland and then down the west coast to land at Dumbarton, west of Glasgow, on the River Clyde. On July 29, 1548, five-year-old Mary gave her mother a good-bye kiss and as her mother watched her, walked away to board King Henry II's own royal galley, which stood waiting for her in the Clyde. Another person watching her, a member of the French party that had come to fetch her, remarked, in the extravagant language popular in those times, that Mary was, at age five, "one of the most perfect creatures that ever was seen, such a one as from this very young age with its wondrous and estimable beginnings has raised such expectations that it isn't possible to hope for more from a princess on this earth."[2]

Delayed by stormy weather, the fleet bearing Mary did not reach France until August 13. From that day until she was nineteen years old, France would be her home. She would learn to speak French, live French, become French. She would not be entirely among strangers, however, for she would be attended by a coterie of Scots who had come with her, including the lords Erskine and Livingstone, who had been appointed by the Scottish Parliament to be Mary's guardians while she was in France, and Lady Fleming, an illegitimate daughter of James IV and thus Mary's aunt, who would be her governess. Also with her were Janet Sinclair, who had been her nurse, and James Stuart, her seventeen-year-old half brother who was to attend college in France, and four of her very best friends and playmates, Mary Beaton, Mary Fleming (Lady Fleming's daughter and thus Mary's cousin), Mary Livingston, and Mary Seton, all about her age and all from prominent Scottish families. Those girls would become known as the Four Marys (or Maries) and would remain her close friends throughout her life.

One of the first of her French relatives whom she met after her arrival was her Guise grandmother, the Duchess Antoinette, who later wrote how Mary impressed her. "She is the prettiest and best for her age that you ever saw. She has auburn hair, with a fine complexion, and I think that when she comes of age, she will be a beautiful girl, because her skin is delicate and white. . . . She is graceful and self-assured. When all is said and done, we may be well pleased with her." Catherine de' Medici, wife of the French king, who had mothered a brood of her own, was similarly impressed with Mary. "Our little Scottish queen has but to smile to turn all the French heads," she gushed after Mary and her party arrived at the royal residence near St.-Germain.

Mary and her companions took up residence with the French royal family, and she and Francis, the dauphin, quickly became friends of a sort. Though he was only a year younger than Mary, Francis was considerably smaller, being as unusually short as she was unusually tall. A sickly child, Francis lacked Mary's vivacity, but he worked hard with his teachers to acquire the social skills he needed. Within months of her arrival, Mary had learned enough French to be able to be schooled along with Francis and his sisters. Mary was also getting instructions from her mother, who was keen on directing her education, particularly her religious education. Her mother insisted she attend Mass every day, and to guide her in the Catholic faith, she was given her own French chaplain as well as a Scottish one. She was also provided with her own private communion service so that she could take communion without the risk of being infected by sharing the vessels with the other children. Mary and her mother kept in touch with each other through frequent letters, written in French.

In September 1550, after a separation of two years, Mary of Guise came to France to see her daughter. Her visit was timed to coincide with a French celebration of France's army having at last driven the English occupation force from its forts in Scotland. As regent, she came to join her French ally in the celebration of the defeat of the English on Scottish soil. She ended up staying a year before returning to Scotland.

As Mary grew into adolescence, her education—her life, actually—was taken over by her uncles, the duke of Guise and the cardinal of Lorraine. She got a new, straitlaced French governess to replace Scottish Lady Fleming, who turned up pregnant by King Henry and after bearing him an illegitimate son was embarrassingly shipped back home to Scotland. The influences of Mary's uncles and the new governess, Françoise d'Estamville, the Lady Parois, virtually completed the job of turning the Scottish child queen into a royal French young lady.

On April 19, 1558, when she was fifteen years old, she was formally betrothed to the dauphin, Francis, in an elaborate ceremony held in the new Louvre, the ancient fortress that Francis I had decided to turn into a palace. The speculation is that puny Francis, practically an invalid, was truly in love with his fiancée and that she in turn held a sincere affection for him. Their impending marriage was something he very much wanted and to which she was perfectly agreeable.

Two marriage contracts, prenuptial agreements between the parties, worked out by individuals more calculating and sophisticated than the bride-to-be and her groom, spelled out the political intentions in the minds of the makers of the match. One contract specified that Mary would preserve the traditional freedoms and privileges of Scotland, that Scotland would be ruled by Mary of Guise as regent when Mary was out of the country, that if Mary died without having borne a child, the regnant French king would support the succession of Mary's nearest blood relative to the Scottish throne, and that if Mary and Francis had sons, the eldest would inherit the crowns of both France and Scotland, but if they had daughters only, the eldest would inherit only the crown of Scotland. That contract also stipulated that Francis would become king of Scotland upon the marriage and that when he succeeded his father as king of France, Scotland and France would become one united kingdom and the subjects of one country would become naturalized subjects of the other country. All those provisions were accepted by the Scottish commission charged with ironing out the details, and the contract was duly signed by the parties and their signatures witnessed. The other marriage agreement was executed surreptitiously, without the knowledge of the Scottish commissioners. In it Mary signed away her right to the English crown in favor of the French king if she died without having children. She furthermore promised to turn over Scotland and its resources to France for as long as it took to repay France its costs in defending Scotland.

By the marriage contracts, King Henry II made clear his designs on not only Scotland but also on England, and Mary's two uncles, with an eye to expanding the Guises' influence, had helped manipulate Mary into agreeing to the French king's plan.

The wedding was held on Sunday, April 24, 1558, in the Cathedral of Notre-Dame in Paris. Mary Queen of Scots by that event became also queen-dauphine of France, wife of the king-dauphin.

Seven months later, on November 17, 1558, England's Queen Mary—Bloody Mary—died. When that news reached Paris, Henry II, seeing opportunity, immediately pronounced his daughter-in-law the new queen of England. The claim was repeated by French writers and propagandists. It was not really far-fetched. Except for Elizabeth's claim to the throne, Mary's was eminently valid, she being the granddaughter of Henry VIII's older sister. If Elizabeth were deemed illegitimate because of Anne Boleyn's clouded status, Mary's claim would be superior to Elizabeth's.

France's King Henry and the Guises ostentatiously promoted the idea that Mary had indeed become queen of England—and consequently, her young husband, Francis, had become England's king. At the wedding of Henry's daughter Princess Claude in early 1559, Francis's and Mary's attendants' uniforms displayed a coat of arms that included the arms of England and France. Official correspondence and documents bore inscriptions that declared Francis and Mary the "king and queen dauphins of Scotland, England and Ireland." The couple's furniture and flatware bore a coat of arms that included the emblems of England. As Mary strode toward the royal chapel, attendants ushering back onlookers shouted to the crowd, "Make way for the queen of England!" Mounted above the display of Mary's coat of arms was an inscription in French that read:

> The arms of Marie, queen-dauphine of France,
> The noblest lady on earth. For to advance
> Of Scotland queen. And of England also,
> Of Ireland also. God hath provided so.[3]

Elizabeth's ambassador, Nicholas Throckmorton, took notice of it all (and translated the above verse into English), and he reported his observations to William Cecil, Elizabeth's wary secretary of state who had begun building a damning dossier on Mary.

It was on June 30, 1559, that Henry II became the victim of the jousting accident that rammed a large splinter from a shattered lance through his left eye and into his brain. He died ten days later, on July 10. Francis instantly succeeded his father as king, and sixteen-year-old Mary Queen of Scots became queen of France as well. Francis's coronation, at which he became King Francis II, was held in the cathedral at Reims on Monday, September 18, after being postponed from Sunday because of the illness of the duke of Savoy, a high-ranking French noble whose attendance at the ceremony was obligatory. The ceremony was conducted by the archbishop of Reims, Mary's uncle Charles, the cardinal of Lorraine.

At the instigation of the Guises, the new royal couple's display of the emblems of England in their coats of arms became more flagrant A new official seal of Scotland was devised, with images of Francis and Mary on it and an inscription that read, "Francis and Mary, by grace of God, king and queen of France, Scotland, England and Ireland." The emblems of England were included in the coat of arms inscribed on the royal couple's new silver flatware, off which Elizabeth's ambassador was obliged to eat while a palace guest. The Guises were not merely flaunting symbols. They were increasingly interfering and asserting their influence, grown enormous with Mary enthroned, over affairs in both Scotland and France. Fifteen-year-old Francis they patronized and shunted aside from governmental policy making.

Mary seemed one of the first to be persuaded by her uncles' campaign to claim for her the crown of England. She began warming to the idea of being queen of England. She started sending personal messages to Elizabeth through Nicholas Throckmorton. She offered to send Elizabeth a portrait of herself if Elizabeth would reciprocate with one of herself. She told Throckmorton that she sought friendship with Elizabeth, if for no other reason than their kinship. "I am the nearest kinswoman she hath," Mary said. "We be both of one blood, of one country and in one island." Her reminder of their kinship also served, intentionally or otherwise, to stake out her claim to the throne Elizabeth occupied.

Meanwhile, on March 31, 1560, Elizabeth, stung by Mary's pretensions to the English throne and urged on by William Cecil, had sent some eight thousand troops across the border to Scotland to aid a revolt of Protestant lords against Mary of Guise, now the sole regent. The English army joined the Scottish rebel force and besieged Leith, outside Edinburgh, where the main French force protecting Mary of Guise was posted. In May an attempt to storm Leith's defenses was thrown back by the French garrison, the English suffering heavy casualties, and with fresh troops sent as reinforcements, the English and Scots resumed the siege. By the end of May, the French seemed ready to negotiate.

Then, at midnight on June 10, Mary of Guise, suffering some chronic disease, died. With her died much of the French resistance to English terms. On July 6, Scots, English, and French representatives signed the Treaty of Edinburgh, in which the French agreed to honor Scottish liberty and to withdraw their troops from Scotland. They also agreed to have their queen, Mary, renounce her claims to the English crown. What was more, the treaty provided that in the event Mary and Francis refused to ratify the treaty, England would be entitled to invade Scotland again in order to secure the Protestant faith and bar French and Catholic influences from the country. As a result of having negotiated the treaty, the Protestant Scottish lords took control of their country's government while their Catholic queen, who had been left out of the negotiations, still resided in France.

Not surprisingly, Mary balked at ratifying the Treaty of Edinburgh, but did so with such grace that Nicholas Throckmorton commented that he wished that either Mary or Elizabeth could be transformed into a man so that the two could "make so happy a marriage as thereby there might be a unity of the whole isle." William Cecil, however, steadfastly maintained to Elizabeth that Mary posed a persistent and deadly threat. "We do all certainly think that the Queen of Scots and for her sake her husband and the house of Guise be in their hearts mortal enemies to Your Majesty's person," he wrote to Elizabeth. The danger would remain, he told her, "as long as Your Majesty and the Scottish queen liveth."

Meanwhile, Francis was not doing well. He was suffering from a number of ailments, including a rash on his face, a nearly constant discharge from his ear, mysterious fevers, headaches, times when he could not speak, and at least one fainting spell, during which he collapsed one Sunday and a large swelling was noticed behind his left ear when he fell. The primitive medicine of the sixteenth century further debilitated him with frequent bleedings and purgatives. On November 27, Throckmorton reported to Elizabeth that Francis's physicians did not expect him to live. Mary, along with Francis's mother and brothers, were going to churches in Orléans, where the royal court was then residing, to pray for the young king, the apparent victim of a brain tumor. Their desperate entreaties for divine intervention failed. On Thursday, December 5, 1560, Francis fell into a coma and died, at age sixteen years and eleven months.

Mary was now more alone than she knew. Francis was succeeded by his ten-year-old brother, Charles, and his mother, Catherine de' Medici, widow of the late King Henry II, was appointed regent to rule until Charles came of age. Although Catherine had years earlier been taken with Mary, she had in the meantime seen how the Guises used Mary to help themselves to increasing power and privilege and she had come to resent Mary as well as Mary's Guise relatives. When the Guises suggested that young Charles should marry Mary, to continue the Guise influence, Catherine quickly squashed the idea, and the Guises started reading the signs. They were being removed from the loop. With their supporters, some seven hundred persons in all, they left Catherine's court in April 1561 and withdrew to their estates in eastern France.

Mary, no longer queen of France, could read the signs, too. She handed over the royal jewels to Catherine, vacated her royal apartments, and went into seclusion. After forty days practically by herself, she emerged with new resolve. She would go back to Scotland, where she was still queen in her own right. On August 14, 1561, after a round of prolonged farewells to her French family, she boarded her galley at Calais and with a party of escorts, aides, and companions, including the four Marys, sailed for Scotland, through the eastern end of the channel and up into the North Sea. She arrived at Leith five days later, back home after an absence of thirteen years.

She took up residence in the Holyrood palace in Edinburgh and within days of her arrival she formed a Privy Council composed of twelve of Scotland's most influential nobles, seven of them Protestant, five Catholic. Her half brother James Stuart, who had been the de facto regent since the overthrow and death of Mary of Guise and whom Mary would soon name earl of Moray, had guided Mary's selections, advising that she look primarily to Protestants for counsel.

At her court and in her public appearances she was generally welcomed with warmth by her subjects, nobles and commoners alike. One exception was the Calvinist firebrand John Knox, whose pugnacity and doctrinal zeal made him a constant irritant to the Catholic queen, now returned to rule a country he wished to be Protestant. Privy Council member William Maitland, who was to serve as Mary's secretary of state, wrote to his English counterpart, William Cecil, about Knox's resistance to Mary. "You know the vehemency of Mr. Knox's spirit," Maitland said, "which cannot be bridled, and yet doth sometimes utter such sentences as cannot easily be digested by a weak stomach. I would wish he should deal with her more gently, being a young princess unpersuaded."

Mary had made known her stand on religion shortly before leaving France. She had told Elizabeth's ambassador, Nicholas Throckmorton, "The religion which I profess I take to be the most acceptable to God. And, indeed, neither do I know nor desire to know any other." Although to be counseled by Protestants, Mary was of no mind to become one, political considerations and Knox's unsettling fulminations notwithstanding.

Still refusing to ratify the Edinburgh Treaty and renounce her claim to Elizabeth's throne, despite Elizabeth's urging her to do so, Mary instead sought to have a private meeting with Elizabeth so that the two of them, sister queens, could sit down and get to know each other better, work out their differences, and begin a continuing relationship. Mary was determined to establish herself as Scotland's monarch in more than name only. She wanted the same sort of authority in Scotland as Elizabeth had in England, and she persuaded herself that she would gain it if Elizabeth would accept her, Mary's, right to succession to the English throne, making her a more important person, she thought, in the eyes of Scotland's people. If she became the recognized heir apparent to England's throne, she believed, rebellious Scottish Protestant appeals to England for help in deposing her would be unavailing.

Elizabeth, though, was as loath as ever to name a successor, Mary or anyone else, as she was to take a husband, believing either to result in an immediate diminution of her power. Besides, as long as Mary harbored the hope that Elizabeth would eventually name her as successor, Mary would be, from Elizabeth's viewpoint, more manipulable. If Elizabeth did name her as successor, Mary would likely be considerably less so. Mary was believed to be Elizabeth's choice to succeed her, but Elizabeth would gain no advantage by officially designating her, even while the English Parliament was becoming increasingly keen on a successor being named in order to avoid a crisis in the increasingly likely event Elizabeth died without an heir. Characteristically, Elizabeth dithered.

As for Mary's repeated requests for a private meeting with Elizabeth, they were repeatedly stalled. Mary was making her requests through her representative, William Maitland, who was meeting in London with William Cecil to arrange the proposed meeting of queens. Cecil, however, was opposed to such a meeting, believing Mary might actually charm Elizabeth into some sort of agreement, and he balked at setting up a royal tête-à-tête.

To make matters worse for Catholic Mary, while Maitland was in London meeting with Cecil in May 1562, her uncle the duke of Guise committed an outrage against a large group of Huguenots, shocking Protestants everywhere. The duke, while returning to Paris accompanied by an armed force, had had his musketeers fire on several hundred Huguenots holding a worship service in a barn near the village of Vassy. Twenty-three of the worshippers were killed, and about a hundred were wounded.

Alarmed at the prospect of the Guises exporting such a Protestant pogrom across the channel, Cecil implored Elizabeth to forget about cozying up to Mary, whom he saw as a constant danger, by granting a private interview. Conscious of the public relations fallout from the massacre, Mary hurriedly sent for Elizabeth's current envoy, Thomas Randolph, to let him know that she "lamenteth their [her uncles'] unadvised enterprise, which shall not only bring themselves in danger of their own persons, but also in hatred and disdain of many princes in the world."

At the same time, Maitland was doing such an effective job lobbying the vacillating Elizabeth that he managed not only to get her okay of a meeting, despite Cecil, but also got the long-awaited portrait of Elizabeth that Mary had requested. It was delivered to Mary in Edinburgh in mid-July 1562, and she was ecstatic over it. "I honor her in my heart," Mary exclaimed to Randolph, "and love her as my dear and natural sister."

By the end of July, however, Mary learned that her beloved Elizabeth had changed her mind again and called off the meeting. Cecil apparently had brought Elizabeth around to his thinking. By October, Elizabeth had gone so far in her support of French Protestants as to send an army to Normandy to help them. She did so with some regard for Mary's feelings, though, and she sent Mary a letter poetically explaining her action. "We have no choice but to protect our own houses from destruction," she wrote, "when those of our neighbors are on fire."

The next big blow to Mary came in January 1563 when she learned that Elizabeth had called her Parliament into session and that an attempt would be made to have Parliament pass legislation that would exclude Mary from the English succession.

Mary countered by taking a new tack. She determined she would find a husband who would help her gain a firmer hold on the Scottish crown and bring England's within her grasp. Her first choice was Carlos, Philip's sixteen-year-old degenerate, deformed, epileptic son and heir. Philip had done a good job of concealing Carlos's physical, mental, and personality defects from public view, and as far as Mary knew—and in her naïve and romantic mind—Carlos was a gallant, dashing young prince, just what she thought she needed. As Carlos's wife, she could become queen of Spain—the superpower of Europe—as well as of Scotland and, with Spain's enormous Catholic influence, queen of England also, whether Elizabeth willed it or not. She began negotiations with Philip to make it happen.

In 1562, however, Carlos had fallen down a flight of stairs and landed on his head, suffering brain damage that left him even more abnormal than previously. Philip, at last providing Mary a definite answer, let her know that a marriage with Carlos was out of the question.

Catherine de' Medici, the French regent and Mary's former mother-in-law, who feared the mere prospect of a Spanish-Scottish-English alliance and who formerly had opposed having her son, the boy king Charles, wed Mary, now proposed such a marriage. It was Mary's turn to reject the proposal.

A surprising candidate was offered by Elizabeth. Astonishingly, she suggested that Mary marry Robert Dudley, Elizabeth's close companion and suspected lover. By then, in mid-1563, Elizabeth had given up—if she had ever seriously considered such a thing—on marrying Dudley herself, an event that had become even more improbable following the suspicious death of Dudley's wife three years earlier. Elizabeth's suggestion of Dudley did, however, indicate the strength of her trust in Dudley, whose loyalty to her and to England remained steadfast. She was confident that as king of Scotland, Dudley would keep Scotland both friendly and Protestant. To encourage Mary to accept

Dudley, Elizabeth hinted that she would be willing to name Mary her successor if she married him.

Mary had another idea. She had become interested in Henry Stuart, better known as Lord Darnley (from the name of one of his family's estates), who had been one of those suggested as a possible husband for Mary shortly following Francis's death. At the time, Darnley was only fourteen years old and failed to interest Mary. Since then he had grown into a six-foot-one, pretty-faced, athletic young man whose godfather was King Henry VIII, for whom he was named. His bloodlines were impressive. He was a descendant of King James II of Scotland through James's daughter, Mary, and a descendant of King Henry VII of England through Henry's daughter Margaret, which made him a not-too-distant cousin of both Mary and Elizabeth. In 1563 he was eighteen years old and had a reputation not only for courtliness, sophistication, charm, and abilities as a sportsman but also for immaturity, petulance, a menacing temper, arrogance, and flagrant sexual promiscuity that embraced both women and men. He was also a Catholic, which Mary found to be in his favor.

By February 1564, Mary had decided on Darnley, ignoring Elizabeth's offer of Dudley, whom Elizabeth had recently created earl of Leicester to enhance his status. Mary and Darnley, who was living in England, began a correspondence. Because Darnley needed Elizabeth's permission to leave England, it took patience and persuasion—mostly by Cecil and Dudley (now called Leicester)—to let him go to Scotland and woo Mary face-to-face. He arrived in Scotland in February 1565 and was received by Mary on February 17. According to one account, Mary "took well with him and said that he was the lustiest and best proportioned long [tall] man that she had seen."

Mary still had hopes that Elizabeth would name her as successor and she turned down Darnley's proposal, made within a few weeks after his arrival, keeping herself free to marry Leicester if Elizabeth would finally declare her to be her successor. On March 16, it became obvious to Mary, however, that Elizabeth was merely playing games with her. Mary received from Elizabeth's ambassador, Thomas Randolph, the clear message that Elizabeth "could not gratify her [Mary's] desire to have her title determined and published until she [Elizabeth] be married herself, or determined not to marry."[4] Leicester then ceased to be a possibility for Mary.

Against the advice of many of her lords, especially including her half brother, James Stuart, earl of Moray, who saw Darnley as a threat, Mary decided to marry Darnley, defying Elizabeth, who persisted in her attempts to have Darnley brought back to England, under restraint if necessary. To quash rebellious propaganda that she and Darnley would reverse the Reformation in Scotland and to prepare her people for her marriage to the Catholic Darnley, Mary on July 12, 1565, issued a proclamation stating that her marriage would not result in any change in her religious policy.

On July 28, acting without the required consent of her Parliament, Mary proclaimed Darnley king of Scots. The next morning in the royal chapel at Holyrood she married him.

Within days of the wedding, Thomas Randolph, Elizabeth's perspicacious envoy, had observed the Scots' lack of respect for their new king and the hostility of many of them toward him. "His words to all men against whom he conceiveth any displeasure, however unjust it be, are so proud and spiteful that rather he seemed a monarch of the world than he that not long since we have seen and known as the Lord Darnley," Randolph reported. "He looketh now for reverence to many that have little will to give it to him, and though there are some that do give it to him, they think him little worthy of it."

Randolph's comments augured grimly for the fate of Mary's new husband, who through arrogance, conceit, and treachery quickly made enemies of most of Scotland's influential lords. His worthwhile accomplishments as king totaled but one: He sired a son who would become King James VI of Scotland. The child was born June 19, 1566. Eight months later, on February 9, 1567, at age twenty-one, Darnley was assassinated, apparently strangled to death, and the palace where he was staying, Kirk o' Field, was blasted into rubble by a massive amount of gunpowder placed at the structure's foundation.

Many were suspected. Even Mary was rumored to be involved. Wearied of the outrages of Darnley, who was then in the second stage of syphilis, a year earlier she had taken up with James Hepburn, earl of Bothwell, seven years older than Mary, a ruddy, rugged soldier and womanizer whose father, Patrick Hepburn, had tried to marry Mary's widowed mother. Bothwell was described to Elizabeth by Nicholas Throckmorton as "a vainglorious, rash and hazardous young man." But he had come to Mary's aid in the summer and fall of 1565 when Moray organized a rebellion to thwart Mary's enthronement of Darnley, and had helped Mary turn back Moray and his rebel allies in a campaign that came to be known as the Chase-About Raid. From then on, Mary viewed the rascally Bothwell as her protector. He had married Lady Jean Gordon in 1566, but he was not one to let a wife stand in the way of opportunity, which Mary soon presented to him.

Suspicion for Darnley's assassination fell hard on Bothwell, who by now was believed to be having an affair with Scotland's queen and who had his eye on even grander things. Mary made no real effort to apprehend and punish Darnley's murderers, prompting Elizabeth to write, in her own hand, an accusatory letter to Mary:

> My ears have been so astounded, my mind so disturbed and my heart so appalled at hearing the horrible report of the abominable murder of your late husband and my slaughtered cousin, that I can scarcely as yet summon the spirit to write about it. . . . I will not conceal from you that people for the most part are saying that you will look through your fingers at this deed instead of avenging it, and that you don't care to take action against those who have done you this pleasure. . . . I beg you to take this thing so far to heart that you will not fear to touch even him whom you have nearest to you if he was involved.[5]

That person "nearest to you" was, of course, Bothwell. With Darnley out of the way, Bothwell and his chief allies—James Douglas (earl of Morton), Archibald Campbell (earl of Argyll), and George Gordon (earl of Huntly)— had taken over Scotland's government, with Mary's acquiescence. For public relations reasons, Bothwell was made to stand trial for the assassination of Darnley, but the trial was conducted by Argyll and Huntly; Bothwell, not surprisingly, was exonerated. His next bold move was to invite Scotland's lords, who had just adjourned a session of Parliament, to a banquet at a tavern in Edinburgh and there have them sign a petition addressed to Mary that affirmed his innocence of the assassination and that urged Mary to marry him. Bribed with grants of property, most of the lords signed, some of them Bothwell's coconspirators in the assassination.

Growing bolder, Bothwell on April 24, 1567, abducted Mary as she was riding from Linlithgow back to Edinburgh after having visited her son, ten-month-old James, who was being kept in the safety of Stirling castle. Her abduction, however, was apparently accomplished with her consent, as was the purported ravishing that occurred once she had been taken to Bothwell's castle, where she stayed for twelve days. "She was minded to cause Bothwell to ravish her," according to William Kirkcaldy of Grange, one of the influential lords, "to the end that she may the sooner end [Bothwell's] marriage, which she promised before she caused [the] murder [of] her husband."[6]

The lords who opposed him had the next critical move. Three days after Mary's abduction, Morton and Argyll deserted him and joined other rebellious lords in a pact to free Mary from Bothwell—who, they declared, was holding the queen in captivity. Banding together and calling themselves "the Confederate Lords," they promised to "preserve the prince and the commonwealth" and pledged themselves to kill Bothwell. To legitimize their actions, they set up a royal court at Stirling in behalf of young prince James, soon to have his first birthday.

On Thursday, May 15, 1567, after Bothwell had cut a deal with his wife, Lady Jean, to divorce him, and after the divorce had been granted by Scottish judges and an annulment had been granted by the Catholic archbishop of St. Andrews, at Mary's request, Bothwell and Mary were married in a sparsely attended Protestant service at Holyrood.

Meanwhile, the Confederate Lords, whose numbers had reached about thirty, were marshaling an army at Stirling. On June 12 they held a secret judicial session and pronounced Bothwell "the principal author and murderer of the King's Grace of good memory and ravishing of the Queen's Majesty." They thus overturned Bothwell's earlier not-guilty verdict and set the stage for armed confrontation. On the morning of Sunday, June 15, the army of the Confederate Lords and that of Mary and Bothwell, each numbering around three thousand men, marched toward each other and drew up within sight of each other at Carberry Hill, a ridge about two miles southeast of Musselburgh, on the east side of Edinburgh. Both poised for battle, but neither was willing to make the first move. Over several hours, as attempts at mediation failed and Mary's troops, at last tired of the waiting and of the summer heat and their thirst, began to desert the field. In the end, Mary surrendered, without the armies having engaged. The terms of her surrender were that Bothwell would be permitted to flee with a handful of his followers and Mary would return to Edinburgh in the custody of the Confederate Lords.

Mary bade Bothwell good-bye, never to see him again. She was led off the field, astride her horse, down to where the Confederate Lords' troops stood for the historic moment of their queen's defeat. "Burn the whore!" some of the troops shouted as she neared them. Mary hoped for an eventual turn of events that would put her back in control, and on the ride back to Edinburgh she repeatedly spoke her intentions to hang all the rebellious lords. She was taken to Holyrood and kept there till dark. Then she was moved by ferry across the Firth of Forth and into a castle that rose from an island in Loch Leven, near Kinross, northwest of Edinburgh. There she was given a room in the castle's turret. Another resident of the Loch Leven castle was the mother of William Douglas, the lord of Loch Leven. His mother had been the mistress of King James V and was the mother also of Mary's half brother James, the earl of Moray, who was now in self-imposed exile in France.

Elizabeth was automatically opposed to such treatment of any fellow monarch, particularly one who was kin to her. Seeking to restore Mary to the throne, she wrote an impassioned protest to the Confederate Lords and dispatched Nicholas Throckmorton to Scotland to see what he could do to free Mary. Elizabeth's secretary of state, William Cecil, though, working against his queen as well as against Mary, dictated to Throckmorton the terms under which Mary could be freed. They amounted to an abdication. They allowed her to be called "queen" but divested her of all authority.

On July 24, 1567, Mary, under threat of death, signed documents that gave Cecil and the lords what they wanted. She abdicated in favor of her son, then one year old, and five days later at Stirling he was crowned king. On August 22, 1567, Moray, having returned from France, was named regent, just what he had in mind all along.

When Elizabeth heard what had happened, she flew into a monumental rage, berating Cecil and threatening to declare war against the Scots. Cecil took her angry harangue patiently, knowing it was a storm that would soon pass.

Nine months later, with the help of a sixteen-year-old boy whose sympathy she had won, Mary escaped the island castle in a rowboat and rode off with another who chose to help her. A force of supporters, including the earl of Argyll, who had abandoned Moray, quickly formed to reinstate her, but was defeated by a rebel army in a battle at Langside, near Glasgow, on May 13, 1568.

After the disastrous defeat, riding as fast as her horse could carry her, Mary fled to Dumfries, then to Dundrennan. On May 16 she boarded a fishing boat and crossed Solway Firth, landing on the opposite side around seven o'clock that evening. She was now in England, about thirty miles from Carlisle, temporarily safe from the Scottish lords, but not from William Cecil.

She wrote twice to Elizabeth, urging her help in forming a new army to put down the rebels and restore her to the throne. Elizabeth's heart said, "Help her." Her head—and Cecil—said, "Don't." Mary was still a danger, Cecil maintained, particularly in the north of England, where she now was and where strong Catholic sympathies persisted. She might easily become a rallying point for a Catholic uprising, which Elizabeth feared.

With no help coming from Elizabeth, Mary in desperation wrote to Philip in September 1568, asking his help. He felt sympathy for her, and although Elizabeth's professions of friendship between England and Spain were sounding increasingly hollow, he would not oppose Elizabeth while his problems in the Netherlands continued. From Spain he wrote to Alba in the Netherlands for advice, saying that he was "willing to help her [Mary] in her sufferings," but that before he answered her letter, he wanted Alba to tell him "what you think of her business, and in what way, and to what extent, I should assist her."

By February 1569 Philip had grown bolder. He had apparently thought over the possibilities offered by Mary's situation and wrote to Alba about "the good opportunity which now presents itself to remedy religious affairs in that country [England] by deposing the present queen and giving the crown to the queen of Scotland." He instructed Alba to give him an opinion as to "what success would probably attend such a design, as, if there is anything in it, I should be glad to carry it out."

Alba let Philip know he didn't think much of the idea and considered military involvement in England to be unwise and dangerous.

On the other hand, the pope thought involvement in England was a good idea. A militant zealot and suppressor of the Reformation, Pius V had gained the papacy in 1566. In February 1570, his antagonism toward Elizabeth having become more intense, he issued a papal bull, titled *Regnans in Excelsius,* in which he excommunicated Elizabeth, calling her "the pretended Queen of England, the servant of wickedness," and deposed her, insofar as the Catholic church was able. The bull urged Elizabeth's Catholic subjects to overthrow her and kill her.

Philip was furious when he learned what Pius V had done. He promptly wrote to Elizabeth to explain that he had had nothing to do with the pope's action. He also wrote to his ambassador in England, Guerau de Spes, to have him make it known in England that "his holiness has taken this step without communicating with me in any way, which certainly has greatly surprised me, because my knowledge of English affairs is such that I believe I could give a better opinion upon them and the course that ought to have been adopted under the circumstances than anyone else." He allowed that he was afraid that "this sudden and unexpected step will exacerbate feeling there and drive the Queen and her friends the more to oppress and persecute the few good Catholics still remaining in England."[7]

His forecast would prove accurate.

Meanwhile, Mary, although provided with all the comforts of home in her captivity, was living every day under a sword, whose holders would strike her a swift and mortal blow at the first sign of an uprising or invasion.

12. THE TRAGEDIES AND TRIUMPHS

Philip was in Ghent, in the Netherlands, on June 22, 1559, the day he was married to the thirteen-year-old French princess, Elizabeth of Valois, at a ceremony in Paris, with the duke of Alba standing in for him. About six weeks later, he began his journey to return to Spain after an absence of five years. Elizabeth—or Isabel, as she was called in Spain—would meet him there.

He and his royal entourage arrived in the Netherlands port city of Vlissingen on August 11, and he toured the area while killing time waiting for a favorable wind. On the afternoon of August 25, after he had bidden formal farewells to the luminaries who had come to see him off, a group that included his half sister, Margaret of Parma, who would rule as regent in his absence, his ship slipped away from the dock and before a light, easterly wind, headed toward the Strait of Dover and the waters of the English Channel, accompanied by a fleet of nearly one hundred vessels.

The voyage was speedy and uneventful, the fleet arriving in Laredo on the evening of September 8, but the next day, while the ships were being unloaded, a storm struck the Spanish coast, and a number of ships were capsized, and men as well as cargo were lost. After resting from the voyage, Philip and his party set out for the southward trip to Valladolid. He arrived on Thursday, September 14, welcomed royally to the gaily decorated city.

There were pressing matters to attend to, one of the main ones being fiscal, others concerning the Inquisition and religious affairs, another involving the continuing military threat from Turkey. A week after having returned, he ordered a legislative session—a Cortes—to be convened in Toledo a month later to help him handle the nation's affairs. He was wasting no time getting down to business.

As arranged, Elizabeth and her entourage in December 1559 crossed the Pyrenees from France and entered the northeastern Spanish province of

Navarre, where she was met by the seventy-year-old duke of Infantado and a huge host of his attendants and noblemen, to be escorted to Castile, in central Spain. She spent a few days in Pamplona, then continued the trip and arrived in Guadalajara on January 28, 1560. There she was treated to a warmly welcoming, lavish reception by Philip's sister, Princess Juana, and there she and Philip would take their marriage vows again, this time together, in person.

She was welcomed to Guadalajara by the local magistrates and escorted through the main streets of the city in a colorful parade. Dressed in ermine, she rode a white palfrey. On one side of her rode the duke of Infantado, and on the other, the cardinal of Burgos. The procession stopped at the local church, where Te Deum was sung in celebration, then proceeded to the duke's palace, where the wedding would be held. Unwilling to wait till she was formally presented to him, Philip, as he had done before meeting his first wife, Maria, disguised himself and mingled with the throng of well-wishers to catch glimpses of his bride and to share the excitement of her reception.

When Elizabeth at last arrived at the ducal palace, Princess Juana affectionately greeted her and led her to the palace saloon, where Philip, with his son, Carlos, was waiting for her. She then saw him for the first time, looking at him so closely that Philip, no doubt conscious of the years between them, asked her, in good humor, if she was looking for gray hairs in his head. She was almost fourteen; he was thirty-two.

Philip was seeing her up close, too, for the first time. She was tall, taller than most Spanish girls, and she had dark eyes, a dark complexion, long, thick black hair, and delicate features. She was attractive, but in the judgment of the ambassador from Venice, "not greatly beautiful." What she had going for her, though, was more than her looks and youth. There was an appealing quality of feminine sweetness in the way she spoke and the way she conducted herself. According to a contemporary biographer, Pierre de Bourdeille, lord of Brantôme, who knew her well, she was "a true daughter of France—discreet, witty, beautiful and good, if ever woman was so."

For the wedding ceremony, held on the morning of January 31, she wore a silver dress edged in pearls and other gems and about her neck wore a lovely diamond necklace. Philip wore a white doublet and crimson cloak. After the ceremony came the reception banquet, with tables set up in the town's public squares, laden with food and drink, free to all. Fireworks, music, and dancing added to the celebration, which continued the next day with bullfights and a jousting tournament. Not long after the Guadalajara celebrations, the couple left for Toledo, where they arrived on February 12 and where more celebration awaited them. On the plain at the outskirts of the city, a mock battle was staged between three thousand Spanish infantry and a troop of Moorish cavalry, all colorfully uniformed and caparisoned. Then a program of dances by girls from Toledo was put on for the royal couple's entertainment.

That done, Philip and Elizabeth were ushered into the city beneath a canopy of cloth of gold and entered a parade of local magistrates, military leaders, officials of the Inquisition, and many of the nobles of Philip's court, including the duke of Alba and Ruy Gómez de Silva, Philip's two chief lieutenants. They proceeded through the lavishly decorated streets, passing under ornamented arches, hailed by throngs of well-wishers who cheered them as they rode by, on their way first to the cathedral, where they stopped for a time of devotion, then to the Alcázar, Toledo's storied fortress palace. There they were greeted by Philip's son, Carlos, Philip's half brother, John of Austria, and Philip's nephew, Alexander Farnese, son of Philip's sister Margaret. All three were about Elizabeth's age. Inside the palace the celebration continued with dances and banquets, and outside, for weeks following their arrival, they and the city's residents were entertained with bullfights and tournaments.

In the meantime, Philip and Elizabeth started settling into their life together. Elizabeth had not yet reached puberty and did not have her first menstrual period till August 1561. Philip by then, beginning sometime in 1559, had acquired a paramour, Eufrasia de Guzmán, one of the ladies-in-waiting to his sister Juana. There may have been others, too, since Philip was well-known for his fondness for the ladies. His three favorite forms of recreation, according to a member of his court, were hunting, tournaments, and women. But even so, he normally spent his nights with Elizabeth. Over a period of time he apparently stopped his philandering, according to his close friend Ruy Gómez, who told the French ambassador that Philip's "love affairs have ceased, and everything is going so well that one could not wish for more."

Elizabeth was no scholar, but she enjoyed reading, poetry especially. She was a quick learner and within a short time was speaking Spanish with a charming French accent. She not only adopted the language of the Spanish but many of their customs as well, which helped her capture the hearts of the people. "No queen of Castile," the biographer Brantôme wrote of her, "with due deference to Isabella the Catholic, was ever so popular in the country."

Whenever she appeared in public, she drew an admiring crowd. To attend her and provide companionship, she had brought with her several noble ladies from France to be her maids of honor, but when she became established in the palace, she was also provided with Spanish ladies to attend her. After a while, the two groups of women developed a rivalry, and to forestall continuing contention between them, Elizabeth unselfishly let most of her French maids of honor, those with whom she was more familiar, return to France, rewarding them with generous gifts and making peace with them and within the royal household. Coincidentally, because her marriage to Philip had been agreed to as a stipulation in the Cateau-Cambrésis treaty of peace with France, the Spanish fondly called their young queen "Isabel *de la Paz*"—Elizabeth of the Peace.

A more serious crisis arose when she was suddenly stricken with smallpox. Apparently her life was not threatened, but there was great concern—in the Spanish palace and in Paris—that the disease would leave her pretty, young face forever scarred. Her mother, gravely concerned and calling on the help of French physicians, ordered couriers to take to her medications that were believed to prevent disfigurement They may have actually helped, for she managed to escape the effects of the disease with her face unmarked, her beauty intact.

Philip by now had come to feel great affection for her and, according to observers, he treated her with moving tenderness. In 1564, when she was eighteen, she became pregnant but suffered a miscarriage. In 1566 she became pregnant again and this time gave birth to a daughter, Isabella Clara Eugenia. The French ambassador commented that during the birth process Philip was "the best and most affectionate husband that could be imagined." It seemed obvious that he had fallen in love with his young wife. A year later, in 1567, Elizabeth gave birth to another daughter, christened Catalina Micaela.

Elizabeth evidently had had problems following each of the births. When she conceived again, not long after Catalina was born, she suffered a tragic miscarriage four months into her term. Within hours of miscarrying, and apparently losing a lot of blood, she slipped away. As life ebbed from her, she apologized to Philip for not giving him a son. She died on October 3, 1568, at age twenty-two.

Philip—and Spain—had lost their beloved, lovely young queen. Philip was heartbroken. He had sat beside her bed, holding her hand, comforting her as she grew weaker. He had heard a Mass said for her after she died and stayed while her body was prepared for interment at the Escorial. Then, with no more to be said or done, he left the palace and moved into the monastery of St. Jerome in Madrid, where he remained in seclusion for more than two weeks, refusing to see anything connected with the business of the nation, refusing to see any government officers or foreign emissaries, but attending Masses held by the monks for the repose of the soul of his dead queen. He dressed in mourning clothes for a year after her death and said sadly that his two young daughters were his only consolation "since Our Lord deprived me of the company of the queen their mother."

Elizabeth's death was the second tragedy to strike him that year. On July 24, 1568, his son, Carlos, had died. Carlos's life, however, had been more tragic than his death. Mental problems ran in the family, attributable no doubt to generations of inbreeding. One source points out that instead of the eight great-grandparents that most people have, Carlos had only four, and instead of sixteen great-great-grandparents, Carlos had only six. His defects were more than mental, however. Portraits of him painted in 1557 and 1564 show his twisted face and deformed legs. His intellectual problems had first become noticeable when as a young boy he proved to be a slow learner, significantly slow in learning to read and write. In 1558, when he was thirteen, his tutor, who had also been Philip's boyhood tutor, at last let Philip know that Carlos was unteachable. There was nothing the tutor, Honorato Juan, could do to have Carlos learn his subjects. In the years following, his disabilities became more obvious. Eating, drinking, and making merry with the girls who were available to him were all that seemed to interest him.

Philip tried to treat him as if he were normal, having him attend court social functions, having him sworn in as heir to the crown of Castile, having him sit in on meetings of Philip's council, all with disappointing effect. Carlos did find acceptance by his young stepmother, though. Elizabeth apparently considered this boy her own age an enjoyable companion, and they played cards, for money, in the queen's chambers, all of course under the watchful eyes of her attendants. Often, however, Carlos locked himself in his rooms, staying out of touch. He started taking strange medicines. He also began suffering mysterious fevers, and his health became generally poor.

Then, on April 19, 1562, when he was sixteen, he was in the town of Alcalá, staying at some sort of guesthouse, and on his way to seek out a serving girl, fell down a set of stairs and struck his head, knocking himself unconscious and suffering a head laceration. He developed a fever, and applying the usual treatment of the times, his doctors bled him, which of course helped not at all. Word was sent speedily to Philip, who immediately left Madrid and hurried to Alcalá, taking with him his own physician and Alba and Ruy Gómez. Others of his council swiftly followed them.

Following a trepanning operation to relieve pressure on Carlos's brain—and some other treatments that reflected beliefs of the times—the boy came out of his coma, and by May 20 his fever was gone. By the middle of June, he was able to get up and walk.

In 1564, two years after his accident, when he was nineteen, he was described by the ambassador of the emperor, Philip's uncle Ferdinand: "Brown curly hair, long in the jaw, pale of face. . . . One of his shoulders is slightly higher than the other. He has a sunken chest, and a little lump on his back, at waist height. His left leg is much longer than his right. . . . His voice is harsh and sharp, he has problems in speaking." Another ambassador to Philip's court described him as having the mental ability of a seven-year-old. Even Philip admitted that Carlos "lags far behind what is normal at his age."

He had moments of gentleness, which he apparently showed particularly to Elizabeth, but he also went into fits of rage and cruelty that made him a menace to those around him, especially the servants. He picked up a page who angered him and threw him out of a window. He threatened Philip's ministers with a knife. He attacked Alba with a knife, enraged because Philip was sending Alba to the Netherlands instead of him. He picked out from his father's stable a horse that Philip especially liked and talked Philip's master of the horse into letting him ride it. He rode it so hard and treated it so cruelly that it died of its injuries.

Eventually he lost the sympathy of his father, and Philip purposely reneged on his promise to send Carlos to govern the Netherlands, which deepened Carlos's alienation from Philip. In 1567 Carlos wrote letters to several Spanish nobles in an attempt to enlist their support for his plan to leave Spain and go to the Netherlands on his own. He also asked John of Austria to help him. He told John and some others that he intended to kill a man, unnamed but deduced to be Philip. Alarmed, John rode off to find Philip in San Lorenzo and tell him what Carlos was planning.

Apparently at his wit's end, having struggled to know what to do about the prince, Philip on January 13, 1568, ordered prayers said in all of Spain's churches and monasteries, asking for an answer from God for the king's problem, which Philip did not specify in his order. Days later Philip summoned his closest advisers and asked their advice. As a result, on the night of January 19 Philip, armored and armed, led several of his council members and guards to Carlos's chambers, stripped the room of weapons and objects that could be used as weapons, and sealed the windows. Carlos, awakened by the commotion, asked his father if he had come to kill him. Philip told him no, but said that he was going to treat him no longer as a father would, but as a king must. Philip and the council members then exited, leaving Carlos a prisoner in his chambers, a two-man guard posted round the clock to keep a permanent watch on him.

The next morning Philip issued a batch of letters informing government representatives, within Spain and without, of the prince's status. Elizabeth of Valois was one of the first to be told and she burst into tears at the news and cried for the next two days, until Philip ordered her to stop. He also ordered members of his court to no longer mention Carlos's name. The ambassador from France reported that Carlos was "passing into oblivion and is spoken of scarcely more often than if he had never been born." Foreign governments interpreted Philip's action in various ways, apparently not all of them realizing that Philip was barring Carlos from succession. By May 1568, Philip was concerned enough about the opinions of outsiders that he wrote the pope a letter explaining his actions:

> . . . since for my sins it has been God's will that the prince should have such great and numerous defects, partly mental, partly due to his physical condition, utterly lacking as he is in the qualifications necessary for ruling, I saw the grave risks that would arise were he to be given the succession, and the obvious dangers that would accrue. And therefore, after long and careful consideration, and having tried every alternative in vain, it was clear that there was little or no prospect of his condition's improving in time to prevent the evils which could reasonably be foreseen. In short, my decision was necessary.[1]

To Emperor Maximilian, who had succeeded his father, Ferdinand, in 1564, Philip wrote in May 1568 that Carlos's confinement and status were "not temporary nor susceptible to any change in the future."

Carlos did not take his confinement and altered status without protest. At times he refused to eat and lost so much weight that his face became drawn and his eyes bulged from its gauntness. He swallowed objects that he thought would poison him. He made himself sick by overheating himself next to the fire, then dousing himself with cold water. By July his physical condition had deteriorated to the point that he was near death.

Finally, in the early morning hours of July 24, 1568, Carlos died, at age twenty-three, apparently of starvation.

And so in October 1568, following the death of Elizabeth, Philip was without a male heir and without a wife. At first, following Elizabeth's death, Philip professed no interest in remarrying. When his former mother-in-law, Catherine de' Medici, began to promote a match with her daughter Margot, Philip in May 1569 wrote and told her that "I would very much like to avoid talking about remarriage because, having lost the company I have lost and with my sadness and grief still keen, I very much desire to remain as I am."

However, he realized that he should do something to resolve the succession question, which meant he would have to find another suitable wife and try again to produce a son. By the fall of 1569, he had completed arrangements to marry his twenty-year-old niece Anna, daughter of his sister Maria and her husband, Emperor Maximilian, Philip's cousin. Petite, pale complexioned, with blond hair and blue eyes, and described as strikingly elegant, Anna was twenty-two years younger than Philip. She had been born near Valladolid while Maximilian ruled Spain as regent during Philip's absence in 1549.

Accompanied by, among others, her younger brothers Albert and Wenzel, Anna in the fall of 1570 traveled from Austria to the Netherlands, where she would board a ship for Spain. She was received in the Netherlands by the duke of Alba and with great fanfare, which included the arrival of an English flotilla of eight ships sent by Queen Elizabeth with an invitation to have them transport her to Spain, with a stop in England for a royal visit. The invitation was declined. Instead, a Netherlands squadron under the command of Count Bossu, the Netherlands navy's captain general, carried her and her party to Santander, where they landed on October 3, 1570, and where a welcoming throng of some two thousand persons hailed her arrival. From Santander she and her entourage traveled overland to Burgos, where she was given another regal welcome, then continued on to Valladolid and then to Segovia, where the wedding was to be held, arriving there on November 12 and escorted into the city by the gaily uniformed local militia and the city officials, mounted and robed.

The procession, with Anna in her Bohemian dress, a plumed hat upon her blond head, and a mantle of gold-fringed crimson velvet about her shoulders, riding a colorfully caparisoned palfrey, made its way through the ornamented streets, beneath decorated arches, past crowds of curious bystanders and well-wishers, to the city's grand cathedral. There the party dismounted and entered the cathedral for the singing of Te Deum, after which the procession re-formed and proceeded on to the Alcazár, entering to the accompaniment of artillery salutes. She was greeted there by Philip's sister Juana, as warmly as Juana had welcomed Elizabeth of Valois to Castile twelve years earlier.

The wedding was held in the cathedral two days later, on November 14, 1570, a bitterly cold, snowy day, the ceremony performed by the archbishop of Seville and witnessed by an overflow crowd of dignitaries and other guests. The ceremony concluded, the city broke out in spectacular celebrations, including a ball at which Philip and his new bride danced alone while the members of his court respectfully stood by and watched as the newlyweds spun around the dance floor.

On November 18 the royal couple left for Madrid to take up residence there in the capital and begin their life together. Philip, graying and showing signs of middle age, was very much taken with his bride, and by spring of the following year she had become pregnant. On December 4, 1571, she gave birth to a son, Fernando, presenting Philip with a new male heir and the nation with a good reason for joyous celebration.

Over the next ten years, Anna bore four more children to Philip, a total of four boys and a girl. Two other pregnancies resulted in stillbirths. Tragically, only one of the five children she bore—Felipe (Philip), born in 1578—lived to reach adulthood. Fernando died in 1578, another heart-crushing experience for Philip. Carlos Lorenzo, born in 1573, died in 1575. Diego Felix, born in 1575, died in 1582. And Maria, born in 1580, died in 1583.

On October 26, 1580, Philip suffered another devastating tragedy. Anna died, at age thirty, victim of a disease that had attacked both her and Philip and that was probably influenza, which swept across Europe that year and spread into Africa and Asia, creating history's first known pandemic. Philip, fifty-three years old, was thus widowed for the fourth time. He would not marry again.

Fortune was treating him better in the public areas of his reign during those years of personal loss. Ever since the days of King Ferdinand and Queen Isabella, Philip's great-grandparents, efforts had been made to suppress the Moors, the North African Moslems who had overrun Spain in the eighth century and whose domination was largely ended by Christian armies in the thirteenth century. During Ferdinand and Isabella's rule in the fifteenth and early sixteenth centuries, the Moors of Spain were told they had a choice: Convert to Catholicism or leave the country. Those who converted, a great many of them becoming no more than nominal Christians, were called Moriscos. The old kingdom of Granada, lying along the Mediterranean coast, the southernmost part of Spain and the part closest to Moslem North Africa, retained a large, bothersome concentration of Moriscos, estimated at one hundred and fifty thousand, that comprised more than half of Granada's population. Another large Morisco population, some two hundred thousand, was concentrated in the old kingdom of Aragon, Spain's easternmost province, also on the Mediterranean coast and bordering on France. There they constituted about 20 percent of the total population.

Philip's problems with the Moriscos were both religious and political. Philip took it as his divinely ordained mission in life to impose his form of Christianity on all within his realms, resorting to force when necessary, as he did with his enthusiastic support of the Inquisition. The Moriscos would have to embrace Catholicism wholeheartedly and conform or else suffer penalties. The bigger concern, however, was the Moriscos' suspected sympathy for Moslems, which overrode their loyalty to their king and country and which, it was believed, led them to give aid and comfort to Algerian marauders who raided Christian villages along Spain's Mediterranean coast. Philip's great fear was that if the Moslem Turks decided to expand their aggression in the western Mediterranean by attacking Spain, the Moriscos would serve as a fifth column, supporting the Turkish invaders against Spanish defenders. Indeed, three Morisco spies captured in 1565 revealed a plot to seize the coast of Granada in conjunction with the Turks' siege of Malta.

One of the last pieces of advice given to Philip by his late father was to drive all the Moors out of Spain, and in 1559 Philip and his officials, acting on prejudice, zeal, and fear, began a campaign of persecution against the Moriscos that intensified over the following years. Moriscos would no longer receive protection against the Inquisition, despite their offer of a hefty payment for it, and the continuation of their cultural practices would make them suspect. Their titles to property came under rigorous scrutiny. The duty on the silk they exported, a primary source of their income, was increased. They were ordered to turn in their weapons. They were ordered to give up their traditional clothes for Castilian dress. They were ordered to stop their use of the Arabic language and were given three years to learn to speak Castilian instead. The observance of many of their customs was to cease. Violations of those orders were punishable by fines and imprisonment.

As Morisco leaders and some of their Spanish sympathizers predicted, the Moriscos rebelled in reaction. In January 1569 an army of some thirty thousand disaffected Moriscos, mostly from villages in the Alpujarra mountains of Granada, launched their uprising, taking over some one hundred and eighty Granada villages that joined the revolt. With most of his experienced soldiers and officers posted in the Netherlands, Philip had to rely on levies called from across the country to meet the threat. Command of the Spanish forces was assumed by the captain general of Granada, the marquis of Mondéjar, a man sympathetic to the Moriscos' grievances. By March 1569, Mondéjar's forces had recaptured all of the rebellious villages, and the major threat remaining was the rebel units that operated out of mountain refuges.

Philip, however, apparently heeding the advice of the inquisitor general, Cardinal Diego de Espinosa, who considered Mondéjar too soft on the Moriscos, decided to replace him. The replacement was Philip's twenty-two-year-old bastard half brother John of Austria, known to history as Don John, born when Charles V was forty-seven and the girl he seduced was about eighteen.

At the same time, the fighting grew more fierce, the rebels' resolve stiffened by Cardinal Espinosa's publicized proposal to remove all Moriscos from Granada, dispersing them throughout the rest of Spain. The fierceness included a rebel massacre of priests and the slaughter of about 150 Morisco hostages by Philip's Christian army on March 18, 1569. On April 6, John left Madrid to take command of a twenty-thousand-man army. In October, as the fighting dragged on, with few battles but many skirmishes, Philip issued the decree that Espinosa had urged. By the king's command, all Moriscos were banished from Granada. That same month, Philip furthermore ordered that from then on, his soldiers were to wage the war against the Moriscos "with fire and blood."

Although opposed by superior, better-equipped forces, the rebels managed to hold their own until at last their food supply ran out and, driven by hunger, they began coming down out of the hills to surrender. By November 1570 the fight had been decided, the rebellion crushed, and John got much of the credit for the success of the campaign. He had shown himself to be a gallant and competent leader of fighting men. Philip took notice.

John also showed he had a heart. As the Moriscos were forced from their homes and rounded up to begin their long, torturous journey into the Spanish hinterlands, he looked on them in their plight and was moved to remark, "I do not know if one can find a more moving picture of human misery than seeing so many people setting out in such confusion, with women and children crying and so laden with burdens." An estimated ninety thousand Moriscos were displaced from Granada. Perhaps as many as fifteen thousand to twenty thousand of them failed to survive the rigors of removal, succumbing to the bitter cold of the winter of 1570–71 as they were marched through snow and wind or lost at sea when the ships transporting them from Málaga to Seville were struck by storms. Those who did survive were assigned in large groups to the major cities of Castile, where they sought shelter in ghettolike communities, living as a hated and feared minority in places where Moors had not lived for centuries.

To forestall such a rebellion in the future, Philip ordered forts, some eighty-four in all, built and manned in the Alpujarras mountains of Granada and he resettled some twelve thousand Catholic families from Spain's northern provinces in Granada, on land confiscated from the displaced Moriscos. His relocation program, however, had come at a high cost. The economy of Granada, heavily dependent on the skills of the Moriscos, suffered for many years because of their removal, and the Moriscos' rebellious spirit was not crushed but merely carried with them to their new locations, no longer concentrated in Granada but spread throughout the nation. Repeated appeals for Philip to solve the Morisco problem once and for all by deporting all of them were turned down. He was determined to make Christians of them and could do so only by keeping them in Spain. His goal was not merely pacification of the Moriscos but their assimilation into Catholicism and Spanish culture.

His missionary zeal extended far beyond the borders of Spain. To the Americas a fresh wave of Spanish missionaries was sent in the 1560s and 1570s, intent on Christianizing and Europeanizing the natives of the New

World. According to one estimate, by 1570 there were more than a thousand Catholic priests serving in America, sent to minister to some one hundred thousand Spanish settlers and as many of the uncounted millions of natives as they could reach. The natives who *would* not be reached, who would not submit to the Spanish conquerors, often found that the alternative to the Gospel was the sword, as in the case of the Incas of Peru. European Protestants seeking a freer atmosphere in the New World were treated likewise. In September 1565 a large group of Huguenots who were attempting to settle on the Florida coast was struck in a surprise attack by a Spanish force led by Pedro Menéndez de Avilés, and more than 250 Frenchmen were slaughtered and their wives and children taken prisoner. When France's ambassador to Philip's court, Raimond de Fourquevaux, strongly protested to Philip, claiming that never in his forty years as a military man had he seen such an atrocity, Philip replied that although he was distressed that blood had been shed, the attack was "an exemplary punishment" that would discourage other such interlopers on Spanish land.

A much older world also became the target of Philip's proselytizing policies. Portuguese explorer Ferdinand Magellan in 1521 had brought the first Europeans to the lush islands of the Asian archipelago that would become known as the Philippine Islands (*Las Islas Filipinas*), named for Philip by explorer Ruy López de Villalobos in 1542. In 1565 the Spanish conquistador Miguel López de Legaspi, on Philip's orders, had sailed from Mexico and landed at Cebu, the Philippines. His mission, as spelled out by Philip, was to make the Philippines a colony of Spain but to do so as peacefully as possible, keeping bloodshed to a minimum. With Legaspi's army as it marched across the islands were Augustinian and Franciscan friars who would convert while the soldiers conquered and searched for gold. Although resisted by the islands' Moslems (who had first come to the islands in the fourteenth century) and some Buddhist tribal groups, Catholicism became the official religion of the Philippines by widespread acceptance and Philip's decrees.

The might of Philip's Spain was being felt much more impressively closer to home. When a Turkish fleet assaulted the island of Malta, off the coast of Sicily, in May 1565, and the island was in serious danger of being taken by the Turks, a Spanish task force led by García de Toledo, commander of Spain's Mediterranean fleet, landed troops on the island to reinforce the garrison of defenders and by September 1565 had forced the Turks to withdraw.

The Moslem Turks of the Ottoman Empire, having already conquered Asia Minor, Syria, Iraq, Egypt, Arabia, the coastal areas of North Africa, the Crimea, and the Balkans, presented a persistent threat to the Christian nations of Western Europe. Their attack on Malta was viewed as an ominous prelude to things to come in the western Mediterranean. Determined to halt Islam's advance, Pope Pius V shortly after his election to the papacy in 1566 proposed a Holy League, an alliance of Venice, Genoa, Spain—all of them naval powers—and the Papal States, to unite their navies and form a fleet so formidable that it would be a match for the massive Turkish naval force that was menacing the western Mediterranean. Occupied with affairs in the Netherlands and with the Morisco rebellion, Philip put off joining the Holy League until May 1571, after the Turks had threatened Malta and had captured Cyprus in 1570.

The Holy League's participants agreed to give overall command of the combined Christian fleet to Philip's charming, blond half brother, John of Austria, then twenty-four years old, whom Philip had already made captain general of Spain's Mediterranean fleet. The participation of Spain, with its considerable navy, was the key element needed to give the league a chance of success over the fearsome Turks, who since the thirteenth century had seemed invincible, both on land and sea. John's appointment as commander evidently helped persuade Philip to join the league. When Philip named John captain general in 1568, he gave him some instructions, as an older brother might be expected to do, and in doing so revealed something of John's personality. He told John to set a good example, to refrain from gambling, eat moderately, watch his language, and treat others with courtesy. He furthermore told John's aide that John "should not go around at night, because Barcelona is noted for its women, and there's no lack of disease." Following John's appointment as commander of the league's fleet, Philip once more felt he had to tell John's aide to keep him out of trouble.

On July 20, 1571, John sailed from Barcelona, bound for Messina, Sicily, where the ships of the Holy League were to rendezvous. By the end of August, the promised ships of Venice, Genoa, the Papal States, and Spain had assembled at Messina, a total of approximately 207 galleys—the ships of war—about 100 support vessels, and 6 Venetian galleasses, unwieldy broadbeamed merchant ships that had been converted into floating fortresses, each carrying some forty heavy guns capable of wreaking awesome devastation.

The fleet's personnel consisted of some 13,000 sailors, plus about 43,500 oarsmen, and about 28,000 soldiers, a total of about 84,500 men. Eighty-one of the galleys had been provided by Spain, and more than eight thousand of the soldiers were Spanish. To command the Spanish vessels Philip had appointed Alvaro de Bazán, the marquis of Santa Cruz. The Venetian fleet, comprising 106 galleys plus the 6 galleasses, was under the command of Sebastian Veniero; the ships of the Papal States were commanded by Marcantonio Colonna; and the commander of Genoa's fleet was the veteran admiral Andrea Doria.

John dispatched a small squadron to locate the Turkish fleet and discover its strength. The squadron returned with news that the Turks were in the Adriatic Sea, where they had been pillaging and burning coastal villages in Venetian territory. The size of their fleet was later put at more than 300 vessels, including 250 galleys—rowed mostly by captured Christians who had been turned into galley slaves—and about sixty-five galliots, small, swift single-masted vessels that carried no more than about twenty rowers. The fleet's personnel totaled about seventy-five thousand men, about a third of them soldiers.

On September 16 the Christian fleet sailed from Messina and on hearing the Turkish fleet's location, John ordered a course set for Corfu, on the northwest coast of Greece, where the Adriatic opens into the Ionian Sea. The fleet reached Corfu on September 26. There John received supplies and learned that the Turkish fleet, apparently apprised of the proximity of the league's fleet, was anchored in the Gulf of Lepanto, between the Greek mainland and the peninsula of Peloponnesus, as if lying in wait for the Christians. John's first impulse was to immediately take on the enemy, but perhaps with his brother's words of caution resounding in his mind, he quickly called together his chief captains for a war council. Their advice was mixed. Some who had had experience fighting Turks were hesitant to confront so massive a force and instead suggested a safer alternative, such as besieging a few Moslem towns. Doria's idea was to draw the Turks out of the relatively narrow confines of the Gulf of Lepanto and engage them in much wider waters that were more advantageous to the Christians. Most of the council, however, and the majority of those whose opinions carried the most weight, were for engaging the Turks where they lay, trapping them in the gulf with no means of retreat or escape and destroying the enemy fleet. That opinion coincided with John's.

The commanding admiral of the Turkish fleet was Ali Pasha, who, preparing his men for the imminent battle, shrewdly told his Christian galley slaves, on whom he would be dependent in the conflict, "If your countrymen are to win this day, Allah give you the benefit of it. Yet, if I win it, you shall certainly have your freedom. If you feel that I do well by you, do then the like by me."

On Sunday, October 7, 1571, two hours before dawn, the Christian fleet weighed anchor and sailed into a light wind, their momentum borne by their oars. At sunrise the lead vessels came abreast of the rocky islets that shield the entrance to the Gulf of Lepanto. Now the Christian crews searched the sea before them, eager to spy the waiting enemy. Then from the foretop of John's flagship, the *Real,* came a shout from the watch, "A sail!" Soon the entire Turkish fleet came into sight, lying menacingly ahead in the distance. John ordered his personal pennon flown atop the *Real*'s mizzen and then unfurled the standard of the Holy League, given to the fleet by his holiness himself, Pius V, and bearing an image of the crucified Christ. That done, John ordered a gun fired to signal the opening of battle. From the decks of the league's vessels rose a thunderous chorus of shouts of men eager for a fight.

John arrayed his fleet in three squadrons, their front extending a distance of three miles across the water. On the right he positioned the squadron commanded by Admiral Doria, composed of sixty-four galleys. On the left, nearest the shoreline, he placed the squadron commanded by the Venetian nobleman Augustino Barbarigo. In the center he put the squadron he himself would command, composed of sixty-three galleys. Immediately on his flanks he positioned the Venetian admiral, Veniero, and the papacy's admiral, Colonna. To the rear of center he positioned the galley commanded by the veteran Spanish general, Berenguer de Requesens, who had been John's mentor in the art of war. Also to the rear was the fleet's reserve force, thirty-five galleys commanded by Santa Cruz, who had been ordered by John to use his discretion and engage wherever his force was most needed. The slow-moving galleasses, burdened with their tremendous artillery, were towed a half mile to the front of the formation, two of them positioned in front of each of the three squadrons, presenting a bulwark of deadly metal to an oncoming enemy.

When all vessels were in place, John boarded a light frigate and set out to make a last-minute inspection and to give words of encouragement to his fighting men. "You have come to fight the battle of the cross!" he shouted to them over the rails of the frigate, making the fight a holy cause. "To conquer or to die! But whether you are to die or conquer, do your duty this day and you will secure a glorious immortality!" He ordered his men to hold their fire until they were close enough to be spattered by Moslem blood. Then, satisfied that all was in readiness, he returned to the *Real*.

Ali Pasha deployed his fleet in the shape of a crescent, its points foremost, then separated the formation into three divisions when he saw the deployment of the league's fleet. He would take command of the center division. Mohammed Sirocco, the viceroy of Egypt, would command on the Turks' right, and Uluch Ali, the governor, or bey, of Algiers, on their left.

The line of Turkish ships plowed ahead, the foremost vessels firing as they advanced. As Ali Pasha's division closed on John's squadron, the guns of the two center galleasses opened fire, with devastating effect, sinking, according to one report, at least seven of the Turks' galleys. Ali Pasha's repeated attempts to draw up to the league's vessels and board them were repulsed by the murderous hail of fire from the harquebuses of Spanish infantrymen posted on the decks and in the rigging of John's ships, answering the assault of arrows from the Turks. John then ordered Ali Pasha's flagship boarded. A first attempt, then a second were both repulsed by the Turks. A third attempt carried John's men across Ali Pasha's bloody decks, up to the ship's poop, the raised deck at the stern of the ship, where Ali Pasha was found wounded and was beheaded by one of the swarming horde of league soldiers. His severed head was spitted on a pike and held up so that all could see that the Turks had lost their commander. At the same time, the dreaded Turkish battle flag was hauled down from the mainmast, the first time it had ever been captured. The center division of the Turkish fleet then broke apart and sought to flee the Holy League's onslaught.

The Turks' right division, closest to the shore and commanded by Mohammed Sirocco, managed to turn the flank of the Christian line, where Barbarigo commanded. Barbarigo's flagship was surrounded by eight Turkish vessels and captured, and he was killed by a Turkish arrow, but the ship was retaken, taken again, and retaken again, the battle for it concluding when Sirocco's ship was sunk. Sirocco was plucked from the water by league soldiers and beheaded. The attempt by Uluch Ali to turn John's right flank, where Doria commanded, was thwarted, although Ali captured one of the Christian galleys, which was later recovered when Santa Cruz led his reserve squadron against Ali. John then turned his vessels on Ali and forced him to break off and run.

After four to five hours, the Battle of Lepanto came to an end, the air filled with the smoke of artillery and burning hulks, the sea thick with wreckage and corpses. The Holy League's victory was so overwhelming that not more than 40 of the 250 Turkish galleys managed to escape. The rest were either sunk or captured. The Turks also lost an estimated thirty thousand men killed and eight thousand taken prisoner. They also lost the thousands of Christian galley slaves who were restored to freedom, many of whom had burst their fetters to join the fight against their Moslem captors. The Holy League lost an estimated eight thousand killed and sixteen thousand wounded.

One of the wounded was a twenty-four-year-old Spanish soldier named Miguel Cervantes, who was serving on board one of the ships of Genoa. His wound cost him the use of his left hand, which ended his military career, but with his right hand he went on to write one of history's greatest, most enduring novels, *Don Quixote*.

The victory vaulted John into prominence throughout Europe, and Philip, extraordinarily elated, according to the Venetian ambassador, over what his kid brother had done, was quick to give him credit for the achievement. "To you," Philip wrote him, "after God, ought to be given, as I now give, the honor and thanks."

As spectacular as it was, over a forbiddingly formidable enemy, the triumph was also bound to add fearsomely to the reputation of Spain and its dauntless king.

·13. THE NETHERLANDS REVOLT

hilip didn't really want to see the count of Egmont. It was February 1565, and Philip's mind was occupied with the Turkish fleet then menacing the Mediterranean. He didn't want to be bothered with affairs in the Netherlands, which was not an unusual attitude for him even in the absence of a Turkish threat. Egmont had come from Brussels, sent by his fellow Netherlands aristocrats, on a mission to talk Philip into adopting a softer policy on Netherlands Protestants—heretics, in Philip's terms—and to give more authority to the Netherlands advisory body, the council of state, and to appoint additional Netherlands nobles to the council. In short, Egmont had come to negotiate less oversight from Philip and more sovereignty for him and his fellow nobles. Philip knew what Egmont was after, and he was as reluctant to say no as he was to say yes. For the present, at least, he didn't want to have to make decisions on those issues.

The Netherlands presented to Philip a far different situation than did Spain, where his rule was more or less absolute. The Netherlands, also known as the Low Countries, was composed of seventeen provinces, political entities that were designated as duchies, counties, or lordships, which in earlier times had each been a separate state ruled by its own prince. They were the duchies of Brabant, Limburg, Luxembourg, and Guelders; the counties of Artois, Hainault, Flanders, Namur, Zutphen, Holland, and Zealand; the margraviate of Antwerp; and the lordships of Friesland, Mechelen, Utrecht, Overyssel, and Groningen. They extended over the area now known as the Netherlands (or Holland) and Belgium.

The provinces shared a tradition of certain freedoms and rights, which made them considerably more liberal than most other sixteenth-century states. Two of the most important rights were the one stipulating that no tax could be levied on the people without the consent of an assembly made up of nobles, clergymen, and representatives of the province's towns, and the one that barred foreigners in a province—anyone not native to that province—from public office. Those rights were mostly ignored by Philip but not forgotten by the Netherlands people.

Netherlanders were an industrious, prosperous people, their country perhaps the most urbanized in Europe. The people were accustomed to thinking and doing for themselves, and when the ideas of the Protestant Reformation came to them from Germany and Geneva, many Netherlanders saw truth in them and wholeheartedly embraced them. Philip's father, Emperor Charles V, himself a native of the Netherlands but a fierce enemy of the Reformation, in an effort to stamp it out, issued edicts, or placards, outlawing virtually all manifestations of Protestantism and setting forth the punishments for persons found guilty of the specified offenses. Over a thirty-year period, beginning in March 1520, Charles issued eleven placards intended to suppress Protestantism. Under the terms of his final placard, issued in September 1550, all persons found guilty of heresy were to be burned alive, buried alive, or beheaded. The death penalty was to be suffered by all who dealt in heretical books, who bought them or copied them, by all who argued Scripture, whether in public or in private, by all who preached or defended the doctrines of reform, by all who held or attended heretical religious assemblies. The courts were ordered to grant no reduction in punishment, and friends of the accused who sought mercy for them were to suffer penalties also. Informers were promised one-half of the property confiscated from the guilty individuals.

To enforce the provisions of his edicts, Charles had Pope Adrian VI appoint for the Netherlands an inquisitor general, with the authority to investigate persons suspected of heresy, imprison and torture them, confiscate their property, and banish them or put them to death. The man who got the job was a lawyer, a member of the Brabant provincial council, who executed his new office so zealously that he quickly enraged his countrymen and was forced to abandon his post and flee for his life.

To replace him, the pope appointed *four* inquisitors. That brought on such a reaction from the Netherlanders that Charles conceded a proviso that before a person accused of heresy could be sentenced, a member of the appropriate provincial council had to approve the sentence. It was perhaps a small compromise, but it showed that the Netherlanders, by their firm resistance, could effect a change in the emperor's policies.

When Philip succeeded his father as the Netherlands' ruler, he endorsed the religious policies set forth in Charles's placards. Religion in the Netherlands was a major concern to Philip, and he was determined to affix Catholicism more steadfastly upon the country's willful population. Convinced that the Netherlands' five bishops were far short of what was needed to oversee an estimated three million souls, he petitioned Pope Paul IV to create for the Netherlands ten more bishops and three archbishops, which the pope did in 1559, the year that Philip left the Netherlands to return to Spain. That change in the status quo, popularly perceived as a threat to established rights, privileges, and powers of the nobles, drew heavy fire from diverse segments of the population, including some Catholic special interests as well as Protestants, who saw in the change an intention by Philip to impose a Spanish-style religious authority, and even a Spanish-style Inquisition, on a people who were too freethinking to accept such. Many Netherlanders saw the change as an attempt to alter not only their religious freedom but their political freedom as well (which of course it was). In addition, Philip in 1561 named Cardinal Antoine Perrenot de Granvelle, the chief adviser to Philip's sister Margaret, the Netherlands regent, and a man widely disliked by Netherlanders, to head the see of Mechelen, thereby placing his hands on the controls of the church as well as the government and deepening popular suspicion of Philip's intentions. And when Granvelle appointed the new bishops, many were found to be inadequate for the job, which led to further popular resentment.

The Netherlanders would not take Philip's missteps lying down. In July 1561 Egmont and Prince William of Orange, on behalf of the Netherlands' nobles, wrote to Philip to protest the church reorganization that Philip had instituted. When Philip refused to back down, Egmont and Philippe de Montmorency, the count of Hornes, quit their seats on the Council of State to further protest Philip's actions. Obstinately, Philip still refused to seek agreement. In 1562 the nobles dispatched Floris de Montmorency, the baron Montigny, to the Spanish capital to meet with Philip and present their grievances, chief of which were the bishops, the Inquisition, and Granvelle. Philip assured them he had no intention of introducing the Spanish Inquisition into the Netherlands, his assurance being the extent of satisfaction received from Philip. Egmont, William of Orange, and Hornes then sent a bold demand to Philip. Granvelle, whom many saw as the instigator of the church reorganization, must resign his posts, they said. Until he did, Egmont, Orange, and Hornes were withdrawing from the Council of State, refusing to cooperate in the government of the country.

Over the objections of the duke of Alba, who was Granvelle's chief supporter, Philip took the advice of his sister Margaret and in January 1564 wrote to Granvelle telling him to get out of the country on the pretext of having to go see his mother. A month later, having allowed time for Granvelle to relocate, Philip ordered the three recalcitrant nobles back into the Council of State. The nobles had got their way, and the crisis was over—for a while.

The religious situation still smoldered, though. Getting rid of Granvelle had not helped much. The harsh, repressive heresy laws set forth in the placards were still in force, although many of the country's magistrates refused to enforce them. In December 1564, William of Orange, touching the sympathies of his fellow aristocrats, delivered a moving speech before the Council of State in which he urged the exercise of freedom of conscience in religious matters. In response, the nobles decided that their grievances should be presented to Philip and that the person to present them was the count of Egmont, who accepted the assignment.

Egmont arrived in Madrid on February 23, 1565. Far from being a zealous reformer, forty-three-year-old Egmont was a distinguished general, spoke several languages fluently, including Spanish, was suave, charming, and vain. Knowing that Philip didn't want to see him, Margaret of Parma wrote to her brother to ask him to see him anyway. Receive him, Margaret urged Philip, "with a happy face and your majesty's accustomed good will." Philip did as his sister requested, greeting Egmont with an embrace and refusing to let him kneel before him. During their meeting, Egmont turned over to Philip the fifteen-page memorandum that set forth the Netherlanders' grievances and petitions, which had to be translated into Spanish before Philip could read it.

For five weeks Philip stalled Egmont. At the end of March he drafted a response to the memorandum and turned the draft over to his secretary, Gonzalo Pérez, to be written up for Egmont. The response was purposely vague, and Philip let Pérez know that vagueness was intentional. "I have drafted my answer in this way," he wrote in a note to the secretary, "so that Egmont will not be able to force me into a decision. . . . My intention is, as you will have gathered, neither to resolve these demands of the count nor to disillusion him about them, for then he would worry us to death and we would never be finished with him."

On the matters concerning the authority and makeup of the Netherlands Council of State, Philip put off a decision by saying that he would have to consult with Margaret of Parma, the regent, about them. About the religious issues, the really important part of Egmont's memorandum, Philip said he would be willing to form a committee to determine how best to punish heretics. There was to be no concession on the heresy laws themselves, however. "Under no circumstances," he made clear to his secretary, "do I wish the punishment to stop. I only wish the [punishment] method to be examined."

On April 4 Philip again met with Egmont and began the meeting by buttering him up with personal grants and favors that meant a considerable amount of money to Egmont. When Philip got around to the subject of religion in the Netherlands, he told Egmont that only Catholicism was to be permitted, but he allowed as how the situation would be improved by the work of the committee that would be formed. Egmont seemed satisfied, elated even, with what he had gained from his king.

By the end of April 1565, Egmont was back in Brussels, where he delivered to the Council of State a glowing report of his meeting with Philip. He said that Philip had not put his intentions in writing but he had told Egmont that the heresy laws would be eased and that more authority would be given to the council. He also reported that Philip was too preoccupied with the Turks to be able to come to the Netherlands anytime soon.

In June a packet of letters from Philip arrived in Brussels, having been dispatched from Segovia (where Philip then was staying at his hunting lodge) in May. The letters contradicted Egmont's claims of what Philip had promised. Especially damaging to Egmont—and to Philip—was a letter in which Philip denied the appeal for clemency for six Anabaptists who, although having repented of their errors, had been sentenced to be burned. Contrary to what Egmont had reported, there obviously was no change in the king's policy regarding the heresy laws. Protestants would continue to be sent to the stake. Egmont had been duped. In protest of Philip's decision, the nobles on the Council of State once more withdrew from cooperation in the government, and one group of nobles began holding meetings to determine what steps they would take if Philip persisted in his refusal to relax the heresy laws. In the meantime, the committee of religious experts that Philip had promised had been formed and it had recommended easing the heresy laws.

Philip was soon told what was happening. In July, Margaret of Parma wrote him about the situation, saying, "On several matters which Count Egmont had heard from the royal lips, your majesty's letters [the so-called Segovia letters that had been received in June] appear at certain points to contradict the report he has made." Margaret also passed along to Philip the recommendations of the committee.

The confusion over what he had said and what Egmont had told the council members he had said baffled Philip. He could not understand how Egmont could have so grossly misconstrued his statements. As for the denial of the appeal of the six Anabaptists, he thought he was being perfectly consistent with the established law, death by burning being the usual punishment for Anabaptists. The letter denying their appeal, though, had been written not by Pérez, who knew that Philip was trying to seem moderate, but instead by Philip's French-language secretary, Charles de Tisnacq, who detested Protestants and who was unaware that Philip had tried to soft-pedal his position in his conversations with Egmont. Nevertheless, Philip had signed the letter, and presumably read it. The denial was his order. The Segovia letters made clear that he was not in favor of changing anything. The heresy laws that were stated in the placards would remain in force. Inquisitors would continue to conduct the Inquisition. Protestants would continue to be persecuted. Anabaptists in particular would continue to be burned.

Furthermore, Philip in the Segovia letters enjoined Margaret and the members of the council to faithfully obey his commands. By so doing, he said, they would render a great service to the cause of religion and to their country. The matters of religion and religious tolerance in the Netherlands were thus summarily closed—at least in Philip's mind. When Philip's letters were read to the council, reaction immediately began to set in. Prince William's was one of the voices heard as the meeting broke up. "Now," he said to his fellow nobles, "we shall see the beginning of a fine tragedy."

It was not only from the Council of State that outrage rose. In December 1565 Margaret ordered copies of Philip's letters—his restatement of rules for the Netherlands—to be delivered to the governors and members of the councils of the seventeen provinces and she ordered those officials to see to it that the king's policies were carried out. To make sure, monitors were to be appointed to keep an eye on the provincial officials and observe the way they followed their orders. The public reaction was as might have been—and actually had been—predicted. In the words of one of Philip's biographers, the distribution of copies of Philip's letters "created a sensation throughout the country little short of what would have been caused by a declaration of war."[1] All hope, even among the most optimistic Netherlanders, of having their king moderate his policies to accommodate the sensibilities of the people was crushed. The disenchanted included many Catholics in the country, those who were repelled by Philip's display of despotism.

Some twenty militant young nobles joined in a league to resist the king's policies and issued a declaration, called the Compromise, detailing their grievances and defying the king's will and authority. In it they charged, among other things, that Philip had violated his oath and was supporting a religious persecution that had as its sole object the confiscation of the victims' property. When copies of the Compromise were circulated around the country, hundreds of Netherlanders—as many as two thousand, according to one source—added their signatures to it, along with those of the original signers.

Prince William, like his fellow nobles on the Council of State, declined to sign the document, but he made known his objection to Philip's intransigence. On January 24, 1566, he wrote to Margaret of Parma that he would not follow the king's orders. He recited the evils of the Inquisition—which, he pointed out, the king had said he would not introduce into the Netherlands—and summarized the agitated feelings of the people, who were then suffering not only persecution but a general shortage of food, the year's harvest having been a poor one. William warned Margaret that Philip's policies might cost him the loss of the Netherlands. "If his majesty insists on the execution of these measures," he wrote with a touch of sarcasm, "rather than incur the stain which must rest on me and my house by attempting it, I will resign my office into the hands of someone better acquainted with the mood of the people and who will be better able to maintain order in the country."

Other provincial governors wrote similar words of protest to the regent in response to the copies of the Segovia letters she had sent them. The country began to seethe with discontent, exacerbated by widespread famine, partial relief for which was sent by Spain. Rumors arose that Philip was coming at the head of a huge army to smash the resistance to his orders. Others had it that a large German force was being marshaled to march on the Netherlands.

Another, with more substance, claimed that Catherine de' Medici, the regent of France, had plotted with the duke of Alba to wipe out the Protestants of France as well as those of the Netherlands. With that extermination of the Protestants, the rumors alleged, the traditional freedoms of the Netherlands' people would also be eliminated.

Margaret also had heard rumors, the most disturbing of which was that the strength of the rebels' league had grown to some thirty thousand men—confederates, they were called—and that they had armed themselves and were preparing to march on Brussels and seize her if she did not concede their demands. She quickly took steps to reinforce the garrisons throughout the country and ordered additional troops into Brussels. She also wrote her brother a desperate letter, informing him of the expected event. She told him the threat could be met in only one of two ways: Answer the rebels with force, or give them what they wanted. Force meant coming up with large sums of money, which was in short supply at the time, to pay the troops. It also meant devastating the country. Concession meant getting rid of the Inquisition, modifying the placards, and granting pardons to all who had signed the Compromise.

She did not say which option she preferred. She did, however, tell Philip that she would faithfully follow his orders—whatever they were—as best she could. She further told him that she would like his answer as soon as possible and asked him to send it to her by the same courier who had brought him her letter.

On April 3, 1566, two hundred confederates—far fewer than were rumored—each armed with a pair of holstered pistols, rode into Brussels, with Baron Henry de Brederode and Louis of Nassau, Prince William's younger brother, at the head of the column, and were enthusiastically greeted by the city's inhabitants. The next day, they met together at a Brussels hotel and heard a letter from Spain read to them, informing them of the death of a well-known Netherlands nobleman named Morone, whom the Inquisition had burned at the stake. They then drafted a request to Margaret to meet with them on the following day and to allow them to present their petition.

At noon on, April 5, they strode in a solemn procession to Margaret's palace, where they were received by her and the nobles of her council. Despite their menacing presence, Margaret received them graciously. Brederode, picked to be the group's spokesman, made a short speech, then handed Margaret the petition, which, he said, he hoped she would grant, since its "requests" were for the good of the country and the glory of the king. Margaret replied that if that was the case, there should be no problem for her in granting what they were seeking.

On April 6 the confederates, their number swelled by the addition of 150 more of them who had ridden into the city the previous evening, went back to the palace to get Margaret's answer, as arranged. Her answer was in writing, penned on the petition the confederates had given her and now handed back to them. She promised she would try to persuade the king to grant them what they sought and said that they could depend on his doing all that was consistent with "his natural and accustomed benignity"—a nebulous phrase that probably left the confederates wondering. She also said that although she had no power to alter the religious laws on her own, she and her advisers would devise a plan to moderate them and submit it to the king. She would in the meantime instruct the inquisitors to exercise discretion in the performance of their duties.

The confederates decided to push her farther than she had gone in her response. On April 8 they delivered to her *their* reply, also written. They thanked her for her prompt attention to their petition but said they wished her response had been more explicit. They thanked her for her assurance that the Inquisition's proceedings would be halted until word could be received back from the king. (She had not given that assurance; the confederates were putting words in her mouth.) They said that on the matter of religion they were eager to cooperate with whatever the king decided *with,* they emphasized, the advice and consent of the States General, the nation's representative body. The push had some effect, for soon after receiving the confederates' response, Margaret wrote instructions to the provincial officials to suspend action on their proceedings concerning religious matters.

Satisfied that their mission had been accomplished, at least for the present, the confederates, still in Brussels, began celebrating. At one of the banquets they staged, Brederode, in the role of master of ceremonies, regaled them with a story about how one of the council members, a man named Barlaimont, seeing Margaret's anxiety over so many armed confederates in her presence, reassured her by telling her not to worry, that "they were nothing but a crowd of beggars." Brederode found the remark funny, and the confederates, agreeing, adopted the term *"les gueux"*—the beggars—as their nom de guerre and took pride in it. *"Vivent les Gueux!"*—Long live the Beggars!—became their rallying cry.

To take the report of her dealings with the confederates to Philip and to urge his approval of the proposed measures, Margaret commissioned two of the Netherlands nobles, the baron de Montigny and the marquis of Bergen, neither of whom was eager to accept the honor and face the king with troubling news. Montigny arrived in Madrid ahead of Bergen, on June 17, 1566, and was graciously received by Philip, who listened impassively while Montigny presented the confederates' list of suggested reforms, especially including the convening of the States General to iron out the problems.

Montigny met with Philip more than once, but each time, Philip promised nothing more than serious consideration. The consideration came from the king's council of state as well as from the king himself, and Montigny and Bergen were allowed to become spectators at the council meetings in which the confederates' proposals were discussed. The council members, including two or three who were Netherlanders loyal to the king, were unanimous in their judgment of the proposals. They were certain that this latest action by the confederates was merely part of a grand scheme by the nobles to revolutionize the country and assume power for themselves. But, the council members realized, something had to be done. Philip should go to the Netherlands and take charge of the situation, they told him. And in the meantime, some kind of concessions should be made.

On July 31, 1566, after weeks of pondering, Philip, at last wrote Margaret his decision. He began by professing surprise that the Netherlanders were upset by his policies, which, he claimed, were nothing new but merely a continuation of the laws instituted by his father. Yet, because it was his nature to act out of mercy and love, he wrote, he would do his best to meet the desires of his subjects rather than resist them with severity. He said he approved the abolition of the Inquisition in the Netherlands, but its inquisitorial authority would be transferred to the Catholic bishops. He disapproved of Margaret's idea of moderating the placards and said he didn't think anything less than complete religious tolerance would satisfy the people. He asked Margaret to come up with another idea on the subject of religion, making sure Catholicism maintained its position. In the matter of amnesty for the confederates, he told Margaret she could give it to whomever she felt deserved it, except for those who had already been condemned, and on the condition that the confederates would quit their league and enthusiastically support the government.

On August 2, two days after writing that letter to Margaret, he wrote her again, telling her she must not agree to a meeting of the States General and that he would never consent to its convening. But, he said, she should not let it become known that she refused to have the States General meet. Let people think, he told her, that she would agree to it sometime later. He also told her that he was sending her sufficient funds to hire a mercenary German army of ten thousand infantry and three thousand cavalry to be on call in case she needed it.

He then ordered a notary to prepare a document that would be witnessed by the duke of Alba and two others and that would set forth his true intention regarding amnesty for the confederates. The document made it clear that he believed his statement of amnesty, made to Margaret, had been coerced from him and that "he therefore did not feel bound by it, but reserved to himself the right to punish the guilty, and especially the authors and abettors of sedition in the Low Countries [the Netherlands]."[2]

He furthermore sent an explanatory message to Pope Pius V, who, as a tireless foe of heresy, had taken great interest in religious affairs in the Netherlands and had offered Margaret of Parma men and money to suppress it. Philip instructed his Vatican envoy, Luis de Requesens, to tell the pope that if he, Philip, had had time, he would have consulted his holiness before writing those letters to Margaret, but that the pope shouldn't worry about what the king had said concerning the abolition of the Inquisition in the Netherlands, since, having been ordered by the pope's authority, it could not be abolished without the pope's consent. And as for the decrees set forth in the placards, Philip wanted the pope to know that he would never reduce the penalties for those found guilty of their violation. But, he also wanted the pope to understand, his position on those two matters were to be kept confidential, a secret between Philip and the pope.

In the Netherlands there were outbursts of triumphal excess in response to Philip's publicized altered policies. Throughout the country during August 1566, rampaging mobs, incited by Reformist preachers, attacked Catholic churches, monasteries, convents, and even hospitals in a frenzy of destruction and vandalism, destroying altars, images, paintings, furnishings, books, the clergy's vestments, and, in Antwerp, the cathedral's magnificent pipe organ. In the western provinces alone some four hundred churches were assaulted, and frightened priests and monks fled for safety before the maddened onslaught, taking with them as much of their churches' valuables as they could carry. Reporting the outrages to Philip, Margaret summarized them as "defilements, abominations and sacrileges."

Already ill with some malady, Philip was made sicker by that news. He wrote back to Margaret saying that he had "received the information with immense grief, but have been unable to reply because of my indisposition." By September 22, he was well enough to call a meeting of his council to consider what should be done about the situation in the Netherlands. The council's unanimous advice was to send troops to quash the rebellion. At another council meeting near the end of October, the advice was repeated. The Turkish threat had diminished, and Philip had received a new windfall of South American silver, so he was ready to finance an army and send it to the Netherlands to restore order and the king's authority. He ordered the marshaling of a force of sixty thousand infantry and twelve thousand cavalry to be commanded by the sixty-year-old duke of Alba. By December 1566 the preparations had been completed. The problem then was that the passes through the Alps would be closed by snow before all the troops could get through them, and so the expedition was postponed until the spring.

Meanwhile, during the winter and early spring of 1567, Margaret of Parma, primarily through the efforts of Prince William and with the help of other nobles, had initiated a successful campaign of pacification, partly by peaceful means and partly by military force. In March 1567 government troops literally wiped out a two-thousand-man rebel army in a crucial battle at Oosterweel, just outside Antwerp, and as a result, towns that had been in rebellion returned to the regent's authority. Margaret notified Philip of the action and told him she did not think further armed intervention was needed. On the same day, April 27, that Margaret's representative arrived at Philip's court with her message, however, Alba sailed from Cartagena with his army in the ships of Admiral Andrea Doria, bound for Italy, where they would disembark and begin their march to the Netherlands.

Once Alba reached Italy, the news from the Netherlands caught up with him. He and Philip apparently then decided that an army of 72,000 was vastly more than Alba needed and that 10,500 troops—approximately 9,250 infantry and 1,250 cavalry, the force he took with him—would be sufficient to quash the rebellion and round up its leaders. With all in readiness, Alba's army set out from Asti on June 25.

No sooner had Alba and his troops departed Spain than Philip began having second thoughts about sending them, especially considering Margaret's latest letters. His councilors were evenly split on the matter of military intervention, and most others from whom he was receiving advice were against it. Raimond de Fourquevaux, the French ambassador, reported that the members of Philip's court generally thought the move was a mistake, that Philip's "Turkish-type army," as he called it, would serve only to unite Catholics and Protestants in the Netherlands against Philip. Nevertheless, Philip did nothing to deter the intervention but found new justification for it in the reports from Emperor Maximilian that Prince William had fled the Netherlands to Germany and had joined a military alliance with a number of German princes.

Alba and his army arrived in Brussels on Friday, August 22, 1567. His first stop was the regent's palace, where Margaret and some members of her Council of State received him informally, briefly, and without enthusiasm. On August 25 Alba met again with Margaret, and this time she asked him why he and his army had come. He told her she already knew why he was there. When she demanded that he remove his troops from the Netherlands, he replied patronizingly, "Madam, I have told your excellency that I have come here to assist you." Thwarted, her authority trumped, her pleas ignored by the king, she resigned her office as regent. Four months later she left Brussels.

Alba wasted no time in getting down to his bloody business. He set up a judiciary body called the Council of Troubles, which would weigh the charges against the accused and pronounce punishment, all under the direction of Alba himself. He also posted his troops throughout the country, strategically placing them to establish control in principal cities. On September 9 he began his campaign of repression by arresting Egmont and the count of Hornes at the mansion where Alba was staying, having invited them there as a seeming act of friendship. From then on, arrests were made almost daily throughout the country, the victims imprisoned and their property confiscated.

"The prisons are so full that I don't know where to put the detained," Alba wrote to Philip, "and I am now busy making more space for them." On a single day in March 1568, five hundred persons were arrested. "We are rounding up the sackers of churches, the ministers of the heretical groups, and those who took up arms against your majesty," Alba reported to Philip in April. His reign of repression was to last six years, and before it was over, some twelve thousand individuals were hailed before the Council of Troubles. More than one thousand of them were executed, and some nine thousand had their property confiscated. Among those executed were Egmont and Hornes, both of them beheaded in a public spectacle in the market square of Brussels on June 5, 1568. The people of the Netherlands, Alba told Philip, must be kept in a constant state of fear, "so that every individual has the feeling that one fine night or morning the house will fall in on him." And at one point, Philip wrote back to Alba to tell him, "I am thoroughly pleased and satisfied with everything you are doing."[3]

Alba's repression campaign drew heavy criticism from European capitals, particularly in reaction to the execution of the well-known and respected Egmont and Hornes. In Germany the reaction was so strong that Emperor Maximilian sent his brother, Archduke Charles, to Madrid to try to persuade Philip to moderate his policies. Philip defended his actions on the grounds that there could be no compromise on the issue of religion. "If there is division and disagreement over religion," he wrote in a reply to Charles's memorandum, "neither government nor state nor the authority of princes nor peace and concord and tranquility among subjects can be maintained." Philip remained undeterred and unapologetic.

Netherlanders' attempts to stop Alba by force all proved futile, yet the Netherlanders persisted. Prince William of Orange and his brother, Louis of Nassau, organized invasions from France and Germany in the summer of 1568, but the force from France was easily defeated by Alba, and the huge army led from Germany by William disintegrated after months of Alba's refusal to engage it. William's attempts to organize new campaigns in 1569 and 1570 also failed. Netherlands cities that showed support for William were mercilessly punished by Alba. In October 1572 he let his soldiers pillage the town of Mechelen and massacre its inhabitants. In the following weeks he inflicted similar punishment on the towns of Zutphen and Naarden. Alba reported to Philip the action taken at Zutphen, where his son Fadrique was commander of the Spanish troops: "They cut the throats of everyone they found and many burghers, because Don Fadrique had orders from me not to leave a soul alive and also to burn down part of the town."

The city of Haarlem put up a strong and prolonged resistance to Alba's attack, holding out against his army from December 1572 until July 1573 but finally surrendering after receiving assurances of fair treatment. When Alba's troops entered the city, however, they executed the entire two-thousand-man garrison of defenders by slashing their throats. News of the atrocity shocked many of Philip's advisers, who began to urge peace and pardon. Reports came to Philip from Spaniards in the Netherlands, telling him of the intense hatred felt toward Alba and the detestation for his terrorizing methods, which after more than five years had nevertheless failed to subdue the rebellious spirit of the Netherlanders. There is no way to deal with the situation, one adviser wrote to Philip, other than clemency and pardon. Granvelle, whom Philip had named viceroy of Naples after removing him from power in the Netherlands, told Philip that Haarlem was no triumph, that Spain was still losing the country. Philip's old friend Luis de Requesens, his viceroy in Milan, was strongly critical of Alba's treatment of Haarlem and with his methods in general. Clemency, Requesens insisted, was what was needed.

Eventually Philip got the message. In September 1571 he appointed Juan de la Cerda, duke of Medinaceli, to replace Alba as governor of the Netherlands and as military commander. Medinaceli arrived in Brussels on June 13, 1572, while the revolt raged more fiercely than ever. Alba, although sick, refused to relinquish command, believing Medinaceli incompetent for the job. In frustration Philip recalled Medinaceli and on January 30, 1573, appointed Requesens as the Netherlands governor and commander. Reluctant to accept the post, Requesens dragged his feet in departing, and by August Alba had become so dispirited, suffering with gout, short of money to pay his troops, who had already mutinied over lack of pay, and having suffered two recent embarrassing defeats (at the town of Alkmaar and in the Zuider Zee), that he wrote exasperatedly to Philip, "For the love of God, remove me from this post and get me out of here."[4] Requesens finally arrived in Brussels on November 17, 1573. Alba left Brussels on December 18. He arrived in Madrid on March 28, 1574, gone from the Netherlands at last and for good.

Requesens soon discovered there was not much he could accomplish without money, which had become extremely scarce in Spain. Philip's wars in the Netherlands and in the Mediterranean against the Turks had bankrupted the government. It was costing nearly seven hundred thousand ducats a month—more than eight million ducats a year against the government's annual income of five and a half million ducats—to maintain the Spanish army in the Netherlands. By the fall of 1575, Philip had run out of money and out of credit to borrow more. Following the advice of his financial advisers, in September 1575 he repudiated his debts and declared bankruptcy.

The effects on his army—some members of which were owed pay for as long as six years—were disastrous. With no hope of collecting their wages, the non-Spanish troops in Philip's Netherlands army, mostly mercenaries, mutinied and looted the city of Antwerp, burning hundreds of houses and killing some eight thousand people. Most of the rest of the army simply deserted. The States General, sidestepping Requesens, convened itself and after making arrangements with Prince William and his army in November 1575, approached Philip seeking concessions.

Desperate for a resolution, Philip was ready to concede, stating, "If matters are in such a state that the States demand unilateral concessions, it seems that, safeguarding religion and my authority as much as may be . . . we shall have to concede everything necessary to bring about a conclusion and save what we can. This is the ultimate solution to a problem like this, and we shall have to trust these people, in spite of all the risks involved."

To represent him in making the concessions and restoring his authority as best as could be, Philip in October 1576 sent to the Netherlands his half brother, John of Austria, the celebrated hero of Lepanto. The Netherlanders, however, refused to acknowledge John's authority until he agreed to send the remaining Spanish troops out of the country, which he did. On February 12, 1577, following Philip's instructions, John issued the so-called Perpetual Edict, granting all of the Netherlanders' demands, including the exclusion of Spanish troops from Netherlands soil. The troops marched away in April, bound for Italy, and on May 6, in a ceremony in Brussels, John took the oath as governor-general of the Netherlands.

Feeling weak without the support of the dependable troops of the Spanish army, John decided to strengthen his position by capturing the fortress at Namur, which he seized on July 24, 1577, using the government troops left available to him. A week later, when he tried to capture the city of Antwerp, the Netherlanders, after the surprise attack at Namur, were ready for him and turned him and his force away. John then asked Philip for the return of the Spanish army—and for the return of Alba's harsh policies.

John had another purpose in mind for the Spanish army. He had come up with a plan to invade England, remove Elizabeth, and place Mary Queen of Scots on the English throne. Then he planned to marry Mary, who would be grateful to him for her rescue, and he would become king of England. He had presented the plan to Philip before leaving for the Netherlands, arguing that it would bring peace and stability to Northern Europe and restore Catholicism in England, all of which coincided with Philip's wishes. Philip, however, showed no enthusiasm for the idea.

John's scheme was known to Elizabeth. Spies employed by Francis Walsingham, whom she had named secretary of state in December 1573, had learned of it and reported it in early 1577. The duke of Guise, Mary's uncle, was reported to be involved in the plan. There was nothing for her to do about it, though, for the whole grandiose scheme came to an end when John took sick and died, apparently of typhus, at age thirty-one on October 1, 1578.

Meanwhile, Philip, changing his mind again and with a new supply of money, sent his troops back to the Netherlands under the command of his nephew Alexander Farnese, Margaret of Parma's son, to see what he could do to restore Philip's authority. And so the Netherlands' fight for freedom, Philip's interminable torment, resumed. He would never see it end.

✥ 14. THE HOSTILITIES

Born in the English port city of Plymouth, son of a prosperous sea captain, John Hawkins took to the sea himself in search of his fortune, and in 1562, at age thirty, he found it. He kidnapped three hundred Africans in Sierra Leone, on the west coast of Africa, and carried them in his ships to the Spanish colony at Santo Domingo in the West Indies, where he traded them for pearls, ginger, sugar, and hides. Spain had forbidden its colonists to trade with anyone except the Spanish, but the Santo Domingan colonists were so eager for slave help they ignored the ban.

The transaction turned such a huge profit for Hawkins that two years later he repeated the performance, with similar results. On his third voyage, in 1567–68, however, he ran into trouble. His flotilla of seven ships, which included his twenty-gun flagship, a vessel lent him by Queen Elizabeth, carried some four hundred captured Africans he intended to sell as slaves in the Spanish Caribbean colonies, but he discovered that things had changed since his previous voyage. The Spanish colonial authorities refused to let him do business. Hawkins refused to let them deter him. With his ship's guns to back him up, he forced the unloading of his human cargo into the Spanish settlements. At one point, he made good on his threats and fired on King Philip's fortresses that guarded the harbor of Cartagena, in Colombia.

Leaving the Caribbean, Hawkins's flotilla was battered by two severe storms off the coast of Cuba, and Hawkins decided to put in at the port of San Juan de Ulúa, on the Mexican coast near present-day Veracruz, to repair his storm-damaged vessels before attempting an Atlantic crossing to return home. He was doubtless surprised when the Spanish officials, far from trying to turn him away, actually welcomed him as his ships sailed into the harbor on September 15, 1568. His welcome turned out to be a case of mistaken identity, the colony's officials having incorrectly assumed that his ships were part of a Spanish fleet bringing the recently appointed viceroy, Martín Enríquez de Almansa, to his post in New Spain (Mexico). The next day, with terrible timing for Hawkins, Almansa arrived. Attempting to make the best of a bad situation, Hawkins barred the Spanish ships from entering the harbor until the new viceroy promised that they would not attack Hawkins's vessels. Almansa promised, but after entering the harbor, the Spanish on September 23 attacked Hawkins's flotilla with two fireships, scattering the English vessels, and then attempted to board the English ships. With his flagship's twenty guns, Hawkins managed to fight his way out of the harbor, sinking two Spanish vessels and destroying another in the process, but his ship and one other of his flotilla were the only English vessels to escape the Spanish. The one other was captained by Hawkins's twenty-eight-year-old cousin, Francis Drake, who had sailed away from the fray and on toward home, leaving Hawkins to manage as best he could without him. Hawkins's vessel was so crowded with survivors of the fight that he could not feed them all from his ship's provisions, and to avoid starvation for all aboard, on their request he put a hundred of his crewmen off on the Mexican coast, hoping they could survive. Instead, they became victims of the Inquisition.

Hawkins arrived back in England on January 25, 1569, to report the disaster. He had lost all but two of his ships and three-fourths of his men. Of the crew who stayed with him aboard his flagship, all but fifteen had died of disease or starvation by the time he reached England. Drake also made it back home, somewhat tarnished by his desertion of his commander. As Hawkins put it, Drake "forsooke us in our great myserie." The experience at San Juan de Ulúa, however, was a turning point in Drake's life, for he never again would flee from a fight and he never would forget the viceroy's treachery in breaking his word and reneging on his assurance to Hawkins. For Drake as well as for Hawkins, the viceroy's treachery became Spain's treachery, and both men thereafter became implacable enemies of the Spanish, persistent adversaries who harassed King Philip's fleet around the globe, all with their queen's connivance.

In November 1568 Elizabeth, not at all frightened by Philip's growing might, answered the treachery perpetrated against her captains. Five Spanish ships entered the channel carrying a large sum in silver to the duke of Alba so that he could pay his troops, who were fighting the Netherlands rebels. They sailed eastward, then put in on the English coast near Southampton to seek shelter. (Sources disagree on the reason the Spanish stopped at Southampton. It might have been an imminent storm, the threat of pirates, or another, unspecified form of distress.) Elizabeth impounded the ships and confiscated the silver, and when Philip, through his envoy, Guerau de Spes, protested, Elizabeth replied that it was not King Philip's silver but rather belonged to the Genoa bankers who had lent it to Philip. She said she was assuming his loan and would repay the lenders. Philip was infuriated. To retaliate, he ordered his Netherlands troops to seize all English ships and other property within their reach, and Alba, commanding in the Netherlands, imposed an embargo on all trade with the English.

Up until 1568 Philip had been determined to avoid conflict with Elizabeth. He had resisted any notions to depose her, figuring that a Protestant queen of England friendly to Spain was far better for him than a Catholic queen of England—that is, Mary Queen of Scots—friendly to France. He was sympathetic to English Catholics, but he was unwilling to try to give them a Catholic queen. He instructed his ambassador in June 1565 to "miss no opportunity which offers of encouraging and strengthening the said Catholics by all such means and measures as will not scandalize the queen or her friends." And he continued to forestall Elizabeth's excommunication by exerting political pressure on the pope. The events in 1568, however, made him change his policy. He had already asked Alba to advise him on what action, if any, he might take regarding Mary Queen of Scots, who had appealed to him for help. In February 1569 he asked Alba to look into the possibility of deposing Elizabeth and told him that if the opportunity was then ripe, he was authorized to act on his own. "You may at once," he told him, "take the steps you consider advisable. . . . I am sure I can safely leave the matter in your hands." Alba, though, was focused on the problems in the Netherlands and gave Philip no encouragement for a campaign against Elizabeth. In frustration, unusual for him, Philip wrote Alba again in late 1569, telling him that "we are beginning to lose reputation by deferring so long to provide a remedy for the great grievance done by this woman [Elizabeth] to my subjects, friends and allies." Alba was not moved by that argument either. To make Philip's frustration greater, several Catholic nobles in the north of England had staged an uprising in support of Mary, and Spain had stood by, doing nothing to help the Catholics while Elizabeth's loyal forces crushed the rebellion.

Impatient to do *something* about Elizabeth, Philip conspired to have Mary marry Thomas Howard, duke of Norfolk and Elizabeth's cousin, a marriage that could set off an uprising that would overthrow Elizabeth. Norfolk was more than willing to cooperate. In 1572 Roberto Ridolfi, a Florence financier and agent of Pius V—the pope having joined the plot with Philip—sought to create a new Catholic uprising that summer. According to the plan, the rebellion was to be supported by ten thousand of Alba's troops, an idea to which Alba remained cool. All the while, Francis Walsingham, then William Cecil's assistant and head of a network of English spies, was aware of Ridolfi's plot and was monitoring its development.

In a piece of counterintrigue, Walsingham used John Hawkins to lure Philip into a scheme to subvert the planned invasion. In April 1572 Hawkins sent a representative to Philip with an offer to defect to him with a squadron of ships on the condition that Philip would free the English crewmen who had been taken prisoner at San Juan de Ulúa. Philip apparently considered the offer, thinking Hawkins would be useful in safely shepherding a Spanish fleet bearing an invasion force through the English Channel. Hawkins passed along to Walsingham what he learned in the negotiations, but his offer never got beyond the talking stage.

Although Alba had let Philip's ambassador, de Spes, know that there was to be no invasion of England by his troops, de Spes, with or without Philip's approval, continued to conspire with Catholic nobles in the north of England to raise an army, free Mary, make her the English queen, and marry her to Norfolk. Elizabeth, acting to defeat the scheme, had Norfolk arrested on October 3, 1572, and imprisoned him in the Tower. Nevertheless, in November the northern lords, with a promise of Spanish help, organized a force of more than twenty-five hundred men and began a march on Tutbury, where Mary was being held captive. To thwart them, Elizabeth on November 25 had Mary moved from Tutbury in the north to Coventry, farther south. She also sent twenty-eight thousand troops to confront the rebel force. With their hopes of freeing Mary dashed by her removal and facing overwhelming numbers, the rebels gave up their cause and fled, their army disintegrating in their rush to escape royal vengeance.

Absorbed with the deteriorating situation in the Netherlands, Philip postponed further moves against Elizabeth until conditions in the Netherlands were stabilized. He remained certain, though, that God intended him to get rid of Elizabeth. In September 1571 he had written to Alba, urging Alba's cooperation in the then current plan to invade England, telling him, "I am so keen to achieve the consummation of this enterprise. I am so attached to it in my heart and I am so convinced that God our Savior must embrace it as his own cause, that I cannot be dissuaded from putting it into operation." Alba, evidently less pious, was not convinced and steadfastly refused to launch the enterprise for Philip. And Philip, while waiting for the Netherlands revolt to be satisfactorily resolved, attempted to avoid having Elizabeth do something that would force his hand against her. He told his London ambassador, Bernardino de Mendoza, in June 1577 that he should "continue to deal gently and amiably with the queen and her ministers, this being the desirable course at present."

Elizabeth was neither mollified nor deterred. Francis Drake in May 1572 had begun a voyage to the New World to seek revenge on the Spanish and had returned to England in August 1573 with his goal accomplished and his ships laden with captured Spanish gold and other treasure seized from Spanish ships. Elizabeth was delighted. In 1577 she commissioned him to execute another foray into Spanish territory. On December 13, 1577, Drake sailed out of Plymouth harbor with five ships and about 180 men, ostensibly headed toward the Nile River on a trading expedition but actually on a voyage that would take him through the Strait of Magellan at the southern tip of South America and into the Pacific Ocean. Before he left, Elizabeth met with him, wished him well, and gave him some idea of what she expected of him. "So it is," she told him, "that I would be revenged on the king of Spain for divers injuries that I have received." She also backed his venture with an investment of more than six hundred pounds, with hopes of receiving a handsome return on her money.

Drake sailed to Mogador, on the Atlantic coast of Morocco, then turned for the Cape Verde Islands, where he captured six Spanish vessels, and crossed the Atlantic, making landfall in southern Brazil on April 5, 1578, then, after a month's delay to rid himself of a mutinous element among his crew, sailed down the east coast of South America. The voyage had inflicted such a beating on two of his vessels that Drake abandoned them on his way south. At the entrance to the Strait of Magellan, Drake renamed his flagship, the *Pelican,* and it became the *Golden Hind,* in honor of one of the expedition's chief financial backers, Christopher Hatton (a hind, or doe, was a prominent element in Hatton's coat of arms). Drake entered the Pacific Ocean on September 6, taking the English flag into the Pacific for the first time. Shortly thereafter, the expedition ran into fierce storms that destroyed one ship, which was lost along with twenty-nine crewmen, and that forced another to turn about and head for home. His little flotilla thus reduced, Drake proceeded north, up the Pacific coast of South America.

For the next five months he attacked the Spanish coastal settlements virtually unopposed. He raided Valparaiso and Arica, the shipping point for ore from Philip's rich silver mines at Potosí, in Peru. At Callao, on the coast, west of Lima, Drake discovered that a heavily laden Spanish treasure ship, the *Nuestra Señora de la Concepción,* had left port three days earlier, and he quickly set sail in hot pursuit. He overtook it and captured it off the coast of Colombia on March 1, 1579, seizing a cargo of gold and silver equal to about half of Elizabeth's revenue for a year.

Drake then sailed farther north and on June 17 landed at a place inhabited by friendly natives and which he named Nova Albion ("New England" in Latin). Unknown today, it was above the northernmost point claimed by Spain and is believed by many to be in Marin County, California. Drake claimed the area for England but kept his landing spot's exact location secret, lest the Spanish learn of it and murder the men he left there to colonize it, as the Spanish had done at the French settlement near St. Augustine, Florida.

From the coast of California, Drake set off to find the Northwest Passage, the supposed sea route across the North American continent, from the Atlantic to the Pacific, which turned out to be nonexistent. Giving up, he then turned south and on July 25, 1579, headed west from the coast of California. By October 16 the *Golden Hind* was in the Philippines. From there Drake sailed to the Moluccas, to Indonesia and Java, and then on March 26, 1580, began his return voyage. He sailed nearly ten thousand miles nonstop and reached the west coast of Africa on July 22. From there he set a northward course for England, arriving in Plymouth on September 26, 1580, after a voyage of nearly three years, during which he had sailed completely around the world, a feat achieved only once before, by the famed Portuguese navigator Ferdinand Magellan some sixty years earlier. Drake had also challenged the imperial power of Spain, had helped himself to much of its riches, which he brought home to share with his queen and his other backers, and, most important, had staked out an English claim to most of North America, the territory he claimed extending from sea to sea.

Elizabeth was cautious about making a big to-do over Drake's return, knowing that his exploits had outraged Philip and his councilors. She furthermore ordered all written accounts of his voyage to be classified as top secret and forbade all who had sailed with Drake to give details of the voyage. She wanted Philip to learn nothing more of Drake's business.

Philip's ambassador, Bernardino de Mendoza, delivered Spain's protests, demanding the return of the captured treasures and insisting that Drake be punished. Elizabeth, who later told Drake that Philip wanted him put to death, ignored all the protests. She locked up her share of Drake's loot in the Tower and, after waiting for Spanish tempers to cool and for the consummation of an alliance with France, on April 4, 1581, she made a trip to Deptford, where the *Golden Hind* was then docked, to be entertained by Drake with a banquet aboard the ship and to knight him for his accomplishments. Drake presented her with a map of his voyage and a diary that described everything that had happened to him while on it. Members of Drake's crew put on Indian garb they had brought back and performed Indian dances for the queen. Drake then took her on a tour of the ship and regaled her for four hours with stories of his adventures. Elizabeth seemed fascinated.

Philip meanwhile took steps to make certain Drake's raids on the west coast of South America would not be repeated. In 1580 he ordered two galleons and four small vessels to patrol the Pacific coast and ward off future attacks. That same year, he also went on the offensive to secure for himself the throne—and the possessions—of Portugal. Portugal's king, Henry I, who was also a cardinal and therefore without legitimate heirs, died on January 31, 1580, and Philip, pressing his hereditary claim (his mother was a Portuguese princess) with military force, moved promptly to succeed him. He called the seventy-two-year-old duke of Alba out of retirement to lead an army of some twenty-three thousand men into Portugal and ordered the marquis of Santa Cruz, Álvaro de Bazán, to command a naval force of nearly one hundred vessels and nine thousand men that would support Alba's invasion. On June 30, Alba's army crossed into Portugal and, overcoming all resistance, which was meager, marched to Lisbon, where it overwhelmed a Portuguese army commanded by Antonio of Crato, whom the Portuguese had appointed king to succeed Henry, and by the end of August Alba had captured the Portuguese capital. On September 12, 1580, in Lisbon, Philip was proclaimed king of Portugal.

Portugal's overseas territories accepted Philip without a quarrel, except for the Azores, an archipelago of nine islands on the Atlantic trade route, to which Antonio had fled and where, with the aid of a French force, he was holding out against Spanish rule. Philip ordered Santa Cruz to put down the resistance after an earlier attempt by General Pedro de Valdés had failed. Santa Cruz took a fleet of more than eighty ships to the Azores and on July 26, 1582, off São Miguel, one of the Azores islands, he smashed the fleet bearing the French forces and wiped out the enemy, killing more than twelve hundred in the battle and hanging many of the survivors as pirates.

With the capture of Portugal and its resources, plus new silver shipments from South America to bolster his treasury, Philip experienced a surge of self-assurance, as if he could do nothing wrong. He adopted a new attitude of belligerence toward Elizabeth. He had already permitted Spanish troops to join an eight-hundred-man expeditionary force sent to Ireland by the pope to assist Irish patriots in their revolt against English occupation, and he had ordered a Spanish admiral to command the ships that transported the troops to Ireland, in what became a failed cause. Those moves stopped just short of being acts of war. In March 1581 he became bolder. He haughtily wrote to Mendoza in London and told him to "represent to the queen and her ministers the danger they incur by irritating me and causing me to look to my own affairs by troubling theirs. Whereas if they do not provoke me further, they need have nothing to fear from my forces. . . . You will intimate to them all I say here, so that fear of my forces may somewhat bridle them from further offending me, while at the same time they may not get desperate and lose hope of being forgiven for their past misdeeds and thus be driven into new and pernicious leagues to the prejudice of Christianity and the public peace, and perhaps plotting new evil in Flanders."[1]

In the fall of 1581, Philip threatened Elizabeth with war after she had imprisoned and then hanged a Jesuit missionary priest, Edmond Campion, sent to England to foment rebellion among English Catholics. In delivering the threat, Ambassador Mendoza told Elizabeth that if she failed to heed Philip's words of warning, "It would be necessary to see whether cannons would not make her hear them better."

With no show of emotion, Elizabeth coolly told Mendoza that if his words were intended to frighten or threaten her, she would clap him "into a place where he could not say a word."

By then, following Philip's seizure of Portugal, Elizabeth could see that arresting Spanish expansion was a task that was falling to her, since no other force seemed able to stop Philip. She would have to assume the task for her own protection and for England's. She resolved to do what she could. "We think it good for the king of Spain," she declared, "to be impeached both in Portugal and his islands [the Azores] and also in the Low Countries, whereto we shall be ready to give such indirect assistance as shall not at once be a cause of war." In a showy move to check Philip's threats against her, she told Mendoza in public on November 22, 1581, that he could inform his king that she was going to marry the duke of Anjou, heir to the French throne, who had been courting her for years and was then standing beside her. She immodestly planted a kiss on Anjou's mouth and gave him a ring off her finger.

Such a marriage, wedding England to France, was one of Philip's worst nightmares, and following Elizabeth's announcement, he quickly began making soothing noises to her, offering to forgive her past affronts and to reestablish the old alliance between their countries. The marriage, of course, never came off. Never intending it to, Elizabeth put such conditions on it that the French king, Henry III, Anjou's brother, rejected the whole idea.

The check on Philip didn't last long. In December 1583 Elizabeth learned that Mendoza was involving Spain in a far-reaching, elaborate plot that called for coordinated military invasions of England, a Catholic uprising within England, the assassination of Elizabeth, and the installation of Mary Queen of Scots on the English throne, an operation that came to be called "the Enterprise of England," Philip's term for his mission to eliminate Elizabeth. After a session on the rack, the chief English conspirator, Francis Throckmorton, a Catholic nephew of Nicholas Throckmorton, implicated Mary's Guise relatives, the Jesuits, and the pope. Soon thereafter, in January 1584, Mendoza was ordered by Elizabeth's Privy Council to pack up and get himself out of England within two weeks. In huffy reaction, Mendoza fired back that his king would retaliate with war. After Mendoza's expulsion, Spain would send no more ambassadors to England for as long as Elizabeth lived.

On June 10, 1584, the duke of Anjou, who had provided the French marriage card that Elizabeth had played whenever Philip threatened her, died of tuberculosis in France. On July 10, Prince William of Orange, chief leader of the continuing Netherlands revolt, was assassinated at Delft, apparently at Philip's behest. Elizabeth could now foresee the defeat of the Netherlands revolt by Philip's nephew, Alexander Farnese, the duke of Parma, who was proving himself a formidable foe on the battlefield, and once the Netherlands had been subdued, she feared, Philip would turn his full attention—and Parma's menacing army—on England.

Meanwhile, attempts on Elizabeth's life increased. In the fall of 1584, there were so many reports of plots to kill Elizabeth and crown Mary—including a written, detailed plan for Philip's Enterprise of England found on a Jesuit priest in the Netherlands—that Leicester and a number of other Privy Council members organized a group of Protestant gentlemen who swore an oath to kill Mary if she participated in any plot, knowingly or otherwise, to assassinate Elizabeth. The oath, called the Bond of Association, drew the endorsement of thousands throughout England. To warn her of the fate she would suffer if she became involved in such plots, the oath document was shown to Mary. She steadfastly maintained that she knew nothing of any such plots and, as if to prove her innocence, she signed the oath herself. Within two days, however, she wrote to Philip to spur him on in the execution of the Enterprise.

One attempt to assassinate Elizabeth in late 1584 failed when the would-be killer, a Welsh member of Parliament, William Parry, hiding in the garden of the palace at Richmond, got cold feet when he saw her approach. According to one account, he "was so daunted with the majesty of her presence, in which he saw the image of her father, King Henry VIII, that his heart would not suffer his hand to execute that which he had resolved."[2] Parry had served as an English spy and had earlier claimed that he had pretended to seek to assassinate Elizabeth in order to gain the confidence of the papacy. At his trial he denied that he had intended any harm to the queen. He was convicted of the attempt and in February 1585 was hanged.

Elizabeth seemed unafraid of the plots swirling about her. She rejected the additional security measures that were proposed and refused to alter her routines or adopt any new measures that restricted her movement. "They are seeking to take my life, but it troubles me not," she told a group of subjects who had come to see her. "He who is on high has defended me until this hour and will keep me still, for in Him I do trust."

In May 1585, Philip, anxious to retaliate for the loss of Spanish ships to Drake, ordered the seizure of all English ships in Spanish and Portuguese ports. Among the vessels seized were English ships that had come loaded with grain to feed Philip's subjects, who were then suffering a food shortage. Those vessels had come with the Spanish government's assurance of safe conduct, and the English merchants who experienced their loss protested Philip's treachery, urging the English government to take measures against him.

Elizabeth took action. On July 1, 1585, she commissioned Drake to sail to the port of Vigo, in northwest Spain, ostensibly to negotiate the return of the seized English vessels. Drake, however, understood his actual mission, which was to take the offensive against Philip, to inflict as much damage as he could to Philip's possessions and forcefully demonstrate to him the hazards of engaging English naval power. Elizabeth gave Drake a fleet of more than twenty ships and some two thousand men and made him an admiral in the English navy. On September 14, 1585, he set sail from Plymouth. Arriving at Vigo, he sacked the city. He also attacked the Spanish port of La Coruña and the outlying area of Lisbon. He destroyed twenty or more ships off the coast of Portugal, then turned and sailed into the open Atlantic, headed for the New World, hoping to capture some of Philip's treasure ships as well as intending to smash Spain's naval bases in the Caribbean. He attacked Santo Domingo and accepted payment of twenty-five thousand ducats to refrain from sacking the city, where he also destroyed a number of ships. In Cartagena he took the one hundred and ten thousand ducats the town paid him not to destroy it. He then turned north toward Cuba, attacked Havana, then sailed on to Florida, where he attacked and burned the Spanish settlement at St. Augustine. He sailed on to the new English settlement on Roanoke Island, off the coast of North Carolina, then turned toward home and arrived back in England in July 1586.

Alarmed by the fall of Antwerp to the duke of Parma's army in August 1585, just before Drake had begun his voyage, Elizabeth had agreed to send to the Netherlands a force of more than six thousand infantry and one thousand cavalry to aid the embattled rebels. On October 1, 1585, she issued a twenty-page document to explain England's intervention in the Netherlands, stating it was justified because of Philip's complicity in the pope's invasion of Ireland, an English territory, and because of his repeated conspiracies to assassinate her. To command the English force Elizabeth appointed her favorite, Robert Dudley, earl of Leicester. He and his army set out across the channel on December 19, 1585.

Philip, battling an illness, received the news of England's intervention in the Netherlands while still smoldering over the depredations of Drake's voyage. It was time, he decided, to take direct action against Elizabeth. On December

29, 1585, he wrote to the duke of Parma, who would be expected to lead the invasion force that Philip would send to England, asking him what he would need to execute the invasion. On January 2, 1586, Philip instructed his ambassador in Rome to seek a grant from the pope to help pay for an invasion fleet and spelled out for the pope the reason he planned to launch it. "The justification and purpose of the Enterprise," he explained, "has to be to reduce that kingdom [England] to the obedience of the Roman Church and to place the queen of Scotland in possession of [England's crown]." Philip furthermore told his ambassador, Count Enrique de Guzmán, count of Olivares, that the pope must agree that Mary's successor would be not Philip, to whom Mary had bequeathed her right to the English throne, but rather Philip's daughter Isabella.

The pope then was Sixtus V, who had been Felice Peretti until his election as pope in May 1585, following the death of Gregory XIII, who had succeeded Pius V. Philip apparently had let it be known in Rome that if the church wanted him to regain England for Catholic Christendom, the papacy would have to defray a large part of the cost. Sixtus was willing to do so, albeit reluctantly at first, believing that Philip's motivation was more political than religious. But Philip's designation of his daughter as Mary's successor and the tantalizing prospect of restoring England to the Catholic fold overcame Sixtus's hesitancy and his suspicions about Philip.

Philip's next step was to get the advice of his leading admiral, Álvaro de Bazán, marquis of Santa Cruz, who had received a major share of the credit for the monumental Spanish victory at Lepanto fourteen years earlier. Santa Cruz wrote to Philip on January 13, 1586, and told him, among other things, that he thought the time was ripe for an invasion of England. Philip ordered him to organize a fleet that would be based at Lisbon and would patrol the Atlantic coast of Spain and Portugal, would protect Philip's treasure fleets arriving from the Americas, and would, it was understood, form the core of an invasion fleet to be used in the Enterprise of England. Santa Cruz was told to have his Lisbon fleet in operation no later than early May of 1586. Santa Cruz then submitted to Philip a plan he had drawn up for the Enterprise, and in March, Philip summoned Santa Cruz to talk about it. In April, Philip ordered all the bishops in Castile, Spain's major province, to offer prayers for what he called "the affairs of Christendom." In June, Parma submitted *his* plan for the Enterprise. Philip became caught up in studying and considering plans.

In England, meanwhile, new intrigue was taking place. On Christmas Eve 1585, Elizabeth had had Mary Queen of Scots moved to Chartley, a fortified castle surrounded by a moat, where it would be more difficult for her to smuggle out messages and have messages smuggled in to her. Mary's laundresses, suspected of being used as the smugglers, carrying messages in places on themselves where gentlemen would not look, would be housed within the castle, cutting them off from outside contacts. Walsingham, however, knowing that Mary would still seek some way to reach persons on the outside, devised a way to entrap her and acquire the legal justification needed to execute her. Sometime in December 1585 English authorities had arrested a priest named Gilbert Gifford shortly after he had landed in England, having come from France as a courier working for Mary's agent in Paris, Thomas Morgan. Gifford was taken to Walsingham, who turned him into a double agent. Gifford was instructed to go to the French embassy in London, where letters for Mary had piled up for lack of a means of getting them to her, and tell the French representatives that he had a secret access to Mary and could deliver letters to her. Gifford then was to get Mary's letters and deliver them to Walsingham's office, where they would be decoded and read, resealed, and then sent on to Mary. Mary's outgoing letters would also be diverted into Walsingham's office and similarly read, then passed on, all without the knowledge of senders or receivers. The supposedly clandestine system that Walsingham had arranged for conveying the messages involved putting them into a moisture-proof wooden box that was then placed inside a beer barrel by the brewer who delivered beer every week to Chartley, whom Gifford recruited, for pay, into the scheme. Once inside the castle, the barrel was opened by specified servants and the box retrieved and turned over to Mary's secretary. For outgoing messages the process was reversed. The French embassy tested Gifford by dispatching one of the accumulated letters to Mary via the system, and when she had received and answered it, messages began to flow regularly to and from her, and Walsingham read them and patiently waited for her to incriminate herself.

In May 1586 two particularly interesting letters from Mary came to Walsingham. One was addressed to Bernardino de Mendoza, Philip's ambassador in Paris since his expulsion from England. In it Mary assured him of her support for Philip's invasion. The other was to one of her supporters, Charles Paget, in which she asked him to tell Philip that he should regard the invasion as urgent. When it came, Paget's reply was also read by Walsingham. Paget informed Mary that a priest named John Ballard had recently come back to England from France to organize Catholics in a rebellion that would coincide with the Spanish invasion, which was planned for the summer of 1586, Walsingham's agents then placed Ballard under surveillance, and he led them to a wealthy twenty-five-year-old Catholic named Anthony Babington, an enthusiastic supporter of Mary who once had served as her page and had earlier been implicated in a plot to murder members of Elizabeth's Privy Council. Under surveillance, Ballard and Babington were heard to discuss the plans for Spain's invasion and for the assassination of Elizabeth. Meanwhile, Thomas Morgan, Mary's Paris agent, had learned about Babington and, as if to encourage her, he wrote to Mary about him. On June 25 Mary wrote to Babington, and on July 6 he wrote back and told her of his plot to kill Elizabeth. The assassination would be done by six of his friends while he rescued Mary. "For the despatch of the usurper [Elizabeth]," he wrote, "from the obedience of whom we are by excommunication of her made free, there be six noble gentlemen, all my private friends, who for the zeal they bear to the Catholic cause and your Majesty's service will undertake that tragical execution." He asked Mary for her comments.

They came in a lengthy letter written on July 17. Mary told Babington what must be done before the assassination, which included devising a sure-fire means of freeing her and also acquiring ironclad assurances of foreign assistance before English Catholic rebels were armed and the rebellion commenced. "The affairs being thus prepared and forces in readiness both within and without the realm," she told him, "then shall it be time to set the six gentlemen to work, taking order, upon the accomplishing of their design I may be suddenly transported out of this place."

Those letters were all Walsingham needed to spring the trap. Ballard was arrested and placed in the Tower on August 4. Babington, who had fled after learning of Ballard's arrest, was captured on August 14 and taken to the Tower. Babington's friends were rounded up and also jailed. A total of fourteen persons, including Mary's two secretaries, were arrested. In the Tower, dreading the torture he feared he was facing, Babington confessed to everything. He and his fellow conspirators were put on trial on September 13. On September 20, Ballard, Babington, and five other conspirators were hanged, cut down from the gallows while still alive, emasculated and disemboweled, then beheaded and quartered, suffering the unmitigated cruelties of a traitor's death while a huge throng of spectators looked on in horror. The next day, the seven other convicted conspirators were, by order of the queen, in response to the revulsion of the previous day's spectators, hanged until dead. Then they were disemboweled and quartered.

The question that remained was what to do about Mary, still in confinement at Chartley, her movements now tightly restricted, her personal staff and servants replaced. She was clearly in on the plot to murder Elizabeth and was part of the planned Enterprise of England. Despite the clear proof of her guilt, Elizabeth was loath to put her on trial, and unwilling to condemn her. She even refused to put her in the Tower, but at last consented to have her moved to Fotheringhay, a stout medieval castle in Northamptonshire where she could be more closely guarded from escape and would-be rescuers. She was taken there on September 25, 1586. Elizabeth's councilors, however, persisted in their demand that she be put on trial, and Elizabeth at last acquiesced. She appointed thirty-six commissioners to consider the evidence and pronounce judgment. Among them were Walsingham and Lord Burghley (William Cecil) and two Catholic lords, John Lumley and Anthony Browne, the viscount Montague. The trial began on October 14, despite Mary's protests that she was not subject to English justice, being an anointed queen. The principal charge against her was that she had participated in a treasonous conspiracy to take the queen's life.

She denied everything. She claimed that the incriminating letters had been forged. She denied ever receiving letters from Babington. She denied complicity in the plot to murder Elizabeth. "I would never make shipwreck of my soul," she asserted, "by compassing the death of my dearest sister."

The weighty evidence being contrary to Mary's protestations, the court of commissioners, with a single dissent (Baron Edward la Zouch), on October 25, 1586, found her guilty of "compassing, practising and imagining of Her Majesty's death." The offenses, under the relevant statute of 1585, were punishable by death and disinheritance. Parliament sentenced her to death, and after months of Elizabeth's fretful indecision and Parliament's firm insistence, Elizabeth at last and reluctantly on February 1, 1587, signed the warrant ordering Mary's execution.

At a little past eight on the morning of Wednesday, February 8, 1587, Mary Queen of Scots was beheaded in the great hall of Fotheringhay castle, her last words, spoken in Latin, being those of Christ's final utterance upon the cross, *"In manuas tuas, Domine, confide spiritum meum"*—Into thy hands, O Lord, I commend my spirit.

Gone was a major part of the Enterprise of England, but its removal actually made the Enterprise more appealing to Philip, for gone also was the worrisome possibility that the French-oriented Mary on England's throne would form the English-French alliance that Philip had for so long dreaded. Now more determined than ever, he eagerly pushed ahead with his plan for the invasion and conquest of England—and for the end of Elizabeth.

~⚙ 15. THE PREPARATION FOR CONQUEST

Elizabeth and her government since December 1585 had known about the preparations Philip was making for the invasion of England. By the summer of 1586, she had begun responding to the threat, and as the months passed, she made ever bolder moves to oppose the mounting danger. In late March 1587 Francis Drake, having already harassed Spanish bases in the Caribbean and along the Iberian coast, received new orders from his queen. He was "to impeach the purpose of the Spanish fleet and stop their meeting at Lisbon."[1] His tactics were to include, according to his instructions, "distressing their ships within their havens."

On April 12, 1587, commanding a fleet composed of six of the queen's own vessels and sixteen privately owned ships, Drake, aboard his flagship, the *Elizabeth Bonaventure,* sailed from Plymouth, bound for Spain. Elizabeth mysteriously at the last minute countermanded her orders to Drake, telling him to avoid attacking Spanish ports but to do his best to capture Spanish vessels at sea, but the countermanding message reached Plymouth, intentionally or otherwise, nine days after Drake had sailed, and he was not to be overtaken by the pinnace sent after him with the new orders, all of which has given rise to speculation that Elizabeth was merely playing diplomatic games with Philip, allowing her later to say she had called off Drake's mission and had canceled his flagrant acts of war.

Whatever the case, Drake sailed on with malice aforethought. A storm off Cape Finisterre, in northwest Spain, took one of his pinnaces and scattered his fleet, but pressing on, he continued southward and captured several Spanish and Portuguese vessels as he headed for the Rock of Lisbon, where the fleet would regroup before sailing for Cádiz, near the mouth of the Mediterranean Sea. Cádiz and its harbor were the target apparently because Drake had learned from Netherlands traders whose ships he had met en route that a sizable fleet was gathering there, prior to becoming part of the armada forming at Lisbon.

On the afternoon of April 29, his English colors furled, Drake led his fleet into the channel that gives access to the bay of Cádiz harbor, surprising the defenders of the crowded, bustling port. Quickly Pedro de Acuña, commanding a Spanish squadron in the bay, formed a line of galleys to block the approaching vessels from the harbor and sent out a lone galley, with a complement of seagoing soldiers aboard, to challenge the unknown intruders. As the challenging vessel came forward, still short of hailing distance, Drake, in the lead ship, the *Elizabeth Bonaventure,* opened fire. Its cannonades were soon followed by fire from the ships in *Elizabeth Bonaventure*'s wake. At the first sounds of gunfire, Drake ran up his colors, and the Spaniards learned whom they were facing.

Drake's galleons veered to turn their broadsides, bristling with cannon, toward Acuña's defensive formation and blasted away at the Spaniards, who maneuvered to escape the hailstorm of Drake's round shot and then turned again to return Drake's fire but received more devastating cannonades from Drake. The pounding by the superior firepower of the English vessels at last drove off Acuña's galleys, and with their dead and wounded atop their bloodied, broken decks, they sought shelter on the far side of the harbor bay, miles away from Drake's oncoming fleet, against which they had merely performed a delaying action.

The crowded waters of Cádiz harbor, sheltering an estimated sixty ships, then lay open to Drake, and as he advanced, vessels of many descriptions and several nationalities, including Spanish, Portuguese, and Dutch, both warships and merchantmen, scurried to escape the dreaded *El Draque*—the Dragon, in the Spanish pronunciation of Drake's name. Many of the smaller vessels, light enough to pass safely over the shoals, fled successfully to the harbor's upper bay. The bigger ships were not so fortunate. Taken by surprise, their crews ashore, their sails down, they became easy prey for the attackers. Only one of the harbored ships, large and stout, with forty brass cannon, resisted. Drake's galleons hammered it until it sank, its guns still firing as it began to slip beneath the surface. Drake then went about seizing those vessels he would take as prizes and burning the rest, their flames illuminating the darkening sky as their blazing hulks drifted out to sea.

One Spanish galley managed to recapture a Portuguese caravel being manned by an English crew following its seizure. Members of the prize crew who had survived the galley's guns were taken prisoner. They and their dead shipmates were the only casualties Drake suffered that day.

On the next day, Sunday, April 30, sailing from the Cádiz harbor to an anchorage off nearby Puental, Drake discovered a newly built galleon that had recently arrived from a shipyard on the Bay of Biscay, ready to be outfitted with its guns and destined to become the flagship of the marquis of Santa Cruz and to join the armada Philip planned to send against England. Drake set it ablaze, and it burned down to the waterline. Six galleys that had escaped the previous day's destruction regrouped and attacked the *Golden Lion*, captained by Drake's vice admiral, William Borough, which had become separated from the rest of the English fleet, but Drake quickly ordered several ships to its aid, and its brisk fire and the supporting vessels forced the galleys to back off and seek shelter.

The Spaniards made an effort to fend off the continuing assault with land-based artillery and with fireships launched in the direction of Drake's fleet. Neither accomplished much, and after being becalmed for twelve hours, the English fleet sailed from the bay at Cádiz, back up the entrance channel and into the open sea around midnight. At dawn on Monday, Acuña's galleys, having followed Drake out through the channel, sighted the English vessels and again opened fire on them. Drake responded by positioning his fleet for combat, but Acuña declined to engage and instead sent over to Drake's flagship a gift of wine and delicacies, along with his compliments. When a fresh breeze came up, Drake and his fleet sailed away. By Drake's reckoning, he had burned, captured, or sunk thirty-seven ships in Cádiz harbor. The damage report sent to Philip from Cádiz put the Spanish losses at twenty-four vessels. Philip, as if to downplay Drake's success, commented that "the loss was not very great, but the daring of the attempt was very great indeed."

Drake also commented. He wrote to Walsingham: "This service, which by God's sufferance we have done, will breed some alterations [in King Philip's plan for the invasion of England]. . . ." But, he wrote, "all possible preparations for defense are very expedient. . . . I dare not almost write of the great forces we hear the King of Spain hath. Prepare in England strongly and most by sea!"

From Cádiz, Drake on May 2 set out for Cape St. Vincent, at the southwest tip of Portugal, the southwestern-most point of Europe, two hundred miles west of Cádiz. He apparently had learned that Juan Martínez de Recalde, one of Philip's most renowned naval commanders, was at sea in the vicinity of Cape St. Vincent with a squadron about half the size of Drake's, and Drake intended to find and engage him. He never did. The only Spanish vessel he met, which he captured, had been dispatched to find Recalde and order him to avoid Drake and take refuge at Lisbon, which is what Recalde did. On May 9 Drake quit his search for Recalde and turned again for Cape St. Vincent. He planned to send an armed force ashore to capture the protective fort at the nearby anchorage at Sagres, he advised his captains, and then to establish a base from which to search for and attack Spanish and Portuguese ships.

On May 14, after a storm delayed him and evidently changed his plan, Drake sailed into the harbor of the port of Lagos, some fifteen miles farther east. He anchored in the bay west of the port and the next morning at dawn put ashore a contingent of more than eleven hundred men, harquebusiers and pikemen, drummers and fifers, in an elaborate show of force that amounted to nothing more than a reconnaissance patrol or a feint before taking his troops back aboard their vessels and making an assault on Sagres, which he did shortly thereafter. Drake sent a message to the Sagres fort's commander calling for his surrender, and when he politely declined, Drake burned the fort's wooden main gate to cinders, overran the garrison, and accepted the surrender of its commandant, twice wounded in the assault. Drake's forces then occupied the fort, which at one time had been the castle of Henry the Navigator, the fifteenth-century Portuguese prince who established a school for the study of navigation and geography, which made possible the founding of Portugal's colonial empire.

Drake stripped the fortified castle of its artillery and set fire to the structure, leaving it a smoking ruins. He then took his fleet to Lisbon. He found no opportunity for a surprise attack or for an engagement with ships based there and so returned to Sagres, where he refreshed his ships and his men. He then launched patrols that destroyed or captured every vessel they came across off the cape, the total exceeding one hundred ships, from fishing boats to merchantmen carrying a variety of freight. Many of them were carrying staves and hoops meant to make barrels to contain provisions for Philip's invading army. "The hoops and pipe staves were above 16 or 17 hundred ton in weight," Drake reported to Walsingham, "which cannot be less than 25 or 30 thousand ton if it had been made in cask, ready for liquor, all which I commanded to be consumed into smoke and ashes by fire, which will be unto the

King no small waste of his provisions besides the want of his barks." The destruction of those barrel components would have critical effects later.

On June 1 Drake took his fleet back to sea, sending several vessels back to England with his sick and wounded and sailing with the rest toward the Azores. On the way, he encountered the Portuguese carrack *São Phelipe,* a huge freighter, taller than any of Drake's vessels, heavily laden and homeward bound to Portugal from India. Its main deck was so loaded with cargo that its gun ports were unusable. Drake promptly engaged it, and after a brief fight, *São Phelipe*'s captain surrendered the ship to Drake. Its cargo turned out to be spices, silk fabrics, ivory, gold, silver, and chests of jewels—worth a fortune amounting to one hundred and fourteen thousand English pounds. The queen's share would be forty thousand pounds, Drake's seventeen thousand. The rest presumably would go to the London merchants who had financed the expedition and had contributed most of the ships. According to the estimates of one account, given for the sake of comparison, a galleon like Drake's flagship, the *Elizabeth Bonaventure,* could be built for about twenty-six hundred pounds, and Elizabeth could finance an army for forty thousand pounds. Drake had captured a truly grand prize and, not willing to risk losing it, he ended his forays off and on the Iberian coast and immediately set sail for England.

Behind him he left Philip's captains so fearful of attack that they refused to venture seaward for a month after Drake had sailed for home. Supplies needed by the armada forming at Lisbon were temporarily cut off, and preparations were so disrupted that the Enterprise of England, planned for the summer of 1587, had to be postponed till the next year.

Both the marquis of Santa Cruz and the duke of Parma previously had come up with plans for the invasion. Santa Cruz was confident he could make the operation work, telling Philip that he was willing "to serve Your Majesty myself in the enterprise in the firm hope that, being so much in Your Majesty's service, I will emerge just as victorious from it as in the other things that I have done for you." The marquis's sketched-out plan drew Philip's interest, and he asked Santa Cruz for more details. Santa Cruz responded with a written proposal that he titled "The Fleet and Army That It Would Seem Necessary to Assemble for the Conquest of England," which was more of a detailed list than a detailed plan for the conquest.

The proposal called for 550 ships to take 55,000 troops and their equipment, supplies, and munitions to England. The fleet would comprise 105 merchant ships, 25 Spanish galleons and the other Spanish vessels gathered at Lisbon and Cádiz, 20 Portuguese ships, including galleons, and 400 other support vessels of various descriptions. The mission of the warships of that fleet would be merely to protect the vessels bearing the troops and materiel as they made their way to their intended landing sites in England. To execute the landings, some two hundred landing craft would be built expressly for that task, and the landings would be similar to those successfully made in the Azores, only on a much larger scale. The galleys and galleasses of the fleet would move in close to shore to support the landings with artillery fire against shore defenses and to unload supplies onto the beachheads.

From the beachheads the invasion army, fully supplied, would speedily march on strategic locations and subdue them. The fifty-five thousand troops Santa Cruz called for would be supported by an array of artillery pieces of various sizes and a three-thousand-man corps of engineers that would clear away obstacles and build siege works and fortifications. The envisioned invasion force would also include a medical corps, a unit of military police, and a contingent of civil administrators to handle governmental affairs. The cost of the entire operation, Santa Cruz figured, would be about four million ducats. The proposal covered just about everything, with one glaring—for the sixteenth century—exception. Evidently less spiritually minded than his king, the marquis neglected to include chaplains in his expeditionary force. The fighting men would have to deal with the Almighty on their own.

Parma's plan was a bit more straightforward. He proposed taking from his army in the Netherlands a force of thirty thousand infantry and five hundred cavalry and sending it across the channel aboard a fleet of barges to make a surprise landing on the English shore. He told Philip he thought that if the English could be taken by surprise, the operation had a fair chance of success, "given the number of troops we have to hand here, and the ease with which we can concentrate and embark them in the barges, and considering that we can ascertain at any moment the forces which Elizabeth has and can be expected to have, and that the crossing only takes ten to twelve hours without a following wind and eight hours with one. . . . The most suitable, close and accessible point of disembarkation," he said in his lengthy letter to Philip, "is the coast between Dover and Margate." A site there would allow him to make a relatively short and fast march on London.

Parma put a three-point proviso on his proposal, though. The operation could be launched with hope of success provided that (1) Spain planned to go it alone, "without," Parma stated, "placing any reliance on either the English themselves or the assistance of other allies"; (2) the French were prevented from giving aid to England and from interfering in the Netherlands; and (3) enough troops remained in the Netherlands to defend what Parma's army had recaptured from the rebels. The only role Parma saw for Philip's navy was to assist the landing of the troops and to ward off English warships, either by creating a diversion to pull English ships away from the Strait of Dover, the army's crossing point, or by actually engaging the English vessels in the channel.

Philip had still another plan to consider. It came from a priest who had once been in the Spanish army, had served as an inquisitor, and had become chief of staff to the archbishop of Seville. His name was Bernardino de Escalante, and he often wrote letters to Philip, offering suggestions on a range of subjects, but particularly on how to deal with England. His suggestions apparently were good enough to gain the reading and consideration of the king and his advisers, even drawing invitations for him to come and discuss them with government officials. And so when Philip passed along Parma's written proposal to Juan de Zúñiga, Philip's close confidant and administrative handyman who had been given the job of filling Santa Cruz's list of invasion items, Zúñiga asked Escalante to study the two proposals—Parma's and Santa Cruz's—and give his opinion. Escalante responded with new plans. He offered that the fleet forming in Lisbon could sail up the north Atlantic and land the invasion army in Scotland, its coasts presumably less well defended than the coasts of England but also more hazardous. "The seas are high and dangerous," he wrote, "but through Jesus Christ crucified, everything is possible."[2] As an alternative to the landing in Scotland, he suggested the fleet sail into the Irish Sea and make a landing from there. However, the English navy would likely prove a substantial obstacle in that case. But, he stated, equally risky was Parma's plan to ferry the invasion force from the Netherlands across the channel to attack London, which, he pointed out, was formidably defended by the Tower of London. And so he offered another alternative.

His idea was to combine the Santa Cruz and Parma strategies into a plan that called for an armada of 120 ships that would transport an invasion force of thirty thousand infantry and two thousand cavalry from Lisbon to a landing site either at Waterford on Ireland's east coast or at Milford Haven in

Wales. While Elizabeth shifted her troops to defend against that attack, Parma, reinforced by additional Spanish troops to combat English troops in the Netherlands, would take a second invasion force across the channel and march on London.

Escalante's ideas were sent to Zúñiga, who reviewed them and then offered his own suggestions to Philip. They echoed Escalante's but included some that Zúñiga had added. Zúñiga advised that after the beachheads had been secured, additional troops and materiel should be brought in from Andalusia. When London was captured, he further advised, Parma should set up a temporary government to take charge until a new ruler—a friendly Catholic monarch, he stipulated—could be installed. Zúñiga did not expect that England would become a Spanish territory even if it were conquered. What he proposed was the elimination of Elizabeth and the imposition of someone who met Philip's approval.

Zúñiga was realistic enough to foresee that English opposition to Spanish rule or even continued Spanish influence might prove insurmountable, and in that event, he advised, Parma, following his conquest, should negotiate a settlement that included three key provisions: (1) the toleration of Catholics in England and the assurance of their freedom of worship; (2) the removal of all English troops from the Netherlands and the surrender to Spain of all the positions they currently held; and (3) the payment of an indemnity for the losses caused Spain. As part of the third provision, Zúñiga suggested, Parma's troops should occupy Kent until the indemnity was paid. Zúñiga furthermore suggested that the invasion should be launched in August or September of 1587.

Philip chose the plan of his administrative handyman, Zúñiga, and of the priest, Escalante. On July 26, 1586, he sent it to his general, Parma, in Brussels and to his admiral, Santa Cruz, in Lisbon, and ordered its execution. The mighty armada being assembled in Lisbon would, according to Philip's orders, sail in the summer of 1587, carrying the invasion force and its equipment to a landing site in Ireland, probably at Waterford. There a beachhead would be established as a feint to divert English naval forces from the channel and troops from the channel coast. Two months following their landing in Ireland, the Spanish troops would be re-embarked aboard the vessels of the armada and would sail into the channel. At the same time, Parma would embark a thirty-thousand-man invasion force from the Netherlands aboard small boats and ferry them across the channel under the protection of the armada. With the armada's support, Parma's troops, together with the troops aboard the armada's ships, would then storm ashore near Margate, near the mouth of the Thames, and swiftly march to London and seize it while Elizabeth was still there, capturing her and her ministers.

Parma didn't like the plan and was doubtful of the entire operation. It took him three months to say so, but in October 1586 he at last wrote to Philip to express his misgivings. He worried that the cost of executing the plan would stagger the Spanish economy. "I shall be bold to say, with the freedom your Majesty allows me," he wrote, "that if you find yourself without adequate resources to undertake such a great enterprise as this . . . , I incline to the view that it would be better to defer or drop it."

He especially disliked the plan's inclusion of an invasion of Ireland. "I am afraid," he said, "that the Irish dimension may do us some mischief." He thought an attack on Ireland, rather than reducing Elizabeth's troop strength in England, might cause her to increase her forces by quickly bringing in foreign mercenaries. Besides, he argued, the Irish expedition would subject the armada to the vagaries of the weather, adverse winds or storms preventing it from making its carefully timed rendezvous with the fleet of small craft ferrying Parma's troops across the channel. Philip defended the plan in a letter of reply written in December 1586, but he obviously considered Parma's objection to the Irish part of the operation and asked Parma what he thought about making the feint landing on the Isle of Wight instead of in Ireland. As for the Enterprise itself, Philip curiously defended it on the grounds that since he had gone to the trouble and expense of building his armada, he should put it to good use. He told Parma he must understand that "we cannot avoid building up the Armada we have here, because of the need to defend Portugal and for other things, and that, having thus created it, at so much cost, it would be best not to lose the chance of doing something with it."

In January 1587 Parma wrote again to object to the plan, criticizing a landing at either Ireland or the Isle of Wight and arguing that if Philip had to go through with the Enterprise, he should send the armada directly to the Netherlands coast and have it protect Parma's army during its channel crossing. Philip wrote back that he was considering all the problems. While he was still considering them, Drake staged his raids on Cádiz and Sagres and captured the treasures of the *São Phelipe,* and Philip became seriously ill, but not so sick that he was prevented from sending Parma a new plan, which he did in June 1587. He was then still thinking the Enterprise would be launched that summer. "Because the Armada here must first deal with meeting and protecting the fleets coming from the Americas," he wrote, stating an objective no doubt born out of Drake's depredations, "I do not think it will be possible for it to reach the Channel before your own crossing. . . . The best course seems to me that, almost at the same time or as close to it as possible, we attack in three directions: an invasion by you and your forces; a diversion via Scotland, thanks to the men and money that the Catholics of that kingdom have requested; and an attack by this armada on the Isle of Wight or Southampton."

While Philip was sick, his council members in late June decided that Santa Cruz should take the whole Lisbon fleet and sail off to protect incoming treasure ships, and Philip concurred. Santa Cruz and his fleet sailed from Lisbon on July 16. About the same time, Philip's councilors decided that the ships gathered in Andalusia should be moved to Lisbon and be there when Santa Cruz returned with his fleet, to join Santa Cruz's vessels in forming the bulk of the armada that Philip envisioned. Philip agreed to that, too. Three weeks later the Andalusia fleet sailed into Lisbon harbor to await Santa Cruz's return and the launching of the Enterprise of England. In expectation of that event's imminent occurrence, the crews and troops of the Andalusia fleet were required to sleep aboard their vessels, to be ready to sail at a moment's notice.

However, Santa Cruz and most of his fleet did not return until September 29, with the ships in desperate need of repairs. The last of his eagerly awaited vessels did not return to Lisbon until October 10, 1587. Still, at that late date and despite advice to the contrary, Philip, feeling stronger since he had got over his illness, insisted the Enterprise be launched before the year's end. On September 4, while ships of the fleet were still straggling into Lisbon, Philip had issued new orders for the Enterprise. In them he had canceled the landing in Ireland and the landing on the Isle of Wight, stating that Drake's raids and the diversion of the fleet to protect the treasure-bearing vessels had cost so much time that the diversionary actions were being scrapped. The new plan specified that Santa Cruz and his Lisbon fleet were to be joined by the vessels from Andalusia, commanded by Alonso Martínez de Leiva, and the Biscayan squadron of Juan Martínez de Recalde, plus the squadron of Miguel de Oquendo, from Guipúzcoa province in the Basque country of northern

Spain. Once assembled, those combined fleets, constituting the mighty Spanish Armada, would forthwith "sail in the name of God straight to the English Channel," Philip ordered, "and go along it until you have anchored off Margate head, having first warned the duke of Parma of your approach."

"The said duke," Philip apprised his admirals, "according to the orders he has received, on seeing the narrow seas [the channel] thus made safe by the Armada being either anchored off the said headland or else cruising in the mouth of the Thames . . . will immediately send across the army that he has prepared in small boats, of which (for transit alone) he has plenty." The admirals were instructed that their mission was only to protect Parma's crossing and to do so by attacking any enemy vessels that attempted to prevent Parma's landing. The Armada would, Philip said, foil any English attempt to "concentrate a fleet which would dare to come out and seek ours." The troops aboard the Armada's vessels, according to Philip's new plan, would not participate in the landings, and the vessels themselves were to serve merely a defensive role, a mission that left Santa Cruz, whose fame had come as a commander of fighting ships, seriously disappointed, so much so that he considered resigning his command.

To the duke of Parma Philip sent corresponding orders, informing him of the latest plan. He said Parma would be sent word of the approaching Armada when it neared the Netherlands coast, so that when he could see it in the Dover strait, he would be ready immediately to embark his troops and send them across the channel. He further told Parma that he was not to move from his position on the Netherlands coast until the Armada had arrived in the strait. In his new directive Philip also made it clear that he did not want to hear any more of Parma's objections to the plan. Parma was told, in effect, to quit complaining and do as he was told.

Santa Cruz got a similar message. In a letter dated October 21, 1587, Philip said he was tired of the delays and told the admiral, "I charge and command you most strictly to leave before the end of the month." Santa Cruz responded with more delays and more excuses—many of them, such as need of repairs and lack of adequate provisions, probably legitimate. In mid-November the fleet was still in Lisbon. Philip rejected all the excuses—even the effects of a cyclone that struck Lisbon on November 16 and damaged thirty-nine of the Armada's ships to the extent that repairs would take two weeks.

Questions and reservations remained in Parma's mind. Philip had never spelled out how the troops in the Netherlands were to escape the shallow-draft Dutch coastal patrol craft that had established a virtual blockade and would keep Parma's small boats from entering the open waters of the channel with the invasion troops. What sort of protection from those Dutch vessels would the Armada provide? Would the Armada include shallow-draft vessels that could fend off the Dutch boats? Or would the troops be embarked at a deep-water port where the Armada's galleys and galleasses could protect them? If the latter, which deep-water port was it to be? Maddeningly prone to micromanage, Philip had nevertheless neglected to provide the essential answers to those questions.

Furthermore, after Philip on September 30 had told Parma that if Elizabeth moved her fleet from the mouth of the Thames to the naval base at Plymouth, near the entrance to the channel, Parma could perhaps take advantage of the English fleet's absence and cross the channel without waiting for the Armada, which was still gathering at Lisbon at that point. That suggestion contradicted Philip's previous order that Parma was not to move until he could see the Armada in the Dover strait.

Parma dutifully but tardily replied on November 14 that he would be ready to launch the invasion by November 20 and that he was "entirely resolved, in the name of God and with His holy assistance, to put to sea myself on the 25th" unless he discovered that the English fleet was still in the channel to oppose his crossing.

Afraid then that Parma might make a landing without the Armada to support him once ashore, Philip urgently commanded Santa Cruz, twice, to hasten for the channel even if he had no more than thirty-five ships ready to sail. Nevertheless, as November passed into December, the fleet still did not sail. By then, not well, ridden with anxiety and frustration, Philip seemed to lapse into irrationality. The pressures on him had become enormous. His councilors were urging action. The Armada's crewmen and troops, still confined to their ships, were falling sick at an alarming rate. On December 2 a muster of the ships' crews revealed that more than one thousand of the sixteen thousand–plus seamen were ill. Many others had already died of disease. What was more, the huge expense of maintaining the Armada and its men, plus Parma's reinforced army, was draining the royal treasury, costing some forty-five thousand ducats a day. Philip was driven to sell his late wife's jewels to help meet the expense.

While repeatedly ordering Santa Cruz to sail, Philip was also firing off letters to Parma, trying to find out where the duke was and what was going on. He wanted to know if Parma had indeed crossed the channel. If he was not already in England, why had he not made the crossing as Philip had suggested?

The contradictory orders finally destroyed Parma's patience. Throwing up his hands, he wrote back to Philip and told him, "Your Majesty has the right to give absolute orders . . . but for you to write to me now with a proposal that runs so contrary to the previous express orders and command of Your Majesty causes me great anguish. I beg you most humbly to do me the very great favor of telling me what to do next."

Parma's remarks apparently chilled Philip's frantic thoughts, for following that exchange of letters, Philip set aside his most recent directives and reinstated the plan that called for the two commanders—Parma and Santa Cruz—to link up in the Dover strait, for Parma to make no move till the Armada was in the strait, and for the Armada to forbear seeking to engage the enemy before it rendezvoused with Parma's invasion force.

Philip could stop worrying about getting his Enterprise in motion before the end of the year. It was now the middle of December 1587 and it was only too obvious that the invasion was going to wait until 1588. As Christmas approached, he ceased his vain efforts to make the Enterprise happen immediately and took to his bed to recover his battered health.

While the king's plan was being made and remade and Spain's war preparations continued, other events were occurring to spur on Philip's grand Enterprise of England. In 1584, when Francis, younger brother of the French king and Elizabeth's onetime suitor, died, Henry of Navarre became heir apparent to the French throne. Henry, however, was a Huguenot, as his mother had raised him to be, and the Catholic League, a powerful religious-political organization headed by Henry, duke of Guise, one of the uncles of Mary Queen of Scots, refused to accept a Protestant as heir and persuaded the king, Henry III, not only to bar Henry of Navarre from the succession but also to revoke concessions that had been made to France's Protestants. The result was civil war. Henry of Navarre took his case to the battlefield. The conflict became known as the War of the Three Henrys and was eventually successful, but while the battles raged and Henry of Navarre was forced to flee Paris, he was also prevented from making trouble for Philip by intervening in the

Netherlands revolt on the side of the rebellious Protestants. Philip felt no fear of an army from France marching across the Netherlands frontier while Parma's army was occupied in England. The situation in France had become a green light for Philip and the Enterprise.

Meanwhile, in Rome another green light went on. Pope Sixtus V had recently shown reluctance to support the Enterprise, even though earlier, when he became pope, he had urged Philip to depose Elizabeth and had offered to pay a third of the cost of doing so. In a new lack of enthusiasm for the Enterprise, the pope had gone so far as to have the French king, Henry III, use his offices in an attempt to talk Elizabeth into embracing the Catholic church, thereby foreclosing an invasion and denying Philip the opportunity to aggrandize the British Isles. Speculation had it that Sixtus, with a reputation for tightfistedness, simply wanted to avoid making good on his offer to help finance the invasion.

But on July 29, 1587, in a treaty consummated between the papacy and Spain, the pope agreed to pay one million ducats toward Philip's costs of removing Elizabeth. The grant, though, would be payable only after Philip's troops were on English soil. Philip's ambassador to Rome, Enrique de Guzmán, count of Olivares, did his best to get the pope to let Philip have an advance on the million ducats, but the pope steadfastly refused. Getting money from Sixtus, Olivares told Philip, was like taking his life's blood from him.

In the treaty with Spain, the pope had at least shown he had no political agenda for England. He allowed that once Philip had seized the crown from Elizabeth, he could place it on the head of whomever he chose, so long as that person could be depended upon to restore Catholicism in England.

Also encouraging Philip's execution of the Enterprise was the absence of an imminent threat from the Turks, the menace of the Mediterranean, who at the time were busy fighting the Persians. Philip had seven years earlier signed a one-year truce agreement with the Turks, and in January 1581 the term of the truce had been lengthened to three years. However, apparently no responsible person in Spain expected the truce to go on interminably. Philip worried about a Turkish attack, and so did his ministers, who figured that with Spain's Armada at sea in the Atlantic or the English Channel, the Turks were likely to see a golden opportunity to strike Spain or its possessions, or both.

Their worries, though, were not sufficient to change Philip's mind about the invasion of England, which was, according to one report,[3] overwhelmingly supported by the Spanish public, which was another reason to execute the plan. Spaniards generally saw the conquest of England as necessary for the security of their country and its territories. It had to be done.

◦֍· 16. THE DEFENDERS

E lizabeth was fifty-four years old in the autumn of 1587, far past the time when she could use hints of marriage to a powerful foreign prince to manipulate her nation's adversaries, forcing them to alter their hostile intentions. She was still able, though, to give them mixed signals, offering peace with one hand and at the same time making mischief with the other. Seeing that the English campaign to aid the Netherlands, ineffectually generaled by the earl of Leicester, was not going well and was costing her much more than she wanted to continue to pay, she used a well-placed Italian businessman in the Netherlands to approach the duke of Parma about an armistice, while at the same time making war on Philip's shipping.

What she apparently had in mind was an informal exchange with Parma, in which he would outline what he believed would be terms acceptable to Philip, which she could then accept or reject. Parma, though, gave her a make-me-an-offer response, telling her that she would have to initiate the peace proposal—the terms of which *Philip* could accept or reject—and that once she did so, he would see what he could do to get Philip to approve it. Refusing to yield the upper hand, she fired back a hot answer to Parma. "We hope our actions," she said, "have not led the world to believe us of so base a mind as to seek him who has first offended us." That was the end of that attempt at a treaty, and with other tries at a Netherlands peace also failing, in December 1587 she abandoned the fruitless Netherlands campaign and ordered Leicester back to England, where he could face the larger menace of Philip's Enterprise. She kept her contacts with Parma alive, though.[1]

The seas that have for eons made Britain an island have for centuries proved more an avenue for invasion than a barrier to it, beginning with the Celts of prehistoric times who crossed the channel from mainland Europe in primitive coracles and displaced the Stone Age inhabitants. After the Celts came the Romans in A.D. 43. Four hundred years later came the Angles, Saxons, and Jutes.

After them, beginning in the eighth century, came the Vikings, then, in 1066, the Normans, led by William the Conqueror. By the time of King Henry VIII, who built a formidable English navy, it was clear that England's first line of defense against invasion had to be established upon the sea.

Elizabeth determined to do so. Her best fighting admiral was Francis Drake, but she would not name him the commanding admiral of the English fleet. Instead, that appointment, as lord admiral, the naval commander in chief, went to Elizabeth's cousin Charles Howard—Lord Howard of Effingham. Although keen on rewarding merit, even that of the son of a farmer-turned-preacher, as Drake was, Elizabeth was bound by propriety to bestow the highest honor on one of her own noble class. Howard came from a long line of lord admirals, being the fourth in his family to hold that title in his nation's navy, but his experience was insignificant in comparison with Drake's. At fifty-one, in 1587, he had no experience in naval combat and only limited experience in leading a fleet at sea. But like his queen, he could recognize the merit of subordinates and stood ready to endow them with responsibility and trust. He would, he once promised, "yield ever unto them of greater experience."

So it was that after considering the lengthy argument made by Drake, who was then admiral of the section of Elizabeth's fleet based in the west of England, Howard agreed to move the navy's main base of operations from Greenwich and the mouth of the Thames to Plymouth, near the western entrance to the channel. Drake had argued that Philip would very likely send a substantial fleet to protect Parma's army as it attempted to cross the channel in the area of Dover, since Parma's crossing would be nearly impossible without a protective escort to ward off English warships. Therefore, Drake insisted, it made great sense to shift as many English vessels as possible to an accommodating port as far west as possible, from which they could take advantage of the prevailing winds to gain the weather gauge of an enemy fleet entering the channel from the Atlantic Ocean and assail it practically the whole length of the English Channel.

His argument having persuaded his fellow admirals as well as Howard, in February 1588 Drake moved a squadron from the main fleet to the base at Plymouth and assumed command of it. Drake had also urged Elizabeth to provide more ships, asking for eight royal galleons to add to his command. Elizabeth instead decided to send to Plymouth fourteen of her mightiest galleons and most of the armed merchant ships that had been pressed into service. Drake's command eventually grew to some sixty ships. On April 29 Howard wrote to the queen's council to propose exactly which vessels he would move to Plymouth and which would remain stationed in or near the Strait of Dover, under the command of Lord Henry Seymour, to contest the duke of Parma's crossing. On May 10 Howard received authorization to shift the fleet as proposed.

Days later the entire fleet, excluding the vessels under Drake's command, assembled in the channel off Margate for a reorganization exercise. Seymour's squadron received several more ships, boosting its total to twenty-nine, and Seymour took over the *Rainbow* as his new flagship, transferring from the *Elizabeth Bonaventure,* his former flagship and once Drake's as well. The remainder of the assembled vessels, an estimated thirty-eight ships and several pinnaces, after receiving new provisions, then took advantage of what Howard called "a pleasant gale" and set sail for Plymouth on May 31, arriving there on the morning of June 2, 1588.

Drake, far from showing resentment over what was for him a sort of demotion, his western command having been absorbed into the fleet under the direct command of the lord admiral, put on an elaborate welcoming ceremony for Howard, who with good judgment had already named Drake vice admiral, making him the combined fleet's second in command. Drake took his sixty vessels out into the channel in a formation of three files, sending his pinnaces out ahead of them. As Howard's contingent approached, Drake had his crewmen line up on the decks and yards while their ships' guns boomed salutes, and to stirring sounds of drumbeats and trumpet calls Drake had his own flag lowered and Howard's raised in its place. The ceremony was apparently Drake's idea, unexpected by Howard. According to some accounts, it was Drake's way of showing that he was yielding to the lord admiral voluntarily rather than merely through obedience, a point apparently important to Drake's pride. In any case, Drake evidently never gave Howard reason to believe Drake resented him. "I must not omit to let you know," Howard wrote of the relationship, "how lovingly and kindly Sir Francis Drake bears himself, and also how dutifully, to Her Majesty's service and to me."

Operating out of Plymouth now were, according to one estimate, some one hundred and five vessels, including nineteen royal galleons and forty-six large support ships. Philip had received intelligence—from an exiled but supposedly knowledgeable English Catholic priest, William Allen—that

Elizabeth's warships were mostly rotting tubs. But actually the ships of the English navy were in sound fighting condition, many of them having been made so only recently. Howard made it his business to inspect every nook and cranny of the fleet's ships and he reported to Elizabeth that hers were "the strongest ships that any prince in Christendom hath" and that her vessels did not know the meaning of "leak." After the *Elizabeth Bonaventure* had accidentally run aground, imperiling its keel and planking, it was refloated and inspected by both Howard and William Wynter, who as surveyor of the navy was in charge of the fleet's construction and maintenance. Howard reported that despite *Elizabeth Bonaventure*'s accident, "there never came a spoonful of water into her well. . . . Except that a ship had been made of iron, it were to be thought impossible to do as she had done; and it may be well and truly said there never was, nor is, in the world a stronger ship than she is." His report was a reassuring tribute to the soundness of the English vessels and the competence of their builders. Howard was so pleased with the ships that he told Francis Walsingham, "Were it not for her majesty's presence, I had rather live in the company of these noble ships than in any [other] place."

The good condition of England's navy was largely due to the work of Wynter and John Hawkins, whom Elizabeth had appointed treasurer of the navy in 1577. Hawkins had rebuilt much of England's fleet, transforming older vessels, with their awkward "castles" towering fore and aft, into so-called race-built (or raze-built) craft, with lowered—or razed—castles and sleeker, trimmer lines that gave them more speed and maneuverability. The design of the rebuilt vessels, also incorporated into the new ships ordered by Elizabeth, gave them a longer gun deck, allowing them to carry more and heavier artillery, thus providing them with significantly more firepower. The new design permitted the warships to be armed with ordnance totaling in some cases more than 10 percent of the vessel's displacement. The *Elizabeth Bonaventure* carried fifty-one and a half tons of ordnance—not counting the guns' carriages or ammunition—artillery that amounted to more than 8 percent of the ship's displacement of six hundred tons. The *Revenge*, which Drake would use as his flagship when he faced the Armada, had a displacement of five hundred tons and carried forty-two guns weighing a total of forty tons, exclusive of their carriages, or nearly 9 percent of the vessel's displacement.

In contrast, the Spanish flagship *San Cristobal*, with a displacement of 700 tons, carried only 3 percent of its tonnage in ordnance, and the huge galleon *San Juan*, displacing 1,050 tons, carried only 4 percent in ordnance.

The guns of the English ships furthermore were able to be fired more rapidly than those of the Armada's vessels, owing to the design of the gun carriages. The English had forsaken the two-wheel carriages with trails, similar to the type used by field artillery, that impeded reloading of the muzzle-loaders, making a laborious task of hauling the guns back from their gun ports to be reloaded after they were fired, and occupying considerable deck space. Instead, the English guns were mounted on boxlike, four-wheel truck carriages that were more mobile and more easily maneuvered. After a gun was fired, it could be quickly wheeled back from its port and reloaded, then swiftly returned to its port to fire again. The truck-mounted guns also required less deck space.

There were two big reasons for the advantages of the English ships in gunnery and design. One was that they were not designed for extended voyages across the Atlantic and back, requiring holds crammed with provisions to nurture their crews during their months at sea. The weight of those provisions and the space consumed by them could be used for armament or eliminated on English warships, which generally were designed to stay close to home and safeguard the nation's shores, as they were about to do against Philip's Armada.

The second, more significant reason was that England had decided to fight a different kind of naval warfare. For many centuries combat at sea meant boarding enemy vessels and fighting hand to hand on their decks and belowdecks as if on land. It was the kind of naval warfare to which Spain was accustomed and at which its seaborne soldiers had shown themselves so proficient in their monumental victory over the Turks in the Battle of Lepanto. The Armada's warships would carry troops not as passengers but as a combat force to oppose English ships they supposed would be similarly freighted with fighting men. But Elizabeth's navy, since around the 1570s, had evolved from the boarding tactic of the past, and the design of its ships reflected the new tactic of having them serve primarily as artillery platforms. Able to prevent the enemy from coming come close enough to board them, the sleek English ships were designed to outmaneuver enemy vessels and with superior firepower hammer them into destruction, submission, or flight.

The new English warships were smaller, lighter, and faster than the bulky Spanish warships, not needing space for the seagoing soldiers and provisions to feed them at sea. The smaller vessels were preferred by many of Elizabeth's fighting commanders, including Sir Walter Raleigh, who as vice admiral of Devon and Cornwall, remarked that "the greatest [largest] ships are [the] least serviceable, go very deep to water and [are expensive to build]. A ship of 600 tons will carry as good ordnance as a ship of 1,200 tons and . . . the lesser will turn her broadsides twice before the greater one can once." Sacrificed in the ships' redesign and the new emphasis on heavy ordnance were the lighter guns, usually mounted on the ships' castles and employed as antipersonnel weapons, capable of firing down on the decks of an enemy vessel before it was boarded, a tactic used by the Spanish.

Ironically enough, Philip had helped England develop its navy. While he was still the husband of Elizabeth's sister, Queen Mary, and was no doubt thinking ahead to a time—which never came—when he would become England's sovereign, Philip in 1555 had responded with alarm to Mary's Privy Council's report on the rundown condition of England's navy. "Since England's chief defense depends upon its navy being always in good order to serve for the defense of the kingdom against all invasion," he told the council members, "it is right that ships should not only be fit for sea but [be] instantly available." And foreshadowing Drake's advice concerning the positioning of the fleet, Philip recommended that "as the passage out of the River Thames is not an easy one, the vessels ought to be stationed at Portsmouth, from which they can more easily be brought into service." His recommendations resulted in the construction of three major warships, each displacing five hundred or more tons. Those three ships, rebuilt under John Hawkins's updating program, now in 1588 were part of the fleet that would oppose the Armada that Philip was about to launch against the nation he had formerly meant to protect.

All told, the English fleet that would face the Armada was reported to total 197 vessels, 34 of them ships of the royal navy and 163 ships privately owned, including 7 owned by Howard, 3 by Hawkins, and 2 by Drake, most of which had been operating as privateers and were captained by relatives or business associates of the owners. England's ships generally were commanded by skilled officers, chosen for their ability rather than their social rank. Only five of the commanders of the fleet's thirty-four major warships were lords, including one who was an experienced privateer. Some, like Drake, were knighted, but they had received that honor for their naval merits. All others were commoners.

Drake, moreover, with a decidedly democratic spirit, made a point of having the gentlemen who were officers on his ships perform the same tasks as lesser men. "I must have the gentleman to haul and draw with the mariner, and the mariner with the gentleman," he declared. "Let us show ourselves to be of a company. I would know him that would refuse to set his hand to a rope, but I know there is not any such here." Setting the example, as a commander he joined his men in hauling and drawing himself. He also was quick to suppress any display of a lack of equalitarianism or unity aboard his vessels. "Such controversy between the sailors and the gentlemen and such stomaching [resentment] between the gentlemen and the sailors," he asserted, ". . . does make me mad to hear it."

There *was* inequality, of course, particularly in the matter of pay. Pay for admirals depended on their social status. Howard, the queen's cousin, received three pounds, six shillings, eight pence per day, plus a handsome food allowance. Henry Seymour, in command of the fleet stationed off Dover, a son of the earl of Hertford, was paid two pounds per day. Drake, vice admiral of the entire fleet but son of a farmer, received thirty shillings per day. Ordinary ship captains were paid half a crown per day, or twelve and a half pence. Common seamen received four pence per day, or ten shillings per month. Until John Hawkins had prevailed upon Elizabeth to give ordinary seamen a raise three years earlier, they had made just six shillings and eight pence per month. Hawkins's argument for the raise was one of practicality. "By this means," he pleaded, "Her Majesty's ships will be furnished with able men, such as can make shift for themselves, keep themselves clean without vermin and noisomeness which breeds sickness and mortality. . . . The wages being so small cause the best men to run away . . . and unskillful persons supply the[ir] place." The sailors' regular pay, however, was often augmented by their shares of captured or pirated vessels and goods.

Life aboard English ships had its horrors, for which pay was little compensation. Besides the normal hazards of seafaring and of naval combat, there was sickness—particularly scurvy, typhus, and dysentery—and a stern code of justice to keep the seamen, often an undisciplined lot, in line and their ships under their captains' control. Falling asleep on watch was one of the more serious offenses, and the punishment for it increased with the frequency of its occurrence. After the fourth time a sailor was caught sleeping on his watch, he was placed in a basket with a ration of beer, a loaf of bread, and a knife and suspended from the ship's bowsprit, where he was left to dangle till he starved to death or cut himself loose and plunged into the sea before the oncoming prow of the vessel. Sailors caught stealing were tied to a rope and put overboard to be hauled behind the ship to the next port, dead or alive. A sailor who drew a weapon on a fellow crewman was punished by having his right hand nailed to the mainmast, or cut off. One who committed murder was tied to the corpse of his victim and heaved overboard to drown. For other serious offenses, keelhauling was the penalty, which in many cases resulted in drowning.

Adequate food to keep a man healthy was a persistent problem aboard English ships. Often it was in short supply, and what there was to eat was rotten. Water and beer, the two main beverages of crews, were often as foul as the food. The prescribed daily diet called for each sailor to get either salted beef or dried fish plus a pound of biscuit and gallon of beer, and on some days butter and cheese. Rations were frequently cut, though, and what was supposed to feed four sometimes fed six. Like other soldiers and sailors over the centuries, English sailors voiced their gripes about the food. One of the seamen who sailed with Drake on his Cádiz raid in 1587 complained about the "weak victualling and filthy drink." "What is a piece of beef of half a pound among four men," he asked in protest, ". . . or half a dry stockfish [unsalted, dried fish] [and] a little beverage [that is] worse than the pump water?"

At least part of the problem of inadequate provisions had to have been Elizabeth's niggardliness, but England's lack of an efficient system to supply its navy, particularly in wartime, has been blamed as a much bigger cause. The English system had the ships provisioned monthly, and new provisions were not issued until the current month's rations had practically run out. The lord admiral himself complained about the system. "We shall now be victualled beginning the 20th of this April unto the 18th of May," he wrote before shifting his base to Plymouth. "The likeliest time for the coming out of the Spanish forces is the midst of May, being the 15th. Then we have three days' victual. If it be fit to be so, it passes my reason." What was needed, especially in wartime, was a system that would supply the ships with enough provisions to last two months or more. Elizabeth's navy, however, accustomed to duty that nearly always had its ships only days from an English port, had no experience at providing for many weeks at sea.

It was not only food and drink that were in short supply. Gunpowder was so scarce that officials asked that ceremonial artillery salutes be curtailed and Elizabeth was moved to criticize Drake for wasting powder and ammunition in target practice. His supply of that vital materiel was reduced, allowing his ships to fight no more than a day and a half. He wrote Elizabeth to warn her of the problem: "Powder and shot for our great ordnance in Her Majesty's ships is but for one day and a half's service. . . . I beseech you to consider deeply of this, for it imports the loss of all." He argued that the fleet was receiving only a third of the amount of gunpowder it needed and urged that the supply be increased, ". . . for if we should want it when we shall have most need thereof," he told her gravely, "it will be too late to send to the Tower for it."

In the Tower's magazines, however, there was not enough powder to meet Drake's request, because of Elizabeth's penny-pinching. She had been warned as early as 1562 about the importance of keeping a reserve supply of gunpowder. "It will be only that thing she shall lack if wars should chance, which should be foreseen in time, because our forces and ships," she was told, "be nothing without powder."[2] She had ignored the warning then, but later, in the 1570s, a supply of saltpeter, the essential ingredient of gunpowder, had been obtained from Fez, on the North African coast, but at a cost—about one hundred English pounds per ton of saltpeter—that Elizabeth found daunting, and getting her to release it from the Tower for the use of her ships had become a major undertaking.

Elizabeth also was scrimping on her navy payroll, to the point that in April there were not enough sailors to man all the ships that were available to face the Armada, even though the cost of keeping a galleon, the navy's prime warship, on active duty was less than four hundred pounds per month. But the expense of national defense came out of the queen's own budget, and Elizabeth could be frugal to a fault. Besides, she still clung to the belief that outright war with Philip might be avoided, making further defense spending unnecessary. The lord admiral with increasing ardor implored her to spend enough to man the navy's idle warships that could prove critical against the Spanish fleet. "I do warrant you [that] our state is well enough known to them in Flanders [i.e., Parma and his Spanish army]," Howard wrote to Elizabeth, "and as we were a terror to them at first coming out, so do they now make little reckoning of us; for they know that we are like bears tied to stakes, and they may come as dogs to offend us and we cannot go to hurt them. I have a good company here with me, so that if the Queen's Majesty will not spare her purse, they will not spare their lives."

Again he urged her: "Before these ships can have their full number of men again it will be a month to gather them, do what we can. And I pray to God we shall have them when we shall need [them]."

And again: "Men we must have or else the ships will do no good." And still one more warning: "Sparing and war have no affinity together."

The other, lesser, arm of England's defense was its land forces. Apparently having learned little from Leicester's lack of military success in the Netherlands, Elizabeth appointed him to command those forces, awarding him the grand title of Lieutenant and Captain General of the Queen's Armies and Companies. Shire militias had already been alerted to the emergency and instructed to prepare themselves. As early as February 1587 instructions had been sent to the commanders of military groups in the counties, directing them to notify their subordinate leaders "and charge them without delay to warn all persons under their charge, from man to man, to be ready in their armour and weapons" for an inspection to be held in March. After the inspection, the militiamen were to be drilled to march and those who had firearms were "to be taught to shoot at certain marks to be devised with boards to be set up to shoot at, which the captains may see weekly done."[3]

Militia commanders in the counties bordering the sea were ordered to study their coastline, decide which sites were the "most dangerous for any number of enemies to have landing,"[4] and then construct defensive works at those sites, erecting barricades and parapets, digging deep pits and ditches, and implanting other obstructions along the beaches. Arrangements were made for artillery, shot, and gunpowder to be sent to the coastal militia units, and orders were issued for the militias to have their artillery pieces and powder ready to be quickly shifted to wherever the militia commanders directed. Draft horses were also to be kept ready to move the artillery "when and where need of service shall require."[5]

Orders were issued for militia troops to be readily shifted to engage the invaders at the point of their assault. The militia commanders were told to organize their men into three divisions: "some to repair to the sea coast, as occasion may serve, to impeach the landing . . . of the enemy upon his first descent; some other part of the said forces to join with such numbers as shall be convenient to make head to the enemy after he shall be landed (if it shall fall out); and another principal part of the said trained numbers to repair hither to join with the Army that shall be appointed for the defence of Her Majesty's person."[6]

The troops assigned to protect Elizabeth were to stand ready to move out on an hour's notice. Elizabeth's advisers had a list made of the invasion force's most probable landing sites, and fortifications were erected at those locations. A signal system was also devised, consisting of braziers mounted on tall poles set atop prominent hills, ready to be lighted to warn distant militia forces of the approach of the enemy.

Concerned that a fifth column might spring into action at the coming of the Catholic Spaniards, hampering the nation's defense, Elizabeth ordered her county officials to make a list of suspects in their areas—persons who refused to accept the Church of England and attend its services. The county officials were "to cause the most obstinate and noted persons to be committed to such prisons as are fittest for their safe keeping. The rest that are . . . not so obstinate to be referred to the custody of some ecclesiastical person and other gentlemen well affected."[7]

The defense plan for land forces seemed to take care of the need, but actually it was no better than the troops who would serve. England had no standing army of any great size, certainly nothing to match Parma's army in numbers, weapons, training, and the experience of its fighting men. For its involvement in wars on foreign soil, England might rely on mercenary armies, particularly those hired from Germany, but to defend itself at home, the nation looked to its militia, the citizen soldiers who would be called out in time of need, a system that dated back to fyrds mustered by England's magnates under the Anglo-Saxon kings, before the Norman Conquest. Militiamen came in degrees of competence and training. The largest group included all the "substantial honest men" between the ages of sixteen and sixty from every county. They were called out periodically for a general muster, held on holidays or designated working days, during which they received the most rudimentary kind of training. On the first of the two days of activity, they practiced marksmanship, though few had weapons with which to practice. On the second day they drilled, going through the motions of forming battle formations. After that, they went back home.

Apart from the general muster there was the special muster, or particular muster, which included only those men who showed some aptitude for things military, as decided by their captains. Those men, formed in units called "trained bands," were called out several times a year and given instruction in the use of weapons and were generally relied upon to serve as the nation's army in defense of England. Excluded from their ranks were Catholics, whose loyalty to their Protestant queen was doubted. The exclusion was extended to the Irish veterans of the force that Elizabeth had recalled from the Netherlands, men who had constituted the bulk of Leicester's four-thousand-man army and had gained valuable combat experience that could have been used to train others. The bands were characterized by the spottiness of the quality of their training and discipline, some units being praiseworthy and many incompetent or unreliable. Some members of the bands, after being issued costly new weapons, took them and disappeared from further service.

Weapons were another part of the problem of the militias' inadequacy. The bands had only begun to replace the infantryman's traditional weapons of choice—the longbow and the bill—with the most modern handheld weapons of the day, the musket, harquebus, and pistol. The shortage of ordnance was even worse, and few individuals in the bands were even trained to use artillery, except for units assigned to specific sites where it was believed the enemy might land. According to one account, the artillery committed to defend the shores of southern England in 1587 amounted to six pieces—two five-pounders, two four-pounders, and two three-pounders—for each county along the channel coast. Furthermore, the scarcity of gunpowder that Elizabeth's navy suffered was felt no less by her land forces.

At the close of 1587, it had been estimated that England could mobilize an army of 45,000 trained infantry and 3,000 cavalry, with an additional 130,000 general-muster militiamen available. How well they would perform against the proven prowess of Parma's army was anybody's guess.

While some were satisfied that all was in readiness for the Armada's arrival, the aggressive Francis Drake grew restless at having to sit and wait. He wanted to take the fight to the coast of Spain, to strike the Armada's vessels while they were tied up in port or when they emerged into the open sea, long before reaching the channel. Drake argued before the queen's council that "the advantage of time and place in all martial actions is half a victory." He claimed that "with fifty sail of shipping we shall do more good upon their own coast than a great many more will do here at home." Howard at first was opposed to Drake's plan, as was Elizabeth, but he later came around to

Drake's position. Howard's adoption of Drake's plan apparently worked an effect on the queen, and she was won over, but only temporarily. It also worked a salutary effect on Drake, who now saw the inexperienced Howard as an ally rather than an obstacle.

With Elizabeth's agreement, Howard took his fleet out of Plymouth harbor on May 30, 1588, and set sail for Spain. The voyage was cut short, however, by fierce storms, as bad as any that might arise in winter, and Howard was forced to turn around and head back to port, there to wait till the weather improved so that the fleet could sail again for Spain. In the meantime, though, Elizabeth changed her mind, once again opposing the fleet's leaving the channel. Her fear was that Philip's ships might get past the English fleet unnoticed and sail into the channel while it was undefended, or underdefended. On June 9, before Howard could sail off again, Elizabeth ordered that his ships, instead of heading for Spain, only patrol England's coasts.

The order so angered Howard that he fired off a bitingly sarcastic note to the queen. "I must and will obey," he wrote, "and am glad there be such there as are able to judge what is fitter for us to do than we here." Perhaps because of his note, Elizabeth changed her mind again and let him sail for Spain once more, which he did on July 8. He was again thwarted by the weather, however, the wind shifting to southerly two days after he had left port, and rather than battle the headwinds and run the risk that the Armada's vessels might dash past him, he turned the fleet toward home again.

Elizabeth meanwhile still showed signs that she held a hope of avoiding all-out war with Philip. In April she had sent her former ambassador in Paris, Valentine Dale, to Parma to make new exploration of the possibility of a peace agreement. Philip's receptivity to her move, however, was perhaps indicated by the loading aboard his ships of printed copies of a papal bull that excommunicated Elizabeth all over again and that urged her subjects to depose her, copies intended to be circulated throughout England by Philip's invading army. Another indication was the publication in June of a pamphlet by the Spanish-supported English cardinal, William Allen, titled *An Admonition to the Nobility and People of England,* which demonized Elizabeth, calling her "an incestuous bastard begotten and born in sin of an infamous courtesan." Both the pamphlet and the bull came to Elizabeth's attention, and when she had Dale complain to Parma about both, Parma shrugged off the protest by claiming he knew nothing of the bull and had not read the pamphlet. He was, he said, just a soldier who was bound to follow his orders, however wronged Dale's queen might have been.

Even so, Elizabeth persisted in the talks with Parma, writing to him on July 8 that "if any reasonable conditions of peace should be offered," she was ready to accept them.[8]

Such a response to the rising threat exasperated Lord Admiral Howard. "For the love of Jesus Christ, Madam," he wrote to Elizabeth, "awake thoroughly and see the villainous treasons around you, against your majesty and your realm, and draw your forces round about you like a mighty prince to defend you. Truly, Madam, if you do so, there is no cause to fear. If you do not, there will be danger."

Finally, on July 17, 1588, Elizabeth at last gave up on the prospects of peace and called off further negotiations with Philip. She was now resigned to the war that was on its way.

⟶❦⟶ 17. THE GRAND ARMADA

Alvaro de Bazán, the first marquis of Santa Cruz, was a fighting naval officer, a sea warrior whose success in combat had won him the job of commanding King Philip's grand Armada—assembling it, equipping it, sailing it, and fulfilling its mission to sweep away England's naval defenses and land the duke of Parma's invasion army safely on English soil. He had begun his task with enthusiasm, but as time wore on, he wore out. Struggling to cope with failing logistics, sick crews, and damaged vessels, he repeatedly missed the deadlines for sailing set for him by Philip.

When on December 2, 1587, he held a muster of the Armada's personnel, he learned that nearly 1,200 of the fleet's 16,260 sailors and seagoing soldiers were ill. His pleas to Philip to let him remove the crews and clean his ships for hygienic purposes were refused. His reasons for not sailing when ordered were summarily dismissed by Philip, who grew more strident as he grew more frustrated with the delays. "I direct you and expressly order you," Philip commanded him on January 18, 1588, after many postponements, "that without losing an hour, you should have the whole armada in the river [sailing for England]."

To make sure Santa Cruz obeyed that order, Philip sent an enforcer, the duke of Alba's no-nonsense nephew, Pedro Enríquez, count of Fuentes, who took with him Philip's authorization to relieve Santa Cruz of his command. Fuentes arrived in Lisbon on January 30 and saw firsthand the chaos into which the Armada's preparation had degenerated. The ships' ordnance was not in place, maintenance of the ships was not completed, supplies were still lacking, provisions were rotting, sailors and soldiers were dying at an appalling rate, surviving seamen were dispirited. There was nothing grand about Philip's Armada when Fuentes saw it.

Even in the best of times, Spanish ships were beset with problems that made conditions on them squalid and life aboard them only slightly better than wretched. William Monson, an Englishman who studied Philip's fleet, wrote a report of his findings, which he titled, "The Ill Management of the Spanish Ships." In it he wrote that "their ships are kept foul and beastly, like hog sties and sheep cots in comparison with ours." The organization of shipboard life assigned no one the duty of swabbing the decks to keep them clean. Belowdecks, in the ships' galleys, there were too many cooks. There was no single set of galley workers to provide meals for a ship's entire complement. Rather, Monson reported, "each man is his own cook and he that is not able to dress his meat may fast." In other words, those who could not cook had a good chance of not eating. Soldiers stationed aboard the ships were organized into squads of eight or ten men, and each squad drew its allotment of rations from a central storeroom and took its turn moving into the ship's galley to cook and eat, each squad using its own cooking and eating utensils. Cleanup duty apparently was not included in the rotation of squads in and out of the common galley, and ships grew filthy and fetid belowdecks. Aboard the galleys and galleasses, both partly powered by oars, the enslaved rowers, chained to their benches, not only slept where they sat but also were often forced to defecate and urinate there, adding to the ships' stench and squalor. In those and other unsanitary conditions aboard the Spanish vessels, sickness became commonplace. Little wonder that the Armada's crews and seagoing soldiers suffered a high rate of illness and death.

By the time Fuentes reached Lisbon, the sixty-two-year-old Santa Cruz was desperately striving to get everything necessary aboard the ships and the ships themselves in readiness to finally sail in February, Philip's latest deadline. On February 9, however, Santa Cruz collapsed and died, apparently of typhus, or ship's fever, as it was often called, a disease frequently associated with unhealthy conditions aboard ships and which had taken the lives of many of the Armada's men. Days later Santa Cruz's vice admiral, the duke of Paliano, also died.

The death of Santa Cruz was a severe loss to the Enterprise, if not in its preparation, certainly in its planned execution. Philip, though, evidently felt some relief at Santa Cruz's having been removed from the scene, making way for someone Philip thought could do a better job. He even went so far as to suggest that Santa Cruz's death was a sort of divine blessing. "God has shown me a favor," he commented, "by removing the marquis now, rather than when the Armada is at sea."

Philip's next move was to replace Santa Cruz. Having anticipated Santa Cruz's removal by Fuentes, he had already picked a successor and on the same day that he received news of Santa Cruz's death, Philip sent notification to Lisbon that he was appointing a new Captain General of the Ocean Sea to command the Armada. His choice for the job this time was his cousin Alonso Pérez de Guzmán, the thirty-seven-year-old duke of Medina Sidonia and captain general of the Spanish province of Andalusia, a man of imposing credentials and impressive wealth. Passed over were such experienced naval commanders as Juan Martínez de Recalde and Alonso Martínez de Leiva, both of whom had applied for the job.

Medina Sidonia had an interesting personal life, having married a ten-year-old princess when he was twenty-one. Once she had become old enough to consummate the marriage, he went on to father sixteen children by her. He also had a military record. He had commanded an army that had helped Philip take over Portugal in 1580. He had led the force that had arrived at Cádiz in time to prevent Francis Drake's sacking of the city in 1587. He had a reputation for keeping a cool head under pressure and had shown his ability as an administrator in managing his extensive estates—which comprised one of the largest landholdings in all of Europe—and in organizing and equipping the treasure-laden convoys that sailed between the Spanish province of Andalusia and America. He furthermore knew something of navigation and seamanship, although it was largely book knowledge. What he lacked was experience as a naval commander, the sort of combat credentials that had given eminence to the late marquis of Santa Cruz.

For that reason, and some others, Medina Sidonia begged off the appointment. "My health is not equal to such a voyage," he wrote to Philip's secretary, Juan de Idiáquez, "for I know by experience of the little I have been at sea that I am always seasick and always catch a cold. My family is burdened with a debt of nine hundred thousand ducats, and I could not spend a *real* [as he would be expected to do] in the king's service. Since I have had no experience either of the sea or of war, I cannot feel that I ought to command so important an enterprise. I know nothing of what the marquis of Santa Cruz has been doing, or of what intelligence he has of England, so that I feel I should give but a bad account of myself, commanding thus blindly, and being obliged to rely on the advice of others, without knowing good from bad or which of my advisors might want to deceive or displace me." He concluded the letter with a recommendation. "The Adelantado Major of Castile [Martín de Padilla, who had commanded a squadron at Lepanto] is much fitter for this post than I. He is a man of much experience in military and naval matters, and a good Christian, too."

Philip dismissed the protest. Not well himself, he was in no mood to argue. He had collapsed during Christmas 1587 and had been confined to his bed for four weeks after that. Exhausted by the stress of planning and preparing for the invasion, he remained, in the words of one report, "languid and weak" through February.[1] Besides, he apparently thought Medina Sidonia was merely being gallantly modest. He answered Medina Sidonia's objections by telling him that he was exhibiting "an excess of modesty" and further told him that, "It is I who must judge of your capabilities and parts and I am fully satisfied. . . . Prepare yourself to the performance of this service in the manner I expect from you."

Medina Sidonia tried again. He wrote another letter on February 18. In it he became more insistent, to the extent that he sharply criticized the Enterprise, revealing his belief that the whole idea was a mistake and that the expedition was bound to fail, the Armada lacking the necessary overwhelming superiority over English naval forces. The critical letter came to Idiáquez and to another of Philip's confidants, Cristóbal de Moura, who, reading it, were shocked by Medina Sidonia's words and balked at passing the letter along to Philip. Instead, they wrote back to Medina Sidonia, upbraiding him for his attitude as well as his words. "We did not dare to show his Majesty what you have just written," they informed him. They told him he was resisting not only the king's will but God's. "Do not depress us with fears for the fate of the Armada," they said, "because in such a cause God will make sure it succeeds."

They let him know he was treading dangerous ground by refusing to accept this honor from the king's hand. "Remember," they warned him, "that the reputation and esteem you currently enjoy for courage and wisdom would entirely be forfeited if what you wrote to us became generally known (although we shall keep it secret)." In the face of their threats and blackmail, and after being refused an audience with Philip, Medina Sidonia caved in and accepted the dubious honor.

He arrived in Lisbon to take on his new responsibility on March 15, 1588. Waiting for him there was a peppy note from Philip. "If I were not needed so much here [in Madrid], to provide what is necessary for that [Enterprise] and for many other things," Philip wrote, sounding very much like a politician, "I would be very pleased to join [you and the Armada] and I would do so with great confidence that it would go very well for me."

Showing the perspicacity that had helped gain him the job, Medina Sidonia had had Philip order Santa Cruz's secretary to let him take a look at the late captain general's papers before they could be removed beyond Medina Sidonia's access. Those papers included the Armada's battle plans, intelligence reports on the enemy, and administrative records, the complete fleet files of the former commander, essential to the new commander. Another of his first actions was to assemble a cadre of advisers. To that group he appointed Diego de Maldonado and Marolín de Juan, both experienced naval captains, along with three of his best squadron commanders—Pedro de Valdés, Miguel de Oquendo, and Juan Martínez de Recalde—and an Italian naval artillery expert. He later would add Diego Flores de Valdés, who was still stationed in Cádiz when Medina Sidonia arrived in Lisbon.

He sought their advice and lent an ear to their complaints, particularly their belief that the Armada lacked sufficient ordnance. The fleet's galleons and galleasses were underequipped with heavy guns, and the ordnance of the vessels that had been seized to bolster the royal fleet consisted almost entirely of light guns suitable only as antipersonnel weapons or for damaging the enemy's rigging, not nearly heavy enough to match the big guns of the English in an artillery slugfest. Medina Sidonia quickly began trying to acquire more and heavier artillery for his captains. He pressed as hard as he could to expedite delivery of promised new brass and bronze pieces from the foundries, a matter that had plagued Santa Cruz. He ordered pieces that had been captured in earlier engagements—including trophies taken in the battle of St.-Quentin in 1557 and in the battle at Pavia in 1525—to be brought to Lisbon, as well as the seventy or so pieces confiscated from foreign ships docked in Spanish ports. He ordered a redistribution of the available ordnance, a move that proved only partly effective, for ships commanded by men who were highest in the aristocratic hierarchy tended to keep their hold on a disproportionate share of the guns, without regard to the ships' purpose or mission or the abilities of their commanders.

The Armada's firepower presented a continuing problem, defying resolution by even the best efforts of such a redoubtable administrator as the duke of Medina Sidonia. Part of the problem was caused by the common idea that proper naval warfare was waged by the ancient tactic of closing on enemy vessels and boarding them, fighting face-to-face using handheld weapons, thus obviating the need for guns big enough to destroy ships rather than only men. It was not until the voices of younger, fresh-thinking commanders were heard that the Armada's lack of sufficient firepower became a worrisome, urgent issue. The crash program to manufacture and otherwise acquire additional ordnance contributed its own weight to the problem. Spanish and Portuguese foundries, suddenly urged to produce more heavy weapons, discovered shortages of iron and copper, ordnance's necessary materials, as well as a shortage of experienced metalworkers. As a result, production time lengthened, and quality greatly suffered. One contemporary account complained that "some of their pieces (and not a few) are bored awry . . . some are crooked . . . other of unequal bores . . . or full of honeycombs and flaws. . . . [They] will either break, split, or blowingly spring their metals and (besides that mischief they do) will be utterly unserviceable ever after."[2]

Ordnance and ammunition made elsewhere, some of it originating in England and smuggled out of the country, some of it seized from enemies, particularly the Turks, in past engagements, were also a part of the problem, turning the ships' weaponry into a collection of miscellaneous, mismatched pieces. There was no standard of caliber to measure the guns' bore and no standard for the weight or size of their shot. Guns and shot manufactured in, say, Italy, although ostensibly of comparable caliber, weight, or diameter to those produced in Spain, differed because the unit of measurement also differed. The Armada's cannonballs commonly were up to an inch and a half smaller in diameter than the diameter of the bore of the cannon from which they were to be fired. Hitting an intended target with shot that literally careened through the barrel of the gun that fired it was much more a matter of luck than skill. One of the Armada's vessels, the *Nuestra Señora del Rosario,* according to one report, was found to be using seventeen different calibers of shot, making the firing of each round an unpredictable shot in the dark.

Overruling Philip's chief of artillery, Juan de Acuña Vela, Medina Sidonia ordered new shot to raise the Armada's supply to fifty balls per artillery piece, considerably more than the thirty per gun that had been recommended by

Acuña Vela, an amount that Medina Sidonia's senior general, Francisco de Bobadilla, had complained was inadequate for the Armada's task. "There was a great scarcity of cannonballs," Bobadilla wrote. "The count of Fuentes can bear witness how much I pleaded in the matter with Don Juan de Acuña, telling him that if the enemy did not allow us to board them and if the artillery fight lasted four days, he might tell me what we might do on the fifth if we carried so few rounds." With Philip's approval, Medina Sidonia ordered the additional ammunition. He also procured more powder for the ships' ordnance, creating an additional problem, for the new powder was stronger than what the gunners had been using and in some cases would burst the barrels of poorly cast guns, killing or maiming the gun crews.

Medina Sidonia ordered more weapons for the Armada's seaborne soldiers, too—muskets, harquebuses, calivers, and pikes—and body armor as well, all to prepare them for the expected close-and-board battles.

Provisions to feed the men of the Armada were another problem. The biscuits, salted meat, and fish that were packed in casks and loaded aboard the ships in the fall of 1587, when the Armada had been expected to sail that October, had spoiled and had to be replaced, while at the same time seamen and soldiers had to be fed during their long wait for the Armada's sailing.

The shortage of food, lack of adequate clothing, and the want of money to meet the Armada's huge payroll, together with the miserable months of confinement aboard the idle ships, set off a steady stream of desertions, and as many as two thousand peasants from the Portuguese countryside had to be conscripted under threats of death to replace the deserters. The conscripts, however, did little or nothing to relieve the fleet's increasing shortage of able-bodied seamen and skilled gunners.

When Medina Sidonia ordered a report on the Armada's personnel, as well as an inventory of the ships and everything they carried, he learned there were some 33,000 men intending to sail aboard the fleet's ships. That number included 8,450 sailors, 2,088 galley slaves, 19,295 soldiers, and about 3,000 miscellaneous passengers—noblemen, their servants and retainers (Medina Sidonia himself was taking sixty servants), priests, friars, physicians, and an assortment of administrators and officials. About half of the fleet's soldiers were trained professionals, many of them battle veterans. The rest were recruits who before joining the Armada's fighting force had been simple farmhands, shepherds, or peasant workers, strangers to life at sea. Seamen and soldiers comprised a motley lot of nationalities—Italians, Sicilians, Nether-landers, and Germans as well as Portuguese, Castilians, and Basques, and even, according to one report, some two hundred Englishmen, either expa-triated recusants seeking to reclaim their property, their careers, or the prac-tice of their faith in the land of their birth, or else unavoidably going as galley slaves. Each nationality group spoke its own language and tended to regard those of other groups with suspicion. Command of the individual ships was vested in the senior officers of the fighting force rather than in the ships' cap-tains, and the seagoing soldiers tended to treat the sailors as their inferiors, which frequently led to fights between the two groups. Many of the officers had been given their commands because of their social status and connec-tions, merely "because they are gentlemen," the veteran naval commander Juan Martínez de Recalde complained. "Very few of them therefore are sol-diers or know what to do." As many as a thousand of them were simply for-tune hunters, hoping to lay claim to the property of vanquished English heretics.

One of Medina Sidonia's first actions after arriving in Lisbon was to in-spect the Armada's ships and determine their condition and expedite repairs. There were then approximately 104 vessels that comprised the Armada, and after having been in Lisbon only three days, Medina Sidonia decided that more ships were needed. He wrote to Philip to ask for more. Within six weeks, by the end of April, the vessels in greatest need of repair had been put in shipshape and Medina Sidonia's plea for more ships had been answered with an additional thirty vessels, bringing the Armada's total to 134, includ-ing twenty galleons, four huge galleasses, and four galleys. In the process of making the fleet ready to do battle against the English, the old heads of Philip's navy had prevailed upon Medina Sidonia to allow alterations to the newer ships that had been designed along lines similar to those of the English fleet's sleek race-built vessels. The naval traditionalists, clinging to the old close-and-board tactic, did not like the new design and pushed for the accus-tomed castles to be erected on the new ships' sterns and bows, from which the crews of enemy vessels could be fired on. Apparently unaware of the im-portant disadvantages those forecastles and sterncastles presented to the ves-sels' speed and maneuverability, Medina Sidonia let the old heads have their way. Merchant ships that had been pressed into service in the Armada also were altered to provide them with the awkward castles.

Medina Sidonia, with the help of his cadre of advisers, organized the Armada into a front line composed of the four powerful galleasses and three squadrons of ten ships each, and a second line composed of four squadrons of ten ships each. Those two lines comprised the awesome fighting front of the formation. Positioned behind them were the four oar-powered galleys, shallow-draft craft that were susceptible to swamping in rough seas. Another squadron was formed from the fleet's thirty-four pinnaces, the smaller, faster vessels that would be used for scouting and as dispatch bearers. The remainder of the Armada's vessels, twenty-two hulks, were positioned at the rear of the formation, freighted with everything needed to equip, arm, and maintain Philip's invasion army, including massive siege guns and their carriages and ammunition, lumber to construct fortifications, construction tools, and a staggering variety and quantity of supplies. One of the hulks, the *Santiago, la urca de las mujeres,* the ship of the women, carried the wives of some of the ships' officers.

As a further act of preparation, Medina Sidonia provided his ship captains with charts—not altogether accurate—showing the Armada's intended route and the English coastline, something the late marquis of Santa Cruz had not thought to do.

By the end of April 1588, the Armada was all but ready to go. It was christened *"Felicissima Armada"*—the most fortunate fleet—but those who saw it approaching readiness called it *"la Invencible Armada"*—the invincible fleet. So menacingly mighty, so frightful, did Philip consider it that he had a written summary put together listing each of the Armada's ships, describing them, detailing their armament, and giving the names of their officers, and had the document printed and copies of it distributed in Rome, the Vatican, Naples, Milan, Venice, Cologne, Paris, and elsewhere in Europe, all to impress both enemies and friends. Venice's ambassador to Madrid, for one, was not all that impressed. He sent a report to his government saying that "the Englishmen are of a different quality than the Spaniards, bearing a name above all the West for being expert and enterprising in maritime affairs, and the finest fighters upon the sea. . . . The English never yield; and although they be put to flight and broken, they ever return athirst for revenge, to renew the attack so long as they have breath."

Pope Sixtus V, ever spiritually minded, did what he could to encourage those who sailed against England's heretical queen. He issued a special indulgence to everyone aboard the Armada's vessels. Those who stayed behind and merely prayed for the Armada's success also received an indulgence. The latter extension of grace presumably applied also to Philip and his family, who were reported to be praying for the Armada's success three hours a day, in relays in the Escorial. Throughout Madrid people marched in religious processions and took part in religious ceremonies every Sunday, assailing the Almighty with demonstrations of their ardor, imploring His favor for the success of the Enterprise of England.

In Lisbon the religious fervor whipped up for the Enterprise was especially directed toward the men who would sail with the Armada. One prominent Jesuit priest, Pedro de Ribadeneira, wrote what he called an "Exhortation to the Soldiers and Captains Who Sail on This Campaign to England," in which he assured his readers and listeners that "We are not going on a difficult enterprise, because God our Lord, whose cause and most holy faith we defend, will go ahead, and with such a Captain we have nothing to fear."

To make sure they were not behaving in ways inconsistent with their spiritual mission, the Armada's crews and troops were issued instructions specifically prohibiting blasphemous oaths, gambling, fighting among themselves, sodomy, and other sinful offenses, and their ships were carefully searched for women who might have been smuggled aboard. What was more, the Armada's entire complement was required to go to confession and to take communion before the fleet was to sail.

Early on the morning of April 25, 1588, as the day of departure grew nearer, Medina Sidonia, accompanied by Philip's Portuguese viceroy, who was also his nephew, Cardinal Archduke Albert, proceeded from Lisbon's royal palace at the head of a stately parade of Spanish grandees, brightly uniformed harquebusiers, and drably clad priests, all marching to the city's cathedral to seek a blessing on the Enterprise now so imminent. Noticeably absent from the procession were virtually all of Portugal's nobility, who apparently had little interest in their conqueror's plan to seize Elizabeth's England and purge its soul. At the cathedral's entrance, ready to receive Medina Sidonia and the cardinal archduke, stood Lisbon's archbishop, who welcomed them and led the paraders inside, where he then dutifully celebrated Mass and pronounced his blessing upon the Enterprise. After that, Medina Sidonia made his way to the altar and took from it the banner woven, it was said, by the ladies of Portugal to be used as the Armada's official standard, emblazoned with the arms of Spain at its center, flanked by a crucifix on one side and an image of the Virgin Mary on the other. Beneath the arms and the images was a Latin inscription, *"Exurge Domine et vindica causam,"* words drawn from Psalm 74:22—Arise, O God, and defend your cause.

The banner was carried from the cathedral and across the city's main plaza to the Dominican convent where Medina Sidonia laid it upon the convent's altar as an act of consecration. It was then taken outside again and carried between lines of kneeling sailors and soldiers as the Armada's friars intoned the absolution and indulgence granted to the men of the Armada by the pope. From there the banner was taken aboard Medina Sidonia's flagship, the *San Martín,* expropriated from the Portuguese navy, and as the Armada's commander came aboard, to the booming sounds of artillery salutes, the banner was hoisted to the top of the mainmast where it fluttered brightly in the stiff breeze.

It had all been a dramatic and moving ceremony, a sacred send-off for the fleet about to embark on its holy task, a mission so important to Spain, its king and, in his mind at least, the cause of Christianity. Yet Philip failed to show up for the event, not bothering to travel from Madrid to Lisbon to participate, to exhibit his support, give his own blessing to the undertaking, and inspire the men who would bear the burden of accomplishing his aims.

As the ships lay in a mile-long line in the Tagus River, awaiting departure, the boys of the crews stood around their ships' mainmasts every day at dawn and dusk to sing matins and the Ave Maria, and the ships' priests celebrated Mass, all in keeping with the spiritual nature of the venture. Just in case the spiritual motivation failed to provide enough impetus for them in their task, the officers, crews, and fighting men of the Armada were promised an earthly reward by their king, who ordered that each ship summon its personnel with drums and read to the men his proclamation stating that although any of Queen Elizabeth's ships captured by them would become Spanish royal property, all other English ships they captured would become theirs. And for the Armada's commander, Philip, still in Madrid, offered words of pious encouragement, telling Medina Sidonia that "as all victories are the gift of God Almighty, and the cause we champion is so exclusively His, we may look for His aid and favor, unless by our sins we render ourselves unworthy."

Not all of the officers of the Armada, although perhaps no less spiritually minded than their king, were so confident. The pope's representative at the Lisbon send-off ceremony asked one of the expedition's chief officers, unnamed in the representative's report to the pope, "If you meet the English armada in the Channel, do you expect to win the battle?"

"Of course," the Spanish officer replied,

"How can you be sure?" the pope's envoy asked.

"It's very simple," the officer answered, with a hint of sarcasm. "It is well known that we fight in God's cause. So, when we meet the English, God will surely arrange matters so that we can grapple and board them, either by sending some strange freak of weather or, more likely, just by depriving the English of their wits. If we can come to close quarters, Spanish valor and Spanish steel (and the great masses of soldiers we shall have on board) will make our victory certain. But unless God helps us by a miracle," the officer went on, "the English, who have faster and handier ships than ours, and many more long-range guns, and who know their advantage just as well as we do, will never close with us at all, but stand aloof and knock us to pieces with their culverins, without our being able to do them any serious hurt. So," the officer concluded, "we are sailing against England in the confident hope of a miracle."[3]

On May 9, everything at last in readiness, the ships raised their anchors and began their descent of the Tagus, but most got no farther than the fortress at Belem before contrary winds, blowing in from the Atlantic, halted the vessels in the river. There they waited for a change in the weather, which over Western Europe that year was unusual for May. Heavy rains, hailstorms, and high winds made it seem more like December. For three long weeks the ships were idled, bobbing at anchor near the river's mouth.

While they waited, Philip, micromanaging from Madrid the fleet he had never seen, wrote to Medina Sidonia to tell him that according to his latest reports—apparently received from Bernardino de Mendoza, the onetime Spanish ambassador to Elizabeth's court and now ambassador in Paris—the English fleet was very weak and that Drake perhaps would not even engage the Armada, but if he did, he would attack it from the rear after the Armada had passed Plymouth or he would attack only after the Spanish invasion force had been landed. Philip told Medina Sidonia to be careful not to weaken the Armada before taking Drake on, that after meeting up with Parma he could attack the English fleet but until then he should avoid battle unless forced into it, and that no matter what occurred, including an assault by Drake on the Spanish coast, Medina Sidonia was not to be deterred from keeping his planned rendezvous with Parma's army. "Even if Drake should have sailed for these waters," Philip wrote, ". . . you should not turn back but continue on your course, not seeking out the enemy even if he should remain here. If, however, he should pursue and overtake you, you may attack him, as you should also do if you meet Drake with his fleet at the entrance to the Channel."

Philip told his captain general that the English ships were faster than his, as if he didn't already know it, and that they carried more long-range ordnance, which he also already knew, and so he must be careful not to get too close, but he should maneuver to gain the wind advantage, bear down on the English vessels, close on them, board them, and take the fight to their decks—instructions repeated from an earlier dispatch in which he told Medina Sidonia, "There is little to say with regard to the mode of fighting and the handling of the Armada on the day of battle . . . [but] it must be borne in mind that the enemy's object will be to fight at long distance, in consequence of his advantage in artillery. . . . The aim of our men, on the contrary, must be to bring him to close quarters and grapple with him, and you will have to be very careful to have this carried out." It was all easy for Philip to say, but how exactly Medina Sidonia was to make it happen Philip never mentioned.

Medina Sidonia begged to differ with Philip on parts of his instructions and while the Armada continued to await a wind change, he wrote to Philip saying, "The opinions of those whom I have consulted here is that the best course would be to break up the enemy's sea forces first. When this is done . . . the rest will be safe and easy." Philip conceded that the Armada would have to do battle with the English fleet, but he insisted that Medina Sidonia make straight for the channel, without diversion, distraction, or unnecessary delay. The massive battle between the two fleets, he figured, could come soon enough when the Armada reached the Cape of Margate, England's southeasternmost point, which projects sharply into the upper end of the Strait of Dover, where Elizabeth's fleet was expected to stand in an attempt to prevent the Armada's passage. Ultimately doing battle with the English fleet, Philip allowed, was "the essence of the business" of the Armada, but he instructed Medina Sidonia that he absolutely must keep his appointment with Parma.

On May 28 the wind shifted enough to allow the Armada's vessels to continue their descent of the Tagus after their frustrating three-week wait. Medina Sidonia's flagship, the *San Martin,* led the way, sailing smartly before the royal galleons, which fired an artillery salute as they glided past St. Julian cas-

tle on their way into the open sea. Still contending with the wind, the remaining vessels took another day to clear the mouth of the Tagus and
emerge into the Atlantic. Now a stiff breeze was blowing from the north-
northwest, and as the ships formed up to begin their voyage up the coast of
Portugal and northwestern Spain, they were sailing directly into the wind.
Movement was extremely slow, the ships being careful to hold the Armada's
planned formation and thus making no better speed than that of the slowest
vessels, the freight-carrying hulks that were bringing up the rear. So slow was
their progress that two weeks after they had cleared the bar at the mouth of
the Tagus, the ships had reached only Cape Finisterre, on the coast of Spain's
panhandle, some 160 miles distance.

Now Medina Sidonia faced a problem as threatening as the weather. The
Armada was running out of food. The three-week delay while idled by the
contrary wind in the Tagus and the snaillike pace of the ships in the ocean, together with the enormous spoilage of food in barrels and casks stored aboard
the vessels, had created a serious shortage of provisions. Those cargoes of barrel staves that Francis Drake had captured and burned at Sagres were proving
crucial in the feeding of the Armada's personnel. To replace the seasoned oak
staves lost to Drake, the Spanish victualers had had to use green wood that
warped out of shape, leaving the barrels neither airtight nor watertight. The
barrels' contents of biscuit, grain, and other dry food had become fouled by
mold and maggots. Much of the cheese and salted fish and beef and bacon had
become rancid. The casks of wine had soured, and much of the stored water
had become foul-tasting and undrinkable. Many of the men who in desperation ate and drank the spoiled provisions became sick, and ultimately the rotten food and foul drink had to be thrown overboard. Medina Sidonia's concern
over the water shortage was expressed in a letter he wrote to the duke of
Parma. "What I fear most," he said, "is lack of water. . . . I do not see where
we can obtain any more. It will be necessary . . . to have all the casks that can
be obtained got ready and filled with water to send to the Armada."

Shortly after putting to sea, Medina Sidonia sent letters to the governor of
Galicia province, in the northwest corner of Spain, asking him to provide the
Armada with a fresh supply of food and water when it reached Cape Finisterre. The Armada's slow northward voyage, however, had kept the governor's supply ships waiting so long that the new provisions also had begun to
rot, and the supply ships returned to their ports without meeting the Armada.

Meanwhile the wind shifted. It began blowing so strongly from the south that Medina Sidonia sent a message to the duke of Parma, waiting in the Netherlands for the Armada's arrival, saying that he hoped to effect the rendezvous within fifteen days after his message was delivered. Expecting to see action soon, Philip's seagoing army officers conducted an inspection of their troops, and ship captains cleared their decks to prepare for action. Medina Sidonia was torn between pressing ahead while the wind was at his back and holding his ships off Cape Finisterre to await the supply ships he expected at any time. Prudence and the advice of his council moved him to wait, which he did for five days before giving up on the supply ships and in desperation deciding to head for La Coruña to take on the needed food and water.

By the evening of June 19, Medina Sidonia's *San Martín* and thirty-five other ships of the Armada had anchored in the La Coruña harbor, and the remainder of the fleet, including the freight-carrying hulks as well as the galleasses and Juan Martínez de Recalde's entire squadron of fighting ships, was standing at sea, near the harbor entrance, waiting for the light of the next day's dawn so that the vessels could pass the headland and safely enter the harbor.

During the night, however, a fierce gale came up suddenly from the southwest, its winds so strong that even ships in the shelter of La Coruña harbor were blown from their anchorages, some suffering damage in collisions with other vessels. The Armada's ships that had anchored off the headland were forced to haul up their anchors and run before the menacing wind, widely scattering across miles and miles of open sea. The storm lasted two days, and it wasn't until the afternoon of June 21 that the winds had calmed enough for Medina Sidonia to order out some of the fleet's pinnaces to search for the scattered parts of his invincible Armada. He also dispatched searchers to see if any of the vessels had made it into nearby ports. Some had. Two galleasses were found at Gijón, on the Bay of Biscay, and ten other ships had sheltered at Viveiro, also on the Bay of Biscay. Recalde arrived back at La Coruña on June 22 with two galleons and eight other vessels.

Even so, on June 24, four days after the storm, two galleasses and twenty-eight other vital warships, including two of Recalde's best ships, remained unaccounted for. Among the missing were the ships bearing the army's artillery. Moreover, many of the vessels that had returned to La Coruña or had been found elsewhere had suffered severe damage, including lost masts, spars, and anchors, and many of their hulls had been so strained by the heavy seas that they had begun leaking. Besides the loss of ships there was the enormous loss of the men aboard them—some six thousand soldiers and sailors from the Armada's effective force of twenty-two thousand men. To make matters still worse, many of the remaining sixteen thousand men had fallen ill with typhus or scurvy or dysentery. And there was still the matter of providing the Armada with the needed food and water.

To Medina Sidonia the Armada's situation—and that of the Enterprise itself—seemed so dire that on June 24 he wrote Philip a long letter detailing the fleet's woes and making a two-pronged argument—one theological, one pragmatic—for calling off the entire venture. Showing extraordinary courage, he reminded Philip that from the very beginning of his taking command of the Armada he, Medina Sidonia, had had doubts about the probable success of the Enterprise, that from the start the Armada had had no better than an even chance of accomplishing its mission, and that staking a nation's fate on a force no more than equal to that of its enemy was generally considered to be an imprudent risk. The storm, moreover, had so reduced the strength of the Armada that it was now not even the equal of the enemy. "I recall," Medina Sidonia wrote, "the great force Your Majesty collected for the conquest of Portugal, although that country was within our own boundaries and many of the people were in your favor. Well, Sire, how do you think we can attack so great a country as England with such a force as ours is now?"

The storm, Medina Sidonia argued, had theological significance. It was extremely unusual for such a storm to have occurred in June, ordinarily the best time of year for sailing, and the fact of its occurrence, he suggested, must have had something to do with God's will. "Since this is the cause of our Lord," he wrote, "to Whose care it has been—and is being—so much entrusted, it would appear that what has just happened must be His doing, for some reason." Maybe, just maybe, the Armada commander deduced, God was telling them that the Armada's mission should be scrubbed and its ships and men turned back.

In view of all that, Medina Sidonia asked as humbly as he could, would it not be better to pull the plug on the whole operation and try to find a way to make peace with Spain's enemies through diplomatic negotiation? Certainly, he concluded, the Armada's situation made it "essential that the enterprise we are engaged in should be given the closest scrutiny."

On June 27, while waiting for Philip's response to his letter, Medina Sidonia held another council of war to talk over the Armada's situation with his chief officers. Following a lengthy discussion, nine of the ten council members agreed that the Armada was now too weak to continue with its mission. Medina Sidonia forwarded the council's recommendation to the king.

Despite another spell of illness, the sixty-one-year-old Philip gave Medina Sidonia's letter long and hard consideration, then dictated his reply to his "Duke and cousin," which began: "I have received the letter written in your own hand, dated 24 June. From what I know of you, I believe that your bringing all these matters to my attention arises solely from your zeal to serve me and a desire to succeed in your command. The certainty that this is so prompts me to be franker with you than I should be with another."[4]

Philip then handled the duke's theological argument. "If this were an unjust war," he asserted, "one could indeed take this storm as a sign from Our Lord to cease offending Him; but being as just as it is, one cannot believe that He will disband it, but will rather grant it more favor than we could hope."

He then took up the Armada's lack of overwhelming strength. "It is true," he said, "that if we could have things exactly as we wished, we would rather have other vessels, but under the present circumstances, the expedition must not be abandoned on account of this difficulty." He ordered Medina Sidonia to make repairs as best he could and take aboard whatever provisions were available. "But," he warned the commander, "you must take great care that the stores are really preserved and not allow yourself to be deceived as you were before."

Finally he told Medina Sidonia grandly that "Every great enterprise is beset with difficulties, and the merit lies in overcoming them. I have dedicated this enterprise to God. . . . Stir yourself then, to do your duty."[5] Having brushed aside all of Medina Sidonia's arguments, the king commanded him to sail on.

Medina Sidonia meekly replied, "Your Majesty may rest assured that no efforts of mine shall be spared." Sail on he would.

To make certain he did, Philip ordered Diego Flores de Valdés, commander of the Armada's Castilian squadron, to station himself aboard Medina Sidonia's flagship as the captain general's principal naval adviser, and he dispatched one of his royal officers from Madrid to see to it that Medina Sidonia followed orders.

ᐊᔥ 18. THE RULERS OF THE SEA

On July 21, 1588, with most of his storm-scattered fleet reunited and the ships' damage repaired, Medina Sidonia took the Armada to sea once again, sailing smartly out of La Coruña, heading northeastward through calm waters, a southerly breeze at his back. After four days of steady progress, however, the storm-battered fleet was struck by more heavy weather, and ships were again scattered and damaged. When at last the storm abated and the sun rose bright on July 28, more than forty ships were missing from the vast formation. Medina Sidonia sent out a pinnace to see if any of the missing vessels, blown before the gale's winds, might have already reached the designated rendezvous location at the western entrance to the English Channel. In the meantime, the fleet resumed its voyage, and repairs were made to the damaged ships as they sailed.

The next day the pinnace came back with news to gladden the commander's harried heart. Most of the missing ships had gathered off the Isles of Scilly, at the rendezvous point, and were there waiting for him and the rest of the Armada.

The fleet caught up to the waiting vessels late that afternoon, and at about 4 P.M., as his flagship continued on, Medina Sidonia caught sight of the Lizard, the headland near the southwestern tip of England. After so many days of toil and having suffered so many of the sea's perils and torments, the Armada had arrived at last at the land it had come to conquer for God and Spain's king. His spirit enlivened by the sight of it, Medina Sidonia ordered the Armada's blessed banner, the symbol of his holy mission, raised on the *San Martín*'s mainmast and Philip's royal standard raised on the foremast, an act that set off the hoisting of provincial and personal standards and battle flags on other vessels of the fleet. Medina Sidonia also ordered signal guns fired to call every man of the expedition to prayer, thanking the Almighty for the Armada's safe arrival and, as he said, "beseeching Our Lord to give us victory against the enemies of His Holy Faith." At 7 P.M., as his vessels drew closer toward land, he issued orders to his fleet to shorten sail about ten miles from the English shore. There they would hold up and wait for daylight.

At dawn of the next day, July 30, Medina Sidonia could see the signal fires newly lighted by English sentries posted along the coast. In the light of the new day, the sentries had spotted the Armada and were signaling smoky warnings to their compatriots up the coast. Before setting sail again, Medina Sidonia summoned his squadron commanders to the *San Martín* for a council of war and conferred with them about how to proceed from their present position off the Lizard. The council members decided that the fleet should advance no farther eastward than the Isle of Wight until the details of the rendezvous with Parma had been worked out. Their reason was that once the Armada's ships passed the Strait of Dover, there would be no deepwater port in which they could find shelter in case a storm suddenly blew in and threatened to run them aground on the shoals along the Netherlands coast. Medina Sidonia and his commanders wanted to be sure Parma's army was ready to be embarked immediately upon the ships' arrival, so that the Armada would not be unnecessarily exposed to potential ruin from a storm. Their decision, of course, was contrary to Philip's order that the Armada should not stop till it met Parma's army.

Twenty-four-year-old squadron commander Alonso Martínez de Leiva, eager for battle, argued for an immediate assault on Plymouth, where, according to the crew of a captured fishing boat, the English fleet now lay in port, vulnerable to a massive, sudden Spanish attack that could cripple England's naval defenses. Leiva's proposal was supported by Oquendo and Recalde, two of the Armada's veteran commanders. They proposed that if the council decided against a Plymouth assault, however, the Armada should proceed directly to Dunkirk. Other members of the council argued that the channel into Plymouth harbor was too narrow to allow more than two or three ships to enter abreast, denying the Armada a massive assault, and the shore batteries at the harbor entrance posed too great a threat. In addition, such an attack, made before Parma's troops had been landed in England, would also be a violation of Philip's orders. All things considered, Medina Sidonia decided to forgo an attack on Plymouth.

The council of war having concluded, the squadron commanders returned to their ships, and the Armada got under way once more. Its massive formation put the galleasses and the squadron commanded by Martín Jiménez de Bertendona in the van and behind it came the Armada's main body, including a squadron of galleons, with Medina Sidonia's flagship in the lead. The squadrons from Andalusia and Guipúzcoa followed the main body, forming two wings, with the hulks positioned between them. In the rear came Recalde's squadron and the rest of the galleons, the entire mass of vessels making a cautious advance up the channel, presenting a fearsome sight to watchers on the shore and the crews of fishing boats and other small craft caught in its path as it sailed deeper into enemy waters.

In the early light of Friday, July 29, a lookout atop the mainmast of the bark *Golden Hind,* one of several English vessels patrolling the channel's west entrance, had spied a large gathering of Spanish ships off the Isles of Scilly, as many as fifty, bobbing on the Atlantic's swells, sails furled, as if awaiting the arrival of another part of its fleet. The lookout shouted his observation down to his captain, Thomas Fleming, a privateer who had answered the call to his country's defense (and to the possibility of enemy prizes). With great haste, Fleming's sleek, speedy vessel made straight for Plymouth, about a hundred miles to the east, to deliver the urgent warning that the Spanish had arrived.

Around 4 o'clock that afternoon, about the same time that Medina Sidonia was sighting England's shore, the *Golden Hind* anchored in Plymouth harbor, and Fleming immediately went ashore to find his squadron commander, Vice Admiral Francis Drake, and give his report. He found Drake on Plymouth's bowling green, absorbed in a game of bowls. Hearing the details of the report, Drake, with characteristic self-confidence, reportedly replied to Fleming, "We have time enough to finish the game and beat the Spaniards, too."

Actually, there was little the English fleet could do at the moment. With the tide flooding into Plymouth harbor and the wind holding against it, the fleet would have to wait till the tide turned, which was expected to occur around nine o'clock that evening. Nevertheless, the ships' crews were soon standing ready to put to sea at the earliest opportunity, some having assumed their stations so hurriedly that they had not finished loading their provisions aboard. While darkness crept over the bustling harbor, the tide began to turn, and the contrary southwesterly wind moderated somewhat. Orders were then issued for the fleet's crews to begin warping their vessels out of the harbor, a laborious process by which a ship's anchors were placed in the ship's longboats and rowed out as far as allowed by the length of the cables—the thick hawsers, or warps, to which the anchors were attached—and then heaved into the water to sink and grasp the sea's bottom while crewmen aboard the ship strained around a capstan to haul the warp back in, thus slowly, tediously moving the ship forward toward the position of the anchor on the sea floor. When the anchor was raised, it would again be loaded into the ship's longboat, and the process repeated. Other ships were simply towed out of the harbor with lines fastened from the ships to their longboats, strenuously propelled by stout rowers.

Once out of the confines of the harbor channel and in the broad waters of Plymouth Sound, the bay that leads to Plymouth harbor, the longboats returned to their ships, which now anchored in the lee of Rame Head, waiting in the dark for the emergence of the rest of the fleet. While they waited, lookouts aloft, peering into the night, kept a watchful eye to the southwest, whence would come the Spanish menace, the time of its approach a matter of guesswork only. As the fleet continued to snake out from Plymouth harbor, the night slowly passed into the dawn of July 30. The sun was hidden above low, dark clouds, from which fell a squally rain, but there was light enough to reveal the empty sea to the southwest.

With fifty-four of his ships now clear of the harbor and ready to sail, Lord Admiral Howard moved the fleet out of the sound and into the open water of the English Channel, sailing off to the south and west in the face of the southwesterly wind, tacking and zigzagging against it, mindful that with the wind at the Armada's back, as it was, the enemy would hold the weather-gauge advantage in battle, a situation every fighting sailor wanted to avoid. Howard's progress against the wind was slow, and it was not until about three o'clock that afternoon that the fleet reached Eddystone Rock, the craggy islet jutting above the channel waters fourteen miles south-southwest of Plymouth.

Not long after the fleet had passed Eddystone Rock, lookouts high atop the fleet's masts first sighted the enemy, visible only in brief glimpses through the low clouds and the veil of rain. "One hundred and twenty sail," the report came, "whereof there are four galleasses and many ships of great burden."

It was then that Howard began the execution of a remarkable maneuver. Rather than approach the Armada in the face of the wind, he slid across the front of its van, taking advantage of the poor visibility, then waited unseen while the wind carried the Armada farther eastward and past the English fleet, allowing Howard to turn the Armada's right flank and sail in behind the entire

Spanish formation, thereby gaining the weather gauge, all without Medina
Sidonia's knowing it. At the same time, Howard sent a decoy squadron to advance along the English coast, on the Armada's left flank, to let the Spanish see
something of the English fleet and believe it lay ahead of them, when actually
the main body of it was threateningly arrayed behind them.

By dawn of July 31, the maneuver had been accomplished. Then Medina
Sidonia could see what he was facing. His enemy was at his rear, to windward.
He quickly ordered the Armada into its planned combat formation, which took
the shape of a huge crescent, not unlike the formation the Turks used at Lepanto. The two tips of the crescent, two miles or more apart, pointed toward
the English formation, and in between them, forming the thick middle of the
crescent, was positioned the bulk of the Armada. Leiva commanded on the left,
or seaward, side, with about twenty ships. Recalde commanded on the right,
nearest the English shore, with about another twenty ships. Medina Sidonia
commanded in the middle, with the rest of the fleet, which proceeded eastward as the English pursued it.

The formation presented an awesome sight to the English sailors and commanders, providing them a powerful demonstration of the Spaniards' own
skill at naval maneuvers. The rationale for the crescent shape was to guard the
weaker vessels, positioned in the center, with the formation's two arms, composed of the fleet's strongest warships, positioned to entrap between them
any enemy ships daring enough to attack the center and therefore leaving
only the Armada's strongest ships exposed to an attack, which was what
Howard immediately proposed.

Before commencing the fight, however, the lord admiral followed an old
naval tradition by dispatching one of his barks, the *Disdain,* to issue a challenge to the Spanish fleet, signaling the English intention to do battle. The
Disdain raced out from Howard's formation, drew up to the closest Spanish
vessels, and fired a defiant shot into the Armada's formation, then swiftly
turned and beat back to rejoin its fleet.

Now the English ships maneuvered into their battle formation while the
Spanish commanders stood watching, witnessing something they probably
had never seen before. The English were forming up in a straight line, single
file, broadside toward the crescent. The conventional wisdom of sixteenth-
century naval warfare was that ship commanders should place their heavy
ordnance at the bow, with only lighter pieces on the broadside, and avoid

offering their broadsides to the enemy. Fernando Oliveira, a Portuguese naval tactician, had authored the then authoritative book on naval combat, *The Art of War at Sea,* and in it he declared, "It is never safe at sea to allow opponents on your beam; rather you should always keep them ahead when you are fighting. Never expose your broadside to them."[1] Another accepted expert on the subject, Alonso de Chaves, a Castilian, assuming that warships would carry their main ordnance in the bow, wrote that the vessels "must not sail in line, since only the ships in the van can fight" when formed in a line.[2] Now, surprisingly, the English were doing exactly what the experts had forbidden. The men of the Armada were about to see, according to one account, "the first true line-ahead attack in the history of European naval warfare."[3]

Leading the formation, the first ship in the line, was Howard's flagship, the *Ark Royal,* and the rest of the fleet maneuvered in behind him in single file, each vessel following the one in front of it, sailing straight ahead when the ship ahead sailed straight, turning when it turned, or as the flagship ordered. When the line reversed itself, on the flagship's command, the vice flagship, positioned at the other end of the line, would then become the lead vessel, and the fleet would follow it. That way, the English ships, with their heavy guns firing from broadside ports, could each deliver a broadside salvo against the enemy, then wheel about and fire another broadside salvo from the opposite side of the ship while the side that fired first reloaded and prepared to fire again. Walter Raleigh had written his own manual on tactics. His idea was that the enemy should be kept "under a perpetual shot," which was exactly what the line formation was designed to do.

The line of English galleons first assaulted Leiva's side of the Spanish formation, then briskly sailed across the gap between the two arms and attacked Recalde's ships on the shoreward side. A number of vessels in Recalde's squadron, recoiling from the intense assault, pulled away from their positions and sought the protection of the Armada's main body, but Recalde, for one, in the *San Juan de Portugal,* defiantly held his position even while most of the English fire was aimed at his ship. Recalde reported that more than three hundred rounds were fired at the *San Juan,* damaging the mainmast, the foremast, and essential parts of the rigging.

The attack lasted about two hours, during which the English fired an estimated 2,000 rounds, answered by some 750 Spanish rounds. The English then broke off and fell back to a distance of about four miles behind the

Armada. At least some of the English commanders seemed to deem the engagement as merely minor. "We had them in chase," Drake reported, "and so coming up unto them there passed some cannon shot between some of our fleet and some of them." John Hawkins called it "some small fight." The lord admiral allowed that the English fleet had been able to do little damage to the Armada because his vessels could not get close enough for their guns to be effective. "We durst not adventure to put in amongst them," he wrote to secretary of state Francis Walsingham, "their fleet being so strong." The commander of the bark *Talbot*, Henry White, gave perhaps the gloomiest assessment. "The majesty of the enemy's fleet," he observed, "the good order they held, and the private consideration of our own wants did cause, in mine opinion, our first onset to be more coldly done than became the value of our nation and the credit of the English navy."

Recalde, however, offered a different view. His ship, the *San Juan*, had been so severely damaged that it had to withdraw from its position into the safety of the Armada's main body so that his ship's carpenters could make repairs. The next day he wrote that if Leiva "should receive the bombardment that I received yesterday, he will not be able to resist, because he carries no heavy artillery with which to resist." A supporter of the proposal to attack the English fleet while it lay in Plymouth harbor, Recalde now criticized the failure to do so, saying that it had allowed the English to gain the wind advantage and launch their attack on the Armada. He commented that "there are some very experienced people out there [the English], and we were like novices. . . ." He saw more significance and strategy in the engagement than the English comments indicated and warned that "it is very necessary to make sure that in the future they do not consume us little by little, and without any risk to themselves."

The Armada was suffering more loss than the English realized. On the same day the English attacked the fleet, July 31, the *San Salvador*, one of the Armada's most powerfully armed warships, was wracked by an explosion that destroyed two of its decks and its sterncastle, crippled its steering mechanism, and killed or severely burned half of its four-hundred-man complement, some of the men drowning after jumping overboard to escape the flames. Medina Sidonia's *San Martín* went quickly to the rescue, and its crew managed to put out the fire before it reached *San Salvador*'s main magazine, where some seven tons of gunpowder were stored. The stricken ship was then towed into the main body of the fleet, in the center of the crescent-shaped formation. Most of the injured were removed to other ships, as were the ship's officers and the fleet's payroll, which San Salvador was carrying, and after Medina Sidonia's experts the next day decided the ship could not be restored to sailing condition—and it could not be scuttled because about fifty of the most seriously burned crewmen were still aboard—the ruined vessel was abandoned as the Armada sailed on. Later that day, Monday, August 1, John Hawkins found it and sent a crew to it to claim it, but finding conditions aboard it so unbearable, the prize crew returned to their ship, and the San Salvador was then towed by Thomas Fleming's ship to Weymouth, farther east on the English coast. Its store of gunpowder would help replenish England's limited supply.

Another costly loss to the Armada occurred through a series of accidents. While surging to the aid of Recalde's San Juan, which had been under heavy fire from the English fleet, the Nuestra Señora del Rosario, assigned duty as a troubleshooter, a part of Medina Sidonia's reserve force that would rush to any position where help was needed or where there was an advantage to be exploited, encountered serious misfortune, made more so by the fact that the ship was freighted with fifty thousand gold ducats drawn from Philip's treasury. Rosario collided with a ship of the Biscayan squadron and suffered damage to its bowsprit, which cost it the use of its spritsail, which affected its steering, which in turn caused it to ram into the Santa Catalina. In that collision the Rosario's foresail and the yard that held it came crashing down, and the stays of the foremast were severed by the falling debris, causing the foremast to break off at the deck and topple onto the mainmast, fouling its rigging. Rosario then was dead in the water. Its commander, Pedro de Valdés, sent a boat to Medina Sidonia to ask for help, but help was refused for fear that stopping to repair the Rosario would endanger the entire Armada, the first consideration being to keep the Armada moving toward its rendezvous with Parma's army. And so the wallowing Rosario was left to the mercy and designs of the oncoming Englishmen.

The first English vessel on the scene was the Margaret and John, a merchant ship serving as a combat vessel. It reached the Rosario about nine o'clock that evening, July 31. When it came alongside the crippled vessel and fired musket rounds into it, the Margaret and John was turned away by two shots from Rosario's guns and sailed away toward the English fleet. Early the next morning, August 1, Drake mysteriously appeared in the *Revenge*, a galleon much more formidable than the *Margaret and John*. Pedro de Valdés came aboard Drake's menacing ship under a flag of truce and after Drake made it clear to him that there was no way out but destruction or surrender, Valdés capitulated, and Drake's crew took over the *Rosario* and its burden of fifty thousand ducats, only half of which reportedly reached Queen Elizabeth's treasury, the rest vanishing into unknown hands.

How Drake happened to be there to take advantage of *Rosario*'s misfortune is another matter. He was supposed to be holding *Revenge*'s place in the English fleet's formation, displaying the light of a lantern on his stern so that the fleet's other ships could follow him in the darkness. He had instead neglected his orders and gone after the Spanish prize, staying close to it all night, till dawn gave him opportunity to take it. The effect of Drake's dereliction was the scattering of the English fleet, which was not reunited until late in the evening of August 1.

Meanwhile, the Armada, temporarily unopposed, continued eastward toward Parma's army. Its progress was soon stifled, however, when during the night the wind died, and the fleet was becalmed several miles off Portland Bill. The next morning, though, a new wind came up, this time from the east, giving the Armada the weather gauge and bringing alarm to England's lord admiral, who quickly moved to the north-northeast to position his fleet between the Armada and England's shore to bar a landing. Medina Sidonia then maneuvered the Armada to thwart the English move and force Howard into a fight. The English vessels now opened fire on the Spaniards as they attempted to close on them and board them. For more than two hours Medina Sidonia's vessels persisted in their attempts while the English kept their distance and staved off the Spanish ships' approach with menacing cannonades.

At the same time, the Spanish caught several English vessels becalmed close to shore. They were mainly merchantmen, but among them was the biggest ship of the English fleet, the mighty *Triumph,* commanded by Martin Frobisher. Medina Sidonia ordered Hugo de Moncada to take his four galleasses to attack the Englishmen, isolated from their fleet. Moncada, commanding from the *San Lorenzo,* led the approach toward *Triumph* and one of its consorts. The Spanish vessels approached warily, advancing to within range of the English heavy guns as the tide turned against Moncada's ships and the wind shifted to the south. Howard then turned several of the royal galleons and a number of other vessels toward Frobisher's position to help him. Seeing Howard's move, Medina Sidonia decided to attack him and led sixteen of the Armada's ships toward the English line, but before they were close enough to engage, Medina Sidonia could see behind him that Recalde's *San Juan,* which had reentered the fight after undergoing repairs, was cut off and under attack by a host of English ships. Medina Sidonia then ordered his squadron to turn around and head for the *San Juan* to rescue it. He, however, aboard the *San Martín,* continued on toward the English line.

As Howard's *Ark Royal,* at the head of the line of his squadron, started to come up to the *San Martín,* Medina Sidonia turned broadside to it and struck his topsails, challenging Howard to close and board the *San Martín* for the traditional hand-to-hand combat, fleet admiral against fleet admiral. Howard declined and instead gave him a broadside of shot at close range, passed him, and was followed by the entire English line, each of the royal galleons giving the *San Martín* a broadside as it passed in turn. The line then came about, and each ship again let Medina Sidonia have a broadside. They then turned about again and fired a third round. The *San Martín* was firing back in hot exchange, forcing the English to increase their range. The battle went on for about an hour, until a line of Spanish galleons led by Oquendo approached and gathered around their beleaguered admiral to fend off the English assault. Howard then broke off. By then Moncada's galleasses had given up their fight against the *Triumph,* and now both Spanish contingents withdrew to reform the Armada's crescent formation and resume its eastward march.

The prolonged English bombardments of the Armada's vessels that day, August 2, had exacted a considerable cost, not in men or ships but in shot and powder, without which all the advantages of Elizabeth's ships would be wasted. John Hawkins wrote to Francis Walsingham that "a good part of our powder and shot" had been expended in the engagement off Portland Bill. He said he did not think it would be prudent to further engage the Armada until the English ammunition supply had been replenished.

That evening, Admiral Howard, reacting to his fleet's inability to halt the Armada thus far, reorganized the fleet, dividing it into four squadrons that could act more or less independently. Drake, Hawkins, Frobisher, and Howard would each command a squadron. Howard hoped the new organization would prove effective in preventing the Armada from entering the Solent and seizing control of it and the Isle of Wight as well. The aim was to force the Armada eastward, past the eastern entrance to the Solent, past Selsey Bill.

The English spent much of the next day receiving the supplies, ammunition, and new volunteers brought to them by small craft while the fleet lay off England's shore. The captured Spanish ammunition was also added to the English stores. During the morning, Drake, aboard the *Revenge,* spotted one of the Spanish hulks, the sluggish *El Gran Grifon,* lagging behind the Armada's formation, several miles off the western entrance to the Solent, which separates the Isle of Wight from the English mainland. He headed straight for the *Grifon* and when he pulled abeam of it, he fired a broadside into it, then came about and gave it another broadside, then slid across its stern and fired again, pounding forty or more balls into it, inflicting casualties on its seagoing soldiers, who were standing on the deck waiting for a chance to board the enemy, but doing little noticeable damage to the ship itself. After Recalde's *San Juan* and Medina Sidonia's flagship, the *San Martin,* entered the fray, taking many rounds themselves as Drake's squadron engaged them, a larger battle followed, during which the mainmast of the *Revenge* took a direct hit. Neither fleet was seriously damaged, though, and after a while, the English withdrew, and Medina Sidonia ordered his fleet to turn about and resume its formation and sail on.

During the night and the following early morning, August 4, as the Armada reached a position off the tip of the Isle of Wight, the English again spotted stragglers from the Spanish formation, the galleon *San Luis* and the hulk *Duquesa Santa Ana.* The wind had died, however, immobilizing the English warships, and Hawkins ordered his squadron, the closest one to the stragglers, to lower their boats and tow their ships into the range of their guns. Three Spanish galleasses, one of them towing a fourth vessel, maneuvered to protect the straggler, and the English opened fire, inflicting minor damage on three of the Spanish ships, which returned the fire and at the same time took the stragglers in tow and hauled them and themselves away from the engagement, and the battle ended.

Closer to shore another fight was going on. Frobisher in the daunting *Triumph* had led his squadron to a position near the eastern entrance of the Solent in order to prevent Spanish vessels from entering. The channel's current was running strong along the coast, in excess of a mile per hour, taking the

English vessels as well as the shoreward side of the Armada's formation somewhat briskly eastward while they were without wind. As the ships drifted eastward, they exchanged fire, but with little effect. When the wind came up again, though, more Spanish vessels moved in to support Medina Sidonia's flagship in an assault on Frobisher's squadron. The *Triumph*, which had drifted farther east than the rest of his squadron and also farther than the rearmost ships of the Armada, was caught leeward of the Spanish, cut off and unable to maneuver against the oncoming enemy. In desperation, Frobisher put his boats over the side to tow the *Triumph*. The English vessels closest to him then put their boats in the water, ten in all, to assist in the towing. Two English galleons, the *Bear* and the *Elizabeth Jonas*, also came to the *Triumph*'s aid, seeking to stave off the Spanish attack. Medina Sidonia in the *San Martín*, Recalde in the *San Juan*, and the other Spanish vessels, however, brushed past the English ships and continued their course to the stalled *Triumph*, expecting at last to close and board one of the English warships, and a great one at that.

That was when the wind shifted. Its sails filled by the fresh breeze, the *Triumph* swiftly cast off the lines to its boats and slipped away from the Spaniards' course and rejoined its waiting squadron. At that point, Medina Sidonia, seeing Drake's squadron beginning a fierce attack on the Armada's seaward arm, fired a signal gun to call off the attack on the *Triumph* and the rest of Frobisher's squadron and veered off to meet the new challenge. Medina Sidonia received sharp criticism from Recalde for calling off the engagement with Frobisher, but one of those aboard a vessel under assault by Drake expressed a different view. "We who were there were cornered," he wrote in an anonymous report, "so that if the duke had not gone about with his flagship, . . . we should have come out vanquished that day."[4]

With its seaward arm reinforced and Drake's attack fended off, the Armada proceeded eastward with the wind at its back. The bad news for the Spanish was that by disengaging from Frobisher's squadron at the eastern entrance to the Solent, they had lost their opportunity to secure a deepwater haven from the perils of the weather and the channel's tides and currents. They had sailed right past it, which was a large part of Recalde's complaint. "Nor was it wise," he wrote, "to sail with our fleet beyond that anchorage, near to the Isle of Wight, until we had heard from the prince of Parma, because it was the best anchorage in the whole Channel for every circumstance."

The Armada made no progress on the following day, August 5. The wind had fallen again, and both fleets lay becalmed, the Spanish using the time to make repairs on their battered vessels, the English, positioned some three miles to the Armada's rear, also making repairs and doing what they could to renew their woefully diminished supply of gunpowder and shot.

August 6 saw the wind rise once more, blowing from the west, and as the Armada resumed its voyage, Medina Sidonia wrung his hands over what he should do next. He was trying to decide between following Philip's explicit instructions to anchor off Cape Margate, as the king called it, meaning the North Foreland, at the northern extreme of the Strait of Dover, there to await Parma's army coming to the Armada in small boats, or instead sail for Dunkirk to anchor there and embark Parma's troops from the Flanders coast. When he consulted his senior officers, Medina Sidonia got conflicting advice and in the end he made the decision he felt was the most prudent. His ship's log records the dilemma he faced that day, and its resolution: "There were different opinions on whether to anchor in that roadstead [at Calais], and most favored going on; but the duke [Medina-Sidonia], understanding from the pilots he had brought with him that if he proceeded farther, the currents would force him out of the Channel and into the North Sea, determined to anchor before Calais, seven leagues [about twenty miles] from Dunkirk, where Parma could come and join him. And so at 5 p.m. he ordered the whole fleet to drop anchor."[5]

He then wrote again to Parma. For a month now he had been trying to make contact with Parma with messages sent by dispatch boats from the Armada. He had written as the Armada neared Finisterre on June 10 and had written again on July 25 as the Armada set out from La Coruña, both times informing Parma of his progress. He had written as the Armada approached Plymouth on July 31, asking Parma to send him pilots familiar with the coast of Flanders. On August 4 he had written again, this time asking to be resupplied with ammunition and powder and notifying Parma that the Armada was about to arrive. A day later, he had sent word once more of his position. As his fleet now stood virtually at Parma's doorstep, Medina Sidonia still had received no reply from him. When he wrote again on August 6, Medina Sidonia let Parma know his feelings. "I have constantly written to your Excellency," he told him, "and not only have I received no reply to my letters, but no acknowledgment of their receipt."

The failure to communicate was not all Parma's fault. The vagaries of wind and weather made communication from and to ships at sea chancy, particularly when ships were on the move, their location changing from day to day, and their destinations uncertain. In any case, Medina Sidonia had not received responses to his earliest letters, and the later letters had only just reached Parma. Parma had received Medina Sidonia's July 31 message on the morning of the day the Armada anchored off Calais, August 6, and later that day he received the letter that Medina Sidonia had written on August 4.

On the evening of August 6, Medina Sidonia at last heard from Parma. In a letter written on August 3, Parma gave him distressing news. As of that date, nothing was ready to be embarked aboard the transport vessels—not one barrel of beer, not one soldier. It would be at least the following Friday, maybe longer, he said, before his troops were ready to be loaded onto their flat-bottomed barges.

Medina Sidonia now faced his worst-case scenario. The Armada lay exposed to the channel's currents, the weather, and the enemy, whose fleet was strengthened by the thirty-five ships of Henry Seymour's squadron, which had been guarding the Strait of Dover and which now joined the main English fleet. What was more, the English, upwind of the Armada's anchorage, held the weather gauge. Moving the Armada westward would mean having to beat against the wind into the teeth of the English fleet. Shoals along the Flanders coast prevented the Armada from moving far shoreward. The only possibility, other than standing where it lay and suffering the English fleet's inevitable assault, was movement eastward, which would eventually take the Armada away from Parma's army and into the currents that would sweep it northward into the North Sea, with little chance of ever making a rendezvous with Parma.

Philip's grand Enterprise of England was now beginning to unravel. Parma was unwilling to mass his troops for embarkation until Medina Sidonia arrived to protect them from attack by the Netherlanders, who with a squadron of light shallow-draft warships controlled the coast of the Netherlands, including Flanders. Even if Parma could manage to embark the bulk of his army while under attack by the Netherlanders' vessels, his troops, put to sea aboard the unarmed, unseaworthy barges, would be sitting ducks without the protection of the Armada's guns. The problem, now grown enormous, was that the ships of the Armada were too large and drew too much water to get across the shoals and come close enough to shore to protect the transport barges.

Philip, the inveterate micromanager, had never come to grips with that problem, apparently believing that the only danger to the invasion force came from the English fleet, and so he had left that bothersome detail to Medina Sidonia, who had no solution other than to let Parma's troops take substantial losses while they embarked and moved across the open, shallow water to reach the protection of the Armada miles away. In his letter to Parma dated June 10—and received on June 21 but never answered—Medina Sidonia had asked Parma to tell him when he could put his troops to sea and where the Armada could meet them, indicating that he expected Parma to accept Medina Sidonia's harsh solution.

Parma refused it. He wanted Medina Sidonia somehow to destroy the Netherlanders' threatening squadron so that his troops could board their transports and sail safely to the rendezvous. He had protested Medina Sidonia's plan in a letter to Philip. "Medina," he wrote, "seems to believe that I should set out to meet him with my small ships, which is simply impossible. These vessels cannot run the gauntlet of warships; they cannot even withstand large waves." Philip's only known response, written in the margin of Parma's letter, which he read on August 7, was an appeal to the Almighty. "Please, God," he scribbled, "don't let there be some *embarazo* [embarrassing misfortune] here."

While Medina Sidonia was trying to decide what to do next, Lord Admiral Howard and his fellow admirals were planning action of their own. On the morning of August 7, they held a council of war aboard the *Ark Royal* and, fearful that Medina Sidonia and Parma were about to link up, decided to assault the anchored Spanish fleet with fireships that night, before the rendezvous could be effected.

Fire was the great dread of the captains and crews of wooden ships. Practically everything that formed them and that was carried on them was combustible. Freighted with large quantities of explosive gunpowder, warships were particularly vulnerable to flames, and experienced commanders were always aware of the possibility of a fireship attack. Medina Sidonia had guessed that Howard might launch fireships into the Armada's tightly packed formation and had ordered measures to defend it. He had designated a number of his pinnaces and other small craft to establish a protective shield by sailing or rowing up to any approaching fireships, taking them in tow with grappling hooks, and pulling them out of the path to the mass of anchored vessels. He had warned his ships' commanders that if fireships managed to avoid the shield, the commanders should slip their anchor cables and buoy them, move out to sea, and let the fireships drift to shore on the current, then return at daylight and retrieve their anchors.

Eight vessels of the English fleet were chosen to be set afire, including one owned by Drake and one by Hawkins. The eight ranged in size from ninety tons to two hundred. Crews removed their belongings and foodstuffs, then placed additional combustibles aboard them and loaded their guns so that they would automatically fire when the flames got them hot enough. The ships were then set afire and abandoned to their deadly mission. Conditions were ideal. The tide, wind, and current were all moving toward the gathered Spanish fleet. The blazing ships would be swiftly carried into the midst of the Armada.

Shortly after midnight the watches aboard the Spanish vessels saw them coming, eight fiery, phantomlike shapes fast approaching through the darkness, bearing down on the anchorage. Within minutes the shapes could be made out: tall ships, their sails set, with flames glowing menacingly from their hulls and masts and rigging. They advanced in a tight line, close abreast, grouped so close together and coming so fast on the wind and current that when the Armada's protective pinnaces raced out to intercept them, only two of them could be grappled and towed from their course. As they quickly drew nearer, their fearsome flames illumining the night sky, their guns started firing, setting off pandemonium aboard the Spanish vessels.

From Medina Sidonia's flagship a signal gun sounded, and the *San Martín* slipped its cable and moved out to sea, close-hauled against a contrary wind. Four others, including Recalde's *San Juan,* sailed out to stand by Medina Sidonia. The rest of the Spanish vessels, however, their commanders desperate to escape the flames, cut their anchor cables and fled to safety, the westerly wind swiftly bearing them away. The disciplined formation that had proved so formidable a defense against the English enemy was now shattered, its vessels scattered over miles of open water.

The one ship that did not escape was Hugo de Moncada's *San Lorenzo.* In the light of the new day, August 8, as Howard led the English fleet, 150 vessels strong, for a mighty assault on the Spaniards, he could see that the Spanish ships were gone from their anchorage. They had vanished from sight, except for the *San Martín,* the four ships that stood with it, and the galleass *San Lorenzo,* which had lost the use of its rudder and had suffered damage to its mainmast. Thus crippled, it was hobbling toward Calais harbor to seek protection from the advancing English, its galley slaves straining at their oars against an ebbing tide. Then suddenly it ran aground on the shoals, the efforts of the oarsmen only driving it more firmly into the sea bottom, and as the tide swept seaward, the great galleass turned over on its starboard side, lacking enough depth to float. Howard's squadron moved in to finish it off, but the water was too shallow for *San Lorenzo* to be approached by his warships, and he ordered his ship's boats into the water with a boarding party. The *San Lorenzo*'s ordnance was unusable, its portside guns pointing skyward, but its crew held off the English with small-arms fire, inflicting several casualties on the English seamen in their boats, who answered the Spaniards' fire with their own. In that exchange, Moncada was killed when struck in the head with a musket shot. At that, the *San Lorenzo* crew and soldiers forsook the defense of their vessel, scrambled over the starboard rail, and hurriedly waded ashore. The English sailors then swarmed over the stricken ship and stripped it of everything of value before returning to their waiting ships.

While Howard's squadron was occupied with the *San Lorenzo,* which eventually rotted to pieces where it lay, the four other English squadrons, led by Drake, pursued Medina Sidonia's flagship and the four other Spanish vessels. The wind was now coming from the south-southwest, perhaps at gale force, and the five Spanish ships had run before it, driven northward in the Strait of Dover. By the time Howard's squadron had withdrawn from plucking the valuables, including twenty-two thousand ducats, from the *San Lorenzo* and satisfying themselves that it would never fight again, Medina Sidonia had managed to round up much of his fleet and was attempting to reshape its battle formation, which though ragged now, still constituted a formidable force. Racing northward to rejoin his fleet, Howard caught up with it off Gravelines, between Calais and Dunkirk. Drake had already overtaken the Armada and engaged it. Howard sailed in to join the battle.

Medina Sidonia was doing his best not only to maintain a defensive formation but also to avoid being drawn completely away from the Flanders ports that still might be used by Parma to embark his invasion army. The English were striving to batter the Spanish vessels at closer range than ever, and with the weather gauge, force the Spaniards leeward onto the shoals, where they would run aground, becoming motionless targets and prisoners of the sands.

The first assault on the Spaniards was by Drake's *Revenge,* which headed the file of his squadron's ships as they moved in to engage the Armada. Drake closed to within about a hundred yards of the *San Martín* before opening fire, first with his bow guns, then turning to deliver a broadside salvo against it. The *Nonpareil,* commanded by Captain Thomas Fenner and sailing right behind the *Revenge,* was next to open fire on the *San Martín,* followed by the rest of Drake's squadron. After blasting Medina Sidonia's flagship with thunderous broadsides, the entire squadron followed Drake's course that led northeastward, farther leeward of the *San Martín,* where a number of Spanish galleons apparently were struggling to avoid being swept onto the shoals.

Frobisher, in the *Triumph,* and his squadron picked up the fight with the *San Martín,* delivering a murderous hail of shot against it. Then Hawkins, commanding the *Victory,* came up and joined the fray as the *San Martín,* despite taking great punishment, defiantly answered the English ships' fire, aided by the *San Marcos de Portugal,* which, as the English approached within musket range, replied not only with its big guns but with small-arms fire. As the rest of Hawkins's squadron came up, other Spanish ships entered the engagement, including the galleons of Castile and of Portugal, Leiva's and Bertendona's carracks, Oquendo's flagship, and others. Gradually a force of some twenty-five of the Armada's vessels rallied to oppose the English squadrons, forming something less than their defensive crescent but nevertheless presenting a formidable front to their attackers. By the time Seymour's squadron entered the battle and William Wynter, commander of the *Vanguard,* one of Seymour's ships, could observe them, the Spaniards had gone "into the proportion of a half moon," Wynter reported, "their admiral and vice admiral in the midst and the greatest number of them; and there went on each side, in the wings, their galleasses, armados of Portugal and other good ships, in the whole to the number of sixteen in a wing which did seem to be of their principal shipping." In a remarkable feat of seamanship, the Armada's scattered ships, under the leadership of their undaunted captain general, had restored their broken formation, though diminished.

The battle raged on for some nine hours, the Spaniards bravely withstanding the English onslaught while struggling to resist being forced upon the threatening shoals at their back, cautiously husbanding their dwindling, unreplenished supply of shot and gunpowder. One Spanish eyewitness, Pedro Calderón, aboard the *San Salvador,* gave his account of the action:

The enemy inflicted such damage upon the galleons *San Mateo* and *San Felipe* that the latter had five guns on the starboard side and a big gun on the poop put out of action. . . . In view of this, and seeing that his upper deck was destroyed, both his pumps broken, his rigging in shreds and his ship almost a wreck, Don Francisco de Toledo ordered the grappling hooks to be got out and shouted to the enemy to come to close quarters. They replied, summoning him to surrender in fair fight; and one Englishman, standing in the maintop with sword and buckler, called out, "Good soldiers that you are, surrender to the fair terms we offer you." But the only answer he got was a musket ball that brought him down in sight of everyone.[6]

The *San Mateo* became, according to one eyewitness, "riddled with shot like a sieve" and like the similarly crippled *San Felipe* dropped out of the Armada's formation and, lagging behind, ran aground in the shoals off the Netherlands coast. The next morning, August 9, after a ferocious two-hour fight, they were captured, along with their defiant commanders and crews, by the Netherlands rebels. The noblemen among the captured Spaniards were held for ransom; the rest were forced overboard to drown.

The *Vanguard*'s captain, William Wynter, wrote about the fierceness of the fight at sea and the close range at which it was fought. "Out of my ship [alone]," he reported, "there was shot 500 shot of demi-cannon, culverin and demi-culverin; and when I was furthest off in discharging any of the pieces, I was not out of the shot of their harquebus, and most time within speech of one another."

The English bombardment had inflicted heavy damage on the Armada. Medina Sidonia's flagship, the *San Martín,* had taken a reported 107 direct hits on its hull, masts, and sails, several of which had smashed holes in the hull near the waterline, requiring emergency underwater repairs by two divers to prevent the ship from filling with water. The *San Juan de Sicilia* was nearly shattered, being hit along its entire length, both above and below the waterline. The *Santa María de la Rosa* was wrecked, with the loss of all hands but one, after being severely shot up. *La Trinidad Valencera* and *El Gran Grifon* incurred such damage to their hulls that both were forced to run ashore to avoid sinking. The *San Pedro* and the *Santa Ana*, Oquendo's flagship, were both severely damaged, the latter having to keep its pumps operating continuously to keep it afloat. The *María Juan*, encircled by a number of English vessels, was pounded so relentlessly that its commander offered to surrender, but the ship sank while the surrender was being negotiated, most of its complement going down with it.

The losses were in men as well as ships. Some of the vessels' decks were reported to be awash with blood, so much so that blood poured from their scuppers. One account[7] places the number of Spaniards killed in the action at Gravelines at more than one thousand, with eight hundred wounded. The Spaniards themselves reported six hundred killed and eight hundred wounded. Another account[8] estimates the number of wounded at nearly six thousand. Many of them would later die of their wounds. The Armada also lost men, many of them not from Spain, because of desertion. They stole away in their ships' boats or, as their ships neared the shoals, leaped overboard and waded or swam ashore.

Around four o'clock that afternoon, as the English fleet began to run out of ammunition and tapered off its attack even while the Armada's formation was threatening to break up, a squall blew in with heavy, blinding rain. Medina Sidonia used the opportunity to lead his fleet away on the only path of escape, to the northeast, toward the shoals, the exact location of which was unknown to him. Many aboard the Spanish vessels expected to run aground at any minute and lose their ships to the pounding waves. They spent a fearful night, braced for disaster, praying and making confession to the ships' chaplains. Among those at confession were Medina Sidonia and his officers.

Through the night the English pursued, though refusing to renew their attack. At the rate the Spaniards were moving and on the course they were sailing, the sands of the shoals along the Zeeland coast would soon do the English defenders' destructive work for them. Wind and current were steadily driving Medina Sidonia's vessels toward the shoals, and Howard and his commanders, familiar with the Netherlands coast, knew what lay ahead for their enemy. It was then only a matter of an hour or so, perhaps only minutes, before they had the Spaniards trapped on the sands, powerless and ready for annihilation.

Then, in the early morning of August 10, the sort of Enterprise-saving phenomenon that King Philip had hoped and prayed for came at long last and just in time—a miracle, the relieved Spaniards believed. The wind, which had been blowing from the northwest, driving the Armada into the coast, suddenly shifted to west-southwest, allowing Medina Sidonia and his beleaguered fleet to veer northward, away from the perilous sands and into the deep of the North Sea, sailing away from the coast of Flanders and from Parma's waiting army.

The English, their shot and powder too depleted to mount another battle, let them go. Philip's Armada was escaping, but in abject failure of its purpose and of Philip's Enterprise of England. There would be no invasion of England now. There would be no deposing England's queen. There would be no hegemony for Philip, no restoration of power for the pope. Britannia ruled the waves, and the invincible Armada was sailing away, broken and beaten.

·⚙· 19. THE RUIN AND THE RENEWAL

O n August 8, the same day that her navy was engaging Philip's Armada off Gravelines, Elizabeth boarded her royal barge in London and descended the Thames to the town of Tilbury, on the north bank of the river, not far from where it flows into the channel. She came to Tilbury at the special invitation of Robert Dudley, the earl of Leicester, who was commanding the army assembled there to prevent Parma's expected invasion army from marching on London. He had urged her to come and inspect her troops, which had been undergoing training with good effects and which he thought she would find impressive. "You shall (dear lady) behold as goodly, as loyal and as able men as any Prince Christian can show you," he wrote to her with some exaggeration. She came despite the fears of some of her advisers that she could be placing herself in grave danger by exposing herself to such a vast and mixed assemblage of her subjects at a time when, at least for some, loyalties were likely to be in conflict.

Leicester had assured her that she would be safe, as safe as she was at St. James's Palace, and declared he would guarantee her safety with his own life. She was apparently eager to come and see the troops, to be among them and talk to them, those stalwarts on whom her life and her crown might soon depend. She had welcomed Leicester's assurance and accepted his invitation.

She spent the night of August 8 at the house of Edward Ritche, about four miles from Tilbury, and the next morning—at the same time that Philip's Armada was escaping into the North Sea, leaving Parma's invasion army behind—she passed among her soldiers as they stood for inspection. There was no mistaking her. Mounted on a handsome steed, she was wearing a conspicuously white velvet dress, over which was fastened a silver breastplate, as if to do battle herself, and she held a ceremonial truncheon in her hand, symbol of her high office. Seeming "full of princely resolution and more than feminine courage . . . she passed like an Amazonian empress through all her army." When she had seen the men of that army, she was moved to give them cheering words, which, although written beforehand and carefully rehearsed, seemed to come spontaneously and straight from her heart:

> My loving people, we have been persuaded by some that are careful of our safety, to take heed how we commit ourselves to armed multitudes, for fear of treachery. But I assure you, I do not desire to live to distrust my faithful and loving people. Let tyrants fear. I have always so behaved myself that, under God, I have placed my chiefest strength and safeguard in the loyal hearts and good will of my subjects. And therefore I am come amongst you, as you see, at this time, not for my recreation and disport, but being resolved, in the midst and heat of the battle, to live or die amongst you all, to lay down for my God, and for my kingdom, and for my people, my honor and my blood, even in the dust.
>
> I know I have the body of a weak and feeble woman. But I have the heart and stomach of a king, and of a king of England, too, and think foul scorn that Parma or Spain or any prince of Europe should dare to invade the borders of my realm—to which, rather than any dishonor shall grow by me, I myself will take up arms. I myself will be your general, judge and rewarder of every one of your virtues in the field. I know already for your forwardness you have deserved rewards and crowns, and we do assure you, in the word of a prince, they shall be duly paid you.[1]

Her stirring words so roused the troops that, according to one witness, they "all at once a mighty shout or cry did give."[2] Leicester reported that she "so inflamed the hearts of her good subjects, as I think the weakest among them is able to match the proudest Spaniard that dares land in England."

She then retired with Leicester, now gray haired, paunchy, and ailing, to his tent for a noontime dinner, during which a report came that Parma's army had embarked on the spring tide and was moving toward the English shore. Elizabeth resolved to stay with her troops and face the enemy with them, despite Leicester's pleas that she return to London for safety. As night came on, without any sign of a Spanish invader, it became obvious that the report was false, and Elizabeth at last agreed to go back to her London palace.

Indeed, invasion was then no closer than was the Armada, and the threat of it grew ever more distant as Philip's vaunted navy continued to flee through the North Sea. On the morning of August 10, the day after Elizabeth's speech to her troops, Medina Sidonia summoned his senior commanders to the *San Martín* for a war council and after briefing them on the condition of the Armada, its personnel, and its supplies, asked them to vote on whether they should turn around and try again to link up with Parma's army or head for home. The war council, according to the account written by Juan Martínez de Recalde, who favored trying again to reach Parma, decided to return to Spain. And so the Armada continued northward, intending to round Scotland and sail down the Atlantic, past the west coast of Ireland, and on to Spain. With food and water running out, with many sick and wounded, Medina Sidonia wanted to get back to Spain as fast as possible, but since the English fleet, which followed the Armada as far as the Firth of Forth, prevented the Spanish from returning through the channel, they would have to take the long way around.

Preparing for that long haul, Medina Sidonia ordered individual daily rations cut to one pint of water, a half pint of wine, and a half pound of biscuit, much of which was barely edible. To conserve water, he had the horses and mules that were meant to serve the invasion force shoved overboard.

Days at sea began to take a toll on the Spanish vessels. Their hulls, already severely battered by English cannonades, suffered new damage from the pounding waves and soon were leaking dangerously. By August 21 four crippled ships, including *El Gran Grifon,* flagship of the fleet's transports, fell so far behind that they lost contact with the rest of the Armada. Ten days later, on September 1, one of them, the *Barca de Amburg,* signaled that it was about to go down, and its 250 men were removed to the *Grifon* and *La Trinidad Valencera* just before it sank, its supplies going down with it.

The *San Martín,* riddled by shot, including a fifty-pounder that smashed a hole in its side just above the waterline, was leaking badly. The *San Marcos,* so severely battered that it was threatening to come apart, was held together by cables passed beneath its keel, the ship thus tied up like a package. The *San Juan,* the vessel captained by Recalde, who wanted to return to face the English fleet again, was also riddled and leaking, and its mainmast was so badly damaged that it could no longer carry its sails. In fact, all of the Armada's fighting ships were damaged to some extent. Three of the Armada's huge carracks, riding low in the water, their commanders apparently despairing of completing the voyage, left the formation and turned eastward, toward Norway, seeking refuge. They all apparently went down before reaching it. They were never heard from again.

To add to the Armada's miseries, the wind shifted to the southwest as the fleet was making its way down the coast of Ireland, and with the wind change came one storm after another. The headwinds were so strong that in two weeks the fleet had made virtually no progress southward but had been blown dangerously eastward, toward the Irish coast. By September 3, seventeen more ships were missing from the formation.

Medina Sidonia had warned his commanders to steer clear of Ireland "for fear of the harm that may happen to you upon that coast." But for many of the vessels, there was no choice, and the Armada suffered its greatest losses upon the shores of Ireland, many of its vessels driven helplessly by wind and wave. As many as seventeen ships in desperation headed for the Irish coast in hopes of finding food and water and to make repairs. Only two of them sailed away again. The rest either fell victim to the rocks along the coast, their crews drowning, or making land, where the crews were slain, most by England's occupying forces. More than six thousand thus perished. A relative few of the stranded Spaniards, perhaps no more than several hundred, did find aid from the Irish, who sheltered and fed them and helped many of them escape to Scotland, a neutral nation. Others, fewer still, avoided capture and remained in Ireland.

On the *San Martín,* hobbling toward home, Medina Sidonia was bedfast, suffering the delirium of a raging fever as well as dysentery and seasickness, his command of the ship taken over by someone else, who heroically piloted the vessel through storms and contrary winds to at last reach Santander, on Spain's north coast, on September 21. Eight other Armada galleons sailed into Santander behind him. In the next few weeks forty-three more of the fleet's vessels made it into Santander; nine made port at San Sebastián, east of Santander, and six reached La Coruña. A total of 67 Armada vessels—of the 134 that had sailed from Lisbon in May—had survived, and about half of them were so severely damaged that they were no longer fit for service. One sank soon after making port. Others were later demolished, their guns and timbers salvaged for reuse.

The loss in men was still greater. Only about a third—an estimated ten thousand men—of the Armada's sailors and seagoing soldiers had survived, and many of them were dying even as their ships rested in Spanish ports, victims of disease and starvation as well as of battle wounds. Among those who succumbed to disease within a month of their return were two of Spain's most able and distinguished naval commanders, Juan Martínez de Recalde and Miguel de Oquendo.

Medina Sidonia struggled to regain his health and strength while still aboard the *San Martín,* doing his best to fulfill his responsibilities to his king and his men, dictating letters to Philip and to Philip's secretary to plead for help for crewmen who were sick, wounded, starving, ill clothed, and unpaid—and still shipbound because there were no accommodations for them ashore. There were days when, in his fever, he was incoherent, and others when, though lucid, he was too weak to sign his name to the letters he had dictated. He felt the pain of defeat deeply, tortured by the belief that the blame for the expedition's failure was his. In one letter to Juan de Idiáquez, Philip's secretary, he as much as said, "I told you so," pointing out that he had warned the king that it was a mistake to place him in command of the Armada. He vowed that he would never accept a command at sea again, even if refusal should cost him his life. Philip, briefed on Medina Sidonia's conduct of the expedition and on his medical condition, found less fault in him than Medina Sidonia found in himself. Philip relieved him of his command and permitted him to go home without first coming to see Philip and pay his respects. Escorted by a few of his servants and traveling in a curtained litter, Medina Sidonia unobtrusively made his way to his estate at Sanlúcar, taking care to avoid the public eye lest he be confronted by angry protesters en route. By the spring of 1589 he had regained his health and later would serve Philip again.

The English fleet had suffered nothing like the Armada's losses. Except for those deliberately burned as fireships, not one ship had been lost to the enemy, though some ships had lost their longboats. Damage to the English fleet's vessels was slight compared to that incurred by the Spanish, though many had to have their hulls patched where the Armada's guns had breached them. Drake's *Revenge* suffered the worst damage known to have been inflicted on any English vessel, that being a mainmast "decayed and perished with shot."[3] English crews, moreover, which had totaled about sixteen thousand men at the beginning of the battles, still had some twelve thousand men in service when the fleet returned to port following the Armada's flight into the North Sea.

English crewmen, however, fared no better than the Spaniards once the fighting had ended. They suffered from deadly disease and lack of medical treatment, from lack of food and lack of adequate clothing. According to one account, half-naked seamen, victors over the mighty Armada and saviors of their queen and country, lay sick, starving, and dying on the streets of Dover and Rochester. Like their Spanish counterparts, they also went unpaid. With no money, they were unable to buy food, shelter, or passage home. Elizabeth's pledge to reward those who served her and the nation, made at Tilbury, proved as false as any promise made by a politician seeking public support. Defeated in his attempts to get his men paid and feeling their pain, Lord Admiral Howard wrote to Walsingham in frustration, "I would to God I were delivered of the dealing for money. . . . God, I trust, will deliver me of it ere long, for there is no other hell." And again he wrote that it would "grieve any man's heart to see them that have served so valiantly die so miserably." He also warned Elizabeth that "if men should not be cared for better than to let them starve and die miserably, we should hardly get men to serve."

Elizabeth had left Tilbury on August 9, but traveling at a somewhat leisurely pace did not arrive back in London until about August 13. By then she had received reports of the victory at Gravelines and of the flight of the Armada and had realized that the threat had passed. On August 17 she ordered the army camped at Tilbury to be disbanded and ten days later, in an act of cost-consciousness, most of her navy was likewise ordered discharged from further service.

During the weeks that followed the spread of the great news, thanksgiving services and victory celebrations were held throughout England. To make the celebration official, a National Day of Thanksgiving was ordered to be observed on November 29, with "a general concurrence of all the people in the Realm in repairing to their Parish Churches and giving public thanks" and "celebrating the return of the English Navy; the defeat of the Spanish Navy . . . wherein is remembered the great goodness of God towards England."[4] On December 4 Elizabeth attended the last of the big celebrations, a service at St. Paul's Cathedral, where she made a public display of kneeling in prayer on the steps outside the west door. Inside, she watched as Spanish flags and banners, captured during the English fleet's battles with the Armada, were paraded down the aisles. She listened, too, as some lyrics she herself had penned, rather self-consciously, were sung in celebration of God's blessed intervention:

He made the wind and waters rise
To scatter all mine enemies . . .
And hath preserved in tender love
The spirit of his turtle dove.[5]

Parma meanwhile had long since given up on embarking his troops and taking them across the channel to depose God's turtle dove. At the end of August word had come from Flanders that Parma had withdrawn his army from the coast and gone on to other objectives. The main one turned out to be the capture of the city of Bergen op Zoom in the Netherlands. By the end of October, that attempt had also failed, leading Elizabeth to gloat that Philip's military forces had received "no less blemish . . . by land than by sea."

In Spain the mood was one of mourning. The disaster of the Armada was all the more shockingly depressing because the early reports, sent to Madrid by wishful-thinking Bernardo de Mendoza from France, had it that Drake had been defeated off the Isle of Wight and that all was going wonderfully well. One of the monks posted at the Escorial, Jerónimo de Sepúlveda, wrote that the Enterprise's failure was a catastrophe "to be wept over forever . . . because it lost us respect and the good reputation among warlike people which we used to have. The grief it caused in all of Spain was extraordinary. . . . Almost the entire country went into mourning. People talked about nothing else."

Philip's secretary, Idiáquez, told Parma how much Philip had been affected by reports of the Armada's reverses. "His Majesty has felt it more than you would believe possible, and if there were not some remaining hope in God that all this might have achieved something for His cause . . . I do not know how he could bear such a great blow."[6] After Recalde had at last made it back to La Coruña on October 7, he had sent Philip his ship's journal, some of the letters that had passed between him and Medina Sidonia, and his own critique of the expedition's strategy. When he had had time to go through the material, Philip confessed that, "I have read it all, although I would rather have not, because it hurts so much." According to one account, Philip's appearance began to change following the Armada's disaster. His complexion took on a pallor, his beard whitened and grew unkempt, his face sagged.[7] His habits also changed. He stayed inside more, made contact with fewer people, kept to himself more, and worked longer hours, alone in his palace study.

Unable to accept the fact that English ships, English firepower, and English tactics were all superior to those of the Armada, Philip put his defeat down to divine displeasure, or at least God's withholding of the needed miracles. "We are bound to give praise to God for all things which He is pleased to do," Philip wrote with a brave face to Spanish bishops in October 1588. "Now I give thanks to Him for the mercy He has shown. In the storms through which the Armada sailed, it might have suffered a worse fate, and that its ill fortune was no greater must be credited to the prayers for its good success." In a statement a bit more revealing of his disappointment with the lack of divine assistance, he was reported to have said, "I sent my ships to fight against men and not against the winds and waves of God."

His despair, however, was not long-lasting. Certain that he was still on God's side, he asked his councilors what they thought of renewing the effort to overthrow England's Protestant queen. He left open for his councilors the possibility of some sort of negotiated settlement with the English, but in a note written in November 1588 he disclosed his royal wishes: "I was moved to undertake the Armada campaign for the service of Our Lord, the defense of His Cause and the advantage of these realms. And I still feel the same now and greatly desire that our efforts should achieve what has become all the more necessary because of what has happened." When his councilors rejected the possibility of negotiations and told him that the war should continue, Philip was elated and let them know he enthusiastically agreed with them. "I, for my part," he told them, "shall never fail to strive for the cause of God and the good of these kingdoms." By the middle of November, Philip's desire for more war was evident in Madrid. Venice's ambassador to Spain reported that, "In spite of everything, his Majesty shows himself determined to carry on the war."

Indeed, not long after he had learned the extent of the Armada's losses, Philip began programs to replace them. He would increase Spanish shipbuilding, cannon manufacture, and the recruitment of new crewmen. He promised himself and the ambassadors of his court that he would build a new armada, greater than the previous one, with financing provided by silver from America, new taxes, new loans from the bankers of Genoa, and, if necessary, by melting down the Escorial's silver service and silver candlesticks.

Philip apparently intended to bet everything on the overthrow of Elizabeth, so single-minded was he in his enmity of her. He swore an oath, according to the English spy Anthony Copley, "that he would waste and consume his

Crown . . . but either he would utterly ruin Her Majesty and England, or else himself and all Spain become tributary to her."

In the years 1589 to 1598 he had more than sixty major ships built to add to the royal navy. Between 1588 and 1591 alone he built twelve one-thousand-ton galleons, which came to be called "the Twelve Apostles." His new fleet was based primarily in La Coruña, Cádiz, and Lisbon, to protect the Atlantic coast of Spain and Portugal as well as the routes to and from the West Indies, along which his New World treasures flowed and which since the Armada's defeat were more threatened than ever.

Elizabeth was not standing idle while Philip reconstructed his fleet, though she had suffered the loss of her dearest associate, the earl of Leicester, who, stricken with several ailments, died at age fifty-five on September 4, 1588, while on his way to the medicinal waters at Derbyshire. In one of his last letters to her, he spoke of his illness and of her health as well, asking "how my gracious lady doth, and what ease of her late pains she finds; being the chiefest thing in the world I do pray for, for her to have good health and long life."

At age fifty-five herself, Elizabeth felt robust enough to order attacks on the surviving ships of Philip's Armada in the havens where they lay while undergoing repairs, hoping to finish the task of their complete destruction, which had been left undone in the channel. Short of funds, however, she gave the task not to her navy, the costs of which she would have had to pay, but to a collection of privateers and adventurers. The expedition she ordered included some 180 ships, some of them from the Netherlands, and twenty-three thousand men, most of them soldiers. She intended them to smash Philip's fleet first, then help themselves to whatever booty and prizes were left available. Her orders to the commanders were explicit: "Before you attempt any thinge either in Portugall or in the [Azores], our express pleasure and commaundment is that you first shall distress the shippes of warre in Guispuscoa, Biscay, and Galizia and in any other places that appertayne either to the kinge of Spayne or his subjects."[8]

She had received intelligence that more than forty of the Armada's battered vessels lay at Santander, a harbor so vast that it could not be adequately defended by its harbor guns. The expedition, led by Francis Drake and John Norris, was to go to Santander first and take care of the business of demolishing the remnants of the Armada.

Instead of following the queen's orders, Drake came up with what he considered a better idea, as was his wont. The expedition sailed from Plymouth on May 8, 1589, and headed straight to La Coruña, where, according to reports that Drake and Norris said they had received, a large group of Spanish galleons was anchored. When Drake and Norris arrived, however, they found the port practically empty. The English troops went ashore and raided the town and the surrounding area with no lasting effect, but giving the enemy warning to prepare Lisbon for an attack. The only losses to the Spanish fleet were Recalde's *San Juan,* Bertendona's *Regazona,* both survivors from the Armada, and one other vessel.

From La Coruña the expedition's fleet sailed to Portugal and landed at Peniche, north of Lisbon. The subsequent march on Lisbon proved fruitless, and if Elizabeth had expected the Portuguese to rise up against their Spanish occupiers at the sight of English troops, there was disappointment all around. Far from joining the English to overthrow Philip's viceroy, Cardinal Albert, the Portuguese decided to sit out the attack and did nothing to help themselves or the English. The assault on Lisbon led by Norris was decisively repelled by Cardinal Albert's forces, and the English were compelled to march back to their ships after suffering more than two thousand casualties.

As the English fleet sailed away, it was struck by a violent storm that scattered its vessels, many of which made it to the port city of Vigo, which Drake burned, perhaps out of sheer frustration. He then attempted to reach the Azores, but strong headwinds forced him to turn back. He sailed back into Plymouth at the end of June. He returned with eleven thousand fewer men than had left Plymouth with him some six weeks earlier. Their lives had been wasted, for nothing had been gained. Drake fell into disgrace, and Elizabeth gave him no new command until 1595, when she ordered new attacks on Spanish trade and vessels.

On September 17, 1595, Drake, with John Hawkins, led six of Elizabeth's galleons across the Atlantic to raid Spanish holdings. Hawkins, however, fell ill and died off the coast of Puerto Rico on November 12. After capturing the city of Nombre de Dios, a settlement founded by Christopher Columbus on the northern coast of Panama, Drake, too, became sick and died on January 28, 1596, near Puerto Bello, Panama. The area came to be considered too unhealthy, and the English abandoned Nombre de Dios in 1597.

Elizabeth sent Lord Admiral Howard to attack the port of Cádiz, where some sixty Spanish ships lay, about half of them galleons loaded with cargoes intended for Spain's colonies in the New World, plus six other galleons to be used to protect the convoy on its crossing. Howard's fleet of 120 vessels arrived off Cádiz on June 30, 1596. Howard launched an assault on the galleons, four of which were Philip's new "Apostles." Two of them, the *San Felipe* and the *Santo Tomas,* Howard burned, and the two others, the *San Mateo* and the *San Andres,* he captured and added to Elizabeth's fleet. He decided to negotiate the seizure of the merchantmen and their cargoes, but while negotiations were going on, the Spanish burned more than thirty of the ships rather than surrender them to the English. Altogether, an estimated two hundred Spanish ships, large and small, were burned in Cádiz harbor, the major port for Spain's New World commerce.

Howard then put ashore the army that had come with him, ten thousand English troops commanded by the young earl of Essex and five thousand Dutch troops commanded by Count Louis of Nassau, brother of the murdered Prince William of Orange. The city's Spanish defenders fled, leaving Cádiz in English control for the two weeks they and the Dutch occupied it before burning much of it and sailing away on July 16, infuriating and shaming the proud Spaniards.

Through the eminent failure of Drake to destroy Philip's battered and vulnerable fleet in the raid of 1589, the surviving Armada had been allowed to repair and refit for a new assault on England. But then events in France, which drew Philip into a new war, and events in the Netherlands, which led to the replacement and death of the duke of Parma in December 1592, had prevented Philip from executing a new campaign against England and its queen, despite the urging of some advisers to do so. Bernardino de Mendoza, whose hatred for Elizabeth was practically pathological, was one of those urging action. It was important, he wrote to Philip, "to show the Queen of England that Your Majesty intends to assail her on all sides."

Undeterred by the English fleet's demonstrated superiority, one adviser told Philip that the blame for the Armada's failure lay with its commanders. "If the Armada had been conducted as it should have been and its commanders had taken advantage of the opportunities offered to them, the King of Spain would now be as much King of England as he is King of Spain."[9]

Writing from England, Marco Antonio Micea of Genoa wrote to Philip that, "If the King of Spain wishes to see the Queen of England dead . . . if he wants to stop them [Elizabeth's councilors] from molesting them in the Indies or Portugal, let him send 3,000 or 4,000 men to Ireland . . . this is the only thing the English fear and the real true way to take this country with little risk and trouble, and if a part of the [new] Armada were to effect this, they would find it a very different matter from attacking this country [England]." Philip seemed to like that idea and penned a note next to it in the margin of Micea's letter: "This would be a very important matter."[10]

Another adviser pressing Philip for action was Martín de Padilla, one of Philip's top naval commanders and the man whom Medina Sidonia had proposed to command the first Armada. Incited by the Spanish humiliation at Cádiz, Padilla urged that a force of men and ships be assembled for a decisive new assault on England. He claimed that Spain would thereby win peace with England on Spanish terms and that Philip's reign would then "with reason be called a Happy and Golden Century."

Philip, now sixty-nine years old, sick, in pain, and seeming to survive on willpower alone, finally took action. He ordered Padilla to organize a fleet, and in October—an odd time of year to be launching a major campaign—of 1596 Padilla's fleet, composed of eighty-one major vessels and a number of smaller ships, set out from Lisbon and La Coruña, its destination ostensibly Ireland. The mission had begun despite Philip's having been warned by Padilla and his commanders that the fleet was not yet properly prepared for the campaign. Philip, as he had done in 1588, rejected the appeals of his naval experts and ordered Padilla to sail anyway. Within days after its departure, the fleet was assailed by a fierce storm in the English Channel and its ships scattered. All but forty-nine of the eighty-one ships were lost to the storm, including the one carrying the force's payroll of thirty-six thousand ducats. The second Spanish Armada had thus been defeated without a fight. Its mission was ended.

Philip's determination, however, remained firm, and in September of the following year, 1597, a third armada, again commanded by Padilla, put to sea. This one was composed of ninety-eight ships, including twenty-four galleons, that carried more than seventeen thousand men. Padilla's orders were to capture the port of Falmouth, on the channel, near the western tip of England. Shortly after sailing from Ferrol, Spain, on September 19, the fleet ran into bad weather that forced it to take shelter at La Coruña. It left La Coruña on October 18, and after four days it again sailed into heavy weather. The storm that struck it scattered the fleet, and after Padilla had found as many of his ships as he could, he regrouped and turned back to Ferrol, there to await the return of the rest of his fleet. After a week of waiting, he had but forty-one vessels in his fleet, only three of which were galleons. His mission was canceled.

Padilla, a moderate man, judging from his correspondence, had something more to say to his stubborn king. "If Your Majesty decides to continue the attempt on England," he told Philip, "take care to make preparations in good time and in good quantity, and if not, then it is better to make peace."

·<20. THE FINAL DEFEAT

Things were not going well for Philip. He was steadily losing ground against the Netherlands rebels. Rebel troops had recaptured the provinces of Drenthe, Groningen, Overijssel, and Gelderland, and Philip's prospects for victory and peace there seemed more distant than ever. His allies in France, the Catholic League, who received enormous financial aid from him as well as the support of a substantial Spanish military force, had been unable to prevent the accession of Huguenot Henry of Navarre to the French throne following the assassination of Navarre's cousin, King Henry III. Philip was appalled that a Protestant would be king of France. He viewed such a situation as a danger to Spain and a disaster for all Christianity. "I am greatly grieved when I look at the present state of Christendom," he wrote in 1591, two years after Henry III's death. Despite its costs to Spain, Philip had been unwilling to quit his war to keep Navarre from assuming the throne. "The religious issue involved," he said, "takes priority over everything."

Navarre had successfully led an army against the forces of the Catholic League and Spain and he was at last crowned king in February 1594, after his politically wise conversion to Catholicism in 1593. Nevertheless, Philip kept his Spanish troops in France, fighting on behalf of the Catholic League and against Navarre, now King Henry IV. Queen Elizabeth had allied herself with Henry by signing the Treaty of Greenwich on May 24, 1596, and had sent four thousand troops to northern France to support him. In October 1596 the United Provinces, the rebel government of the Netherlands, joined that alliance, thereby uniting Philip's three great enemies in Northern Europe against him. In May 1598, Philip, weakened by repeated reversals, was at last forced to give up the fight and get out of France, agreeing to a peace treaty that restored to France everything Philip's armies had taken from it during nine years of war, including the important port city of Calais.

The news from the New World was not much better. Spanish military forces seeking to quell uprisings by the native populations were thwarted in Mexico and Chile. Spanish ships carrying the commerce of America were relentlessly preyed upon by more than a hundred English privateers that robbed Spain of needed revenues. In Spain itself trouble loomed like a dark cloud. Higher taxes brought on by Philip's continuing wars, and widespread food shortages, even starvation, caused by huge crop failures, threatened to spread throughout the land the isolated revolts that Philip had already sternly suppressed.

The years, the infirmities, the stresses and disappointments of a lifetime had all added up, and the total was expressed in Philip's appearance, in his diminished activity, and in his failing health. One of his biographers says that as early as December 1592, when Philip was sixty-five, he looked like a dying man and those who saw him were shocked to see how old he looked and how feeble he had become.

Realizing the end was drawing near, Philip started turning over to his son, Prince Felipe, some of the document-signing chores and letting the boy, sixteen years old in 1594, appear conspicuously in some public ceremonies. On March 7, 1594, Philip put his signature on his final testament, which at some length specified the rights he was passing on to his son. A month later he found that paperwork so wearied him that he instructed his aides, "From now on, don't send me anything unless it is before lunch, because afterwards I am already burdened with work for the afternoon." Most of the administrative tasks had been taken on by his secretaries, who had become in effect ministers in his government, Juan de Idiáquez and Cristóbal de Moura. His council of advisers, the Council of State, had apparently become too cumbersome, too tiring for him to continue to work with, and it was shifted aside. Idiáquez handled foreign affairs, Moura domestic affairs. For a time Philip continued to annotate papers that were sent to him by those two chief aides, but as he grew ever more feeble, he ended his practice of making notes in the margins and instead orally told Idiáquez and Moura what his wishes were. One of them would then pass on the king's instructions in notes that began, "His Majesty says . . ."

Yet Philip's proclivity to micromanage seemed invincible, and at times, though having skipped the paperwork, he stepped in to make pronouncements on policy matters. "As usual," Moura commented, "His Majesty does just what he wants, no matter how much we lecture him."

To make him more comfortable during the day, a sort of portable couch was constructed for him in 1595. It was as much chair as it was couch, seven feet long and thirty inches wide, with a horsehair mattress. It could be adjusted to allow him to sit up, as if in a chair at a desk, or recline and take naps. After getting out of bed in the morning, he immediately moved into the chair. He sometimes spent the entire day in it, returning to his bed at night.

In May 1595 he was stricken by a new fever that lasted more than a month. According to one report, "The doctors say that his body is so withered and feeble that it is almost impossible that a human being in such a state could live for long."[1]

Nevertheless, in February 1596 he left the palace to celebrate Carnival and in March felt strong enough to go hunting. In April, however, a new attack of gout struck him with such intensity that he was unable to use his right arm. He was also suffering from dropsy, an abnormal accumulation of fluid that, in his case, caused his abdomen and legs to swell up. By the middle of May, though, he felt well enough to move his court to Toledo, where he stayed till the end of the summer. There he displayed his micromanagement tendency once more. A section of the city's commercial center, including houses as well as other structures, had been destroyed by fire and had become an eyesore. Philip could not stand to look at it and ordered it rebuilt. A plan for doing so was drawn up and approved by Philip, who then declared that the plan must be followed by everyone intending to rebuild. "If the owners of the houses in the square do not wish to rebuild according to the plan," he decreed, "and there are other people who are willing to do so, let the present owners be forced and encouraged to sell, receiving for the property the just price." Defending his decree, he said he was issuing the order "because it is my will and because it accords with reason and justice that it should be done, since it is to beautify such a principal and important city."

Gradually, however, he began to lose touch with what was going on around him. He spent more and more time sleeping and was prevented by long periods of disabling illness from attending to government affairs. In early 1597 illness kept him confined in Madrid. In May he managed to get out for a short visit to El Pardo, then moved on to San Lorenzo for the summer. He even worked up enough energy to go hunting from a coach. But another wave of gout forced him to stay inside and during that time he wrote a codicil to the testament he had drawn up in 1594. The addition instructed that the keys to certain of Philip's private papers be given to Moura and that Moura was to burn "all the papers of my late confessor fray Diego de Chaves, written by him to me or by me to him." Philip also now authorized Felipe to sign all government documents in Philip's name.

In late 1597 he was further dispirited by news that his daughter Catalina had died in childbirth on December 7 at age thirty.

On May 6, 1598, four days after Spain had at last made its humiliating peace with France, Philip signed a document turning over the Netherlands to his daughter Isabel and Archduke Albert, who were to be married (in April 1599) and who would, according to the terms of the document, rule the Netherlands jointly. Prince Felipe was directed to sign papers indicating his relinquishment of the Netherlands as part of his expected inheritance.

By now Philip's physical condition had deteriorated dramatically. Even so, around the end of June he insisted on being taken to the Escorial, at San Lorenzo, some twenty-five miles northwest of Madrid, where he meant to die. His doctors warned him against the trip, believing he would die en route. He insisted anyway. Borne in his couch-chair, which also could be extended to form a litter, and accompanied by, among others, the couch-chair's designer, Jean Lhermite, he made the journey in four days in almost unbearably hot weather. When he arrived and was asked how he felt, he grittily replied, "Very well." He was doing so well, in fact, that some were encouraged to think his condition might improve.

Then he suffered a relapse. The journey, which he had bravely suffered, had so weakened him that he was struck by a fever that persisted through July. Aching with arthritis, he was carried from his couch-chair to his bed on July 22 and there he remained. Suppurating sores and boils, attributed to a blood infection, developed over his body as he lay flat on his back, unable to bear being touched. Skin began to peel away from the bedsores that soon afflicted him. The running sores on his body gave off a foul smell, which was increased by his incontinence. He was in such pain that he could not stand to be washed, preventing his attendants from cleaning him thoroughly. The attendants finally cut a hole in the mattress to let his excrement and urine drain from the bed. The stench in the room was so overpowering that, according to one report, one of his physicians became ill from it.

In August, Philip made plans for his funeral, assisted by his priest, Francisco

Terrones, and the Escorial's monks. Still micromanaging, despite all his misery, he planned the ceremony, according to one account, "down to details such as which door of the church his coffin was to go in and go out."[2] He also had his coffin brought to his bedside so that he could inspect it. He called for the crucifix that his mother and then his father had held as they died, so that he too could hold it in his dying moments. He had himself surrounded by the many relics he had collected over a lifetime, as if to be encompassed by the great cloud of Christian witnesses that the writer of the New Testament book of Hebrews mentions.

When he was lucid and in less pain, he spent time with Terrones, receiving the priest's counsel, comfort, and instruction. He prayed that his last moments would come while he was fully conscious. He called his children together at his bedside and urged them to be good governors of their people, and he presented Felipe with a sealed envelope that was not to be opened until after his death.

On September 3 he was so weak that those who were at his bedside thought he had died. The attending priests gave him extreme unction, the Catholic church's sacrament for one who is about to die, to strengthen his soul. He awakened and asked to be handed his mother and father's crucifix. At that, Moura asked him if he was ready to turn the government over to Felipe. Grasping his power as long as he could, he refused to surrender sovereignty. On September 11 he was still issuing orders, dictating a letter to Archduke Albert to tell him that he, Philip, accepted the pope's offer to conduct Albert's marriage to Isabel.

Philip also instructed Felipe to be at his bedside when he died. He wanted his son to see how his reign ended. He had other instructions for Felipe, much like the ones his father, the Emperor Charles, had given him. As the end drew ever closer, Felipe and Isabel both stood by their father's bed while he gave them his blessing. When he allowed them to go, with tears in their eyes they kissed his hands and told him good-bye.

He awoke from a deep sleep early Sunday morning, September 13, 1598, and apparently realizing he was in his last minutes of life, smiled, as if happy that his prayer to be conscious at the moment of death had been answered. About five o'clock that morning, as an Escorial seminary choir began to sing the Mass and as he grasped his parents' crucifix, King Philip II of Spain died.

"He died slowly," one eyewitness, a monk, reported, "so that with only a faint motion, giving two or three small gasps, his saintly spirit left him."[3] Without being embalmed, his body was interred at the Escorial the next day in a simple ceremony.

The bitter rivalry, the lasting enmity, the holy cause were all for Philip now ended.

In England, Elizabeth, his foe, remained queen.

·❦· EPILOGUE

Philip's death, although expected, nevertheless came as a blow to Elizabeth. He had been involved in her life for more than forty years. When she was young, he had been her friend. He had been her protective brother-in-law. He later had been her suitor. He had been one of her correspondents. As a fellow prince, he had been her colleague. When he contended with her, she had found a sort of enjoyment in being his adversary. She had taken pleasure when her sea captains bested him, capturing or destroying his ships and stealing his treasure, as if she were playing some outrageous game with him, as if their ships were pieces on an extraordinary chessboard. It was a game in which he was a consistent, hapless loser and she the exultant winner, a fact that made playing it all the more pleasurable for her. So influential was he, though, so powerful in other ways, that he had required consideration, by her and by rulers throughout Europe, including the popes, in most matters touching other nations. For good or for ill, in the dozen years or so before his death he had stood as a nearly constant presence in her mind. He had presented a continuing challenge that drew from her the best that her wits could supply. She would miss him, in an odd way. When she was brought the news of his death, tears came to her eyes, and she secluded herself until the wave of sorrow had passed and she could compose herself.

Her desultory war with Spain continued, as it would for the remainder of her reign. King Henry of France wearied of the fight, and despite France's promise that it would not make peace without England's concurrence, it had concluded the Treaty of Vervins on May 2, 1598, ending its war with Spain, four months before Philip's death. Elizabeth too wanted to quit the war, but her Privy Council, or most of its members anyway, and the Netherlanders, who saw disaster for their cause if England left the fight, urged her to stay in it, which she did.

But although the conflict continued, Spain was no longer a threat to make a successful invasion of England or to depose its valiant queen. The defeat of Philip's grand Armada and the failures of its successors had validated the misgivings of Philip's military leaders concerning his Enterprise of England. Were it not for his fanatical belief in his holy cause and his despotic insistence that it be executed, his Enterprise likely would not have been attempted in the first place.

England's victory at sea had saved not only a nation and a queen, though. It had saved the Protestant movement in Europe. The defeated Philip would not be able to stamp out Protestantism and its adherents as he had done in Spain and was trying to do in the Netherlands. He would not be able to impose Catholicism on those who rejected it, neither upon the people of England nor upon the peoples of Northern Europe who were their allies. Freedom of conscience had prevailed over tyranny.

For many in Europe, the English victory also settled a big, bothersome issue. As historian Garrett Mattingly puts it in his epilogue to his monumental work, *The Armada*, "The Protestants of France and the Netherlands, Germany and Scandinavia saw with relief that God was, in truth, as they had always supposed, on their side. The Catholics of France and Italy and Germany saw with almost equal relief that Spain was not, after all, God's chosen champion." Although Spain would remain a power for another generation, its time of preeminence, in the public mind and in fact, was over.

Elizabeth went on to face other problems, including a mountain of debt (incurred as the cost of her nation's defense), a revolt in Ireland—aided by a sizable Spanish army, but handily defeated by an army led by Lord Mountjoy—and the treason of the earl of Essex, Robert Devereux, who conspired to overthrow her and take the crown for himself. Essex was put on trial, found guilty, and beheaded. He had been a favorite of Elizabeth, for a while perhaps the most favorite of all her courtiers, and his execution in February 1601, at age thirty-four, deeply affected her, sending her into a prolonged state of melancholy. By early 1602 she seemed to have emerged from her depression, but the years were showing in her appearance and even more so in her behavior. The French ambassador described her: "Her bosom [revealed in low-cut dresses] is rather wrinkled. . . . As for her face it is . . . long and thin, and her teeth are very yellow and irregular . . . on the left side less than on the right. Many of them are missing, so that you cannot understand her easily when she speaks."[1] Beneath the red wig that she wore in public her hair was thin and gray.

For special occasions she still dressed elegantly, though, clothing herself in strikingly beautiful gowns and elaborately bedecking herself with dazzling jewelry.

Her behavior became increasingly fitful and at times bizarre, her emotions subject to a wide range of expression. Without warning she would launch into tantrums, would harangue and abuse her attendants, and yet at other times she would be as captivatingly charming as she had been when young. She had outlived most of those once dearest to her and when she spoke or thought of them, she often would openly cry. In a display of paranoidlike fear she kept an old, rusted sword near her bed and would rise to grasp it in the night and stab it into the draperies behind which she thought assassins might be hiding. As time went on, she kept more and more to her private chambers and was seldom seen except for holiday appearances.

At Christmas of 1602, three and a half months after her sixty-ninth birthday, she seemed well and vigorous enough. The holiday celebrations at her Whitehall palace included dances, the presentation of several plays, and, among other things, of course considerable feasting. She even attended two dinners outside Whitehall, one put on by her cousin Charles Howard (who had commanded her navy against the Armada) at his house in London and one by Robert Cecil at his. Four weeks later, on January 21, 1603, as winter deepened, she moved to Richmond, believed to be the warmest of her palaces. The weather was terrible, cold and wet, and a bitingly severe frost set in once she was there. By late February she had taken ill and fallen into a state of depression. She refused to take the medicines her physicians prescribed, and those closest to her grew ever more concerned. Her cousin Robert Carey came to see her to try to brighten her mood. Cheerfully greeting her, he told her he was glad to see that she was in good health, but she grasped his hand and earnestly replied, "No, Robin, I am not well." Carey later described the meeting that day and the day following:

> She discoursed with me of her indisposition and in her discourse she fetched not so few as forty or fifty great sighes. . . . In all my lifetime I never knew her [to] fetch a sigh but when the Queen of Scottes was beheaded. . . . This was upon a Saterday night, and she gave command that the great closet [a chamber in the palace chapel] should be prepared for her to go to chappell the next morning. The next day, all things being in a readinesse, wee long

expected her coming. After eleven o'clock, one of the grooms came out and bade make ready for the private closet. . . . There we stayed long for her coming, but, at last, she had cushions lay'd for her in the privy chamber, hard-by the closet door, and there she heard service. From that day forwards she grew worse and worse.[2]

Another visitor was John Harrington, who in an effort to cheer her recited some humorous verse he had written. She gave him a smile and told him, "When thou dost feel creeping Time at thy gate, these fooleries will please thee less. I am past my relish for such matters."

She was running a fever and felt "a great heat" in her stomach. She also suffered a loss of appetite, insatiable thirst, swollen glands, and insomnia. She refused to undress or to lie in her bed, resting instead on cushions scattered around the room, silently staring at the floor, often with one finger in her mouth, her emaciated body fetid from neglect or disease.

Charles Howard came to see her on March 22 and managed to persuade her to rest in her bed. There she lay silently on her side while prayers were read to her. The next evening, March 23, the archbishop of Canterbury, John Whitgift, came to pray, as she had requested. He prayed for half an hour, on his knees, then blessed her and started to rise to leave. She motioned for him to continue praying. After praying for another half hour, he again rose to leave, and she again motioned for him to continue, which he did for another half hour. "She would not hear him speak of hope of her longer life," Robert Carey recalled, "but when he prayed or spoke of heaven, and those joys, she would hug his hand." She then fell into unconsciousness, and the sore-kneed archbishop was at last able to get to his feet and ease from her bedside.

Without again awakening, Elizabeth died sometime between two and three o'clock the next morning, March 24, 1603.

At ten o'clock that same morning, James Stuart, king of Scotland, the son of Mary Queen of Scots and Lord Darnley, was proclaimed king of England.

Elizabeth's body was removed from Richmond palace and transported on a black-draped barge down the Thames to Whitehall, where it lay in state. On April 28 an elaborate funeral was held for her, and her body, contained in a lead coffin, was interred at Westminster Abbey beside that of her grandfather, King Henry VII.

✦ NOTES

1. THE PRINCE

1. Kamen, *Philip of Spain*, p. 3.
2. Prescott, *History of the Reign of Philip the Second*, 1:20.
3. Kamen, *Philip of Spain*, p. 4.
4. Parker, *Philip II*, p. 7.
5. Kamen, *Philip of Spain*, p. 4.
6. Parker, *Philip II*, p. 6.
7. Ibid., p. 9.
8. Ibid., pp. 18–19.
9. Ibid., p. 19.
10. Kamen, *Philip of Spain*, p. 11.
11. Ibid.
12. Prescott, *History of the Reign of Philip the Second*, 1:25.

2. THE PRINCESS

1. Starkey, *Six Wives*, p. 260.
2. Williams, *The Tudors*, p. 32.
3. Starkey, *Elizabeth*, p. 17.
4. Somerset, *Elizabeth I*, p. 6.
5. Ibid.
6. Williams, *Elizabeth the First*, p. 5.
7. Ibid., pp. 5–6.
8. Ibid., p. 6.
9. Starkey, *Six Wives*, p. 602.
10. Marcus, Mueller, and Rose, *Elizabeth I*, pp. 5–6.
11. Hibbert, *The Virgin Queen*, p. 28.

3. THE PREPARATION FOR A CROWN

1. Kamen, *Philip of Spain*, p. 20.
2. Walsh, *Philip II*, p. 74.
3. Kamen, *Philip of Spain*, p. 17.
4. Walsh, *Philip II*, p. 79.
5. Prescott, *History of the Reign of Philip the Second*, 1:33.
6. Kamen, *Philip of Spain*, p. 38.
7. Ibid.
8. Ibid.
9. Ibid.
10. Ibid., p. 41.
11. Prescott, *History of the Reign of Philip the Second*, 1:41.
12. Walsh, *Philip II*, p. 106. Walsh uses Leti's quote to contradict biographers, such as Prescott, who cast Philip as making an unfavorable impression on his Netherlands subjects. Leti's account is a "fanciful compilation," according to twentieth-century biographer Geoffrey Parker, who writes that "Leti once acknowledged to a friend that he thought fiction could be more entertaining than fact when it came to writing history" (*Philip II*, p. 202).
13. Kamen, *Philip of Spain*, p. 44.
14. Prescott, *History of the Reign of Philip the Second*, 1:42.
15. Ibid., pp. 42–43.
16. Kamen, *Philip of Spain*, p. 49.
17. Ibid., p. 51.
18. Ibid., pp. 52–53.
19. Walsh, *Philip II*, pp. 123–124.

4. THE BLOODY QUEEN

1. Prescott, *History of the Reign of Philip the Second*, 1:61.
2. Erickson, *Bloody Mary*, p. 353.
3. Prescott, *History of the Reign of Philip the Second*, 1:63.
4. Erickson, *Bloody Mary*, p. 371.
5. Ibid., p. 372.
6. Prescott, *History of the Reign of Philip the Second*, 1:79.
7. Erickson, *Bloody Mary*, p. 405.

5. THE SUSPECT PRINCESS

1. Marcus, Mueller, and Rose, *Elizabeth I,* pp. 41–42.
2. Foxe, *Foxe's Book of Martyrs,* pp. 362–63.
3. Starkey, *Elizabeth,* p. 141.
4. Ibid., p. 145.
5. Williams, *Elizabeth the First,* p. 37.

6. THE NEW SPANISH KING

1. From an account by the ambassador of Venice, Giovanni Micheli, quoted by Erickson, *Bloody Mary,* p. 426.
2. Kamen, *Philip of Spain,* p. 63.
3. Prescott, *History of the Reign of Philip the Second,* 1:12–13.
4. Ibid., p. 103.
5. Ibid., p. 117.
6. Ibid., p. 121.

7. THE END OF REIGN

1. Erickson, *Bloody Mary,* p. 464.
2. Ibid., p. 485.

8. THE NEW QUEEN

1. Weir, *Life of Elizabeth I,* p. 35.
2. Williams, *Elizabeth the First,* p. 57.
3. Ibid., p. 63.
4. Somerset, *Elizabeth I,* p. 82.

9. THE NEW PROPOSAL

1. Marcus, Mueller, and Rose, *Elizabeth I,* pp. 59–60. Another version of her remarks has her saying, ". . . in the end this shall be for me sufficient, that a marble stone shall declare that a queen, having reigned such a time, lived and died a virgin."

2. Waldman, *Elizabeth and Leicester,* p. 69.

3. Ibid.

4. Ibid., p. 83.

10. THE RELIGIOUS DIVIDE

1. Schwiebert, *Luther and His Times,* p. 150.

2. Ibid.

3. Ibid., p. 153.

4. Bainton, *Here I Stand,* pp. 49–50.

5. Ibid., p. 54.

6. Schwiebert, *Luther and His Times,* pp. 308–09.

7. Ibid., p. 315.

8. Bainton, *Here I stand,* p. 61.

9. Ibid., pp. 61–62.

10. Ibid., p. 62.

11. Ibid., pp. 62–63.

12. M. U. Edwards, "Martin Luther," *World Book* Online Reference Center.

13. Durant, *The Reformation,* p. 390.

14. Prescott, *History of the Reign of Philip the Second,* 1:252.

15. This quote appears in one translation or another in several works on Philip, including Kamen, Prescott, Patrick Williams, Parker, and Roth.

16. James Anthony Froude, "English Seamen in the Sixteenth Century," lecture given at Oxford University, 1893–94.

11. THE CATHOLIC RIVAL

1. Guy, *Queen of Scots,* p. 57.

2. Ibid., p. 39.

3. Ibid., p. 93.

4. Weir, *Mary, Queen of Scots,* p. 67.

5. Guy, *Queen of Scots,* p. 299.

6. Ibid., p. 317.

7. Williams, *Elizabeth the First,* p. 127.

12. THE TRAGEDIES AND TRIUMPHS

1. Parker, *Philip II,* p. 91.

13. THE NETHERLANDS REVOLT

1. Prescott, *History of the Reign of Philip the Second*, 1:353.
2. Ibid., 2:40.
3. Kamen, *Duke of Alba*, p. 84.
4. Ibid., pp. 123–24.

14. THE HOSTILITIES

1. Williams, *Elizabeth the First*, p. 175.
2. Weir, *Life of Elizabeth I*, p. 354.

15. THE PREPARATION FOR CONQUEST

1. Mattingly, *The Armada*, p. 88.
2. Martin and Parker, *Spanish Armada*, p. 91.
3. Ibid., p. 98.

16. THE DEFENDERS

1. Weir, *Life of Elizabeth I*, p. 389.
2. Hanson, *Confident Hope of a Miracle*, p. 182.
3. Somerset, *Elizabeth I*, p. 454.
4. Ibid., p. 455.
5. Ibid.
6. Martin and Parker, *Spanish Armada*, p. 30.
7. Somerset, *Elizabeth I*, p. 455.
8. Weir, *Life of Elizabeth I*, p. 389.

17. THE GRAND ARMADA

1. Williams, *Philip II*, p. 196.
2. Hanson, *Confident Hope of a Miracle*, p. 105.
3. Mattingly, *The Armada*, pp. 216–17.
4. Martin and Parker, *Spanish Armada*, p. 143.
5. Hanson, *Confident Hope of a Miracle*, pp. 125–26.

18. THE RULERS OF THE SEA

1. Martin and Parker, *Spanish Armada*, p. 148.
2. Ibid.
3. Ibid.
4. Ibid., p. 160.
5. Ibid., p. 161.
6. Ibid., pp. 177–78.
7. Ibid., p. 180.
8. Hanson, *Confident Hope of a Miracle*, p. 328.

19. THE RUIN AND THE RENEWAL

1. Neale, *Queen Elizabeth I*, p. 302.
2. Somerset, *Elizabeth I*, p. 464.
3. Hanson, *Confident Hope of a Miracle*, p. 367.
4. Ibid., p. 385.
5. Ibid., p. 386.
6. Martin and Parker, *Spanish Armada*, p. 238.
7. Mattingly, *The Armada*, p. 389.
8. Williams, *Elizabeth the First*, p. 211.
9. Hanson, *Confident Hope of a Miracle*, p. 427.
10. Ibid.

20. THE FINAL DEFEAT

1. Parker, p. 182.
2. Ibid., p. 198.
3. Ibid.

EPILOGUE

1. Hibbert, *Virgin Queen*, p. 253.
2. Ibid., pp. 261–62.

Andrews, Kenneth R. *Elizabethan Privateering*. London: Cambridge University Press, 1964.

Bainton, Roland H. *Here I Stand: A Life of Martin Luther*. New York: Mentor Books, 1955.

Barrow, John. *Memoirs of the Naval Worthies of Queen Elizabeth's Reign*. London: John Murray, 1845.

Beckinsale, B. W. *Elizabeth I*. New York: Arco Publishing, 1963.

Black, J. B. *The Reign of Elizabeth, 1558–1603*. Oxford: Clarendon Press, 1936.

The Book of Common Prayer. London: Everyman Publishers, 1999.

Boyden, James M. *The Courtier and the King—Ruy Gómez de Silva, Philip II, and the Court of Spain*. Berkeley: University of California Press, 1995.

Chamberlin, Frederick. *The Private Character of Queen Elizabeth*. New York: Dodd, Mead, 1922.

Clapham, John. *Elizabeth of England*. Philadelphia: University of Pennsylvania Press, 1951.

Cruickshank, C. G. *Elizabeth's Army*. 2d ed. Oxford: Clarendon Press, 1966.

Dunn, Richard S. *The Age of Religious Wars, 1559–1689*. New York: W. W. Norton, 1970.

Durant, Will. *The Reformation*. New York: Simon & Schuster, 1957.

Elliott, J. H. *Imperial Spain 1469–1716*. New York: Penguin Books, 1990.

Erickson, Carolly. *Bloody Mary*. New York: St. Martin's Press, 1997.

Fernández-Armesto, Felipe. *Philip II's Empire: A Decade on the Edge*. London: Hakluyt Society, 1999.

———. *The Spanish Armada: The Experience of War in 1588*. New York: Oxford University Press, 1988.

Foxe, John. *Foxe's Book of Martyrs*. Peabody, MA: Hendrickson Publishers, 2004.

Fraser, Antonia. *Mary Queen of Scots*. New York: Delta, 1993.

Grierson, Edward. *King of Two Worlds*. New York: Putnam, 1974.

Guy, John. *Queen of Scots*. Boston: Houghton Mifflin, 2004.

Haigh, Christopher. *Elizabeth I*. Boston: Addison-Wesley, 1998.

Hanson, Neil. *The Confident Hope of a Miracle*. New York: Alfred A. Knopf, 2005.

Hay, Millicent V. *The Life of Robert Sidney, Earl of Leicester (1563–1626)*. Washington, DC: Folger Books, 1984.

Hibbert, Christopher. *Tower of London*. New York: Newsweek, 1971.

———. *The Virgin Queen*. New York: Addison-Wesley, 1991.

Howarth, David. *The Voyage of the Armada*. New York: Penguin, 1982.

Hughes, Philip. *The Reformation in England.* New York: Macmillan, 1954.

Hume, Martin. *The Courtships of Queen Elizabeth.* New York: Brentano's.

Johnson, Paul. *A History of the English People.* New York: Harper, 1985.

Kamen, Henry. *The Duke of Alba.* New Haven: Yale University Press, 2004.

———. *Philip of Spain.* New Haven: Yale University Press, 1997.

Lynch, John. *Spain Under the Habsburgs.* New York: Oxford University Press, 1964.

Maass, Edgar. *The Dream of Philip II.* New York: Bobbs-Merrill, 1944.

MacCulloch, Diarmaid. *The Reformation.* New York: Viking, 2003.

Marcus, Leah S., Janel Mueller, and Mary Beth Rose, eds. *Elizabeth I: Collected Works.* Chicago: University of Chicago Press, 2000.

Martin, Colin, and Geoffrey Parker. *The Spanish Armada.* 2d rev. ed. New York: St. Martin's Press, 1999.

Mattingly, Garrett. *The Armada.* Boston: Houghton Mifflin, 1959.

McDermott, James. *England & the Spanish Armada.* New Haven: Yale University Press, 2005.

McKendrick, Melveena. *Spain.* New York: American Heritage, 1972.

Melchiore, Susan McCarthy. *The Spanish Inquisition.* Philadelphia: Chelsea House, 2002.

Morgan, Kenneth O., ed. *The Oxford Illustrated History of Britain.* New York: Oxford University Press, 1988.

Neale, J. E. *Queen Elizabeth I.* Harmondsworth, England: Penguin Books, 1960.

Palmer, Alan. *Kings and Queens of England.* London: Octopus Books, 1976.

Parker, Geoffrey. *The Grand Strategy of Philip II.* New Haven: Yale University Press, 1998.

———. *Philip II.* 4th ed. Chicago: Open Court, 2002.

Prescott, William H. *History of the Reign of Philip the Second, King of Spain.* 3 vols. Philadelphia: Lippincott, 1902.

Read, Conyers. *Lord Burghley and Queen Elizabeth.* New York: Alfred A. Knopf, 1960.

Ridley, Jaspar. *The Life and Times of Mary Tudor.* London: Weidenfeld and Nicolson, 1973.

Roth, Cecil. *The Spanish Inquisition.* New York: W. W. Norton, 1996.

Rowse, A. L. *The England of Elizabeth.* Madison: University of Wisconsin Press, 1978.

Schwiebert, E. G. *Luther and His Times.* St. Louis: Concordia Publishing House, 1950.

Simpson, Helen. *The Spanish Marriage.* New York: Putham, 1933.

Smith, Lacey Baldwin. *The Elizabethan Epic.* London: Panther, 1969.

Somerset, Anne. *Elizabeth I.* New York: St. Martin's Press, 1991.

Starkey, David. *Elizabeth.* New York: Harper, 2001.

———. *Six Wives.* New York: Harper, 2003.

Sugden, John. *Sir Francis Drake.* New York: Henry Holt, 1991.

Waldman, Milton. *Elizabeth and Leicester.* Boston: Houghton Mifflin, 1944.

Walsh, William Thomas. *Philip II.* New York: Sheed & Ward, 1937.

Weir, Alison. *The Life of Elizabeth I.* New York: Ballantine Books, 1998.

———. *Mary, Queen of Scots and the Murder of Lord Darnley.* New York: Ballantine Books, 2003.

Westminster Abbey. New York: Peebles Press International.

Williams, Neville. *Elizabeth the First, Queen of England.* New York: Dutton, 1968.

———. *The Tudors.* Berkeley: University of California Press, 2000.

Williams, Patrick. *Philip II.* New York: Palgrave, 2001.

ACKNOWLEDGMENTS

Material for the story told here is drawn from many sources, and I acknowledge with deep and sincere gratitude all the help I received from those authors and editors whose works made this book possible. I am especially indebted to the biographers of Queen Elizabeth and the English-language biographers of King Philip. I am also especially indebted to the authors who wrote about the Armada and its battles with Elizabeth's fleet. To those and all others from whose works I borrowed I hereby express my hearty thanks.

Hearty thanks, too, to all the readers who have come this far in the book.